Scent

~~~

By K.R. Smith
~~~

~ **Acknowledgments** ~

"Cheers Greg," for being an awesome flatmate. Thanks for sharing your huge CD collection, which in turn was written in as my characters' tunes. Thanks too for letting me run ideas past you on my make-believe tribe and the information you shared on your favourite animal; the wolf.

To my other second family; through catch-ups and entertainment, you kept me on earth rather than floating off into space. Here's to my fiancés Darianne and Nicole. To my old Student Res pals, Paul and Karen. Last but not least, to Gaylynn and Brenden. The 'KGB' lives on!

To my parents, who offer refuge and respite during our holidays together. Dear ole Dad and Coral, for our fish and chips on the beach and our long drives. To my darling Mumsy, who's responsible for turning me into a Trekkie, to which I returned the favour by introducing her to 'Dexter'.

I feel fortunate for the amazing artist who did the cover and illustrations of my first novel 'Circulate', to do the graphics of 'Scent' too. Thank you Isabel de Sequera, using your talents again adds a sense of continuity to the Circulate Series.

I'd like to thank Nina Ackerman and Leesa Montague for letting me use one of their photos taken on their Alaskan holiday for the front cover. I'd also like to thank Nina for lending me her books on her favourite state. I hope you had a blast at 'Moosefest'!

Last but not least, I want to thank my friends in the online community Storywrite. Coming from all over the world, you left encouraging feedback on the chapters I posted. I actually experienced giddy excitement when sharing my characters with you... giggle. Thank you for being some of the first to read and comment on B and Declan, my fantastical characters who've become very real to me.

- K.R. Smith 2010

~ Contents ~

~~~~~~~~

"Men do not roar. Women roar. Then they hurl heavy objects. And claw at you."
-- "What does the man do?"
"He reads love poetry. He ducks a lot."

(Worf and Wesley on Klingon mating rituals Star Trek: The Next Generation)

~~~~~~~~

~ 1 ~

1st September 2084

Man, this Iggy Pop album is awesome! Our heads bopped along to the tune of 'Lust For Life' in time to the beat and in time with each other.

"B."

Hmm, what was that?

"B!"

Is that Mum?

"BIANCA!"

Derik and I looked to each other, each of us wondering if the other had heard that? as we laid on our stomachs on top of my bed, listening to the old CD play on the second-hand CD player that used to be my Dad's.

"I think your Mom is calling you." Derik turned down my music.

Just then Mum blew into my room and stood in the doorway with her hands on her hips.

"Bianca Grace I have been calling out your name for the past ten minutes!" She announced.

"Yes?" I looked up inquiringly.

"Will Derik be staying for dinner tonight?" Mum rolled her eyes and then she looked his way.

"No thanks Aunt Jess, but thanks anyway. My Mom is expecting me home." He answered in his usual polite manner.

"Thanks for answering that Derik. Now I have to go all the way back downstairs and continue making Bianca's dinner. Next time B, keep the music to a less deafening level and save my legs the hassle, OK?" Mum glared as she started to leave.

"So? Phase." I shrugged.

"Excuse me?" She stopped to look back.

"Instead of using the stairs and coming all this way to ask us that one question, just instantaneously phase up here." I pointed out.

"Oh right! Because I'm already in the custom of instantaneously phasing in and out of my 17 year old daughter's bedroom at my leisure. No never mind if you were up here with a boyfriend or you were getting undressed for a shower or if..." She prattled on.

"Mum!" I cut her off as I blushed.

"I'll be sure to pass on your open invitation to your father so he knows that he too can suddenly appear inside your bedroom at his preference." She added on sarcastically. "We'll post an 'open' sign on your bedroom door, shall we?"

With that she was gone, and Derik was left chuckling in her aftermath.

"Your parents are cool." He said for his millionth time since I've known him.

"No they're not." I rebuked for my billionth time.

"Your Mom is much more flexible than my Mom." He remarked.

"That's because my Mum was 19 years old when she had me and your Mum was 24 when she had you. I think it's an age thing." I shrugged.

"Your family is cool." Derik said for his zillionth time.

"No they're not." I sighed for my gazillionth time.

"You've got a pretty cool Mom and Dad, you've got a cool Uncle and Grandparents and Great Grandma. Your Dad, Uncle and Grandfather are Werewolves...but they're cool Werewolves. They're not interested in hunting humans. And your Dad and the rest of the tribe makes sure Declan doesn't either even though he's a different kind of Werewolf." Derik went on.

"Declan is an asshole – he would frickin' eat Bambi if he saw it all helpless and alone in the woods." I said unimpressed.

"He's not that bad, it's just around a full moon he gets a bit tetchy." He defended his older brother.

"Your older brother is 'tetchy' even when there isn't a full moon... which means every night of the frickin' year." I retorted.

"It's only because of this Werewolf business."

"Declan has been a Werewolf since he was three years old when he was attacked." I arched an eyebrow back.

"Yeah, but see? The Lokoti Werewolves don't turn until they're ten years old or older, when a male relative like a grandfather or a father dies, which triggers their Werewolf DNA. Declan was turned into a Werewolf by the European Werewolf that attacked him and Dad, when our Dad died. Plus he's a different breed of Werewolf, so he has different symptoms. It's not his fault if..." Derik went on but I cut him off.

"He's socially inept."

"No he's not..." He tried to argue, but then I shot him a tired look and he stopped himself, "...well alright, so he's a little on the defensive side and he keeps people at arms length. But that's only so he won't accidentally turn anybody else by biting them. He hardly ever hugs Mom because he's scared of hurting her. How do you think that makes him feel?"

"Oh poor Declan, he's just misunderstood." I whined in a funny voice. He tickled me for that! "Derik, cut it out!" I laughed and rolled away from him. But he didn't cut it out, he kept at it! "Derik no! Stop it!" I squealed, rolling off the bed to get away from him.

He cracked up laughing when he saw me land on the floor.

"Are you OK?" he chuckled, reaching over and pulling me back onto the bed.

"You know I hate being tickled!" I hit him hard on the arm.

"Oow!" Derik guffawed, flinching. "Your right hook has really been beefing up in the last month or so. Are you working out or something?"

"No." I gave him a look as if he were mad for even suggesting it.

"Hmm." He squeezed my arms to check the muscles for himself. "I guess not, they still feel pretty flimsy."

"Hey!" I whacked him a second time.

"Ouch!" he rubbed his sore shoulder where I hit him. "You may look like a pipsqueak, but you hit almost as hard as Declan."

"I thought you said he treated you and your mother with kid gloves or something." I gave him a funny look.

"He's punched me now and then." Derik smiled ruefully.

"I thought he was worried about accidentally turning you."

"Well, yeah he is." He shrugged. "But when he punches me his hand is in a fist so his nails are tucked in. Besides he can only turn someone if he bites them... I overheard your Grandfather and my Mom talk about it."

"Typical." I rolled my eyes. "The guy is afraid to hug his own mother but he'll still male bond with his brother by beating him up now and again."

"Yeah, that's about right for us men." Derik said in humor. Then he looked at his watch before he looked back. "I'd better take off. So, will I see you later on tonight down at Ben's bonfire?"

I gave a nod before he stood up first and out of politeness so did I, as I walked him to my bedroom door.

Just as I started to open the door to let him out, Derik stopped us. He quickly leaned in and kissed me softly on the lips. At first this took me by surprise and for a couple of seconds I froze... but then I recovered.

"Derik." I frowned.

"Yeah I know, you don't know if you're ready for anything more than friends yet." He gave a guilty smile. "But I couldn't resist."

"Try."

He sighed wistfully as he left my bedroom and he walked down the small corridor to the stairs. After throwing me one last look, he jogged down my small staircase. I closed my bedroom door behind and leant on it whilst sighing myself.

I've known Derik forever...he's one of the few boys of the tribe that's my age, although he's not a Native Alaskan nor is he Lokoti by marriage. Derik, his older brother Declan and his mother Aunt Susan, are the only non-Lokoti invited to live on this land as one of us, who weren't married into us.

Aunt Susan who was pregnant with Derik at the time, came here to live when Declan was just three years old. On the night of her arrival, her husband died from the European Werewolf attack which had also mauled and ultimately changed Declan. My Gran helped the Lokoti Werewolves fight the foreign Werewolf which was a different and more dangerous breed of Werewolf, a man-eater. Then Gran found out that Susan had been married to Anthony Sabre who was killed by the foreign Werewolf? That was that, Susan and her kids were declared family and were taken in by the tribe. Apparently Anthony's Great Grand Uncle was Mike Sabre, who was turned into a Circulator by my Great Great Grandmother, Elisha Worthall.

The female lineage of Elisha Worthall all became Circulators, including my grandmother and mother. They used to be part of the Circulate, but when the Circulate evolved to exist as pure energy and light to take their place in the space time continuum? It left behind only my Gran and Mum, who later met the last Calculator Vincent Moher, who was our distant cousin.

I'm meant to be the last Circulator although I haven't circulated yet, which means that I can't put myself into phase. In layman's terms it basically explains that I can't turn my biological body into one of light and pass through time and space, as you do...! I'm turning 18 years old in a month's time and all I've had are the dreams and visions. Sometimes I wonder if I'm a Circulator, or a Calculator? Vincent who's our Calculator can't put himself into phase; but he has a highly attuned mind that is able to calculate temporal causalities. He can 'see' how we affect the timeline, or what's in store for us.

"I wouldn't worry about it, B." Mum said for her trillionth time when I voiced my reservations about my ability. "I didn't phase for my first time until I was 18 years old and pregnant with you."

"How old were you when you phased for the first time, Gran?" I asked her over the dinner table.

She, Grandfather, Great Grandma, Uncle Julian, Aunt Danika, and my younger cousins would often come to dinner, or I would go to Gran and Grandfather's house with my parents and see everyone there.

"I phased for my first time when I was 13 years old. My mother phased for her first time when she was 16." Gran shrugged so casually it was as if we were talking about learning how to do a handstand.

To say that my family was 'unique' would have been an understatement. With Mum and Gran being Circulators; their bio-electromagnetic frequencies are in temporal flux so they hardly aged. Both my Mum and my Gran had the appearance of human women in their twenties. But their husbands, Dad and Grandfather didn't mind this one bit. Since Dad, Grandfather and Uncle Julian were Lokoti Werewolves, they could live until they're 200 years old. My 56 year old Grandfather looked like a man in his early forties as my 39 year old Dad had the appearance of a man in his mid twenties. As was the custom of our tribe except with my family, the Lokoti Werewolves outlived their human wives.

Whereas we lived on the hill, the Sabre's (pronounced *Sar-bra*, if you ever want to see Declan's Werewolf eyes glow then mispronounce his surname) lived in the central community of our tribal lands where the sports field, general store/ gas station, garage, meeting hall and small library/ school were. The Lokoti community centre was like a village primarily made up of residential homes on small streets, with simplistic gardens and greenhouses for families to grow their own fruit and vegetables. All of the buildings here were made from wood which came courtesy of the surrounding forest.

Our tribal lands were safely tucked away in a small corner of the vast Lokoti National Park in the Alaska Range. We were situated 4.5 hours north of Anchorage and 1.5 hours south of Fairbanks. The small township of Alma is 7 km's away where before the War, the Lokoti kids went to school and families shopped in the supermarket there. However since the War, Alma like many towns or cities of this planet, either turned into a ghost town or a crime hotspot thanks to looting.

Aunt Susan and Gran helped run our make-shift school which primarily went from when you were 7 – 15 years old. But there were some kids like Derik and I, who continued our schooling by concentrating on different areas. Derik loved studying science and I just loved studying history, so our parents continued to tell us what additional books we could read. They even set us 'assignments' which we occasionally had to write up to show if we understood or not, the books which had been recommended.

"He doesn't just look like his Great Great Grand Uncle, Mike Sabre but he has disposition too... maybe Derik will become a Medicine Man? Mike Sabre was a doctor." Gran shrugged to Aunt Susan. She and Grandfather were especially close to Aunt Susan and her sons, as they helped the widow raise her young.

My aunt was equally proud of her two boys, although they were as different from each other as chalk and cheese. Derik had brown hair, brown eyes and was academic, sensitive and easy to talk to. He had been my playmate ever since we were babies as our birthdays were only two weeks apart.

However Derik's older brother Declan, was another story. He stopped going to school when he was 13 years old to become an apprentice mechanic instead. Declan is soon to turn 21 and he's the rudest, most arrogant boy in the tribe... with dark blonde hair, bright blue eyes and a constant scowl. He bosses Derik around a lot, seeing himself as head of the family. The only people I've ever seen him be nice to, are adults such as his parent, my parents and to my grandparents. When Declan changed, the Lokoti Werewolf pack took him under their wing. By taking him hunting every full moon in the National Park, they taught the young European Werewolf to replace his craving for human flesh to animal instead.

When Lokoti Werewolves change they still look humanoid; as their muscles bulk up, their eyes change colour and glow, the nails on their hands and feet turn long and hard, like claws. Their teeth become elongated and sharp as they have lightening fast reflexes and supernatural strength. But when Declan changes, he completely morphs from man to beast. He looks like a huge, hulking, hairless wolf with his height and weight doubling; which means he's bigger and stronger than the Lokoti Werewolf. His bright green eyes would glow in the dark and from the few times I'd seen them in Werewolf form, they still unnerved me.

The fifteen Lokoti Werewolves are highly esteemed members of the Lokoti tribe. Three of our nine Tribal Elders are Werewolves. The Lokoti Werewolves were seen as our guardians. World War Three occurred three years before I was born and from then, the Lokoti Werewolves have patrolled our tribal lands, keeping us safe from looters during the outside world's sickness and lawlessness. They even fought foreign Werewolves who still feasted on human flesh, like the European Werewolf who killed Anthony Sabre and turned Declan.

Our tribe has become accustomed to the mish-mash of different breeds of Werewolves, or Circulators and other humans with special gifts. To the humans, it became easy to spot a Werewolf in the crowd due to their towering height and strong build. To the Werewolves, it was easy with their infrared sight, to spot the Circulator or the psychic, because of the auras they produced.

And me...? I'm nobody special, not really. I'm the daughter, granddaughter and niece of Lokoti Werewolves but that's it. Oh yeah, I'm supposed to be a Circulator but I can't circulate. I'm the last Circulator in all of human history, so my family says. My appearance is nothing out of the ordinary either. I'm 160 cm's tall with typical straight, black Lokoti hair but I have my mother's and my grandmother's blue eyes. My skin wasn't bronzed like the Lokoti natural skin colour either and neither is Mum's. I think my mother and I get our colouring from my grandmother who is English.

Gran has bright blue eyes, pale skin and wavy, chestnut brown hair. Grandfather and Dad are either half or three-quarter Lokoti with the typical straight black hair. But Grandfather's grandmother was Caucasian so he has her blue eyes. Nana, who is my Dad's Mum, is Chinese-American so Dad has her pale skin and dark, sharp eyes. With my blue eyes, they were darker than my family's for some reason. Maybe because my father's Lokoti-Asian dark brown were mixed in?

"B!" I heard Mum call out.

"Yeah?"

"Dinner's ready!"

I opened my bedroom door and skipped downstairs to take my place at the table. I found Dad was home from his meeting with the Tribal Elders and the pack and he helped Mum serve dinner. They shared the jobs around the house like cooking and cleaning in equal measure, which included raising their beloved only child.

"How are you B?" He smiled.

"Good thanks Dad. What's for dinner?" I watched my parents serve up in the kitchen.

"Roast Duck and vegetables." He answered. "We've got plenty of food here, it looks like we have enough leftovers for the next two nights."

"I was expecting Derik would be staying for dinner." Mum said.

"That boy's got the appetite of a Werewolf alright, although he's human." He let out a laugh.

Dad carried our plates over to the table and placed mine in front of me before taking his seat. Mum followed after him and she poured us all a glass of milk each.

"Is this Great Grandma's special gravy recipe?" I paused before I picked up the gravy boat.

"Of course." She answered.

I picked up the gravy boat, poured a generous amount over my plate and then I started to pass it to Dad.

"Your mother first." He nodded towards his mate whom he doted upon.

I held the gravy boat for Mum as she finished doling out our glasses of milk. She took it from me, poured it and then passed it to Dad, coupled with a small smile. He beamed back, before he cleared his throat and turned my way.

"Are you going to Ben's bonfire tonight?"

"Yep." I answered as I picked up my cutlery.

"You'll be home by midnight, OK?"

"OK."

"Ask Derik to walk you home." He added on.

"Why?"

"Because I'm old fashioned." He said simply.

"Huh?" I gave a funny look.

"In the olden days it was the custom for men to walk women home." Mum informed.

"Why?"

"Well, safety was the primary issue." She shrugged.

"But I'm safe as nothing ever happens here. The pack keeps out strangers and outsiders." I scoffed as I ate. Dad shared a knowing look with Mum, which I caught. "What is it?"

"How did the meeting with the Tribal Elders go?" My mother asked my father.

"Remember how we were talking a couple of months ago how Alma is starting to become repopulated again? Apparently there is a bad element brewing in the town. The Elders have been approached by a representative of the town who asked if the pack will remove the trouble makers." He told her.

Mum arched her eyebrows in surprise. "What's the consensus of the Elders?"

"They're thinking about it." Dad said. "What happens in town does affect our tribal lands. A couple of times when we've been on patrol we've had to warn off some of the new townspeople who've been poaching on our land."

"What's poaching?" I asked.

"It's when somebody hunts game or wildlife on somebody else's land... so in fact that they're killing somebody else's animals to eat." She explained.

"Isn't that stealing?"

"It's definitely trespassing." Dad said staunchly. "They feign ignorance, but twice I've caught the same group of men doing it."

"The same group of men who are the bad element?" She guessed.

"Your father and brother told me when they've been on patrol how they've also moved this group of men on, when they've been drinking on our land." He said unhappily. "The last six months we've had the most problems with these particular guys."

"So how many people are we talking about here, that the pack has been asked to play law enforcers by removing?" She asked concerned.

"Around twenty." He answered.

"And the townspeople have tried asking them to leave?"

"The townspeople have."

"And what happened?" She pressed.

"They beat up the town's representatives of the three men and one woman. A week later the hoodlums reopened the old Bar and are serving moonshine, attracting more of a bad element." He said flatly.

Mum glared down at her plate, losing her appetite which I could tell as she just pushed the food around instead of eating it.

"They hit the woman?" I looked at my father in alarm as he gave a nod. I wanted to clarify, "they actually beat up the woman?"

Dad looked like he was regretting talking about this now, as he looked on guiltily.

"Hang on." I put down my cutlery. "They – the men – the baddies in the story, HIT the woman?"

"Unfortunately that's what baddies do, B." Dad said softly, as he reached over to put his hand over mine.

Flabbergasted, I looked back... I hadn't heard of men physically harming women except in the books I've read. Aside from the tribe's story of the second last time a Lokoti Werewolf feasted on human was 300 years ago in vengeance of the English soldiers who had kidnapped six Lokoti women; the very last time a Lokoti Werewolf tasted human flesh was three months before I was born. A group of over 500 invaders who were sick, starving and desperate, tried to invade our tribal lands since unpolluted land safe from nuclear fall out was precious and rare.

I had grown accustomed to the blissful domesticity that our tribe had worked hard to create. Ours was a world where doors were left unlocked, everyone knew each other's names and we had many tribal celebrations. Sure, things got sad when somebody died? But with the miraculous skill of our Medicine Man my Grandpa, he used his Werewolf supernatural senses to accurately diagnose and offer treatment. The highest cause of death in the tribe was simply old age.

Our festivities centered around the change in the seasons, or when it was somebody's birthday, or when the tribe threw a Housewarming for a couple whom moved in together. Ben's bonfire tonight was to commemorate the last night of the summer. All the tribe's young people would be there to 'hang out' and sip soda which was only served on special occasions since it was becoming a rare commodity now.

"So I would prefer it if Derik walked you home after the bonfire tonight." Dad patted my hand before he returned to his eating.

"Why?" I asked again. "No baddies or strangers make it past our boarders with the Werewolves patrolling."

"Call it peace of mind." He said coolly.

"But Derik lives at the bottom of the hill, twenty minutes away. So he'll have to walk me home, twenty minutes up the hill and then back home again, twenty minutes back. That's over half an hour out of his way." I debated.

"I don't think Derik will mind." My mother smirked to my father.

"Not if he's hoping for a kiss for his effort." He smirked back.

"Mum! Dad! Shut up!" I turned bright red. My parents cracked up laughing at how quickly my face's colour changed. "Besides as my father, aren't you meant to be chasing my suitors away?"

"If your 'suitor' was a hoodlum or a baddie, yes I would chase him away. But this is Derik we're talking about here. He's been your best friend from the age of 0 – 16 and your boyfriend since." Dad shrugged. "He's a good boy."

"He's NOT my boyfriend." I looked down to concentrate on cutting up my food. "Derik's my best friend but that's it."

"What is with the women in your family?" Dad looked on Mum, who looked inquiringly back. "Your father took a while to woo your mother, it took me a while to woo you and now Derik is up against the same wall around our daughter?"

"Stop exaggerating!" She rolled her eyes. "My Mum had me when she was 19 years old and I had B when I was 19 too. I wouldn't call that strong opposition!"

"Ah, but your father fell in love with your mother when he was 14 and I fell in love with you when I was 2 years old." He arched his eyebrows. "It took me sixteen years to finally make a mark or put a dent in your exterior."

"Oh excuse me for not becoming pregnant when I was 13 years old!" Mum said sarcastically.

"I saved your mother's life when she was 5 and I was 7 years old." Dad began the old story.

"Here we go." She sat back and folded her arms.

"She nearly drowned when the river flooded after a bad storm. She was down there by herself, which she wasn't allowed to do when she was that age. I sensed she was in danger and I reached her first." He recanted the tale.

Mum and I exchanged smiles of amusement as we listened to him retell the story I've heard repeatedly since I was a little girl.

"I've always known that your mother is the woman for me. But getting your mother to see this point of view was another story." He gave her a goofy grin. "When your mother was 7 years old, she started running away and hiding from me. When she was 14, I asked her out on a date but she turned me down. From the ages of 14 to 18, I kept asking her out and she continued to turn me down. She was so stubborn, she would probably still be doing that; but then I saved her life a second time when she was 18 and I was 20 years old and from that day on, I could finally call her my mate."

"Now I'm stuck with him for another 100 years." She pulled a face, making me laugh.

"But she secretly loves every minute that we're together." He pulled a face too, continuing the laughter.

"Your father has his bearable moments." She conceded with a sigh.

"My heart still races when your mother walks into a room." He sighed too.

My parents shared one of their typical meaningful long glances across the table.

"Er, kids in the room." I said uncomfortably as I stood up from the table and carried my plate into the kitchen. As I put my plate in the sink, I enquired, "do you want me to wash up?"

"No, you go on to the bonfire." Mum said.

"And remember, let Derik walk you home." Dad ordered.

*****

I arrived at the bonfire in Ben's back yard just before seven o'clock and found a large crowd of young people, between the ages of 12 to 22 already here.

Ben was two years older than me and was a mechanic along with Declan and Uncle Finn. The garage they worked at was beside the general store/ gas station. The boys called themselves 'grease monkeys' and played loud rock music all day as they worked on a car or motor bike or boat engine. Declan may have been an arrogant asshole, but Ben was pretty cool. He was human, funny and charismatic. He's been holding bonfire parties in his parent's large back yard since he was 14 years old.

"Hey Ben." I greeted him first, since this was his party.

"Hey B!" He smiled exuberantly, as he shook my hand. "Welcome! Grab yourself a soda. My Mom and Dad are over there, doling them out."

"Thanks." I walked away to let him continue his conversation before I interrupted. Ben was talking to Feather, one of the tribe's prettiest girls.

"Hi B."

"How's it goin', B?"

"Good to see you, B."

I smiled as I said the expected pleasantries back to the familiar faces that I grew up with as I walked to the drinks table. I saw Derik was talking to Pan, a boy who was a year older than us. He noticed my arrival and waved me over. I waved back and mouthed 'in a minute'. He understood and turned back to continue his conversation.

"Hi Mr. and Mrs. Shallow Water." I greeted, approaching Ben's parents.

"Hi Bianca." She smiled warmly. "How are you? How is your mother?"

"Good thanks."

"Say hi to her for me, won't you." Mrs. Shallow Water said. "Now what soda would you like?"

I looked at the bottles of root beer, creaming soda, lemonade and cola.

"I'll go the cola please." I pointed.

"Wise choice." Mr. Shallow Water smiled and then he jokingly went on. "It's a good year and was picked during a good harvest. It has a sweet flavor with a fizzy bouquet. Perhaps madame would like to sniff the beverage before consuming it?"

"Oh Cliff!" She laughed at her husband. "Take no heed of him Bianca. Here, enjoy your drink." She passed me my plastic cup with the soda inside.

"Thank you." I giggled at the both of them and then I turned around and I was about to head towards Derik, when I almost ran into Daniel.

"Bianca!" his eyes widened.

"Oh, Daniel! Sorry!" I laughed. "I didn't mean to walk into you."

"No harm done, you can walk into me any day." He joked.

OK... I thought that was a bit of an odd thing to say.

"So, what are you drinking?" Daniel asked, looking at my cup.

"Um, cola."

"Good choice, I think I might have the same." He looked at Mr. Shallow Water who nodded and poured him a cup. He passed it to Daniel who immediately took a large mouthful, before he asked, "what have you been up to, B? I haven't seen you in a while."

"Oh um, I'm studying a lot." I shrugged.

"That's right." Daniel nodded. "History, right?"

"Yeah."

"When was the last time you went swimming in the river?" He next asked.

"Wow, what a good question... um, since ages?" I pondered.

"I'm going tomorrow with the usual gang." He nodded towards his small group of friends standing off to the side, who like Daniel, were two years older than me. "You should come along."

"I don't know..."

"Come on, before it gets cold." He recommended.

"Um, I'll see." I smiled uneasily.

Daniel has never asked me anywhere before, he's always just been a friendly acquaintance and nothing more.

"OK then." He half turned away. "Well, I've gotta go back and join my friends. Feel free to come and say hi to them. You'll see that we're actually not that scary."

"OK." I laughed lightly.

"See you around, Bianca." He squeezed my arm and gave a meaningful look, the same kind of look I had seen my Dad give my Mum only half an hour ago…

I stood still to watch him walk off, but as soon as he rejoined his friends he looked back my way. That IS weird! Why is Daniel, this older boy who I hardly talk to, who I thought has never noticed me before, paying attention to me now?

Just then Justin and Leaf walked past to the drinks table.

"Hey B." Justin greeted.

"How's it goin', B?" Leaf asked politely.

"Oh um, what?" I snapped out of it. "Oh, I'm fine thanks. How are you two goin'?"

"Not bad." Justin shrugged.

"I can't complain – no one listens." Leaf said the old joke. Then he paused to look on closely. "Are you wearing mascara?"

"No." I gave him a funny look and so did Jack.

"Oh, sorry! It's just that your eyes looked different for a second then." Leaf blushed and looked down.

"Were you going to try to get some beauty tips or something there Leaf?" Justin laughed and nudged his friend.

"Aw, shut up!" Leaf nudged him back.

"So B, what have you been up to lately? We don't see you around as much anymore." Justin asked.

"Studying." I answered.

"What are you studying?" Leaf asked.

"History."

"What kind of history?" He asked again.

"All kinds of History. I'm reading about Ancient Egypt and Ancient Greece and Rome." I told him.

"Rome? Oh yeah, like gladiators and stuff." He nodded.

"Yeah, something like that." I sipped my drink.

"Do you have a favourite part in History that you like?" He inquired.

"Um no, not really." I shrugged. "I like all of it."

"And how did you get interested in that sort of stuff?" Leaf looked on with wide eyes, almost as if he were drinking in the sight of my face.

I looked from him to Justin, wondering what was going on here? He appeared just as surprised at his friend's sudden interest in me as I was. Justin and Leaf were cool guys, who were two years younger than I was. Leaf was like a little cousin since he was Uncle Ian's son. His father was my father's best friend and another Lokoti Werewolf. But like Daniel, they were just casual acquaintances. Until tonight, I had hardly said 'boo' to them except for polite acknowledgements at social gatherings such as this.

"How did I get interested in History? Um, I don't know... I've always enjoyed hearing the stories about our tribe. I also liked finding out about my Mum's family line from England and Australia." I looked downwards as I felt antsy to get away.

"So what are you doing tomorrow, B?" Leaf asked. "Justin and I and a couple of the guys were going to have a game of soccer..."

...but before he could finish, he was interrupted.

"Alright small fry." Declan suddenly appeared beside me. "The lady's taken. Skedaddle!"

Justin and Leaf's eyes widened by the sudden appearance of the tribe's most dangerous Werewolf, even if he was in human form. They quickly turned around and left to talk to someone else.

"Declan!" I whacked him on the arm as I felt my cheeks burn.

"What?" He gave a funny look.

"What did you do that for?!"

"Oh, you mean you like having all the guys at this party fall over themselves for you?" He looked on unimpressed.

"I don't know what you're talking about!" I felt my cheeks turn from red to crimson.

"No?" He arched his eyebrows. "Either you're the most popular girl here that everyone's inviting to swimming in rivers or to soccer games...but I'm thinking that these guys aren't exactly inviting you to these events for the sport, or that kind of sport anyway."

Declan was looking about with his eyes narrowing and I looked around to see what he was looking at. Beside Leaf and Daniel's eyes looking my way, I actually noticed two other boys doing the same.

"Your popularity has certainly gone up around here." He said stroppily. Then he gave me a peculiar look, "are you wearing a new perfume or something?"

"What?" I took a step away from him. "No!"

"Hey, don't flatter yourself princess." He sneered at my reaction. "I'm here looking out for my brother's interests."

"Excuse me?"

"Derik is just a human so he can't smell the elevated testosterone around you." He sneered as he looked about again.

"Don't be disgusting, Declan."

"Go and stand with my brother and stop flirting with the other boys, would you?"

"Drop dead Declan." I said icily before I walked away.

Instead of walking to Derik, I went over to Rachel and Mandy, two girls my age whom I used to hang out with in school and I still got together with.

"Hi B!" Rachel smiled. "How are you?"

"I'm good thanks Rach. How are you?" I kissed her cheek and then Mandy's.

"I'm OK." Rachel answered congenially.

"How are your studies going?" Mandy asked.

"Pretty good." I gave a nod. "How about with you guys?"

"Yeah, OK. Your Grandpa keeps lending me books to read, to study up on Naturopathy." Rachel shrugged.

"Mr. Lightfoot is lending me text books and stuff as he and Aunt Susan teach me how to do lesson plans. Next year I could start teaching one or two days a week." My other friend informed.

"Gees Mandy, why do you want to go BACK to school for?" Rachel joked.

"Hey at least it will be different this time, as a Teacher I won't have to do homework." She shrugged.

"I wouldn't be so sure about that if I were you." I smirked. "I see my Gran marking stuff all the time when she's at home."

Rachel cracked up laughing and pointed tauntingly at Mandy, who bad-temperedly hit her hand away.

"At least I'll be marking it instead of doing it." She came up as her excuse and then she changed tact. "B, have you ever thought about going to University to study History?"

"University?" I echoed in surprise.

"I saw on the internet that a couple of Universities have reopened, including Cambridge in England. You're part English or something, aren't you?" She remembered.

"Yeah."

"Hence her Lokoti dark hair and her English blue eyes." Rachel laughed.

"You could probably study History at Cambridge." Mandy shrugged.

"Yeah!" My eyes lit up at the idea. "That would be cool! I could study History in a place full of history! And I have relatives in England I could visit."

"You're all set then." Rachel laughed.

"But my Dad says University education is expensive." Our friend warned.

"Mandy, I've heard her English relatives live in a frickin' castle! A CASTLE! I don't think money - or English money - will be a problem." Rachel jibed.

"Plus I'm supposed to be a Circulator." I shrugged. "When my ability to phase starts up, I'll be able to travel back in time, pinch relics and bring them back here to sell for heaps of money."

"Yeah, there's always that." Mandy shrugged.

Just then we were interrupted by Roger a boy who was three years older than us, when he walked up to our small circle.

"Hi Rachel. Hi Mandy. Hi Bianca." He greeted nervously.

"Hi Roger." Mandy gave his sudden appearance a curious look.

"Bianca." He turned to look my way. "Hi... I mean er, how are you?"

What the...? What the hell is going on here?! Is this some kind of joke or a prank or something, with the guys at this party tonight? Am I secretly being filmed as apart of a 'Candid Camera' skit?

"I'm good thanks Roger. How are you?" I replied as I forced myself to be polite, although I felt like taking off and running out of here.

"Me? Oh um, I'm good." He looked down into his drink, which was trembling slightly in his hand. "Um Bianca, can I ask you a question?"

"You just did." Rachel said dryly, making Mandy giggle.

"Oh yeah, I did." He laughed nervously. "But um, Bianca, are you going out with Derik?"

"What?" I looked from him to my other friends, embarrassed. "Um, no. Why?"

"Then would you like to come over to my place for a movie night tomorrow? Or I could bring the movies over to your place...?" He asked hastily, almost forcing it out.

"Um..." I felt my face heat up, "...no, I'm sorry Roger but no thanks."

"Oh..." he looked completely crestfallen, "...um, why?"

"Look Roger, you're a nice guy. But um, I've never seen you more than as a friend." My face flushed as I looked from him and then into my drink. To be honest, I've never seen him more than a casual acquaintance!

"Really?" He looked on pleadingly. "Why not?"

"Because um, I don't know you that well..."

Suddenly I was saved by the bell when Derik walked over and joined us.

"Derik!" I cried out in relief.

My best friend stood next to the intruder, giving him a warning look. But Roger refused to be scared off by Derik who was three years younger than him so he glared back. But then Declan appeared beside him and he looked on Roger... and he skedaddled out of here with out being told.

"I'll see you later Bianca." Roger said annoyed, before he turned around and walked off.

"Wow, you're popular tonight." Derik frowned, watching the back of Roger disappear into the party.

"Is this some kind of joke? Is this a prank? Did somebody arrange this or something?" I looked from Mandy to Rachel then to Derik. "Are people going to next yell out, 'April's Fool'!"

"What's a joke?" Rachel gave a peculiar look.

"I don't know, but that was my first guess. Besides my blind younger brother, I don't know who would see you as attractive." Declan scoffed.

Derik turned around and whacked him! Older brother growled at younger brother, as the two stood tense and angry with each other for a minute or two.

"I told you Daniel was checking her out." Mandy nudged Rachel, inferring me.

"What?" Derik's eyes widened in alarm, as he next looked over to where his competition was standing with his friends.

"But I'm sure it's nothing to worry about, Derik." Rachel laughed and clapped him on the shoulder. "Daniel may be older than you? But you've got way more years in experience by knowing B and by knowing what makes her tick."

"Now that's not something he can boast about, nor would be something difficult to do." Declan muttered into his drink before he was whacked him on the arm again. Then he tossed his plastic cup into a bin two meters away. "Alright, I'm outta here."

"Thank God for small favors." I said sarcastically.

"I'm on patrol tonight." Declan glared at me before he looked at his little brother. "Tell Mom I'll be home at dawn."

"See you." Derik watched his brother leave as did Mandy.

I caught her checking out the back view of his strong build, as he walked away...

"Mandy, no way!" I looked on askance.

"What?" She shyly looked away, but Derik sprung her.

"Why Mandy, I never knew." He teased.

"Shut up." She blushed whilst taking several large mouthfuls of her drink.

"This is just like Shakespeare's 'A Midsummer Nights Dream' with all the awry love going on here." Rachel remarked.

"And Declan is the ass that the Fairy Queen falls in love with." I nodded in agreement.

*****

The rest of the evening passed relatively free of incident, but I grew bored around 10 PM.

"I think I might head off." I excused myself.

"OK then." Rachel said, as I gave her another kiss on the cheek and then on Mandy's.

"We should catch up soon." She said sincerely.

"Yeah, that would be cool." I agreed.

"I'll walk you home." My best friend threw away his plastic cup.

"No Derik, it's OK -" I began.

"I'll walk you home." He repeated as he took hold of my hand. "G'night guys."

"G'night Derik. G'night B." Rachel and Mandy waved back.

I noticed that Roger, Daniel and Leaf, watched us leave as they stood apart with their different groups of friends. I looked away from the party as I focused my gaze on the road ahead. We left Ben's place and headed towards the wood-encrusted hill, where I lived. At first we walked in a comfortable silence, as I looked upwards and stared at the stars...

"I can't wait for the day when I can travel to Mars and Taurus Six by myself." I sighed.

"Really?" Derik frowned. "Why are you so anxious to leave?"

"I'm not 'anxious' to leave... I just can't wait until I can phase there and not rely on my Mum or my Gran taking me." I shrugged.

"OK." He looked on ahead whilst tucking his free hand into his pocket.

"Oh." I remembered something else on this note. "Mandy told me tonight that Cambridge University in England has opened again."

"B, I know where Cambridge University is." Derik chuckled.

"Sorry!" I playfully poked him. "But anyway, have you ever wondered what it might be like to go away and study somewhere like that?"

"Um, yes and no... I don't know." He shrugged. "I mean, sure I want to further my education, but I don't know if I could live overseas to do it."

Then we turned quiet for a couple of minutes. We walked along the dirt road in the dim light, but in the starlight I could make out the pot holes so I knew when to step over them. But Derik seemed to have a harder time making anything out in the darkness and at one stage he nearly tripped over!

"Aagh!" He cried out, but I quickly caught him.

"Are you OK?" I held him steady.

"Er, yeah... good reflexes you've got there." He said, impressed. "I can't see the pot holes in the road properly."

"Really?" I asked in surprise. "I can see everything pretty well in the starlight."

"Are you kidding?" He sounded further surprised. "It's so dark, especially with the trees blocking out most of the light."

I stopped us in our tracks. "Derik, you don't have to walk me home..."

"B, don't be stupid." He said adamantly as I caught him blush. "Of course I'm going to walk you home."

I laughed as I shook my head, "no wonder my Dad likes you; you seem a lot alike."

"Yeah?" He sounded surprised.

I shrugged, but he didn't see me shrug. Actually, I don't think he could see much of anything. I had to take hold of his hand and guide him, as he was veering off all over the place.

"You know what?" I started to slow. "I don't think you should walk me home, as you can barely see where you're going."

"I'll be fine...." He started, but then he tripped over a rock on the road! I caught him a second time as I helped him return to his feet. He laughed, embarrassed. "Woah! You ARE strong and you see well in the dark! Are you sure Lokoti women can't turn into Werewolves?"

"Yeah, I'm sure." I giggled. I stopped us in our tracks and when he tried to pull me onwards, I ended up pulling him back. I said firmly, "Derik, this is the end of the line for you. I don't want you to walk back by yourself and break your neck."

"Yeah, I guess you have a point." He chuckled. "Or I could walk you home and maybe borrow a torch for the walk back?"

"There's no need. You've walked me more than halfway home now. You should go home yourself." I said resolutely, but Derik sighed disappointedly for some reason. I watched his nervous look appear on his face. "What?"

"This isn't the walk home that I imagined taking you on." He sounded regretful. I gave him a funny look, thinking that this was an odd thing to say, but I don't think he saw that either. "B, do you remember that afternoon by the river a few months back?"

"Derik, we've spent many an afternoon by the river."

"Yeah, I know. But I mean the afternoon we kissed for the first time, our first French kiss for the both of us." He said awkwardly, shoving his hands deep into the pockets of his jeans. Oh oh... my stomach lurched as I felt tension tighten my shoulders. He went on, "I know we kissed just so we could get out of the way our first kiss with anyone? But I liked it and I liked kissing you that way. I know that you see me as your best friend, but don't you think that's good grounds to base a relationship on?"

"What, am I next going to start kissing Rachel and Mandy like that?" I laughed at his logic as I gave a playful shove.

Derik laughed uneasily before he rolled his eyes, "just in case you do, make sure Declan isn't around. Otherwise he'd probably lose his self control."

"Huh?"

"Never mind."

We turned quiet again and I noticed how we fell into an uncomfortable silence which was unusual for us. I caught Derik looking away, frowning deeply. Oh oh, don't tell me that I'm in jeopardy of losing my best friend, because I don't want to kiss him?

"Look." He spoke in a low voice. "B, couldn't we just try it?"

"Try it? Try what? We've already tried kissing..." I said confused.

He took hold of my hand to pull me to him. "Try seeing me as more than a friend even if it's just for a moment, or even for a little while. Just see me as grown up Derik, instead of childhood friend Derik."

Now he put his arms around my waist...Frickin' hell, what do I do? Do I push him away? Can I turn around and run home? But most importantly, do I really want to hurt my best friend?

This was the thought which stayed me. I forced myself to remain still when he bent his head forward to kiss me. I had to use all of my self control and staying power to not gross out. It's not like this was deliberately torture, but I didn't feel that way about Derik... I just didn't.

BANG!

We pulled apart to look about in fright.

"Did you hear that?" He asked worriedly.

"That was a gun shot." I said anxiously. "It sounded far away, like it was coming from the border between Lokoti land and Alma."

BANG! BANG! BANG!

I ended up clinging onto Derik's top as he held me tighter.

"Come on, let's get you home!" He turned us around to speedily walk us up the hill with his arm about my shoulders.

BANG! BANG! BANG!

The shots rang out through the still night, echoing through the trees... the noise seemed to wash over the woods and reverberate through the darkness.

"What the hell is going on down there?" I uttered out, afraid.

My stomach knotted as I fretted about which two Lokoti Werewolves who were on patrol tonight, were up against THAT?

Suddenly I stopped, "oh no!"

"What?"

"DECLAN is on patrol tonight!" I cried out. Derik froze as a look of utter dread spread across his face. I grabbed hold of his hand as I began to run us back down the hill. "Come on!"

"Where are we going?" He objected.

"To your house!" I barked back. "If anything has happened to Declan, the Lokoti Werewolves will bring him there where Grandpa will treat him!"

Now he ran faster and we bolted whilst holding hands, all the way to his house.

*****

He barged through his front door, with me right behind. We found his mother dressed in a nightgown and robe, pacing up and down in their small lounge room.

"Derik!" She tearfully held out her arms and her youngest son rushed into them to comfort her. "Did you hear that?"

"Yeah, I heard it." He said unhappily.

"I had just turned off my light and settled down to sleep when I heard it!" Aunt Susan's eyes watered. "It's Declan's turn to patrol tonight."

"Yeah, I know." He walked her over to the couch to sit her down. "But remember what Uncle Em says about European Werewolves, which Declan is? They're stronger and faster than Lokoti Werewolves so I'm sure he'll be OK."

I nodded encouragingly, "Grandfather says Declan is the strongest and fastest of the pack."

"And he's a fast healer." Derik went on. "Remember the time he accidentally nearly cut his finger off when he was helping you cook last year? Remember how much blood there was? Declan completely healed from it in two hours and he was right as rain."

She turned away to quietly cry into her hand which was in a tight fist, pressed against her mouth. Poor Aunt Susan, I felt bad for her. She lost her husband and now her eldest could have been harmed?

I too was worried, not just for Declan but for the Lokoti Werewolves who were family members or friends, who took turns patrolling the borders. I know Dad wasn't rostered on tonight, since he patrolled last night. Two Werewolves patrolled at a time, to cover our vast territory. I hoped it wasn't Grandfather or Uncle Julian's turn tonight. I sank onto the couch which was opposite Derik and Aunt Susan's seat.

"This damned, damned war..." Aunt Susan sniffed, "...I thought moving up here, would have got us away from the looting and the chaos."

"Well, it has." Derik squeezed her shoulder. "I mean, how many times has something like this happened since the whole time we've lived here?"

"Declan's not even 21 years old." She trembled with emotion. "He may have been patrolling the border since he was 16 years old, but he's too young for this kind of responsibility and danger!"

I kept my mouth shut, as I recalled the fact that Uncle Julian and Dad began patrolling the borders when they were 16 or 17 years old. They started as soon as they were turned, right after the war. Their Lokoti Werewolf genes were activated from the deaths of their grandfathers, who died in altercations with marauders. Aunt Susan saw my uneasy look and shook her head at herself.

"I'm sorry B." She said weakly. "I must sound like an ingrate sitting here and complaining. Your family and the Lokoti people have done a lot for us. But when you've already lost your husband and now something like this happens to your son?"

"Shhh." He pulled her into his arms. "Shhh...Mom, it'll be alright."

I kept quiet as my legs jiggled nervously. I exchanged a worried look with Derik before we both looked away at the same time.

*****

I contacted Mum on Aunt Susan's walky-talky to let her know where I was . In return, she told me Dad had rushed out of the house before the first gun shot was heard, to be back up. She had used the walky-talky to contact Gran, who told her that Grandfather had done the same thing. Aunt Susan's eyes widened as she and Derik listened in.

"Oh no! Oh no!" She panicked as she cried harder.

"It's alright, it doesn't mean anything's happened to him. It's standard procedure." I quickly reassured. "Every time there's trouble, the whole pack runs to help. Usually when they fight altogether, nothing bad happens."

Then I sat back down on the couch to wait with them.

*****

One hour stretched to two...two hours stretched to three...the clock on the wall read the time as 1.30 AM. My eyes were stinging and I felt cold because I was tired. I curled up on the Sabre's old, beat-up couch, as the three of us continued to wait it out.

I recalled my earlier conversation with my parents over dinner. I frowned as I remembered what Dad said about the trespassers and poachers. Next, I shuddered as I relived Dad telling me that the baddies hit the woman, who went with her male colleagues to ask them to leave town. I wonder if what was happening tonight because of the same element?

The longer we waited, the worse Aunt Susan's shaking became. I felt bad seeing her like this since she was usually a strong, independent woman. Her chastisements could even put Declan's ferocious temper, in its place!

My Aunt raised her sons with a loving but iron fist, with the help of my Gran and Grandfather whom Derik and Declan appreciatively called 'Uncle Em' and 'Aunt Arabella'. Sometimes even Mum and Dad helped out with babysitting duty, as Derik and I spent many hours either building cubby-houses in the woods, or playing games. Grandfather was probably the closest to Declan though, with the amount of time the older Werewolf took the younger one out hunting to placate Declan's demanding European Werewolf bloodlust.

Gran once told me that Grandfather felt the most responsible for Declan. I think it's because of the night the Sabre family arrived on tribal lands.

It was Grandfather who shared his blood with the dying Declan, because his mate declared the Sabre's family. The pack were at first reluctant to have a foreign Werewolf in their midst, as at first they doubted they could train his bloodlust to hunt animal instead of human. But it was through an incredible amount of will power, stubbornness and most of all love; that Grandfather succeeded where the pack thought that he would fail.

Aunt Susan, Gran and Mum got on like a house on fire, as the three of them would sit together at tribal gatherings and laugh until the cows came home. My Aunt was a strict but sometimes funny teacher, who I greatly respected. So to see her sit there, shaking like a leaf? This was a new experience seeing her this way. I wish I had a better handle of my abilities as a Circulator, so that I could just make all of this somehow go away.

Yet she could still surprise me, because although she was in the throws of panic about the safety of her first born? She still noticed how cold I looked.

"Derik, get B a blanket from the linen cupboard, would you?" She broke the silence.

"No, I'm fine." I sat up, but he was quick to jump to his feet and obey her command.

He smiled warmly as he returned with the blanket to put over my legs, which I appreciated. Then he returned to his mother's side as they sat, holding hands... but he snuck lots of looks in my direction.

By 1.30 AM Declan hadn't come home yet nor had the Lokoti Werewolves carried him home.

"I think this is a good sign." I told them. "If something had happened to him, they would have brought him home by now."

Aunt Susan nodded vaguely, but she didn't look convinced. I snuggled under the blanket then I lay my head on the arm rest to let myself doze for a little while.

*****

It was still dark when I woke up from hearing the backdoor open in the kitchen. I sat up as I watched Aunt Susan and Derik jump to their feet.

"Declan!" His mother cried out as she threw her arms about her eldest.

I watched the family reunion through the kitchen doorway. Declan had just pulled on the spare bathrobe which always hung on the back of the kitchen door, when his mother pounced on him.

He would pull off the robe just before he changed into his shape of a European Werewolf and then he would put it on again, when he reverted back to human. Unlike the Lokoti Werewolves who could still wear jeans in their humanoid werewolf bodies, when Declan changed his form completely altered. It was because of this, he couldn't wear any clothes since they were torn apart.

"Declan, is that blood?" Aunt Susan cried out as she pulled back to look on.

I saw his left shoulder had dried blood on it, which was rubbing off onto the white bathrobe.

"Relax Mom, it's almost healed." He sighed.

"What happened?" Derik asked his older brother.

"Those stupid drunks from Alma - that's what happened!" He growled unhappily. "I'm OK, but Jack isn't."

Aunt Susan and Derik turned quiet as my stomach sank.

"Is Uncle Jack badly injured?" I asked from the couch.

Declan looked past his family as his eyes settled on my position in a grim look.

"Jack took two bullets to the brain, removing half of his head as another tore through his heart." He said unhappily. "He didn't survive."

My eyes filled with tears as my throat tightened. Uncle Jack... is dead? I mean, he wasn't literally my Uncle; we used the term 'Uncle' as a sign of affectionate respect. Being one of the pack was more than just belonging; Mum once told me that the Lokoti Werewolves were not just empathic with their mates, but also with each other. There was even a rumor that they had limited telepathic ability. It was why Dad would suddenly leave the house and run out the front door with no word where he was going, like what happened tonight.

The European Werewolf released his human brother and mother and started to walk past where I was sitting, when he stopped to look down.

"I'll just get some clothes on and I'll drive you home." He said flatly.

"No." I tearfully shook my head. "There's no need and you're wounded anyways. I want to walk."

"I can drive B home." Derik offered.

"I said I'd do it so I'll do it!" He suddenly said angrily, startling us all. Then he left the lounge room and went into his bedroom to dress.

*****

Neither Declan nor I said a thing, as he drove me home in his old, light blue, pick up truck. The sky was just starting to lighten with the onset of dawn and I felt cold, tired, hungry and emotional. Tearfully, I stared out the window for the short trip and couldn't wait to get home so I could cry openly.

His vehicle chugged up the steep, dirt road as we drove past my families houses before Declan turned into the driveway of Mum and Dad's. He pulled up in front of my veranda and left the engine running.

Just as I was about to hop out, Declan suddenly put his hand over mine. He squeezed it tightly which made me pause, as my breath caught and my heart began to race... I didn't look at him nor did he look at me.

The heat of his hand actually began to travel up my arm and magically warm me all over, his grip was strong as it was tight. I even began to feel his thumb start to caress my palm, putting butterflies in my stomach. I sat there unmoving, not breathing and not blinking. Neither of us said a thing, leaving an eerie quietness in his truck.

Next, I felt his fingers entwine with mine, making my eyes widen as I stared ahead out of the windscreen. My butterflies grew worse, flying into a flurry; making me tremble when his fingers pressed into my palm and massaged it with his finger tips. His touch was both direct and yet tender.

Unconsciously, I started to squeeze his hand back but then my front door opened and Dad walked out. Automatically, he pulled back his hand as he still didn't look my way.

"Go get some sleep." He said shortly.

Finally I started breathing again, almost hyperventilating when I quickly opened my door and climbed out. I accidentally slammed the door shut, as I walked around the truck and up my veranda steps. Dad gave a nod to Declan, who quickly reversed out of our driveway to drive off back down the hill.

I collapsed into tears in my father's waiting arms and he squeezed me tightly before leading me inside the house.

~~~~~~
~~~~~~

~ 2 ~

4th September 2084

Uncle Jack's funeral was held in the traditional period three days after a Lokoti's death. Dad drove Mum and I down to the Holy Grounds, by the river just off to the side of the community centre. There, the rest of the tribe had convened where I saw the typical scene of a Lokoti funeral. In the grassy glade before the three Sacred Totem Poles sat a large, rectangular, wooden funeral pyre.

The council of nine Tribal Elders which included Grandpa, were dressed in the traditional way. They were wearing old suede clothing with face paint, of the Lokoti Wolf claw mark going down the side of their faces. Dressed as such, they led the funeral chant to a drum beat.

Uncle Jack's family stood at the front of the crowd, as everyone stood in a semi-circle about the pyre.   Four members of the Lokoti Werewolf pack, carried Uncle Jack's body up to the pyre on a stretcher made from two branches with a large, leather pelt in the middle. We couldn't see Uncle Jack's body though, as it was wrapped in the woven, funeral shroud.

The funeral was held at sunset of the third day of death, because of spiritual reasons. It had to be exactly in this period, to guide the deceased's spirit into the next life. The funeral ceremony could go for an hour, but the body would burn all night. Then in the morning, the deceased's ashes were sprinkled into the river. The river was very important to my people, as it was vast and interconnected to the other major rivers in Alaska. Eventually, it made its way to the Bering Sea and then the Pacific Ocean. But the river wasn't just vital to geography, but it was seen to represent the ongoing nature of life, in relation to our beliefs.

The Circulate which was once made up of Circulators and Calculators, believed that the timeline is the surface of the space time continuum. Those that have special gifts and have been trained like Circulators, Calculators or those with ESP, can 'see' what was ahead in the timeline. Another belief the Circulate and the Lokoti had in common, was reincarnation. By sprinkling the deceased's ashes into the river, it was the metaphor of returning the person's spirit into the timeline so that they can be reborn, further down stream in another era.

I watched the four carefully place the body on top of the pyre. Then Grandpa lit the wood with a fiery torch that he was holding. I looked away when the flames approached the body, before it was completely engulfed in heat. As the body burned, the nine Tribal Elders stood in between the pyre and the three Sacred Totem Poles, continued to sing the Lokoti funeral chant to the beat of the drum.

I couldn't watch the body catch on fire, I just couldn't. Even if it was wrapped in the woven funeral shroud, it seriously creeped me out! As I looked away, my eyes fell upon the people standing up the front of the crowd, just across. To be honest, I wasn't really looking, but I was staring blankly ahead. I could have been gazing upon Julius Caesar, without even noticing.

Just as my blurred vision started to come into focus, I realized that I was staring at Declan. My worst enemy was staring right back, which gave me a jolt in surprise. I was looking directly into his bright blue eyes which made me embarrassedly look away.

Frickin' hell, if he wasn't the worst person in the world I could have been staring at? Attila the Hun would have come a close second. But when I had to look away from the pyre again, I found myself gazing his way once more.

Declan was still staring in my direction, or was he glaring? He was wearing his traditional scowl with his hands shoved deep into his jeans pockets, as he stood beside his mother and brother. He didn't look away either. Declan didn't seem to care if anybody noticed who he was looking at or scowling at, rather.

Isn't this just great? So far my only two options are to stare at a dead guy on fire, or the rudest boy in the tribe. I gave up on looking at either, as I closed my eyes and turned to bury my face into my father's arm. I think Dad must have thought I was overwrought with grief, as he next kissed the top of my head and squeezed my hand tighter.

As the Tribal Elders sang, I used this opportunity of self-imposed privacy to think about Uncle Jack.   I remember him coming to my house a couple of times, to talk about pack business with my father. The two would leave the house and go stand at the end of the driveway to talk privately. Sometimes Uncle Ian as well as Ian's younger brother Grant, would be with them for these conversations since they were members of the pack too.

I remembered how Uncle Jack was devoted to his wife and family just as all of the Lokoti Werewolves were. Uncle Jack and his wife were something like 70 years old; but because he was a Werewolf he aged slower than his human mate. It looked kind of funny seeing them together about the community, at how this man who appeared in his forties held hands with an elderly woman, or even when they kissed. As was customary with Lokoti Werewolves and their 'mate for life' policy; they in no way looked on their wives with any less love. When their mates died of old age, they mourned them deeply. It became the custom that Lokoti Werewolves didn't take another mate after the death of their first.

Opening my eyes again, I looked on the elderly Aunt Meg who was being comforted by her grown children. Poor Aunt Meg, I guess she and Uncle Jack had always expected that he would outlive her. As I looked on his surviving family, I started to realize something else... What was usually the way, the eldest son's Lokoti Werewolf gene would be activated upon the death of their father or grandfather. But the typical age bracket for a change to take place was between 10 – 25 years old. Uncle Jack's son was 30 years old, so he was too old for the change and his son whom was 9 years old was too young.

Hmm, I wondered who else could be activated instead? I guess I'd find out on the next full moon, when a human Lokoti changed to become the fifteenth member of the pack. As my eyes started to scan the other male members of the tribe between 10 – 25 years old my gaze met Declan's once more.

He was still glaring at me for some strange reason. It was seriously starting to make me feel VERY uncomfortable. I shot a scowl back his way, before I concentrated on staring at the tips of the flames, as they danced in the evening sky.

~~~~~~

<div style="text-align: right">7th September 2084</div>

Last night I went with Mum and Dad to dinner at Gran, Grandfather's and Great Grandma's house.

They lived in the old Riverclaw family home which looked like a huge log cabin. Uncle Julian lived with Aunt Danika and their children in another house built at the bottom of the hill. Mum, Dad and I lived in a house which had been in Dad's family for several generations. All four of our houses along with Grandpa and Nana who were Dad's parents, were situated on the same road on the forest encrusted hill.

Their house was just slightly down from ours and was a seven minute walk. But Dad and his Lokoti Werewolf overprotectiveness, we still ended up driving there for a whole two minutes, including the time it took to reverse out of our driveway and into theirs.

As we pulled up, we saw Uncle Julian's four-wheel-drive before us in the driveway which meant he, Aunt Danika and my cousins Phoenix and Phoebe were here. When we went inside, I also found Grandpa and Nana were here too.

"B!" My father's parents were the first to greet. I rushed into their awaiting arms to receive numerous kisses.

Nana cupped my face as she examined me closely. "You're looking taller every day! You're even bigger than me now!"

I smiled in good humor on my slightly shorter, Chinese-American Nana when Grandpa distracted me by pulling me into another embrace.

"Bianca Grace, I swear you are looking a little taller and since I'm the tribe's Medicine Man my diagnosis is usually right." Then my Lokoti Grandpa affectionately messed up my hair.

"Grandpa!" I complained as I pulled away from his roughing-up.

"Fern, stop it!" Nana joking chastised. "Don't you know that hair is very important to a young woman?"

"My bad, sorry Ling." He smiled in good humor as he apologized to his mate before he tweaked my nose. "Sorry B."

I giggled back as I was next pulled away from Grandpa's arms and into my Uncle Julian's.

"B!" He boomed. "You little heart-breaker! What's this rumor I heard that you and Derik Sabre are engaged?"
~~~~~~

Uncle Jules was doing his typical ribbing, but my parents didn't look like they appreciated that particular joke.

"Shut up Uncle Julian!" I poked him in the side.

"Give her a break, Jules!" Mum glared at her twin brother. "She's not even 18 years old."

"But that didn't stop Hunter." He laughed as he nudged my father.

Dad threw him a warning look when I was pulled into my fourth embrace so far with Aunt Danika. She was also English and she had pale skin, brown eyes and dark brown hair. She and Mum were actually third cousins. I guess that was the type-set for my family, we either had blue eyes or brown.

"B!" She kissed both of my cheeks in the French style as her great grandmother had been this nationality as well as a telepath.

It was thanks to her great grandmother that she was bilingual as well as a mind-reader. Belle Dupont met my great, great grandmother, Elisha Worthall when she researched ESP for SSIT – Supernatural Scientific Investigative Team. Belle married Xavier Bell, her work associate who ran SSIT with her. Ironically, their daughter later married Elisha's son, Bastian Worthall. However she had more in common with Elisha than marriage; all of their supernatural abilities were carried on genetically. Now with Aunt Danika's marriage to a Lokoti Werewolf, their daughter was a mind-reader like her mother and their son was destined to join the pack.

"Bonjour Aunt Danika." I greeted.

"Bonjour madamemoiselle Bianca." She returned. "Comment allez-vous?"

"Bien." I managed to remember the reply.

My 12 year old cousin Phoebe next looked up from her drawings as she sat at our grandparent's dining table.

"Salut!" She gave a little wave.

"Bonjour petite belle." I walked forwards to plant an affectionate kiss on top of her head.

I hope I just said, 'hello little beauty' otherwise I could be in trouble. But as I saw Aunt Danika next fall into a catch-up with my Mum, I assumed I was in the all-clear.

"Hi bitch-features." Phoenix said casually, as he didn't look up from his homework he had brought.

Ah yes… here was Phoebe's 14 year old brother. Our relationship was an affectionate enmity which was similar to sibling rivalry. If I had been standing any closer I would have whacked him and given him 'what for' with his use of language. But then I didn't have to.

"Phoenix!" Grandfather growled at his grandson as he came out of the kitchen to lightly punch him on the arm as a warning.

"Oow!" Phoenix instantly complained as he rubbed the spot where his fist had landed.

"Grandfather." I smiled as I walked into yet another embrace.

"B." He squeezed me affectionately. "How are you?"

"Good thanks." I answered before I pulled away to walk into one last hug.

"B." Gran rubbed my back as she held me firmly. "How is the 'Last Circulator'?"

"I still can't phase." I sighed as I looked on defeated. "I swear it just isn't gonna happen Gran."

"Of course it's going to happen!" She spoke in her English accent which could sound very crisp sometimes. "You're the 'Last Circulator'. You certainly wouldn't be called that if you couldn't very well circulate, would you?"

It was thanks to our international ties, we were some of the few families in the tribe to call our mother's 'Mum' instead of the American custom, 'Mom'. Gran's English accent remained constant, but sometimes she could slip into Australian slang as her grandmother had been this nationality. Elisha had married the English Jarrod Worthall, who had been the Lord of Blythe Castle.

"Mom, B's here." Grandfather turned his head to speak to Great Grandma who was busy cooking in the kitchen.

Great Grandma now came out of her favoured domain to give a smile and a kiss on the cheek before doing the same to Mum and Dad. She didn't talk much and she was one of these old-fashioned types who never complained. She just did what had to be done and she knew what her strength was, her wonderful cooking. Great Grandma's recipes were renown through out our tribe, in particular her gravy recipe.

She was full-blooded Lokoti and her deceased husband had been a Lokoti Werewolf whom died in saving Grandfather's life when he was a boy. Great Grandfather was run over by a Logging Truck which from the size of the vehicle, not even a supernatural creature such as the Lokoti Werewolf could survive. After his demise Grandfather took his father's place among the pack. It was also because of this Grandfather and his mother were close. When my grandparents married, Gran simply moved in them and the family welcomed her with open-arms.

I looked past my grandparents who were standing in the kitchen entranceway; at the food that was in mid-preparation sitting on top of the kitchen bench. "What's for dinner?"

"Roast caribou and vegetables." Grandfather answered.

"And Great Grandma's special gravy?" I asked hopeful.

"Of course." He smiled with a twinkle in his eye.

Then I stood back to let them greet my parents. Grandfather kissed his daughter on the cheek but when he shook Dad's hand, he mouthed the words; "we need to talk." My father looked from him to Uncle Julian and Grandpa, as he immediately guessed it was about 'pack business' then he nodded.

"Excuse us." Grandfather now turned to the rest of the room. "We just have to duck outside for a moment but we'll be right back."

He led the way with Grandpa walking a close second and then Dad and Uncle Julian behind, as they departed via the front door. I noticed how the older women didn't look surprised by their sudden exit.

Once they were gone, Aunt Danika whom could read the men's minds, said; "it's about Jack's death and the bad element brewing in Alma."

"I thought so." Mum frowned. "Hunter said that the Tribal Elders had been considering the town's representatives request to move the bad element on."

"I guess Jack's death only confirmed their decision." Gran sighed.

However Great Grandma redirected the conversation to protect the Werewolves private talk. The elderly woman looked on my youthful grandmother. "Arabella, can you please check on the bread rolls in the oven? Danika, can you please help me shell the peas? Jess, you can cut up the pumpkin."

"And me, Clara?" Nana stepped forward to volunteer her services.

"Ling, can you please peel the potatoes?" Great Grandma requested.

Next, I moved out of the way as all of the older women streamed into the kitchen to busy themselves with matters other than worrying about their husbands playing law keepers.

"Ha ha!" Phoenix teased. "Women belong in the kitchen."

"Phoenix!" Aunt Danika barked at her son. "You can set the table thank you very much!"

"D'oh!" He complained 'Homer Simpson' style.

"Ha ha!" I pointed at him .

Since Phoebe had to tidy up her drawings so Phoenix could set the table for dinner, I took her outside to sit on the veranda steps with me. I also brought her as I had a secret agenda and she knew this, as she was used to me 'borrowing' her telepathic abilities now and then.

We looked out at the woods that surrounded the house as we pretended to talk about something when really we were eavesdropping. The male Werewolves were standing at the end of the driveway and talking quietly, well outside our hearing range. Phoebe and I deliberately didn't look their way as we whispered.

"So, what's up?" I prompted my little cousin.

She frowned as she stared at a particular tree across the driveway, "they're talking about fighting."

"Fighting the bad element in Alma?" I queried as I too stared at the tree.

"Uh huh."

"When is this going to be done?"

"Soon...they had been planning to wait until the next full moon when a new Werewolf turns to make the fifteenth member of the pack? But they decided that they can't wait that long." She whispered.

"Do they know who's going to be activated?"

She shook her head, "they don't know for sure but they think it's gonna be Uncle Ian's son, Leaf."

"It makes sense." I thought out loud. "He would be the right age."

Just then she added on, "oh, they already removed half of the bad element the night that Uncle Jack died. They're planning moving on the rest."

"OK." I purposefully kept my eyes averted. "How many bad people are they going to be sending away?"

"Um..." she frowned, "...I don't know. They're not thinking specific numbers."

Suddenly we were interrupted by Aunt Danika walking out of the front door to give us a warning look.

"Phoebe," she started, "what did I tell you about eavesdropping on deliberately private conversations?"

"I'm sorry Mummy but B asked me to." She pouted.

Aunt Danika held open the door and motioned us to come inside. Before I disappeared into the house, I looked over at Dad standing in the distance. I saw him frown when he saw what my Aunt was doing. Frickin' hell, I'm probably in for a 'what for' now.

A couple of minutes later he, Grandpa, Grandfather and Uncle Julian returned to the house. As Grandfather went into the kitchen to help his wife and mother with the cooking; Dad walked over to where I was sitting on the couch with Phoebe and he didn't look happy.

"You and I are going to have a conversation when we get home, at how it's not only rude to eavesdrop but how it can be for safety reasons as well." He said gruffly.

Then I watched him go and stand with Grandpa and Nana.

"Frickin' hell." I rolled my eyes. "I'm gonna get it now."

"Yeah well, at least you're older than I am." Phoebe said annoyed. "You're old enough to leave home if you wanted to. I'm gonna get it much worse than you."

Hmm... leave home? That notion reminded me of what I had wanted to discuss with my family tonight. I wondered what the reaction would be to the idea of me going away to study History at Cambridge University? Would my parents or my grandparents object?

Phoebe's mouth fell open as she stared in surprise, having just read my thoughts.

"Shhh!" I hissed at her. "I'll ask them over dinner so don't say a thing!"

"Oh, now you want me to be quiet?!" She stood up in a huff before she flounced off to go and be picked up by her father. Uncle Jules readily did as he put her on his back whilst he talked to the other adults.

I'll give it to Phoebe, even though she was probably in just as much trouble as I was over the 'eavesdropping' thing? She could certainly work the room. She was cute and she knew it and all she had to do was give her father or grandfather a certain kind of look and they would scoop her up into their arms whether they were angry or not.

Twenty minutes later, everyone sat down to a set table that was laden with food. A huge haunch of roast caribou sat at the head of the table as several dishes followed, full of home-grown vegetables or bread rolls and of course, there were two large gravy boats for Great Grandma's special gravy.

Grandfather sat at the head of the table with Great Grandma sitting on the other end and the rest sat in between. As he busied himself with carving up the meat, we all took turns to serving ourselves with vegetables or bread rolls. I broke open my roll before I reached for the butter when I soon found, Phoebe wasn't just good at divulging people's secrets to me but she was also good with sharing out mine too.

"Where's Cambridge University?" She asked her father.

"Cambridge University?" Uncle Julian echoed. "Well it's in Cambridge, in England."

"Hence the name, Cambridge University." Phoenix snickered.

"It's where many of your ancestors studied." Grandfather explained. "Like Elisha Worthall, Xavier Bell as well as Jarrod and Bastian Worthall."

"Oh." Phoebe pondered on his words then she looked my way.

Now everyone else looked my way too, suspecting that she asked this question as it was on my mind instead.

"Thanks Phoebe." I rolled my eyes before I slightly changed the subject, "Mandy told me and then I saw it for myself on the internet today that Cambridge University is open again."

"Yeah, Mum told me last week that Oxford has reopened too." Aunt Danika added on. "As has Kings and a few other of the old private schools and colleges in the UK."

"Why are you asking about Cambridge, B?" My grandmother asked.

"Didn't you go to Cambridge, Gran?"

"No, I did my Environmental Economics degree at the University of London." She answered. "Why, are you thinking of doing a degree?"

Now was the moment, I looked from Gran to Mum as I announced, "I'm wondering what it would be like to study History at Cambridge."

Suddenly Grandfather dropped the carving knife which clattered loudly onto the table as he, Uncle Julian, Dad and Grandpa looked my way in alarm.

"I think that's a wonderful idea!" Mum said brightly. "I always wanted to study Literature at a place like Cambridge but I couldn't because it was too soon after the War."

"It still IS too soon after the War!" Dad said indignantly.

"No it's not." Mum disagreed.

"Yes it is." Uncle Julian agreed.

"No Julian, it's not." She glared at her brother.

"It is, Jess." Grandpa said seriously.

Mum looked in surprise his way and then to Dad whom she next asked, "why is it too soon?"

"Come off it Jess!" He sounded annoyed. "Eighteen years ago you took us to Blythe Castle in England to scare off looters from attacking your English family! Now you're going to let our daughter live there?"

"It's not safe." Grandpa frowned.

"But the Worthall's haven't had problems with looters for years." She tried as next she looked at her English cousin, "it's safe now, isn't it Danika?"

"It's safer than what it used to be." My Aunt shrugged. "When I talked to Mum last month she said that since the reinstatement of the police force; crime has really cut back."

"Sweetie." Uncle Jules turned to his wife, "we don't think it's a good idea that B leaves tribal lands."

"But why?!" Mum cried out in frustration.

"Because Jack was killed by the bad element in Alma, the same kind of people who could be in England." Grandfather said unhappily. "The same kind of people would see a healthy young woman who is unaffected by sickness or starvation and try to claim her like they have tried to the other lawless towns about this planet."

Mum's face fell as she deflated at her father's words.

"It doesn't mean that B can't study." Dad was quick to put his hand on her shoulder. "She can study while living here."

"Yeah I mean, if Cambridge University has opened up then surely it or other universities would, have courses people can do via correspondence." Uncle Julian shrugged.

But my mother wasn't going to be dissuaded easily and she kept up the fight.

"B," she looked my way, "what did it say about safety at Cambridge University? I mean if students are going to study there, what did it say about that?"

"That half of the Colleges at Cambridge like Holy Spirit College which are open again, have extra security in the dormitories... like state of the art alarms and locks." I recited from memory. "And the University has security guards walking around campus 24 hours a day."

"Oh yeah, I feel better now." Dad said sarcastically. "I'm really going to be able to sleep well, knowing that an alarm is able to fight off attackers for my daughter."

"So far the crime rate in Cambridge is keeping down." I told him. "I mean if it wasn't then I doubt that the University would have opened again."

"Nor would it be attracting any students who were afraid for their lives." Mum glared.

"I could ask my my mother when I talk to her tomorrow night via satellite phone about the safety of Cambridge." Aunt Danika offered.

"No." My father put his foot down. "If B is going to study History at Cambridge University then it's going to be done via correspondence!"

"No!" My mother fired up. "B is a free young woman, who can't be chained to a kitchen sink or tied to her parent's apron strings! She's nearly 18 years old! She's intelligent and she's good at studying. If she wants to go to University then she'll go to University!"

"Jess!" He growled at her.

"Hunter!" She growled back.

Frickin' hell, my parents were fuming at each other! I've seen Mum fire up at Dad plenty of times and usually he could calm her down or use jokes to diffuse the situation, but not today.

As all of this went on, I noticed that Great Grandma remained silent as she usually did. She calmly continued to serve herself then she patiently waited for Grandfather to finish carving up the meat.

"It's not safe Jess!" Dad said adamantly.

"How would you know if it's safe or not in Cambridge?" Mum crossed her arms.

"Because I've patrolled these lands for the past twenty-one years since the War and I've battled what's on the outside trying to get in!" He said vehemently. "And you should remember what is trying to get in, Jess! You should remember very clearly what nearly happened to you nineteen years ago!"

"THAT was nineteen years ago!" She shot back. "So what now, Hunter? Is my daughter now going to be victimized because of what happened in the past? I'm not going to let her turn into a prisoner!"

"Um, guys?" Uncle Julian put up his hand. "Besides safety being the main issue here, how about money?"

"Money?" Mum echoed. "What money?"

"Exactly." Grandpa said pointedly. "What money can be found to pay for Cambridge University?"

Now Nana looked sad over this topic, "I had a savings account before the War which had a couple of thousand I inherited when my grandparents died. I was saving it for Hunter's future." She passed her son a rueful look. "It could have been used for B. But with the collapse of the economy after the war and the bank going bankrupt? I think everyone's in the same boat."

"Money wouldn't be a problem." Gran said simply.

Everyone but Grandfather looked on in surprise.

"Why won't it be a problem, Mum?" Uncle Jules queried.

"There's one multinational corporation that survived the collapse of the world's economy and it's under Circulate control." She continued.

"Hodge Endeavor?" Grandfather guessed.

"Hodge Endeavor." She confirmed.

"Hodge Endeavor!" Mum's face lit up. "Of course! Whenever I fetch Vincent from Circulate HQ on Mars, to take him to Blythe? He says he sends commands to the company. He's said he's even sat in a couple of the board meetings in London!"

Dad moaned as he rubbed his face hard, as a sign of frustration.

"So if B wants to go to University in Cambridge or study elsewhere, then it won't be finances stopping her." Gran passed a smile my way.

I grinned back as I allowed myself to feel hope. Grandfather sighed loudly as he knew his wife long enough despite their deceptively young appearance; that once Gran's mind was made up there was no changing it.

"But can we please make sure that Cambridge University is safe first?" He tried.

"Of course. I'll ask Mum tomorrow and I'll get back to you immediately." Aunt Danika promised.

Phoebe looked from her mother to her grandmother who was sitting on the right from her grandfather.

"Can I go to Cambridge too?" She asked brightly.

"Of course you can sweetheart." Gran declared. "When you're 18 years old and you want to do a degree too? We'll support you in whatever decision you make."

Now Uncle Julian let out a loud groan, "thanks B, thanks Jess and thanks Mum. I think you've just doubled the work load for the Lokoti Werewolves because now we won't just be patrolling Lokoti land? But we'll also be patrolling Cambridge University as well."

I accidentally let out a snicker as I briefly pictured my topless and changed Werewolf relations, stalking across the University campus at night. Then so did Phoebe when she saw what I was imagining.

"What is with the men in this family?!" Mum snapped. "Why do you think it's only the Werewolves that can protect my daughter? Has everybody forgotten that they also have two Circulators with a silver sword each and the access to advanced weaponry?"

Again Dad moaned as he rubbed his face hard with both of his hands... Again Uncle Julian groaned... Grandfather and Grandpa remained quiet as they wore grave expressions.

"Oh great, this just keeps getting better and better." Uncle Julian shook his head. "Now it's not just B and Phoebe who will need protection off tribal lands but it's my sister and mother too!"

"I don't need your protection, I can kick your butt!" My mother turned on him. "I can fight more men than you can without supernatural strength or claws!"

"Oh we can see that Jess." He smirked. "After all, we see you do it every day to poor Hunter."

Just then Dad burst out laughing, as did Grandpa, Grandfather and then the rest of the adults at the table.

"Shut up Julian." She picked up her bread roll to throw it at his head.

~~~~~~

9th September 2084

I waited to cross the road as a familiar black jeep drove past. Behind the wheel, Grant gave a friendly wave and I was quick to return it.

Grant Elm is a nice guy and was one of the few 28 year old men in the tribe who were still unmarried. Since he's an old family friend, he even babysat me once when my parents went to Australia with my grandparents to catch up with our relatives. He was also one of the pack and changed after the death of his father, who died fighting the European Werewolf which changed Declan. He had the Elm sense of humor, but as Uncle Ian was loud and boisterous, Grant was more of the polite type.

Once his jeep was well away, I crossed the quiet road since there was no further sign of traffic. I walked up Derik's driveway and to his front door. When I rang the doorbell, nothing happened. Yep, it's still busted.

I was just about to knock instead, when all of a sudden the door swung open. Declan stood there, looking on unimpressed. I guess he heard me with his Werewolf hearing?

"Oh, it's you." He said flatly.

"Hi Declan." I rolled my eyes as I pushed past him.

"Please, come in." He said sarcastically, slamming the door shut behind.

I walked through their small entranceway and looked into their living room but I couldn't see Derik. So I turned down the tiny hallway to walk towards his closed bedroom door.

"Help yourself." Declan muttered as he watched me go.

I ignored him as I knocked loudly. I could hear loud grunge music playing on the other side, which instantly turned down before the door opened. Derik's eyes immediately lit up when he saw me.

"B! Hi!"

"Hey Derik." I smiled whilst I walked into his bedroom.

I could feel Declan's frown as he watched me go into his little brother's room. Derik immediately shut his door behind to ensure our privacy as I went and sat on his bed. I pulled out my laptop from my bag as soon as I was seated.

"I have to show you." I said as he moved to sit beside.

I rested my computer on my lap after dropping my bag. I turned it on and instantly opened up the wireless connection to the internet. I went to my
~~~~~~

'Favourites' and selected the Cambridge University website as Derik looked over my shoulder, interested.

"Mandy was right." I told him excitedly. "Cambridge is open again and has been for a couple of years now. We can apply if we wanted to!"

"Really?" His eyes widened.

"And check this out," I went to the History Department's page, "I've read the entry requirements and with the War, not many people have a High School Diploma. But they're accepting copies of the applicant's academic work like essays and stuff with the application papers to review them case by case!"

"Oh my God..." he looked impressed, "...that's ah, that's something."

"We could apply together!" I gushed. "We could even start studying there next year!"

"Um, B?" He pointed out something on the screen. "It says here the University currently doesn't have any scholarship programs, that they only accept cash upfront. Um, we don't have any money."

"Derik, money doesn't matter." I said as I knew he was talking about his family specifically.

"It doesn't?" He gave a funny look.

"No because you're a Sabre."

"And?"

"You're part of the Circulate too."

"Er, what does that mean?"

I shook my head impatiently, "it means that your Great, Great Grand Uncle Mike Sabre was a Circulator. He was a member of the Circulate and they have access to Hodge Endeavor funds!"

"Who's Hodge Endeavor?"

I huffed as I went to my 'Favourites' again and next I opened the homepage for the multinational company. Then I had to smile at his gaping as he read about the large corporation.

"How the hell do I have access to THAT company's money?" He asked in disbelief.

"The Circulate controls Hodge Endeavor!" I punched him on the shoulder as if he should have known. "Your Great, Great Grand Uncle who was a Circulator, sent your family here to live with us. Hodge Endeavor will pay for your education!"

"It will?" He looked on in amazement.

"Sh-yeah!" I punched him on the arm again.

"Oow!" He laughed as he punched me on the arm back. "That hurt!"

We laughed as we began to play fight, with the two of us whacking each other. Abruptly there was a knock on the door and Derik immediately jumped up from the bed to answer it. When he opened the door, I found Aunt Susan standing there.

"Hi B." She customarily smiled warmly.

"Hi Aunt Susan." I smiled as I gave a little wave.

"I thought I heard your voice." She walked into Derik's bedroom. "How are you?"

"I'm good, thanks." I nodded.

"How are your parents?"

"Good thanks."

"How is your Great Grandma?" She asked next, smoothing back her graying blonde hair as her blue eyes sparkled.

"Good thanks." I nodded.

Aunt Susan didn't have to ask about my Gran or Grandfather, as she saw my grandparents on a regular basis with teaching. Grandfather may not have taught in a classroom, but in the summer months he wasn't adverse to taking the younger members of the tribe on nature walks, through the National Park.

She looked at her watch before she looked back, "you'll stay for dinner, won't you B? It's getting close to that time."

"Um..." I frowned, as my parents were expecting me home.

"There's tiramisu for dessert." She taunted.

"I'm in!" I said quickly.

She and Derik laughed at how quickly I snapped at her bait.

"Dinner will be ready in thirty minutes." Aunt Susan announced before she left his bedroom.

"Thanks Mom." Derik saw her out and closed his door behind to give us privacy again.

"Why didn't you tell her?" I gave him a funny look.

"I'll tell her and Declan over dinner." He shrugged, before coming to sit beside again. He looked momentarily at the website for Hodge Endeavor before he looked back my way. "So, how is this big corporation going to give me money again?"

"Gran is in contact with them." I explained. "She's always remained in contact with the company. She even has a special liaison that sees to any of her requests, kinda like a PA or something."

"She does?"

"She'll tell the liaison about you." I shrugged casually. "The liaison will sort out both of our course fees."

"You're kidding."

"No."

"Just like that?" He marveled.

"Basically." I shrugged again. "But we may both have to write formal letters with our applications, like a cover sheet explaining why we want to study at Cambridge."

"What courses can we do?" He angled my laptop his way.

"I'm going to do Ancient History." I said gleefully. "What are you going to do, science?"

"Um," he hesitated before he answered, "I'd be interested in studying Medicine."

"Medicine?" I echoed in surprise.

"Well, yeah." He admitted. "I've been thinking about it for a while now."

I looked on in shock as Derik is my best friend and I never knew this!

"Why didn't you say anything before?"

"I was going to tell you soon. Grandpa Wisetail said he would take me on as his apprentice and our tribe could have two Medicine Men. But if I could do an Undergrad course in Medicine first, I would be stoked!"

As I watched his excited expression, I started to piece it all together. Derik was always particular to Biology as well as Chemistry. I recalled him talking to Grandpa in private a few times at tribal gatherings, or family dinners when the Sabre's were invited to mine or my grandparent's houses. He's even lent my best friend a couple of medical books upon occasion.

I looked on impressed, "Derik that would be awesome!"

"Thanks." He chuckled. Then he looked at my computer for a moment before he looked back my way. "So this Hodge Endeavor would really pay for me?"

"Sure." I verified. "Remember, you're related to the Circulator Mike Sabre. I wouldn't be surprised if Hodge Endeavor already knew about you guys. I'm sure all my Gran would have to say, 'Mike Sabre's family needs this' and they would open up the company vault immediately."

"Yeah, right!" He snickered, before he looked on with this funny expression on his face. "You and I could actually live at Cambridge together?"

"Yeah." I smiled. "Cool, isn't it? Even though we'll be on the other side of the world, we'll still be best friends and still together."

Derik looked downwards as he picked up my hand in his. "B, I've seen you more than just a friend for two years now."

I felt my face start to heat up as nervously I glanced away. I felt awkward when he talked like this, or looked at me that way. It's hard to think of him romantically other than 'the brotherly type', which really made me feel awkward.

He lifted up the computer from my lap to put aside so he could have all of my attention. However my eyes remained downcast, as Derik moved in closer and then he gently cupped my face. He pressed his lips against mine as I forced myself to remain still, although I wanted to pull back.

I mean I loved Derik, just not in the same way he felt for me. If I push him away, I could lose the best friend I've had my whole life, so I guess I would have to put up with this kissing nonsense now and then.   At least he hasn't tried anything else.   I've heard that two other girls who were my age, have had sex before! Then I wondered if I spoke too soon, as he used his lips to part mine and push his tongue into my mouth! I almost shuddered as I really wanted to stop.

Awkwardly, I tried to move away but he must have thought I was just making myself comfortable or something. He started to push me backwards onto his bed! Oh oh...Quickly I turned my face away, so he started to kiss my neck. Frickin' hell, now what do I do?

Suddenly there was a loud knock and Declan's voice suddenly boomed out, "hey, pipsqueaks!" He had knocked once and then walked into the bedroom.

"DECLAN!" My best friend yelled as he quickly released my waist.

I jumped up from the bed embarrassed! It was almost in light speed, I leapt to my feet with my face burning bright red.

"Dinner's ready." Declan gave a steely-glare, before he turned around and walked out again.

Has it been half an hour already? I had lost my appetite, but I was the first to walk out of the bedroom as I went straight into the bathroom and shut the door behind. I used their sink to wash my hands as I suddenly felt really unhygienic. I even washed my face and neck where Derik's mouth had been. Then I dried off using the hand towel before I took a deep breath and opened the bathroom door again.

Frickin' hell, I wish Declan hadn't sprung us... the worst person in the world who could have seen that, would be him.

When I walked out to the dining table, I saw he was sitting on one side of the table glaring at Derik who was sitting on the other, glaring back. Aunt Susan sat at the head of the table as the matriarch of the family. I sat at the place setting beside my best friend where my plate of spaghetti bolognaise was waiting.

Derik and Aunt Susan hadn't started eating yet, as they were waiting for me to sit down but my enemy was already shoveling food into his mouth.

"Declan." She glared at her eldest. "It's polite to wait until everybody is seated before we begin our meals."

He threw his mother a tired look, but he dropped his fork and sat back into his seat as he chewed on his mouthful. Er, I was sitting down now so can't he eat? Aunt Susan smiled at Derik and I and then she picked up her cutlery which prompted us to follow suit. Declan glared my way next, as he picked up his fork and continued on feeding his face, not even stopping for air!

Whereas the humans politely cut up the spaghetti, the European Werewolf was merely swiveling his fork through it, picking up a huge amount and shoveling it into his oversized mouth. I looked on in disgust... and Mandy finds THAT attractive? He noticed my unimpressed look as he raised his eyebrows. I shook my head as I looked down at my plate.

"B's got a point, Declan." His mother commented.

"Oh yeah, like B's the picture of politeness and morality in this tribe." He sneered.

Derik dropped his cutlery loudly onto his plate as his objection whilst he sent his older brother the look of death.

I quickly changed the subject. "Aunt Susan, do you still make your own pasta? I noticed that the Store never has any."

"Ah yes I do B." She answered. "Speaking of which, I've got some extra lasagna sheets you can take home to your mother. She told me that she wanted to try making lasagna soon."

"Cool." I gave a nod.

"Your Mom said your Gran has an old family recipe of lasagna. But when she was telling me about the method, I didn't think there was enough cheese in it. Now, I know we can't get any parmesan cheese around here, as the only cheese that this tribe makes is tasty. However I recommend that you put extra cheese into the béchamel sauce as well as on the top of the dish." Aunt Susan instructed.

"OK." I nodded, before I turned quiet for a minute or two as I thought on how Aunt Susan and Great Grandma were alike. "You know, you and Great Grandma are the only two women I know who has a list of old family recipes. I mean, Gran has the recipe for lasagna and toss salad dressing from her Australian family, but that's it. I don't think the Worthall's passed down any recipes to Gran, as before the War the family had Housekeepers or Cooks and chose from different menus."

"Cooking is an important tradition in many Italian families." Aunt Susan pronounced. "When my family as well as Anthony's left Italy after World War Two, they brought the recipes with them. In the old culture, cooking was a family activity as well as social ritual."

"Mom told me that in the old days, they would let the bolognaise sauce stew all day, whilst they made the pasta by hand." Derik turned my way.

"Really?" I looked on in surprise.

"It's true." She verified then she smiled on her sons. "Derik isn't really interested in that part of his heritage, but Declan's got a gift for it. Declan and I can sit at this table for hours, making spaghetti, fettuccine, lasagna sheets or pasta spirals."

"Declan?" I looked on the great oaf sitting across in further surprise.

"How do you like your pasta tonight, B?" He returned smugly. Then he shot off a look to his little brother. "If Mom, heaven forbid, dropped dead tomorrow... Derik would be screwed. He can barely boil an egg!"

"Yeah well Declan, there are more important things to life than just thinking with your stomach." Derik said coldly.

"You and your books," he sneered, "like THAT'S going to get you anywhere!"

"How about Cambridge?" Derik said gloatingly.

Declan paused in his eating to look on in surprise. "Say what?"

"Derik?" Aunt Susan gave her youngest an inquiring look.

"Cambridge University is open again and B will be applying to study History there." He boasted, causing Declan to throw me a shocked look next.

"You're leaving?"

Huh? Why is he taken aback by this? I was expecting a smartass retort like, 'good riddance' or something from him.

"B says I could go with her and do an Undergraduate's course in Medicine." Derik told his mother. "I don't need to do a Masters or a PhD because Grandpa Wisetail said he'll take me on as an apprentice Medicine Man."

"Say what?" Declan's mouth fell open as he looked back at his little brother.

"Derik!" My Aunt beamed proudly on her youngest son.

"Since the War, not many schools are open so kids like us, can complete their High School Certificates. But we're able to submit assignments with our application papers to be reviewed on a case by case basis." He went on.

"I'll help you pick your best work to put together." She quickly agreed. "Your biology essays were always the best in the tribe, especially your last on the immune system. I don't think we can submit them in your handwriting, but we could borrow Arabella's laptop and portable printer and type them up -"

"Hang on hang on hang on!" Declan interrupted before he strangely laughed to himself, "Mom, I'm sorry to be the slap of reality here, but how exactly are we going to pay for all of this?"

She looked on her eldest as if his words really were a slap and her face fell.

"No problem." Derik said coolly.

"No problem?" He arched his eyebrows. "I don't think the University operates on a barter system like we have here in the tribe, Derik. You won't be able to trade in dead moose or caribou to pay your way through." He looked coldly my way before he looked back on his brother. "B as I understand, has English relatives that live in a castle full of rich and expensive old things that can pay her way. But what have you got, Derik? What has this family got which will pay for all of this?"

His little brother looked away to tell their mother, "B showed me this website for a company called Hodge Endeavor which will pay my way."

"Hodge Endeavor?" Her eyes widened with recognition. "They will pay for your tuition, like a scholarship or some such?"

"We came to Alaska to live because a letter from our Great, Great Grand Uncle told us to. He was a Circulator in the Circulate. The Circulate run Hodge Endeavor. Because of Mike Sabre, B was telling me that we have access to Hodge Endeavor money. They'll pay for Cambridge." Derik explained.

"Who's Hodge Endeavor?" Declan asked skeptically.

"They're one of the few multinational companies which survived the War." Aunt Susan said, before she looked my way in confusion. "B, I understand that with you being a Circulator in the Circulate along with your Mom and your Gran that Hodge Endeavor will pay for you. But why will they pay for Derik?"

"Because of who you are." I told her. "Your late husband Anthony was Mike Sabre's Great Grand Nephew. Because you're related, you have his access to Circulate funds through Hodge Endeavor."

Declan dropped his fork loudly onto his plate and pushed it away, looking cranky for some reason.

"So, my brother is a millionaire because of a distant relation?" He asked in disbelief. "Well, I don't need my job at the Garage anymore!"

"You have access to that money too Declan, if you should ever need it or even if you had some kind of inkling towards bettering yourself!" I snapped.

He stood up in a rage so suddenly, his chair fell backwards onto the floor! I blanched as his blue eyes flashed glowing green, with his circular pupils turning into narrow slits. Then he growled under his breath before he turned around and stalked out of the room...

... BAM! I think he slammed his bedroom door behind him so hard that the wood started to split! I looked guiltily to Aunt Susan, who actually didn't seem surprised by her eldest's temper tantrum, but just a little sad instead.

"Sorry." I said uneasily, then I looked to Derik. "I just thought he was wrong to put you and your dreams down like that."

He smiled appreciatively as he put his hand over mine.

"No B, it's alright." She sighed. "I think Declan is jealous. Not about Derik's education, since he's never been one for school or homework. But he can't leave Lokoti tribal lands, like Derik is being offered the chance to. Being a Werewolf, there aren't many places he can go where he can change and hunt freely like he can here."

Now I really felt bad. I pulled my hand out of Derik's grasp to stare down at my plate as I lost my appetite.

*****

I didn't stay much longer than that. After dinner, I helped Derik with the washing up. Since I wasn't hungry anymore, Aunt Susan put a piece of tiramisu into a tupperwear container for me to take home. She kindly threw in an extra two slices for Mum and Dad.

Derik tried to insist on walking me back, but I didn't feel like kissing him again which I knew he would try if he did. So I firmly told him that I would be fine and I began my trek alone towards the hill.

I walked out of the community centre and up the steep, dirt road towards my house. The road was well-lit under the light of the full moon and I looked at my watch. It was just after 8 PM, I wasn't sure if Dad would be home by the time I returned, or if he would have left for the hunt with the rest of the Werewolves. Declan had departed as Derik and I were washing up, leaving the house in his bathrobe.

As I walked, I noticed that I started to feel a little crampy in my stomach, as if I had indigestion or something. That's weird, usually my stomach was solid as a rock. Even my immune system was better than most kids in the tribe, as I never got the stomach bug. I didn't even get food poisoning the time the Store accidentally sold bad cheese! I never got the flu either. The only thing that could lay me out was bad period pain, which happened frequently. Yep, the hot water bottle and supply of strong pain killers from the Medical Lab at Circulate Headquarters were my best friends when that happened.

Grandpa as our Medicine Man, would worry over how many painkillers Gran, Mum or I would take when the curse was upon us. He said that we took so many, our bodies were building up a resistance to the drug which was why we had to keep upping the dosage. He tried to replace it with herbal remedies, but they didn't work as well or as fast as the 25th Century drugs our Calculator Vincent was happy to keep us stocked up on.

My indigestion grew worse, as the discomfort was harking on the painful side. But then I wondered if it was indigestion, as I felt my mouth water and I craved something. It was as if my stomach was experiencing was hunger pains. I'm not hungry AGAIN am I? I don't get it, pasta always fills me up and I only ate an hour ago. What's going on here?

I stopped walking to pry the lid off the tupperwear container I was carrying. I sniffed at the tiramisu, tempted to eat some right now. But then my stomach lurched in an objectionable manner. My taste buds told me that my body didn't want something sweet, but it wanted to eat something savoury. It wanted something like – like - like a huge thick piece of red meat that was cooked at such a rare state it was still bleeding freely...

Now that IS weird! Usually I prefer my meat well-done. Where the hell is all of this coming from? Why do I feel this way?   My shoulders were tense and I could feel my heart begin to race. I felt like sprinting the rest of the way home, so I did.

I shut the lid on the tupperwear container before I broke into a run. I easily ran the rest of the way up the hill, not breaking a sweat let alone becoming breathless. I ran up my driveway, easily high jumped over my veranda railing and I threw open my front door to go inside.

Mum looked up startled from reading a book on the couch.

"Has Dad gone hunting?" I asked as I walked past into the kitchen, to put the tiramisu in the fridge.

"No, he's at your Uncle Ian's place." She answered.

"Why is he there?" I walked back into the lounge room.

"With Jack's death, the pack thinks it'll be Ian's son Leaf who is going to change instead of Jack's grandson Meadow since he's only 9 years old."

"Ah," I raised my eyebrows, "and the pack want to be ready to initiate him or something?"

"Yeah, something like that." She sighed. "I think when a human changes into a Werewolf for the first time, their bloodlust has to be controlled. The pack want to be ready to help Leaf so he doesn't take off from the tribal lands and into Alma, to try to eat a townsperson or something."

"Eugh!" I shuddered at the thought. "But mind you, after what happened to Uncle Jack? Maybe we should let Leaf go nuts, particularly on the bad element of town."

"The Tribal Elders along with the pack have decided to help the people in Alma remove the bad element." Mum looked up from her book again. "This will be the first time that the Lokoti will be policing off their land. The people of Alma have always had suspicions the Lokoti Werewolves existed, with the odd eye-witness report here and there. When the invaders tried to take over our land when I was pregnant with you? That confirmed their existence."

"So the people in Alma aren't scared of the Werewolves?" I asked curiously.

"They are wary, yes. But since no good townsperson has ever been attacked by a Lokoti Werewolf, they trust them. The only time they've injured a townsperson was if the they were on our land, doing something they shouldn't. The people of Alma know this. It was one of the reasons why they asked the Tribal Elders if the Lokoti Werewolves would remove the trouble makers." Mum went on.

Her eyes widened in worry when she noticed I was slumped over the back of the easy chair, rubbing my tummy. She asked, "B are you alright?"

"Cramps." I flinched.

"Go to bed and I'll bring up the hot water bottle and some pain killers." She put aside her book to stand up.

"It's not those kind of cramps." I said weakly. "I feel like I've got indigestion or something like it."

She frowned as she walked over to my position to put her hand over my forehead. "Right now your skin does feel rather hot."

"I'm going to go lie down." I turned away. "There's tiramisu in the fridge that Aunt Susan told me to bring back for you and Dad."

"Thanks." Mum watched with concern as I slowly walked over to the staircase.

Whilst gripping onto the banister hard, I slowly made my way up to my bedroom. I didn't even bother to shower or change into my pajamas. Instead I simply lay down on top of the covers as I curled up into a ball. I started to tremble as I experienced hot flushes whilst the pain grew worse.

My mother came into my bedroom carrying a glass of water as she came to sit on the side of the bed to help me drink from it.

"Drink lots of water." She advised. "Maybe your body needs to flush out a toxin of some kind." I nodded weakly, but then I emitted a small smile in appreciation as she began to rub my tummy to ease the pain. She continued, "if you don't start to feel better in a couple of hours, I'll take you to the Medical Lab at Circulate Headquarters. I'll get Vincent to do a scan and check you out."

I gave a final nod, before I squeezed my eyes shut and tried to concentrate on the massage instead of the pain itself. I could feel a layer of cold sweat appear over my hot skin, which made me feel worse...

*****

~ 3 ~

I just managed to fall asleep, but it was such a light sleep that I kept waking up. Every single noise inside the house or even outside, bothered my ears. Even the light of the full moon agitated me and I growled in frustration at the brightness filling my bedroom.

Frickin' hell, I actually growled at it! I sounded just like Dad or another Werewolf when they growled about something. It was deep and guttural as it traveled from my chest, up my throat and through my clenched teeth...speaking of which, they were all aching for some reason.

I'm not talking about just one or two teeth but ALL of them were hurting. Actually come to think about it, my hands were sore as well. It was primarily the skin around my nails which were stinging. I lifted up my hands and looked on them in the moonlight.

Before my very eyes my nails grew longer! My eyes widened as my breath caught in my throat... oh my God! Did I just see that then? Did I just watch all of my nails grow an inch longer in seconds?! Oh oh, they weren't just longer, but they were pointier as well. When I ran my fingers over them, I noticed that they didn't bend and that they were suddenly a lot stronger too.

What the hell is going on here?! What's happening to me...?

My breathing was so hard and fast, it sounded like panting. I began to pant harder as I felt my clothes and especially my blouse, grow tighter and tighter on me as if they were shrinking! Next, I heard the material begin to tear...my blouse is magically shrinking while it's still on me?!

I sat up startled, as I looked down on myself. My eyes bulged when I saw that it wasn't my blouse that was shrinking - it was me that was expanding! I suddenly looked like a bodybuilder or something, as my muscle tone was huge.

Oh my God oh my God oh my God oh my God!

My eyes filled with frightened tears as I gaped at the long, sharp nails and my huge body. However as my lips parted over my teeth, I noticed that my teeth felt sharper against my lips! My hands flew up over my mouth as I felt that all of my teeth were longer and jagged, in particular my canine teeth.

Next, I felt my toenails begin to change. I literally felt the nails on my feet grow long and sharp as they tore out of my socks. Within minutes, I was looking on claws at the end of my feet poke through the tops of my sneakers!

"MUM!" I screamed out... but I didn't just scream, what came out of me was a ROAR! Even my voice had changed! It was deeper and more growly, rumbling out like thunder. "MUM! MUM! MUM!"

"B?"

The sound of her footsteps exited her bedroom and crossed the hallway. She flung open my bedroom door when she looked on in complete and utter horror... Mum looked as if a strange creature had taken the place of her daughter.

"Oh my God B...!" she stood petrified in my bedroom doorway.

I could hear her heart pound as loud as a drum. I could see clearly in the dim bedroom her expression of fear. Hell, I could even smell the blood pump beneath her skin! We stared on each other in terror... I didn't just feel afraid, but I felt wretched that my own mother could look on me if I were a monster and I couldn't stand it!

Quick as lightening, I leapt up from the bed and ran to my window to open it and jump out. But I didn't know my own strength and I broke the glass. Screw this, I'm outta here! I smashed through the remaining shards as I leapt from my upstairs window. I easily landed on all fours, as I wasn't harmed in the slightest.

In awe, I looked back up at the broken window which Mum had now rushed to as she looked out for me. Then her eyes further widened when she saw my crouched position on the ground. I growled at her, angry and hurt that she could be so repulsed by my appearance before I took off into the woods!

Running swiftly barefoot in only my jeans and bra startled me at first. However my heightened instincts guided me safely, as I wove through the trees. I ran in supernatural speed, leaping over fern, bush, log and rock in a single bound.

I was starting to like this, my strength and speed gave me a new sense of empowerment as amazingly I could see everything as clear as day! I ran down the forest-encrusted hill towards the river, with my sensitive ears picking up the noise of the flowing waters hundreds of meters away.

As I leapt onto the river bank I landed on all fours again. I remained in my crouched position, panting not because of the exercise, but because it felt normal to breathe this way. I looked back over my shoulder at the direction I came from. Frickin' hell, I had just run a 25 minute walk from my house to the river within one minute!

I sniffed at the air as I listened to the noises of the night, like the crickets and frogs which reverberated loudly in my ears. But then I smelled something other than the river, or the moist earth surrounding it or the trees and other vegetation of the forest... and it smelled good.

The smell made my hunger pains return as agonizing cramps ripped through my abdomen! I have to eat, I have to placate this horrible hunger! I leapt to my feet and took off through the woods towards the delicious smell.

As I ran in supernaturally fast speeds through the wood, my mouth watered as the delicious smell lured me further on. Right now, it was more tempting than one of Great Grandma's roast dinners with her special gravy. The smell seemed to hypnotize me, as my craving got worse and my stomach pains drove me to run faster.

Oh I need it - I want it - I want to eat raw red meat tonight!

These painful urges continued to drive me onwards as I picked up speed. I was running so fast through the trees towards a direction I know not what, but all I knew was that the smell was this way. But then something else started to happen... I sensed I wasn't alone.

I picked up the sound of footsteps of something or lots of things, chasing me. When I briefly looked back over my shoulder, I saw the forms of my Grandfather, Grandpa, Uncle Julian, Uncle Ian, Grant and the eight other Lokoti Werewolves come through the trees. I spotted their different coloured glowing eyes first and then their topless forms second, as they only wore jeans or tracksuit pants.

They were running after me in a supernatural speed which matched my own. As they were running, they began to fan out to surround me. Oh no, they were coming to stop me, I could feel it. I suddenly felt afraid like I was in trouble for doing something wrong as my Lokoti Werewolf kin came closer. I even heard their unhappy growls.

Suddenly Dad in Werewolf form leapt out in front, cutting me off! His eyes glowed red as he snarled loudly! I stopped dead still, as I faced him off.

"B!" Grandfather growled as he leapt beside, with his glowing blue eyes glinting warningly.

Grandpa landed on all fours on the other side, as Uncle Ian and Uncle Julian took the direct rear of me and the eight other Lokoti Werewolves encircled them. I was completely surrounded...all of their different coloured glowing eyes burned in anger. My heart raced and for the first time in my life, I felt scared of my father and Werewolf relations.

"B, you must come back with us." Grandfather growled.

NO! The scent of the delicious food was getting stronger the closer I came to it and the pains in my stomach were not going away...

"B, you must control your bloodlust!" Grandpa roared. "You have to fight it and you have to learn to master it!"

Bloodlust, what bloodlust? What the hell were they talking about? I wasn't experiencing any kind of bloodlust... all I wanted to do was track down that delicious smell, to make the pain go away.

My heart raced as I sniffed the air. The delicious aroma smelled so close I could almost taste it. I looked from my father to Grant, who was standing behind him as my mind began to work of ways of getting around them.

"B, come home." Uncle Julian growled next, with his glowing yellow eyes.

I shook my head as my refusal then I jumped in fright when Dad edged closer! His red Werewolf eyes hypnotically tried to hold my own as they burned into my very soul... No! Go away! Get away from me! Don't come any closer!

"B, you must come with us." Grandfather ordered.

His glowing blue eyes narrowed, as he watched me suspiciously. All of them started to move in closer, making me feel trapped in and very, very scared...

You're faster than them**,* a new voice spoke inside of me, taking me by surprise. It sounded cold and cunning, ***you're not just Lokoti Werewolf but you're a Circulator too!

The pains in my stomach were so bad that it felt like I was being stabbed! I cried out as I almost sunk to my knees... oh the smell, the smell! I need to eat!

"Come home with us B." Grandpa growled softly.

Run towards the smell the strange, cold voice goaded. ***Run and eat your fill and the pain will go away***

Dad edged even closer as I saw him reach out towards me with his clawed hand...

"NO!" I roared.

In lightening fast speed I first jumped backwards from Dad. When both Uncle Julian and Uncle Ian tried to grab me from behind I leapt forwards as I completely leap-frogged over Dad's crouched form. Next, I streaked past Grant who too tried to catch me.

I bolted away from the Lokoti Werewolves who turned and ran after. I ran so fast that the trees looked like a blur! But trusting my new Werewolf instincts, I was able to weave between the tree trunks in my path.

I ran so fast that even the other Lokoti Werewolves couldn't keep up! I sensed they dropped further and further back until I could no longer hear or smell them anymore. I ran and ran... bolting out of the woods and into a clearing on the south border of our land which separated us from the township of Alma.

Oh, now I knew where I was going and where the intoxicating smell was leading me - straight to Alma. I slowed to a stop as I started to wonder if I should go any further? What if this IS the bloodlust making me feel this way? What if I wasn't running towards an actual food, but towards a person? Was I craving townfolk to eat?

EAT! My stomach hurt so bad, I whimpered as I bent over in pain. ***FEAST! FEED! RED MEAT! FRESH MEAT! HUMAN MEAT!***

Oh no, my mouth didn't just water but my teeth grew longer at these very thoughts. This strange voice kept goading me on. It made me fall forwards onto the ground, as if an invisible hand had pushed me from behind. It was like the voice itself was trying to take control of me.

However, my new Werewolf instincts were also whispering something else... that I wasn't alone. I smelled him before I looked up and saw him.

Declan in European Werewolf form, stepped out of the tree line to the side. My eyes widened with fear as they took in the sight of his huge, hulking, hairless, monstrous body.

I've never seen Declan in European Werewolf form this close before. A couple of times in the past when I was over his house, I had vaguely caught sight of him morphing in his dark back yard before he quickly disappeared into the night. But his size was intimidating as Declan was twice my height when he walked on his hind legs and three times as wide with his muscle bulk, which rippled underneath his hardened hide.

He started to stalk towards me as his razor-sharp teeth glinted in the moonlight, inside of his canine jaws. His bright green eyes with the black slits for pupils were trained my way. He was a light-tanned colour all over, almost the colour of cream. The claws on his hands and feet were black and sharp. He settled on all fours as he engaged me in a face off, ready to pounce in either direction I might run.

Oh oh, now what do I do? I'd heard he was not only stronger than the Lokoti Werewolves but he was faster as well... can I outrun him too? Declan snarled warningly, his glowing green Werewolf eyes flashing as if he meant to say, 'don't even think about it!'

Has he come to stop me from crossing the border too? I guess so, as he walked on all fours to stand directly in front, as if to use his large size to block the way.

In a lightening fast move I tried to duck sideways but in another lightening fast move Declan jumped in front. I jumped sideways in the other direction and immediately he appeared right in front of me again! I jumped backwards a couple of times, to get some distance between us so I could try to run past? But he sensed this and jumped forwards, closing the distance again.

What do I do? I certainly didn't want to get into a fight with him, he would tear me apart! Frickin' hell, now what?

Declan snarled viciously in my direction as he came even closer. He slowly stalked forwards on all fours, tense and ready incase I made any further sudden moves.

In desperation I roared out "NO!" as I took a swipe at him with my right claw! He easily ducked from my blow before he leapt upon me! "NOOO!" now I roared in fear as I couldn't move from his overbearing weight!

I was scared that this was it and that I had gone too far. I was scared that this was my punishment for trying to make it into town to eat a townsperson; of being eaten by Declan. I honestly thought that the punishment for my crime for the attempted eating of a human was to be eaten myself.

Declan's hot breath on my face felt so scorching it could have scalded. His glowing green Werewolf eyes burned into mine and I heard him snarl and snap his jaws! As he lowered his head over mine, I closed my eyes, thinking that this was it. I thought that today was the day I would die...but I didn't.

Just as I was expecting to feel his huge jaws rip into my face or my neck; instead I felt something hot, wet and strong lap at my ear.

When I opened my eyes, to my surprise I found it was Declan's large tongue. He was licking my ear before he moved across my face and over my lips! What was this, a Werewolf kiss? Was I going to get licked to death as Declan slobbered all over me?

My mouth opened in surprise just as my eyes did, when his tongue went right into my mouth and lapped at mine. My heart was already racing in fear for my life; but now I felt it start to pound in my chest because I liked what

Declan was doing. I couldn't stop myself as my tongue started to lap back at his.

He whined softly as he kept me pinned to the ground. Strangely, I even started to like the feel of his claws digging into my skin, which heated up by doing this with him. His two hot, heavy front claws released my shoulders and brazenly rested over my breasts instead. I growled hungrily as I tried to kiss him back, not just by lapping like we really were two wolves licking each other, but I wanted to use my lips. However as I found out, it was frickin' hard trying to passionately kiss something with a snout.

Declan sensed what I was trying to do, so he turned his head sideways and opened his large jaws wider. He set them over the bottom half of my face with his sharp teeth digging into my cheeks. But I didn't mind the discomfort as instead I liked this... especially how his tongue could go deeper into my mouth, which never stopped moving against mine.

As I excitedly clawed at him, it occurred to me; this is what I had been secretly wanting that Derik as my best friend couldn't give. I wanted passion that I just didn't feel for my closest childhood friend. I certainly felt no inclination to do this with him instead.

Declan released my face from his jaws as he lifted up his head and his glowing green eyes glared down. His tongue darted out twice more, as I stuck out my tongue to meet it. Then he moved his large jaws away as he begin to sniff around my face and my hair before he ducked his head to nuzzle my neck. I growled in a satisfied manner as I felt him teasingly use his sharp teeth to even chew on my ear.

This turned me on so I twisted my head around to kiss him again, but for some reason he raised his head higher away. Declan started to snarl again, as if he was angry at me for doing this with him. His Werewolf eyes flashed brighter still...when suddenly he ducked his head in lightening fast speed.

Using his stronger jaws, he gripped the side of my neck and began to bring his teeth down. It sent a sharp, blinding pain up the muscles of my neck and into my brain and – and – and – I think I blacked out?

*****

As I started to come to, I felt myself lying on a cold, hard surface. I opened my eyes and for some reason the first thing I saw was the side of my bath tub. I raised my head as I looked about myself in confusion.

I'm lying on the bathroom floor? What am I doing, sleeping on the bathroom floor like this? I sat up and when I looked down, I found myself still in my jeans and bra and I was covered in dirt. My feet and my hands were the dirtiest and my hair was mangy with leaves in it. I examined my dirty nails, which thankfully looked normal again and I saw that my body was its human size once more.

Slowly I stood up, flinching from my sore neck which felt like I had pulled a muscle, to look on my reflection in the bathroom mirror. My normal face looked back... Did last night really happen? My dirty appearance and my missing clothing like my top, confirmed it did.

I shivered as I hugged myself, as I recalled how the Lokoti Werewolves surrounded me in the woods. A cold chill shot down my spine as I knew why they had acted that way last night - to stop me from running into town and eating a townsperson. My stomach pains along with the craving for human flesh must have been the infamous bloodlust I'd heard of.

Then I remembered something else about last night; I had kissed Declan – if you would call that kissing – while we were in Werewolf form.

I KISSED Declan?! Eugh! B, are you nuts? You frickin' hate the guy! And rightly so, as he was a jerk most days and a complete asshole in between! Then after he made out with me, by probably leaving more slobber on my face than inside his own mouth, he bloody well bit me.

He bit me! He knocked me out cold! But how the hell did I get here, in my bathroom, passed out on my bathroom floor?

I wanted to see my parents and ask them what happened. However when I walked over to my closed bathroom door and I tried to open it; to my surprise, it wouldn't move. It was locked from the outside, which meant somebody had locked me in here.

I've been locked inside the bathroom? Surely this must be some kind of mistake...

"Hey!" I cried out worriedly as I shook the doorknob. "Mum! Dad! I can't get out!"

Just then I heard two voices outside the bathroom door, of Dad and Grandpa talking.

"It sounds like she's changed back." Dad said.

"Let's hope so." Grandpa said unhappily.

After a moment I heard the door unlock and my father slowly opened it as he looked on warily.

"Dad!" my eyes widened when I saw the fearful expression on his face.

"B," he said seriously before he and Grandpa stepped aside to let me pass.

I walked towards my bedroom to get ready to have a shower to wash all this dirt off. But I stopped in my bedroom doorway when I saw Grandfather and Uncle Julian standing in my room, examining my broken window. Oh shit, I had forgotten about that.

Grandfather and Uncle Julian glanced my way, not looking too happy either.   When I turned around, I found Dad and Grandpa right behind as if they were guarding me. I looked from them, back to my relations, confused.

"How are you feeling, B?" Grandfather asked.

"Fine."

"Do you remember what happened last night?" Dad asked.

I tried to joke, "either I went to one hell of a party," I inferred my missing clothes and dirty skin. "Or I turned into a Werewolf last night."

"Can you remember what happened to the window?" Grandfather asked next.

I vividly recalled Mum's look of horror on me, her daughter, changing into a monster, yes. I remember that I felt so sickened at frightening my mother that way that I had to run away from her. Since she was in the bedroom doorway, the window seemed the only other option. My eyes watered as I felt everybody's unhappy expressions which seemed to look on with disappointment.

Do they always look like this when a new Werewolf is created? Or is it just me that's earned this? Are they really angry with the way I behaved last night?

"Mum looked at me like I was a monster... the same way you're all looking at me now. I couldn't bear her disgust, so I jumped out the window." My voice wavered.

"You're not a monster B." Dad said sadly as he put his hand on my shoulder. "But you are the very first female Lokoti Werewolf in the history of the tribe."

"And you're a Circulator." Grandfather frowned. "Last night you ran away from us in the speed of light."

I did?

"It's going to make it harder for us to help you control the bloodlust because we can't contain you." Grandpa said gravely.

I looked back in surprise at them before I echoed, "I ran at the speed of light?"

"You did." Grandfather verified. "I've only seen your mother and your grandmother, other Circulators, move that fast."

This was news to me! So last night I didn't just change into a Lokoti Werewolf, but finally my abilities as a Circulator were also kick-started! No wonder I was able to outrun them last night.

"It's why we had to lock you in the bathroom." Dad said seriously. "If we can't catch you, we can't stop you."

"Stop me?" I gave him a funny look. "Stop me from what?"

"Bianca, you were running right for Alma." He said gravely. "You were hunting human. You would have attacked the town folk, if Declan hadn't of caught up to you."

This hit me like a physical slap in the face; I was hunting HUMAN? That was the delicious smell last night? I nearly killed a townsperson? Declan was the only one who was able to stop me?

I nearly killed last night... I nearly became a murderer... I nearly cannibalized a human being stop the horrible pain!

Eat! My stomach hurt so bad, I whimpered as I bent over in pain. *FEAST! FEED! RED MEAT! FRESH MEAT! HUMAN MEAT!*

Like a blow to the stomach, my legs suddenly gave away and I landed on my arse on the floor. I felt all the blood drain from my face as I stared at my broken window in horror. Mum was right to be afraid... because I'm a killer.

Dad knelt on the floor beside as he tried to put his arms about my shoulders, but I pushed him away.

No wonder they all hate me... I'm dangerous! I felt worse than horror, I felt worse than terror, I even felt worse than wretchedness or guilt. I felt like the Judge and Jury in a high-profile murder case, listening to the sins of the convicted. I was surrounded by evidence that I was now a murderer! And like any murder trial, which I now found myself in... it was time to accept my charges. It was time for my punishment and since bars probably wouldn't hold me for long, it was time to consider capital punishment.

When I thought Declan was going to eat me last night, I realized it was because I was thinking that I deserved it. The bloodlust... it hurt me, tormented me, made me lose my self control. If it wasn't for Declan's actions last night, I could be very well covered in blood as well as dirt.

I'm a killer... I'm a stone-cold killer... I'm even an abomination to the other Lokoti Werewolves!

"Dad!" I grabbed his arm as I looked at him fearfully. "You've still got that hunting rifle, haven't you?" He looked on, askance. "You have to shoot me in the head!" I cried out. "I nearly killed a person last night! The voice and the pain and the hunger... it nearly made me do it! I very nearly did it!"

My father's eyes watered as he looked on worriedly. "We know about the hunger B, and the cold voice that comes from it. It's called the bloodlust. We can teach you to control it -"

"No! No!" I shook my head as I dug my fingers into his arm. "You don't understand - you don't know how powerful it is!"

Grandpa knelt down besid as he looked rueful, "we know exactly how powerful it is, Bianca Grace Wisetail. And we're going to teach you how to control it and in battle, to use it when you fight for your people and your land."

Maddeningly, I shook my head. They don't get it! They don't see my point at all. I'm more dangerous than them!

"But how can you teach me self control when you can't control me and I can't control IT?!" I yelled.

"Bianca Grace!" Grandfather growled fiercely, as his blue eyes flashed brighter in anger. He walked over and knelt by my other side and he cupped my face to force me to look at him. He growled fiercely, "you will NEVER talk that way again! You are now the fifteenth member of our pack. You are one of us! What happens to you affects us all. We felt you change last night. We feel your fear now. We CAN help you and we will! And one of the ways you can start learning to control what's happening to you is to stop fearing IT and yourself!"

Uncle Julian came over to crouch beside his father. "We're all in this together, B." He put his hand on my leg. "The Lokoti Werewolves are more than animal. We're more than human. We are one, it's how we stay strong."

"Welcome little wolf." Grandpa smiled sadly as he reached out and stroked my dirty, matted hair.

No! I don't want this, I don't! The immense power and the freedom that I felt last night as I ran through the woods in the speed of light, using my Werewolf reflexes to weave between the trees? The exhilaration which rushed through me because of it, no longer seemed worth it.

"I don't want this!" I turned to Dad. "Activate someone else! I don't want this! You were at Uncle Ian's house last night, I thought Leaf was going to turn, not me!"

"We can't control whose genes are activated and whose are not." My father said tearfully. "The spirit of the Lokoti Wolf that's combined with the spirit of Aru, the tribe's first Lokoti Werewolf, are the ones who pick the warriors to make up the pack, just as they did in the beginning."

"But it wasn't much of a choice then." I remembered the story of old. "Aru picked the remaining fourteen warriors who were still alive. There are way better choices than me."

"Maybe and maybe not." Grandpa disagreed as he exchanged a look with Grandfather. "Em told me that the Circulate once had a rule that no other Circulators were meant to be born after 1985. But your Great Great Gran, Elisha broke this rule when she gave birth to your Great Gran, Alexandrina, another Circulator. Alexandrina had your Gran Arabella, another Circulator and your Gran had your mother, Jessica yet another Circulator. Now Jess and Arabella tell us that you will be the last Circulator in human history. Perhaps this is the reason why the Lokoti Wolf picked you to become the first female Lokoti Werewolf."

Grandfather nodded back and then he, Uncle Julian and Dad looked on with grave expressions.

"B? B!!" Mum's frantic cry interrupted us, as suddenly she came rushing into my room with Gran right behind her. Both women also crouched down beside with Mum almost knocking Dad out of the way as Grandfather considerately moved aside for his mate. Mum pulled me into her arms and squeezed tightly in relief.

"Mum!" I cried in her arms. "I'm a monster, Mum! I'm a monster!"

"No you're not sweetie," she instantly disagreed, as she released me to look on with motherly love. "You're not a monster, you're a Circulator. Now you're a Werewolf too? Some adjustments have to be made, that's all."

"Adjustments?" I raised my eyebrows.

"Let's find out first what we're dealing with here." Gran said firmly as she looked from me to Mum. "Let's take B to Circulate HQ and get her checked out by Vincent."

"Good idea." My mother nodded enthusiastically.

She and Gran instantly acted upon their idea as they stood up and then they too pulled me up from the floor.

"We'll come with you." Grandfather said.

"OK." Gran gave a nod. "Gentlemen?"

The Lokoti Werewolves were well used to Gran and Mum's mode of travel as Circulators. They had the ability to instantaneously phase to anywhere and anytime of their choosing. As Gran and Mum placed their hands on my shoulders; Dad, Grandfather, Grandpa and Uncle Julian placed their hands on theirs.

In a bright flash of light, all seven of us disappeared from my bedroom in Alaska to find ourselves standing instead, in the Medical Lab of the ultra-futuristic Circulate HQ.

We were inside the habitation dome on the green surface of Mars. The HQ was constructed using 25th Century technology, ironically 250,000 years in the past when the planet still had vegetation. This little hypocrisy, were one of the many that these time travelers could revel in.

Usually I loved to travel by phasing or instantaneously phasing with Mum or Gran. I loved the feeling of having my biological body turned into light as even my very molecules were altered. I liked the rush of warmth and the tingling sensation. I loved the momentary floating feeling of being free from such constraints as gravity or even the laws of physics.

Just as much as I enjoyed traveling like this, I also enjoyed my visits to Circulate HQ. I liked to marvel at the technology of the future integrated with the smooth lines of the uber-modern lay out of the base. Aside from the black floors, glass was everywhere as it was used for doors and of course, the dome that the HQ was inside, allowing as much natural light to come through. Even the computers here were glass-like with specialized crystal chips which had computer programs etched into them that were accessed by concentrated beams of light.

Once upon a time the Circulate was made up 696 people, with two thirds of its members being Calculators and one third were Circulators. This figure increased when Elisha Worthall began a female lineage joining the ranks. What was truly marvelous about this, was the fact that the ability to circulate or even to calculate was not an ability which can be passed down genetically.

'Mother Nature', 'fate', 'destiny' or whatever you wanted to call it, decided on which minority of humans on planet Earth could turn their biological bodies into ones made of light to pass through time. Spread across all cultures and races, Circulators and Calculators were born different. This was supposed to ensure that the Circulate remained an elusive and highly exclusive club. Did this stop Elisha who bore Circulators and even changed a man into a Circulator? Nope! With her ongoing light, she continued to rewrite the history books as she recreated the future.

With the onset of World War Three, the Circulate departed Earth as they evolved from their human existence to one of an eternal nature inside of the space time continuum. As their parting gift to mankind, they were able to dissipate over a quarter of the nuclear blast which protected their remaining human families from fall out.

Our Calculator Vincent Moher, preferred to spend the most of his time here alone, as he and the Circulate Mainframe monitored the timeline of human history. With Vincent as the only Calculator left, he had the task of watching over the last three Circulators in Gran, Mum and me.

Vincent Moher was named after his forefather Vincent Worthall whom Elisha became romantically involved with. In an alternate timeline, Elisha married and procreated with the World War Two Spitfire pilot. However Elisha decided not to follow that timeline and she instead married Jarrod Worthall, a Med student she met at Cambridge who was Vincent Worthall's Grand Nephew. Elisha was such a strong force in the timeline with her bio-electromagnetic frequency being in temporal flux; her progeny to Vincent Worthall didn't cease. They continued to exist apart from the timeline, almost in temporal flux themselves.   The good thing about this was that Gran, Mum and I have a Calculator now in our distant cousin.

Within a minute of our arrival, Vincent who must have foreseen this next walked through the automatic doors of the Lab to greet us.

"Arabella and Jess? I need to talk to you..." he began but he pulled up the moment he saw my disheveled appearance, "...good god B, what happened to you?"

The male Werewolves glared dangerously upon our blonde haired, blue eyed English cousin.

"What's the wrong Vincent, can't you 'see' what happened to B?" Dad growled out.

"Funny you should say that, Hunter." Vincent growled back. "But no I can't. That's what I need to talk to Arabella and Jess about."

"Well what a stroke of luck, coz we came here to talk to you about B." Mum sung sarcastically.

Vincent became aware that all seven unhappy faces were aimed his way.

"What did I do?" He asked, taken aback.

"What didn't you do more like!" Dad fired up. "You call yourself these girls Calculator? Why didn't you see this happening to B?!"

"And if you did see it, why didn't you tell us?" Gran asked in a low voice.

"Hold up a minute people." He held up his hands. "Before we all tie the Calculator to a stake and burn him for either Witchcraft or Heresy, how about I hear the charges first?"

"B's a Werewolf!" Mum cried out.

Silence... Vincent blinked and then he blinked again as he looked on in disbelief.

"You're a Werewolf?" He looked my way.

"She's the first female Lokoti Werewolf in the history of the Lokoti tribe." Grandfather advised.

"You're a Lokoti Werewolf?" Vincent wanted to clarify as he stared in my direction. "So you weren't bitten and changed that way?"

"One of the pack died and B's Lokoti Werewolf genes were activated last night, the first night of the full moon." Uncle Julian put his hands on his hips.

"I thought you understood from the SSIT notes on Lokoti Werewolves that our bite or blood can't turn a human into one of us." Grandpa's eyes narrowed.

"I do remember that fact thank you, Fern." Vincent said in annoyance. "But I also remember that females can't change into one of you and that only the males in the tribe can."

"Well don't just stand there, examine her!" Dad demanded.

"Then if you lot get out of the way, maybe I will!" He snapped back.

The male Lokoti Werewolves all stepped aside from standing protectively around. This enabled Vincent to lead me over to the bench underneath the main scanner to begin his examination. I sat up on the bench and just before I laid down, he handed me a papery smock to wear. Then he helped me to lie in position underneath the scanner.

Vincent gave a curious look before he observed, "B you're taller, plus you're more bulky. I think your height and your weight have changed."

"Has it?" I raised my head in surprise.

My Calculator pushed my head back down then he walked over to the control panel and activated the machine. It hummed to life as a green light ran over my body from head to toe, as the technology collected its readings of my physical changes.

"B, when you changed into a Werewolf last night, did anything else strange happen?" He inquired.

"She ran away in the speed of light." Grandpa told him.

"That explains her higher bio-electromagnetic frequency." Vincent thought out loud. "It appears when your Werewolf genes were activated, it also triggered your Circulator's ability to phase."

Gran and Grandfather stood together, holding hands as they looked on; Mum and Dad stood together holding hands as they looked on; Uncle Julian and Grandpa stood side by side with their arms crossed, listening in to the results.

"Aha!" Vincent remarked. "I was right! You're now 10 cm's taller. You've gone from 160 cm's to 170 cm's tall and your weight has changed from 60kg's to 70kg's with your new Werewolf muscle."

"Am I fat?" Anxiously I raised my head.

"No, but you are bulkier." He replied. "Even your shoulders look broader."

"What, do I look masculine?" Now I sat upright in alarm.

"I wouldn't say 'masculine' but definitely more athletic." Vincent mused.

I looked worriedly to my parents, "but I don't want to look athletic!"

"You've always been a bit of a tomboy growing up." Dad gave a rueful grin. "You always played soccer with Derik and the other boys of the tribe instead of dolls with the other girls."

"Do I look 'butch'?" I looked Mum's way in concern.

"Nah, of course not!" She was quick to reassure as she and Dad came to stand beside, as I was sitting up on the bench. "You've always given the boys a run for their money, so now you can always beat them at sport being a Werewolf."

"Derik's never minded that you were always as strong or as fast as him." He tried to use as his consolation. "I'm sure he won't look on you any less now that you're stronger or faster."

"Don't worry B, it just means that a guy has to work extra hard to impress you." Uncle Julian gave a wink.

Vincent next came back to where I was sitting as did the rest of my family.

"Well." He took a deep breath. "From the read outs, I can see a change in her dental structure, her muscle tissue, the calcium deposits around her nails and even with her irises and her ocular sensory input, which confirm her change into a Lokoti Werewolf."

"My irises?" I echoed confused. "My ocular sensory input?"

"It means that now you can see better in the dark." Vincent put it simply.

"Oh yeah, I could see through the dark woods last night as if it were daylight." I confirmed. Then something occurred to me which made me look at the other Lokoti Werewolves, "did my eyes change colour like yours do?"

"They did." Grandpa confirmed.

"What color did they turn?" I asked out of curiosity.

"Turquoise, like your great, great grandfather Flint Riverclaw's eyes." Grandfather announced.

"They did too!" Mum recalled as she looked from Grandfather to Uncle Julian. "I forgot what colour Great Grandfather's eyes were."

"Same coloured eyes is a family trait in Lokoti Werewolves." Uncle Julian informed his twin. "I have yellow eyes like another Riverclaw ancestor had. Dad has blue eyes like his Dad did. Now, B has Great Grandfather's turquoise colour."

"At least she's keeping it in the family." Mum joked.

"At least we know she's a Riverclaw Werewolf that way." He chuckled back.

"And not a Werewolf from the 'Milk Man' or something?" She laughed.

"THAT'S not even funny!" Dad rolled his eyes at his wife and brother-in-law's sense of humor.

This just made the twins laugh even more as they elbowed each other in their brotherly/ sisterly banter.

"C'mon kids." Grandfather smilingly pulled them up. "Let's focus here."

"The 'Milk Man'!" Mum couldn't stop laughing.

"Actually that IS pretty funny." Vincent even ducked his head as he chuckled. "Pity the poor man should he ever have an affair with a Werewolf's wife!"

My father emitted a low and dangerous growl as he glowered at our Calculator.

"It wouldn't happen." He said staunchly. "We would smell it as well as sense it. Hell, I can smell your testosterone stink on Jess after you hug her or kiss her on the cheek."

That quickly put an end to the laughs, from both his tone of voice and the dangerous look he was giving Vincent.

"Moving right along now." My Calculator cleared his throat as he straightened. "B should start her training as a Circulator now that her ability to phase has started."

"Yes, about that." Grandpa spoke up. "We need to find a way to stop her."

"Stop her?" Vincent gave the older Werewolf an incredulous look for suggesting it. "Now I see where Hunter gets it from when he tried to stop you from training your ability." He looked to Mum.

Grandpa ignored this as he glared, "last night B ran right for Alma. She ran as a new Werewolf from the bloodlust as she ran as a new Circulator in the speed of light."

"Oh." His face fell as he now caught their meaning.

"We need to find a way to stop B from running in light speed to Alma until we teach her control over the bloodlust." Grandpa said firmly.

"I see." My Calculator frowned as he thoughtfully stroked his chin.

"Vincent, what did you have to talk to Mum and I about?" My mother queried.

"What?" He gave her a funny look.

"When we first arrived and you walked through the door to the Lab, you started to say that you needed to talk to us about something." She reminded.

"Oh right! Yes!" He suddenly remembered. "I needed to talk to you about B."

"What about me?" I asked.

"I can't calculate for B properly using the Viewing Room or with the Circulate Mainframe because her energy signature in the timeline keeps disappearing at odd intervals." Vincent announced. "And now that I've found out she's now a Werewolf? That might explain it."

"What do you mean her future keeps disappearing?" Mum asked concerned.

"B is the Last Circulator." Vincent began to explain slowly.

"Yep, we got that memo." Gran said coolly. "What's your next point?"

"And now she's the first female Lokoti Werewolf." He went on.

"Yep, we also got the notification for that too." Dad crossed his arms.

"I didn't see this happening to B." He said, looking flustered. "I can't see half of what's going to happen to her, because there's something blocking my sight as well as the Circulate systems. B's future is cloudy because her bio-electromagnetic frequency is not just high - it's not just in temporal flux - but because of this Werewolf business, it's like there's something that's not permitting us to see her future."

Grandfather and Grandpa sucked in their breath sharply.

"Our father the Lokoti Wolf is guiding her." Grandpa decided.

"It would explain why the Last Circulator would be picked to be the tribe's first female Lokoti Werewolf." Grandfather agreed.

"Oh yeah THAT would really explain the meaning of life!" Vincent sneered.

Suddenly he was met by the sound effects of the dangerous growling being emitted by four unhappy male Lokoti Werewolves.

"Vincent." Mum raised her eyebrows. "Please don't diss somebody else's religious beliefs. That's one of the reasons why War is fought."

"True." My grandmother said coldly as she gave him the 'skunk eye'.

"Quite." He cleared his throat once more as he looked downwards.

"So you're saying you didn't see B turning into a Werewolf just like other parts of her future are cloudy to you?" Mum wanted to reconfirm.

"Yes." Vincent clarified. "I can calculate your future, Jess. I can see what's in store for you, Arabella." Next he looked my way. "But B's future is hazy. I could no more see her turn into a Werewolf like I can see if tomorrow she gets hit by a truck."

Gran was the first to notice the threatening growl to come out of her mate as Grandfather looked on Vincent in displeasure at his choice of words... especially since his own father died this way.

"OK." She said firmly to take control of the situation. "Let's take affirmative action here." All of the male Lokoti Werewolves looked on her for leadership. "Vincent, I think Fern is hoping to borrow some DYSTAR to give to B during the full moon to prevent her from running away and eating somebody before they can train her." Grandpa gave a nod to show his agreement to this. "Jess, we should be on stand-by since we're the only two that can catch B."

"Right." Mum gave a nod as she and Dad put their arms about my shoulders.

"Em." She looked to her husband next. "Jess, Vincent and I can try to contain the Circulator element in B, but you should keep the pack updated. Just incase we need them as back-up."

"The pack are already aware of the situation and are ready." Grandfather said seriously.

"Very well then." She said primly, before she looked our Calculator's way again. "Vincent?"

"Yes?" He stood to attention.

"The DYSTAR if you please."

He frowned but after another moment he reluctantly turned away from our circle. He walked over to a medical cabinet on the other side of the room. When he returned, he was holding a tiny glass vial of blue liquid and a futuristic spray/ syringe.

"There is enough DYSTAR in this vial which should weaken her ability to phase for at least seven days." Vincent spoke gravely as he placed the spray/ syringe and the vial into Gran's awaiting hands.

I felt my stomach shrink as my shoulder muscles tensed up. "What's DYSTAR?"

"It's a drug which can temporarily halt a Circulator's ability to phase. This also means you won't be able to run in light speed either." She stated.

"Oh." I looked down at the blue liquid in the tiny glass vial. My eyes widened as I blanched upon the sight of the deceptively small medicine bottle. "Um, do I really need it?" I tried to point out, "I mean it's not like I've actually gone into phase yet. All I can do is run really fast."

Grandfather's face was a mask of consternation, "that's part of your ability to phase, B."

"It is?"

"You have the ability to change your biological body into one made of light." Gran said matter-of-factly. "From this, you can phase through time and space. It's also linked to your ability to move in the speed of light since you become light."

"Oh." My mouth turned sickeningly salty. "Well um, how about I just promise never to do it again?"

The male Lokoti Werewolves all looked worried as Grandpa spoke; "when the bloodlust controls you, you lose control over your body."

"B." Uncle Julian looked wary, "the pack can train you as a new Werewolf but we can't contain you as a Circulator."

"But first things first," Dad said gruffly, "first we ride out the full moon's pull on the bloodlust of a new Werewolf. Second, we temporarily stop a Circulator from using their new ability to phase just as the moon goes through its phases. Then we'll begin your training as both a new Werewolf and a Circulator."

My shoulders slumped as I looked on the blue liquid. "If you say so."

"Fine then." Vincent said in annoyance as he looked on my male relatives. "We'll do this your way but I want to come with you. I want to be the one who administers the DYSTAR to B. This drug can be dangerous if handled incorrectly."

"As you wish." Grandfather gave a nod.

*****

Our Calculator prepared a medical kit to take with him before we instantaneously phased back to my house in Alaska.

"Before we can give B the DYSTAR she has to be unconscious." Vincent advised, as he loaded up on more drugs to take with him.

"How come you didn't say that before?" Dad watched him suspiciously.

"Why didn't you tell me that the Lokoti Werewolf gene was in every Lokoti, even if it were only the males who were usually activated?" He retorted.

Dad rolled his eyes before he turned back to Mum, however she had to quickly look away to hide her laughter. She had always thought it was funny, the constant fighting between her Lokoti Werewolf husband and Calculator.

When we were all transported back to my house in Alaska, Vincent was holding onto Mum's arm too.

The sight of the futuristic Medical Lab disappeared and reformed into the semblance of my living room. Medical beds and the sterilized smell of the Lab were replaced with the vision of couches, the dining table and the smells of recent cooking from our kitchen.

Our house was decorated almost the same as Gran and Grandfathers; Nana and Grandpa's or even Uncle Julian and Aunt Danika's was... country style with a pine furniture and second-hand couches in the living room. Our house was simplistic, spartan and yet homey as it was kept warm with life, food and company. Plenty of family photos adorned shelf space or sat over the mantle piece.

Everyone released their hold on Mum or Gran as Vincent immediately set to work by opening up his medical kit on our dining table. I watched hesitantly as he prepared two futuristic syringes which would spray the drugs at high pressure into the applicant's skin. One syringe was filled with a knock-out drug and the other with DYSTAR.

"Um, do we need to do this right now?" I asked nervously.

"It's best to, especially since you need to be asleep for the procedure." Vincent replied as he filled the futuristic syringe/ sprays with the drugs.

I subconsciously took a step backwards away from the scary looking blue liquid... when I accidentally walked into Dad who was standing behind.

"It's only temporary B," he squeezed my shoulder, "as it's only for two more nights of the full moon cycle."

"Uh huh." I tried to swallow but my throat felt constricted.

Just then I jumped when we heard; KNOCK KNOCK KNOCK!

It was pretty loud too, so loud that our front door shook from the impact. Uncle Julian went to answer it. He didn't say a word as he simply stood to the side and held the door open.

My eyes widened when I saw the ten other members of the Lokoti Werewolf pack led by Uncle Harry, walk into my living room. Oh and Declan was here too.

He walked in last as the honorary member of the pack. Declan threw me a quick glare before he went and stood behind Uncle Fin to avoid eye-contact with me. That bastard! He's the one who kissed me and HE'S the one who's acting like it's the other way around!

"B." Uncle Harry greeted with a nod.

"Uncle Harry." I gave a polite nod back.

"You are the first female Lokoti Werewolf." He said.

"Yeah, so I heard." I almost rolled my eyes but Dad nudged me to mind my manners.

Uncle Harry smirked, "and you're the last Circulator born in human history."

"Um yeah, I heard that too." I muttered and this time it was Grandfather who gave a warning look.

"You are the fifteenth member of the pack." He continued, unperturbed by my petulance.

I looked from him to the other members, but I purposefully skipped over Declan. To be honest I felt a little self-conscious standing there in my jeans and the papery smock. Especially now I would be the only female in a male dominated pack.

"So." I forced myself to sound cheerful. "Do I get a membership kit or something? How about a name tag that says, 'Hi I'm Bianca the First Female Lokoti Werewolf?"

"Yeah, it's in the post." Uncle Ian snickered and then so did several other members of the pack.

Considering that postal deliveries were sketchy at best since the War? It made me smirk at the, 'don't hold your breath' quality of the answer. I pressed my lips together as I quietened.

"The Lokoti Werewolves have a long history as well as a noble one." Uncle Harry said seriously. "We uphold the tradition of protecting the Lokoti Tribe. We were created to protect all that a Lokoti Wolf holds important, his mate, his young and his territory." Uncle Harry's chest expanded in pride. "As Circulators have the responsibility to protect the timeline, you Little Wolf are now part of history by becoming one who fights as part of the pack."

"OK...?" I tried to swallow again but my throat was too dry.

Next, he stepped up so he could place a heavy hand on my shoulder. "You will always be remembered in stories of the pack, just as you will be remembered as one of the tribe's Light People. You are both the Last Circulator born to the human race as you are the first female Lokoti Werewolf to the tribe. You are legacy, Little Wolf."

My breath caught in my throat as my eyes widened, before I looked from Uncle Harry, to Ian, to Grant, to Fin, Quinn and the rest of the pack until my gaze ended with the males in my family. With the Werewolves differing ages, some in their twenties to others over a hundred, I truly did see history in my very own living room.

"I am First." Uncle Harry proclaimed. "Your Grandfather is Second to the Lokoti Werewolf pack."

I nervously licked my lips, "OK...?" But I was completely clueless what all of this meant?

Uncle Ian recognized the lost look in my eyes, "it means B that when Harry gives an order, we follow it."

"Oh." I said puzzled. "But I always thought that you lot were empathic and operated on a group consensus or something."

"All organizations need a leader, do they not?" Uncle Harry smiled in amusement.

Next I looked at Grandfather, "so what does Second do?"

"I make sure the will of the First is adhered to." He said simply.

Oh...then for some reason I next found my eyes sneaking towards Declan to see how he reacted to all of this. I couldn't imagine him obeying just one person. I always thought it took the entire will of the pack to keep him in line. To my surprise, I found Declan looking on Grandfather with the same kind of respect of a son looking on his father in admiration.

"So um," I tried to keep my voice from wavering, "does this mean that I'm going to start patrolling the borders of Lokoti land too?"

Suddenly the reaction from not only Uncle Harry, but all of the male Werewolves took me off-guard. They all growled loudly by the very idea!

"No." Uncle Harry proclaimed as if his word was law.

"No?" I echoed.

"You are the pack's one and only female Lokoti Werewolf. You may be faster than us also being a Circulator, but we are stronger than you. As a female, you will not patrol." He declared.

As uneasy I was feeling being the only female Werewolf in this room full of males, I was also curious. So like a beginner, I put up my hand to ask my questions.

"But why?" I queried. "Mum helped the tribe fight off the 500 marauders just before I was born. Gran helped ready the tribe for the Third World War and she was the one who took down the European Werewolf which turned Declan. So why can't I patrol?"

"Because you are female." Grant spoke.

"Because not only are female Werewolves rare in this world, let alone this tribe..." Uncle Quinn added.

"...healthy human females are fought over thanks to radiation sickness." Uncle Fin ended.

"You will not be seen by outsiders or strangers." Uncle Harry said firmly.

"No non-Lokoti may know of your existence." Grandpa agreed.

"Just as the identity of the Lokoti Werewolves are protected by the tribe..." Dad spoke up.

"...as are the identities of the tribe's Circulators are hidden from outsiders," Grandfather finished, "the tribe's Last Circulator and first female Lokoti Werewolf must never be known to the rest of the world."

Then all of the male Werewolves in the room including Declan, gave a firm nod in agreement.

In the pack, I saw uniformity as well as a hierarchy which served as a support structure. The male Werewolves in the room shared a comradeship from years of fighting together in their roles as the tribe's protectors. To be honest, right then I didn't want to make waves especially since I was the first and only female Lokoti Werewolf, which really threw a spanner in the works. So I too gave a nod to show that I would obey the will of the First.

Grandfather, Grandpa and Dad came to stand behind me as they placed their hands on my back. Then Uncle Harry gave me a wink before he turned and departed from my house. The eleven other members, all followed him out as they left as a group.

Declan was the last one out as he closed our front door behind himself. He passed me one last look, before he gave Grandfather a nod. Then he too disappeared.

"Oh well then." Mum looked to Gran. "That was nice wasn't it, by welcoming B like that?"

"If that was a 'Welcome' party remind me never to become a female Werewolf in this tribe." My Calculator sneered.

"Trust me Vincent," Dad said dryly, "if you ever turned into a female Werewolf? We wouldn't greet you like that in fact we would actually turn and run the other way."

*****

Before I was drugged with DYSTAR, my captors were at least good enough to allow me to shower and change into an old tracksuit with even a meal prepared. But I didn't eat, I couldn't. As I sat at the table pushing around the food with my fork, the syringe of DYSTAR seemed to stare up at me from the middle of the table.

Eventually I was led upstairs by Mum, Dad, Gran and Grandpa who as the tribe's Medicine Man, wanted to observe. Grandfather and Uncle Julian remained in the living room, as they milled around restlessly.

I noticed that my bedroom was now looking tidier with the broken glass vacuumed up thanks to my mother's cleanliness. I lay down on top of my bed, as Vincent and Mum and Dad sat beside. Nervously, I looked at each of them individually whilst the whole room looked back.

"What's going to happen?" I asked worriedly as Vincent readied the syringe with the sedative first.

"You're going to sleep for a couple of hours and when you wake up you won't be able to phase." He replied. "Don't worry B, it's just for seven days and then your ability will come back."

I looked on my parents, feeling so scared, I was shaking.

"Does it hurt?" I asked my mother.

"I don't think so sweet heart." She promised. "All it does it make you stop phasing for a little while."

"This is only temporary B." My father rested his warm palm against my cheek. "As soon as this full moon cycle is over, we can start training you to be ready for the next."

"I'll be watching." Grandpa tried to reassure as he stood at the end of my bed. "You have two Medicine Men looking out for you."

"Just relax." My Calculator tried to give an encouraging smile to put my fears at ease.

He placed the syringe/ spray against my neck and next I felt a tickling sensation as I heard the tell-tale HIIISSSSS...!

"Woah..." my eyes started to close by themselves, "...that was faasst..." and then I didn't get to finish my sentence.

All of the muscles in my body simultaneously went loose as a heavy black curtain fell over my eyes. I was more than 'out like a light', I frickin' well didn't have a light bulb anymore to turn on!

*****

To be honest, I don't remember the next two evenings very well let alone at all clearly. I think the first night I woke up on the bathroom floor again. I remember waking up on the cold, hard surface and wondering why I was locked up once more?

Wouldn't being drugged with DYSTAR mean that I don't have to be shut away? But I soon got my answer as I felt my chest quickly rise and fall as I was panting. When I caught sight of my hands, I saw my nails were long, sharp and claw-like. Oh... I'm changing again.

I think it was night time, as the bathroom was partially dark but for the light of the full moon spilling onto the white tiles. I hated the bright, eerie light of the full moon because of what it brought...pain. I felt excruciating, horrible, agonizing pain!

Oh my gosh, I think there's a fire burning in my stomach! It hurt! It hurt so much I couldn't lie still! I writhed on the bathroom floor in complete and utter hideous torture. I felt like acid was eating me up inside and out! Did they inject me with DYSTAR or frickin' poison?!

"MUM! MUUUUMMM! THE PAIN! WHAT DID YOU DO TO ME?! THE PAIN!!" I thought I was screaming in anguish but what came out of me was a thunderous Werewolf's roar!

I want my Mum and Dad! Where are my parents? I want them to take away the hurt!

My tracksuit top tore as my body expanded with Werewolf muscle and my teeth grew long and sharp just like my nails. I cried as my entire body ached from my change. Even the bathroom seemed to turn brighter, as my human eyes switched to my Werewolf night vision.

"did my eyes change colour like yours do?" "They did." "What color did they turn?" "Turquoise like your Great, Great Grandfather, Flint Riverclaw's eyes."

As our previous words reverberated inside my head, I had to see it; I had to see what I had become. Using the bathroom sink for support, I pulled myself up from the floor and onto my unsteady feet. As my eyes lifted upwards I saw IT.

I saw a female Lokoti Werewolf look back in the small bathroom mirror. Two glowing turquoise eyes stared with an open mouth full of jagged, elongated teeth which looked threatening. I saw the tops of my broad, muscled shoulders peeking through the torn tracksuit top.

I look hideous! I look absolutely disgusting! I really am a monster! Declan kissed THIS?!

"YOU FREAK!" I roared out with my thunderous voice.

My clawed hand jutted out to punch through the mirrored door of the medicine cabinet!   Glass went flying everywhere, as the shards landed with a 'tinkling' noise onto the bathroom floor.

I don't remember much after that, but I think Dad must have come inside the bathroom with me at some stage. I recalled for part of the night he sat with his back against the tub, holding me in his stronger Werewolf form. His bigger arms were wrapped tightly about my torso as he held me firmly against his chest, his glowing red Werewolf eyes filling with tears as I writhed in pain. He desperately tried to hold me still to try to soothe the pain somehow.

My father couldn't ease the pain as he couldn't do a thing to help. The bloodlust was boiling the very blood in my veins, as my dangerous mouth watered by the very thought of meat...human meat. Fresh, juicy, bleeding meat off the bone that belonged to one of those delicious humans in the township of Alma which was 7 km's away.

As much as these thoughts taunted my Werewolf senses...a tiny remaining human part wanted to throw up in disgust.

~~~~~~

12th September 2084

I survived...somehow I managed to pull through the transition into a new Werewolf.

The first night I changed, I broke my bedroom window and I tried to eat a townsperson but I was stopped by Declan. The second night I changed, I was locked inside my bathroom, unable to phase thanks to the DYSTAR with Dad sitting with me. On the third night I changed, again I was locked inside my bathroom, unable to phase with Grandfather sitting with me.
~~~~~~

I slept all day as I writhed in agony thanks to the bloodlust, all night. During the day I had Mum, Gran, Great Grandma and even Aunt Danika to tend to me. The women fussed about as they took away my torn clothes to be mended and they tried to feed me the meals they had prepared. But I wasn't hungry and all I wanted to do was sleep.

Then during the night I had Dad, Grandfather, Grandpa and Uncle Julian to tend to me in their roles as jailors. They kept me locked inside the bathroom so I couldn't escape and try to make a run for Alma again. As either Dad or Grandfather sat with me, I heard the whispering of Grandpa and Uncle Julian on the other side of the door.

This was the worst experience of my entire life. It was even worse then the first day I got my period when I was 14 years old. It happened during a game of soccer with Derik and the other boys when Rachel and Mandy waved me off the field so they could whisper that a red patch was beginning to form on the back of my shorts. That day I thought I would die of embarrassment, as Mandy calmly tied her jumper around my waist then she and Rachel walked me home. However that day now paled in comparison, when I rued the facts of life for being a female human? These days I rued being the first female Lokoti Werewolf.

Yet somehow I survived, although I thought I would die from the pain the murderous bloodlust brought upon for not indulging its dangerous craving. But I didn't die, instead I carried on. Albeit, a broken bathroom mirror, a broken bedroom window and three sets of torn clothes later; I survived the change into my new existence.

Last night, I went over to my repaired window after I had showered and changed in my PJ's for bed. I examined the handiwork of my father and Uncle Ian as I admired their skill. The new glass was perfectly cut and installed. I sighed wistfully as I looked on the shiny new glass... if only my life could be repaired so easily.

I didn't want this because I was scared of who I now was. The pack along with my Werewolf relations were right there and willing to train me. The pack felt proud, even if they were apprehensive that I was the new Lokoti Werewolf.

I was the first female Lokoti Werewolf just as I was the Last Circulator. Boy, what a contradiction! I'm both the first and last...oh no, that's not complicating my life at all, is it?

Just as I took a step back from the window to pull the curtains closed, I saw something. Or, I think I saw something... Hang on a minute, what is that?

My eyes squinted and I think my Werewolf-vision must have kicked in, when I could suddenly see clearer into the dark woods. I spotted a pair of glowing green eyes, watching me from the forest. Uncle Quinn, one of the Lokoti Werewolves had glowing emerald green eyes but these glowing green eyes were a different kind of green. They looked brighter and burned more fiercely, hungrily even. They were Declan's European Werewolf eyes, I knew it.

He was watching me from the woods, via my bedroom window but why was he spying on me? Was Declan guarding me somehow, to make sure I didn't make another run for the townspeople in Alma? Why was he here? But as my heart began to pound, I started to think differently...

I remembered his kiss three nights ago, when he stopped me on the border. I felt warm and a little giddy, as I recalled the heat which was generated between us...that was until his huge jaws clamped down on a nerve in my neck. Declan knocked me out cold, to carry me back home. Bastard! I bet he probably enjoyed rendering me unconscious even more than the kissing part!

As my way of saying 'get lost!', I whipped the curtains closed before I climbed into bed and switched off my lamp.

~~~~~~
~~~~~~

~ 4 ~

14th September 2084

I was sitting at the dining table reading a book on Ancient Greek Mythology, when Mum walked out of the kitchen carrying her shopping list.

"OK." She spoke to both me and Dad, who was sitting on the couch with another book. "I'm going down to the store to pick up a few odds and ends. I hope that you both remembered to write down anything you needed."

Normally Dad would volunteer to go with her to hold the carry basket as she strolled up and down the small aisles, but today he didn't. For the past five days, he's stayed home to keep an eye on his daughter, the new Lokoti Werewolf in the family.

I've been housebound these past days, so much so I might as well have been in jail with all of these new restrictions! I couldn't have visitors; I couldn't go out and visit; I had to meditate or study, to get my mind off the bloodlust.

Grandpa gave me these meditation exercises, but to be honest I found them as about as useful as small puncture repair kit whist trying to plug up a hole in an inflatable life raft, whilst being tossed about a storm-driven sea... In other words, they did diddlysquat in helping me try to ignore or even control the menacing voice of the bloodlust.

Mum had just started to walk towards the front door when I jumped up and cried out, "can I come too?"

That made Dad quickly stand up with apprehension, "I don't think so B."

"Why not?" Mum turned his way. "It's just to the store."

"I don't think it's a good idea Jess." He said.

"But we won't even be leaving tribal lands!" She argued back.

"B's supposed to be meditating right now." Dad said simply.

"She's been 'meditating' for three days straight." Mum stated. "Even Buddhist Monks leave the temple now and again from their 'meditation'. When she comes back from the store she can 'meditate' again."

I started to snicker at the tone of voice she used every time she said the word 'meditate'. But I stopped when Dad turned his unhappy look my way.

"Sorry." I quickly sat back down again.

"No." She said firmly and pulled me towards the front door with her. "C'mon B, you can help me shop."

"Jess..." Dad started to object.

"We'll be home in thirty minutes!" She called back as we left the house.

As we walked over to Dad's truck parked out the front, the outside sun warmed my skin. Along with the gentle wind blowing through the trees, the weather instantly picked up my spirits as I felt glad to get out of the house for a little while. Mum hit the remote to release the truck's central locking and then we climbed in.

"Thanks Mum." I said appreciatively at her stubbornness which could stand against a Lokoti Werewolf's resolution.

She gave an affectionate pat on my arm, before she started the engine and reversed out of our driveway. I caught sight of Dad standing on our veranda with his hands on his hips as he reluctantly watched us leave. The frown on his face was so deep, it not only made his face look grave but it looked older.

*****

After we pulled up into a free car space by the store, I hopped out before Mum. With my new strength and energy, I started to notice she moved slower than I did. She closed the door behind herself, locked it and dropped her keys into her handbag as she pulled out her shopping list.

Whilst Mum spent a few seconds doing all of this, my head turned towards the garage beside the store.

I could hear music playing loudly, as 'The Cult' belted out of the speakers of the portable stereo that I had once seen on a shelf inside the garage. I could see a pick up truck was parked halfway inside of the garage, with its front half out in the open air. I guessed it was parked as such so the mechanics could use the sunlight to see into the motor's dark crevices. I saw that a mechanic who looked to be Ben, was lying underneath the truck and somebody was leaning over the top of it, with the bonnet propped up.

My heart picked up speed, as I recognized the familiar male body wearing scuffed black boots, dirty jeans and a tight grey t-shirt, also covered in dirt and grease. My breath almost caught in my throat, when I recognized the large muscles straining underneath the fabric. I think I stopped breathing as if by sensing me, Declan's head rose and he turned my way. As quickly as his eyes widened by the sight of me, they next narrowed into a glare.

"OK, let's get this over and done with." Mum sung, with the shopping list now in her hand. "This shouldn't take long and besides, your father is probably timing us on his watch!"

Quickly, I ducked my head as I followed her into the Store, with Declan's eyes following us.

I picked up a carry basket from beside the door and held it for her as she walked ahead. She was almost speed shopping as she didn't stop, she just simply grabbed as she passed. The basket quickly began to fill up. I started to appreciate my extra Werewolf muscle, as the basket began to strain under the load.

"Bread...milk...butter...eggs...cheese...juice...toothpaste." Mum read out the list under her breath, as she breezed down the small aisles.

As I walked behind her, I noticed how we attracted a lot of looks from passersby. But then I realized that people weren't looking at her, they were looking at me. They were all watching with curiosity in their eyes.

Frickin' hell, word travels fast in this tribe! Does everybody know that I'm a Werewolf? It looked like it, as I ducked my head to walk quickly after.

As we passed a group of teenaged boys who were hanging around the sweets shelf, their eyes widened as they took me in. I think I even overheard one of them inhale deeply as I walked past. I stopped and turned to give the youth a peculiar look, whose eyes bulged because I looked in his direction.

"Oh, hi B!" The 14 year old raised his hand to give a small wave.

"How's it goin'?" His 13 year old friend asked next.

"That's a nice er, top that you're wearing." The other 14 year old boy standing with them, fumbled out.

I looked on the kids as if they were nuts! I was wearing a two year old, faded and stretched, red woolen jumper that Grandpa had made as a Christmas present. Not to degrade Grandpa's workmanship, but there was no way that this jumper looked 'nice' anymore, especially with all of the holes I accidentally put in it.

"Come on B." Mum grabbed hold of my arm to pull me after her.

Just as I was yanked away, I overheard one of the youths critique the one who remarked on my top; "you don't say nice top you dumb-ass! You're supposed to compliment women on their shoes!"

When I turned my head back around to give the three a funny look, they instantly stood to attention and waved back. I continued on, shaking my head to myself as I followed Mum to the counter.

I placed the basket on top and began to pile everything onto the surface. This way, the elderly Mr. Barley who owned the general store could mark it off in his book what we were 'purchasing'. He would put it on our family account for us to make up in a future barter or trade. Since the War, no-one in the tribe used money anymore, as the majority of our money went to trading with outsiders.

"How are you, B?" He asked politely.

"Good thanks Mr. Barley."

"I suppose with your change, carrying this load isn't a problem anymore." He joked, meaning the large amount that Mum was shopping for today.

"Um, no." I answered awkwardly.

"B's been stronger than me since she passed her sixteenth birthday. After she turned sixteen, I was getting her to take lids off jars whenever her father wasn't around." Mum laughed jovially.

Mr. Barley laughed along with her, before he looked on me closely. "I swear you look taller, as it usually happens to a Lokoti who goes through the change."

"I think you might be right." Mum agreed. "I swear she used to be my height, now she's ten centimeters taller."

He nodded in acknowledgement as he finished up writing a tally of what we were 'purchasing' today. "Here." He threw in a bonus chocolate bar as he gave a wink. "A new Werewolf needs to keep up their strength."

"Oh, isn't that nice!" Mum smiled on his gesture. "Thanks Mr. Barley!"

"A Circulator for a mother and a Lokoti Werewolf for a father; now we have our tribe's first female Lokoti Werewolf who's a Circulator." He said proudly.

Just then I noticed that the other people in the store smiled and nodded in agreement, as they were watching this transaction take place. The three teenaged boys by the sweets shelf waved at me again.

I could feel my cheeks start to burn as I ducked my head in embarrassment at being the centre of such attention. I was relieved to pick up the shopping in the cotton carry bags Mum brought, as I walked out of the store first. But because my head was lowered, I didn't see where I was going and I walked into somebody who was coming in as I was going out.

"B!" Roger's eyes widened and I caught him suck in his breath and hold it as he looked me over. He stood almost stuck to the spot whilst he stared, as we were standing outside of the store.

Mum passed by and she took one look at Roger's face and I caught her snicker, before she walked over to Dad's truck.

"Um, how are you?" He asked, reaching out his hand to place on my arm. "I heard what happened, are you alright?"

I passed him a look that questioned his sanity, as I moved away from his touch.

"I'm fine thanks Roger, how are you?" I forced out to be polite.

"Me? Oh, I'm fine." He gulped nervously. "But I've been thinking about you a lot, especially now that I've heard what's happened."

"I'm a Werewolf Roger, I'm not dying from rabies." I said uncomfortably.

"Oh yeah, I know that. But um, is there anything I can do to help? I mean, can I get you anything? I guess what I'm trying to say is, is there anything you need?" He prattled off.

"No thank you Roger, I'm fine." I stood there holding four carry bags of groceries. I thought he was being a bit rude, making me stand here and talk to him when he saw my hands were full.

"Oh, can I get those for you?" He started to reach out for my bags of food but I quickly pulled back.

"No thank you Roger, they're not heavy but my Mum's waiting for me -
"

"Oh, that's right." He nodded quickly. "Lokoti Werewolves are a lot stronger than humans and I guess so are you, now that you're one and all." I opened my mouth about to excuse myself, when he interrupted again. "I know that when a Werewolf goes through their first change and all, they're supposed to be in training or whatever and you can't socialize much. But um, I could come over if you like? I could bring a couple of movies over to your house and -"

However he was interrupted from a low, dangerous growl coming from the garage. Our heads quickly turned, to see Declan standing beside the truck he was meant to be fixing. His head was lowered but a fierce look was directed right at Roger. His teeth were bared and I swear they were looking sharper and I guess so thought Roger.

"See you later B." He almost flew through the glass door of the Store as he quickly darted inside.

A laugh escaped as I watched him take off and then I turned back around to look on Declan in amusement.

"Did you forget that you already have a boyfriend, B?" He asked sulkily. Then he turned back around to continue his work on the engine of the truck.

I knew he was inferring his little brother but it pissed me off by him saying this. He just acted like Roger's behavior was my fault! I shook my head in disbelief at his primitive behavior as I marched over to Dad's truck where Mum was waiting inside.

After I placed the shopping bags in the back, I walked over to the passenger's side door to climb in. Mum turned the key, started the ignition and she reversed out onto the road. However as she pulled out, I caught Declan watch us leave. I quickly turned my head away to glare out the windscreen, as Mum drove back around the sports field and headed towards the hill we lived on.

She abruptly laughed, "I haven't noticed that much attention to Werewolf pheromones since I married your father."

"Shut up Mum." I said darkly as I felt myself blush, which made her laugh again.

As I stared out at the trees whizzing past, I couldn't get Declan out of my mind. He was the one who put his hand over mine that morning he drove me home. He was the one who kissed me on the borders of Lokoti land when he stopped me from running into town. And HE has the hide to remind me of MY loyalty to Derik...?

Mum was still laughing about what happened when we arrived home. As I put away the groceries in the kitchen, I had to relive the experience as she told Dad all about it. Whereas she could laugh about it, I noticed he didn't. In fact, this just made him look more unhappy.

"B, I don't think you should go out again where people will be, not for a while at least." He frowned.

"Hunter." She looked on unimpressed. "What's that going to prove? B didn't try to EAT anybody while she was away."

Dad frowned even deeper, "THAT'S not what I'm worried about."

"Hunter - " She began to object, but I interrupted.

"It's fine with me!" I huffed as I turned away.

Speedily, I left the kitchen to run upstairs to my room to hide underneath the cover of another history book.

~~~~~~

15ᵗʰ September 2084

I read and re-read all of my books about Ancient Greece, Ancient Rome and even Ancient Egypt. I studied the ancient myths of Greek Gods and their cousins, the Roman Gods. I daydreamed about what it would be like to study these at Cambridge University.   I either read on my bed or downstairs sitting at the dining table with an ever-watchful Dad hovering nearby.

This morning when I was in my bedroom reading a book on Tutankhamen, I overheard a knock on the front door downstairs.

Since becoming a Werewolf, my hearing has become sharper than what it used to be and I could eavesdrop a hell of a lot better. As soon as I heard the knock, I looked up from my book as I next listened to what took place when Dad answered the door.

"Hi Uncle Hunter." Derik's voice sounded.

Derik? He's here? I sat upright in anticipation of seeing him.

"Hello Derik." Dad said formally.

"Um, is B home?" He asked.

"Yes she is."

"Can I um, see her?"

"No you can't." He said gruffly. "I'm sorry Derik, but since B's change she can't have any visitors for a while."

"Oh." I heard the disappointment in his voice. "Well um, can I leave something for her?"

Pause... and then Dad said; "I'll see that she gets this."

"Thanks Uncle Hunter." He sighed reluctantly as he prepared to leave.

"Bye Derik." Dad said. "Send my regards to your mother for me."

"OK." He spoke as his voice grew more distant... sounding like he was stepping down from our front veranda.

Derik! Quickly I jumped up from my bed as I raced over to my window to watch my best friend slowly walk down my gravel driveway. Derik! Anxiously I knocked on my window, minding the glass with my increased strength, then I waved furiously hoping that my best friend would see.   But he didn't turn around as his eyes or ears didn't pick up my efforts to attract his attention since he was only human...
~~~~~~

...only human...

...I was no longer human and I felt like this Werewolf business was pulling me away from my bestest friend in the whole world because he was.

Just as I was about to open my window to yell out, Dad walked into my room. He saw me standing by the window and he immediately guessed what I was looking at.

"Here." He placed on my bed what Derik had given him. "He left this for you."

"Why did you turn Derik away?" I cried out, upset. "He's my best friend!"

"I'm sorry B, but you can't have any visitors right now." He said gravely. "Not friends and not even family. It's why you haven't seen your Gran or your Aunt or your cousins for a while. They know you're supposed to be using this time to learn self-control."

Then he turned around and left me alone in my bedroom. I watched the back of my father disappear down the stairs before I walked over to my bed and I picked up what was left for me.

It was a square envelop with Derik's writing scribbled on it. On the front of the envelope was a huge 'B' and I quickly and yet carefully opened it up when a CD and a letter fell out. I picked up both as I unfolded the letter to read;

'Hi B, I'm not sure if I'm going to be allowed to visit you so I wrote this just in case. Declan says as a new Werewolf you're going to be in 'lock down' for a little while as you train. I just want you to know that I'm thinking about you and I miss you. I was really worried about what happened to you as Declan won't tell me about the first night you changed. I wish I had walked you home from our place now so maybe I could have been there for you and helped you somehow. Please know that as soon as your Mom and Dad tell my Mom that you're allowed to see people again that I'll be there in a flash. Rachel and Mandy say 'hi' and they came over yesterday. Mandy was getting books about teaching from my Mom and Rachel helped me to put together my assignments that I'll be submitting to Cambridge. She brought her laptop with her so I could type my stuff out in an email to Cambridge with my application letter. Mandy and Rachel are worried about you too and when they asked Declan what happened since he was there the first night you changed, he refused to talk about it and stormed off into his room again... like he always does. Your Grandfather only repaired Declan's broken bedroom door from where the wood split with Declan always slamming it two days ago... what's the bet he's going to have to fix it again? LoL! Anyways just know that I'm there with you in spirit and that my thoughts are with you always. I made you this CD of our favourite songs for you to listen to and think of me. I love you B... Your best friend Derik.'

My heart hurt as my eyes filled with tears whilst I stared on those last four words; 'Your best friend Derik'.

I miss my best friend so much, it was part of the reason why I couldn't concentrate on the meditation exercises I was given to do. It was even part of the reason why I wasn't enjoying studying either, because I was so used to studying with Derik.

My best friend and I always studied together. We sat together in school and when school finished we went to the library together, to get more books to self-school ourselves. We either sat at his dining table or mine, reading and making notes. Aunt Susan as well as Gran, would set assignments for us and together Derik and I would do them and hand them in to be marked. Derik would do something scientific and I would write up a paper on a topic in ancient history. Half of the time, Rachel and Mandy joined in. As Rachel began to study Naturopathy, Mandy would brush up on a broad range of subjects to become a teacher.

Occasionally, he and I would go to either Rachel's or Mandy's houses, but most of the time we hung out at his place. Aunt Susan would come home from teaching the tribe's younger generations and then she would check on our independent studies. Her patience and 'welcome one and all' view on education ran at levels which verged on sainthood. Sometimes Declan would complain when everyone stayed for dinner at Aunt Susan's invitation.

"What, you're not only educating them but we're feeding them too?" He whined when she checked that he was cooking enough for six people instead of three.

Derik's patience with my mischievousness or even my temper, came from his mother. I knew I had it good, having a best friend like him as he always supported me in everything I did. He never ridiculed my 'tom boy' ways or he never felt that his masculinity was threatened by me occasionally beating him in running races. He always jumped at the chance to be on the same soccer team with me. Derik and I were nicknamed 'the terrible two' by our parents or even the tribe. He became my partner-in-crime in everything... even when I used to misbehave.

One Sunday afternoon at the Sabre's house when I was 10 years old, I remember being babysat by a 13 year-old Declan along with Derik, Mandy and Rachel. Our parents were attending a meeting held by our Tribal Elders in the hall. I think it was during the period of the full moon so Declan was not just his grumpy self, but he was also tired from hunting all night with the pack. He repeatedly yelled at us to shut up as he wanted to nap on the couch in the lounge room so we went to play in the back yard.

It was a quiet Sunday afternoon in the middle of summer and we were bored. Then I had happened to notice a large bag of flour that Aunt Susan had recently picked up from the store, I guess to use to make bread and pasta. It was sitting just inside the kitchen by the back door.

I don't remember the specifics now, but there were no adults around to stop us; so Mandy, Rachel, Derik and I got into a 'flour and water' fight! White flour went everywhere! White flour was sprinkled over not just our clothes, but all over the back yard and it was spilt all over the floor in the kitchen as well!

We had a wonderful time, not only throwing flour at each other but water as well, which made the flour congeal and turn into glue. So four 10 year olds had flour-glue all through their hair, their clothes and over the walls of the back of the house! When Declan woke up from our shouting...to say 'the shit hit the fan' would have been an understatement!

"What the frickin' hell have you done?!" His blue eyes turned their Werewolf state in anger. "When Mom sees this she's gonna freak!"

Declan's temper scared Mandy and Rachel as they froze in fear. But since my Dad and Grandfather were Werewolves, I knew that he wouldn't be allowed to hurt me. I marched up to my best friend's bigger brother with his enraged glowing green eyes and I threw a handful of wet flour over his flannel shirt!

"B, no!" Derik blanched, terrified of his older brother's supernatural temper.

Declan slowly looked down at his messed-up t-shirt and then he slowly looked back up, as I started to hear a low growl build up in his throat...oh oh!

When I turned to run away, he grabbed me with his faster reflexes. He picked me up and slung me over his shoulder! With my worrield friends looking on, Declan carried me over to the tap where he dropped me onto the grass. He held me down with his strong foot, as he sprayed a torrent of water over me from the garden hose!

"Derik!" I screeched. "Derik, stop him!"

My best friend tried to run to my aid but Declan turned the hose on him, sending him scurrying away! Then he did the same to both Rachel and Mandy! His eyes returned to their human blue colour as he stood there, laughing at us. He kept me on the ground with his foot on my stomach, as he washed all four of us down with the hose. Once he had washed off the flour from us and the back of the house, he yelled at Derik; "you're on clean up duty!"

The European Werewolf marched all four of us in our wet clothes, into the house to clean up the spilt flour from the kitchen floor. He sat up on the kitchen bench to supervise and any time we complained or started to slack-off, he growled dangerously which prompted us to clean faster.

"I'm cold." Rachel whined as she shivered.

"You were already wet before I turned the hose on you." Declan said coolly.

"We should change out of these clothes so we don't catch our deaths." Mandy tried to talk like an adult.

"I wish!" He scoffed at the idea.

"They can borrow my clothes to put on." Derik said helpfully.

"Change later and clean now!" Declan barked loudly.

He scared Mandy and Rachel, sending them frantically sweeping with the dust pan and brush.

"I hate you." I glared at our bully of a babysitter.

Declan looked long and hard on me before he eventually said back, "likewise."

As I angrily returned to our cleaning, Derik tried to give me a goofy grin as he gently nudged my side.

"It was worth it." He smiled my way, which made Mandy and Rachel giggle in agreement.

Then all four of us burst into laughter as we looked on each other's wet hair and soaking wet clothes with the white flour sticking to us...

...and as I returned to the present, I still laughed at the memory of that day.

I picked up the CD which Derik had burned and put it in Dad's second hand CD player I had 'inherited'. As I lay on my stomach on top of the bed, I listened to bands like Nirvana, Pearl Jam, Live, Blur, Oasis, The Verve and of course Iggy Pop, play.

We grew up with these old 20th Century bands thanks to hearing our parents or our grandparents play this music. Declan was a 'grunge band' enthusiast so he was always listening to this kind of music at home or at the garage. I think when Derik came over with these CD's, he must have been borrowing them from his older brother's collection.

This fact came to light another time when I was at the Sabre house. Declan came storming out of his bedroom over to where Derik and I were studying at the dining table, with his eyes glowing green in anger.

"Have you got my U2 CD?!" He demanded of his little brother.

"Er, which one?" Derik asked back.

"'Rattle & Hum'!"

"Yeah, but you said I could borrow it."

"I said that last month Derik!" He growled out. "That was over four weeks ago! When you borrow my stuff, you frickin' return it or else!"

With that, he spun on his heel and stalked off to retrieve it from his little brother's room himself.

"Meeeoow!" I commented to my best friend about his older brother's behavior.

"Er, Declan's a Werewolf." Derik said in good humor. "I think it's more like, 'woof! Woof!'"

"Shut up you little pipsqueaks!" Declan roared back before...

...SLAM!

He closed his bedroom door so loudly that we felt the vibrations from where we were sitting.

~~~~~~
~~~~~~

16th September 2084

I walked along the muddy track with the wet ferns brushing against my jeans. It was still drizzling, but at least the rain was light and I didn't mind my clothes turning damp.

I just had to get out of the house! I had to get away from my parents. I had to get away from their quiet talks and their worried glances. I couldn't stay a prisoner inside my bedroom forever.

Being inside for too long always gave me a head-ache, even in the dead of winter. Mum could sit in front of the fire, snuggled up with a book for hours. As much as I shared her love for reading, I had to take regular breaks and go for walks, even if it was in below freezing temperatures. So being cooped up inside in fall with winter coming, depressed me. Although it had been raining all day, I just had to get out.

"I won't go anywhere near town, I'll go down to the river." I snapped at their concern.

"I'll come with you." My father made a move to stand up from the table.

"No Dad." I glared at him. "I want to be alone."

"B - " He started to object.

"I promise I won't eat anybody while I'm away!" I rolled my eyes.

That was it, I was storming off into the woods before my parents knew it.

I had to walk off this anxiety, this tetchiness, this caged-in feeling. The bloodlust was making my heart pound so hard it made me shake, even when I was sitting still. I could smell the blood in my mother's veins, as I noticed the blue lines under her soft white skin. I could hear her heart beating. I could smell her at the end of the driveway when she came home from visiting family or friends.

Not that I wanted to eat my mother, but she reminded me of those delicious townspeople on the other side of the border. It was driving me insane! So I thought I could walk off these cravings.

Once I came to the river, I probably stood there for like two minutes. However I couldn't sit and think like I usually liked to do, I had to keep moving...so I turned around and deliberately took the longer way home.

I was trudging up the muddy path, in the drizzling rain. The woods were silent, with no bird noise from the trees which dripped with the odd raindrop. Even the frogs were quiet, like everything else. I started to think that perhaps everything was a little too quiet. I thought I was alone, but now I wondered?

Just then I stopped as I couldn't explain it, but I knew I was being watched by the skin on the back of my neck tingling. I sniffed the quiet air as I could vaguely smell something. I listened with my keen hearing and I heard the quiet footsteps of something large, stalking me.

Then I heard it, a faint growl. I couldn't see it as it expertly hid, but I sensed that it stopped moving because I had stopped moving. It was watching me and it knew that I was aware of its presence.

"Grrraaaaaaaawwwllll!!!"

I barely caught sight of the lightening fast figure leap out, before I felt my feet leave the ground as I went flying through the air...

...something had just leapt upon me and this something made me land on the ground over five meters away from where I had been walking. This big strong creature was suddenly a naked man, lying on top and he was doing something to me with his hands.

It was Declan, he had reverted back to his human shape. He was unbuttoning my jeans, unzipping them and shoving them halfway down my thighs, which stopped me from moving my legs. All of this was done so quickly in lightening fast speed, I was barely aware of what was happening. I didn't cotton on to what was going on until he started pushing himself inside.

He was moving so quickly as he grunted was like he was in some kind of pain, or that the pain was leaving him somehow. I was lying there on the wet ground almost pinned, as I started to become aware that this was called something. This was happening to me right now, in fact.

I was having sex... I was having sex with Declan... or he was having sex with me... it did seem rather one sided.

What, this is sex? I laid there almost unimpressed by the mundanity. This is what all the fuss is about, with our parents telling us to be careful with? He held me so taught, I couldn't move. It felt so strange that I realized if I could, I wouldn't know what to do anyway because I've never done this before.

He cried out - he literally cried out - and when I caught sight of his face? He had tears in his eyes as his face was bright red. At first he kept his face turned away as his movements were mechanical, but the way he was holding me seemed desperate. At first it felt strange, having this foreign body part being pushed into me over and over again... then it started to hurt a little... and then it went back to feeling strange. Now I felt really warm and wet down there, but I didn't know if that was because of my body? I suspected it could be because of Declan.

As he slowed down, gasping and making helpless noises; finally he looked down and his face was a mask of fear and regret.

"Are – are you OK?" he asked weakly.

"I can't move."

Declan immediately raised himself, pushed my jeans now past my knees and down to my ankles. As he did this, he opened my legs as he raised my knees on either side before he started to move again.

"Is that better?" he checked.

I nodded as I looked past him. It did feel better this way because when he pushed, I started to push back by using my hips. It felt more... natural this way. I started to like it.

As we moved, I stared up through the trees, at the grey sky. My back felt wet from lying on the cold, wet ground. But I stopped noticing this so much as something else started to happen... I started to feel warm and tingly.

To my surprise, I was starting to really like this. I felt something strange but nice happen inside my abdomen and then I felt like I couldn't stop. It felt like I had to go on, to reach somewhere. I grabbed hold of Declan's arms and pushed harder against him. As he watched my face in partial surprise, he began to push faster as if to help somehow.

The harder and faster Declan pushed, the more these feelings intensified. It occurred to me that this was pleasure, no this was RAPTURE that I was feeling! I couldn't stop and I liked feeling this way so much so that I wanted it more and more...

Abruptly these sensations felt like they took off and it actually gave me a spasm! A brilliant spasm! A wonderful spasm! I accidentally made this whimpering noise as I dug my fingers into his skin.

"Oh gees...oh yes...oh no...oh shit!" he winced as he seemed to push extra hard.

He closed his eyes and turned his face away as he kept on moving. It was like he was powerless to stop and he didn't look happy about it. He gripped onto my thighs, squeezing them against his waist. He kept pushing himself harder as he moaned whilst he kept his eyes shut.

Being this close together, I smelled his body odor or his 'scent' as my Dad or Grandfather would call it. Declan smelled like – like - like a food or something, I tried to think of it. He smelled like something that was sweet and buttery, something like maple syrup...

...Declan smells like maple syrup?!

I looked on the scar of the teeth marks near his left shoulder, as well as the long white scar that looked like a claw mark going down his chest. It reminded me of the story of the night a three year old Declan and a pregnant Aunt Susan arrived. The tale of the European Werewolf which followed them here and killed his father and nearly Declan as well, came alive inside my mind from seeing the monster's marks it had left behind.

He came six times, I counted. I almost stopped counting after five, because I thought that we had finished when he stopped moving for about fifteen seconds, before he started up again. He moved so quickly, it was like this was a release for him, a long held release that he could finally let go of. This coupled with how tight his fingers were digging into my thighs? Or the helpless noises that came out of his mouth?

"Take off your top." He asked in a pleading voice. I unzipped my parker and unbuttoned my shirt, before I slowly opened it. "Yeeesss..." he breathed, instantly ducking his head. He used his teeth to pull away the cup of my bra to get at my breasts.

He started to slow down as he sucked and bit which sent my pleasure sky high! The feel of his sharp teeth scraping over my nipples, followed by his hot tongue? It was like the icing on the cake, with his rhythmic movements which were already sending warm, waves of pleasure through my body.

"Oh my - oh what the - oh shit Declan!" I cried out, throwing back my head.

And that was number six...he made himself stop after that. Declan rolled off and onto his back, lying on the wet ground beside me. We were both panting and I guessed he was feeling the same way as I was; fading glory and extremely wet.

"I really am an animal." Declan said unhappily when I didn't say anything. "I should go straight to hell." He moaned which made me looked over and watch as he rubbed his face with his hands and growled, angry at himself. "Since your stupid pheromones started up, I can't get you out of my mind! When we fought on the border, I liked it. I liked knocking you unconscious. I liked carrying you back, because I got to hold you..." He rubbed his face harder. "Argh! Why the fuck do I feel this way?! You're my little brother's girlfriend!"

I looked away to stare up at the canopy of trees, with my feelings of bliss quickly dissipating as the horror set in... I just had sex with Declan... I just had sex with Derik's older brother, with the guy that I hated the most in the world. This happened behind Derik's back and Derik loves me...I blanched upon my betrayal.

With trembling hands, I sat upright as I started buttoning up my shirt again. Just as I was about to stand so I could pull my pants back up, instead I jumped when Declan quickly grabbed my arm.

"What are you doing?" He gave a funny look.

"I'm getting dressed, what does it look like I'm doing?" I returned the look.

"Not yet." He sat upright too. "I filled you to the brim, now I have to make sure that you don't get pregnant."

"Excuse me?"

"Up the duff! A bun in the oven! With child! Do you want me to spell it for you?!" He snapped.

What an asshole! Indignantly, I tried to stand up, but he wouldn't let me. In fact, he pushed me back down to the ground!

"Declan!" I cried out annoyed as he moved over me again. I put out my hands to stop him. "What about the feelings of remorse you were just talking about?!"

"Shut up and stay still!"

He pushed open my legs and then to my shock, he went down on me! What the...?! I didn't know what to do that was until I felt a sharp pain and I tried to move away.

"Oow! Declan!" I objected.

"Do you want to get pregnant and have everybody to find out about us?" he looked up in annoyance. The very fear of that idea made me pause... "That's what I thought." He glared, before he lowered his mouth once more.

He went back to whatever it was he was doing and when the pain returned, I bit into my fist as I forced myself to stay still. However the pain didn't last long...actually the pain very quickly turned into something else. I had to remove my fist as I sucked in my breath from surprise!

"Oh Declan, don't stop." I uttered out as I felt him chuckle in amusement at my change in mind. "Oh Declan... don't stop... oh Declan... don't stop... oh Declan...don't stop don't stop don't stop don't stop!"

A lot faster and a hell of a lot stronger, the pleasure rushed up through my abdomen and spread through out my entire body like a tidal wave! It left tremors of ecstasy in my crotch as I felt my body open itself inside out.

"Frickin hell that was awesome...!" I moaned.

I vaguely became aware his mouth had left that area of my body. He began to kiss his way up my torso, tearing open my shirt and helping himself to my breasts again. I looked down as he used his hands to squeeze my breasts before kissing them.

Declan paused when he realized that I was watching him. "It's not like I'll be doing this again, to you or any other girl in this tribe. I might as well enjoy it while it lasts." He shrugged.

"What?" I asked in further surprise.

"It's not like I have a lot of options, with you being the only girl around that I can do this to, without accidentally killing her or worse, turning her."

"Thanks a lot!" I pushed him off, offended.

Now I stood up as I pulled my jeans back up and then I re-buttoned my shirt before zipping up my parka.

"And it makes it a whole lot worse when you're my brother's girl." He glared as he stood up too.

"Well don't worry, because it's not like I'm proud of what we've done!" I glared back.

"Then you won't tell Derik?" he asked warily.

"What?"

"Then you promise that you won't tell Derik?" Declan demanded. "I would quite happily live with this guilty secret and he'd never know about us."

"There is no 'us'!" I shouted as I turned to walk towards the muddy path again.

"Good because that's exactly what I want to hear!" He followed after.

I returned to trudging up the path when abruptly I was pushed off it once again. This time I was pushed up against a tree! Declan looked longingly on my face as he held me pinned with his greater strength, before he leaned in to kiss hungrily.

Oh shit that felt good and as much as I hate to say this? He was even a better kisser than Derik! His entire mouth smothered mine whilst we had a wrestling match with our tongues; of him trying to be the dominant, with me fighting back. We kissed over and over again, as my heart raced and I began to feel hot and bothered once more!

"There." He pulled back. "If we really had to cheat on my brother, then at least we did it properly." Huh?! I looked on him in disgust as he released his hold. "And don't tell your girlfriends about us either! I know how you chicks like to talk."

"You're a pig!" I rolled my eyes as I turned away to continue walking again.

"This was a one time thing!" He called out. "Don't come looking for it again!"

I don't believe this...I really don't believe this! He pounced on me and he's carrying on as if I were the one who started this?!

"I'm serious! This can never happen again! Even if I'm the best lay you'll ever have..." he went on. I hurried away by power walking up the muddy path, up the hill in the direction of my house as Declan raved like a loony; "...even if you're the only chick I can touch, I can control myself!"

Finally I turned around to shout back, "go and put some clothes on, would you?!"

Declan was standing naked amongst the ferns like he was Adam in the Garden of Eden. He laughed before he morphed into his huge, hulking, hairless European Werewolf shape once more. Like this, he snarled with his sharp teeth glinting in the poor light, with his glowing green eyes flashing.

Lastly, he leapt away from the track to disappear into the trees and just like that, he was gone.

*****

As I walked out of the woods and onto my property again, I hastily straightened my clothes as I worried over my appearance.

My heart was pounding so hard, I was scared that my Lokoti Werewolf father would hear and then he would ask what was wrong? Which I certainly couldn't tell him! Just as I felt guilty about what I had done, I was also worried about anybody finding out.

Nervously, I walked up my veranda steps before I cautiously opened my front door to see where my parents were. I heard Mum banging around in the kitchen but I couldn't see Dad. I quietly came inside, shutting the front door behind then I began to creep over to my staircase...

"B?"

Frickin' hell! I almost jumped out of my skin as I whirled around to find Mum looking up, questioningly.

"B, why is your back all wet like that?" She asked, concerned.

"I slipped over." I lied automatically.

"Oh," she frowned, "are you alright?"

"I'm fine." I said hastily. "Um, where's Dad?"

"He's in the greenhouse planting some new vegetables." She implied that he was right outside. "Did you want to give him a hand?"

"Um, not today." I shook my head, which earned a peculiar look from my mother. "I'm going to have a shower now."

"OK." Mum gave a funny look as she watched me quickly run up the rest of the stairs.

Hurriedly, I stripped off my wet and dirty clothes in the bathroom before I turned on the shower. I stepped under the scalding hot water in an attempt to wash my transgressions away.

My behavior was probably seen as suspicious because Mum knew that I enjoyed working in our greenhouse. My family would put on music and work away to the tunes in a comfortable silence. Mum and Dad knew that I drew great enjoyment from planting, watering and then harvesting my efforts, as the vegetables grew to delicious perfection.

Before World War Three hit, Gran prepared the Lokoti by organizing that every house on tribal lands had a greenhouse to grow fresh fruit and vegetables in; as other kinds of food were put into secret underground bunkers. That way during and after the War, the Lokoti were able to survive the ensuing years of chaos and looting, safe and well-fed.

However if my father found out what I had done this afternoon, there would be another War – between enraged Lokoti Werewolf father and European Werewolf cad.

That day in the shower, I used my strawberry-perfumed shower gel and loofa twice. I sponged myself down a second time to make sure I had removed the last traces of maple syrup scent from my skin.

*****

After dinner as I lay on top of my bed in my pajamas, instead of reading the book I stared vacantly at it. My eyes were looking at the words but my brain was in no way processing them. I couldn't concentrate as my thoughts were elsewhere.

Absentmindedly, I traced my fingertips over my lips which were still tingling from Declan's hot, stronger ones smothering them when we had our tongue-wrestling match. When we were on the ground amongst the ferns he didn't kiss me then, well not on the lips anyway. Now I wondered why? Why did he kiss me afterwards and not during…?

Frickin' hell B...why are you even thinking about this?! You hate the guy, remember? You can't stand the arrogant asshole. He was still rude to you after he did what he did. I mean, I should have wolfed-out then and there and swiped at his smug face with my claws!

Then my eyes squeezed shut, as my body vividly recalled the hypnotizing pleasure I felt with Declan Sabre. I remembered his blue eyes were wide and watching me as he moved, like he wanted to see me come... Oh my gosh!

My face turned bright red as I fell face first into my pillow from lying on my side. I can't believe I just used those words in the same train of thought with Declan Sabre! Hell, I can't believe that I actually had sex this afternoon.

It's strange because I had deliberately never thought about it much. I used to hear about it from either Rachel or Mandy, as we exchanged gossip who was secretly 'doing it'? But I always thought to myself that it would be ages until I 'did it'. Now that I have 'done it' I felt half elated and yet half let down. In the beginning I thought to myself, so THIS is sex? THIS is what the big deal is? But it wasn't until the second round that I started to like it when Declan changed our positions so we could both move differently.

Oh why? Why did I have to do what I did with HIM? I should have done what I did this afternoon with his little brother Derik who was in love with me. It would have been what he would have wanted...but I just don't feel that way for Derik.

I don't feel that way about Declan either, so what was the difference? If I had to choose between two evils, I would pick my best friend over his bullying older brother every day of the week and twice on Sundays. Then how come it was Declan and not Derik who could make me feel all funny inside? How come I didn't like to kiss Derik but I liked kissing Declan?

Maybe somehow my internal wires have been crossed because of this stupid 'bloodlust' thing? Maybe it was what was making me feel this way? I growled in frustration when I knew that it couldn't be true because of the butterflies in my stomach, which appeared the morning Declan drove me home and he put his hand over mine. This happened before I turned into a frickin' Werewolf, so what now?

I sighed in defeat, as I sat upright and slammed my book shut. I stood up from the bed and made a move towards my bedroom window to close my curtains...when I paused.

Through the glass, I spotted in the dark woods a pair of glowing green eyes from Declan watching my window...again. My heart raced, making my face flush and I quickly pulled my curtain shut before I backed away.

What's he doing here? I thought he said he could control himself. So why is he here in the woods outside my house - again? However what really scared me was the compulsion I felt to run outside to relive this afternoon all over again. No, I can't risk this turning into a 'thing'.

I turned off the lamp on my bedside table before I crawled under my covers as I tried to ignore my pounding heart or how my skin was heating up.

"No Bianca Wisetail. This isn't a 'thing' you're having with Declan Sabre. It isn't." I said firmly to my dark bedroom.

Ignore him and ignore your feelings... do this for Derik. This is just some weird Werewolf thing, I know it is. We can ignore it and we will.

~~~~~~
~~~~~~

~ 5 ~

21st September 2084

I trudged up the forest-encrusted hill from the river towards home after being granted a temporary reprieve from my 'house arrest'.

It's been five days since what happened with Declan in the woods and I still felt restless because of my guilty conscience. Usually sitting by the river and listening to the quiet whispers come from the water helped... but not today; not for the past eleven days since I changed; not since this stupid Werewolf business started.

Why me...? Why does it have to be ME to be both a Circulator and a Werewolf? Why does it have to be ME to be the first female Lokoti Werewolf in history? Why can't I just be a Circulator like my mother, my grandmother, my great grandmother and my great, great grandmother? Why do I also have to be a Werewolf like my father, my grandfather, my great grandfather and my great great grandfather...?

Why do I have to be the only girl on tribal lands to have the bloodlust burning on the inside? Why does it have to be me, who turns animalistic and gorge herself on fresh kill? Why do I have to be physically the strongest woman in the tribe? Why does it have to be me to have the potent pheromones to attract the opposite sex? I'm not even interested in relationships!

This completely and utterly sucks! This has even alienated me from the best friend I've had all my life; all because I accidentally shagged his older brother instead of him, which Derik had been hoping for in his unrequited love. I mean, I don't even LIKE Declan, I downright despise him! So why was it with him that I did what I did? Declan doesn't even like me either. What did he say to me afterwards?

"It's not like I have a lot of options, with you being the only girl around that I can do this to, without accidentally killing or worse, turning her..."

As much as we detested each other, we were able to agree that we wouldn't do it again out of respect for his brother...no matter how much our bloodlust turned us towards each other.

We would keep the incident under wraps. No-one must ever know what we did for two reasons, with the most important to spare Derik's feelings. The second was that if the tribe or our parents found out what we had done, they could call us 'mates'. We could be expected to live together as husband and wife... eugh!

Blech! Gross! Disgusting! Me permanently tied to Declan...? We would probably kill each other within the first week of 'marriage'. I would as soon as rip his face off to get rid of his smug expression!

When I returned home from my walk, I saw Dad's truck parked in its usual spot, by the side of the house. Then I slowed my steps when I saw several more trucks and one familiar black jeep, parked out the front. I recognized that the vehicles belonged to Grandpa, Grandfather and one of the other Tribal Elders, but I wasn't sure about the jeep. I had seen it around the community center before, but I couldn't remember who drove it.

Why were the Tribal Elders at my house? They only convened at the meeting hall or on the Holy Grounds for ceremonies. What business did they have here? As I came closer to the house I heard a heated discussion, so heated it sounded like arguing. I picked up Mum's voice first and she didn't sound happy about something.

"She's not even 18 years old!" She said angrily.

"But she'll be 18 in a month." Aunt Beth, one of the Tribal Elders spoke calmly.

"She's talking about going to University!" She exclaimed.

"Jess, you know that B can never leave our lands now. She's tied to her hunting grounds, the place of her ancestors. It's in her blood." Grandpa stated.

"Bianca's future changed the moment she did." Aunt Beth declared.

"But she's a Circulator too! She's going to live longer than 200 years like the other Lokoti Werewolves. She can't stay here for the next 1,000 years or until she evolves, it's unfair to expect that." Mum debated.

"Right now, it's too dangerous for her to leave our land. The first night she changed, she went hunting for human. With her speed as a Circulator coupled with her Werewolf bloodlust, we nearly couldn't catch her before she reached town. She needs to be trained, to curb her bloodlust towards animal and not human." Dad said matter-of-factly.

"It took Declan, who is stronger and faster than us, to catch her when she escaped." Grandfather noted unhappily.

"By B taking a mate and an older Werewolf at that? One who has experience and training, he would help her contain her bloodlust." Grandpa explained. "By B bonding to an older Werewolf, it would help her learn control and give her peace."

What the…? Did they just say that they wanted me to take a MATE?! I froze, as I was dumbfounded by the very idea!

"How is an early marriage supposed to bring her peace?!" Mum retorted. "And an ARRANGED marriage at that?!"

There was an awkward moment of silence, before Dad tried to explain it to her. "Jess, when a Lokoti Werewolf takes a mate, it brings out more of their protector instincts which in turn lessens their predator inclinations. Since the mating process is very much a biological and empathic bonding ritual, if B took another Werewolf as a mate? They would become attuned to each other. B's mate would help her crave animal flesh because that's what he would crave. Then the older Werewolf would be able to sense when B is about to change and be there for her to take her hunting."

"Hunter you're talking about marrying off our 17 year old daughter!" Mum cried out in frustration.

"Jess, do you really think that I would be in support of this if this was a bad idea? Do you think that I would allow the Elders or even the pack tell me what to do with my daughter, if what they were recommending would hurt B? You know I only want the best for my daughter, my little one...and what the pack and the Elders are advising is the right thing." Dad sounded frustrated too.

Mum moaned as I heard the floor boards creak, indicating that she was doing her customary pacing up and down which she always did, when she was unhappy about something.

My mouth turned dry as my stomach churned in a sickening way. My parents, as in my very own Mum and Dad; were letting the pack and the Elders try to marry me off? Just who am I expected to marry...?

"Jess, think back to the day that Hunter saved you from those strangers." Grandfather spoke. "Do you remember when he was gravely injured and I told you that you had to make your decision? Do you remember when I told you that I knew Hunter would make a good mate? I wasn't wrong, was I? You and he have been very happy together. Now we are telling you the same thing about your daughter. I know that this is the right decision for B."

"So you're saying that you're 100% certain that this person here is going to make my little girl happy?" Mum asked in disbelief. "But what about Derik?"

I heard Dad sigh in resignation. "Derik would have made a good mate for B...if she had remained human. But he can't help her with controlling the bloodlust or take her hunting."

Then who are they talking about MATING me to? Oh no, they're not talking about Declan, are they?

"But – but – but can we at least give her a bit more say of who she would like to marry in the pack?" Mum started to argue again. "Since the pack is her only option in the choice of husband material?"

"There are only two males in the pack who are unmarried and they are both older than Bianca. But we have decided on this particular Werewolf because we think it would be risky if she were mated to the other." Grandpa said.

"So basically she only has the one alternative? That's not much in the range of choice!" Mum scoffed.

"She can't consider Declan as a mate for two very obvious reasons." Grandpa spoke as the tribe's Medicine Man. "One, it would cause a rift in his family between he and his brother. Two, is because he isn't a Lokoti Werewolf, he's a European Werewolf. Declan is still battling to keep his bloodlust under control and we aren't sure of the mating habits of his breed. As far as we know, his species isn't designed for long-term mating. His breed of Werewolf doesn't live in packs and his species has never been sighted with a long-term mate. His Werewolf gene may or may not be passed genetically from him to his children? But more importantly, he could harm the woman who is not of his breed when he mates with her."

My eyes fell as my hands clenched into fists. Hang on a sec...I don't feel disappointed that they're not talking about mating me with Declan, am I? I should be happy about this! Even if I don't want to take a mate, at least it wouldn't be him. Then who the hell were they talking about fixing me up with?!

"Fine, I can see that Declan would be a bad choice because of Derik...but still. Isn't there some way of giving my daughter a bit more of a choice? Or what about you, wouldn't you prefer to choose who you would like to be your mate?" Mum asked somebody.

"Who me?" a familiar male voice asked back. "It's OK, Jess. I'm unmarried because I don't have anyone in mind."

"Then wouldn't you prefer to remain single a bit longer?" Mum asked this person. "Until you make up your mind yourself on whom you would like to spend the rest of your life with?"

"Um, I don't mind really." I heard this person say bashfully. "I respect the advice of the pack and the Elders although I've never seen B that way before, I guess because she's much younger than me. But she's friendly, polite and pretty. I know what the mating process entails, so I don't imagine myself being unhappy or B either."

Is this person inside the house, now? The voice was so familiar, I could almost picture whoever it was that's speaking. Right, that's it! My curiosity got the better of me, I have to find out who this person is!

"Bianca's home." Grandfather spoke, hearing my approach.

This silenced everybody as I reached the veranda steps. I threw open the front door and as I walked in, I immediately spotted Mum who was pacing up and down. Dad was sitting down next to Grandfather on one couch and on our second couch, sat Grandpa and Aunt Beth who were on the council of Tribal Elders... and Grant Elm stood by himself in front of our fireplace.

My eyes widened as I looked on Grant...of course! It was his voice that I heard talking and it's his black jeep parked on our drive way. He's the younger brother of Uncle Ian, Dad's best friend so he's like a cousin or something. He's the one I'm expected to MATE with?!

"B..." Dad began.

"Grant is 10 years older than me!" I said indignantly. "He babysat me once when I was 13 years old when you, Mum, Gran and Grandfather went to Australia for a night!"

"B..." Grandfather began.

"What's his hourly rate going to be as my husband, the same when he was babysitting me?!" I exhorted, hurt. "But it seems like he's still going to be babysitting me, isn't he? And that's why you picked him!"

"B..." Grandpa began.

"No way!" I cried out. "I'm going to Cambridge to get a Bachelor of Arts in History! I'm NOT getting MARRIED!"

"B..." Mum began.

But I didn't hang around to hear what they had to say, instead I turned around and took off through the front door! I leapt from the veranda, down onto the drive way and I high-tailed it back into the forest. Everyone else in the room looked to each other uncomfortably, as Grant frowned thoughtfully.

"At least she's a good runner." Grandfather tried to look on the bright side.

"She must make a good hunter, being able to outrun her prey." Aunt Beth agreed.

"Is she wearing a new perfume?" Grant mused.

"No, those were the pheromones you could smell." Grandpa smirked.

"Oh." He pondered this. "She smells good."

"All of the young available men of the tribe would agree with you." Dad sighed wearily as he rubbed his face.

"I'll go and talk to her." Mum started to leave.

"No, I should." He stopped her.

"I don't think that she'll want to talk to you, Hunter. You're apart of the pro-marriage party." She said coldly.

"That's why I should talk to her, instead of you making this any harder for her than it has to be." He replied.

"I'M making this hard for her?" She glared at him. "I'M not the one trying to palm her off!"

"If she knows that it's because the Elders and the pack are concerned for her welfare, then she'll realize that this is the right thing to do." Dad said strongly.

"It's only going to make her feel cornered and more upset!" Mum disagreed.

While they were arguing, Grant walked around them towards the front door. "I'll go talk to her." He volunteered. "She'll probably have lots of questions to ask me."

"Grant..." Mum began to object.

"That's a good idea." Dad said firmly.

Grant left the house, easily leaping from the veranda as he made his way to the tree line of the woods...

... as I ran through the forest in a direction I wasn't sure of, but all I knew was that I had to get out of there and fast. I ran down the hill and found myself back at the river but I didn't stop, I kept running. I ran upstream towards another hill, five kilometers away.

I ran to Sunset Point which was a hill that was just as big as the one that my house sat on top of, but it had a steep, rocky top with a cliff face. Dad has taken me there a couple of times during my summers growing up. We would sit and look over the valley with the river snaking below. It was quiet and peaceful and had the best view of our tribal lands at sunset, hence its name.

One of the good things that I've noticed about being a Werewolf, running was easier now even in human form. I closed the five kilometers distance within minutes before I ran up the steep side like a mountain goat. In the ten minutes I had left my house, I was sitting just over ten kilometers away on the rocky overlook.

I sat huddled in a ball whilst hugging my legs as I looked out over the view. The multiple tree tops looked like a green, uneven carpet contrasted against the dark blue river which flowed through our snow-tipped mountainous land. Everything looked deceptively peaceful, which was in direct contrast to how I was feeling.

Grant...I can't believe they picked Grant! I mean, he's not an asshole like Declan, but he's like an older cousin. Well OK, I admit that I didn't see him very often growing up, except for the couple of times he would come over with his older brother. Dad, Uncle Ian and Grant would fix the roof together and Dad would thank them by providing cans of soda he had saved up, as well as a packet of pretzels or peanuts or something. Then the three of them would remain on the roof to eat and drink their rewards. Or occasionally, he would come over for dinner after fishing with Uncle Ian and Dad. Or I would see him now and then in the meeting hall during tribal functions.

The only time that I really talked to him was the night he babysat me when I was 13 years old. Grant kept me entertained by playing cards as he taught me Poker and Black Jack. He brought a couple of cans of soda as a special treat and he let me stay up until midnight. I remember thinking that night how he was a pretty cool guy.

"Did you brush your teeth?" He quizzed as he stood in my bedroom doorway when he put me to bed.

"Yes." I answered, pulling my covers up. "I thought you were a Werewolf."

"I am a Werewolf."

"Can't you smell the toothpaste?" I asked. "Dad says he knows when I haven't brushed my teeth because he doesn't smell the toothpaste."

"Yeah, I can smell the toothpaste." Grant chuckled.

"Then why did you ask?"

"Hey, give me a break as this is my first babysitting job. All I know is that adults ask kids that question when they put them to bed." He said lightly.

"Oh, OK." I yawned.

"If you want me, I'll be downstairs." He switched off my light as he turned to go.

"Grant?"

"Yeah?" he looked back.

"How old are you?"

"I'm 23 years old."

"When did you turn into a Werewolf?"

"When I was 10 years old, after my father died." He said.

"Oh…" I immediately felt sorry for him, "…Uncle Ian's a Werewolf too, isn't he?"

"Yep."

"How come Uncle Ian is much older than you?"

Grant laughed at my questions. "Because my parents had him 10 years before me with a couple of girls thrown in between."

"Are you the youngest in your family?"

"Yep."

"Is everyone in your family married?"

"Yep."

"Why aren't you married?"

He laughed again as he scratched his head. "Because I haven't met the right one yet, I guess."

"How will you know if she's the right one?"

"I dunno." he mused. "Why is Derik your best friend?"

"Because he is." I shrugged.

"I think it's something similar when I meet the right one." He shrugged.

"Oh OK… g'night." I rolled over onto my side.

"Sweet dreams." He shut my bedroom door behind him.

Grant only babysat me that once and his visits remained sporadic and always in the company of Uncle Ian.

"Hi B." He would grin when he bumped into me at the general store or at family or tribal functions.

"Hi Grant." I smiled back, still thinking that he was one of the coolest adults around because he gave me two cans of soda and taught me Poker and Black Jack.

That would be it as we wouldn't say anything else to each other. I was usually with Derik or Rachel or Mandy and he was with Uncle Ian or somebody else. At tribal functions in the meeting hall when there was a bit of dancing, I noticed he never seemed to run out of dance partners. When I used the ladies bathroom on one occasion, I overheard a couple of older girls talking about him.

"Grant's certainly got that Lokoti Werewolf pheromone thing going for him." Shelly tittered.

"I feel like I'm overheating every time he comes near!" Flora giggled back.

I was 14 years old when I eavesdropped whilst washing my hands. At the time I had no idea what 'pheromones' were, or how Flora could possibly be 'overheating'. I just shrugged and put it down to weird romantic behavior that I didn't see the point in.

"What are pheromones?" I asked my friends when I came back out.

"I don't know." Derik shrugged.

"Where did you hear that word?" Mandy asked curiously.

"Shelly and Flora were talking about Grant and his pheromones." I told them.

"I think it's something to do with sex." Rachel said.

As soon as she said the 's' word, Mandy and I screwed up our faces in distaste. "Eeew!" we cried out at the same time.

"Jinx!" Derik laughed at us. Then he and Rachel watched as we did the jinx finger wrestle which I won as I always did.

Now I knew why I was stronger and faster than Rachel and Mandy, because I was on my way to becoming a Werewolf. It was why I could see better in the dark than Derik. It was why I suddenly started attracting more attention from the opposite sex, when my Lokoti Werewolf pheromones kicked in. They were the prelude for my upcoming change.

I became an anomaly. I became the first female Lokoti Werewolf. I became the fifteenth member of the pack, after Uncle Jack's death. When you included Declan, the pack was sixteen members big but he wasn't a Lokoti Werewolf, he was adopted by the Lokoti Werewolves. Declan was trained by them as he hunted with them before he patrolled our lands alongside of them.

I wonder if one day I'll start patrolling like the other male Werewolves? I wondered what I would do if I came across strangers on our territory? The very thought of it actually made me shiver!

My eyes closed as I thought on how since my change, the smell of human flesh smelled as appealing as a roast dinner. Except the meat was extremely rare and hold the vegetables, so really it was just raw meat off the bone. My mouth watered just thinking about this, which also disturbed me.

I didn't want to eat any of the human tribal members, at least that was something. But the urge I felt that first night I changed; the compulsion, the agonizing desire that drove me to run as fast as I could, off tribal lands and towards town to munch on town folk. I remember the smell of human flesh on the wind, wafting towards me like the smell of a banquet to a starving person.

I remember feeling scared when the pack surrounded me, trying to cut me off from reaching that delicious smell. I also remembered the elation I felt when I escaped from them. Then I remember Declan in his huge, hulking, hairless Werewolf body, catching up to me on the border. I remembered fighting him, with the bloodlust burning in my veins, driving me onwards to even attempt to fight my way past a European Werewolf. My heart still raced as I recalled making out with him after he easily won. Then Declan knocked me unconscious and I remembered waking up on my bathroom floor because the bathroom was the only room in the house that my family could lock me in until I changed back.

"Bianca, you were running right for Alma." Dad said gravely. "You were hunting human. You would have attacked the town folk, if Declan hadn't of caught up to you."

I recalled the look of concern on Dad's face as well as the look of horror on Mum's. Have I really become a disappointment to them? Is that why they're marrying me off? Is that why they don't want me anymore?

Just then I jumped from the sound of footsteps behind! I turned my head sharply, to see Grant easily leap up the steep rocks. He casually came and sat beside, to also look out at the view.

"Sorry, I didn't mean to startle you." He greeted. Nervously I looked away, back over the forest, as I felt shy for the first time in his company. Grant said seriously, "I thought we should talk."

"I don't want to talk." I said petulantly.

"Yes you do." He said evenly. "I'm sure you have lots of questions."

"Only one; how much do my parents hate me to be doing this?" my eyes welled with tears.

"Thanks a lot!" Grant burst out laughing. "I'll try not to take offence." I didn't say anything else, so he spoke again. "I was a bit surprised when the pack and the Elders first spoke to me about the idea. But I can see their logic."

"There's logic?" I asked bitterly.

"You're the first female Lokoti Werewolf. Because you're also a Circulator, you're faster than any member of the pack. You need to be trained and if you took a mate, it will help settle your bloodlust as you would be driven to hunt with your mate. He would guide you towards other quarry than the forbidden fruit."

"I don't see how marrying me off to somebody is going to stop me craving human flesh." My head dropped to stare on the fungus-stained surface of the rock.

"It will help."

"But you're not married so how would you know?"

"If I was married, then we wouldn't be engaged." He tried to joke, but I didn't laugh. "I know this is so because of the experience of the pack and from a millennia of knowledge down our bloodline."

"But I'm the first female Lokoti Werewolf in history, so a millennia of knowledge doesn't seem helpful." I looked out at the view once more.

"You have the same bloodlust that a male Lokoti Werewolf has, so we know it to be true." He answered patiently.

We sat quietly for a couple of minutes, the both of us looking out at the forest underneath.

Grant spoke again, "Look B, I can understand how you're nervous about this...it's taken you by surprise, that's all. When Lokoti Werewolves mate, it goes beyond simple marriage that you've read about in your books or seen in your movies. We would bond together in a way that we would become attuned to each other's thoughts and feelings. When we take a mate, it's a rewarding experience which is why it's held with reverence and it's taken very seriously among our people."

"But I'm not the one." I ducked my head.

"What was that?"

"I'm not the one."

He paused for a moment, before his eyes widened in recognition. "You remember that conversation?"

"It's a bit hard to forget! That night you babysat me was the only time that we ever talked."

"We've talked plenty of times."

"No we haven't. We've said 'hallo' plenty of times, but the night you babysat me five years ago was the only time that we talked." I said as I stared at my shoes.

"I remember that night...I taught you a couple of card games which you picked it up pretty quickly and won a few hands too." He gave a playful nudge.

"You brought over soda and let me stay up until midnight." A smile escaped.

"So how did I go for my first babysitting job?" He asked in good humor.

"Not bad." I shrugged. "Ten out of ten."

"Cool." He sat back as he leant on his hands. "After I looked after you, my older sisters and brother all roped me into looking after their kids now and then too. I think the fact that you managed to live through the experience spoke well of my child care skills. Mind you, they're not so impressed that all their kids are card sharks now and can even fleece half the adults in the tribe."

That made me laugh and I almost relaxed in his company, which I guessed it was what Grant was trying to do.

"What made you think of our conversation on why I wasn't married?" He asked as I shrugged back. "Because our marriage will be arranged?" he guessed before I nodded. Grant moved closer, which made me feel awkward. "Did you know that in our tribe's history there have been other arranged marriages?

I shook my head to show that no, I didn't know that. I briefly looked back his way to show that I was listening, before my eyes skipped away once again.

"There has never been a case where an arranged marriage in our tribe has turned out badly." He started to rub my back, which the gesture surprised me. "And I doubt that we would be the first."

"But I'm our tribe's first female Werewolf." I said in a small voice as I fidgeted with my shoes.

"That just adds to exoticness of our situation. And B?" Next, he used his forefinger to turn my face towards him. "You're not being married to me as a punishment. I see myself as lucky to be marrying you. I know that we'll be happy together and in a way, I feel like I've won a prize in a competition I didn't even know I had entered."

Oh no! Now I felt really rotten, as I tearfully turned away. I should tell him that I was in no way like that, instead I was like a booby prize!

"B?" He looked on, puzzled.

"Grant..." I began.

"Yes?"

"Grant I'm – I'm – I'm..."

"Yeah?"

"I'm not a prize!" my face burned. "I'm not a virgin!"

"OK." He raised his eyebrows but he didn't remove his hand from my back. "Er, would it be helpful for you to know that neither am I?"

I looked his way in surprise, "I thought we weren't supposed to have sex unless it's with the one who is meant to become our mate?"

"That's what our Elders would prefer, sure." He shrugged. "But I guess you've come to realize yourself that certain things happen by their own accord."

"How did you manage to have sex without mating yourself to somebody?" I asked bluntly.

Grant cracked up laughing again. "You've still got a curious mind." I quickly looked away, embarrassed. "No, it's cool." He cleared his throat. "Um well, male Werewolves can hold themselves back."

"Oh." I thought on this in befuddlement.

"If you don't mind me asking, what was it like for you?" He queried.

"What?!" I looked on him in alarm as I had no idea how to answer that! He leaned in to sniff me. I leaned away shyly. "What are you doing?"

"Phew! You don't smell like you've mated with anybody." He said in relief.

"Huh?" I wondered what the hell he was going on about?

"If you were mated to somebody, I would have smelled him on you." Grant said plainly. "If I had smelled him on you, it would have been a little embarrassing to return to our families and say that you already had a mate."

"Oh...!" My eyes widened in horror at the idea of everybody finding out about Declan.

"Since I can't smell him on you, it means that the last time you were with this person was a while ago. If you had mated with this person, his smell on you would be strong because you would see him frequently. If you were mated to this person, you wouldn't be able to go for long periods of being separated from him."

"OK..." My eyebrows rose as my brain digested this piece of information.

This would explain how Gran and Grandfather, Nana and Grandpa and even Mum and Dad behaved as if they were joined at the hip. I had always thought that Werewolf couples were the soppiest in the tribe, which was in direct contrast to the Werewolf's dangerous bloodlust. Does this mean that this could one day be me too?

"Smell me." He suddenly offered.

"Excuse me?"

"Smell me." Grant said simply.

"Why?"

"Just smell me!" He laughed at my hesitation. I leaned over closer and inhaled. He looked expectant, "well?"

"Well what?"

"What do you smell?"

"Um, I don't know..."

"Did you smell perfume or human female scent or anything like that?"

"No."

"Then you know I haven't got a mate either." He stated. "Or you would be able to smell her on me."

"Oh, OK." I raised my eyebrows, impressed at learning something new about myself. "Can humans do this?"

"Some can, but it's generally just Werewolves because of our keen sense of smell."

"Cool." I smiled.

"See?" Grant grinned. "It's not so bad being a Werewolf, is it?"

"Um no, I guess not."

"There are many benefits in being who you are," he rested his hand on the back of my neck, "and when you take a mate? You'll find out many more things that make you special and what you have with your mate is unique."

~~~~~~

22nd September 2084

This morning after eating a huge, hot breakfast that Dad cooked up; I helped Mum with the washing up. He was finally leaving the house since my change.

"I'm going to help repair the Lightfoot's roof." He announced as he put his wallet and his keys in his pocket.

"You're not playing 'jailor' today, Dad?" I teased as I grabbed the tea towel to do the drying.

"Nope." He smiled to show that he wasn't offended. "Besides in another week, that will be Grant's job."
~~~~~~

Then to show that he was joking, he tweaked my nose before he placed a kiss on his wife's cheek.

"I'll be home around 5 PM." He told her.

"Don't fall off the roof." She said coolly as she didn't look up from her task.

Dad paused on his way out when he heard that and he shot off a hurt look towards Mum but she didn't see.

I felt awkward as I realized that she was still upset over the idea of my arranged marriage, which put her in direct disagreement with Dad. I also came to the realization that he had cooked up the huge hot breakfast of bacon, eggs, grilled tomato, mushrooms, hash browns and toast this morning; as a nice gesture to try to bring back some peace in our household.

He didn't say anything else as he looked from Mum to me and then back to her. He turned and left the house without another word. I heard the sound of his truck start up and I remained quiet as I listened to him reverse out of the driveway.

From remaining quiet, I began to hear Mum mutter angrily as she washed up our plates, cups and cutlery so fast that her hands were a blur.

"What is this, the 21st Century or the 1st Century?" She fumed. "Where women are property or cattle to be owned? Where women can't decide on their future? Where women can't even decide who they're gonna marry or when they're gonna marry?!"

She showed little regard as she dumped the crockery into the draining rack so hard that I thought that our plates might crack! The angrier Mum got, the faster she whizzed through the washing up almost moving at the speed of light with her ability as a Circulator. I struggled to keep up and I was barely a quarter of the way through the drying when the dish rack strained under the entire wash load. She drained the dirty dishwater out of the sink, before she grabbed the sponge and the multipurpose spray. As I continued to dry, she wiped down the stove top and the kitchen benches.

"I'm tempted to instantaneously phase you somewhere time where the stupid Lokoti Werewolves will never find you!" She grumbled in a low voice. "My own daughter - a Circulator - being told who to marry, before her 18th Birthday just because she's also a Werewolf!" Next, she stormed out of the kitchen to wipe down the table. "This is ridiculous! My daughter who's a month away from her 18th Birthday is being forced into adulthood by a fucking arranged marriage?!"

I paused in surprise at my mother's language. "Did you just say 'fucking'?"

"I said 'fricking'!" She quickly tried to cover. "Fricking is not a swear word!"

"No, but the word 'fucking' is." I smirked.

"Bianca Grace Wisetail you will not use that kind of language!" She pointed the multipurpose spray my way.

"OK then Jessica Grace Wisetail." I tittered. "I won't if you won't."

Just then there was a loud knock on the door which made us look on each other in surprise.

"Is that for you?" Mum queried.

"It can't be for me as I'm not allowed to have any visitors, remember?"

Out of curiosity, I came to stand in the entranceway of the kitchen so I could watch her answer the door...as soon as she did though, I jumped backwards to hide myself! Aunt Julienne and her two married daughters, Vine and Hannah stood on our front veranda. They were Uncle Ian and Grant's mother and sisters. What the hell are THEY doing here?

"Aunt Julienne." My mother greeted and I heard the surprise in her voice too.

"Jess." She returned. "Can we come in?"

"Er, of course." I heard her move back to let them enter the house.

"I expect that you know why we're here." She came straight to the point.

"I suppose so." Mum forced herself to be polite. "Because of B's upcoming arranged marriage to Grant."

"You might as well come out, Bianca." Aunt Julienne called. "I saw you duck into the kitchen."

Frickin' hell, I've been sprung! Reluctantly, I came into plain sight as I moved to stand beside my mother. Although I was now taller than her, she still placed a protective arm about my shoulders.

"Jess." The older woman saw this. "Ian tells us that you're worried about your daughter's union with my son."

"You could say that." Mum said diplomatically.

"I suppose you're thinking that B is too young for this." Vine spoke.

"You could say that too." She said crisply as her hold on me tightened.

"Jess," Aunt Julienne started, "your husband and my eldest have been best friends all their lives. They became Werewolves just a few months apart when their grandfathers died in protecting their homes and the tribe. I saw you grow up from knee-high to the Circulator you now are, when you helped save this tribe from the Invaders."

"Our families go back awhile." Hannah summed up.

"Grant knows this." His mother stated. "He's fought as one of the pack for the past thirteen years for his family and his people. Your husband helped initiate him after he turned from the death of his father, my beloved Yule." I caught Aunt her eyes turn misty from the mention of her late husband, but she stood steadfast as she cleared her throat. "Grant in some ways is like a little brother to Hunter as well as to Ian. So you can be damn sure that my youngest is going to take good care of your little one!"

Mum took a deep breath as she planned her words carefully; "thank you Aunt Julienne. I appreciate your words as I appreciate you coming over to say them, but -"

"But nothing!" She interrupted. "Jess, I think in many ways you're more 'Light Person' than you are Lokoti!" she eluded to Mum being a Circulator which the Lokoti called 'Light People'.

"You may be right but - " Mum started but she was interrupted again.

"Your daughter is a Lokoti Werewolf!" Aunt Julienne fired up. "B is the first female Lokoti Werewolf in the history of the tribe. It's only natural, right and proper that she ends up with another Lokoti Werewolf like Grant. Someone who will be patient, kind and understanding with her since he went through the same thing when he changed."

"I'm not disputing that but - " She tried again.

"We all know about B and Derik." Vine said. "The whole tribe does."

They do? I pondered what exactly it was that they thought they knew? Does everybody think that Derik and I were a couple? The Elm's looked on in sympathy.

"We know the transition will be hard for you B," Vine continued, "and we know a person can't just switch their feelings like that."

Huh? What feelings were these per se?

"But we also know that you'll grow to love Grant," Hannah added on, "and that our little brother will take care of you."

I exchanged a puzzled look with Mum as she too wondered what the hell they were going on about?

"Derik and I are best friends but nothing more!" I quickly put in.

However I don't think they believed me as Aunt Julienne next looked Mum's way, "we know that the Sabre's are old friends to the Riverclaw family. We know that you, your mother and Susan Sabre were hoping for a union between B and Derik instead. But consider this Jess, the Elm family are just as much old friends to the Wisetail family. With the experience of the pack which goes back for hundreds of years, we know that this marriage is a good thing for B. Otherwise the pack and the Tribal Elders wouldn't have suggested it in the first place!"

I could sense the anger building up inside of my mother, if she were a Werewolf she probably would be growling right about now! However Vine recognized the dangerous look in her eye so she tried a different approach.

"Let's all sit down and talk about this calmly." She suggested.

"Yeah, like a negotiating table." Hannah agreed.

Next we found ourselves hustled towards the dining table. We were sat down with Vine sitting at the head of the table like the mediator as she sent Hannah into the kitchen to procure coffees for everyone. I think she was hoping to use the caffeinated beverages as a 21st Century version of the 'peace pipe'.

"Now Mom." Vine looked towards her elderly mother. "Nobody is saying that Grant isn't a suitable husband." Aunt Julienne looked away offended by the very idea. "Now Jess." Vine looked towards her. "Nobody is saying that you're reaction to B's early marriage is unreasonable." Mum looked away in annoyance too. "But let's all agree on one thing, shall we? That B's unique situation has called for a very unique solution."

I groaned as I fell forwards to bang my head on the table, "I don't want to be a Werewolf!"

"Now aside from the over-dramatic moaning and groaning." Vine threw me a wry look. "Let's try to come up with an amicable arrangement between us women."

"Too true sister!" Hannah called enthusiastically from our kitchen.

"A bunch of males may have come up with the idea of B's early marriage," she rolled her eyes, "and now it's up to us women to try to smooth out the bumps to their less than cunning plan."

"As women typically do." Hannah readily agreed as she prepared the coffees.

"So." Vine clapped her hands together. "B, you are a Circulator and a Lokoti Werewolf, is that correct?"

"Um yeah, I guess my torn clothes can confirm that."

"Grant can sew!" Hannah called out. "He's an expert from years of experience of doing his own!"

"B," Vine continued to look my way, "when you change into a Werewolf, I hear that you can outrun the pack because you're a Circulator too."

"I guess." I shrugged.

"I see." She continued in her role as the negotiator. "Your mother and your grandmother being Circulators could catch you because they're as fast as you, but you would be stronger than them as a Werewolf. When it comes to the male Lokoti Werewolves, they're strong enough to stop you but they can't catch you, am I correct so far?"

"Uh huh."

"Go the girl power!" Hannah cheered as she poured in the milk.

"So," Vine went on, "the pack have recommended that if you mate with a male Lokoti Werewolf who will become attuned to you, he will sense when the bloodlust is upon you and take you hunting for animal instead of human."

"Supposedly." Mum rolled her eyes as she stubbornly crossed her arms.

"Jess." Vine looked on her. "Has Hunter ever been a bad husband?"

"Excuse me?" She retorted. "Of course not!"

"Has Hunter always sensed what you were feeling?" Vine asked again.

"Well yes he has but - "

"When your father told you that he believed that Hunter would be a good mate, was he wrong?"

"No but - "

"Then we can promise you the same thing, Jess." Aunt Julienne said firmly. "Grant will cherish B for as long as he lives."

Mum jumped up from the table to start pacing up and down once more as she wrung her hands.

"Coffee's ready!" Hannah sung cheerfully as she carried over the mugs. "Aren't I a silly goose? I should have brought the choc-chip cookies I made yesterday."

She sat down in the seat beside her mother before we all picked up our cups, all except Mum that is.

"Look," she spoke as she paced, "I'm NOT discounting the kind of husband Grant will make for B or for any girl for that matter. But I'm concerned about B's age and her future."

"Aren't we all?" Vine tried to point out.

"Jess, the Lokoti aren't a group of people who just happen to inhabit the same land - we're one. We're strong because of this fact. What happens to one person affects us all." Aunt Julienne said formally.

"We all want to help B." Hannah agreed.

"At the moment this means marriage to Grant." Vine said simply.

"But why?" I spoke up. "How is marrying me off going to help curb my bloodlust?"

Vine next exchanged looks with Hannah and her mother.

"I'll answer this one." The older woman told her daughters. "After all, I was married to a Werewolf and I have two sons who are Werewolves."

Vine and Hannah's husbands were human so they let their mother go right ahead. They quietly sipped their beverages, occasionally snickering at their mother's words.

Aunt Julienne began, "B, you never knew my husband who was Ian's, Vine's, Hannah's and Grant's father, since he died fighting the European Werewolf that turned Declan Sabre. When I first met Yule Elm and before I knew he was a Werewolf, I thought he was arrogant, immature and a compete smartass."

Her daughters erupted into giggles and even Aunt Julienne had a chuckle, before she pressed onwards. Although she spoke humorously, I still detected a great deal of emotional attachment especially by the expression on her face.

"Yule Elm thought he was the 'bees knees' and because he had a small gaggle of giggling girls thanks to his Werewolf pheromones? He got quite a shock the first time he asked me out and I refused him. He didn't believe his ears so I had to scream the word 'no' to make him go away!"

Now Mum let out a snicker as her pacing began to slow and she listened to Aunt Julienne tell her story.

"I moved to Alma with my parents when I just entered my teens. As you may know, I'm not Lokoti by birth but my mother's from the Haida Tribe. I met Yule when we attended school in Alma, long before the War. Yule was in the year above and he didn't pay much attention to me until he was in his Senior year. I happened to wear a new perfume one day as well as my hair differently to attract the attention of a boy in my year? But I ended up attracting a teenaged Lokoti Werewolf instead. I didn't know he was a Werewolf of course as I wasn't a part of the tribe then. All of a sudden this physically attractive but obnoxious boy kept throwing himself into my face and into my life at every possible chance he could. Before we married we fought about how much time he spent with his friends, or the stupid dare-devil stunts he used to pull or his secretive behavior around a full moon, when he would disappear for three days straight and I had no idea what was going on! But somehow or rather I took leave of my senses and I agreed to marry him... and my word the transformation he underwent made me even wonder if he was the same man!"

I noticed in the corner of my eye Mum had returned to her seat and picked up her cup of coffee, as she listened with interest. Aunt Julienne saw that she had captured all of our attention so she went on.

"After we married, Yule told me he was a Werewolf. He had to, as one week after our wedding day it was a full moon. He assured me as did the tribe that Lokoti Werewolves don't hunt human and since I grew up in Alma and we didn't have any people go missing, I believed them. But the first time I saw Yule as a Werewolf? I very near fainted, which of course hurt his feelings. As it came to be when you're married to one of his kind, I was soon with child and Yule's attentiveness during those nine months was legendary...! For the first three years of our marriage I didn't even open a door for myself – I kid you not! If I was walking towards a door then Yule would suddenly appear and open it for me. He wouldn't let me carry anything remotely heavy and he was always rushing about, buying whatever food that he sensed I craved."

"Our Granny said her son turned into a new man." Vine joked.

"The whole tribe was astounded by the transformation in him once we married. Sure, his wise-cracks remained which consequently Ian inherited from his father." Aunt Julienne flashed a smile to Mum.

She knew all about Uncle Ian's loud sense of humor, as his jokes would usually be about her. They delighted in ribbing each other as they exchanged many a taunt, which made Dad laugh at the two.

The older woman spoke candidly, "but what amazed me was here was this Werewolf; who had this thing called the bloodlust, which demanded that Yule partook in feasting on fresh kill every full moon. Yet he was also the most loving, kindest and gentlest of husbands and fathers."

Mum ducked her head as she stared at the table. I caught a small smile play on her lips, as I guess she saw Dad in the same way. The elderly woman wore the same nostalgic look, thinking back on her late husband.

"So you see B," Vine turned my way. "The reason why the pack and Elders have suggested that you mate with Grant is because of this; by becoming your mate he will sense you craving flesh the way Dad sensed when Mom craved chocolate. He will be able to take you hunting every full moon as you take your place among the pack."

"The change that Yule went through when he took a mate, it calmed his wild ways which is what we expect will happen to B. This in turn, will help her control the bloodlust." Aunt Julienne finished.

Oh...I see. I stared into my coffee as their words slowly sunk in. The Elms turned quiet as Mum and I considered carefully what they had said. In turn, our visitors watched our faces closely.

Mum looked my way, "well, what do you think, B?"

I continued to gaze downwards, which probably caused some concern. The air was thick with anticipation, as I sensed everybody's plans hung on my acquiescing to the pack and the Elders' decision.

"I guess I'm going to get married." I said as I still stared into my mug.

~~~~~~
~~~~~~

~ 6 ~

25th September 2084

I knocked on his front door... Nothing. I knocked on his front door again... Still nothing. I knocked on his front door a third time, then I leaned forward to listen. I didn't hear footsteps or a single noise at all. Hmm...I know he's home as I can smell his scent.

I stepped off his tiny patio before I walked around the small, wooden house. I helped myself through the side gate, where I found him in the backyard. He was hanging out washing on the clothes line.

"B!" Derik beamed as soon as he saw me approach.

"Hey, I thought you were home." I smiled back as I walked up.

"Did you knock on the front door?" He guessed. "Sorry I didn't hear you. We tried fixing the doorbell, but it's still busted."

"No problem." I shrugged casually, which belied my racing heart.

I picked up some wet laundry out of his washing basket to help him hang it out.

"How are you?" Derik asked with a serious expression on his face.

"Oh...you know." I shrugged again.

"How's it going?" He asked sympathetically, "I mean, with your change."

"You mean what it's like being a Werewolf?" I asked to which he gave a nod. "Oh...you know." I repeated, my stomach knotting. I was starting to chicken out, but the fear of him finding out about my news from another source than me and hurting him even more, made me go on. "Um Derik, I came to tell you something."

"Yeah?" he bent over to pick up a shirt to hang next.

"Um..." I faltered, "...you're probably not going to like this, but I thought you should know anyways."

"Oh?" He gave a funny look, picking up a pair of jeans. I paused as I watched him hang that up next and clip on the pegs. He looked my way inquiringly, "B?"

I gazed back guiltily as my stomach shrunk and my hands started shaking. I had to glance downwards as I kicked at the clothesline post. I wished I didn't have to do this...I would have given anything not to.

"B, what is it?" He asked concerned. "You're not sick or anything, are you?"

"Sick?" I echoed, before I let out a bitter laugh. "Sometimes it feels like that! But no, I'm not sick."

"Then what is it?" he stopped what he was doing to meet my gaze as he waited.

"Derik..."

"Yes?"

"Derik, I'm sorry..."

"Yeah?"

"Derik I'm getting married."

His face fell – literally. His mouth fell open, his eyes bulged outwards and his whole face looked ashen. "You're...what?"

"I'm getting married."

"To who?!" He erupted angrily.

"To um..."

"Yes?"

"Um..."

"Yeah?!" He demanded.

"To Grant Elm."

"Grant Elm?!?" He echoed. "But that guy is ten years older than you!"

"I know that."

"Why the hell are you marrying Grant Elm?!" He walked up to shout in my face.

"Because the Elders and the pack..."

"What about the Elders and the pack?"

"Because my family and the Elders and the pack said so."

"The PACK?!" Derik yelled. "A bunch of Werewolves are telling you to marry another Werewolf?!"

"Yeah, basically." I said helplessly.

"Then say no!" He grabbed hold of both of my arms.

"I wish it was as simple as that..."

"Why isn't it as simple as that? My God you haven't - you haven't MATED with him, have you?!" Derik released me in disgust.

"No! Not yet...but that's what they want me to do."

"Why?"

"Because he's a Werewolf and they think that mating with one of my kind will help control the bloodlust." I poured out.

"What?"

"To help me stop craving human flesh."

"What…?" He stared in shock.

"I want to eat human, Derik." My eyes watered. "The very first night I turned, I tried to run to town and eat a townsperson."

"You tried to what?"

"But Declan stopped me. My speed being a Circulator has made me exceptionally fast. I outran the pack and Declan just managed to catch me before I left Lokoti land. I nearly ate a human being that night…"

"DECLAN stopped you?" His eyes bulged. I stood there as he walked away, shaking his head in disbelief. A full minute passed as I guess he had to process all of this. Then he turned back around to face me, "but why are the other Werewolves marrying you to Grant Elm?"

"By mating with him, it's supposed to help curb my craving for human flesh and calm me down."

"Calm you down?" He looked on, hurt. "But what about me? What about us? I thought that your parents always approved of us!"

"They did…until I turned into a Werewolf." I confessed. "My change has all of the pack and the Elders in an uproar. I'm a freak! I'm not meant to be…now they don't know what to do with me."

"Except to marry you off to another Werewolf?!"

"Yeah, basically."

"You're just going to go along with this?" His eyes filled with tears.

"I don't know what else to do, Derik! I even scare myself! You don't understand the bloodlust! I'm not B Wisetail anymore but I'm a monster! I'm a creature of the night! Even with you standing here right now, you smell like a roast dinner complete with my Great Grandma's special gravy!"

"You want to EAT me?" He blanched.

"Not specifically but generally speaking, yes."

"What?!"

"I don't want to eat you or our tribe but I crave human flesh. I want to hunt. I want to gorge myself on fresh kill." I confessed, "and because I'm fast and hard to catch, the pack and the Elders have decided that it's best that I be bonded to an older Werewolf like Grant who can curb my bloodlust. He's supposed to become attuned to me and take me hunting."

Derik rubbed his red eyes and sniffed, as he looked away, "and I suppose Cambridge is now out of the question."

"For me it is but not for you." I couldn't keep the disappointment from my voice. "Because I'm Lokoti Werewolf, I supposedly can't leave Lokoti land for long periods of time."

"I wish you never turned into a Werewolf." He said miserably.

"You and me both."

"So what you're saying is that if you had remained a human being, then you could be with me? But because of your transformation, you're being married off to Grant?"

"Basically." I shrugged helplessly.

He turned silent once more as he turned to walk a little away. He remained quiet for a good two minutes, making me start to think that this was the end of our conversation. I turned to leave, when Derik faced me once more.

"Say no."

"Say no?" I looked back.

"Tell your family and the Elders and the pack that you're marrying me."

"What?" I gave a funny look.

"Marry me Bianca!" He walked up and tried to put his arms around my waist, but I took a step away.

"Derik?"

"I'll be your mate."

"But Derik, you can't take me hunting."

"Why not?"

"Because you're not a Werewolf!" I stated the obvious. "If you were around when I lost control of my bloodlust? I mean, I would do everything in my power to ensure that you wouldn't come to harm. But if one day something went wrong, or the bloodlust became too much..."

"Bianca you would no more eat me than your father would eat your mother!"

"You're right." I admitted. "I'm bound to protect the tribe, as well as my loved ones which is why I hunger for the flesh of the humans in Alma."

"Then what's the problem?"

"You can't stop me if I did go for a townsperson. I would become a murderer. I would have a human death on my head." I looked downcast.

"Then Declan would stop you again." He thought up.

I flinched at the sound of his name before I said sadly, "I'm sorry but I stopped being the girl who was your best friend all our lives, the night I changed. You wouldn't be able to stop me if I saw a non-Lokoti in my path."

"Then I'll get a rifle with tranquilizer darts!"

My hot tears spilled over, as I half laughed and half cried. "I'm sorry Derik, but that wouldn't work."

"What if you came here and lived with me as my mate? Then if you turned, Declan would be able to take you hunting." He cried out in frustration.

"Derik," my tearful gaze met his, "I'm sorry but that just wouldn't work."

He looked on longingly. "B, I love you."

I rasped out, "I know Derik and I'm so sorry! You're my best friend and the last person in the world that I would ever want to hurt."

Quickly, I threw my arms about him for a second or two, before I released him to hurry out of his back yard.

My face looked like a river of tears as I cried all the walk home. I openly sobbed as I walked out of the community centre to the road which went up the hill to my house. I walked up the hill, barely noticing the cheerful sunny day of the last of the warm weather for fall. I stomped past my relatives' houses as if I blamed my Werewolf relations, as I cried all the way to my house.

When I turned into my yard, I saw Grant's jeep was parked on the driveway, along with two of the Tribal Elders trucks. But I didn't want to see them. I didn't want to listen to their plans for Grant's and my future together...I wouldn't be able to stand it.

I veered off to walk into the woods, when I heard Dad call out; "B, is that you? Can you come inside please?"

Frickin' hell! I took several deep breaths, wiped my face dry with my sleeves and then I turned back around. I weaved between the vehicles before I climbed the veranda steps. As soon as I walked in through the front door, I found not just Grant here with two of the Tribal Elders, Aunt Beth and Grandpa; but I also found Uncle Ian and Grandfather were here too.

Everyone was seated around the dining table like some kind of conference was going on, complete with Aunt Beth and Mum writing notes.

"Hi B." Grant smiled warmly in my direction.

"B." Grandfather nodded.

"Come in, B." Aunt Beth waved me over. "Join us, please."

There was a spare seat at the table, but I didn't take it. Instead I wandered over to the couch and sat on the arm rest, keeping my distance from the instigators of my misery. Everyone frowned at my unhappiness and Mum and Dad exchanged concerned glances. I picked up one of the cushions and began to fidget with the tassels so I wouldn't have to look at anyone.

Grandfather cleared his throat. "Before we go on with the wedding plans, I have some good news for B." However I didn't look up as I began to plait the tassels. He announced, "your Gran has sent off your application to Cambridge University to study via correspondence."

"Really?" Mum asked excitedly. "She can do her Bachelor of Arts in History by correspondence?"

"Uh huh. Your mother thinks that B has a good chance to be accepted too. Apparently the organization Hodge Endeavor still holds some sway over there. Hodge Endeavor will be paying for her education, which Cambridge looks favourably on as her scholarship fund. Last night, your Gran sent off via email one of B's history papers with her application." Grandfather claimed.

"B that's great news!" Dad said chirpily.

In the corner of my eye, I caught my parents take hold of each other's hands and exchange gleeful looks. I bit down on my lower lip as I ducked my head further to hide my face.   Just keep plaiting B... just keep plaiting...the build up of bile in my throat became worse, but I managed to swallow it back.

What would have made me happy was if I still had my best friend to share the 'good news' with. What really would have made me ecstatic, was if my best friend and I could have gone to Cambridge to study together. I just wish I could leave this life of a Werewolf behind; to walk away from my monumental mistake with Declan; walk away from the bloodlust that made me feel perpetually hungry or even angry; walk away from the constant pounding in my ears of everybody's hearts beating along with my own...

"B," Dad frowned, "you could at least say thank you."

"Thank you." I repeated automatically like a robot.

"You know in the library at Blythe, there's Elisha's, Jarrod's, Xavier's and Bastian's old Uni work from their days at Cambridge. Mum kept them. We could have a look through their old notes at the class structure with the lectures and tutorials and things like that." My mother thought up.

"But I won't be going to any lectures or tutorials." I growled in frustration.

"Maybe not, but at least it will give you an idea on how the lessons will be structured." She reasoned.

I bit so hard on my lower lip, forcing myself to remain quiet that soon I tasted blood - my blood.

"Let's continue with our plans." Grandpa said. "We only have five days before the wedding to enable Grant and Bianca to prepare for the next full moon."

"Because of this type of arrangement, the Tribal Elders feel that instead of the usual celebration of a Housewarming that we should formalize this union with a Joining Ceremony." Aunt Beth announced.

"A Joining Ceremony?" Mum echoed in surprise.

"In the old days, when a man or woman or a werewolf and woman coupled, there was a Joining Ceremony. It's when the Tribal Elders acknowledge their joining." Grandpa explained.

"I can't remember when the last Joining Ceremony happened. All the other weddings we've been to were Housewarmings to set up for the new couple." Dad thought aloud.

"That's what happened when we were 'married', we had a Housewarming." Mum agreed. "Why does it have to be different with Grant and B?"

"In the old days, a wedding came in two parts; the Joining Ceremony and then the Housewarming. At the Joining Ceremony the Elders blessed the man and woman's union and then the Housewarming was the tribe's way of helping the new couple set up their home. In the last few decades, the Joining Ceremony has been dropped with just keeping the Housewarming. Since B and Grant's union is arranged, the Tribal Elders thought it should be formalized." Aunt Beth explained.

"When was the last Joining Ceremony?" Dad inquired.

"The last ceremony was last held around 50 years ago, with our last arranged marriage." Grandpa told him.

"Arabella and I had an Anglican Wedding Ceremony to appease her family shortly after we mated. That was a Joining Ceremony as such but different customs." Grandfather shrugged.

"I know what happens during an Anglican Wedding Ceremony, I saw Mum and Dad's wedding DVD." My mother pondered. "But what happens during a Lokoti Joining Ceremony?"

"On the Holy Grounds before the three Sacred Totems, the nine Tribal Elders convene, with the tribe as witnesses." Aunt Beth spoke gravely, showing her reverence towards the ritual. "The man and woman come forward and ask for the Elders blessing. We give thanks to our mother the earth and to our father, the Lokoti Wolf. We tell the man and woman that by this Joining Ceremony they will become like the Lokoti Wolf, by mating for life. Then from the sacred cup that has been kept by the Tribal Elders for generations, the man and woman each mixes a drop of blood into the mead and drink from it, sealing their fates together. By doing this, the Tribal Elders acknowledge the man and woman as Husband and Wife and are empowered by the Lokoti Wolf to bless the union."

There was a moment's silence as the table seemed to contemplate this. However, my stomach felt like it was full of snakes, all writhing and wriggling around inside. I felt like a complete fraud, expected to go through a ritual like that to a man I hardly knew!

"Does the man and woman have to wear special clothes?" Mum asked next.

"The Tribal Elders will be wearing the Lokoti clothing of old and so should the Husband and Wife." Aunt Beth advised.

"What does that entail?" My mother looked to her father-in-law.

"B can wear my grandmother's skins that she wore for her Joining Ceremony." Grandpa offered.

"And Grant can wear our grandfather's skins that he wore for his Joining Ceremony." Uncle Ian patted his brother on the back.

"Good." Aunt Beth said in approval. "By the couple wearing the traditional clothes of their ancestors, this will seal their futures together as they respect their past."

This almost made me laugh, but I managed to stifle the snicker.

"B." I heard Grandfather say in disapproval, catching me out.

"B, come and sit at the table please." Dad ordered.

But I couldn't...I just couldn't sit at the same table as the conspirators. I couldn't bring myself to be in league with their plans. Mum saw that I wasn't going to move, or that I was unable to and she quickly moved along.

"So about this Housewarming," she changed the subject. "Hunter told me you have a house already sorted out?"

I guess she must have been speaking to Grant, as he answered with; "ah yeah, I've bought the old Windchime place up the top of this hill."

"Oh, the one at the end of the road?" Mum sounded happy. "Well, we're all going to remain together on the same hill then. I like that, as it adds a certain sense of familial to it."

"We can make the Joining Ceremony at 10 o'clock in the morning and then at midday the Housewarming can begin." Aunt Beth said. "We'll have all afternoon to celebrate as we set up the new couple's home."

"Sounds like a plan." Uncle Ian agreed. "Grant, Hunter, Em and I will have the place spick and span, repaired and ready by Saturday."

"We certainly will." Dad said confidently.

I sucked on my bleeding lip as my fingers madly plaited away the tassels on the square cushion; I had plaited two sides already. Then there was a pause in the conversation as I sensed Grandfather and everyone else look over in my direction.

"I could show you the house this afternoon if you like, B." Grant offered.

Frickin' hell, I felt the clothes around my underarms become drenched in a cold sweat. I turned the cushion around and began plaiting the third side as I literally felt like I was unable to speak.

"That sounds like a great idea, Grant." My mother spoke for me again. "That way B can get an idea of the lay out of the place, so when the furniture and household goods start arriving, she'll know where to put it all."

Dad frowned; "B, can you please come and sit at the table and involve yourself in the conversation?"

"Hunter." Grandpa said softly and shook his head at him to back off.

"A Housewarming this Saturday may be a bit too soon. Is it enough warning for the tribe to scrape together the furniture for the couple's new place?" Mum wondered.

"It should be fine, Jess." Grandfather smiled on his daughter. "The Lokoti are a resourceful people."

"I've just finished building the couple's dining table and chairs and they'll have two rocking chairs for their lounge room." Uncle Ian boasted about his furniture construction business.

"You build good furniture, Ian." Aunt Beth said in approval. "That tallboy and two bedside tables that I gave to my granddaughter for her Housewarming look great."

"Grant made the two bedside tables." He said proudly.

He did? I listened in with mild interest to keep my temper at bay. It was almost working too...

"Good work Grant." Aunt Beth said warmly. "So have you decided to permanently work with your brother in his furniture construction business? Or do you just help out occasionally with the other odd jobs you do around the tribe?"

"I've been helping Ian with the furniture or Hunter with house repairs around the community." Grant told her.

"Talking about construction." Dad spoke up. "I've now scraped up enough glass for us to start the greenhouse repairs at your new place."

"Cool." He gave a nod and then he threw a sideways glance my way before he spoke again. "I guess we'll have the greenhouse fixed before Saturday. B and I could start potting and planting as soon as we move in."

"Oh and B?" Mum spoke again. "I've bought new packets of seed for you. I've bought something like ten different kinds of vegetables to get you started in your new place."

I turned the cushion around as I began to plait the last side.

"Thanks Jess." Grant said appreciatively for the both of us.

Grandpa cleared his throat. "You certainly seem to be good with your hands, B. Have you thought about taking up knitting or something like it?"

I didn't answer as I just kept working. My hands twisted and moved as I plaited and plaited. The plaits on the cushion looked like they'd always been like that.

"It's a nervous habit." Dad said quietly. "She used to do the same to her ribbons or shoelaces."

I couldn't take much more of this; I had run out of tassels to plait and I tossed the cushion aside as I stood up.

"Excuse me." I bit out, before I turned to head out the front door.

"Good idea B." Grandpa spoke up. Huh, what was that? I paused in the doorway to give a funny look. He said calmly, "now would be a good time for Grant to show you the new place."

"What?" Grant looked on Grandpa in surprise, when his older brother nudged him sharply. "Oh yeah," he quickly stood up.

This is getting beyond a joke! I rolled my eyes as I violently pushed open the door to stomp down the veranda steps.

"That girl is just as skittish as Jess was, when she was growing up." I overheard Uncle Ian chuckle. "Next thing we know, Bianca will start running away and hiding from Grant."

"Shut up Ian." Mum moaned. "That joke is so old."

Grant came down the veranda steps as he unlocked his jeep with his remote key ring, before he hopped in first. Darn it! I didn't know how to get out of this so I would have to go along. I let out a frustrated sigh as I opened the door on the passengers' side and climbed in last.

He didn't say anything as he turned on the ignition. Whilst barely looking behind, he reversed past the surrounding trucks. Grant drove fast, without looking over his shoulder but instead through his rear-vision mirror. He skillfully reversed out onto the dirt road, before he drove up the hill. I have to admit, the way he just made it look so easy then, was impressive.

We drove half a kilometer up to the cull de sac at the end of the dirt road. There we pulled into another dirt driveway of a small, two-story, brown wooden house with a stone chimney. I had seen the old place before, but it was long ago. Old Mr. and Mrs. Windchime lived in the house before they passed away last year. Grant must have bought the house off their children, who had houses of their own in the community centre.

"How did you buy it?" I wondered aloud as I looked through the windscreen. "I mean, since the War the only time we use money in the tribe is when we transact with the outside world."

Grant smiled as he said mysteriously; "a transaction for this property did take place but you don't have to concern yourself with the details."

Next, he hopped out of the jeep and walked around the front of the vehicle to wait for me. I hopped out, shut the door behind and then I walked over to where Grant stood.

"What do you mean that I don't have to concern myself with the details? Either that's a jibe at my sex or my age, like you don't want me to worry about the cost of living. That's stupid because I'm being thrust into adulthood by this marriage." I griped.

"B, this house is my wedding gift to you." He said simply.

My eyes widened as my mouth dropped, as I looked from Grant to the house in shock...this is his present to ME? A house?!

"Come on, I'll show you inside." He laughed at my stunned expression.

He took hold of my hand to lead me up the veranda steps. He only released it to search for the keys in his jacket. I stood back as I watched Grant unlock the front door and then he stepped aside to let me go in first.

I walked into the old, empty place which smelled of freshly sawn wood and lacquer from the repair work currently going on. I even saw a couple of hammers, boxes of nails and sandpaper lying around. The house had a very similar lay out to my home, with the same open-planned living area for the lounge and dining room combined, with a walk-in kitchen. There was a staircase next to the downstairs bathroom-combined-laundry. Next, I headed up the stairs to the second story where I found two bedrooms and another bathroom.

Grant followed me up and retook hold of my hand. Like this, he walked us inside the master bedroom which looked fairly spacious.

"This is our bedroom." He waved his free arm. "The windows face the front of the house. And this..." he next led us out of that room and into the second, smaller room, "...will be the kids' bedroom."

Kids? He's already talking about kids? I'm still a kid!

This made me feel uncomfortable and I pulled back my hand from his. I walked a little away as I folded my arms in front. Like this, I looked at the woods at the back of the house from one of the windows.

"As you can see, there are blinds on the windows which will give us our privacy. But to make it less bare and more homey, my sisters Vine and Hannah are currently making curtains for us." He said chirpily. "Plus we'll be getting my grandparents old rugs to put in the lounge area as well as in the main bedroom, so it will add some coziness."

I nodded, trying to appear enthusiastic when I really felt the exact opposite. Not only did I feel forced into this situation, but I still felt guilty that Grant was doing this for me and not the woman he was meant to be with. I certainly didn't feel like a woman, as I still felt like a teenager.

When he walked up behind to wrap his arms around my waist, it made me feel more nervous. He said good-naturedly, "it will all work out B, you'll see."

I didn't know what to say or do. I mean, sure it was sweet the effort he was making for our future. But I was still unsure if I wanted a future with Grant? I guess there was still some small part of me that was still hoping that I could be an actual University student, attending Cambridge. I didn't want to study by correspondence! I wanted to physically attend class. I wanted to study with other people like me.

But then, I'll never be able to study with people LIKE me, because now I'm a Lokoti Werewolf. I stopped being like everybody else the first moment I changed. I'm not even like the other Lokoti Werewolves, being the only female amongst all males!

Now I'm in an arranged marriage, the first one in 50 years? And I have to go through a Joining Ceremony, another first in 50 years? This Werewolf thing just keeps getting further and further out of my control! I growled in frustration as I pulled out of his arms to rub my weary face.

"B?" he looked on, concerned. "What is it?"

I turned and opened my mouth to tell him? But then nothing came out. So I started to pace up and down, as I wrung my hands as there were no cushion tassels to plait.

"Er, don't you like the house?" Grant asked, worried.

"The house is fine, the house is lovely in fact." I said shortly, pacing faster.

"Then what is it?"

"You should buy this house and fix it up with your brother for the woman you love!" I suddenly shouted. It all poured out of me, as my eyes watered and I trembled with emotion. "You should be going through a Joining Ceremony with the woman you love! You barely know me! We have to dress up like idiots, wearing 'skins', declare to the public that we love each other when we don't. We hardly even know each other!"

"B - "

"I HATE this Werewolf business! I HATE it! My best friend is no longer speaking to me and he said he wishes that I never turned into a Werewolf! Well so do I! Why can't I just be a Circulator? Why do I have to be a frickin' Werewolf?!" I yelled tearfully.

He stood back quietly as he watched me pace up and down.

I ranted, "Grandfather expects me to be happy that I can study via correspondence? Well I'm not happy! Derik and I were actually planning on going to Cambridge together! Now he hates me and I'm being told I can study via correspondence?   CORRESPONDENCE! What the hell does that mean, anyway?"

"It means that you'll be taught online via correspondence; that you'll email your assignments and -"

"If I knew I could give up this Werewolf business by cutting out my heart with a silver knife I'd do it! If I could cut this thing out of me, I would! Why can't I just make it go away...?" I sobbed.

"B." He walked up to hold me firmly by the arms. He frowned, "this isn't the end of the world, in fact it's the beginning -"

"But you don't love me Grant!" I pulled away. "I don't love you! I'm not the one! This is all spinning out of my control and I just want to make it stop!"

I guess at this point, he thought that he could make it stop...when all of a sudden he pulled me in for a kiss!

Grant pushed his lips over mine which effectively shut me up, as the pressure of his kiss made my head go backwards in an uncomfortable manner. He was holding my arms so tightly I couldn't pull back. I turned my face away as I gasped for breath.

He gasped too, "sorry, I had hoped our first kiss would have been a little more romantic than that. But I guess I was just trying to break the ice."

However he hadn't let go either, so I noted when he leaned his face towards mine as I guess he was going to have a second go. This time his lips gently smothered mine, before I felt him slowly push them apart with his and after another moment, I felt his tongue in my mouth.

I froze...I was literally stuck to the spot as I didn't know what to do! With the force he was holding me still, I would have literally had to use my own Werewolf strength to push the guy off!

B, you can't push your future husband off you! But why not? I'm not enjoying this as it felt strange and alien. Derik was a better kisser than Grant and Declan was a better kisser than him...

...eugh! Yuck! You said Declan! Gross! I thought that we had an understanding that we wouldn't think about THAT guy again.

Right, that's it! To make sure I don't think about THAT person again, I'll throw myself into this marriage. If I have to get married, then I'll just have to get used to it. Grant's a nice guy and he's been pretty patient so far. He did buy me a house...so I forced myself to kiss him back.

I responded to his advances and after a minute or so, he let go of my arms as his encircled my waist instead. He ran his hands up and down my back which felt nice. After another couple of minutes we started to develop a style, a technique per se. Then this didn't feel so icky anymore and I even started to like it.

Grant eventually pulled away before he sighed happily whilst bumping his forehead against mine. "Your pheromones B, they're quite alluring."

"My pheromones?"

"Yeah, your scent. You smell like freshly baked choc-chip cookies." He rubbed his nose against mine. "What do I smell like?"

Oh, I hadn't considered it before. I sniffed him again and then again, but I couldn't quite get the gist of it. I don't know if I was doing it right?

"Close your eyes and breathe in deeply and hold it." He held me close.

Using one of his hands, he gently moved my face closer to his neck. I did what he said; I closed my eyes and breathed in deeply as I ran my nose across his skin and held it.

Woah...now I get it! Suddenly I understood what he was talking about. His scent reminded me of a herb garden. He smelled like a combination of herbs such as oregano, thyme, rosemary and even faintly of coriander.

Am I imagining things or is this really his scent? I inhaled him again, with my nose touching his skin. I caught his eyes close as he held onto me tighter. The fragrant herbs filled my senses once more, almost making my head spin! I took the liberty of pressing my nose against his throat and inhaling him over and over.

I heard him growl as simultaneously I felt the rumble in his chest. I think this excited him somehow as he bent his head to kiss me again. This time, I liked it...I really, really liked it! I even playfully bit down on his lower lip, which made him chuckle.

"Do you still hate everything Werewolf?" Grant murmured.

"Shut up." I breathed as I grabbed hold of his long, black hair.

I pulled his head in to kiss him again. We kissed passionately for a good couple of minutes, even losing our balance at one stage! We stumbled sideways with Grant steadying us with his greater strength.

"Woah!" He laughed, "I can't say that's happened before; a girl sweeping me off MY feet."

This made me laugh along with him, which made me start to fall into ease in his company even more.

*****

It was late in the afternoon when Grant drove me home. As he parked his jeep in my driveway, I noticed the other trucks and vehicles had gone, indicating that my 'wedding planners' had left. My husband-to-be turned off his engine before he turned in his seat to look on longingly.

"Try not to worry so much." He spoke softly as put his hand over mine. "Everything will fall into place, you'll see."

"Hmm." I stared thoughtfully out his windscreen.

"I don't know about you, but I'm looking forward to our future together. I think it could be fun." He gave a wink.

I sighed weary with emotion, "thanks Grant."

"Thanks for what?"

"Thanks for being the optimist in all of this." I turned to give him a small smile. "Thanks for the house too."

"Anytime." He said humorously. "I just hope I haven't spoiled you so when your birthday rolls around, you're not expecting anymore large pieces of real estate."

I laughed out my return, "you mean it was a one time thing?"

He laughed back, "for the moment anyways."

We both turned quiet as his hand didn't want to let go of mine and he was staring again.

"What?" I wondered.

"You're the only girl in the tribe with dark blue eyes, you know that?"

"Yeah I guess."

"Your mother, your grandmother and your grandfather have blue eyes but not dark blue eyes like yours." His voice turned husky as he caressed the top of my hand with his thumb.

"OK...?"

Then he leaned forwards to kiss me softly on the lips and whilst he was sitting closer, I overheard him breathe in deeply.

"Good bye B, for the moment." He sighed like he didn't want to see me go.

"Bye Grant."

I opened the door and climbed out to walk up my veranda steps. I threw him a wave before I disappeared inside. He didn't start his jeep again until he saw me go through my front door. As I closed the door behind, I heard him begin to reverse out.

My parents came out of the kitchen where they had started to prepare dinner.

"Hi B." Dad looked on hopefully. "Did you have a good afternoon with Grant?"

"Um yeah, it was OK." I said as I turned towards the stairs.

"What did you think of the house?" Mum enquired.

"It's OK."

"Well, did you like it? Can you imagine yourself living there?" She stopped at the bottom of the stairs to watch me climb up.

"Yeah, I guess."

"What did you and Grant talk about?" He queried.

"Typical newlywed stuff." I called as I disappeared down the hallway.

Mum and Dad exchanged confused glances but they thought it best to leave it at that before they returned to the kitchen.

I walked into my bedroom and shut my door behind. Then whilst leaning on the wood, I slid down to the floor and sat like that, with my back against the door. I don't believe it...I'm actually engaged to be married! Then the double-whammy is that the groom isn't such a bad guy, nor is he a bad kisser.

Frickin' hell, my Werewolf pheromones just keep on snow-balling...picking up reluctant or willing volunteers along the way. How did the male Lokoti Werewolves cope with their attractiveness before they took mates? I guess their egos expanded as they enjoyed the attention from the opposite sex, but it was going to take me a little while longer to get used to.

It started off with Derik; then the boys at Ben's party flirted with me; then Declan holds my hand before he kisses me and then I do something else with him. Now this afternoon I kissed my fiancé, the man that the tribe set me up to marry because of this Werewolf business.

I felt like a tennis ball, being hit back and forth across the net in a game of doubles. Derik, Declan and now Grant were holding the rackets. But as the Sabre's stood on one side of the net, Grant Elm played as a one-man team on his own. I rubbed my face hard with the palms of my hands as I tried to take control of my raging Werewolf hormones.

As my room changed colours with the oncoming sunset, I tried to stop myself comparing scents; maple syrup or a herb garden, which did I prefer? Whilst the lighting in my room changed from pink to purple, I tried to make sense of my racing heart.

"Stop it B!" I growled out, angry with myself. "Just stop it!"

I decided to get my mind off you-know-who by having a shower before dinner. However as I walked over to the window to close my curtains to undress? In the purple dusk, I spotted his glowing green Werewolf eyes as he sat in his hiding spot in the woods.

This time I paused as I stared back, unsure of what to do. Usually I would close my curtains on him, but today I didn't. Today Declan did something different. Instead of me closing my curtains dismissively, I saw his eyes move away as he turned around to disappear amongst the trees. I sensed that he bolted off down the hill, probably back home.

Oh, I guess Declan knows and I don't think he was happy about my news either.

~~~~~~
~~~~~~

~ 7 ~

30th September 2084

"OK." Grandpa stood up, putting the piece of chalk in his pocket that he had been using to draw lines over the skins. "I'll take it in here, here and here. B is much slimmer than my Grandmother was when she wore these."

I was standing in the lounge area with Nana, Mum, Dad, Gran, Grandfather and Great Grandma all wandering around, sipping tea or coffee whilst watching Grandpa do my fitting. I was wearing the 'skins' which was basically a long suede skirt, suede boots, and a suede tie-up blouse. The shirt and skirt had beaded patterns around the edges and even a couple of feathers. The suede smelled old and I felt a little ridiculous to be honest.

"What's with the feathers?" I cracked up laughing. "It's a bit cliché, isn't it?" Grandpa raised his eyebrows, waiting for me to elaborate. "I mean, c'mon! We're Indian and we HAVE to wear feathers?!"

"We're not Indian, we're Lokoti." Grandfather frowned.

"The feathers are from the Boreal Owl, which are rare." Great Grandma advised. "There aren't many of those birds left so now they're a protected animal."

"Hmm." Nana frowned as she looked on. "B has a point, can we do the outfit without the feathers?"

Great Grandma rolled her eyes as she left the living area to walk back into the kitchen.

"Ling." Grandpa frowned on his wife. "They're part of our tribe's tradition. How would you like it I asked you being Chinese to stop wearing silk or jade or even not to burn incense?"

"But I don't burn incense!" Nana retorted. "Fern, when in our married life have I ever burned incense?"

"But you are fond of wearing silk." He pointed out. "Your favourite evening dress is the long black silk one with the white embroidered water lilies."

"Hey, I like that dress!" Gran retorted.

"Same here." Mum agreed.

"My point being, would you appreciate it if I told you to lose it, as it looked too Chinese?" Grandpa argued.

"Grant being an Elm will be wearing feathers." Grandfather spoke up.

"He surely will." Grandpa agreed. "The Elm family used to be the best hunters for catching Boreal Owl. Their family used to trade in it."

"Are you for real?!" I laughed even louder. "Grant is going to marry me, wearing feathers too?"

"With his height he'll look like 'Big Bird' off 'Sesame Street'." Nana snickered to which Mum and Gran joined in.

"I'll laugh all through out the Joining Ceremony!" I guffawed along.

Dad saw the annoyed look on his father's face so he stepped in. "You will NOT laugh during your own Joining Ceremony, Bianca Grace Wisetail." He growled. "Tomorrow is not just an important day for you, but for the tribe as well."

"Your union is an important cultural event." Grandpa lectured. "You are the first female Lokoti Werewolf and you are marrying a male Lokoti Werewolf. Tomorrow you will be making history as your joining will be leaving a mark in time, as never before has there been a union of this kind."

"The whole tribe is looking forward to this celebration." Grandfather nodded. "I drove past the Holy Grounds today and I saw the last of the decorations being put into place."

"Now if you could please stand still so I can finish making these alterations? I have to prepare my own tribal clothes since I'm one of the Elders marrying you!" Grandpa grumbled, pulling out his sewing kit. "Ling, can you thread the needle for me while I cut the suede?"

Nana came forward to help Grandpa out, as the two began to work in unison.

"Can we cut the feathers off?" I thought I would try, while he was holding the scissors.

Grandpa passed me a glare before he returned to work.

"Bianca." Dad sung warningly. "You're turning 18 years old in less than two weeks. Grow up!"

"Hey, I'm a child bride so I'm going to act like one!" I said sulkily.

"They're not so bad." Gran walked up to put her arm about Grandfather's waist as she looked on. "The feathers are only on the tops of the sleeves and on the bottom of the shirt. It's not so bad, really." She promised.

"Her hair will be braided and some more feathers will hang from the ends of her hair." Great Grandma walked out of the kitchen, carrying her sewing basket. She sat at the table and began to take the hair adornments. I scowled when I saw the old leather hair bands with the feathers tied to them. Great Grandma held up the decorated hair bands. "Your Great Grandfather wore this when he married me."

"Did he look like 'Big Bird' too?" I giggled.

"Bianca please, be serious now." Dad moaned, putting down his cup of coffee before falling backwards into one of couches next to Mum.

"No." I said stubbornly. "Sure, you can tell me who to marry. Fine, you can even arrange the whole thing. But just because I'm being pushed into this wedlock before my 18th Birthday? It doesn't mean that I'm going to behave."

"If you do misbehave, I swear I'm going to throw you over my shoulder and carry you down to the river and drop you in, feathers and all!" He wagged his finger.

"And I'll hold your head under the water." Grandpa agreed, as he looked on dangerously.

"You'll be representing the Riverclaw's and the Wisetail's at the union, when you enter the Elm family. Your behavior will reflect on all of us." Great Grandma spoke crisply.

"So if I screamed out, 'noooooo!' and turned and fled in the middle of the ceremony and stole somebody's car to leave town...?" I ribbed.

"You would be hunted to the ends of the earth." Grandpa growled.

"Then I would circulate to Mars or to somewhere else, sometime else, where you can never find me." I said coolly.

"Then I would find you with your Gran's help." Grandfather folded his arms as he glared, "and I would throw you over my shoulder and carry you back to the river and drop you into the icy waters."

"Great." I muttered, looking downwards. "This isn't an ARRANGED marriage – this is a frickin' SHOTGUN wedding!"

"Language." Great Grandma sung as she organized the beads on top of the table.

"Frickin' is not a swear word. Fucking is a swear word, but frickin' isn't." I pointed out.

"That's something that Declan would say." Grandfather gave a funny look.

I quickly looked away to glance downwards at Nana and Grandpa both cutting and sewing the clothes I was wearing.

"These clothes smell like dead cow." I changed the subject.

"They're made from the pelts of caribou, actually." Grandpa stated.

"Are they going to be washed before tomorrow?" I whinged.

"You DON'T wash suede." Grandpa said staunchly.

"B, could you please stop whinging?" Gran rolled her eyes.

"You could do worse." Mum shrugged. "Grant's a nice guy and he's good looking and he seems to like you for some strange reason. If I'm not mistaking that last kiss I saw you give him, I'd say that you're starting to like him too."

I quickly ducked my head to hide my blush.

"B's heart rate has just jumped from 91 up to 120 and her pheromone level has increased." Grandpa smiled as he worked.

"Grandpa!" I nearly whacked him, but he might accidentally stick me with the large sewing needle.

"Fern, behave." Nana glared at her husband, who began to chuckle.

"Tell me." He mused as he worked. "Why do women hide their attraction when men don't?"

"Rebecca certainly didn't hide it around you." Mum said quietly to Dad, which made him chuckle as he put his arm about her to pull her close.

"Not all women." Great Grandma corrected. "I didn't hide my attraction to David."

"The night I met Ling, I could tell she was attracted to me, which was helped along by my pheromones. But she stood ready for the first half hour of meeting me, gripping onto that tyre iron so hard, ready to bring it crashing through my skull if I made any sudden moves." Grandpa chuckled.

"Fern, what do you expect?!" Nana rolled her eyes. "My car broke down in the middle of the night, when you came out of the woods in only a pair of jeans!"

"With Jess, it was only if there was nobody else around that she spoke to me. If I bumped into her by the river or in the woods, she was almost friendly. But when we were around other people it was when she used to run away from me." My father laughed as he kissed my mother's cheek.

"If you keep making an example out of me, I'll turn very unfriendly in a sec!" Mum poked him in the ribs, making him laugh harder.

I paused for a moment as I looked on the interaction between the three married couples in the room...

Gran and Grandfather stood there with their arms wrapped about each other. Mum and Dad sat there with their arms wrapped about the other. Nana and Grandpa worked in perfect unison, exchanging many a glance or a small smile to the other.

My grandmother looked like she was still in her twenties and my grandfather looked like he was in his early forties when in actuality they were both 56 years old. Mum and Dad looked like they were still in their twenties, even though Dad was 39 and Mum was 37. Grandpa was 69 years old even though he looked to be in his late forties, as Nana was 60 years old and she did look like she was in her sixties.

Nana and Great Grandma were the 'mere mortals' of this eclectic group of Werewolves and Circulators. However as I observed Grandpa and Nana's glances, their deep love for the other was still evident, even if time hadn't been kind to Nana's appearance. But seeing the love in Grandpa's eyes towards his mate, you could see that time hasn't changed the way he looks on Nana. In his eyes she was still the woman that he loved, the mother of his child and the grandmother of his grandchild. I saw the same regard in Dad with Mum and in Grandfather with Gran, although they looked much younger.

Will that one day be Grant and I? Will we one day, dress our daughter or our granddaughter in traditional dress for a Joining Ceremony? Will Grant one day look on me the same way these three male Lokoti Werewolves looked on their mates? A love that not even time could diminish...

Great Grandma lovingly smoothed out the feathers on the leather hair bands, whilst sitting there smiling to herself, as she recalled her late husband. Time may be aging my 74 year old Great Grandma, but it certainly didn't diminish her love for Grandfather's father. She's been a widow for 46 years, but seeing her treat those feathers on the hair band with reverence, I could see her love was still burning strong.

Would that be me one day, in love with the man that I marry? Would I too be in a loving marriage? I hoped so.

"Who was the arranged marriage that the last Joining Ceremony was for?" I suddenly asked.

"Finn and Georgia Ivy." Grandpa informed.

"Uncle Finn?" I echoed in surprise.

Uncle Finn and Aunt Georgia were an arranged marriage? Uncle Finn was also a Werewolf who appeared to be in his late forties although he was 70 years old. Aunt Georgia looked elderly since she was a 70 year old human. I've always looked on their marriage with respect, especially at how Uncle Finn showed so much love towards his aged mate. I've observed them as they shopped in the store and he insisted on carrying everything. I had admired at how fast Finn moved to open doors for Aunt Georgia or by helping her in and out of the car with her bad knees.

"They were an arranged marriage?" I asked in disbelief. "Why?"

"What do you mean, why?" Nana laughed.

"I mean, why were they an arranged marriage?" I asked.

"Their union was to cement the peaceful relationship between the Lokoti and the Lynx Tribe." Great Grandma informed.

"Huh?" I looked on, puzzled.

"In the past whenever something happened to the Lynx's livestock, such as cattle went missing or chickens were killed? The Lokoti Werewolves were blamed." Grandpa shook his head.

"Chickens?" Dad raised his eyebrows. "They actually thought that we would hunt penned-in chickens?"

"They knew that the Lokoti Werewolves existed but they didn't understand the Lokoti Werewolf." Grandpa shook his head. "Whenever their animals turned up dead or missing, we would get the blame."

"But Lynx land is over 300 km's from here and Lokoti Werewolves only hunt on Lokoti land." I frowned.

"You know that, I know that and the Lokoti tribe know that but explaining it to the Lynx people? Many a war over the eons resulted from ignorance. Right up until the beginning of the 21st Century, there were still skirmishes." Grandpa sighed.

"To end the bad blood, a new blood tie was made between our two tribes." Great Grandma went on.

"Finn was chosen by the Tribal Elders to be the groom and Georgia was one of the Lynx Chief's daughters." Grandpa explained.

"Did Finn mind being picked like that?" I raised my eyebrows.

"The pack agreed with the Tribal Elders that it would be a good idea if the groom was a Werewolf, so the Lynx People could be educated in our ways. Since Finn was the only unmarried Werewolf who was the right age at the time..." Grandpa shrugged, "...Finn accepted our decision. He met your Aunt Georgia for the first time at their Joining Ceremony."

"That was the first time they laid eyes on each other, at their frickin' wedding ceremony?!" I gaped in horror.

"Language." Great Grandma sung again.

"But Finn fell in love with Georgia during the first month of their marriage." Grandfather chuckled as he gave Gran a squeeze. "I remember the change that came over him. Before the Joining Ceremony he liked to stay out late, either playing cards or hanging out in Harry's Bar playing pool? He spent all of his days fixing up cars but once he was mated, he completely changed. Except when he hunted during a full moon or worked at the Garage, he stayed home with Georgia."

"He still fixed up that old truck from the 1940's just for fun." She looked back.

"Yeah but it was the last vehicle that he restored. After the antique truck, he completely settled into married life with Georgia, particularly when they began to have kids." He pointed out.

"Six kids." Grandpa raised his eyebrows. "That impressed the Lynx Chief by how productive their union turned out."

"Six kids...?" I uttered in surprise.

"That's the Lokoti Werewolf virility." Great Grandma sighed.

That was true, as the Riverclaw's and the Wisetail's seemed to be the only aversions to this rule. Our two families were the only case where two children or less were produced from a union with a Lokoti Werewolf.

All the other married members in the pack had at least three children and the eldest was always a male, except for Grandfather who had twins; Mum and Uncle Julian. But my uncle was reportedly born first, minutes before my mother so technically he was 'older'. With my birth, I was the first in Lokoti history to be a first born let alone an only child who was a girl. It's no wonder then that I'm also the first female Lokoti Werewolf; I seemed to have the odds stacked against me!

"If one Lokoti Werewolf can be so productive in the bedroom, can you imagine what it's going to be like having two Lokoti Werewolves reproducing?" Nana joked. "In nine months we could all be together again celebrating the birth of triplets or something."

"Nana!" I turned bright red.

"At least B doesn't have an apartment to throw Grant out of, so he should be safe." Gran joked.

"What was that?" Nana looked on.

"When my Grandfather tracked down my Grandmother again, after their one night stand? He told her that she was his mate and that she was pregnant. When Grandmother heard that, she tried to throw him out of her apartment." Grandfather told the room to much laughter.

"I'd believe that, the first Jessica Riverclaw certainly was a fiery one." Grandpa chuckled as he shook his head over the woman who was my mother's namesake.

Then he and Nana stood back with Grandpa putting away his sewing kit.

"All done." She announced. "Turn around for us please B."

I obeyed as I did a little spin on the spot.

"That looks much better." Great Grandma gave a nod of approval.

"Let's go upstairs and show you." Mum stood up from the couch to take hold of my hand and led me up our poky staircase.

"I'll come too!" Gran followed after.

The three of us traipsed upstairs and we went into Mum and Dad's bedroom where her full-length mirror was. There I stared at my reflection in partial surprise...I didn't look ridiculous after all. The grey and white feathers actually complimented the chocolate brown colour of the skins, as well as with the beaded work around the collar. I was pleasantly taken aback by my appearance.

"You look beautiful!" Gran beamed as she hugged me from behind.

"Like a real Pocahontas." Mum agreed as she kissed my cheek.

My face flushed as I gave myself one last look before I turned away. "I suppose the feathers look alright."

When Gran was hugging me, she suddenly screwed up her face and pulled away. "Eugh! You're right about the smell of the suede, B."

"Take the clothes off and I'll put them in a box with some pot pouri. Hopefully they'll smell nice by tomorrow." My mother organized.

I changed out of the skins and put on my jeans and sweater again. Then as I sat down on the side of the bed to pull on my socks and shoes, Mum put the skins into the box Grandpa brought them over in. As she did, she put in a couple of pouches of pot pouri with them.

"That's a good idea, Jess." Gran smiled.

Just then we heard the arrival of more guests downstairs, as Uncle Julian arrived with Aunt Danika and my cousins. I heard Phoenix's and Phoebe's shouting immediately, as Uncle Julian yelled over the top to quieten them down.

"The whole tribe can probably hear those two fight!" Gran snickered about her two youngest grandchildren.

We three returned downstairs, to see a tired Aunt Danika hand over a white cardboard box to Great Grandma, who took it from her to put in the fridge.

"What's that?" I asked as I walked over to give her a kiss on the cheek.

"Your wedding cake, B." She smiled.

"Oh." I echoed in surprise. "I didn't know I would have a wedding cake."

"Yes well, it is customary when somebody has a wedding, B." Uncle Jules laughed as he came over to give me a hug.

"But I thought this wedding was a Lokoti affair, as in the traditional way. I thought the idea of the wedding cake was too...'white'?" I pondered.

"Well, there are going to be 'white' guests at this shindig too." Grandfather laughed at my perspective.

"There are?"

"Some of your English and Australian relatives are coming tomorrow." Mum announced.

"They are?" I asked in further surprise.

"Of course your family is coming for your wedding." Gran rolled her eyes at my clueless behavior.

"A wedding is always a good excuse for a family gathering and we haven't seen our English or Australian kin in a while." Uncle Jules mused.

"Grandfather! Grandfather! Grandfather!" Phoebe ran over to her grandparent with her arms outstretched.

Phoebe was 12 years old but still Grandfather would pick her up and carry her in his arms, which is exactly what he did. With his strength, he behaved like she still weighed the same as a 5 year old and Phoebe absolutely loved it. She was small for her age and very pretty which made her father and grandfather dote on her.

Phoenix roused on his little sister, "Phoebe, grow up! You're not a frickin' 3 year old!"

"Language!" Great Grandma sung out yet again.

"Phoenix!" Uncle Jules whacked his son on the arm.

"Frickin' is not a swear word!" He griped, rubbing his 'injury'. "Declan says it all the time!"

The male Werewolves exchanged raised eyebrows.

"I think we're going to have to have a word with Declan, regarding his influence on the younger generation of this family." Grandfather smirked.

I felt my face begin to burn by the very mention of him, as I quickly busied myself by helping Great Grandma make coffees or teas for the new arrivals. However with my sharper hearing, I caught Gran say softly to both Grandfather and Mum; "well you won't be able to do it tomorrow. I ran into Susan at the store today. Neither she, Derik or Declan, will be coming to the Ceremony or the Housewarming."

Grandfather sighed sadly, "I expected as much."

"Was Susan angry?" Mum asked quietly.

"Not as such, just very disappointed and maybe even a little betrayed. She asked why the tribe felt that Derik would no longer be a good match for my granddaughter? I told her the truth, I had to. We owe her family that much at least." She whispered.

"Hmm." He frowned as he looked from his wife over to his granddaughter.

Gran continued, "but as such, I told her that I sent off Derik's application to Cambridge University along with B's. I told her that because Mike Sabre was apart of the Circulate, her family also had access to Hodge Endeavor funds which can pay for his degree. Susan thanked us and said that Derik was considering living in Cambridge instead of studying by correspondence, to get away for a while."

Derik...he was going away? He was going to Cambridge without me? My marriage to Grant was sending him away? I had just started to hand Aunt Danika her coffee, when suddenly the muscles in my hand gave out...

...and the mug fell to the floor and smashed!

Everyone went quiet, as they looked either surprised or guilty. I stood there, feeling everybody's heavy gaze as I felt my eyes sting but I refused to cry so publicly.

"What are these feathers for?" Phoenix suddenly bellowed, holding up the leather hair band with the feathers. "Is B going to be wearing feathers tomorrow? Hahahaha!"

When Grandpa growled warningly, it made him quickly put down the hair band and step away from the table.

I walked out of the kitchen, past the crowd of onlookers, out of the front door, down the veranda steps, across the gravel driveway and into the woods. I walked quickly, I had to. But then I heard the front door open and Dad call out, "B?"

Quickly I took off so he couldn't come after me. I ran in supernatural speed, down the hill towards the river. My eyes watered from the rushing air as well as from the force of the emotions which were making my chest ache. I picked up with my Werewolf hearing that I was being followed and that Dad was running after, matching my speed...

No, Dad, no! Don't come after me! So I ran faster...I ran at almost the speed of light, as my Circulator ability took over from my Werewolf physical prowess. The woods became a blur as I streaked through the trees. I jumped over log or rock, in between the tree trunks as my hair streamed behind.

I left the path that went down to the river as I ran upstream, past Sunset Point. I ran even faster, going further and further than I had ever gone before. No longer did I recognize the terrain that looked like a blur anyway, as I zoomed along the river bank. I made sure I had lost Dad until I began to slow down, slipping back into Werewolf speed, as I high jumped over a fallen tree to land on all-fours.

When I looked up, I found myself in a pretty glade surrounded by different kinds of ferns next to a quiet part of the riverbank. With the late afternoon, the light in this glade actually looked a curious kind of purple-green. The air smelled sweet and the bird song was constant. This glade was not just full of beauty, it was full of life.

I've never seen this part of Lokoti tribal lands before although my instincts told me that I was deep inside of the National Park. In the years just prior to the War, this land was renamed the 'Lokoti National Park'. Hodge Endeavor sponsored it in the name of the original landowners the Lokoti, or so the press release said.

Just then something moved and I realized I wasn't alone...somebody who was sitting on a large rock with their back to me, now turned my way to show a tearful, angry face. That face belonged to Declan, who was sitting in grease-covered jeans and a dirty grey t-shirt, which had momentarily camouflaged him on the similarly coloured rock.

"YOU!" he shouted, enraged.

Me?

"What are YOU doing here?!?" He bellowed.

I paused, not knowing how to answer that.

"How did you find me? How did you find MY spot? Did you sniff me out to come and gloat about tomorrow?!" He stood up.

This was HIS spot?

"Look, I come here to get away so I don't accidentally eat anybody when I get angry! And now you won't even let me have my space? My privacy?" He charged towards me.

He was sitting here because he was angry?

Declan marched up so he was standing right in my face, tearfully glaring as I tearfully stared back, in shock. What are the chances of me just stumbling across HIS spot like this?

"What the hell are YOU crying for?!" He shouted in my face. "YOU'RE the one who broke my brother's heart! YOU'RE the one who's callously marrying another!"

I couldn't take this - not from him - not right now. I turned around and tried to leave the glade. But Declan as I found, wasn't about to let me leave that easily.

"I made you promise that you would NEVER tell my brother about us so he wouldn't be hurt! And what the hell do you go and do? You get promised to another!" He raged as he followed after. "You still hurt Derik!"

"It wasn't my idea, Declan!" I cried.

"Yeah but I don't exactly see or hear you refusing, either!" he rebuked as he grabbed hold of my arm to whirl me around. "My brother asked you to marry him! My brother's been in love with you since you were 16 years old! He frickin' worships the ground you walk on! And what do you do? You walk all over his heart!"

I ripped my arm out of his grasp as I tried to flee, but Declan stormed after.

"You're a cold, heartless bitch who doesn't care about anybody but herself! I hope your marriage to Grant is a failure! I hope that he hurts you like you hurt Derik!"

My eyes watered so much, I had rivers of tears coursing down my cheeks as I hurried away.

"I hope that you do another first in this frickin' tribe by being the first to die during childbirth to a frickin' Lokoti Werewolf!" He went on. "I hope that you're absolutely miserable and you're in pain! Did you know my brother's not just leaving the tribe, but he's talking about skipping the country because of you!"

Declan meant by Derik going to Cambridge University.

"Bianca Grace Wisetail, you are such a shallow, stuck up bitch! You think you know everything by reading your books! You think you're so good with your Werewolf pheromones and your pretty face! But that's all you've got! You don't have a heart! You don't have a soul! And you certainly don't have a conscience!" He yelled.

I almost tripped over a hidden rock in some ferns, but I stumbled onwards.

"Did you plan this all along? Did you string my brother along on purpose? Did you plan on breaking his heart?" He grabbed hold of my arm once more. "ANSWER ME DAMN YOU! SAY FRICKIN' SOMETHING!"

I sobbed as I struggled to pull my arm back from his strong grip.

"Would you at least tell me why?" He shook me, as his voice cracked. "Why B, why? Why are you doing what you're doing tomorrow?"

Then I realized that this stopped being about Derik, but this started to be about Declan's feelings. This thought occurred when he pulled me close to rub his wet face against mine.

"Why B, why?" He sniffed. "Why are you marrying Grant Elm tomorrow?"

"B – b – because the pack and the Tribal Elders said so." I mumbled.

"I know THEIR reason, but what's yours B?" He looked on, hurt. "When I first heard what they were thinking, I laughed! I actually laughed as I thought there was no way in hell Bianca Wisetail would go along with this. No way in hell, would Bianca let a bunch of old folks tell her who she was going to marry... and then I see the wedding preparations at the Holy Grounds? And what I heard from Derik which you said to him?"

Declan gently shook me once more before he held me even closer, so close I felt his breath on my face. "I could take it when you were with my brother, because he had you first... but Grant Elm? Grant Elm?! That guy is a full ten years older than you!" His voice turned loud again. Then he sniffed me and suddenly pushed me backwards! "I can even smell him on you!"

I cringed as I felt dirty for kissing my fiancé, the man the whole tribe had set me up with.

"You've KISSED him haven't you?" Declan spat out in disgust. "What else have you done with him?!"

I spun around as I tried to get away from him and away from this...

"Grant Elm gets Bianca Wisetail. Grant Elm gets to marry the first female Lokoti Werewolf. Grant Elm gets the prize, the tribe's trophy bride! How does it make you feel, B? To be passed around and to be decided over like you were property?!" He said cruelly, following behind.

I tried to break into a run, but Declan leapt on top of me! He knocked me to the muddy ground. When I tried to get up, he pinned me underneath! My heart raced as we wrestled, with me trying to get up and Declan fighting to stay on top.

"Get off me! Get off me! GET OFF ME!" I screamed, turning afraid.

If he tries to do what I was worried he would do, Grant would smell him on me. Then the shit would really hit the fan! I was frightened Grant and Uncle Ian and maybe even Dad would go gunning for Declan. I was scared how this would hurt Aunt Susan and even Derik would find out.

However as soon as he heard me scream, a change came over him. He instantly froze as he looked down, remorseful.

"I'm not going to hurt you, B." Fresh tears sprung to his eyes.

We both paused as we looked on the other with wide eyes. Declan removed his hands from my wrists, when instead they encircled my waist. He buried his face in my hair as I heard him inhale deeply. He held me tightly in his arms and we laid there like that in the mud, in an embrace.

I turned my head as I closed my eyes whilst pressing my nose against his neck to inhale him deeply. His familiar maple syrup   scent filled my senses, as I held him tighter. As I pondered on how I relished his scent, I wondered what I smelled like to him?

"What do I smell like?" I asked out of the blue.

"Say what?" He raised his head to give a funny look.

"What do I smell like to you?" I asked as I wanted to see if I smelled the same to him as I did to Grant.

Declan bent his head again to run his nose down my cheek to my neck, as I felt his body harden in arousal.

"You smell like a vase of wildflowers sitting in a kitchen while a cake is baking in the oven." He said in a low voice.

My heart raced at his words as I thought that it was the most romantic thing that anyone has ever said to me...!

I kissed him which seemed to be just what he was waiting for because he eagerly kissed back. Our passion not only made my stomach flutter but it made me feel hot all over. I gripped onto his shirt so tightly it was as if my body never wanted to let him go.

Our lips opened to each other's as soon as they touched. Whilst our tongues wrestled, he tried to be the dominant but again, I fought back. Our teeth sharpened, which we both felt as our mouths couldn't bare to be apart. The odd growl escaped, although I wasn't completely sure if it came from me or him or even the both of us?

His right hand moved to my front and I felt it slip inside my sweater to get at my breasts. I had to admit, his technique has improved as instead of just grabbing them, he ran his fingertips over them teasingly. But when I felt his other hand start head for the button on my jeans, in a lightening fast move I caught it.

"No." I said hoarsely. "Grant will smell you on me."

He snarled jealously and saying Grant's name was like cold water being thrown on us. Declan rolled off and onto his back. I noticed he was panting, with his hands clenched into fists and his eyes were squeezed shut. It was like he was using up every bit of control he had to restrain himself.

"I am SO tempted right now to sling you over my shoulder and high tail it out of here, off these damned tribal lands." He growled in frustration.

"But the Lokoti Werewolves would hunt us down." I sighed sadly.

"They don't scare me." He said. "I could take them on! I mean, it took your Grandmother a Circulator, with two silver swords to kill the European Werewolf who killed my father and nearly killed me. Now I'm the bastard Werewolf."

"You are NOT the bastard." I said firmly.

"Yes I am B, I'm an ungrateful bastard. Your Grandfather gave his blood to save my life and your tribe took my family in and provided for us. Your Grandfather, Uncle, Dad and Grandpa all trained me as one of the pack and what do I do? I steal the trophy bride, my little brother's girlfriend, our Second in the pack's beloved granddaughter and the tribe's first female Lokoti Werewolf."

"You're not a bastard because you're not stealing me." I said flatly.

"Say what?" He gave a peculiar look.

I spoke firmly, "tomorrow morning in a Joining Ceremony I will marry Grant Elm as everyone expects it. I will be the first female Lokoti Werewolf to mate with a male Lokoti Werewolf. I will do this for my families as everyone expects this. So not to divide you and Derik as brothers, I will be marrying another man so I won't be between you."

There was a pause as Declan's expression was one of incredulity.

"Oh great! Ladies and gentlemen, may I present Saint Bianca." He said sarcastically. "You martyring yourself this way certainly doesn't make me feel better."

"I'm just trying to do the right thing." I sat up.

"Trust me B, I know all about 'doing the right thing'." He sat up too. "I don't eat human, even though the bloodlust is like acid eating me inside out. Now I have to fight the lust towards you which is just as strong if not stronger. Every time I close my eyes, I picture that rainy afternoon where I got to have you. Then I kick myself over and over again for being so weak by caving in to the carnal desires that made me pounce. I want to shrivel up and die when I wonder if maybe..." his eyes watered once more as he looked on fearfully, "...if I forced myself on you and I hurt you?"

I felt my face flush as I had to quickly look away. "You didn't hurt me, Declan." I said after a long moment. "You didn't."

I nearly confessed that I felt quite the opposite of pain that afternoon. I wanted to tell him that I in no way hated what I did with him when instead, I scolded myself for enjoying it a little too much. But I didn't want to feed his ego as I could imagine his next remarks that might follow. I also didn't want to tempt him into the idea of taking off Lokoti land with me, the day before my marrying somebody else.

Right at that moment, we heard the distant 'snap!' of a stick being broken, from somebody walking over it. I smelled that it was Dad, as he had tracked me all the way here!

"Shit!" We both scrambled to our feet. I even started wiping my mouth on my sleeve, to get rid of Declan's scent on my skin!

"Like that's going to work!" He scoffed, seeing what I was doing.

"Then do you have a better idea?" I growled in annoyance.

He looked from me to the river...

"Oh no...!" My eyes widened as I guessed his thoughts. "No you don't!"

He picked me up and slung me over his shoulder!

"Declan no!" I squealed as I grabbed a handful of his hair to pull!

"Shut up! Do you want your Dad to hear you?!" He shouted in a whisper as he removed my hand.

He walked a couple of steps, before he unceremoniously dropped me...

SPLASH!!

... into the frickin' icy waters of the river!

"AAAARGHH!" I screeched as I leapt out, drenched and freezing!

Declan pissed himself with laughter! He was laughing so hard with his hand over his mouth, so my father wouldn't hear him that he was doubled over!

"B? B!" I heard Dad call out.

He worriedly turned in the direction my father was coming in and then he quickly grabbed my arms to kiss me again.

"And don't you dare die during childbirth or I'll kill you." He murmured, as he gently chewed on my lower lip...and then he pushed me backwards into the frickin' river again!

"DEECC...!!" I started to roar his name in fury, but I stopped myself.

He silently laughed as he pointed at me whilst walking backwards from the river. Lastly he gave me a wink, before he turned around and bolted off in the opposite direction my father was coming. He disappeared into the woods in supernatural speed.

That – that – that BASTARD!!! The water was so cold, it hurt! I dragged my waterlogged self back up onto the river bank, just as Dad appeared.

"B?" He looked on my soaking wet state in surprise.

"I fell into the river!" I snapped.

"How the hell did you do that?" he walked forwards whilst taking off his jacket to put about my cold, wet shoulders.

"I was washing mud off my hands and I guess I lost my balance." I lied feebly.

"Bianca Grace Wisetail," he laughingly shook his head, "you know that your Grandpa, Grandfather and I were only kidding about throwing you in the river. You didn't have to throw yourself in as practice."

"Very funny!" I said curtly.

I shivered uncontrollably as we began the long walk back. His laughter died down when he saw how badly I was shaking and then he looked about at the enclosing night which further chilled the already icy air. He stopped us momentarily, as he took his jacket off from my shoulders. I wondered what he was doing as he next stripped off his shirt and his t-shirt.

"Here, take off your wet top and put these on." He ordered.

"No Dad, I'll be alright." I started to object as my teeth chattered.

"Do it!" he demanded and then he turned away to give me privacy to change.

I removed my wet sweater and t-shirt to put on Dad's dry t-shirt, shirt and jacket. I walked back over to where he was standing, "OK, I'm changed."

"I'll carry you on my back and run us home." He said, as he turned his back to indicate for me to hop up.

"No Dad, it's OK. I can run myself home."

"Your wet jeans and shoes will slow you up." He said gruffly, before he morphed into his supernatural body before my eyes.

Dad turned his hardened, muscled back my way once more and waited for me to hop on. I sighed with resignation, tied my wet t-shirt and sweater around my waist and then I jumped up onto his back. As I wrapped my arms about his neck, he wrapped my legs around his waist before he turned his head to growl my way.

I think that was my father asking in Werewolf if I was ready? It's strange, since my change I started to pick up the different meanings behind a Werewolf's growls or the intonations behind them.

"Yep, I'm ready." I said.

Then he took off running at 200km/h! Dad sprinted through the trees, easily leaping over log and rock before us. It reminded me when I was a little girl and I used to beg him to take me for rides like this, on his back. I found myself laughing just like I did when I was little, as he carried me like I weighed no more than a feather. My legs turned cold and numb from the cold air rushing through my wet jeans, but my top half was warm in his dry clothes.

It took us longer to get back, since we were running at Werewolf speed and not in Circulator speed, but it was a lot more fun this way. To show off, he even leapt over the large rocks we came across instead of simply steering around.

"Go Dad!" I cheered and I heard him lightly growl back, like he was laughing.

We arrived home ten minutes later as the stars peaked through the night sky. He piggy-backed me over to our veranda where he turned around and gently released my legs. I slid off his back but then my legs gave way because they were numb! I landed on my arse, sitting on the top step, before I laughed at myself.

Dad reverted back into his human body whilst he looked on in amusement. "Your legs aren't working B? C'mon then."

He pulled me up and helped me inside and as soon as we walked in through the front door, everyone went into an uproar!

Mum stood up from sitting on the couch,"what happened to YOU?"

"She fell into the river." Dad told her.

"You FELL into the river?" Grandfather's eyes widened in disbelief.

"Best you get upstairs and have a nice long hot bath." Gran organized, coming forwards.

"Best she has a shower instead to wash her hair tonight. We have to get her ready and start on her hair at 6 AM tomorrow." Aunt Danika disagreed.

"Danika's right, we need to do her hair tomorrow when it's dry." Great Grandma agreed whilst she still sat at the table, getting the beads ready.

Phoebe who was sitting at the table with her, was helping her group the different beads together when she looked up.

"You've got mud and leaves in your hair!" She pointed at my head.

"Hahaha! You're wearing feathers! You're wearing feathers!" Phoenix taunted as he pointed too.

"Phoenix!" Uncle Jules growled at his son, which silenced him.

Grandpa shook his head as he rolled his eyes to Nana, "I worry about the future of this tribe sometimes, Ling."

"Why does your sweater have mud all over it?" Mum complained, untying it along with my wet t-shirt from my waist.

I continued to lie, "I fell over in the mud, which is why I tried to clean myself off in the river, when I -"

"When you fell in?" Grandfather frowned in disbelief.

The way the older Werewolves were looking on suspiciously, began to make me nervous. Even Aunt Danika and Phoebe – two telepaths – exchanged a knowing look.

"I'll go have that shower now." I quickly headed for the stairs before I could be cross-examined any further.

~~~~~~
~~~~~~

~ 8 ~

2nd October 2084

Yesterday morning, I was woken up at six o'clock on the dot by Mum coming into my room and shaking me awake.

"Rise and shine 'Sleeping Beauty'. Today's the day you marry your prince." She joked.

"The wedding's not for another four hours!" I griped as I pulled my pillow over my head.

"Nice try but sorry, no cigar." She ripped the pillow off my head to toss away. "Get up and here, you can get dressed in your 'wedding dress'. Your Great Grandma and Aunt Danika will be here shortly to start on your hair."

Mum placed the box with the 'skins' on the end of my bed and then left the room to give me privacy to change.

"Your father is making you a cup of coffee." She promised before she shut my bedroom door behind.

I yawned profusely as I tiredly sat up and looked at the cardboard box sitting next to my legs.

Frickin' hell... today's my 'wedding' day and I felt about as excited as if it were somebody else's wedding instead. It's not that I objected to marrying Grant because I didn't like him. That was just it, he was a very nice person and I didn't deserve him. I should be marrying a bastard who has no qualms about pouncing on me, insulting me and even throwing me into the river. Declan may treat me like crap but with my guilty conscience, I thought that I deserved to be treated like that. Then my chest hurt as I thought of the pain Derik must be in right now, because of Tribal Elders decision.

They were right, I couldn't marry Declan because it would hurt his brother. I would cause a rift between them and I've already hurt Derik enough as it is. No, I'll do the right thing. I'll be joined to Grant and I'll bite my tongue and I'll banish my wicked thoughts that might stray towards another. I'll be good and start by behaving myself and getting dressed for my Joining Ceremony to my appointed husband, Grant Elm.

Rock-hard determination filled me as I stood up with purpose. I busied myself with my first task of the day; I put on my 'wedding dress'. Then amazingly, the rest of the morning began to fall into place. I dressed in the 'skins' and put on the matching suede slippers. I went downstairs to join my parents for a cup of coffee and a few slices of toast.

At 7 AM on the dot, Great Grandma and Aunt Danika arrived to do my hair. I sat in a chair at the dining table as the two women worked. Mum who was sitting at the table, watched with interest. Great Grandma knew exactly what to do as Aunt Danika read her mind so she knew too. The two women worked in unison, dividing my hair into three plaits, with beads woven through them. Then they tied the feathered leather hair bands at the ends.

At 7.30 AM Dad left the house to give Grandfather, Uncle Jules, Uncle Ian and Grant a hand at moving our new furniture into our future home. I was told Vine and Hannah would also be at my new house, setting up the kitchen. They would oversee the delivery of my refrigerator to store some of the food and drinks for the Housewarming.

Around 8 AM, Vine and Hannah and their husbands arrived to pick up my suitcases and boxes of things to take to my new place of residence.

"You sure do look the part, B." Vine smiled in approval over my appearance.

"They haven't painted her face yet, but already B looks the part of a Lokoti woman from the past." Hannah agreed.

Mum fussed about, making sure that I hadn't forgotten anything and that everything was packed, including my toiletries.

"B! Where's your toothbrush?" She called from the upstairs bathroom.

I had to remain in my seat as Great Grandma and Aunt Danika finished up my hair. I called back, "it's in my toiletries bag!"

Pause...before Mum responded, "found it!"

She tearfully handed over my suitcases to the women as their husbands carried out the boxes to their trucks.

"Don't get all emotional, Jess." Vine patted her on the shoulder. "Bianca isn't just a Riverclaw and a Wisetail, but today she'll also become an Elm. We'll take good care of her, I promise."

"Hey, the girl's marrying Grant." Hannah joked. "We trained our little brother well. He'll treat her like she was a precious jewel."

"He'll take good care of your little girl just as he did when he babysat her five years ago." She ended.

"Thanks a lot you guys!" I laughed. "Now I know what a Lokoti Joining Ceremony is – a life long contract for an extremely long babysitting job!"

The room cracked up laughing at my way of putting it.

"You look good B." Hannah gave a wave goodbye. "We'll see you at the ceremony!"

"See you there!" I waved from my chair.

Once my hair was done, Great Grandma pulled out of her bag several small jars of paint which were handmade using natural ingredients from the land. She began to put the traditional colors of white, black, grey and red on my face in the ancient pattern; which looked like a long, colorful claw mark going down the right side of my face.

"This is the mark of our father the Lokoti Wolf." She narrated as she worked. "Our tribe has worn this mark as a sign of respect for his sacrifice in creating the tribe's protectors, the Lokoti Werewolves. We have worn this mark in battle as we have worn this in celebration. Today you wear the mark so he will bless your union to your promised one."

Aunt Danika read my mind and she asked Great Grandma the questions that I wanted to, but I couldn't move my mouth whilst I had to sit still.

"Will Grant also be wearing this mark?" She queried.

"He will," Great Grandma answered, "and so will the Tribal Elders."

She asked my next question, "when Uncle Finn married Aunt Georgia, what was on their faces?"

"Finn wore the mark of the Lokoti Wolf and Georgia wore the mark of the Lynx." Great Grandma remembered.

At 9.30 AM Dad returned from his work as a removalist. Although he had to race to have a shower and change clothes; he stopped still as soon as he saw me. His eyes welled up with tears as he smiled on proudly.

"Bianca Grace Wisetail, you truly look like a Lokoti tribeswoman." He beamed.

"Yeah yeah...our little girl is all grown up and her father is going to make us late for the Ceremony!" Mum started to push him towards the stairs.

"Jess!" He laughingly pulled his mate into his arms. "Look at her, look at our little girl that we brought into this world. Look at how mature she looks!"

Mum softened at Dad's words as she lovingly caressed his cheek, before she started to push him up the stairs again.

"Move it, Hunter Wisetail! You have twenty minutes before you have to drive your daughter to the Holy Grounds for the Ceremony!" She barked.

He tickled her back before he bolted up the steps and disappeared into the bathroom.

At 9.50 AM, I was led out of the house with the paint barely dry on my face. I was in full traditional dress, with my long black hair plaited, beaded and feathered. Mum, Dad, Great Grandma and Aunt Danika, were dressed in their smart clothes.

"Where are our Australian and English relatives?" I asked as I climbed into Dad's truck.

I sat in the middle of my parents as I always have done. Aunt Danika climbed inside of Great Grandma's truck with her to drive in front of us.

"Your Gran instantaneously phased them here an hour ago, to her house. They'll be down at the Holy Grounds now, along with the rest of the tribe." Mum answered.

"OK, let's go." Dad slowly started the ignition to let Great Grandma reverse out our driveway first.

We drove down the hill and turned left at the intersection instead of right. Rather than driving towards the community centre, Dad drove towards the outskirts of our village. The Holy Grounds where the three Sacred Totems sat were in a picturesque, grassy glade by the side of the river.

Up until this point, I had felt calm and determined to go through with this. But as soon as I saw all of those parked vehicles and the size of the crowd that had gathered? My eyes widened as my heart sped up. I had heard even the general store was closed for the celebrations. I wasn't afraid of marrying Grant as I was determined to do that. But to marry him with the WHOLE tribe watching? I got stage fright! My breath sucked in sharply as I grimaced at the sight of all of those people.

Dad drove through the large cluster of parked vehicles and into the awaiting car space, reserved for us up the front with Mr. Barley waving us in.

"You'll be fine." My parents accidentally said at the same time, as he turned off the engine.

"Just breathe." Dad instructed, squeezing one hand.

"Just try to focus on the ceremony." Mum squeezed my other.

"Right." I tried not to blanch.

"Let's get this show on the road." He grinned. "Just remember, you're a Lokoti Werewolf and there's very little that scares us."

"Just don't instantaneously phase out of here because you're also a Circulator." She joked.

"Now THAT would scare us." He chuckled.

My parents hopped out of the truck as I climbed out after Mum. I stood by her side feeling rather conspicuous, dressed and painted up as such, especially when everybody turned and craned their necks to get a good look. I could hear a drum beat as Dad walked around from the driver's side of the truck. He took hold of my hand as she held onto my other and together they walked me forwards onto the Holy Grounds.

Gran and Grandfather joined us as did Great Grandma, Aunt Danika and Nana and they were all dressed formally.

"You look beautiful, B." Grandfather smiled a little tearfully as he kissed the side of my face that wasn't painted.

"Thank you." I smiled nervously.

At that moment Grant appeared and he was dressed similar to me, with Uncle Ian walking beside him wearing jeans and a suit jacket and tie.

Grant wore the same coloured suede clothing, with a suede shirt, a suede jacket and suede pants. His long black hair wasn't in three plaits like mine, but in three loose ponytails which were also tied by leather bands with feathers. He also had the painted claw mark on his face but it was on his left side. My eyes widened as I looked on impressed, as I thought that he looked very handsome and just like a Lokoti Warrior of old.

"Hi B." He smiled softly.

"Hi Grant." I smiled back shyly.

"I formally ask your permission Emanuel Riverclaw as the head of the Riverclaw family; for the hand of your beloved granddaughter, Bianca Grace Wisetail." He spoke in a clear, concise voice to Grandfather.

I noticed the tribe suddenly turned quiet as they stood back to watch and listen. Oh was this apart of the ceremony?

"You have my permission, Grant Elm." My grandfather stepped aside.

"I formally ask your permission Hunter Wisetail, as the father of Bianca Grace Wisetail, for the hand of your beloved daughter." He next spoke to Dad.

"You have my permission, Grant Elm." My father released my hand.

Then Mum let go of my other when he stepped forward and took hold of the hand that Dad let go. Grant turned me around to face Uncle Ian.

"Bianca Grace Wisetail, with the blessing of the Elders today; I formally acknowledge your entry into my family's house. I call you from this day forth, Bianca Grace Elm." My 'uncle' spoke loudly, so everyone could hear.

I could hear the tribe murmur in excitement and admiration, watching this 'handing over' to the beat of the drum.

Then Grant led me by the hand to walk through the crowd. Our tribe parted to allow us passage towards the assembled nine Tribal Elders. They stood also dressed in traditional attire, before the three Sacred Totems. Uncle Ian, Dad, Mum, Gran, Grandfather, Great Grandma and Nana all walked behind Grant and I through the parted crowd towards the Elders. Aunt Danika went to go and stand next to Uncle Jules and their children.

The Council of Elders moved to sit in a half circle before a fire, as Grant led me forwards to kneel on the ground before them. Then all of our families and the rest of the tribe also sat down on the ground, with the people up the back remaining on their feet so they could see what would happen.

Then the drum beat stopped, with Mr. Lightfoot and Mr. Shallow Water lowering their instruments.

"You have the Tribal Elders convened here for you today. What do you ask of us?" Aunt Beth began.

"I have come to ask for the blessing of the Tribal Elders as the Guides of the Lokoti Wolf, to take this woman as my mate." Grant spoke loudly.

I felt him squeeze my hand, which touched my heart.

"And do you have the permission of your family for this union?" Uncle Harry next asked as another one of the Elders.

"He does." Uncle Ian answered.

"And do you have the permission of the woman's family for this union?" Uncle Fred, another one of the Elders inquired.

"He does." Grandfather answered.

"He does." Dad answered.

"Fern Wisetail, do you give your permission for your beloved granddaughter Bianca Grace to mate with Grant Elm?" Aunt Beth next asked Grandpa, who was sitting beside her.

"She has my permission." He said gravely.

"Then Grant Elm, you and your mate may drink from the Sacred Cup. You may prove to us your brave heart and of your mate's love in return. By adding your bloodline to a vessel that eons of Lokoti Warriors, Werewolf and Human, have spilled their life force into; you will be sealing your fates together and start a new bloodline of Wisetail-Elm." Aunt Gail passed the cup around the hands of the nine council member until it reached him.

Uncle Ian handed Grant the Elm family knife. He put down the Sacred Cup, which was an old, painted wooden cup as big as a bowl. When I looked inside I saw a small amount of liquid which may have been mead. I watched Grant take the knife from his older brother and he ran the sharp blade over his forefinger, before he dipped it into the liquid.

Dad leaned forward and handed me the Wisetail family blade that Grandpa had given him. Next, Grant watched me unsheathe the knife and I stuck the pointy end into my forefinger. Then I too dipped my bleeding finger into the mead.

To my surprise, Grant took hold of my injured finger and he raised it to his mouth to briefly suck on it. The stinging subsided as I felt my skin start to heal over thanks to his saliva. I don't think this was apart of the ceremony, but I noticed the Elders looked on in approval. In return I picked up his injured finger to place inside my mouth too. I gently began to suck on it to start his healing.

"The male Lokoti Werewolf has the scent of his mate, as the female Lokoti Werewolf now has the scent of her mate. No matter where either of you should go, you will always have the other's scent." Grandpa announced.

To my further surprise, I found that he was right. Suddenly I could smell Grant's scent much stronger! I smelled his scent like the herb garden, as clear as day.

"Grant and Bianca, you may pick up the cup and drink." Uncle Trevor ordered.

Together we used both of our hands to pick up the Lokoti Sacred Cup. Grant held the cup carefully as I drank from it first and I guess because I was a Werewolf, I tasted his blood in the mead immediately. Next, I held the cup for him as he drank it down lastly.

Grandpa narrated, "when the Lokoti Wolf created the first Lokoti Werewolf Aru; he did this by sharing his blood with the injured Warrior after a great battle. The Warrior fell whilst fighting for his land and family. The Lokoti Wolf smelled that the Warrior had a brave spirit for going up against insurmountable numbers and he thought that the bravery should be rewarded. The Lokoti Wolf understood why the Warrior Aru had risked his life, as the wolf too fought in the wild for its mate and young. In seeing Aru's heart was true, the old Lokoti Wolf gave up his blood to Aru to drink. When the old father wolf died, its spirit merged with the Warrior's. Aru arose healed, as the first Lokoti Werewolf. With the spirit and the blood of the Lokoti Wolf inside him, he shared his blood with the last fourteen Warriors, creating the fifteen members of the pack. With this renewed strength, the first pack of Lokoti Werewolves fought off the invading tribe. From that day on, the Lokoti Werewolf has never feasted on Lokoti flesh, but remained strong as their tribe's protectors. You share blood today from the Lokoti Sacred Cup, just as the Lokoti Wolf shared his blood to ensure that our people would go on."

Uncle Harry said gravely, "you have sat by the fire of the Tribal Elders and have heard the story of your pack's beginning. Your union, Grant Elm and now Bianca Elm, is a new beginning. Bianca Elm you are the first female Lokoti Werewolf and it is fitting that your mate is a male Lokoti Werewolf. Bianca as you are a sign of the new, Grant represents the old. By accepting Grant as your mate, you are undertaking his instruction in the ways of the pack as you are entering under his family's protection."

Then all of the Tribal Elders stood up, which prompted us to stand up too as did everyone else.

"You have the blessing of the Lokoti Wolf over your union. You may leave us to start your new lives together. Go with the blessing of your Tribal Elders." Uncle Donald announced.

And that was it...Grant and I turned around to face our family as well as the tribe, as husband and wife.

All of our families walked up to kiss us on the cheek or shake our hands, which included Grandpa as he left his place on the council. After our families congratulated us, then the rest of the tribe did too...everyone that is except Aunt Susan, Declan or Derik, since they weren't here.

I received kiss after kiss, hand shake after hand shake, as I was congratulated by young and old. All I could do was stand there and smile politely as everyone deigned their goodwill. Even my English and Australian relatives boisterously offered their congratulations...everyone that is, except my Calculator who wasn't here. He was another obvious absentee.

"Where's Vincent?" I asked Gran who stood close by.

"Oh um, he said he couldn't make it because of Circulate business." Gran frowned.

"What Circulate business?" I asked concerned.

"I don't know, he didn't say." She shrugged. "But he made it sound pretty important. He was working on something in the Viewing Room at Circulate HQ when I last saw him."

Oh...a heavy, sinking feeling appeared in my stomach. Now why wouldn't Vincent come to my wedding? Did he know something that I didn't? I bet he was avoiding me because he saw something in my future with Grant.

"I'm sure it's nothing to worry about." Grandfather saw the worried look on my face. "Today is the day you're meant to be happy, B. No frowns allowed!"

Grant partially overheard our conversation as he was talking to Vine and her husband. He turned to give a curious look.

"Who's Vincent?" Vine asked, also listening in.

"Vincent is my Calculator." I told her.

"Huh?" She gave a funny look.

"He's like an observer." Gran told her. "He monitors her time traveling and her changes as a Circulator."

"Oh." Her eyes widened. "Well well! I now have a little sister that can travel through time!"

Grant chuckled at the sound of that as he kissed my cheek, making my grandparents beam at the attention he bestowed.

*****

After an hour of mingling, we could finally leave to start the Housewarming. By now I was starving as well as anxious to change into normal clothes again.

Uncle Ian drove us up to our new house on top of the hill. Uncle Ian - or Ian I should say - laughed out during the drive, "you can stop calling me 'Uncle', I am your brother now!"

As soon as my husband and I walked into our new home, we went upstairs to change.

We opened up our suitcases which awaited us in the main bedroom. Whilst I took out the new, yellow dress that Great Grandma made for me, Grant as casual as casual can be, started to undress in front of me. My face turned bright red, as I quickly averted my eyes.

"Excuse me, I'll just change in the bathroom and wash my face." I left to his surprise.

After I dressed, I used the sink to wash the paint off my face. It was then that Grant strolled into the bathroom, wearing jeans and a black shirt. His hair like mine, was still done up in the traditional way which I thought looked good on him.

"Hey." I moved away from the sink to dry my face.

Instead of immediately removing the paint, he walked up to pull me into his arms.

"That's a nice dress you're wearing." He smiled softly in approval.

"Thanks, Great Grandma made it for me to wear today."

"I wouldn't have minded seeing you put it on, you know." He bent his head to rub his nose against mine.

I blushed again as I uneasily looked away. He saw this which made him sigh as he reluctantly released his hold on my waist. Then he bent over the sink as he proceeded to wash the paint off his face too.

Uncle Ian – sorry Ian – stood patiently downstairs, waiting for us as well as greeting the first of the arrivals. I noticed how easily he mixed in with my Australian and English families, as he seemed to know them. But of course he would, from the time Mum brought them here to fight with the Lokoti against the Invaders before I was born. Ian's wife Bec also arrived with their kids, as more and more people arrived from the Joining Ceremony.

Our new house wasn't big enough to entertain the whole tribe and lucky for us it was a beautiful sunny day outside, with the wind chill at a bare minimum. People sat out the front of the house in fold-up chairs they brought, prepared for this kind of seating arrangement. Grant and I helped our families serve the food and drinks on a couple of fold-up tables outside that had been set up. Everyone had brought a dish and a bottle of soda, so there was plenty of food and drink to go around.

"Grant and B, go sit down!" Hannah ordered. "This is YOUR Housewarming! You can't spend the whole day waiting on people. No-one expects you to serve so let everybody help themselves."

"OK." Grant smiled in relief. Then he took hold of my hand and led me to go and sit with him in two spare seats that were next to Ian and Dad.

They were talking with Mum, Gran, Grandfather, Grandpa, Nana, Great Grandma, Uncle Harry, Vine and her husband; when they instantly paused in their discussion to smile on our appearance.

"Here's the blushing bride." Mum teased.

"Shut up!" I did blush.

"That was too easy! That girl blushes like a strawberry, all it takes is one word and she blushes!" Ian ribbed.

"But she still has a curious mind though." Grant told his brother. "Did I ever tell you guys about the first time B and I ever talked about matrimony?"

"No." Dad gave a curious look.

"It was when she was 13 years old." He announced, still holding onto my hand.

"13 years old, huh?" Grandfather chuckled.

"No way!" I guessed what he was about to do. "Shut up Grant!"

"No Grant, don't shut up. I want to hear this." Ian nudged his brother.

"It was the night I babysat B when you were in Australia." Grant told Mum and Dad.

"You talked to Grant about matrimony when you were thirteen?" Mum raised her eyebrows.

"Shut up!" I felt my face burn. "It wasn't like that!"

"Here we thought that this was an ARRANGED marriage with us doing all of the arranging! But as it turns out, that B has secretly arranged this all along!" Ian pretended to act offended, getting more laughs.

"I was putting B to bed after her beating me at poker." Grant told my family. "'Grant?' she asks. 'How old are you?'"

"Why do kids always ask THAT question?" Grandpa shook his head.

"Now that IS a good question." Uncle Harry smirked.

Grant went on, "'I'm 23.' I tell her. 'When did you turn into a Werewolf?' she next asks. '13 years ago when I was 10 years old, after my father died.' I say. Then she asks again, 'Uncle Ian's a Werewolf too, isn't he?' 'Yep.' I tell her. 'How come Uncle Ian is much older than you?' she next inquires."

"Because our parents knew that Grant would suck at being an older brother so they made him the youngest." Ian added on.

"Be quiet Ian!" Vine rolled her eyes. "Grant would have made an awesome older brother."

He continued, "'Because my parents had him 10 years before me, with a couple of girls thrown in between us who are my older sisters.' I tell her. 'Are you the youngest in your family?' she asks. 'Yep.' I tell her. 'Is everyone in your family married?' she asks. 'Yep.' I tell her and then she asks in this innocent little voice, 'Why aren't you married?'"

Everyone cracked up laughing!

"She had you picked out from the start!" Ian guffawed as I turned as red as a tomato.

Grant laughed, "So I scratched my head and said, 'Because I haven't met the right one yet, I guess.' Then B asks, 'How will you know if she's the right one?' Five years later, when B found out about our engagement? I found her sitting on top of Sunset Point, she says to me in this worried voice, 'But I'm not the one.' She remembered our conversation. So what did I tell you, about how I saw our arranged marriage?" He turned my way. "Ah yes, that's right. I told her that I see myself as lucky to be marrying her. I told her how I felt like I've won a prize in a competition I didn't even know I had entered."

Everyone smiled on his words, then at how he put his arm about my shoulders.

"Grant Elm gets Bianca Wisetail. Grant Elm gets to marry the first female Lokoti Werewolf. Grant Elm gets the prize, the tribe's trophy bride! How does it make you feel, B? To be passed around, to be decided over like you were property?!"

Just then I shuddered as Declan's angry words sent chills down my spine.

My husband looked on in concern. "Are you cold B?"

"Ah yeah." I rubbed my arms to stave off the goose bumps.

"I'll get your jacket." He stood up and went inside the house to retrieve it.

I watched him disappear and when I turned back to the group, I saw everyone was watching his behavior with approval. Nervously I looked down, as I pretended to be pre-occupied with straightening my dress when secretly my thoughts were churning about somebody else.

What would have happened if this had been Declan's and my Housewarming? I could just hear his smartass retort if I said I had been cold; "then you'd better put a jacket on then," and he wouldn't move from his seat.

I mean, this is the boy who tossed me into the freezing river to remove his own transgressions! I inwardly moaned as I closed my eyes...yep, this wedding to Grant Elm was probably for the best. I just hope that I'm up to the task.

*****

Another hour passed of sitting beside my new husband, wearing the cardigan he brought out. I forced myself to smile at everybody who approached.

Most of the time he held onto my hand which earned more looks of approval from our families. I half thought it was kinda sweet at how he was entering matrimony so willingly; whilst the other half of me wanted to cry out, "what's wrong with you?! We hardly know each other!" Aside from seeing him at social functions and that one time he babysat me? I hardly knew anything about him.

OK, so he drives a black jeep. Alright then, he builds furniture with his older brother. Very well, I certainly knew his family. I mean c'mon, growing up in isolation from the rest of the world thanks to nuclear fall-out can really make a group of people bond together. But I had no idea what he liked to do for a hobby? Or I hadn't a clue what kind of music he liked. What if he doesn't like 'Iggy Pop'?

What if we take turns cooking for each other and he doesn't like what I make? What if he never lets me drive his jeep when I need to get groceries? What if he's a chauvinistic pig who tries to make me do all of the housework?

"B?" my thoughts were interrupted when he passed me another cup of soda he had thoughtfully retrieved when he poured himself a cup.

"Oh, thanks." I smiled impressed at his consideration.

Frickin' hell, so far his behavior today has really pushed up his score card. Grant 56 points and Declan 0.

B, this is your wedding day! Stop thinking about the boy you swore to hate for the rest of your life! Instead, think of the man that you're sworn to. Er, hello? Priorities!

When Grant returned to his seat beside mine, I surprised him by abruptly asking, "have you ever pushed a person into the river?"

"Um maybe." He looked on with amusement. "Why? Has Ian been complaining again?" he next looked over to his older brother.

"What's that?" Ian enquired.

"Have you been complaining to B about the time I pushed you into the river when we were fishing?" Grant ribbed.

Vine and Hannah cracked up laughing as they recalled what the brothers were talking about.

"Yeah pull the other leg, Grant!" Ian looked embarrassed. "I slipped!"

"What, at the same time as Grant's elbow connected with your rib cage?" Hannah teased.

"Grant couldn't push me into the river if he tried!" Ian fired up.

"Especially if he were only 13 years old and you were 23." Vine smirked.

"Never in a million years." Hannah winked, which made me laugh.

The Elm's cracked up laughing at their eldest brother as my husband's hand reclaimed mine once more.

"B, you just wait until Grant tries to impress you with his ironing skills. His clothes come out more wrinkled than before he turned the iron on!" Ian retorted.

"At least I didn't nearly set fire to my clothes by leaving the iron turned on!" Grant taunted.

"You did what?!" Mum laughed out loud.

"Oh great, here we go." Ian rolled his eyes.

"You actually left the iron on your clothes and then you walked away?" She carried on.

"Thanks Grant, thanks for giving Jess more ammunition to use on me!" Ian growled at his younger brother.

"And YOU gave ME a hard time for my washing machine breaking and flooding the laundry?" She got all riled up, "and you leave an IRON turned on?"

"Shut up Jess!" He harrumphed. "Hunter told me about the time you forgot to pick up B after school one winter and B ended up having to walk home in a blizzard! Now that's WAY worse than an iron burning through a shirt!"

"What?" She immediately turned defensive as she looked from him to her husband. "That wasn't my fault! I was at Circulate Headquarters on MARS!"

"Oh that's even better! You don't just leave tribal lands but you leave behind an entire PLANET whilst your 12 year old daughter has to walk home from school in a blizzard!" Ian pretended to take the high ground.

"Hunter!" Mum whacked Dad on the arm. "I told you I was going to Circulate HQ. Why is this MY fault?"

"You didn't tell me WHEN you were going to Mars, you just instantaneously phased out of the house when I was away repairing the Huntington's greenhouse." He pointed out. "I assumed you would go AFTER picking B up."

"You walked home from school in a blizzard?" Vine looked on in sympathy.

"Not really." I squirmed uneasily at having been dragged into another round of their sparring. "I didn't make it to the hill coz I couldn't see properly. When the wind nearly blew me over, I went to Derik's where Dad found me."

I spent that afternoon as I spent millions of afternoons, hanging out with my best friend. I recalled that day vividly; I had sat before a roaring fire and Aunt Susan made hot chocolates complete with marshmallows for the kids. We three drank up as we listened to her try to scare us with tales of 'Urban Legends' she grew up with, whilst the gale-force winds howled outside. Such stories of alligators in sewers or escaped killers from mental asylums, barely raised an eyebrow from a teenaged European Werewolf.

"That's not scary!" Declan said as his chest filled out with arrogant pride. "If that psycho-killer caught sight of me as a European Werewolf, he would have turned and run back to the asylum!"

"You're not scary." I pronounced, as I looked on the tall, muscled, supernatural 15 year old in human form.

"I'm not scary, huh?" He smirked as he switched his human blue eyes into their glowing green Werewolf ones, with his circular pupils turning into thin, black slits. Then he chuckled when I shuddered and looked away.

As I reminisced on what happened years ago, I started to become aware that a lull had fallen on the conversation. Mum looked guilty with Dad rubbing her shoulders and all of the Elm's except Grant, now looked uncomfortable. Maybe I shouldn't have said Derik's name? I think they all thought that we had been this big romance or something.

"So anyway," I added on hastily, "Dad picked me up on his way home from work. It's no biggie because I lived, didn't I?"

"Lucky for me." Grant picked up my hand to kiss it.

*****

Our new house fell quiet once all of the guests had left. Upon their departure, they left us with our many 'wedding presents', in furniture and household goods.

My new home was decorated in the typical country-style of mostly pine furniture thanks to the ample trees in the surrounding woods. Our new pine dining table and chairs sat in the dining area and the pine coffee table sat in between two second-hand, green and white checkered couches near the stone fireplace. There was a red rug on the lounge room floor and in the main bedroom upstairs along with home-made curtains of a red and green checkered material, on our windows thanks to Vine, Hannah and even Aunt Julienne.

So far our new home looked a little spartan, but nothing that a few photographs or trinkets couldn't fix. The Worthall's had kindly brought a couple of boxes of antique ornaments or gilt-edged photo frames from Blythe Castle which were still unpacked. Even my Australian relatives brought with them a couple of knick-knacks as well as the token jar of Vegemite.

I pottered around, picking up the last of the rubbish and the errant plate or glass, as Grant stood at the kitchen sink, washing up.

"Today went well." He made small talk as I placed the items on the sink.

"Ah yeah, it did." I said back. Then I caught him look me up and down once again. I wondered why he kept doing that? "What?"

"What?" he looked back at my face.

"What's wrong?" I queried.

"Nothing, you look very nice in that dress that's all."

"Oh, thanks." I said awkwardly as this was the third time that he's said that.

I walked out of the kitchen and went up the stairs to our bedroom. There I changed into my blue coloured flannel pajamas, which had cartoon flying elephants over them. Lastly, I used the bathroom to clean my teeth.

The staircase creaked, indicating Grant was coming. He too came into the bathroom as he grabbed his toothbrush and the toothpaste. I moved aside to give him room, feeling weird about how casually he waltzed in instead of waiting for me to finish. As he brushed his teeth, he looked me up and down as I was standing there in my pajamas. The intensity of his gaze made me feel uncomfortable.

"Are you right there?" I spoke with a mouthful of foam.

"Huh?" he inquired.

I didn't care to reiterate, so I let it go. I spat out the toothpaste before I rinsed my mouth and the toothbrush with water. I brushed past as I left the bathroom to head back into the bedroom. I was putting my lip gloss on when he came in. He walked up behind to place his hands on my shoulders when I jumped in fright!

"Sorry." He moved his warm hands down my arms. "Man, you sure are jumpy."

"Er yeah, I guess." I placed the lip gloss back on top of the bedside table.

"I would say, 'I won't bite I promise' but with our kind it's a given." He joked.

"Uh huh." I said uneasily as I was unable to look his way.

I proceeded to pull the covers back on the bed to climb in, when Grant turned me around so I was facing him.

"B." He said softly as I nervously looked up into his expectant face, but then I had to look away again. He tried to hold my gaze, "it's actually pretty easy what we have to do and usually quite enjoyable too."

I couldn't reply as I didn't know what to say. My heart was racing and I felt like I was trembling like a leaf, which Grant noticed too. I think he must have thought I was cold though, because he began to rub my arms as if to warm them.

He leaned in to kiss me softly on the lips...he tasted like toothpaste and I guess so did I. Then he released me for a moment to pull off his shirt and his t-shirt, so that he was now topless before he leaned in to kiss for longer. He was muscled, almost as much as Declan, I guess like any Werewolf was. Just part and parcel for being part animal I suppose?

His lips gently pushed apart mine, as he eased his tongue inside of my mouth which reminded me too much of Declan doing this very thing only a day or so ago.

"I'm sorry...!" I pulled away with my face burning up. "I'm sorry...!"

"It's OK." He said gently but he didn't move away. "We can go more slowly if you like."

"No." I shook my head as I hid my face in my hands. "I'm sorry Grant, but I don't think I can do this."

"It's fine, B." He removed my hands. "It's natural to be nervous for our first time together."

"No!" I said more strongly this time. "I don't think there can be a first time."

"Because you're thinking of another?" He guessed.

This was it, this was the deal breaker...

"Yes!" I grew tearful.

"Listen B, I'm aware that if you had remained human you would be doing this with somebody else." Grant said evenly. "But since circumstances have changed and even though this hasn't turned out the way either of us had expected? I think we can make a go at this."

"You see? There you go!" I said quickly. "You didn't want this and I didn't want this so we shouldn't do this."

"I'm not saying that."

"But -"

"I'm a Lokoti Werewolf and you are a Lokoti Werewolf. You're pretty and you smell good and I'm fairly sure that I'm not repulsive to you either. Just try to relax and enjoy the moment." He said lightly.

When he leaned in to kiss my neck, I heard him inhale my scent deeply. He wrapped his arms about my waist to hold me against his hardening form. His mouth traveled down to my collar bone, as he pushed aside my pajama collar to kiss my left shoulder.

Oh oh...that felt good! I struggled to hold onto my composure and not become swept up in the moment. I was also trying hard not to imagine doing this with a certain other person instead.

"Fine," I swallowed, "but perhaps we could maybe work our way towards this? You know, by using your 'move slowly' suggestion and do this bit by bit each night...?"

He paused to look back. "We have three days before the next full moon. We need to be mates before then so we can be prepared."

"But um, aren't we mates now?" I gulped as he began to unbutton my pajama shirt.

He craned his head lower to work his lips down to my breasts whilst gently leaning me backwards. "Nah ah."

"But we're living together...?" I shook harder when his mouth took in my left nipple.

"We're not mates yet." He shook his head as his open mouth moved across to my right breast.

"When will we be mates?"

"Trust me, you'll know." His voice dropped an octave as he look up with lust in his eyes.

Grant lifted me up in his arms before he fell onto the bed with me underneath.

"You're getting into the swing of things...!" my eyes widened in further surprise as he pushed open my shirt to give himself free access.

"Ah ha." He scraped his sharpening teeth over my navel.

He began to turn as I picked up the soft growls being emitted which excited me even more!

"Mmmmrrrrrrrr!" A growl crept up out of my throat! Embarrassed, I quickly put the both of my hands over my mouth to silence myself.

Grant looked back with glowing silver eyes and he smiled with his sharp, elongated teeth.

"Don't hold back on my account." He spoke in his deep Lokoti Werewolf voice which was like rumbling thunder.

Then whilst holding my gaze, he used his claw-like hands to pull down my pajama pants, spread apart my legs and he went down on me!

"MMMRRRRAAAWWW!" a roar came up, out of my chest!

I could feel my mouth tingle as my teeth grew longer and sharper whilst my back buckled in pleasure. I felt my body heat up in both ecstasy and in excess muscle bulk. I lifted up my hands to see my nails turn long and sharp. When I turned my head to catch sight of my reflection in the mirror on the dresser, I saw my glowing turquoise eyes look back...

Oh shit! Oh no! I'm turning! My fear was as great as was the urge to toss him onto his back and pounce on him!

"Oh no - oh no - I've changed - I've changed!" I growled out in my different voice which was thunderous as his. I sat upright as I grabbed him by the hair, to catch his attention.

"And do you want to eat human?" He asked in his rumbling tone.

"No, I want to eat you instead!" I tugged on his hair to pull him closer.

"Good." He pushed me back down with himself on top.

I tried to roll out from under, but just as I managed to sit on top, Grant flipped me over to pin me underneath. As we wrestled, we clawed and bit into each other. I don't know why, but it seemed really important that I tasted his blood and it seemed like it was the same for him. We both left deep, bloodied teeth marks in each other's shoulders.

As my ecstasy grew, I realized that amongst all of this growling, biting and clawing, he was managing to shag me as well. He was doing a pretty good job of it too, as I certainly wasn't lying still in my frenzy. Our sheets were victimized as they were accidentally shredded from our claws. This mating behavior went a little longer than I expected it to, as Grant was showing no sign of tiring, even when he came which happened several times.

Was this normal? Well I guess that was a stupid question, of course this wasn't normal! We're frickin' Werewolves for crying out loud! If a human just happened to accidentally walk in on us, they would probably run screaming from our house. So I guess what I meant to say, was this normal behavior for Lokoti Werewolves?

When I was with Declan it was wham bam thank you ma'am, with a couple of insults thrown in and a "don't tell my brother about this". Now here I was, with my husband or mate or whatever you wanted to call him... mating with him?

"Are we mates now?" I growled out as I grabbed hold of his hair once again.

"We're getting there." He growled back as he removed my hand.

*****

Two hours later, I lay as a tired human being in the arms of another tired human being, amongst torn linen with even my pillow case having a couple of holes in the shape of bite marks. I started spluttering and Grant chuckled as he watched me remove a piece of yellow cotton from my teeth; the same yellow cotton that the pillow case was made from.

"Great Grandma's gonna kill me when she sees what's happened to her wedding present of the bedding!" I momentarily raised my head to survey the damage.

"Not if I sew it all up before she sees it." He held me closely.

"You know how to sew?" I remembered Hannah saying something as such.

"It's a requirement of going through the change..." he said casually, "...I went through quite a lot of clothing when I accidentally turned before undressing."

"Yeah, I tore my favourite top the first night I changed," I sighed, "and my sneakers and my socks were K.I.A."

"You looked pretty hot, running through the woods in your bra and jeans." He snickered.

"Oh shut up!" I put my hands over my face as I rolled onto my back, embarrassed.

"Why do you think I didn't mind the idea of marrying you?" Grant grinned as he kissed the bite mark on my right shoulder. The mark which was already half healed, as was his.

"So what happens now?" I asked softly, looking back into his dark brown eyes.

He gazed for a while into my dark blue ones, before he replied. "We're mates, Bianca. We hunt together and we sleep together and we live happily ever after."

~~~~~~
~~~~~~

~ 9 ~

7th October 2084

For the first three days of marriage leading up the full moon, I found my new husband's behavior surprising. He was still extremely nice and polite and he even acted overprotective sometimes. He threw himself into our marriage with gusto while I myself dawdled.

When we began to set up the greenhouse, he insisted on carrying anything that looked remotely heavy, even though we both knew my Werewolf strength almost matched his physical prowess. He quickly found out what music I liked, which was similar to the music he liked. He would set up his iPod with mini-speakers in the greenhouse for us to listen to as we worked.

For the first two nights Grant insisted on cooking for us, which was basically warming up left-overs from our Housewarming in the microwave. He had this strange idea that I had never cooked before? I had to explain to him that it was thanks to all the cooking lessons I had with my Great Grandma, whenever she looked after me over the years.

He also started out by doing ALL of the housework, also under the misinformation that I didn't know how to do this either. But I showed him I certainly knew how to vacuum a house or mop the kitchen and bathroom floors. I even corrected him when he was doing the washing on when to put in the laundry softener.

"Oh." He looked on impressed that I stopped the machine in time.

"See?" I pointed out on the controls. "It's the last rinse cycle."

"Right!" he bashfully laughed. "I knew that!"

However what particularly surprised me about Grant, was how he acted like he couldn't get enough of the physical side of our marriage. I have to admit, it started to cause me some concern. Consummating the marriage bed could go for hours and don't get me wrong, it was pleasurable. But he started to expect more and more.

What I mean is for the first three nights, we'd have dinner and afterwards we'd read or watch a DVD. Then we'd brush our teeth and lastly go to bed.   But it got to the stage where I no longer bothered to put on my pajamas, because I knew that they weren't going to stay on.

On the third night, as he washed the dishes and I dried and put them away; half way through the washing up he stopped to start to kiss my neck.

"Mmm...you smell better than Hannah's choc chip cookies that she bakes." He said hungrily.

"Er, Grant? What about the washing up?" I laughed uneasily.

"Who cares about the washing up? I want to wash you up!" he growled, tossing aside my tea towel.

"Grant!" I objected when I saw it land in the hot, soapy water.

"Oh B...!" he dropped to the kitchen floor and pulled me down with him.

I remember lying there, staring up at the fluorescent kitchen light, feeling ravaged. I also felt a mass of conflicting emotions that were raging inside...

Half of me was on the side of the 'Pro Grant' party. This voice reminded me in an authoritative manner, 'Grant is your mate as you married him for your tribe. You have a responsibility to fulfill. He's a nice guy and you could be in a worse situation than this.' The other half kicked and screamed and swore, 'kick him off you! Leave this guy! Run away and never come back! Run away with Declan! Derik already lost you to Grant so what if you run away with his brother instead?'

However the good side won as it usually did, by Grant managing to stir my desires. Slowly but eventually, I could finally lose myself in the moment as relief washed over me whilst I started to connect with my husband. There, you said it - your husband. You're frickin' married Bianca, now get used to it!

Afterwards, I lay on top with the both of us half undressed, still on the kitchen floor.

My husband surprised me again when out of the blue he blurted out, "sometimes it feels like there's a war being raged inside of you."

Inwardly I cringed but I managed to swallow before I forced out, "what do you mean?"

He was quiet for a moment before he sighed, "it feels like you're holding back because you're not completely letting me in."

With him saying this, I realized that I was an idiot for underestimating Grant and for telling myself that he wouldn't notice. Now I felt wretched with guilt and I said quietly, "I guess that makes me a bad person, doesn't it?"

"B..."

I rolled off as I quickly got up and went upstairs for a shower.

My guilt turned into anger as I stood under the scalding hot water. I tried to scrub away my past transgressions as I washed off the day's grime. His words made me angrier and angrier which made me scrub harder and harder with the loofa. I mean, what does he expect? We're an arranged marriage! Does he expect me to turn all goo-goo over him, overnight? He knew there was somebody in my past...albeit it wasn't the person he was thinking of, but still.

When I eventually came out of the bathroom, I heard that Grant was in the bedroom, waiting for me in bed with his bedside lamp still on. I didn't feel like going to bed and lying down beside him. I knew he would instantly put his arms about me and right then, I didn't want him to touch me anymore.

Instead, I went downstairs and opened the front door. I walked out into the cold air, as I stood on the small veranda and looked out into the night. It was almost the full moon, I observed.

However I also noticed that the moonlight made my heart pound. I had to suppress the urge to throw off my robe, jump of the veranda and run into the woods! I wanted to hunt and make a kill. The very thought made my stomach rumble. My eyes fluttered closed as I sniffed the night air.

Predominantly I could smell vegetation, but there was the scent of something warm blooded…something that I could hunt…something that I could chase…something that I could kill…something that I could feed on…I could smell the dangerously tempting scent of human again.

This human was a townsperson from Alma which was 7 km's away. As I sniffed the air again I pictured this human, who smelled Caucasian. Instead of being safely ensconced indoors, this human strolled down the street of the township. I could smell the delicious hormones indicating he was male and he could possibly be large, which meant he would be strong.

Good - large quarry. The greater the challenge, the greater the satisfaction would be over the kill. I licked my lips as I closed my eyes whilst enjoying the sensation of my teeth turning sharp as they grew elongated. My nails hardened into claws and I could feel my body change in excitement!

When I opened my eyes again, the night was lit up as clear as day thanks to my Werewolf sight. With my glowing turquoise eyes, I saw into the dark corners and crevices of the woods as clearly as if it were bright and sunny.

"B."

Grant's voice startled me and I whipped my head around to see him standing in the front doorway. He was watching my changes warily. I forced my claws and teeth to retract, as my glowing turquoise eyes dulled to their human dark blue.

"Come inside please." He said firmly, stepping aside. But I remained where I was, as my predator instincts made me eye him up and down, judging the chances of taking him on. His eyes narrowed as he sensed this. His voice dropped warningly, "B, come inside."

My rational human brain knew that Grant wasn't some 'wife beater' as I knew he wasn't about to grab me by the hair to drag me in. However my Lokoti Werewolf instincts also knew that he stood tense and ready, waiting to see if he would have to chase me down if I made a run for Alma.

I knew that it was for the safety of the tribe that my husband would have to stop me, just as it was for the safety of the tribe that Declan stopped me on the boarder. It was for the safety of the tribe that Dad locked me in the bathroom afterwards. It was for the safety of the tribe for the next two nights after it, I was drugged with DYSTAR as well as locked up. If Alma was attacked by a Lokoti Werewolf, the pack as well as the whole of the Lokoti Tribe would suffer for it. It was why I was married off to another Lokoti Werewolf, to prevent this from happening.

"B?"

"I know!" I spat out in frustration. "Hunting human is bad and hunting animal is good! I'm just standing here -"

"Bianca Elm!" He growled out in his rumbling Werewolf voice.

When I turned my head in his direction once more, I saw his glowing silver eyes, glint dangerously. His partial change both excited as well as frightened me.

I could feel it in my blood what Grant was trying to do. He was trying to exert his influence as my mate, over my mind and body; by using our biological bond as my leash. I could feel the pull of his will on my mind and on the blood in my veins, which again divided me into two. One half wanted to obey as the other half wanted to rebel and kill something!

Then I realized something else about my new husband that he was far more cunning than I gave him credit for. While I had been inwardly tossing and turning, he had sidled up and now was firmly holding onto my wrist to prevent my getaway. I may be faster than him, but he was stronger and his grip on my arm was ironclad.

"Let go of me!" I roared in my Werewolf voice.

"Not likely!" He growled back.

Whilst one hand was wrapped around my wrist, his other arm wrapped about my waist. He picked me up and didn't put me down again until I was inside the house with the front door closed behind.

"I was just standing outside!" I raged whilst trying to pull away but he wouldn't let go.

"You could smell the human male walking the streets of Alma over 7 km's away!" He snarled.

My eyes widened in surprise, "you smelled him?"

"Of course I smelled him!" He hissed. "I can control my bloodlust so I may smell him but I'm no longer tempted by him!"

"If you can smell him and I can smell him, then why don't we both just have him?" I tried to loosen his grip. "We could carry him out of the town so fast that nobody would see us! Nobody would know!"

"Because that man could be somebody's mate!" He said strongly. "Because that man could be somebody's brother! That man could be somebody's father! I lost my father when I was 10 years old and I would not put that on another child's head!"

That worked...his words hit home. I stopped trying to wriggle out as my face fell and my guilt overrode the bloodlust.

Grant pulled me close as he growled softly in my ear, "it will become easier, B. It will, I promise you."

I trembled with the excess energy of the bloodlust which wouldn't go away. I felt like it was pushing me closer and closer to the edge of insanity. I cried out as I tried one last time to pull myself free!

Then to the both of our surprise, I momentarily glowed! It wasn't just my eyes glowing turquoise, but my skin lit up with a whitish light. I even looked a little blurry as well as bright, as I started to realize that this is how Mum and Gran looked when they went into phase. When a Circulator phased through time or moved in light speed, their biological bodies were for all essential purposes, turned into light.

I almost phased out of his grasp, but his will overrode my concentration. His mind made my mind cloud over, so I couldn't continue to put myself into phase. Grant was holding onto my wrists more firmly than if they were in handcuffs. His physical strength wasn't just the only thing holding onto me nor was his will, but his scent suddenly became overpowering too.

"Listen to the sound of my voice B and concentrate on my scent. Don't listen to the bloodlust but listen to me. It's why you're angry just as it's why you're restless and hungry, even on a full stomach. Stop fighting me and as soon as you do, it will start to become easier." He spoke in his deep, supernatural voice which rumbled out like thunder.

I turned from his earthy herb garden smell, as I tried to edge away from him.

"Listen to the sound of my voice. You can hear the sound of the Lokoti Wolf in my voice. Listen to what the he's saying to you. It's telling you to be mindful of your people, of your tribe, of your family. By hunting human when it's not in battle, you are putting your people at risk. The Lokoti Wolf created Aru the first Lokoti Werewolf to help his tribe - your tribe B." His voice permeated through my body.

"No!" I growled angrily, leaning as far back as I could.

"Listen to me B, listen to my voice, it's the voice of your mate. My blood is inside of you. You have my scent so concentrate on it. All you have to do is stop fighting me. Stop pulling away, B. All you have to do is stop resisting and the rest will come easily. The rest will come so easily to you. Rest B, rest now."

His deep Werewolf voice rumbled through my head, making my mind spin, along with his hypnotizing scent.

"No! No!" I started to feel my bloodlust die down, as my physical and mental resistance began to lower.

"You see? Do you feel it, B? Do you see how easy it is? All you have to do is stop fighting me. Stop fighting and you will be rewarded. Listen to my voice, inhale my scent and I know you can feel my blood inside you. It's what's telling you to trust me."

"No...!" my arms flopped downwards against my control.

Grant pulled me to him as he let out a deep sigh of relief whilst he held a more pliable wife in his arms. The tension completely slipped away from my back and my shoulders as my hardened Werewolf muscle bulk slipped away. Whilst I morphed back into my human softness, he growled tenderly as he ran his hands up and down my back.

I felt him revert back into his smaller human shape, as he began to gently kiss my neck again. I closed my eyes as I inhaled his strong scent whilst I let go of the last of my misgivings.

"Shhh...shhh...rest B...rest now." He whispered in my ear.

He began to lead me away from the door towards the staircase. The fog that had drifted over my mind now began to blur my eyesight as I felt myself half-carried up the stairs.

"No Grant, no!" I whimpered, as I futilely tried to shake off his will over my mind, just as I tried to shake off his physical hold.

"It's time to sleep now, B. It's time for you to rest." He guided me into our bedroom.

I had never seen a bed look so welcoming before with its snuggly quilt. I slid in between the clean sheets, stretching out into the invitingly warm space before I tucked my face into the pillow. He instantly hopped in behind as he ran his warm hand up and down my back.

"Sleep now, B. You're tired and you need your rest." He spoke softly whilst smoothing back my hair.

Grant's influence functioned like a light switch inside my mind; I 'clicked' from a state of consciousness into one of unconsciousness...

...

... and when I opened my eyes again? For a first in the past three days, I woke up alone. He wasn't in bed, nor was he in the room.

I raised my head to look about, thinking that things looked a little brighter than usual. Hang on, what time is it? I turned my head towards the digital clock on his nightstand which read 10.33 AM. I've certainly slept in! Usually my body clock woke me up at eight as did Grant's so no wonder he's no longer in bed.

When I sat upright, I paused. My keen hearing picked up somebody talking downstairs and I recognized it was Grant.

"Last night was almost a full moon and B changed to go gunning into town again." I heard my husband say unhappily.

"And how has she been besides last night?" I heard Grandfather ask, indicating he was downstairs too.

"Fine," he answered, "she had been adjusting to the transition just fine, until last night."

"Tell us what happened." I heard Dad's voice, showing he was here as well.

"We had dinner and then we did the dishes. We had a slight...well, I wouldn't call it an argument but she got annoyed. She went for her evening shower then after the shower instead of coming to bed, she went downstairs to stand on the veranda. I sensed her bloodlust begin to boil, so I came out. B could smell a townsperson in Alma and when I asked her to come inside; she became confrontational. I had to use my will on her to muddle her mind which bought me time to bring her inside. Then she begged me to let her go or even go with her after the townsperson. I had to use every bit of will power I had, to calm her down enough to put her to bed." He told the older men.

Dad sighed out, "that's the Circulator in her. Whenever Jess gets angry, she gets itchy feet. The Circulator way of tackling a problem is to run away from it. It's why B went outside."

"She probably went out on the veranda to look at the stars." Grandfather added on. "Arabella likes to do that. I think it's because they're

Light People who come from the place of light, just as they're destined to return to that place."

"Jess enjoys that too...stargazing. Circulators belong to the space time continuum however it sounds like the Werewolf part of B kicked in, when she smelled the townsperson." Dad said seriously.

"Bianca isn't ready to go hunting tonight." Grant proclaimed.

"But this will be her second change!" Dad objected. "She has to start learning to hunt animal instead of human."

"Last night when B changed, I nearly lost control of her and it wasn't yet a full moon. With tonight being the first night of the full moon, I don't think my will alone can hold her. I don't think I can steer her towards animal flesh yet." He sighed disappointedly.

There was a minute's silence before Grandfather said concerned, "I'll get Arabella to bring back more DYSTAR from Circulate HQ on Mars."

"Does your bathroom lock on the outside as well as the inside?" Dad asked Grant.

"No, but that fact will change today." My husband promised. "Can a wooden door hold her even if it's locked?"

"With my back against it, it will." Dad said determinedly.

"No Hunter," he interrupted, "I'll stay with her tonight."

"I think we'll ALL stay with her tonight and tomorrow night and the night after it." Grandfather declared. "When the full moon is over, I'll teach her how to control her changing as I start teaching her to hunt animal."

"To prepare her for the next full moon?" Dad guessed his plan.

"It's how my Grandfather taught me and how I taught Julian." He told the younger men. "By teaching B how to control herself without the full moon making her bloodlust peak? She'll be able to concentrate better. When Julian first changed, he wasn't as fast as B, so I was able to take him on his first hunt immediately. With the will of the pack, we were able to convert his bloodlust from hungering human to craving animal. But I think because B is a Circulator and their bio-electromagnetic fields are different, it can disrupt our will so it loses its potency. That's how B escaped the pack the first night she changed, as well as her running away at light speed."

"My Dad taught me that way too." My father agreed. "He taught me how to control my change in between full moons by taking me hunting when the bloodlust wasn't at its peak."

"And that's how you and Ian also taught me when I first changed." Grant said to Dad.

"Grant." He spoke in a serious tone of voice. "What Em just said about a Circulator's bio-electromagnetic field disrupting a Werewolf's will is true as well. Jess is pretty good at deflecting my will over her from time to time. It's how she managed to live away from me during those three months when she was pregnant. Jess became aware of what I was doing and it hardened her resolve. It's why she purposefully avoided me by living and training in England. Jess started to become aware that when she was around me, my will could pervade her mind. B isn't consciously aware of the Lokoti Werewolf will yet, so you have that going for you. But the more you're around her, it will help increase your biological and mental meld with each other."

"I won't let her out of my sight." My husband said firmly.

There was another moment of silence as I heard my grandfather and father walk towards the front door.

"We'll be back at sunset." Grandfather said as his farewell.

I listened to them leave the house, with Grant shutting the front door behind. Next, I overheard their car doors open as they climbed in to start up their engines. I heard both Dad's and Grandfather's four-wheel-drive vehicles roar to life, before they reversed out of the driveway.   Lastly, I listened to the sound of their engines disappear down the hill.

My stomach sunk as my mouth fell open with dismay...I'm still a liability, even after this whole arranged marriage debacle. I'm a shame on my family because I'm still a killer. Mating me to Grant Elm wasn't working - he said so himself! But what was more disturbing, was my own father and even my grandfather, were encouraging him to use some sort of mind trick on me!

Dad was even giving him frickin' pointers on his technique, by using his own experience on my mother! This was so wrong, it was disgusting!   It even sounded like Grandfather wasn't above using it on Gran now and then! Well they can all go to HELL!

I leapt out of bed to quickly change into my everyday clothes. However just as I sat on the side of the bed, to pull on my socks and shoes; the bedroom door opened with Grant carrying in a cup of coffee.

"Good morning." He smiled cheerfully. "I thought I heard you were up, how did you sleep?"

I remained quiet as I finished fastening my boots.

"Oh." His face fell. "Not well, huh? Um, I made you a coffee..." he walked over to put it on my bedside table. He watched what I was doing. "Er B, it looks like you're going somewhere?"

"I'm going for a walk!" I stood up to march out of the bedroom.

"A walk?" He quickly followed after. "OK hang on a sec, I'll just grab my keys. We could walk down to the general store if you feel up to it? I was going to go there anyways."

"Why, to buy a lock to put on the outside of the bathroom door?" I flashed him a hurt look, before I stormed down the stairs towards the front door.

I marched off the veranda and down the driveway towards the road. I was stomping, full-steam ahead with a worried husband trailing after. Grant just managed to grab his keys, lock the front door behind us and then he followed me down the hill.

"Oh, you heard that, huh? Listen B, I can explain -" he tried to offer but I cut him off.

"I'm not listening to you!" I put my hands over my ears.

"Don't be foolish!" He laughed as he easily fell into step beside my angry form. "You've got it all wrong -"

"Don't follow me!" I whirled around to put up my hands to stop him. "Don't talk to me and don't be around me! Do you know what I want to do right now Grant Elm?"

"Er what?"

"March over to my grandmother's as well as my mother's house and tell them what I heard my father and even my own grandfather tell you!" I shouted . "Mind tricks?! Mind control?! What are we, frickin' sheep?!"

"B, you've got it all wrong and if you'd just let me explain -"

"And let you use more of your 'Jedi' mind games on me? No way in hell!!" I yelled in his face.

"B please -"

"These are not the droids you're looking for!" I quoted sarcastically. "Yeah right! How about I go running and tell every single woman who's unlucky enough to be married to you sneaky Werewolf bastards what's really happening in this tribe?!"

"Come on, it's not like that! If you would just let me explain -"

I put my hands over my ears again and started singing loudly, 'Lust For Life' by Iggy Pop to drown out his voice. "Here comes Johnny yeah, with the liquor and the drugs..."

"Come on, B!" He laughed again. "Not that you don't look cute doing that? But I think you should calm down and just hear me out."

I spun around to storm on ahead with my hands over my ears and singing loudly as I went.

STOP!

Huh? I stopped in surprise to look around in bewilderment.

TURN AROUND.

What was that? I turned around as I continued to look about. Where the hell did that come from? Is the bloodlust causing me to hallucinate now?!

LISTEN TO ME.

My hands lowered from my ears as I madly looked about, almost a little fearfully. Don't tell me I'm going insane and I'm starting to hear voices inside my head? Thanks to my hesitation, Grant caught up once more.

"Did you hear that, or did you feel that?" He took hold of my shoulders to make me look his way.

"Did you hear that?" I looked on in shock.

"B, did you hear the words, or did you feel those words just then?" he repeated.

I blanched as I took a frightened step backwards...did HE just do that?!

"You felt my words, didn't you?" He asked knowingly. "You felt them here..." He placed his hand over my heart.

Grant was right, it was as if the words originated from my chest and ended up in my head.

"How did you do THAT?" I demanded.

"I feel the words all the time." He shrugged. "I feel them from the pack, when we receive an order from our First or Second. I feel the words when one of us is on patrol and they need backup."

"You mean we're telepathic?!" I asked in amazement.

"Yes and no." He emitted a small smile. "We're more empathic. I've heard from your Uncle Julian being married to a telepath that he and his mate can have complete mental conversations with each other. I've heard that your Aunt Danika can also see images in other people's heads. When Lokoti Werewolves send mental messages to other members of the pack, we primarily sense the emotion behind them. It takes a lot out of us so we can only send short bursts or commands."

"Is it what you use on your wives?!" I glowered with distrust.

"If you weren't another Lokoti Werewolf, you wouldn't have heard the words but you would have felt the will behind them. Usually we can't hear words from our human mates but we feel it when you're hungry or we feel it when you're tired or ill. I feel it when you're worried about something and I also feel when you're scared...like right now."

"No." I shook my head in disbelief. "I heard those words in my head! I heard the words 'stop' and then 'turn around' and then 'listen to me'!"

Grant's eyes widened, as he looked on impressed. "Usually it can take weeks or months for a new Lokoti Werewolf's mind to fall into line with the rest of the pack. I didn't hear the words, as I only felt the will for the first couple of months of my change."

As I pondered on his words, I realized that he was right. I remembered the times Dad would suddenly leave the house without word where he was going. He would depart in the middle of the night when it wasn't for a hunt nor was it his turn to patrol. Once he abruptly left the dinner table in the middle of a meal and Mum guessed the pack had called on him for a fight on the border.

This also reminded me of something else, of the night I first changed. That night I ran through the woods towards town, the pack just suddenly appeared, sensing where I was going and why. I had always wondered how the other Werewolves managed to appear out of nowhere. Did they telepathically or empathically hear my actions?

"Yes." He answered, as if he even felt my thoughts. "It was how we sensed your change that first night. It was how we knew which direction you were heading in and why."

"What did you hear or feel?"

"FEAST! FEED! RED MEAT! FRESH MEAT! HUMAN MEAT." Grant recited.

My eyes almost popped out of my skull by the accuracy!

"I – I – I had stomach cramps! I felt like I had to eat human to make the pain go away." I said weakly.

"I know just as the pack knows this, B. We've all been there." He said patiently.

My eyes watered as I looked away and took a deep breath to pull myself together.

He continued, "I felt what you were feeling when I was 10 years old. I thought I was losing my mind when I first went through the change! While other boys my age were experiencing growing pains, I had stomach cramps for not feeding on human. While the other boys my age grew tall naturally, my height and strength tripled supernaturally. If it wasn't for Ian, your Dad and the rest of the pack's help? I would have gone insane and let the bloodlust win. I learned that by the will of the pack, they could guide me away from craving human. The Lokoti Werewolf will isn't just used on our mates, but we use it on each other."

"But why would you want to use it on your mates?" I looked on, betrayed.

"Do you see us using it on your mother or your grandmother to make them do all the cooking and the cleaning for us? No. Have you ever see your father try to force your mother into doing something she didn't want to do? No. B, we feel it when you're cold or you're ill, as we sense it in another member of the pack. Just as we would run to the aid of our pack in battle, we want to run to the aid of our mate. The Lokoti Werewolf is exceptionally protective over their mates and their young because of this. When your mother was pregnant with you and she left for England to train; your father could still sense while he was in Alaska, if she was cold or angry or scared. It frustrated him that he wasn't there to help in some way. He tried to use his will to keep her warm and safe on Lokoti land, where he could do something." He explained.

I still didn't like the sound of that, as I looked down the dirt road that headed towards the community centre of our tribal lands.

Grant changed tact, "OK, here's another way to look at how the Lokoti Werewolf might use his will over his mate; during childbirth."

"Huh?" I gave him a funny look.

"When our mate gives birth, we're always there, right beside her. We've been doing this for centuries, even before White Man's medicine started to encourage the husband or the partner to be at the birth. Do you know why?" He arched his eyebrows and I shook my head. "The biological chora is a manifestation of our will. A Lokoti Werewolf can control his mate's heart beat, her blood pressure, her stress level and even share our physical strength. Just say you went through a difficult birth and a complication arose; I can guarantee you that our Tribe's Medicine Man isn't about to ask the Werewolf to leave his mate. Instead, your Grandpa uses us to regulate our mate's heart beat and breathing should he have to perform a procedure."

This made me curious about something else, "is this also somehow related to why Gran and Mum only gave birth once?"

"Exactly!" He beamed at my question. "It's not just our will over the woman, but the woman has her say over us too. If our bodies sensed that it would put our mate in danger if she conceived again, it shuts down our sperm production."

"What?!" I cracked up laughing.

"It's true." He shrugged as he kicked a small stone away with his foot.

"So after Gran had Mum and Uncle Julian; Grandfather's body just stopped? And after Mum had me my Dad's body just stopped?"

"And after my Mom had me, my Dad's body stopped." He said simply.

"Yeah but you're the youngest of four children! Your Dad's body didn't have to stop after one birth. His sperm factory got to keep its job a lot longer then the men in my family." I snickered.

He chuckled at the analogy before giving me a sheepish grin.

"So does that mean that you just stop having sex -" I started to ask when he interrupted.

"No!" he looked horrified by the very notion. "Hell no! We're ready and we're willing and we certainly are operational! We still come but it's what comes out of us that's changed."

"Oh." I looked down at the ground again. I started to draw lines in the dirt with the tip of my shoe as I felt a little shy talking about all of this.

"You maybe only starting to notice this about yourself, B? But Werewolves don't just like to eat but we're animals all around. We like the satisfaction that comes from hunting just as we like the act of procreation, even if there isn't any procreating going on." He gave a goofy grin.

I think I blushed again as I ducked my head whilst I tried to concentrate on drawing a pattern in the dirt. Actually, I had noticed this about Grant and others like him. Then I tried to banish from my thoughts the recollection of a particular rainy afternoon in the woods, with Declan. I vividly recalled the desperation on his face with his own loss of control...

He leaned in to growl playfully in my ear, "and considering the fact that there are two Werewolves in this marriage? I think that's why we haven't had any visitors. Everybody assumes that for the next month or so, we'll be a little preoccupied."

"Yeah, busy sewing up sheets!" I cracked up laughing as I nudged him away.

Grant laughed as well before he threw his arm about my shoulders and began to walk us down the dirt road towards the community centre.

"Come on, let's get that lock from the General Store. The sooner we get it, the sooner we can get in some alone time after I fix the bathroom door." He messed up my already messy hair.

"Hey!" I elbowed him off, "not the hair!"

Feeling in a better mood, I ran off ahead. For a couple of moments he was happy to just stand back and watch me run with my long, black hair streaming out from behind. He smiled softly to himself before he ran after, quickly catching up.

*****

Around 4 PM in the afternoon Grandfather, Gran, Mum, Dad and even Uncle Julian came over. I knew it wasn't a social event by their solemn expressions let alone the absence of any light conversation.

"B." My uncle said gravely.

"Hey Uncle Jules." I tried to swallow but for the lump appearing in my throat.

"I came here via Circulate HQ to get some more DYSTAR off Vincent." Gran held up the futuristic looking medical kit.

I knew well what it enclosed; futuristic syringes and more drugs. My heart skipped a beat as my stomach sank. I wasn't aware that Grant was standing near until he put a supportive hand on my back, as if he could sense my apprehension.

"Alright," I growled out, "let's just get this over and done with."

I turned and started to make my way upstairs when Mum queried; "where are you going?"

"To bed, so you can drug me!" I said sullenly.

Whilst I climbed the stairs, I caught Mum hiss at Dad; "I thought you said this marriage business was going to cure her all of this!"

Grant who overheard, turned his head sharply Mum's way.

"Jess, not now!" Dad hissed back.

"How much longer is this going to go on for?" She glared at her husband.

"As long as it needs to." Grandfather said calmly.

"Considering the fact that B is a Circulator and not just a Werewolf, it doesn't exactly fill me with hope. Circulators can live up to 1,000 years in biological form!" She said grouchily.

"Then I'll do my best to keep up with her, Jess." Grant said simply before he turned to follow me up to our bedroom.

"Mum," my mother turned to look on her mother, "surely we can think of something else besides drugging B every time that there's a full moon?"

Gran stepped up closely to look on with a serious expression. "Yes we can, Jess. After this wretched full moon business is over, I'll train B as a new Circulator." My mother's eyes widened in hope by this piece of news. She said firmly, "as B learns to control her ability as a Circulator, maybe it will also teach her self-control over the Werewolf part of her."

"I'll help." My mother volunteered. "We'll take her to Circulate HQ and together we'll train her."

"Er, Mum?" Uncle Julian spoke up. "Are you sure that's a good idea? To train the new Circulator how to circulate, before we train the new Werewolf how to control the bloodlust? The Werewolf – slash – Circulator could then circulate right out of our grasp and go on a feeding frenzy."

Mum turned to throw her twin a dirty look, "are you saying my daughter is a serial killer?"

"No, I'm saying that my niece is a new Lokoti Werewolf whom needs to be trained." Uncle Julian returned.

"After this full moon is over then that is what we'll do." Grandfather came to stand beside Gran to lend his support. "The Circulate will train B as a new Circulator and the pack will train B as a new Werewolf."

As he stood beside his mate; Dad went to Mum's side.

"As Jess teaches B how to phase, we can train B how to adjust to the moons' phases." He said as he put his arm about Mum's shoulders.

My grandparents exchanged a long look, before they looked on their daughter and son-in-law.

Uncle Julian rolled his eyes, but he still came to stand with the four. "Yeah well, count me in. You're still annoying," he looked Mum's way, "but you're still my sister."

"Yeah and you're an idiot." She smirked.

"I love you too Jess." He said wryly. Then he let out a loud laugh when she whacked him on the arm with her light speed reflexes.

*****

Instead of Vincent and Grandpa as the two men of medicine presiding, it was Gran and Mum as the residing Circulators.

"You know the drill." Gran spoke crisply in her English accent. "We need to give you a sedative first to put you under before we apply the DYSTAR."

I lay on the bed and watched with wide eyes as she prepared two syringes. Grant sat on the bed beside, also watching her closely as he held my hand. Grandfather, Mum, Dad and Uncle Jules stood close by, I'm not sure as guards or witnesses?

"Why isn't Vincent doing this?" I gulped. Mum also looked to Gran for the answer. She continued by picking up the syringe with the sedative. "Gran?" I tensed up as she moved the syringe closer. "Where's Vincent?"

My grandmother gave a pained look, "He doesn't exactly agree to all of this."

"What?" I raised my head. "You mean he doesn't think I have to be drugged?"

"No B." Gran faltered as she shared a glance with Grandfather, "Vincent doesn't understand what's happening here."

"What do you mean, 'he doesn't understand what's happening'?" I demanded, sitting upright.

Grant exchanged a long look with both Grandfather and Dad and I think the Werewolf part of me sensed their silent communication. Then my new husband frowned whilst he looked away and I watched his shoulders turn tense. My accute hearing picked up the low, dissatisfied growl that he emitted.

"B, let's not talk about this now." Grandfather spoke. "Let's just do the procedure and concentrate on getting you through this full moon cycle."

"No." I raised my hands. "Tell me Gran, where's Vincent?"

"Um…" Mum caught on to what Gran was trying not to say. Both women cast an uncomfortable look towards the men in the room as they tried to put it diplomatically, "your Calculator doesn't understand Lokoti Werewolves."

"Huh?" I looked on in surprise.

"Vincent doesn't like Werewolves. Alright, there I've said it!" Mum bit out guiltily. "I don't know why but he just doesn't."

Nobody needed supernatural hearing to pick up the unhappy growls that came from Grandfather, Dad, Uncle Jules and Grant this time.

"Could it be because Vincent saw a Lokoti Werewolf claim the Circulator he was interested in?" Dad unhappily put his hands on his hips.

"I don't know, he's just always had a hard time with the idea of Werewolves." She tried to say innocently. "When I first told him that I was married to a Werewolf, he offered drugs which could treat delusional behavior. When he found out what I said was true, he freaked out and had a panic attack. Next, he accused my Werewolf husband of primitive behavior because you tried to stop me from training my ability as a Circulator."

"You were pregnant when he taught you self-defense!" He cried out in frustration.

"Don't maul the messenger!" She rolled her eyes. "I'm just saying that Vincent's always had a hard time dealing with the idea of Werewolves. He pictures you guys as rampaging monsters, thanks to your strength and your bloodlust. In his opinion, you're a thin line away from joining the character Pat Bateman in 'American Psycho'!"

"European Werewolves may be like that but not Lokoti Werewolves." He scowled.

Oh…Dad just put down Declan. My father just put down Declan because he was a European Werewolf. His words caused a small twinge of pain in my heart, but I tried to cover it when Grant who must have sensed it, looked my way closely.

"Moving right along now," Gran cleared her throat, "Vincent and his prejudice's aside, we have to focus on B right now."

My eyes became glued to the syringe she was holding as I nervously licked my lips. "You know what? We don't HAVE to right now, Gran. We can talk about Vincent a little longer if you'd like?"

My husband gently lowered me back down onto the bed. "I'll be right by your side." He promised as he squeezed my hand.

Gran placed the futuristic syringe against my neck and I heard the tell-tale HIIIISSSS as the drug was pushed through my skin in a compressed spray.

Again, thanks to the powerful effects of the drugs, within ten seconds my vision became blurred as my muscles loosened.

"...it's time to get things started on the Muppet Show tonight..." I uttered out.

Or I think I uttered out? It sounded like my voice but I couldn't feel my mouth move as I couldn't feel anything at all...

*****

I swear I was sitting in the audience of the 'Muppet Show', watching the familiar stage. I saw Fozzy Bear get pelted with fruit and vegetables during his routine. I saw Gonzo get blown up. I saw Animal go nuts on the drums and eat his drum sticks.

Before my very eyes, I watched Animal turn into a pale tanned, hardened skinned, bulked-up, muscled body of a European Werewolf. I saw his eyes turn glowing green. His plastic eyes glowed like they were green lights, with the thin, black slits for pupils.

The muppet version of Declan in European Werewolf form then sat on a fake log howling out of tune to the song, "why are there so many, songs about rainbows and what's on the other side..." As he howled, I saw the Lokoti Werewolf pack also as muppets, come out onto the stage as his back-up singers. Their smaller muscles were made of foam, their different glowing eyes were like multi-coloured light globes like the kind you see on a Christmas Tree.

As if the stage lights were turned off, abruptly all of this turned to quiet darkness...nothing, I couldn't see or hear anything at first but then I started to make out a pale light. I realized that the pale light wasn't stage lighting but it was moonlight. When I blinked to refocus my eyes, I realized I was no longer sitting in a theatre but I was lying down on the bathroom floor of my new house.

The light of the full moon was pouring in through the bathroom window. Then it suddenly looked brighter as my Werewolf eyes took over. I watched the nails on my hands grow longer as I felt the same happen to the nails on my feet. I felt my clothes become constricted as my body inflated with extra muscle-bulk.

Oh no, I knew what was going to come next! No sooner had I finished this train of thought, was I right.

"NNNOOOOOOOOOO!!!" I rolled onto my back to howl in agony!

The pain! The pain! It felt worse than last time! I writhed on the floor, in utter torture. My stomach felt like it was on fire as I had painful spasms across my abdomen! Even my blood felt like it was boiling inside my veins as sweat poured from my skin...!

"GRANT!" I roared out in my thunderous Werewolf voice. "MUM! DAD! GRAN! GRANDFATHER!"

Come and help me! Please! Stop this pain!

"THE PAIN! MUM! THE PAIN IS WORSE THAN LAST TIME! MUM, HELP ME PLEASE!"

But no help came as I laid alone on the bathroom floor, convulsing in hideous physical anguish.

Where is everyone? Where did they all go? I smelled that they were close as I could smell the supernatural pheromones in my Lokoti Werewolf kin just as I could smell the familiar human scent of my mother and grandmother. But why won't they help me?

Surely if they knew how bad the pain was, they would! If only they knew of the agonizing torture I was in, made the words, 'hunger pains' look like a tranquil walk in the park! If they knew, they would unlock the bathroom door and let me go gunning for Alma! Hell, they'd even help me catch a townsperson to eat!

"MUM! DAD! GRANT! THE PAIN! THE PAIN!" I sobbed in my thunderous voice.

I lay there waiting but no help came. Can't they hear me? Don't they know what's happening to me? I rolled back onto my stomach as I pulled myself across the tiled floor towards the bathroom door.

"MUM! DAD! GRANT!" I banged with my fist. "HELP ME!"

Still nothing... Futilely I hit the door as hard as I could, but the door didn't budge. The door didn't even move from my pounding. The door didn't move? Hang on, the door should have moved! In the very least, it should have rattled. Then that means that it's not just the wood preventing my escape.

I sniffed at the air coming in from the gap between the door and the floor when I smelled three male Lokoti Werewolves standing on the other side. They must have their backs against it. They're not helping me, they're hindering me! It's their fault I'm in so much pain!

"MUM! MUUUUUUM!" I tearfully cried out. "I CAN SMELL YOU! I KNOW YOU'RE HERE! HELP ME MUM, PLEASE!"

Downstairs where I couldn't see what was happening but was later told; Mum and Gran anxiously paced around my new living room with Uncle Julian sitting with them.

"I have to go to her!" Mum started towards the staircase.

"No Jess!" Uncle Jules was quick to catch her. "You can't."

"Stop it Julian!" She pushed him off. "My daughter needs me!"

"Jess, right now that's not B." He warned. "It's the bloodlust making her act that way."

"Of course it's her and she's calling for her mother!" She refuted.

"Jess listen to me, please." Uncle Julian held up his hands to stop her. "As soon as you open the bathroom door, B would knock you over and run towards Alma."

"B wouldn't hurt me!" She said indignantly.

"She wouldn't feed on you Jess, but she would feed on others." He said unhappily. "You have to stay here. Please sis, we know what we're doing."

Gran put her arms about Mum, "come and sit down, Jess." She pulled her daughter over to sit on one of the sofas. "All three of us will wait it out until morning."

Mum dissolved into tears as she allowed her mother to seat her. Gran sat beside as Uncle Julian knelt on the floor before them. He took hold of his sister's hands and he tried to give her a brave smile.

"It'll be alright Jess, you'll see. Once we start B's training as a new Werewolf? We'll teach her control so this doesn't have to happen anymore." He promised.

"How come Dad didn't lock you up in the bathroom when you first changed?" She sulked.

"I wasn't part Circulator." He said frankly. "My Mum and my sister are Circulators but I'm a Lokoti Werewolf, like my father and his father before him."

Whilst my grandmother had one arm about her daughter, she reached out for her son. "Oh Julian..." the deceptively youthful Caucasian woman stroked her son's long, black Lokoti hair. To an outsider it would have looked a little odd considering they appeared to be the same age. She said guiltily, "I wish I could have been here to help you when you went through your change."

"It's OK Mum." He caught her hand and held it. "I guess I'm luckier than B because when I first changed, Dad took me on my first hunt immediately. He didn't have to worry about me running away in the speed of light so he could start my training to placate the bloodlust."

Mum groaned as she rose to her feet to begin to pace up and down. "Great, my daughter is a female Lokoti Werewolf. Wonderful, it would have to be MY daughter who's a Circulator too!" She muttered as she paced faster. "She's a Circulator like her mother, her grandmother, her great grandmother and her great, great grandmother. Now she's a Werewolf, like her father, her grandfather, her great grandfather and her great, great grandfather!"

"Just as it is with the eldest males in the Riverclaw and Wisetail families." Uncle Jules sung.

"So much for tradition!" She rolled her eyes. "I wish we could break family tradition by rearranging our genetics!"

"I don't know if it is genetics behind this." Gran frowned.

"Mum?" Uncle Jules queried.

"Vincent says that he can't calculate for B because her energy in the timeline keeps fluctuating. It keeps disappearing at odd intervals and he can't see why..." She speculated from her seat.

"He said there was something blocking his sight." Mum recalled as she paced.

"Genetically speaking, just because her father, her Uncle and her two grandfathers are Lokoti Werewolves; her DNA shouldn't have been activated. I mean, Lokoti women are carriers so they can pass the gene on to their sons. But it's the sons that are activated when a member of the pack dies." Gran recanted.

"Yeah this sounds familiar." He smiled patiently. "Do you have a point, Mum?"

"The ability to Circulate or to Calculate isn't genetic. There is nothing in human DNA that can be passed down to dictate that a person will be able to see through time or to travel through time. But somehow our foremother, Elisha Worthall passed down her ability to Circulate through her progeny to Jarrod Worthall. She also somehow passed on the ability to Calculate through her progeny to Vincent Moher." She thought out loud as she stood up.

Uncle Jules looked on in amusement as he now saw his mother start to pace beside his sister, as the two women brainstormed.

"So you're saying that B is a genetic freak?" Mum raised her eyebrows. "By being a Circulator when it's not meant to be passed down and by being a Lokoti Werewolf when women aren't meant to be activated?"

"Not a freak, but an anomaly." Gran frowned deeper still. "She truly is in temporal flux, an amalgamation of the past, present and future, all colliding into one. It's probably why her future is so cloudy. Think about temporal causalities, Jess. A leads to B and the effect is C. By outward appearances, it would seem that Bianca becoming the first female Lokoti Werewolf as well as a Circulator by having Werewolf and Circulator ancestors is C – the effect. But it's not."

"Because A didn't lead to B so why the hell did we end up with C?" Mum caught on. "Circulating is not a genetic ability and females are only carriers of the Lokoti Werewolf gene. So Vincent can't calculate B's future because C was never meant to happen! She was never meant to be both Lokoti Werewolf and Circulator!"

"Exactly!" Gran clapped her hands excitedly.

Both women stopped pacing and looked on each other like they were about to crack a major conspiracy. Uncle Jules remained quiet as he watched the two Circulators expectantly. Then he saw their faces fall and their shoulders slump as confusion returned to their faces.

"So then why is B the way she is?" My mother asked her mother.

"It beats me." She shook her head. "But I think the space time continuum has something big planned for her, even if we don't know it yet."

Then Uncle Jules saw his twin and mother return to their pacing, as they tried to comprehend life and all of its little eccentricities.

*****

Meanwhile, in the upper part of the house; my husband, father and grandfather all stood outside the bathroom door. Dad was gripping onto the doorknob so hard his knuckles had turned white; Grandfather leaned with his back on the door to use himself as an extra support and Grant stood helplessly by, as his new wife screamed in pain.

They flinched but remained steady as they both heard and felt me bang on the door once more.

"GRANT! DAD! MUM!" They heard me holler. "HELP ME!"

"She's strong." Grandfather remarked.

"She's almost as strong as a male Lokoti Werewolf." Dad agreed.

Then all three flinched in sympathy pain, as they heard a bloodcurdling scream come through the wood that the agonizing bloodlust inflicted.

"If the DYSTAR stops Circulators from phasing through time, shouldn't it stop B from also running in light speed?" Grant asked.

"Theoretically it should." Grandfather answered.

"Then can't we take her hunting if she can't escape from us using her Circulator ability?" He continued.

"No! I won't risk B to that." Dad said fiercely. "She's my daughter and I won't risk her escaping us. I won't risk the people of Alma complaining to the Government, if B eats one of them. I won't risk the Government sending Marines or whatever soldiers they have available with machine guns, to destroy her."

"But if she's dosed on DYSTAR -" he began.

"Werewolves aren't the only supernatural species with regenerative capability." Grandfather interrupted. "Circulators can self-heal, including from DYSTAR. B could suddenly get her ability back while we were taking her on a hunt. Then it would be like the first night she changed all over again, she'll run towards Alma and we won't be fast enough to catch her."

My husband's eyes widened at the older Werewolves worry. His heart hurt as his stomach tightened at the idea of putting his young wife in any kind of danger. His protective Lokoti Werewolf instincts were in direct agreement with their plan.

"But we may not have to worry about the Government coming to destroy her." Dad continued. "The morning after her first change, you should have seen her eyes, Grant. When she realized what she nearly did, B told me to get my hunting rifle and shoot her in the head."

His eyes bulged at this news! His face became a mask of shock, which then turned into one of sadness. He looked from Dad to the door I was on the other side of.

"We're not just saving the humans in Alma from B's bloodlust, but we're saving her as well." Grandfather said sadly.

My new husband looked down at the floor and after a moment, Grant gave a nod to show he understood.

Just then Dad and Grandfather were nearly thrown forwards when I gave the door an almighty thump! They heard the sound of the wood crack and this time even Grant jumped forwards. He was quick to put his hand over where the wood was weakening to stop it from splitting.

"She's getting stronger!" Dad said with gritted teeth, almost turning as he recaptured the rattling door knob.

"Her bloodlust is making her strength peak." Grandfather agreed, pushing his back up against the wood once more.

All three of them stood ready incase the bathroom door completely broke. They knew they would have to restrain a vicious animal; a predator. They waited and then they waited some more...but nothing happened.

The door didn't shake anymore, nor were there any further banging sounds. It turned eerily quiet, like inside the eye of hurricane. Grandfather and Dad exchanged an optimistic look as they wondered if the worst was now over? But their hopeful glances were interrupted when my husband doubled-over, with his face a mask of pain.

"Grant?" Grandfather put his arm out to steady him. "What is it, what's wrong?"

"B's pain..." He groaned, "...the bloodlust is tearing her insides apart and she's in complete agony!"

"My baby B?" Dad asked fearfully.

"I have to go in." My husband moaned. "I have to be with her, to help her!"

"Grant, I don't know if that's a good idea -" Dad frowned.

"She needs me, Hunter." He interrupted. "I'm going in!"

Dad looked conflicted on the younger Werewolf, before he looked questioningly at Grandfather. He watched his Second of the pack give a nod, although he looked a little wary himself.

"Alright then." Dad sighed in resignation. "I'll unlock the door and open it for one second. Em, stand ready incase she tries to bolt."

Grant nodded to show he understood, as did Grandfather. After one more moment as the three exchanged a rueful look, they put their plan into play.

At first my father leaned in close to the door to listen in, trying to hear if I was right on the other side of it.   Then he took a deep breath before his hands moved to the lock to turn it quietly. Grandfather stood ready just as Dad quickly opened the door and he barked out; "now!" Grant leapt through the crack and he immediately slammed the door shut behind!

However my husband soon found out that my father needn't have worried about me making a mad dash as I felt so weak and wretched, I could no longer move. I was curled up in a ball on the cold and hard, tiled floor. I was panting hard in pain as the agonizing cramps ripped across my entire torso! I couldn't even look up as Grant crouched down beside.

"B...?" His eyes watered. "B, come on." He pulled me into an upright position where I was leaning against the bath tub and I growled at him warningly. He smoothed the hair off my wet face, "I know B, I know."

I even snapped at his hands! Not to injure, but to warn him to keep away. However he sat down beside as he tried to pull me into his arms. Instead I pushed them away, as I turned my head in the opposite direction.

The pain was so bad, Grant's scent became as intoxicating as a glass of vintage wine to an alcoholic wine connoisseur. I could hear his heart beat drumming in my ears as I could smell the blood in his veins whilst I could feel the heat emanate from his warm body. I was even tempted to feast on him!

I wanted him - I wanted him bad - but not as a wife should want her husband.

"Grant!" I snarled. "Get out of here!"

"No." he growled back in his deep, thunderous Werewolf voice.

When I looked back, I saw that he had changed and he was gazing back with his glowing silver eyes. His enlarged Lokoti Werewolf muscles bulged underneath his long-sleeved t-shirt which was almost ripping at the seams.

"GRANT GET OUT OF HERE!" I roared, leaning away.

Then I thought that he did the stupidest as well as the cruelest thing I had ever seen a person do; he used the claws of his right hand to place a cut on his left wrist and then he held the injury up to my mouth.

My eyes widened as my nostrils flared at the seductive smell! My already elongated teeth grew sharper, as I stared at the blood hypnotized... Yet some tiny amount of will power enabled me to turn my head away from the temptation.

"What the HELL are you doing! Get it away from me!" I roared in fury.

How can he be torturing me like this?! What was he, a sadist?! Just my luck to be mated to the Maquis de Sade.

"Drink!" He ordered.

He used his uninjured hand to take hold of head then he thrust his injury against my mouth! But I refused to part my lips...

NO B, HE'S YOUR MATE!

My willpower refused to let his red sweetness in, as I locked my mouth shut. As strong as the bloodlust was to feed? So too were the protective instincts which kept my jaw shut.

"You won't injure me." He growled out. "Now drink!"

I tried roll away from him and the delicious aroma of his cut, but Grant pulled me back using his greater strength. Whilst keeping his uninjured right arm about my body, he used his strong claws to force apart my jaw. Then he shoved his injured wrist into my mouth...

Frickin' hell's delight! I had never tasted anything so good before in my entire life! Imagine the most perfect plum or the sweetest peach or even the rarest steak that you have ever enjoyed and times that pleasure by a hundred!

DRINK! – he mentally commanded.

As the mouthwatering sweetness like nectar from the ripest fruit filled my mouth, I couldn't help it...my sharp teeth came down!

Grant's eyes squeezed shut from the pain, but he didn't stop me. The blood flowed freely out of his double wound as I gripped onto his arm. I drank down his life force like I was both ravenously hungry and dying of thirst.

The agonizing stabbing pains immediately began to ease as my heart raced in excitement! My skin warmed all over as I felt renewed energy course through my veins. I drank in his warmth, I drank in his vitality, I drank down his essence. Until this night, I had never quite understood the term 'life force' when applied to blood before now. But drinking Grant's blood? It was like I was truly drinking HIM. He was his blood and that night it also became part of mine.

I started to lose track of how much I was drinking as I reveled in these new sensations...that was until I felt his heart slow and his blood pressure begin to fall.

NO! my protective instinct roared. **HE IS YOUR MATE!***

I sharply drew back my head and gasped, pushing away his wrist. Grant leaned heavily against the bath tub, pale and panting hard. I turned and looked on him fearfully... oh no, what have I done?!

"I'm OK...!" He heaved whilst still keeping his uninjured arm about his wife. "If I remain in my Werewolf form, I will be fully regenerated by morning." I turned around in his arms to cup his face as I sniffed him worriedly. "I'm OK, B." He managed out one more time, before he closed his eyes to rest.

I looked down and saw that his wrist was still bleeding and it wasn't healing quickly as it was meant to. I picked it up and placed it in my mouth once more, not to drink but to heal. He partially opened his glowing silver eyes to watch. I ran my tongue over the broken skin repetitively, to start his healing process. I could feel it begin to work as the bleeding slowed to a stop. By the time I removed it from my mouth again, it was well on its way to healing over.

"Sleep now B, sleep." He held his wife closely.

Guiltily, I wrapped my arms around his torso and I closed my eyes. I listened to his heart beat and as mine beat strongly, I concentrated on bringing his heart beat into sync with mine. After a minute, I felt his heart beat fall into the same rhythm. Next, I focused on his breathing as Grant was still panting hard. I had to concentrate on slowing it down to make him breath more deeply. After another couple of minutes, his breathing began to even out too.

My nose nuzzled against his neck, inhaling his herb garden scent as my eyes remained closed. Within ten minutes of listening to his steady breathing, I was sleeping soundly in the arms of my mate.

~~~~~~
~~~~~~

~ 10 ~

11th October 2084

The full moon period ended, leaving a pair of newly-weds a little worse for wear. Each night that I was locked inside that bathroom with Dad and Grandfather playing jailors, my new husband was locked inside with me. Where for me it was necessity, for Grant it was by choice. He refused to let me go through the agonizing pain brought on by the bloodlust alone.

For three nights, my Lokoti Werewolf husband held onto his Lokoti Werewolf wife as he did his damndest to lessen the pain somehow. At first he would try to soothe as he held me in his arms. Secondly, he would try to talk to me to try to get my mind off my painful situation. Thirdly, he would use his claws to put a gash on the inside of his arm which he would place in my eager yet guilty mouth.

The bloodlust made me eager but the guilt of relying on my husband in such a way, made me reluctant. However Grant made good on his word; by the next morning he was fully regenerated from his injuries. But I did notice the bloodletting could leave him famished, as his body demanded sustenance to replenish his blood level.

Grant would sit at the dining table with Dad and Grandfather, as all three of them eagerly scoffed down their huge, hot breakfasts that Mum or Gran cooked up. But the sight and the smell of cooked food, after painfully craving raw meat all night, made me nauseas.

"Excuse me." I put down my cup of coffee as I left the table.

I went up the stairs and into my bedroom to curl up on top of the bed. I laid in a fetal position as my abdomen still felt tense and sore from the previous night's proceedings. My eyes watered with self-pity as I stared at the glowing red digits of Grant's alarm clock.

Time seemed like a cruel joke, only reminding me that I may have survived my second full moon cycle as a new Werewolf but the next full moon was only twenty-seven days away. It meant I would have to go through all of this again and again, for all my existence as a Werewolf.

However I soon realized, my family had a plan to tackle what would happen the next full moon. As I came to realize, it wasn't just the Lokoti Werewolves that were the embodiment of the Chumbawumba 'Tub Thumping' song, it was the Circulators too. "I get knocked down, but I get up again, you're never gonna keep me down..." as the song goes; and so did my husband, mother, father, grandfather and grandmother.

On the fourth morning when I came down the stairs, dressed to start my day; I found in my living area the aforementioned people all gathered around my dining table.

"Oh," my eyes widened in surprise, "hallo."

"Hey B." Mum smiled.

"It's a nice day outside," Gran grinned, "it's the perfect weather to start your training."

"What training?" I queried.

"Your training as a Circulator." She announced.

"But before we begin, I propose that we eat first." Grandfather recommended.

"Yep." All of the male Werewolves in the room eagerly agreed.

"I can't concentrate on an empty stomach." Grant admitted.

"Me neither." Dad shook his head.

Then he, Grant and Grandfather all went into the kitchen to start cooking up breakfast for one and all. Within twenty minutes, everyone was seated at the dining table in my new house; guzzling down scrambled eggs, bacon, hash browns, grilled tomatoes and toast, the men had procured.

"Good eggs, Em." Gran complimented as she finished off her plate. "You can really take after your mother in the kitchen."

"Yep, Clara Riverclaw's culinary expertise is legendary in the tribe." Grant smiled to Grandfather. "Even my Mom borrows recipes from your Mom."

"So does mine." Dad chuckled. "I think my parents were secretly waiting for me to marry Jess, so Mom had an excuse to visit Clara Riverclaw in the kitchen more often on the pretense to talk about us."

"That's alright," Grandfather laughed, "because my Mom also had a cunning plan about your coupling. She couldn't wait to get her hands on your Dad's knitting patterns."

On this, Grant looked at the white woolen turtle-neck jumper I was wearing. "Did your Grandpa knit that for you?" he asked.

"Yep." I nodded.

"A Lokoti Werewolf who likes to knit; if outsiders only knew?" He joked as Mum giggled in agreement.

"You'll need to change out of your jumper before we start your training, B." Gran warned. "You don't want to put a hole in it."

I thought that was a little odd, as I pondered on what kind of training were they planning? "Why?"

"Today, your mother and I are going to start off your training in fencing." She announced.

"You can move in the speed of light." Mum stated. "So it's a good place to start teaching you fencing before we move onto phasing through time."

My eyebrows rose warily, "um, do you really think I'll be able to phase? I mean, running really fast is completely different to passing through mirrors or glass without breaking them."

"You looked bright like your skin was glowing, when you ran." Dad advised.

"I did?" I echoed in surprise.

"I guess your grandmother and your mother think it's related to how you phase through time." Grandfather shrugged.

"It is related." Mum proclaimed. "By moving in light speed, you're effectively turning yourself into light. I'd bet a hundred bucks that says you're probably running in phase rather than in your biological body."

"I'll agree to your wager." Gran smiled in amusement. "Let's make it two hundred quid that says Jess is right."

"I'm on your side." Grandfather grinned to his beloved mate. "I've learned never to underestimate what a Circulator says about the timeline or even about other Circulators."

"So if I'm going to learn fencing, does that mean I'm going to get a sword of my own to play with?" I asked hopeful.

I have always admired Mum's and Gran's swords. Ever since I was a little girl, I liked to swing them around as I imagined that I could sword fight in the speed of light, like they could. I had many imaginary battles, taking down monsters like the European Werewolf that attacked Aunt Susan and turned Declan. However the battles would end when either Dad or Grandfather would chastise, "that sword is NOT a toy, B." They would warily come to take it away, always careful to hold the weapon by the hilt and avoid the blade as it was silver folded over steel and as we all know, Werewolves are allergic to silver.

"To 'play' with?" Dad's eyebrows rose unimpressed as he repeated, "swords aren't toys, B. They're deadly and dangerous weapons."

"Especially when they're silver coated." Grandfather frowned my way, before he looked at Gran. "B's sword isn't coated with silver, is it?"

"It is." Gran said simply.

Just then the table turned quiet as the male Werewolves eyes bulged at this piece of news.

"But Arabella," he began, "B is a Lokoti Werewolf and Werewolves are allergic to silver."

"Yes, I know that other Werewolves are allergic to silver." Gran smirked.

"'Other' Werewolves?" Dad immediately caught what she said.

Then Gran stood up and momentarily left the table. We watched her walk over to where I now noticed three sheathed swords stood, leaning against the wall. I recognized two of them as Mum and her silver-coated Katanas, which were Japanese style swords.

I was once told that the Circulate's collection of Katanas were indeed made in Japan in the medieval times. Gran told of how they were collected by a Japanese Circulator who had left Earth with the majority of the Circulate in the 'Final Phase'. The swords were left as a part of the collection of weapons through the ages, on display in the self-defense training room at Circulate HQ.

The Katanas complimented perfectly the European swords, crossbows or longbows through the ages which also hung on the wall. There were even futuristic laser rifles, next to the polished antique muskets.

My heart picked up speed in excitement when Gran picked up the third sword to carry over. "This is for you, B." she smiled. "Consider it an early birthday present. But don't lose it, because not only is it a priceless antique, but one day it's going to save your life."

I practically snatched it from her as I giggled with anticipation! I immediately unsheathed it to behold the long, sharp, silver-coated Katana gleaming in my hands...

"Woah!" Grant, Dad and Grandfather instantly leapt out of their seats and away from the table.

"Arabella!" Dad looked on worriedly. "B is a Werewolf! Can't she get a sword that's NOT coated in silver?"

Hmm, if I was a Werewolf then shouldn't I feel apprehension around silver too? But I don't and I wondered why. The women watched intently as the men looked on in horror; as I reached out my other hand to touch the actual sword.

"NO, B! DON'T!" The male Werewolves yelled in alarm.

But nothing happened... I was touching the blade, but nothing was happening from the contact with my flesh.

"Are you sure it's silver?" I checked with Gran.

"Yep," she clarified, "it's silver alright."

"But I thought Werewolves are allergic to silver?" I frowned, confused.

"We are allergic to silver." Grant stated.

"Then you touch it." I moved the sword towards him.

"NO B!" He leapt further backwards in a lightening fast move.

Huh? I don't understand, why won't Grant go near but I can hold it?

"Gran?" I looked to her for an answer.

"Arabella?" so did Grandfather.

"I just had this feeling." She shrugged.

"Actually, so did I." Mum smirked. "B is the first female Lokoti Werewolf, but because she's also a Circulator..."

"...silver doesn't have the same effect on her." Gran finished.

Now Mum clicked her fingers as something else occurred to her, "I bet it has something to do with her higher bio-electromagnetic frequency! Circulator's don't age the same way as humans do because we're in temporal flux. I bet it's the same with silver."

"Her heightened bio-electromagnetic frequency is harmonizing with her Lokoti Werewolf regenerative ability. So as a Circulator, she's faster than Werewolves and now, she's also not allergic to silver." Gran pronounced.

I looked on the two older women impressed, "did you two just 'see' all of that then?"

They stood back smugly and nodded. Although I believed them, I also sensed there was something missing to the equation.

"Hang on." I said and then I surprised everyone by morphing into my stronger Lokoti Werewolf shape.

In my supernatural form, I touched the silver on the sword again...still nothing. So this time I ran my finger along the sharp edge and that got a reaction for sure!

"OOOOWWWW!" I roared in pain!

Simultaneously I dropped the sword which clanged when it landed on top of the table, as I jumped backwards recoiling in pain.

My finger didn't feel like I had a simple cut, but it felt like it was burning too! It was like somebody had poured acid into the wound! I nursed my injured hand whilst reverting to my human shape, as I backed so far away from the table that I knocked into the wall.

"Let me see." Grant was quick to rush to my side. He carefully held my hand and we both looked down to see blood almost pour out of the tiny cut.

"There's so much blood!" I whimpered, afraid.

"As a human which is also her Circulator form, B can touch the silver. But in Werewolf form if the silver breaks her skin? Then silver causes just as much injury to her as it does to us." He proclaimed.

"So she's not as allergic to silver as we are, but she's still allergic." Dad pondered as he and the rest of my family crowded around to see.

"But it's just a tiny cut! Why is there so much blood?" I complained.

"Silver is deadly to Werewolves." Grandfather spoke softly. "In weapon form, it can kill us."

"We can't regenerate easily from silver-caused injuries." Dad added on.

"It's why you're bleeding so much and why the cut isn't healing itself immediately." Grant finished. "But Em and Hunter look at the cut, do you notice anything different?"

Dad's breath sucked in sharply as his eyes widened, "there's blood but no smoke."

"Smoke? What smoke?" I gave him a peculiar look.

"Silver burns us. It not only weakens our flesh, but a small amount of red smoke can appear which is a chemical reaction to the silver." Grandfather explained.

Next, Grant raised my injured finger to gently place it inside of his mouth. I felt his tongue tenderly lap at the cut, sending it numb with his regenerative ability. As he did so, my parents and grandparents moved a little away to give us privacy.

My eyes met with my husband's, as my stomach felt all fluttery from the contact. After a minute, he took my finger back out of his mouth and we both looked on. The cut had completely healed over and was now just a small, pink line.

"Thanks!" I looked at my husband like he was a hero. Grant gave a small smile, before he turned to look warily on my silver sword on top of the table. "What would happen if you touched the sword?" I asked him.

"I can't touch it." My husband stated. "I can't touch silver at all...not as swords, not as bullets, not even as jewelry."

"Why?" I asked. "I mean, what would happen if you touched silver jewelry?"

Grant exchanged rueful looks with the other males, before Grandfather explained, "when your grandmother and I were 14 years old, she used to wear a silver crucifix that her father bought her."

"Oh oh." Gran's face fell. "I remember this story."

"I wasn't aware she had it on, as it was hidden under her blouse. But when I hugged her and a small part of my skin touched it?" Grandfather still winced from the memory, "it left a swollen, red welt which lasted for a week. It felt just like a burn does."

"I never wore that necklace again." Gran looked on Grandfather guiltily. "I'm so sorry Em..."

"It's OK." He smiled patiently. "It happened in the first month we met. You were still getting used to the idea of having a Werewolf as a playmate."

Gran giggled as she put her arms about her husband's neck, "you became my playmate alright." Then the two laughed softly before they exchanged a kiss.

Mum cleared her throat, "erm, back to B's training?"

"Yes," she turned back around as Grandfather's arms remained about her waist, "back to B's training. So how about we go to the usual place we train in?"

"Cool!" I gave an excited jump. "The self-defense room at Circulate Headquarters?"

"Not yet." Gran smilingly shook her head.

"You have to work up to that part." Mum joked.

*****

Sixty minutes later, once the dishes had been washed and teeth had been cleaned; Mum and Gran instantaneously phased us to my 'training area'.

"Huh, this is it?" I looked about, feeling let down.

We were standing in one of the grassy glades inside of the Lokoti National Park. I mean, sure it was pretty...the grass was long and soft, we were surrounded by woods, which in turn were surrounded by mountain ranges. But seriously, this is it?

"Why are we training here?" I whined. "Why not at the futuristic Circulate HQ?"

"I trained here with your grandmother." Grandfather smilingly shrugged.

"I watched your mother train here with your grandmother." Dad winked at his wife.

"When did you train, Grandfather?" I looked on in disbelief. "You're a Werewolf, not a Circulator!"

"I taught Em self-defense and fencing." His wife informed.

"Grandfather knows how to fence?" I looked on my big, strong grandparent. "But he's a Werewolf, so why does he need to use a sword?"

"European Vampires fight with swords." She said simply.

"They do?" my eyes widened at her words. I guess Vampires would exist just like Werewolves exist, but it still felt strange to hear about them.

"European Vampires aren't as strong as Werewolves, so they fight with silver-coated swords." She advised. "They also fight each other with those swords. Vampires, like Werewolves and other Shape Shifters, are allergic to silver too."

"Really?" my eyes widened in surprise. Then it dawned on me, "so you want to train me with a silver sword, so I can fight European Vampires and European Werewolves, like the one who changed Declan?"

"Bingo." Mum smiled.

"Think of the Boy Scout motto B; always come prepared." Gran said humorously. "By the time your training with us is finished, you'll be able to fight in armed and unarmed combat in the speed of light. Plus, you'll be able to incorporate these fighting skills with your ability to phase."

"I liked it when Arabella taught me. I also liked it when she flipped me to the ground and landed on top." Grandfather laughed to the other men.

"I don't mind helping Jess out with her training now and then either." Dad snickered back.

"B, observe." Gran ordered.

I stood back carrying my sword sheathed, in a special holster on my back. Gran and Mum unsheathed their swords from the holsters on their backs as they began to circle each other. I watched them carefully, noting their foot work and their stances; one in an attack posture and the other poised in defense. I was looking forward to seeing this, since it didn't happen often that I got to watch them practice. I guess it was because they were always busy with other things; Gran with helping Aunt Susan and Mr. Lightfoot teach and Mum was always doing something else, like phasing to England or to Mars.

The two women circled each other carefully, not taking their eyes off their opponent. As I studied their movements, I saw that everything was deliberate as well as calculated. It was almost like watching dance partners, as they each adjusted their movements when they saw the other change. They watched the other warily for any sudden strikes.

Just then Mum swung the first blow which Gran easily parried and then the two women fought each other so fast, they both looked like two bright blurs!

"No way!" my eyes widened. I'm supposed to be able to do THIS one day?

The Circulators were fighting so fast, the sound of their swords clashing were constant and loud that I had to put my hands up over my ears!

Clang clang clang clang clang clang clang clang clang claaaaaaannnng!

They moved so fast that they seemed to instantly appear in their new positions and I couldn't keep track of their arm movements.

Suddenly Mum's sword went right through a bright and blurry Gran who went into phase! My hands flew up to my mouth in shock...! But just as suddenly, Gran now appeared behind Mum and she started to swing her sword when Mum spun around to block her!

"No way!" I watched the two women in wonder.

The two Circulators continued to fight like this for another thirty seconds. Since they were fighting in light speed, in those thirty seconds they probably made so many movements it would be the equivalent of two humans fighting over thirty minutes. It almost seemed like a stale-mate with neither Circulator able to get the upper-hand as their abilities matched the others. It was when abruptly Mum landed on her back on the cushioned, grassy ground, with Gran standing over her that the fight was over.

"No way...!" I stared at Gran, taken aback. She's pretty spry for an old guy! She doesn't just look like she's still in her twenties, but it was physically as well.

"How many times do I have to tell you Jess? Watch your footwork." She lightly scolded as she offered her hand. Mum was pulled to her feet before the two women looked over my way.

Subconsciously, I took a step backwards... "There's no way I can fight like that!"

"Not at first, no." Gran laughed at my apprehension. "Hence the lessons."

"C'mon B, don't be a chicken." Mum teased. "I learned how to fight when I was pregnant with you, so how hard can it be?"

"Bianca Elm, come on down!" Gran sung like I was a contestant on the 'Price Is Right'.

I took a deep breath as I unsheathed my sword which made the males take a couple of steps away and gingerly, I came forwards.

"First of all, let's look at your leg work." She started.

"And how to hold your sword in a defensive posture." Mum added.

I looked back at Grant, who was standing in between Dad and Grandfather and he gave an encouraging grin.

"If worse comes to worse, you have three Lokoti Werewolves here that can share their blood, or put your cuts inside their mouths to heal you." He joked.

Oh yeah that really made me feel better...NOT!   I looked helplessly from the Lokoti Werewolves in the shapes of my husband, father and my grandfather. You would think being around Werewolves, it was natural to be wary around such dangerous creatures. But when you saw your mother and grandmother as Circulators who were significantly weaker than they were, but were such masters of instruments of death? Now I didn't know what was scarier! I took a deep breath before I joined them. OK here I go...

Over the next sixty minutes, I was instructed to always mind my footwork and how to carry my sword. I felt like I was learning how to waltz with a dangerous dance partner. I learned how to circle and by holding my sword correctly, how to parry and to block.

The men ended up sitting in the grass and watching this way. I noted that although Grandfather and Dad could casually lean back on their hands in a relaxed manner, Grant could not. My husband sat forwards, watching us carefully. His protective instinct to guard his young bride was in full-force. His long, black hair blew playfully in the wind, but his face was a mask of concern as he never took his eyes off us, in particular me.

Within ninety minutes, I learned to fight Gran or Mum, as they took turns at coaching. When I fought Gran, Mum stood back and called out her advice on how to move or what to do. Then the same would happen when I fought Mum, with Gran issuing instructions.

After two hours, I fought my mother as my grandmother now stood quietly beside my grandfather, looking on. We circled the other, with our swords raised and our footwork planned.

"Be careful Jess." Dad frowned as his own overprotective nature kicked-in. "Do I need to remind you that B is our ONLY child?"

Mum ignored him before she made her strike, which I parried. Then she swung again and again, each time her sword clanged against mine.

"Good work B." Gran said encouragingly. "Just keep your tip up."

My mother tried to throw me off guard by suddenly ducking right and then swinging left, but again I was able to block. Then she sped up her attack, moving faster and faster...and somehow I could keep up. I could see that she was going faster, especially by how bright she turned. Yet I was able to block everything that she threw my way.

Clang clang clang clang clang clang clang clang clang clang claaaaanng!

I could hear the noise and hell, I could even hear the 'whir' in the air from how fast she swung her sword around! Yet I was able to block and parry, minding my foot work and also keeping my sword high and ready.

Suddenly she stopped and broke off her attack. When she stepped back and lowered her sword, her bright, blurry form returned to her solid shape. She beamed, looking proud as punch.

"Not bad for a beginner." She commended.

"Really?" I wanted to check.

"Hell yeah!" Mum laughed. "I don't know if you realize it B, but you just fought me in the speed of light."

"No way!" I looked over at our audience for clarification.

"Way." Dad smiled.

"You were faster than a speeding bullet." Gran giggled.

"You could give 'Road Runner' a run for his money." Grandfather chuckled as he put his arm about his mate's waist.

Lastly I looked on my husband, who seemed to be in shock for some reason. He was standing completely still, with a blank expression on his face.

"Grant?" I turned worried. "What is it? What's wrong?"

"Huh?" he snapped out of it. "Nothing's wrong, it's just that I never expected to find myself married to a 'Light Person'."

"Welcome to the club." Dad clapped him on the back.

Mum leaned in to say cheekily, "I'm sure if you put away your sword, your husband would give you a kiss."

"Oh!" I blushed at her words, "of course."

As soon as I sheathed my sword, Grant came forwards. He tenderly cupped my face to stare into my eyes before he said huskily; "I feel like I've won a prize in a competition I didn't even know I had entered."

In retrospect, it was may have sounded a little cheesy? But at the time it made my heart race and my body tremble. Then as his lips molded to mine, I felt a strange heat build up inside of my stomach and radiate outwards... Yep, I'm definitely starting to get used to this 'arranged marriage' kinda thing.

*****

The sun set and turned the light in our bedroom into a reddish-orange glow, which was observed by the newlyweds, from their bed.

We were lying naked in each other's arms, with the wife's cheek resting on top of her husband's chest. I was starting to get used to his body, as I enjoyed how constantly warm he felt. I also liked how his heart beat would fall into sync with mine.

I wondered if it was the same with Grant, was he still getting used to the feel of me too? He was always using his hands to stroke my skin as he looked on my form. Now was one of these moments as I smiled softly, enjoying the feel of hi's hands running over my shoulders and down my back.

"That was good." He commented.

"Mmm..." I smiled in agreement.

"It felt different today."

"It did?"

"It felt like somehow I helped you win the war and now we were fighting on the same side."

I looked long and hard into his eyes which held mine and this time I didn't look away. "You're right, you did help me win the war. You tended to me when I was sick. You healed the cut on my finger. You're continually showing me all of the benefits to being one of our kind, just as you showed me how wonderful you are as a husband."

"B." He placed his forefinger underneath my chin to ensure he held my gaze. "I meant what I said in the week leading up to our wedding. I'm looking forward to our future together. We have much to look forward to. The future holds so much promise for you both as a Light Person and a Lokoti Werewolf and I will always be by your side to greet it with you."

This made me falter, "but I'm not an angel, Grant."

"I know." He spoke plainly. "You have the light of a Circulator but you battle the darkness just like the rest of us. I think it would be harder to be your mate if you were the embodiment of perfection," then he kidded, "and it would definitely be more boring."

"Boring, huh?" I raised my eyebrows.

He roared with laughter as next I took several playful bites of his torso, before he could stand it no more which made him roll back on top.

"Careful B, teeth and nails are powerful aphrodisiacs to our kind." His dark brown eyes glinted their glowing silver supernatural colour.

"Oh really?" I began to chew on his neck.

I heard a deep growl build up inside of his chest and rumble up, through his sharpening teeth. He bent his head to tenderly bite my ear as I overheard him inhale my scent.

"Grrrr!" he growled louder, which sounded like frustration.

To my surprise, Grant gently pushed my head back as he raised himself up. Puzzled, I watched him climb out of bed as he proceeded to get dressed.

"Where are you going?" I asked, wondering if I had done something wrong?

"Downstairs to the kitchen, I'll make a sandwich before I go." He answered as he buttoned up his jeans.

"Go where?"

"I'm on patrol tonight."

"You are?"

"Yep." He answered before he turned and left our bedroom in just his jeans.

Oh, patrol... I had almost completely forgotten about it, let alone the dangerous world outside of our blissful one. Grant was going out tonight to risk his life for the safety of his home, family and tribe. Now I was his wife? I was part of the family he fought to keep safe.

A couple of minutes later I came down the stairs dressed, with my sword's sheath strapped to my back. I found him in the kitchen, making me a sandwich too. He placed cold slices of caribou meat on the bread with some mayonnaise, lettuce and tomato in a manner that said 'one for me and one for B'.

"What's the sword for?" He gave a peculiar look.

"I'm coming with you."

Suddenly the knife he was using to spread the mayonnaise was placed loudly on the plate. He stopped what he was doing so he could frown my way. "No."

"What do you mean, no?"

"It is the will of the pack as it is also the direct order of the First that you will not patrol." He said firmly.

"So you as the husband can fight, defending his home and land, but me as the wife, can't?" I asked unimpressed.

"Yes."

"I'm not letting you go out there alone -" I began.

"B!" he interrupted. "It may be the will of the First that you will not fight, but it is the wish of your husband that you obey."

"Then it's the wish of your wife," I crossed my arms to glare, "that you don't go out there alone."

"I won't be alone, two members of the pack patrol each night. Tonight I will be patrolling the borders with Ian."

I huffed as I momentarily looked away before I met his steely-gaze once more. "Grant, it's not fair that I just sit around looking pretty because I'm a female! Why should only the male Werewolves risk their lives? I'm faster than you so -"

"You may be faster but we're stronger." He interrupted. "You as a female will also one day, be with child. Also the world doesn't know that a female Lokoti Werewolf exists. All of these reasons have been taken into consideration by the pack when the First decided that you will never patrol."

I felt angry at his stubborn determination. "It's so sexist!"

"It is." He admitted. "But it also puts my fears at rest for your safety."

"So you can feel safe that I'm stuck at home, but I don't have that luxury about you?" I argued.

"Have you been shot before?" he suddenly asked.

"What?"

"Have you been shot before?"

"No of course not!"

"I have, six times since I started patrolling when I was 15 years old." He said unhappily. "As a male Lokoti Werewolf I'm stronger than you so I don't know how you would fare, if you were shot. But then what if you were shot in the abdomen when you were pregnant?"

This thought disturbed me so much that I turned away, when Grant caught my arm. He pulled me into his arms before cupping my face to make me look his way.

"I patrol for the safety of my mate, my family and my tribe. I patrol so my future children lives will not be in danger." He said in a low voice.

I didn't know what to say to that and I couldn't look into his eyes either. My head ducked so I could stare at the floor instead, when he gently rested my cheek against his chest so I could hear his strong heart beat.

"I'll come home to you, B." He promised.

"I bet Uncle Jack said the same thing to Aunt Meg the night that he was shot." I said sullenly.

"Jack was killed by two bullets removing half of his head and the other which blew a gaping hole through his chest where his heart used to be." He spoke candidly. "But it takes a lot to kill us B and right now I have a lot to live for. I'm looking forward to our future, remember?"

I sighed unhappily because I knew there was nothing I could say to change his mind. "It's still hypocritical since I'm one of the pack, aren't I?"

"You're a Light Person first, you're my wife second and you're a female Lokoti Werewolf third." Grant said strongly. "Three very good reasons why you will never patrol."

Eventually he released his hold to return to finishing up our dinner. I leaned on the fridge to watch him complete the sandwiches. I realized arguing about this would do me as much good as yelling at the sky for being blue.

"How about a glass of milk with our food?" Grant next gave a playful grin, which was his way of asking me to pour him one.

I set about pouring two glasses of milk as he carried our sandwiches over to the table. I asked as I joined him with the drinks, "what time will you be home?"

"Patrol usually goes until dawn."

He was right, I recalled growing up, I'd hear my father come home about the time my bedroom would lighten with a new day. Now I was in the same boat as my mother and my grandmother. We were forced to sit on our Circulator hands as our Lokoti Werewolf husbands fought outsiders without us.

"Just be careful Grant." I looked long and hard whilst I sat across at the table.

"Like I said B, I have a lot to live for." He reached out to put his hand over mine. "Don't worry, you'll be stuck with me for a few years yet."

When he released my hand to pick up his sandwich, he gave a cheeky grin.

*****

I tossed and turned in bed that night, as every little noise made my eyes snap open and my heart turned cold with dread.

Please don't let that be a distant gunshot! Please don't let him be harmed, fighting for me! Grant – Grant – Grant – please be safe!

Somehow or rather, I think out of exhaustion, sleep finally claimed my mind. I don't think I slept long, maybe just an hour or two? However the next time I awoke, the bedroom was a pale grey colour with the onset of dawn.

When my eyes swept over the quiet room, they fell upon my husband who had used his predatory skills to sneak up. He was kneeling by my side of the bed without making any noise. Grant smiled softly, as he gazed down.

"I'm home safe," he greeted, "just like I promised."

I flung my arms about his neck in pure relief!

He held me back just as tightly and as he did so, he murmured into my ear, "Happy Birthday."

Happy Birthday? Why would he wish me...oh, today must be the 10th October. My childlike habit of counting down the days until Birthdays, Christmases or Easters had ended when I started counting down with dread, the days in between full moons instead.

"I'm legal now." I joked which made him shake with laughter.

"My 17 year old wife turns 18...damn!" He pretended to sound disappointed. "I liked having the reputation of a cradle-robber."

Next, he pulled away slightly so he could hold out my present. It was wrapped in old newspaper thanks to rationing after the War, but I didn't care. I excitedly unwrapped my gift before I let out a happy giggle.

"A new MP3 player!"

"I noticed that yours looked scratched and the battery life wasn't very long." He observed. "With this model, it can last for up to 72 hours of continual playback before you have to charge it again."

"I love it!" I hugged him so suddenly our heads accidentally bumped, but he was quick to laugh it off.

Grant was sitting in only his jeans from patrolling in Werewolf form. He was perched on the side of the bed, holding me against his bare chest. Once I relinquished the hug, he remained close.

"There's already a couple of songs stored in its' memory." He implied my gift. "When you were doing the laundry, I used your laptop to transfer the music onto it. I noticed you had a lot of 'Iggy Pop' and other old bands on your hard-drive."

Oh oh...I tried not to tense up otherwise he would sense it. I tried not to panic over if he saw any of the diary entries, which were also stored on my computer.

"Um yeah." I carefully kept my voice neutral. "Those songs were given to me by Derik when he used to borrow Declan's CDs."

"Hmm," he frowned thoughtfully. "I have a couple of 'Greenday' and 'The Killers' songs on my iPod which I also converted to put onto your MP3 player. You should listen as I think you'll like them."

Although I only liked a couple of songs from the bands he mentioned, I managed out a smile, "OK."

Grant pulled off his jeans to climb into bed beside. Together we snuggled under the covers, with me ensconced in his strong arms. It wasn't just his strength or his generosity that I appreciated then, it was the fact that he had come home alive.

"Your family will be coming over around eleven to cook you up a birthday brunch." He informed. "So until then, I might catch up on some sleep."

"Sounds like a plan." I readily agreed as I settled into his embrace.

This surprised him which he turned this expression my way. "You didn't sleep while I was out on patrol?"

"Not much." I closed my eyes.

Lastly, I felt his lips place several appreciative kisses on my forehead whilst his hand rubbed my back. I think we even fell asleep at the same time. Just as our Lokoti Werewolf hearts would fall into sync, so did our consciousness.

But as much as I appreciated this closeness with my husband, I realized I would also have to be wary of it, especially with my secrets.

~~~~~~

13th October 2084

I sat at the dining table polishing my new silver-coated sword with jewelry cleaner and an old rag until it shone. I smiled to myself whilst admiring the craftsmanship...I liked the fact that I got another Circulator's sword. It made me feel more like a Circulator myself, by handling a weapon that was over a thousand years old from an era long since forgotten. It added a sense of continuity to all of this.

Grant came inside from the greenhouse when he stopped to look on. He smiled to himself to see my happiness with my new 'toy'. I held the sword up to slowly move it around to catch the reflection of the ceiling light.

"I think it's clean, B." He said in amusement before he walked over to the kitchen sink to wash the dirt off his hands.

"I like my sword." I joked. "I'm tempted to even name it."

"Mr. Pointy?" he joked back.

"Nah, I'd want to give it a female name." I disagreed. "It's an elegant sword as it's not big and bulky like the European swords."
~~~~~~

"I think this is love at first sight." He jested as he leant on the entryway of the kitchen. "Just please don't try to take the sword to bed with us."

I noticed he was standing a respectful distance from the silver-coated weapon.

"Oh, sorry." I returned the sword to its sheath.

"Thank you." He now came forwards once the danger had been removed. He rested his hand on my back, "I was about to run down to the store to pick up a few things if you wanna come?"

"What things?" I queried.

"Milk, bread, butter, toilet paper…just a few odds and ends to tie us over until the end of the week." He shrugged.

"OK." I stood up. "I'd like something sweet, like more biscuits or ice cream or maybe some chocolate. I get the munchies for something sugary after dinner."

"So I've noticed," he smirked, "you finished off Hannah's choc-chip cookies in three days."

"Hey, you helped!" I turned around to poke him.

Grant laughed as he pulled me close for a quick kiss before we prepared to leave.

*****

We walked hand-in-hand, up and down the small aisles of the general store. In his other hand, he held the carry-basket for us as he told me what to grab. When we walked past a couple of older women, I noticed their looks of approval by seeing us behave like we really were a married couple.

"Hi B and Grant." Old Mrs. Huntington smiled as we passed by, whilst she was shopping with her grown granddaughter.

"Hi Mrs. Huntington." My husband greeted the elderly woman. "How's your elbow treating you?"

"Good thanks, Grant." Old Mrs. Huntington answered before she smiled in my direction. "The cold compress your Grandpa gave me to use works like a treat."

"That's good." I said politely.

Mrs. Huntington just stood there, grinning at us then she looked down to obviously stare at our holding hands. It was almost like she was bestowing her approval, which made me uncomfortable.

"Well then, we'll be seeing you." He excused us.

Even if we weren't Werewolves with our sensitive hearing, we still would have heard old Mrs. Huntington say as she watched us walk away; "the Wisetail-Riverclaw girl and the Elm boy, now there's a good match! Three branches of the tribe's oldest families have come together to create one strong tree. They'll breed good stock."

My eyes widened as Grant tried not to snicker. He pulled me along to prevent me from turning around and staring back at the nosy old woman! I felt my cheeks burn as I tried to refocus on the task at hand, whilst he didn't seem offended at all.

"Come on B." He squeezed my hand. I gave him a funny look, which he caught so he spoke quietly, "when my family first announced our engagement, I got a lot of that. I had people stopping me on the street to offer their congratulations. They all told me how they thought we're the perfect match being two Lokoti Werewolves marrying another, let alone a Wisetail-Riverclaw and an Elm union."

I gulped as I quickly looked away and tried to look preoccupied at the bottles of sunflower or olive oil.

Not that there was any pressure or anything! Boy, if this is how the whole tribe feels about our nuptials, I wonder what would have happened if I had refused to go ahead with the wedding? Or if I had ended up with Declan instead...

Grant grabbed the bottle of the olive oil before he moved us along. I sensed that he wasn't bothered by any of this in the slightest. He may have been amused but I started to wonder if he saw our union as something else; fate perhaps?

"Yum!" I stopped in front of the different confectionary and I was relieved to change the subject. "Should we get choc-chip biscuits or just a bar of chocolate?"

"I think Hannah will be giving us some more biscuits soon, so we probably don't need any of the bought kind. How about a couple of bars of chocolate instead?" He shrugged.

"OK." I readily put two bars of chocolate inside the basket.

Just then we heard the rattle of the bell over the door, of somebody else coming into the general store. Before I turned my head to see who it was, I smelled his maple syrup scent.

I looked up sharply just as Declan stopped in his tracks when he saw me. I watched his eyes widen, before they narrowed into a look of pure resentment when he saw Grant standing beside. His human blue eyes even began to look a little green...

...when he quickly turned around again and walked back out. Oh, just like that he was gone. As I watched his abrupt departure, I noticed his huge muscles under the dirty white t-shirt looked tense. The poor guy, since he worked next door at the Garage, he probably came in to get a can of soda or something when we put him off.

My heart hurt but to hide this from my husband, I quickly busied myself by grabbing another two blocks of chocolate off the shelf before moving us on again. However what I really wanted to do was let go of Grant's hand and run after Declan, to comfort him.

I wished I could somehow ease his pain, because the pack and even the tribe thought that it was a much safer bet to pair me off to Grant Elm instead of

Declan Sabre. Just because he wasn't a Lokoti Werewolf and because his family wasn't as old in the tribe as the Elm family was...it did seem a bit unfair.

"I think that's it." Grant said cheerfully, acting oblivious to Declan's sudden appearance and disappearance. "Are you ready to go home?"

Quietly I nodded before I walked with him over to the counter for Mr. Barley to mark the things out in his book.

"And how would you like to make up for this trade today?" Mr. Barley asked congenially.

"Ian and I are currently working on some new pieces of furniture." He began.

"I've seen your work, it's good. I especially liked that dining table set you did for the Lightfoot's. I can give you two month's worth of groceries for a dining table set with a buffet unit." Mr. Barley bartered.

"Deal." He smiled on the arrangement and the two men shook on it.

Grant placed a happy kiss on my forehead, as I watched Mr. Barley write this down in his book underneath the items we were checking out. As I looked on the book which kept records of all the family accounts, I realized that this was a new section of the book that he had created for Grant and I. My name was no longer under the 'Hunter & Jessica Wisetail' account, but it was now under the 'Grant & Bianca Elm' account.

Frickin' hell! I really am a married woman and the tribe firmly saw me this way. I stared at my name scribbled next my husband's – Bianca Elm. We had our own family account as I was officially seen as Mrs. Bianca Elm.

No wonder Declan couldn't bear to be in the same room with my husband and I...because I was another man's territory.

~~~~~~
~~~~~~

~ 11 ~

16th October 2084

It was late in the afternoon and I was in the lounge room, organizing my books on the new set of shelves Grant had made, as my husband was sitting on the couch reading the old Stephen King novel 'Cujo'. We were both listening to a Cranberries album called 'No Need To Argue' which was playing softly in the background.

I was grouping together all of my old books on ancient history, with the new books I had recently purchased for my degree.

Five days ago, after Mum dropped off Vincent at the Hodge Endeavor Head Office in London; she instantaneously phased herself into my living area. Mum suddenly appeared in a bright flash of light, startling Grant and I as we were sitting at the table eating our dinner. She came to deliver two things, an acceptance letter from Cambridge University and a proud grin.

Both her and Gran were eager to assist in any way possible with my University education. So yesterday morning at 9 AM Alaskan time, they instantaneously phased the three of us to the Hodge Endeavor London Office at 9 AM London time. From there we caught the Underground to a large bookstore to buy the books on my reading list. They also purchased anything else they deemed useful for my course work. Gran bought me a personal organizer to keep track of my assignments as Mum bought a calendar to stick on my fridge.

I truly enjoyed our outing in London, as the city was one of the most organized places during the recovery after the War. England's police force has been reinstated rather than just relying on its over-worked military. London, just like Cambridge and the majority of the country, was no longer prey to looters. However as I walked down the busy streets with Mum and Gran, we still had to hold onto our handbags tightly especially after we witnessed a bag-snatching happen to the person walking in front.

As a special treat, Gran shouted Mum and I lunch at an outdoor café by the Thames. We ate our food whilst protectively nursing our handbags in our laps; as we enjoyed the scenery of Big Ben, Parliament House and other notable London landmarks.

"Thanks for today, Gran and Mum." I smiled appreciatively on the older women.

"You're most welcome, B." Gran replied warmly in her English accent.

Then we watched her pay the bill using her Hodge Endeavor credit card. Mum and I also had our own company credit cards, just as Vincent did. I think it was largely thanks to Hodge Endeavor's influence that Cambridge University accepted Derik's and my late applications although the semester had already started. Hodge Endeavor sponsored Cambridge University, Oxford University, London University and several other educational as well as health institutions during the financial crisis after the War. This made the UK Government particularly appreciative so they quickly waved through Derik's and my student visas. Speak of devil...

"How is Derik?" I queried, as it was my understanding that Gran had instantaneously phased him to Cambridge University, two weeks ago.

"He's settling in at Holy Spirit College." She nodded. "The Worthall's have already visited him to let him know he has 'family' in England. They said he's attending lectures and tutorials and making firm friendships."

This made me feel a little jealous, as I wished I could have been one of his friends who lived in student accommodation or went to one of the libraries to study with him. However just as I was inwardly sulking over these things, a delicious smell captured my attention.

I looked around whilst discreetly sniffing to track the scent which was so tempting, it made my stomach rumble even though I had just indulged in a two-course lunch. It was then that my eyes fell upon the couple who were sitting at the table next to us. A chilly breeze brushed past, which made the couple pull their coats about them tighter, but it didn't mask their delicious aroma...

"OK, time to go." Suddenly Mum stood up and Gran was quick to follow her. "C'mon B, let's get you back to tribal lands."

"Huh?" to my surprise I found myself yanked to my feet and hastily pulled away from the café.

"There's an alleyway over there, where we can instantaneously phase back and no-one will see." Gran led us across the street via a pedestrian crossing.

As soon as we were half way down the dirty alleyway and away from prying eyes, Gran instantaneously phased us back to Alaska. In a bright flash of light we disappeared from London to reappear in another bright flash of light in my living area, on tribal lands.

To my surprise, I found Ian was with Grant and the two men stood upon our arrival. That's strange, I thought they'd be at work in his large shed making furniture.

"What is it, Gran? What's the hurry? Is there something wrong?" I asked puzzled.

I watched the two women share their unhappy glances as they offloaded the cotton carry bags of books and stationery, onto my dining table. I even caught Grant and Ian exchange a wary look.

"Would somebody please tell me what's wrong?!" I demanded.

"Did you have a nice lunch, B?" Ian asked in a serious tone of voice.

"I ate grilled chicken, avocado and cheese on focaccia and then sticky-date pudding with caramel sauce and thickened cream for dessert." I announced as I placed my hands on my hips. "So what's the big deal?"

"B, you were sniffing the humans at the table next to us and your teeth began to look longer and sharper." Gran said unhappily.

"They did...?" I blanched.

"We sensed, as did your Dad, Grandfather and Grandpa that your bloodlust began to rise." Grant informed.

"But you did so well today." Mum tried to look on the bright side. "You were walking down crowded city streets all morning, before your bloodlust raised its ugly head."

"Oh yeah that's real reassuring, Jess." My brother-in-law rolled his eyes.

"Shut up Ian! When you first turned, you couldn't step foot off tribal lands for months until your bloodlust was under control!" She snapped back.

"Then maybe it should be the same with B until she can contain hers." Ian said gravely, turning away to give me a long, hard look.

The nice day I was having abruptly turned sour, as my mouth fell open aghast. Hastily I turned around and ran up the steps to my bedroom. The hot tears were already making my eyes sting when I fell face first onto the bed.

This was the reason why I can't go to University with Derik...because I'm a killer. My stomach gets turned on by the smell of non-Lokoti humans. How the hell could I live away from tribal lands with this?

"B?" Grant followed after and moved to sit on the bed beside.

"Please go away!" I bit out.

"B, come on." He said gently as he sat down. "Ian doesn't mean you have to turn into a prisoner, it's just that we have to be more careful."

"GO AWAY Grant!"

I felt the bed rise as he stood up and I heard him leave the room. I listened to my husband and his brother leave the house, probably to return to work but my mother and grandmother remained. The two women began to organize a couple of things downstairs as I could hear them talk softly whilst they worked.

"I don't care what these stupid male Werewolves say, my daughter is going to get an education damn it!" Mum said stubbornly.

"Jess, your father, husband and the other Lokoti Werewolves are doing the best they can in this difficult situation." Gran reasoned.

"Oh yeah?" She let out a bitter laugh. "Oh I know what we'll do with the tribe's first female Lokoti Werewolf; let's marry her off to another Lokoti Werewolf to supposedly lessen the infamous bloodlust! Oh gee, what a surprise it's not working."

"I like Grant." Gran declared. "I'm surprised you can't see it for yourself Jess that he's already developing feelings for B."

"Yes I know Grant is a nice guy, Mum." My mother said tiredly. "But have you ever wondered what the timeline would have been like if B married Derik instead?"

"B wouldn't have married Derik." She returned. "She doesn't love him like that."

Pause...before Mum said quieter still, "I know. Sometimes I wondered if there was somebody else as B could act pretty secretive."

I wished I didn't have the sensitive hearing of a Werewolf as their gossiping was something that I didn't want to hear right now. I rolled my tearful eyes, took a deep breath and then I moved to go back downstairs. Not surprisingly on my return, they instantly talked about something else.

"Look at this, B." Mum waved her arm towards the calendar she stuck to my fridge door. "Now when you go down to the kitchen to start your day, you can see what's ahead of you; 'Mesopotamia Paper Due', 'Dinner with Aunt Julienne', 'Ancient Egyptian Gods Paper Due', 'Baby-sit Phoenix & Phoebe', 'Dinner with Nana & Grandpa', 'Ancient Greek Marriages Paper Due' etc etc..."

"Oh." I managed out whilst wiping at my wet eyes once more. "That's a good idea."

I walked over to the calendar to check the oncoming social engagements and due dates of assignments she had put down were correct. Then Gran also put them down in my personal organizer she had bought. I really liked the personal organizer, it wasn't electronic but it had a pink leather covering with removable daily planner pages and a separate address book. It also had plenty of pockets to put in business cards.

Once the calendar and personal organizer were sorted, we then turned our attention to the many books we had bought according to my course's reading list.

Mum looked from the piles of books on the table, to my one and only bookshelf which already looked overcrowded; "me thinks it's time for more shelves."

"Me thinks you might be right." I smirked.

It took several minutes for the three of us to tote the books over to sit in two neat piles on the floor, next to the shelves. We put the largest books on the bottom with the smaller ones on the top. They looked relatively tidy, all things considered.

Around 4 PM, they went home and I walked into the kitchen to start preparing dinner. I was feeling especially hungry which I think was caused from the bloodlust, as the smell of those humans back in London still taunted my Werewolf senses. I tried to distract myself by cutting up some vegetables as well as some raw moose meat to cook up a casserole.

As I chopped, I overheard the sound of Grant's jeep which indicated his homecoming. However I also heard the sound of Ian's pick up truck follow him into the driveway. The next series of noises which arrived with them astonished me.

"Come on Grant! You're taking longer than an Alaskan winter!" Ian griped.

I heard the front door loudly open as it banged against the wall. The two men puffed and I heard something hit the doorframe. I walked out of the kitchen whilst wiping my hands on a tea towel to find the two Lokoti

Werewolves using their supernatural strength to carry in a massive set of wooden bookshelves!

"What's this?" my mouth fell open in shock.

"Your new bath tub, what do you think?" Ian growled out. "Do you mind moving those piles of books that are in the way of putting down your new shelves?!"

Quickly I darted forward and crudely shoved the piles aside which knocked the books all over the floor. Then they placed the larger bookshelves against the wall next to our smaller set. As soon as they did, Ian let out a loud sigh of relief as he pretended he had hurt his back.

"Yeah pull the other one, Ian." Grant snickered before he put his arm about my shoulders. "Well B, what do you think?"

"Er..." my mouth wavered as I didn't know what to say, "...thanks."

I was touched by his gesture. Grant saw his wife required more shelves so he brought her home just what she needed. It was almost as if he was trying to do a small part in helping with my University education, himself.

"New bookshelves for your new books which are for your new degree." Grant smiled then he preened, "my wife is going to have a Bachelor of Arts in three to five years."

"Great." Ian rubbed his lower back. "When you earn lots of money, you can pay for the medical bills to get my back reset."

"Nah, I'd rather just watch you live with the pain." I joked back.

"Yep, you're your mother's daughter alright." He grumbled as he turned to depart. "I'm going home to my wife who's a lot more sympathetic than yours, Grant."

"See you, Ian." My husband closed the front door behind, before he turned back my way. "I hope you like the shelves. They're constructed from pine but I stained it a mahogany colour to give them an antiquated appearance."

I walked up to wrap my arms about his waist, "I love the shelves, Grant Elm."

"That's good Bianca Elm." He smiled in relief as he held me closer. "Mmm, something smells good."

"I just started making 'Burgundy Beef Casserole' but with moose meat instead of beef." I announced.

"I wasn't talking about the smell coming from the kitchen." He grinned mischievously, before his mouth smothered mine...

...

...now it was the day after and I was putting all of my history books new and old, onto the new set of shelves my husband had made.

As the 'Cranberries' played softly as mood music, Grant occasionally looked over his book to watch me work. He quietly observed me separate all of my books on history and mythology from my novels and shelve them in alphabetical and categorical order. I was so fastidious, it took me most of the afternoon. I was almost done when we were interrupted by unexpected guests.

Knock, knock, knock!

"Come in!" He called out immediately, as if he were expecting the intrusion.

I watched my front door open with the entry of Ian, Dad, Grandfather and even Grandpa walking into my living room.

"Oh." I stood up worriedly from the floor. "What's wrong?"

"Why do you think something is wrong?" Grandpa smiled in amusement.

"Then what's with the mini reunion?" I pondered.

"We're declaring class is now in session." Dad announced.

"Class, what class?" I looked his way in befuddlement.

"Tonight, tomorrow night and for the next couple of nights, you'll be training with Lokoti Werewolves." Grandfather grinned. "Your mother and grandmother as the Circulators within the family are your 'lecturers' in time manipulation. Now you have us as your tutors for your Werewolf abilities."

"I do?" my eyes widened, before they narrowed when they turned towards Grant who came over. "You knew about this?"

"Of course." He shrugged. "The pack have been talking about this for the last couple of days. When you fall into sync with us, you'll hear as well as feel the pack consensus too."

My heart skipped a beat as I felt dwarfed by being the only female amongst all of the males in the room.

"Where's Mum and Gran?" I took a step backwards. "Are they coming too?"

"Your grandmother and mother can advise you on Circulator matters, but they can't train your bloodlust as a Werewolf, B." Dad said gravely.

"But I don't want to wolf-out and go all yucky!" I took another step backwards with apprehension. "It hurts being a Werewolf and I always get into trouble for it!"

"If you start your training as soon as possible, you can be taught to control the bloodlust, B." Grandpa said patiently. "The longer we leave it, the harder it will be."

"It's not a full moon so I don't want to change!" I objected. "I don't want this! I don't want to be like you!"

"B..." Grant looked pained, "...it will be alright, I promise."

"Yeah but when I turn into you, I get locked up as my clothes tear and I feel the worse pain imaginable!" I objected.

"Then we'd better get you trained as soon as possible, so you don't feel the agonizing stomach cramps anymore." Ian said calmly.

Suddenly in a bright flash of light, Mum and Gran instantaneously phased into my living area, to the surprise of the male Lokoti Werewolves.

"Arabella?" Grandfather looked on his mate.

"Jess?" Dad had to blink at Mum's abrupt appearance.

"Hi Hunter." She smirked. "We just came to drop something off for B."

"For me?" I wondered out loud. "Like what?"

Gran walked forwards holding a small pile of neatly folded up clothes in her hands. As she came forwards, she unfolded the garments and soon we were looking on several elasticized black tops and bottoms of what looked to be like gym clothes.

"You need elasticized clothing which won't tear when you change." She announced. "Here's a couple of pairs of work-out clothes you can wear which will handle your increased muscle bulk."

I looked on the two other females in the room which coupled with their consideration; it was like they were the light in all of this darkness. I walked up not just to accept my gift, but I pulled both older women into my stronger arms in a grateful hug.

"Thank you!" I uttered out in a tight voice. "Thank you so much!"

"They're just clothes, B." Mum laughed at reaction, but Gran understood.

"Of course we'd be here for the first female Lokoti Werewolf who's still our beloved B." She rubbed my back in a soothing manner. "Now how about you go upstairs and change?"

"You mean you'll be coming too?" I asked hopeful.

"Er, perhaps not." She tried not to laugh.

"We'll stay here though." Mum promised. "Go off and do your 'Werewolf bonding' or whatever the males have planned? And when you come home all hunted out, we will be waiting for you."

"Really?" I held onto their hands.

"Truly." Gran verified. "Now off you go and change."

I gave a nod before I headed upstairs for my bedroom. However on my way up I overheard with my sensitive ears;

"Thanks Arabella and Jess." Grant acknowledged.

"It looks like B just needed the feminine touch being the only female Werewolf in a pack of males." Grandfather said humorously.

"Be gentle with her, Em." His wife said in concern. "She's scared because she still doesn't understand everything's that happening to her."

"We know, Arabella." Dad said seriously. "We feel her fear being one of the pack just as we feel it when our mates are cold or scared."

Then I didn't hear anything else when I closed the bedroom door to change into my unusual kind of 'hunting clothes'.

*****

Soon I was standing barefoot on the dirt driveway in my elasticized gym clothes. Grant stood barefoot beside me, as did Dad, Grandpa, Grandfather and Ian. The male Lokoti Werewolves were also topless for their oncoming change.

I watched Grant change first, as his upper body expanded with his increased muscle bulk and the nails on his hands and feet turned strong and claw-like. His dark brown eyes turned glowing silver as his elongated, sharper teeth jutted from his mouth.

Next, I watched Dad change, as did Ian, Grandfather and Grandpa. Dad's eyes glowed red, Grandpa's orange, Ian's turned pink and Grandfather's eyes glowed a bright blue. All of their glowing eyes turned my way, as they waited for my transformation.

Grant emitted a soft growl of encouragement as if he empathically sensed my heart pound with anxiety. I allowed my heart to beat faster, as I felt the elasticized gym clothes feel tighter because my upper body bulked up with Werewolf muscle. I looked down at the nails on my hands and feet and watched them turn hard and long. I felt my teeth poke out of my lips, which tingled at their sharpness. I assumed my eyes glowed turquoise as the poor light of the oncoming night suddenly seemed so much brighter and clearer.

I stood as the first female Lokoti Werewolf amongst the male Werewolves...

"Tonight we hunt grizzly!" Grandfather rumbled out in his deep, growly Werewolf voice.

Then abruptly he took off into the surrounding woods! Hot on his 'tail' ran Grandpa and then Dad, with Ian right behind his best friend.

"Come!" Grant barked in his thunderous voice before he too leapt into the tree line.

I took a deep breath as I watched the males disappear in supernatural speed, before I leapt after them. As the four ran down the forest-encrusted hill, I realized they were running in some kind of formation with Grandfather out in front with Dad and Ian flanking him. Grant was running behind with Grandpa when I caught up. I wonder if everyone was deliberately letting Grandfather go first because he was Second in the pack? Uncle Harry who was First, if he was here he'd probably be running out in front.

I thought this was a little stupid, especially how I was faster and I easily surpassed them. I ran out in front, but I was careful not to lose them since they were supposed to be leading the way on this 'hunt'. I sensed when they were about to swerve left so I would swerve at the same time, whilst retaining my position in the lead.

SLOW DOWN B – Grandfather thought my way – *THE GRIZZLY WE'RE TRACKING CAN SMELL YOUR APPROACH*

It can? Whoops! I immediately slowed down to allow the males to catch up, as we ran into a small clearing in the woods on the south east side of tribal lands. I found myself slowing to a stop when they did and just as I was about to ask why? I saw the reason...

A huge, adult, female grizzly who was scratching up a tree to reach inside the trunk for something, turned upon our arrival. She faced us off, roaring in anger! She even tried to declare her dominance by doing a short charge towards us.

Two months ago if I was still human and I happened to come across a grizzly in the wild? I would have turned and run away screaming to be rescued. But now I felt my heart pound with anticipation instead of fear, as my Werewolf muscles turned tense and ready for combat.

The female grizzly did another short charge towards us whilst roaring louder. I flexed my claws as I bared my sharp teeth, just waiting for her to come closer. I was barely aware of Grant, Ian, Dad, Grandpa and Grandfather dropping back to allow me to have this fight.

My opponent saw I stood my ground which made her rise to my challenge. She stood upright on her hind legs to attempt to intimidate me with her greater size but I growled back to show her she couldn't frighten me. It was then that she took the first swing which I easily ducked with my faster reflexes.

Grant watched our fight warily as his overprotective instincts for his mate made him stand ready to come to my aid, but I didn't need it. I was loving every minute of this! It reminded me of the childhood chastisement, "don't play with your food," because it was exactly what I was doing.

The grizzly swung at me with her claws or tried to bite me with her strong jaws but I ducked and swerved so fast, I looked like a bright blur. When the bear had to pull back to swing again, I delivered my own blows. My claws coupled with my supernatural strength staggered her.

I realized I wasn't just using my Werewolf strength, but I was also using my speed as a Circulator. It was like I was seeing the bear's attack in slow motion and the creature just couldn't keep up. I saw her brown fur turn red as my claws shredded her!

Before I knew it, the female grizzly collapsed to the ground too injured to fight any further. I stood tall as the victor whilst looking down on what was about to turn into my meal. My mouth watered from the smell of her injuries, as her bleeding flesh also made my stomach rumble.

FEAST! FEED! RED MEAT! FRESH MEAT! FEAST ON YOUR VICTIM'S FLESH!

Huh, what was that?

FEAST ON FRESH KILL!

Oh no...not that horrible, cold, cruel voice again!

FEED ON FRESH KILL! MAKE YOUR HUNGER GO AWAY! DELIGHT IN THE FEAST!

My eyes widened in fear at what I had done as I looked down on the poor animal which was groaning in agony. Then I looked up at the tree she had been clawing when I saw some kind of insect hive inside of the broken trunk. The female grizzly had been happily minding her own business, trying to feed herself when I stumbled along and massacred her!

"Do it, B." Grant growled out softly in his deep, rumbling Werewolf voice.   He walked up to stand beside, as did Ian, Dad, Grandpa and Grandfather. "Kill her and put her out of her misery."

"Then we will feast on her flesh." Ian eagerly licked his lips as his glowing pink eyes stared hungrily on our prey.

"Make the kill, B." Grandfather ordered.

No, no, no! I don't want to! I shook my head as I stepped back from the scene of my crime. I'm disgusting! I shouldn't feed on her as I don't deserve it!

Dad's glowing red eyes narrowed in what I thought was disappointment as he watched me back away. He must feel so let down that he didn't have a son to turn instead. He must think I'm a disappointment to the entire pack...

Ian saw that I wasn't going to do it, so he dropped down to his knees and took hold of the grizzly's huge head in his supernaturally strong arms.

SNAP!

The grizzly's head dropped to the ground lifeless, with her eyes staring blankly as her blood continued to ooze out of her many cuts and scratches.

Dad lowered to the ground beside his best friend, as both Grandpa and Grandfather followed. My mouth fell open in a mixture of horror and yet hunger, as I watched the male Lokoti Werewolves begin to feed. They used their claws and teeth to pull away her fur to reach the warm, succulent flesh underneath.

"B?" Grant held out his clawed hand to me.

"NO!" I roared before I turned around and took off out of there!

I ran in a direction I know not... The trees flew at me so thick and fast, I felt the odd scratch of a low branch or a bush that grazed as I concentrated on missing the tree trunks. I ran faster, slipping from Lokoti Werewolf speed to Circulator light speed. My skin turned bright as all of me and not just my eyes glowed. I tried to run faster than I had ever run before, even faster than light speed!

Something odd happened as I no longer felt my bare feet touching the cold, hard earth anymore. I was running so fast, I felt all light and tingly like I could have been floating. When I looked down at my bright body, I saw straight through myself! Oh my god I look like a ghost! Then that means I'm in phase! I looked just like Gran and Mum did when they went into phase being Circulators.

Just then I looked up when I saw I was about to hit a huge tree...! Frickin' hell, this is gonna hurt! I 'closed' my eyes as best as I could, being all bright and see-through as I tried to prepare for the impact...but it never came.

I stopped, or I think I stopped. My body of bright light reformed back into it's solid, Werewolf shape and I could feel my feet touching the ground again. When I looked around, there was no sign of the tree I was supposed to hit. Hang on, where am I?

Feeling completely lost, I looked around the surrounding wilderness which I had never seen before. I was in some kind of huge, grassy plain which stretched for a couple of square kilometers. But I knew I was still in the vast Lokoti National Park by recognizing the distant trees as well as the familiar backdrop of mountains in the Alaska Range.

The real question though, was how the hell did I get here? Oh my god, I think I must have instantaneously phased! It would make sense, I was running so fast I went into phase. When I thought I was about to hit the tree and I closed my eyes, somehow I instantaneously phased myself out of danger to another part of the National Park. Only how do I get back? I'm lost! I don't know my way home from here.

My muscles turned to jelly because my body was depleted of energy and I slipped to the cold, grassy ground. I tried to remain in my Werewolf body for the supernatural body heat as I was wary of the icy cold air. Next, I tried to calm my racing heart by admiring the view of the snow-capped mountains which looked a haunting white under the starry sky.

Just then I heard a noise and my head snapped around to track it. My nose caught wind of a familiar scent...maple syrup? Off in the distance I spotted Declan in European Werewolf form. He stepped out of a section of wood carrying some kind of large, dead animal in his strong canine jaws.

On all fours, he trotted over to where I was sitting in the grassy plain. His glowing green eyes stood out in the night, with his jaws dripping with blood from his hapless victim. The closer he came, the sight of his huge, hulking, hairless supernatural body made him a sight for sore eyes!

"How did you find me?" I wondered.

I WASN'T LOOKING FOR YOU – he telepathically replied – *I WAS HUNTING WHEN I CAUGHT YOUR SCENT.*

"Oh." I said flatly, looking on his prey.

Declan ceremoniously dumped the carcass he had been carrying in his mouth, which I saw was a male Elk? Then he sat down on his hind legs to look down on me as the weaker Werewolf.

"Elk?" I queried in my deep, rumbling voice. "How the hell are you hunting Elk? They're not native to Alaska."

SOMETIMES THEY STUMBLE INTO OUR TERRITORY, ESPECIALLY TO MIGRATE AWAY FROM THE RADIATION – Declan shrugged with his bulky shoulders – *SO WHERE IS GRANT AND THE OTHER LOKOTI WEREWOLVES?*

"I don't know." I answered.

AREN'T THEY SUPPOSED TO BE TEACHING YOU TO HUNT OR SOMETHING? – he gave a funny look with his monstrous face– *IT'S WHAT THE PACK HAD BEEN PLANNING*

"They did take me hunting." I said dismally. "I'm a failure."

IS THAT WHY YOU'RE SITTING HERE SULKING? – he chuckled which came out as an odd kind of panting noise.

"They took me hunting and I hurt a bear." I said guiltily. "I think I disappointed Dad when I couldn't finish the kill so Ian did it. Just as Grant tried to get me to eat with them, I chickened out and ran away."

STOP BEING SUCH A PRINCESS BY WASTING GOOD FOOD – he rolled his glowing green eyes – *GRIZZLY IS RARELY HUNTED AS THEIR NUMBERS ARE FEW SO YOU JUST TURNED DOWN A DELICACY.*

"Thanks for the sympathy!" I looked away in annoyance. However when I heard some kind of strange, wet, crunching noise? I turned my head back around to find Declan eating his prey. "You're eating that now?"

WHEN THE MEAT TURNS COLD AND IT STARTS TO DECOMPOSE IT'S NO GOOD – he thought with his mouthful – *NEED I REMIND YOU THAT WEREWOLVES FEAST ON FRESH KILL?*

I paused for a moment as I watched his huge, strong, canine jaws chomp through both bone and muscle. "What does Elk taste like?"

GO KILL YOUR OWN FOOD! – Declan moved his meal away.

"Why are you out hunting Elk anyways?" I snapped back. "It's not a full moon and I thought the only Werewolves out hunting tonight were me and my small group of teachers."

I HAVE TO HUNT IN BETWEEN FULL MOON CYCLES TO PLACATE MY EUROPEAN WEREWOLF BLOODLUST – he thought unhappily.

"Really?" this took me by surprise. "How often do you hunt?"

AROUND ONCE A WEEK – he answered as he crunched on some bone.

"Do you mind?" I queried and when he stopped eating to give a peculiar look I continued, "I mean, do you hate the bloodlust for driving you to hunt once a week? In winter it must get annoying."

THE COLD DOESN'T BOTHER ME – he shrugged with his huge, muscle-bulked shoulders once more.

"But do you hate the bloodlust for making you hunt once a week?" I pressed.

B, I'M A EUROPEAN WEREWOLF AND HAVE BEEN SINCE I WAS THREE. WHY BOTHER KICK UP A FUSS AND HOWL AT THE MOON IN SELF PITY? – he looked me in the eyes with his narrow slits for pupils – *BESIDES I ENJOY HUNTING AND MORE SO THE DELIGHT OF EATING WHAT I DESTROY.*

"Charming." I said unhappily as I looked away.

GO HOME TO YOUR HUSBAND AND LET ME EAT IN PEACE – he thought grouchily.

"I'd love to but I don't know where home is." I admitted. "I accidentally instantaneously phased here when I was running away."

YOU MUST BE THE MOST PATHETIC WEREWOLF IN THE WORLD – he chuckled again with more weird growling – *EVER THOUGHT OF USING YOUR SENSE OF SMELL AND TRACKING YOUR WAY HOME?*

"Shut up!" I barked out. "Man it's a good thing I didn't marry you, as you're the most inconsiderate male around! A gentleman would escort a lost lady home."

This made him pause in his eating and he looked sharply my way.

LOOK AT ME B – Declan thought grimly – *I'M A FRICKIN' EUROPEAN WEREWOLF AND TRUST ME, WE AIN'T GENTLEMEN!*

"So I've noticed." I shivered whilst not looking his way.

YOU SHOULDN'T BE SHIVERING IN YOUR WEREWOLF FORM – he noticed what I was doing. Then he leaned in to sniff me – *YOU SMELL WEAK*

"I think it's from going into phase." My sharp teeth chattered from the cold. "I used up a lot of energy by turning into light."

To my surprise, Declan moved up against me to share his body heat. His muscle bulk coupled with his hardened hide almost felt like I sitting up against a rock, but a hot rock nonetheless. He felt so warm! I almost threw my arms about him to indulge in his excessive heat.

LET ME AT LEAST EAT HALF OF THIS AND THEN I'LL TAKE YOU HOME – he let out a sigh of resignation which sounded like a long pant.

I turned quiet to allow him to eat his prey in peace, whilst I tried to ignore my rumbling stomach from the smell of fresh kill.

*****

Declan reluctantly stood up from his half-eaten meal and then he waited for me to stand. I had to lean on him whilst I pulled myself to my feet, as my legs wobbled horribly. I feel so weak and hungry!

FRICKIN' HELL, YOU LOOK USELESS – he telepathically taunted – *HERE'S A TIP B, MALE WEREWOLVES ARE ATTRACTED TO STRONG WOMEN.*

"Man am I relieved that I'm not married to you!" I grumbled.

CLIMB UP AND I'LL CARRY YOU HOME TO YOUR HUSBAND – he thought bitterly.

He was so big in his European Werewolf body that even standing on all fours, he was almost the height of a horse. He was too high to climb in my weakened state! When I pointed this out, he growled unhappily and lowered himself to the ground. As soon as I'd clambered up, I wrapped my legs about his wide, muscled waist. I leaned over to hold onto his bulky shoulders which also enabled me to bask in his excessive body heat.

The monster raised himself once more to his four clawed feet, but he stood still for a minute or two as I sensed he appreciated our contact. Then after turning his beastly head to make sure I was holding on tightly, he took off out of the grassy plain! Declan bounded along on all fours at typical European Werewolf speed which was something like 300 km/h which was 100 km's faster than what Lokoti Werewolves run.

We ran through the forest, with Declan expertly dodging the trees in our path as he simultaneously leapt over log, rock or bush. I must admit, I was enjoying the ride...! I felt as warm as toast thanks to his greater body heat and I also enjoyed the feel of his huge muscles ripple. However it took him twenty minutes running in supernatural speed, for him to reach the hill that my house sat on. I didn't know I had gone so far...

WHEREABOUTS WERE WE? – I wondered when he slowed to a jog.

YOU MEAN IN THE NATIONAL PARK? ALL THE WAY ON THE NORTH SIDE OF THE BORDER – he answered.

NO WONDER I HAD NEVER SEEN THAT PART OF OUR LANDS BEFORE – I marveled.

It was here that the ride ended when he leapt out of the tree line of the woods and landed on my dirt driveway. There we found Grant, Ian, Dad, Grandpa and Grandfather standing by the veranda steps talking to Mum and Gran. Everyone looked relieved to see me, but puzzled by the method of my arrival.

"B?" Mum came forwards, as did Dad and Grant.

"Hallo." I growled out in my Werewolf voice as I gave a little wave with my claw-like hand.

Declan lowered himself to the ground once more, to enable me to climb off. When I did so, my legs gave away but Grant was quick to catch me. The European Werewolf looked on my husband jealously, before he abruptly turned and leapt back into the woods! Mum and Gran looked surprised by his sudden appearance and then disappearance, but I sensed he did it to stop himself from mauling the man who had become his rival.

"B, what's wrong with you?" Mum cried out concerned as I had trouble standing on my own two feet.

"I instantaneously phased tonight." I managed out, looking on their astonished faces. "I ran so fast in light speed that I accidentally turned myself into light. I looked bright and see through as I was running and when I nearly ran into a tree? Suddenly I found myself on the north side of the border, having instantaneously phased there without realizing it."

"Hunter!" She whacked her husband on the arm. "You take our little girl out on a hunting trip as a Werewolf and she circulates for her first time without us!"

"You're weak and tired at the moment, which happens to a Circulator who circulates for their first time." Gran frowned. "Let's get you inside and warmed up."

"Actually," I looked on in a pleading manner. "I'm really, really hungry...could I please have some bacon and eggs?"

"Of course you can!" She quickly agreed. "I was famished after the first time I circulated."

Grant was about to scoop me up into his arms to carry his weakened wife inside, when I stopped him. I looked apologetically into his concerned eyes, before I next looked to Ian, Grandpa, Grandfather and then lastly, Dad.

"I'm sorry I disappointed you tonight and I'm not a very good Werewolf. I know if you had a son instead of a daughter he'd probably make a much better Lokoti Werewolf -"

"You think I'm disappointed in you?" He interrupted in an incredulous voice, before he crossed over to stand closely. "B I'm damn proud of you! I'm proud that you're my daughter just as I'm proud of the fact that you're the first female Lokoti Werewolf."

"But," I said in confusion, "when I couldn't kill the bear you seemed angry or something."

"Tonight I saw a new Lokoti Werewolf not let the bloodlust get the better of her. If that bear had been human, you managed to run away from the temptation of the kill and the human would have lived." He said strongly.

"The human would have lived?" I asked amazed. "The human really would have lived because I ran away?"

"As long as Ian doesn't snap its neck, sure." Grandpa joked, making the men chuckle.

"Hey, how often do we get to eat grizzly?" Ian tried to justify himself. "The bear was just lying there like that..."

"I really can't take you anywhere." Grant mockingly shook his head at his older brother.

Just then Gran shuddered from the cold as Mum rubbed her arms in agreement.

"Er guys? Can we have this heartfelt moment inside where it's heated?" My mother complained.

"Bacon and eggs do sound good right about now." Grandfather smiled on Gran, before he escorted her up the veranda steps and into the house.

"But I thought you guys fed on grizzly tonight?" I looked at Grant.

"Never underestimate a Werewolf's appetite, B." Mum rolled her eyes. "They're ALWAYS hungry."

"Yeah well, it's not just for food." Dad laughingly pulled her close, before they followed her parents inside.

"C'mon then, let's get some 'human' food inside of you." Ian joked. He stepped back as he watched Grant pick me up to gallantly carry me over the threshold. As he trailed in after, he mused, "but what about Declan though, I've never seen him give anybody a ride on his back before."

"With his European Werewolf temper, he would soon as maul whoever would even suggest such a thing." Dad agreed.

Grant sat me down in a chair at the dining table before taking the seat next to mine, as Gran and Grandfather helped themselves to cooking in my kitchen for one and all. Mum even went in to help, as Dad set the table.

"Declan's always been protective over B." Mum mused, overhearing their conversation. "I remember how he used to pick her up and carry her everywhere when she was little."

"He did?" I looked up, taken aback. "I must have been really little then, because I don't remember it."

"I remember." Gran smiled softly. "You, Derik and Declan all used to be quite close until you and Derik hit seven years old."

"That's when the fighting began." Mum chimed in. "Suddenly you and Declan went from best friends to worst enemies, almost overnight."

Just then Grant frowned as he leaned in and sniffed me, "his scent on you is strong."

"Oh, I had to hold onto him tightly so not to fall off." I tried to say casually.

"Anyways that's enough about Declan." Dad said narkily.

"Agreed." Ian declared. "Mmm that bacon smells good, Em and Arabella."

All of our heads turned at the delicious smell of bacon frying and the creamy, cheesy scrambled eggs being cooked to perfection. As Gran and Grandfather were concentrating on these, Mum made the toast as Dad put out the butter, salt and pepper.

I was relieved when the conversation was changed and as soon as we were all sitting at the table eating; I was able to shrink back into my human body. My prior thoughts of Declan slipped away just as my Werewolf muscle bulk did.

~~~~~~

30th October 2084

"Are you ready?" Grant's glowing silver eyes felt like they burned into my soul.

"Yes." I gulped.

"I feel that you're ready tonight B." He rumbled out in his thunderous voice. I looked at him expectantly when he said simply, "come."

Then in his Werewolf form, Grant leapt from our front veranda, clear over the driveway and he disappeared into the woods in a single bound. In one leap, in my Werewolf form I joined him. He ran out in front as I ran right behind, so close I was almost treading on his heels.

We ran through the darkened woods so fast that the colours seemed to stream into each other like army camouflage of green, grey and black.

My husband streaked along, running up to 200 km/h as I deliberately hung back, not engaging my faster speed thanks to my ability as a Circulator. Although Grant's supernatural strength was more than my match; my
~~~~~~

Circulator speed was greater than his. My instincts slowed me from overtaking him as I played out the role he were First and I were Second of our personalized pack.

Grant ducked left and instantly I ducked left. He ducked right and automatically so did I. I mirrored his movements and together we bolted through the woods as he was Yin to my Yang. I smelled his scent as clear as day as I felt his heart beat and I felt his hunger... Tonight I hunted as a Lokoti Werewolf with my mate.

TONIGHT WE HUNT ANIMAL AND NOT HUMAN – Grant willed to his Werewolf wife.

TONIGHT WE FEAST ON ANIMAL FLESH – I willed back to my husband.

My body copied exactly what my mate's did. I ran at his pace and I panted when he panted. Hell, even my heart would beat to the same rhythm as his.

Then I sensed what he sensed, as I smelled what he smelled. I picked up that we were closing in on the pack, as they chased down a small group of moose. I smelled the scent of our prey which made my stomach rumble.

The thirteen other members of the pack all closed in on the four moose who were running for their lives. I felt exhilaration with my predator instinct delighting in their fear. I could almost taste the fresh kill!

However as my mouth watered, another instinct knew that this wasn't the National Park's only moose. I sensed that I wasn't hunting a species to the point of extinction. If this had been the case, then our instincts would have steered us towards other prey.

As my mate and I left the tree coverage, we spotted the Lokoti Werewolves running up a mountain ridge behind our targets. Out in front of the pack, ran Declan in his European Werewolf form as our honorary member.

My heart skipped a beat, as it picked up in speed from seeing Declan's large supernatural form running on all-fours. Like this, he chased down the Alpha male moose. Don't ask me how and don't ask me why, but although this was my first hunt with the pack; I sensed that the pack allowed him to take down fighting, the largest and the strongest. If it were moose than Declan would challenge and take down the alpha male or if it were caribou it would be the same. The pack would chase other quarry to let him combat alone. I sensed that his European Werewolf bloodlust demanded that he didn't share his prey.

My greater speed as a Circulator engaged, thanks to the rush of exhilaration I experienced from seeing him out in hunt. I streaked past Grant as I spotted the fastest female moose. As Declan challenged the strongest male to combat, I wanted no I needed, to chase down the fastest. My bloodlust wanted to feel the satisfaction of being not only stronger but faster than my meal.

As the female moose ran out in front, I streaked past the entire pack to chase her down. The female tried to shake me as she ducked left so I did too. The female next ducked right and so did I. Next, she bolted towards more trees to try to hide but before she reached the tree line I leapt upon her.

My bloodlust boiled as my heart was pounding and all I could smell let alone breathe was the scent of my kill. I smelled her fear, her racing heart and her adrenaline rush as she tried to escape from death - from me.

I leapt into the air and landed upon her outstretched, engaging my supernatural strength to dig my claws into her tough hide. The female moose made a last-ditch attempt to bolt with all of her might...but by instinct, I knew exactly where her jugular was in her larger neck and I brought my dangerous jaws down. I felt her mangy fur against my tongue, as my elongated teeth drove through her tough pelt. I tingled all over as soon when I felt her warm blood gush into my ready mouth.

With her jugular pierced she immediately came crashing into the ground with me right on top of her. Then as her legs flailed uselessly in the air, I kept my jaws over her crucial artery which both expedited her death and made it as painless as possible.

In the corner of my eye, I caught Grant also pounce on her fallen form, indicating that he had run right behind. Then so did Grandpa, Dad and Ian and share my kill they did. Grant's elongated teeth dove into the artery in her chest, right next to her heart. Dad also bit into another major artery. Ian and Grandpa bit into the moose's upper legs which were still trying to kick us off. As soon as I saw my kin do this, the sooner I felt the female moose's heart stop as she no longer inhaled air...she was dead.

The female moose who was my first kill on my first full moon hunt with the pack, was extinguished. As if guided by my predator instincts, my elongated teeth now began to pull away her pelt to reach the warm, soft flesh underneath.

This even tasted better than my Great Grandma's roast dinners with her famous gravy! This was more fulfilling than I could have ever dreamed possible! The taste was both sweet and yet savoury, with the fresh kill both placating my hunger and my thirst. My heart raced as I felt giddy over the exquisite delight!

Frickin' hell, this both excited as well as satisfied me in a way that I have never experienced before. This was more than pleasure, this was more than delight, this WAS fulfillment. For a brief couple of moments as my bloodlust was purged; I felt more than satisfaction but I felt almost euphoric as I addressed my yearnings.

As I feasted, I caught Grant's silver eyes watching as he hungrily ate. Then I felt something else...I felt a rush of pleasure and appreciation in my Lokoti Werewolf husband that he got to share this with his wife. I sensed the relief that he felt for being able to share the hunt and the kill with not only another Lokoti Werewolf, but it was with his mate.

My glowing turquoise eyes met his glowing silver ones. Grant growled satisfactorily as he ripped open the chest cavity with his clawed hands. I couldn't see Dad's or Grandpa's bloodied faces, as they were eating their way through the moose's abdomen. Ian tore off a leg to eat, like it could have been a giant chicken drumstick instead.

The males feasting encouraged my own as we didn't have to worry about table manners. I didn't care about being 'lady like' as I was permitted to gorge on fresh kill. My dangerous mouth became covered in blood, just as Grant's, Ian's, Dad's and Grandpa's did.

I am Lokoti Werewolf who is mated to another Lokoti Werewolf. I AM the fifteenth member of the pack and for a coherent moment all of the basic principles of life and my existence made perfect sense. I AM a predator, just as I AM a killer. I need to hunt when the full moon piqued not only our bloodlust but our lunatic tendencies.

Luna which means the moon...lunatic which means made crazy by the moon...the light of the full moon which stirred my bloodlust and I must hunt and I must kill and I must feed. That was all there was to it, so why fight it when I could hunt with my kin; animal instead of human?

The circle of life and death; the universe expands, the universe contracts and the cycle of existence continues to renew itself. My Lokoti Werewolf instincts were part of this; able to hunt a species where numbers were not endangered so it harmonized with nature.

As I contemplated all of this, my life started to make sense because I now made sense. I am the first female Lokoti Werewolf and I am the last Circulator. I am the beginning and I am the end but I am not alone. I had my Mum, Gran and Vincent, as members of the Circulate; I had Grant and the rest of the pack to guide me as one of Earth's dangerous predators. But in a small way I also had Declan...

He was the male whom my secret desires lay with; he was the male who secretly desired me; Declan who as another breed of Werewolf, could never completely be one of us, just as I would always be different as the first female of the pack. Declan, who after combating the strongest male moose, he ate his kill alone. The rest of the pack numbered four to six Lokoti Werewolves per prey. As the Lokoti Werewolves could hunt in a pack, his European Werewolf bloodlust demanded that he ate his conquered alone.

Declan raised himself from his already-eaten meal, thanks to his greater appetite. I felt his burning gaze as the green-eyed monster looked my way. I overheard the satisfied growl he emitted, seeing me covered in blood as I sensed inside of him a different kind of hunger build...

Just then he caught sight in the corner of his glowing green eyes, another male moose come into the clearing. It looked enraged at my feasting on one of its females. The male moose made a charge towards me, but Declan swatted the animal with his strong, sharp claw when it charged past the tree that he was standing behind.

His second kill went crashing bleeding profusely, into the ground. As Declan's large canine head and ever-hungry jaws lowered to eat his second meal, he never looked away from my direction.

~~~~~~
~~~~~~

~ **12** ~

20th August 2085

I felt hot…I felt extremely hot…I felt so hot, that the heat made me light headed and therefore I felt dizzy.

I was standing in a strange place with red rocks and soil, with only small patches of green that surrounded a small, bluish-green river in a deep gorge. I vaguely recognized this place, but I couldn't place where. It did seem familiar somehow however I knew I wasn't in Alaska.

Navigating my way between the large, red boulders towards the water, I desperately needed to feel the coolness of the breeze coming off the surface. Growing up in Alaska, I wasn't used to this heat and I didn't like it. I preferred the cool air and the musky scent of pine trees.

I arrived at the water's edge and just as I was about to kneel down and splash some of the coolness onto my face? I became aware that I wasn't alone. I turned my head to see Great Grandma sitting casually on a big boulder, swinging her legs and she looked different, somehow she looked younger.

"Hi B." She smiled.

"Hey Great Grandma, how are you?" I asked brightly. I felt relieved to see a familiar sight in this strange place.

"Warm," she answered, "it's warm here."

That was my Great Grandma, never a complaint but her observations were always full of truth.

"Yeah." I agreed. "So um, where are we exactly?"

"Australia."

"Australia?" I echoed in surprise.

"We're in the Northern Territory to be exact, near Katherine."

"Oh." I thought on her words. "So er, what are we doing here?"

"I'm not here."

"You're not?"

"No."

"Then where are you?"

"I'm just visiting."

"OK." I pondered on her words. "Um, Great Grandma?"

"Yes?"

"Is this a vision?"

"Do you mean are you seeing prophetically in your dreams while you are sleeping in Alaska?"

"Yeah."

"Yes, then this is a vision." She smirked.

"Oh." I looked about, wondering why the hell I would be having a vision about this place?

"It's very dry, isn't it?" I commented.

"That's because it's Dry Season." She said simply.

"Oh." I shrugged. "That would make sense."

"B?" she looked my way.

"Yeah?"

"I came to tell you something before I go away."

"OK." I waited.

"You're here for several reasons." She advised. "You're here to remember your past whilst you learn something about your future."

"My past?" I looked about the strange gorge, wondering what this had to do with the price of fish?

"You're Lokoti, but you're also English, just as you're also Australian. Lokoti blood flows inside you, just as Elisha's blood does. Elisha is Australian and and she married an Englishman. They're apart of you as everything is part of something. We are all connected."

"We are?" I listened with interest.

"Your cousin Vincent who is called the Last Calculator, is English and he came from Elisha. You are the Last Circulator and you are living in Alaska with the Lokoti and you too come from Elisha."

"Oh yeah." I saw her point.

Great Grandma looked around, "her present day relatives live not far away, near the border of Western Australia."

"OK." I nodded as I started to see her general direction in all of this.

"B?"

"Yeah?"

"This country..." She gazed about the hot rocks with the sparse greenery poking through, "...is your body."

"It is?" I looked at the surroundings in surprise.

"It's full of history just as it's timeless." Great Grandma spoke with reverence. "Look at the trees and the bushes, springing up between the rocks. They have to live in harsh conditions, as they have to deal with floods when the river rises, as they have to deal with six months a year when it doesn't rain. Although there is some kind of life here, a different kind of life... some people might say that it's barren."

"Oh." That hit me like a slap in the face! "Barren?"

"You aren't meant to produce new life, B." Great Grandma looked on in sadness.

"I'm not?"

"You are the Last Circulator, which means you are the last on the line. The buck stops with you."

"Why?"

"Because no other Circulators were meant to be born after 1985." She sighed.

"So can't I reproduce without reproducing more Circulators?"

"Apparently not."

I turned away as my heart ached and my stomach wrung itself out. "Is it why I've been married to Grant for the past eleven months and I haven't fallen pregnant?" I whispered.

"Yes."

My eyes stung with tears over her words and they also reacted to the dryness.

"But – but - but I'm Lokoti Werewolf and we're supposed to be fertile!"

"Just as you are the first female Lokoti Werewolf, you are also the Last Circulator. You are the beginning and the end. I'm sorry B, but you are not meant to breed." Grandma said.

"But – but – but why?!" I turned on her. "Why Great Grandma? Why?"

"It's not meant to be." She looked downcast.

Great Grandma tossed a pebble into the bluish-green water of the river. Then something fierce looking, with sharp teeth and scales swam up to the water's surface! It's pointed reptilian nose pocked out of the water before it ducked back into the murky depths. Although my teeth could turn just as sharp, it still gave me a fright!

"What was that?" I frightenedly took a step back.

"It was a fresh water crocodile. Don't worry B, they don't eat humans. It's the salt water crocodiles you have to watch out for." She warned. "But they're here as a reminder that life can be cruel."

Then she stood up from where she had been sitting to turn around to walk up, out of the gorge.

"Where are you going?" I followed her, as I didn't want to be left alone in this place.

"I have to go now B, but I just wanted to say good bye first." She stopped to give a sad smile.

"Go, Great Grandma? Go where?" I complained.

"You can't come with me B, not yet anyway. Your Great Grandfather is waiting for me and he's going to take me to the place of our ancestors. I'm going to the Holy Hunting Grounds." She said happily.

"You are?" I asked sadly. "Please don't go yet, Great Grandma...!"

"I'm sorry B, but as they say, 'it's been fun while it's lasted'. Say goodbye to your Grandfather for me. Tell him his father and I will always be watching over him, even when he leaves with your Gran."

"When Grandfather leaves with Gran? What do you mean?"

"To go and exist as soul mates in the space time continuum." She said simply, walking onwards. "When he goes to be with your Gran in the space time continuum as her mate for all time, we will see him then."

I watched her steadily climb up the steep pathway out of the gorge, towards the bright sunlight which was streaming over the cliff tops. The light was so glaring, it was as if you were blinded by a setting sun. I vaguely made out Great Grandma's shape walk towards another shape, waiting for her up the top of the gorge. The shape of a man took hold of Great Grandma's hand and together they disappeared over the blinding white edge...and then I woke up.

Blinking repeatedly, my eyes had to readjust to the blackness of my bedroom, as it was the middle of the night in Alaska. It was as if I really had been blinded by a sunset and it even took me a couple of minutes to get my bearings. After a little while, I was comforted by the physical sensation of my husband's warm arm about my waist and I started to feel grounded again.

Was that really a vision of things to come? I'm barren...Great Grandma told me that I couldn't have children. All because I was the last of the Circulators and that was it, the buck stops with me. I remembered the fresh water crocodile swimming along the surface of the water with its' sharp teeth, to show the cruelty of life. As much as my head was spinning if I really was experiencing heat stroke from the hot surroundings in my dream? My gut instinct told me that what I had 'seen', truly had been a vision of the future.

I turned my head to look on Grant slumbering away. My heart hurt even more as I looked on his peaceful expression. I was so scared of disappointing him if it were true and I had to know for sure.

Carefully, I lifted up his arm to slide out of bed. Then quiet as a mouse, I put on some clothes, before I tip-toed out of the bedroom. He was still sleeping soundly when I instantaneously phased in a bright flash of light to Circulate Headquarters.

*****

It was just as late at Circulate HQ on Mars 250,000 years in the past as it had been when I left Alaska in 2085 AD. I marched up to Vincent's Personnel Quarters and never-minding they were dark, probably because he was asleep? I hit the 'doorbell'.

"Bianca Elm, requesting entry." The electronic female voice of the computer announced.

My foot tapped impatiently on the floor as I waited. Eventually through his frosted-over glass door, I made out that a light came on. I had to wait a full minute until his door slid opened. An unimpressed Calculator stood in a pair of navy coloured, silk boxer shorts.

"B, it's nearly 2 AM and you're a time traveler. You couldn't have phased here at 8 AM in the morning?" He glared.

"Good morning." I said curtly. "I woke up in the middle of the night in Alaska so I thought I would extend the same courtesy."

"You're a bloody Werewolf! You're supposed to be a creature of the night! I am NOT!" He snapped back.

"Yeah and you're my frickin' Calculator so start Calculating! This is a medical emergency!" I barked in his face. "Now put some clothes on and I'll meet you in the Medical Lab."

"The Medical Lab? Why the Medical Lab? B…?"

However as he spoke, I had already spun on my heel and was marching off down the corridor.

*****

As I walked down the dimly lit, futuristic corridors with the computer interfaces along the walls; the Circulate Mainframe which was a 'smart computer' was considerate enough to engage full-lighting to the HQ. Its motion sensors detected my presence which in turn not only activated the lighting, it took the computers out of 'sleep mode' to full operational status.

By the time I walked through the automatic sliding doors of the Medical Lab, the technology which awaited was beeping expectantly.

I helped myself to sitting up on the main examination bench that was directly underneath the huge medical scanner and diagnostics system above. It was the bench that patients – when there were patients – were treated by both a doctor and the computer. Operations used to be performed here, as this Medical Lab was fully equipped to handle any emergency. These days, it primarily functioned just as a diagnostics device as Vincent used it to run check-ups on the Circulators in his care.

Within five minutes Vincent too, entered the lab. His sleepy eyes widened when he noticed where I was sitting. He grumbled as he walked over to the main controls to engage the machine.

"Are you going to tell me what I'm looking for?" He asked sarcastically. "Or is it a surprise?"

"I want to know if I'm barren." I said coolly.

"Huh?" that gave him pause. "Barren? Why on earth would you think that?"

"Precisely, why on 'earth' would I?" I quipped, before I lay down.

"I see." Vincent's voice softened. I heard the hum of the machine start up as the scanning commenced. He spoke from behind the controls as he oversaw the procedure, "you had a vision, I take it?"

"Yes." I tried to keep my voice calm. "But all things considered..."

"Yes?" he waited for me to continue.

"I've been married for eleven months to a Lokoti Werewolf and I'm a Lokoti Werewolf. It's kind of weird that I'm not pregnant yet." I said uncomfortably.

"Not really." He spoke in a conversational way. "There are dozens of reasons why, such as it may not have been the right time in your cycle?"

"We have sex pretty much every day." I stated.

"Oh." I caught the surprise in his voice. "Well er, I guess that blows that reason out of the water. Look, I'll concentrate my scans over that particular region of your body. But B, even when I run my yearly check-ups on you, your mother and your grandmother? If you had ovarian cancer or any other medical problems with your reproductive organs; the scans are so thorough with this futuristic technology, I would have picked up something."

"You didn't pick up the changes to my body before I turned into a Werewolf." I rolled my eyes.

"To be fair, that wasn't mine OR the system's fault! You can blame your deceptive Lokoti gene pool for that matter. After my investigation when you first turned, did you know what I found out?"

"No, what did you find?" I asked obligatory.

"That the Lokoti Werewolf DNA is in EVERY member of the Lokoti Tribe! Although it's usually the males that are activated, the females are still carriers! I guess it's so they can pass on the genes to their male progeny, but still. After reviewing your past medical history, I saw that you too always had the genes. When Jack died, you were activated instead of a male member of the tribe."

"If the females are meant to be carriers so they can have sons who can turn into Werewolves, then how come I'm not having babies to pass this on to?" I asked in a small voice.

Pause...Vincent's frown faded as he looked on this supposedly powerful patient lying on the examination bench, who appeared scared.

"I don't know B, but I'll find out." He promised. "If there's something medically wrong with you? I'll find it."

*****

Two hours passed as my Calculator ran every test he could think of. He did close-up scans of every part of my reproductive organs. I had to lie on my back, lie on my side and even lie on my stomach. Sometimes I had to lie so still that if I moved, he would lose his patience when he had to run the scans again. He even took a blood sample, to get a reading of my hormone levels in my bloodstream.

In the end, I was still sitting up on the bench when Vincent carried over my results on a PDA. He wheeled over a stool to sit on, before he faced me. I almost wished he didn't, as I didn't like the expression he wore. He looked well and truly baffled...which as a Calculator and his ability to supposedly calculate for every contingency? This was what you DIDN'T want to see.

"Alright." He sighed tiredly. "Um, I don't know what to tell you because according to the computer? There's nothing wrong with you."

"Vincent!" I cried out frightenedly. "You're supposed to be my Calculator! You're supposed to 'see' what's wrong with me!"

"I wish people would stop saying that!" He rolled his eyes. "Do you know how NOT funny that and the 'what are the winning lottery numbers' barbs are?"

"Would you please stop whinging and just frickin' diagnose me!" I felt like hitting him over the head!

"Fine!" He flared. "You don't have Ovulation Disorder, as you ovulate each month like clock work and your eggs are biologically sound. You don't have Tubal Disease. You don't have Endometriosis. From the scans I took of your womb, there is no scarring or tears, indicating that you have never had a miscarriage. Even the high levels of hormones in your bloodstream confirm that you're ready to go!"

"Then if I'm ready to go, how come I'm not going anywhere?!" I whined.

"I don't know." He rubbed his face. "From the left over sperm samples I found inside your womb which I assume come from your husband..." he said snidely, "...indicate that there's nothing medically wrong with him either."

"Vincent!" I squealed embarrassed and this time I did hit him, but on the arm.

"Oow!" He dropped the PDA from the force of the blow. He threw me an annoyed look when he had to pick it up. "B, as a Werewolf you're stronger than me so would you mind refraining from beating up weaker individuals?"

I was about to really let him have it, when I stopped myself. Vincent was just the messenger so I shouldn't shoot him for it. Instead I drooped forward as I buried my face in my hands.

"Look," he sighed as he watched my reaction, "there are things we can try, such as certain medical procedures. We can try IVF, there's also ICSI, Blastocyst Culture and Assisted Hatching. I can put you on drugs that can increase the amount of eggs that are produced by your ovaries -"

But I interrupted, "did you say you scanned Grant's sperm that's still inside my womb?"

"Er, yes...?"

"And there's nothing wrong with it?"

"That's right."

"Then what are they doing in there, lounging around the pool and drinking cocktails? Why aren't they mingling with my eggs?"

This gave him pause, as I watched his eyes widen as he caught on to my line of thinking.

"Lie down again and I'll have another look." He quickly stood up to walk over to the scanner's controls. Next he asked; "when did your last period finish?"

"Um maybe ten days ago?" I tried to remember as I lay back down on the examination bench.

"Then you're almost midway through your cycle, in the stage that's supposed to be the most fertile." Vincent thought out loud. "Now lie as still as you can as these are very delicate scans that I'll be taking whilst I try to have a close look as possible."

I ended up lying there for nearly thirty minutes, barely breathing as I didn't want to screw up the tests. I lay tense, nearly jiggling my foot but I stopped myself in time. I was silently hoping that this was all just inside of my mind and not in another part of my body.

*****

Half an hour later, I was standing beside my Calculator looking on the large diagnostics screen on the wall which showed the results. We were looking on something which completely baffled us, my Calculator especially.

"Well, I'll give the Lokoti Werewolves this; it's not just their muscles that's strong it's also their reproductive systems. I've never seen such active sperm in my life!" He declared.

When I gave him a funny look, I saw his face was earnest even if he sounded sarcastic.

"Why, what's the big deal?" I pondered.

Vincent turned to give me an incredulous look, "B you're joking, right?"

"No...?"

"Look!" He raised his voice, before he caught himself and he spoke in a calmer manner, "er, B? When a man reproduces with the woman, it's usually one sperm that penetrates the egg as most of them die. But if you look at this?" He tapped on a control to make the close-up even closer. "There are TWENTY sperm all trying to penetrate the egg. They're stubborn little buggers too, as they don't give in easily."

"Yeah, but see? Why aren't they getting in? If the sperm is supernaturally strong, how come they can't crack the egg? How come I'm not getting pregnant?" I asked concerned.

Vincent frowned as he hit the control again to make the egg appear even larger on the screen. "I don't know, B. From where I'm standing, it appears to be a normal, healthy, functioning egg. There are no cellular defects, but I see what you mean. It appears that the sperm and the egg are coming into contact with each other however for some reason, conception isn't occurring."

"Then can you please find out why?" I asked in annoyance.

Vincent gave a long look, "if I do, you do know what has to be done, don't you?"

"What?"

"I have to take the egg as well as the sperm out of you to run further tests."

My eyes widened as my mouth fell open in dismay... I watched Vincent turn to walk a little way away to pick up something that was folded up on a shelf. He walked back over with it as he held it out. I looked from it back to him, as he tried to wear a professional expression.

"I need you to put this on for the procedure." He spoke crisply. "You can go over there, behind that screen to change."

After a long moment, my hands took hold of what he was offering. It immediately fell open in my clumsy grip, to reveal a papery hospital smock that left little to the imagination. I looked horrified at my Calculator who was like a male member of my family.

"Can't we just...um, can't we just 'beam' it out of me?" I asked with a red face.

"This isn't 'Star Trek', B. We may have the Gate that can transport a Circulator's light waves to different locations on earth, but we can't turn the matter into light and then transport it, that's your job. Unless your Circulator training is going so well that you can do this? It's still the human way unfortunately." He said perfunctory.

"Then I'll go to a doctor in my time frame -" I began.

"Sure you can!" He laughed bitterly. "If you can find any fertility specialists left that aren't reassigned to treating radiation sickness instead; in hospitals that are not only understaffed but have had most of their medical equipment and supplies stolen from the looting."

"Then I'll go to a hospital that's in a different time frame." I thought up.

"You may want to aim for one in the 24th Century or later, as removing eggs let alone sperm from a womb is a delicate procedure. You'll certainly need futuristic technology to take these out without damaging or destroying them." Vincent pointed out.

Frickin' hell, this was getting so complicated! I was about to call the whole thing off but then I couldn't face going home to Grant and telling him that I couldn't have his child because I didn't find out all the answers. What if something could be done? What if I had to do this, to find a treatment?

In frustration I growled under my breath as I stomped off behind the screen with the useless smock.

*****

Another hour later, I paced around and around the examination bench, fully clothed again. Vincent was sitting at a specialized computer, with the samples he took. He was deep in thought which left me with just myself for company.

With a pink face, I enquired; "so if you're a doctor and you know how to do all of this; why aren't you working in a hospital somewhere?"

"I was a third year medical student when the War started twenty-three years ago." My deceptively youthful Calculator answered. "I was drafted from medical school and an Army Medic uniform was slapped on me. Simultaneously as they were issuing me with a First Aid Kit, they were pushing me out onto the battle field. While I served King and Country in the Middle East, a missile landed on my parent's house back in London. I couldn't save my parents just as I couldn't save the soldiers being used for canon fodder."

His harsh words stopped my pacing as I looked back in surprise. His back was still turned, as he was running his tests. I looked him over speculatively, as he still looked like he was in his twenties even though he was actually in his forties. Calculators aged slower than humans, but they couldn't manipulate their ages like Circulators could.

I came to lean beside him on the bench he was working at, "so you became disillusioned at the prospect of becoming a doctor?"

"Not at all, I became disillusioned with the humans in my time period. After the War, I followed my visions from war-torn London to the looted countryside of England as I searched for the castle in my dreams. By finding Blythe Castle, the Worthall family became my saviors. Then meeting your mother, a Circulator and finding out I was a Calculator? It gave me a renewed sense of purpose. I was quite happy to continue my medical studies here at Circulate HQ, training on a 25th Century computer. You may not believe it, but the Circulate Mainframe is a good companion. She answers politely every time that I ask her a question and she always has an explanation." Vincent looked up to smile.

"You visit the Worthall family at Blythe Castle often enough, but you hardly ever visit us in Alaska. Why?" I queried.

"I have my reasons." He answered elusively as he looked back down.

"Mum says it's because you don't like Werewolves." I accused.

"True." He shrugged as he didn't look up. "I'm not a fan Werewolves."

"But the Lokoti Werewolves DON'T eat people! They're upstanding members of the tribe, just as they're loving husbands and fathers. They only fight to protect their land and loved ones." I tried to point out.

"B," he stopped working to look directly into my eyes, "do you know how your husband or your father or even your grandfather, 'protect' their loved ones?"

"Yeah, they patrol." I shrugged.

"And do you know what happens while they patrol?"

"Yeah, they turn away outsiders and strangers."

"And do you know how they turn away these people?"

"Um..." I tried to think, "...I guess they ask first. But when the strangers turn violent, I guess they have to as well."

Vincent's eyes narrowed, "the next time your husband comes home from his 'patrol', ask him how many people he has killed."

"But they don't eat people! It's against the rules! It's tribal law that we don't eat humans!" I cried out in alarm.

"I never said anything about eating people, B. I know the Lokoti Werewolves don't eat people, as they're worried it would trigger their bloodlust into permanently hunting human. But you didn't see what they were like when they fought off the five hundred invaders before you were born. I still monitor them today and I've seen what their claws let alone their teeth can do to human flesh."

"But they fight to defend their territory!" I disagreed. "They only attack in defense, not offense! You don't see them picking a fight, do you?"

"You asked me why I don't like Werewolves and I'm telling you. They're sexist, archaic, primitive beasts who dominate anyone unfortunate enough to fall under their 'care'. Being Circulators, your mother and your grandmother could live in any time frame of their choosing! They don't have to live in your era, during the violent recovery after World War Three. They could be sunning themselves on a tropical beach, in a peaceful era! But instead they're chained to a kitchen sink in Alaska as their Werewolf husbands get to indulge their bloodlust in the so-called 'protection' of land and family." Vincent ranted.

I crossed my arms as I looked away angrily, "then I guess you must think I'm a primitive beast too?"

"B..." he sighed, "...you are a Circulator first and a Werewolf second. What makes me angry about your situation is that instead of scientifically exploring how a female Werewolf was created, what did the male Werewolves do? They bloody well married you off as a child bride! As you are a Circulator, you're not tied down to one piece of geography as the male Werewolves claim they are. You would have the inbuilt urge let alone the ability to travel through time. With your Werewolf strength combined with your Circulator speed, I think the male Werewolves were afraid of you. So what did they do with a powerful female in their midst? They tie a leash around your neck in the form of marriage to another Werewolf!"

I huffed as I looked away, feeling deeply insulted. My 'primitive' Lokoti Werewolf instincts strongly objected to hear my mate talked about as such, let alone my father or my grandfather. In my eyes, I saw that they were doing the best they could in a difficult situation. In Vincent's eyes, he saw them making a bad situation worse.

"Look, we're both tired." He sighed as he rubbed his eyes. "I think I have the results you were looking for. I'll give them to you so you can go home to your precious Werewolves."

He hit a command into the computer, so the picture would be displayed on the larger diagnostics screen on the wall again. However when I looked at it, I just saw the same picture as before. I saw my egg with several different sperm trying to break into it.

"What am I supposed to be looking for?" I pondered.

"Let me show you." He hit another control. Somehow this changed the colours of the screen, so now my egg looked red and the sperm looked blue.

"Why did you do that?" I wondered out loud. "What are the different colours supposed to mean?"

"Do you know anything about astronomy, like Red Shift or Blue Shift, which shows if light from a star or a galaxy is moving either towards or away from us?" He asked.

"Kinda..." I frowned, confused, "doesn't Red Shift show that our universe is currently still expanding?"

"Correct." He answered. "It can also go into time differentials, as some Astronomers believe they can date the universe by Red Shift. I'm using the same principle here with Grant's sperm and your egg."

"You're what?" I looked on blankly.

"Look at the time differential for your egg and the time differential for Grant's sperm." He nodded towards the screen. "Has your grandmother or your mother ever told you about your differences as a Circulator to the rest of the human race?"

"Er yeah, I can turn myself into light and phase through time and space and other people can't?" I gave my glib reply.

Vincent ignored my sarcasm as he continued, "a Circulator's difference to the human race is not a biological one. If a 21st Century doctor examined you, he wouldn't be able to tell you had the ability to phase. Your abilities stem from the electrical impulses in your brain which controls your higher bio-electromagnetic field. Biologically speaking, you are supposed to be 100% human. But B, by looking at the time differential inside your womb? This is the first time I have ever seen a Circulator differ from a human biologically."

"What do you mean?" I asked worriedly. "Am I going to be found out by humans who will want to experiment on me?"

"Not at all, unless they find out you're also a Werewolf." He smirked. "As you know being a Circulator, your bio-electromagnetic field not only registers much higher than a human's, but it's also in temporal flux. Now, using this principle, let's look at your egg again. By outward appearances, it looks like a healthy human egg. So why isn't your husband's sperm able to penetrate it? Blue Shift is light coming towards us and Red Shift is light moving away from us and it's something very similar occurring with your reproductive organs. Your reproductive systems are operating in another time differential. Your husband's sperm is operating in the space time he's physically occupying but your egg isn't. Your egg, your womb, your ovaries, your very body is existing in another time. You have a separate temporal signature than your husband, it's almost like your very cells are in temporal flux, just like your bio-electromagnetic field is."

I stared disheartened at my red egg and my husband's blue sperm.

"Is there a way that I can change my time differential to match Grant's, to make my egg blue as well?" I gulped.

Vincent sighed sadly, "I'm afraid not, as not even 25th Century technology can change temporal signatures. It's scientifically impossible with the laws of physics, let alone in our known universe."

"Funny, that's what some people say about time travel." I said ruefully.

"Not true, as light is known to travel through time. You travel through time by turning yourself into light. This along with your bio-electromagnetic field operating in temporal flux, you could outlast the known universe." He gave a small smile.

"Well isn't that an irony?" My hot tears trickled down my cheeks. "Humans try to make themselves everlasting by procreation as I on the other hand am everlasting but I can't procreate."

*****

I reappeared inside my bedroom distraught. It was now day time and the bed was made, showing Grant was up. I was crying so hard, that my breathing caught in my throat as if I had the hiccups... and then I did start to hiccup!

I had to tell him, I had to confess as I had to give him the option to leave me for another woman who was fertile. I left the bedroom and started down the steps to find Grant serving tea to Mum, Dad and Ian.

"Here she is." He smiled at my reappearance, before his face fell when he saw the state I was in. "Oh, I think she already knows."

Mum, Dad and Ian looked up and I noticed that Mum's eyes as well as her nose were red because she was crying.

"B...?" Dad stood up whilst resting a supportive hand on his mate's shoulder.

No-one looked happy and I suppose that could have been my fault. Not only was I letting down my husband, but I was letting down the family as well. I was probably letting the pack down too!   Hell, with my role as the defective first female Lokoti Werewolf, my being barren was probably disappointing the whole tribe! I stood halfway up the staircase as I looked down to make my confession.

"I'm sorry! It's all my fault, I know." I wrung my hands.

"Your fault?" Dad gave a funny look.

"I'm letting Grant down and I'm letting the pack down. I'm letting the Tribal Elders down because they married us. I'm probably letting the whole tribe down too!"

"B?" Ian gave a peculiar look.

"It's not Grant's fault, but it's my fault and mine alone. As Great Grandma said, the buck stops with me!" I blubbered, as my eyes released an onslaught of tears.

"B...?" My mate took a step towards me, but I held up my hand to stop him.

"No Grant, I can take the blame. I'll take full responsibility of this, I promise. It won't reflect badly on you in anyway."

He turned to throw my father and his brother a look of befuddlement, but all they could do was shrug back.

"I'll make the announcement." I said but then I hiccupped! "I'll tell everyone..." I hiccupped again, "...and I'll make sure everyone knows it's my fault." Then I hiccupped a third time.

"B, I think you'd better come down to sit at the table." My father said gravely.

"No Dad." I stood my ground. "You taught me to always tell the truth and I respect your teachings... (hiccup!) ...it didn't work when I tried to lie when I snuck out of the house the night of the full moon when I was thirteen to watch that horror movie with Derik, Rachel and Mandy... (hiccup!)...You sprung me climbing back through my bedroom window when you came back from the hunt... (hiccup!) ...and I can't lie now." Then I hiccupped again for good measure.

"B, your Great Grandma passed away last night!" Mum exclaimed.

Pause...oh so that's why they were all looking like somebody had just died? But in my emotional state, I blundered onwards.

"I know!" I cried out. "She told me I was barren on her way to the Holy Hunting Grounds!"

Silence...everybody's eyes widened as they looked on in shock.

"This makes it that much worse!" I collapsed to sit on the step to cry. "Great Grandma said I can't produce new life on her way to the after life!"

Nobody said anything, as Dad and Ian exchanged awkward glances, before they looked at Grant.

"So after Great Grandma's funeral I'll start the divorce proceedings. Since I'm the first female Werewolf and now I'm the first woman who's barren after the coupling with a Werewolf? I'm sure it won't look surprising if we're the first to get divorced as well!" I stood up in defiance.

"B...?" He looked on with a hurt expression.

"I'm a dud! I'm worthless! I'm not even a real woman! You've been sold a lemon, Grant! But I'll make sure that you get your money back, I promise!" I bit out, before I raced back up the stairs and into our bedroom.

I slammed the bedroom shut before I fell face first onto the bed. Oh Great Grandma, why? Why couldn't you have left me with a happy ending? Why does it have to be me who is the disappointment in her family? Why can't I be like my mother and my grandmother and fall pregnant to a Lokoti Werewolf? Why does it have to be me, to be the last on the line?

I've tried so hard to be good; I don't eat people and I married who I was told to. Derik never did find out about what I did with Declan that ONE time, so I didn't hurt him that way. Oh please don't tell me this is some kind of punishment for sleeping with Declan...?

"B?" My husband opened the bedroom door to come in and sit beside me on the bed. "B, please." He tried to make me look at him, but I refused to. "Besides your Great Grandma telling you that you were barren on her way to the after life, how do you know it's for sure?"

"Because when I woke up, I instantaneously phased to Circulate Headquarters and made Vincent scan me." I said sadly as I looked in the opposite direction.

"And?"

"My eggs operate on a separate time differential than your sperm, so I can't conceive." My lower lip trembled.

"A separate time differential? What does that mean exactly?" He frowned in confusion.

"I don't know, but I think it's something to do with the universe expanding!" I shook with new sobs. "Basically it means that I'm defective, I'm faulty and I don't work."

"Listen B." He said firmly. "You once told me that this Circulate Headquarters has futuristic technology, maybe this can be treated?"

"It can't, that's what I asked!" I finally sat up to face him. "I'm the last Circulator ever and both the space time continuum AND the timeline want to keep it that way by me never reproducing!" I wailed.

I collapsed face first back onto the bed as I tried to bury my wet face into the quilt.

"Then we'll adopt!" Grant cried out in frustration. He pulled me back up to make me look on him. "We're not the first couple in the tribe that this has happened to B and there's always alternatives."

"But you're a male Lokoti Werewolf, Grant! You're so fertile that all you have to do is walk past a girl and she's pregnant! My Grandmother was pregnant within the first month of mating and my mother after the first night! But me...?" I looked downwards. "I'm the last of the line."

"So what if we don't have kids?" He tried to shrug it off. "Maybe one day we will and like I said, maybe we'll adopt?"

"But Grant," I stopped him, "YOU can still have kids!"

He paused as he looked on baffled, "er how do you figure that, if we can't?"

"Leave me!" I announced. "You're not even 30 years old! You can shag and knock up another!"

"What?!" He pulled away with his hurt expression returning.

"Grant, the Tribal Elders married you to me just as the pack did, to curb my bloodlust to crave animal flesh and it's worked. Congratulations on a job well done!" I clapped him on the arm. "But you shouldn't be hindered by me any more."

My husband suddenly straightened as if I had just slapped him in the face. He did not look happy; Grant did not look happy at all. His eyes even watered.

"B, is that how you honestly think that's the way I see you?" He asked incredulous. I shrugged, not knowing what to say when he grabbed hold of my arms. "Bianca we're mates! WE ARE MATES! We're biologically bound together! I have your scent! I feel your emotions! I have lain with you almost every night for the past eleven months! I hunt with you! I cook with you! I tend our greenhouse with you! I care for you! I've built my future around you!"

He released my arms as he stood up from the bed to walk a little away as he rubbed his eyes and I even heard him sniff. Frickin' hell, did I just hurt my husband so much so that he's now crying? I've never seen Grant this upset before. Now I felt really rotten...

"Do you honestly think that my feelings are arranged, like our arranged marriage?" He turned on me. "Because I can tell you now that after our first night together? We became mates from that moment on! There was nothing arranged between us because of the way you made me feel!"

My husband turned around to storm out of the bedroom, slamming the door behind! It was so loud that the BANG made me jump in fright! After another second, I heard our front door slam too which was so hard, I felt the vibrations up here.

Good one Bianca, now you've done it! Not only do you injure him with the news about your defectiveness but you hurt his feelings too? What's going to be my encore, cheating on him next? Running away with Declan? I moaned as I walked over to the wall next to the dresser where I banged my head against it several times.

Just then I heard the faint sound of the front door being opened once more. Next, I heard the sound of somebody marching up the stairs and then my bedroom door blew open.

"OK." Grant declared in annoyance. "I've never told you that I love you so maybe that's where the confusion lies. But I just assumed by my body language or my demeanor towards you that you would have been able to sense being my mate that the love was there... I love you B."

My mouth fell open as he stood there looking on expectantly, but I didn't know what to say as my jaw had dropped to the floor.

"Um, thanks."

"What the hell?" He now leant on the tallboy with an expression as if I were a complete nut.

"Frickin' hell!" my face burned bright red. "OK, I love you! There, I've said it!"

He was still staring in a way that I couldn't stand so I went to sit on the far side of the bed to get away.

"I was saving it for a special occasion." I confessed. "Don't you think it sounds fake or forced when one person says it and then it's like a social requirement that the other person says it too?"

"Oh, er..." he raised his eyebrows, "...I'd never really thought about it, actually."

Grant wandered over to where I was sitting to sit down beside. I looked from my husband back towards the bedroom doorway.

"Are my parents and your older brother still here?" I remembered we had company.

"No." He smirked. "They made themselves scarce when I followed you up after your announcement."

"Oh no...!" I inwardly cringed; that was another special trick, I became so wrapped up in my own problems that I didn't care that Great Grandma had dropped dead. "Um, how did she die? Was it peacefully?"

"Yes." He sighed sadly.

"I thought so, she seemed at peace when I saw her." I thought out loud. "I think that's why I'm happy for her, because she's with her husband again."

"Did you see him too?" He asked in surprise.

"Well, kind of. She walked off into the sunset and somebody took hold of her hand to lead her into the light." I stared out the window as I relived the image .

"It sounds nice." He conceded.

"Hmm."

"Hmm." He took hold of my hand as he stared out the window too.

We sat in a comfortable silence whilst I remembered the younger Great Grandma in my vision, sitting on a rock and swinging her legs carefree. It was a contrast compared to the old woman I grew up with, who spent years cooking and caring for her family.

"No one in my family can cook like her." I said after a long moment.

"Her gravy was a treat." He nodded then after another moment, he added on, "the funeral is tomorrow and we've been asked to bring a dish to the Wake."

"Do you think it will be a family affair or a big tribal shindig?" I wondered.

"Probably a big tribal shindig, as Clara Riverclaw had many friends." He speculated as he picked up my hand to hold it in his two.

"She lost her husband when Grandfather was 12 years old and that mustn't have been easy. She raised Grandfather with the help of her father-in-law. She saw my Grandfather meet my Gran, as she saw to their courtship. After their mating, she helped Gran out when she came to live with them. Great Grandma always cooked as she helped raise Mum and Uncle Julian, especially when Gran disappeared to the space time continuum for a couple of years from the 'Final Phase'. Then her father-in-law died and Uncle Julian became a

Werewolf whilst Mum was learning how to become a Circulator. She oversaw Mum's marriage to Dad just as she oversaw our marriage."

"Clara Riverclaw had this quiet control over people." He reminisced. "I remember when my Dad died, how she came over with food in tupperwear containers. She was this quiet, calm presence in our house. She even helped me when I went through the change and she was the one who taught me how to sew."

"Really?" I smiled on the idea.

"She told me not to worry, as she had been mending clothes for years. Her husband had been a Werewolf, her son was a Werewolf, her grandson was a Werewolf and now her grandson-in-law was a Werewolf. As she worked, she told me stories about her family which made me feel like I wasn't alone." He recalled.

"It sounds like she helped you out; as she also helped Mum and Dad out, as she helped Gran and Grandfather out." I realized. "She was always helping people."

"It was one of the reasons why I didn't mind the idea of marrying you, B." Grant met my gaze. "My older brother was your Dad's best friend and your Great Grandma helped my family out after my Dad's death. Your family has always felt like my family."

All this talk of families made me sad again, as I stared down at the quilt. "Now we can't have a family of our own..."

"Hey!" He cupped my face to make me look on him. "We ARE family, B. I love you as a husband loves his wife. You are my mate and we are a family of two."

"But we won't have children or grandchildren and what about the pack? There will be no bloodline for you to pass down the Werewolf gene -"

He chuckled as he gently banged his forehead into mine; "Ian has two sons and Finn has three. If I don't have a son, the pack isn't about to become extinct!"

This also reminded me of what Vincent had said, of how the Lokoti Werewolf DNA was in every single member of the Lokoti tribe.

"I suppose you're right." I sighed. "But I don't want to be different, Grant! I'm already the first female Lokoti Werewolf. Now people are going to stare because I'm the first barren Lokoti Werewolf."

My husband tenderly stroked my face, "think of your parents for a moment, B. Your parents had one child – you – a beautiful little girl who glowed because she was a Circulator. But your Mom couldn't have anymore children, otherwise it would endanger her. Your father didn't care about his Lokoti Werewolf genes carrying on, he was over the moon when you were born! He would come to my house to take me hunting with Ian and he'd go on about your first smile, your first laugh, your first word, your first step, you calling him 'Dada' for the first time. Seriously B, concerns about having a son was the furthest thing from his mind."

My tearful eyes overflowed, but they weren't tears of sadness anymore they were tears of joy. I threw my arms about his neck to hug him tightly.

"I love you Grant." I uttered out.

He wrapped his stronger arms about my waist and held me so tightly, if I wasn't a Werewolf, he probably would have broken a rib or two.

"We're mates Bianca, we hunt together, we sleep together and we live happily ever after." He growled affectionately.

~~~~~~

23rd August, 2085

Great Grandma's funeral was held in the traditional Lokoti fashion, on the Holy Grounds before the three Sacred Totems, three days after her death.

I stood up the front of the crowd with my husband and family, as all of the tribe stood behind in a large semi-circle. Great Grandma's body wrapped in the traditional woven funeral shroud, burned on top of the funeral pyre, as the Tribal Elders led the funeral chant to the drum beat.

Grandpa's voice was the loudest, as he sang farewell to the woman whom was greatly respected and admired. Great Grandma's patience, kindness and cooking made quite the impact on the lives around her. In one form or another, she had helped almost every single member of the tribe, as well as her family.

As what happened at another funeral twelve months ago, my eyes skipped away since I was still uncomfortable with watching cremation. Once more, they landed on the person standing opposite in the crowd but this time it wasn't Declan's blue eyes glaring, it was Derik's brown ones.

Derik was here? Did he come back from Cambridge, for Great Grandma's funeral? How sweet! However right then he didn't look sweet, but he was looking very sour...

Then I realized that Derik wasn't glaring at me, rather he was glaring at the sight of me standing with my husband. Grant's arm rested supportively about my shoulders, which had captured his attention. He was looking on Grant with the same loathing I had seen on Declan's face, when he occasionally ran into us at the general store.

Speaking of which, where is Declan? I saw Derik and Aunt Susan were standing together, but he was nowhere to be found. Just as I was about to search him out, Derik's eyes met my own.

My best friend smiled warmly in my direction, albeit sadly from the circumstance which brought us here. I allowed myself to feel hope as I returned it. It felt good to see my best friend again, as it reminded me how once we were partners in crime.

Whether it was inappropriate for a funeral or not, I beamed back. This made him quietly chuckle, before he nodded his head in a particular direction. This made me give a nod in agreement.

"Back in a sec." I whispered in Grant's ear, before I pulled away.
~~~~~~

He turned his head sharply in surprise, but he didn't try to stop me. Instead he silently watched me slip through the gathering. I quietly excused and pardoned my way so much so, I was still doing it when I ran into Derik.

"Excuse me...huh? Derik!" I giggled out. "How are you?"

"I'm good, but look at you! B, you look exactly the same as a year ago when I left!" He laughed.

"Your hair is different, Derik! It's longer and you've grown out your fringe!" I reached forward to ruffle it. "It looks good on you."

However our friendly banter earned some unimpressed looks from the people at the end of the crowd, as we were interrupting the funeral they came to pay their respects. I think they were also unhappy at our behavior, considering the ceremony was in my Great Grandma's honor.

"C'mon." Derik grabbed hold of my arm to lead me away.

Walking hand-in-hand, we left the Holy Grounds and walked along the road towards the sports field in our community centre. Derik and I had been best friends for so long, I already knew what was on his mind so I followed after. We even fell into a comfortable silence as we admired the light of the Alaskan summer.

We headed for the swing set next to the sport's field. I caught Derik looking up at the sky which was still light, but a quarter moon and a couple of stars poked through. The celestial objects were the only giveaway to the late hour of our extended daylight.

"I actually miss the odd Alaskan daylight hours, can you believe it?" He chuckled as he claimed a swing.

"Are you kidding me?" I sat down on another. "But I wanna hear about Cambridge, Derik! What are the dorms like? Are there lots of parties? What are your classes like? What are the students like? Tell me everything!"

We started to slowly swing as we talked, dragging our feet through the dirt just as we did when we were little.

"It's good." He nodded. "It definitely helps me get my mind off things..." he hinted before he cleared his throat. "Yeah um, I like it. I'm living in Holy Spirit College Dorms. During my first week there, the Worthall's came from Blythe Castle to visit. Your Aunt Josephine told me that my room is the same one your Great Great Grandfather Jarrod Worthall lived in, when he was there."

"No way!" I stared in surprise. "Are you for real?"

"Yep." He grinned. "I usually eat a frozen dinner in my room when I'm studying, or I munch on a plate of fries or 'chips' as they call them, in the College Bar. There are all these trophies behind the bar, right? Your Aunt Josephine asked the bartender to pass down these two in particular and I'm not kidding when I say this. On one trophy is the name Vincent Moher with the date 1938, the man Elisha Worthall nearly ended up but whom your Calculator is descended from. On another trophy is the name Jarrod Worthall with the date 2003, the man Elisha Worthall did marry."

"No way...!" my eyes bulged.

"Vincent Moher was a darts champion and Jarrod Worthall was a Rowing Captain or somethin'." He kicked at the dirt beneath.

"Tell me more, Derik! Tell me everything!" I listened animatedly. "What are your classes like?"

"Well, there are lectures and there are tutorials. Plus studying medicine, we have lab work too which I like the most. I'm not as smart as most of the people in my course, as they got to complete their High School Certificates properly with the schools which have re-opened in England. They all think of me as some backwards hillbilly coming from Alaska." He laughingly shook his head.

"They do not!" I whacked him on the arm for putting himself down. "You were always the smartest boy in the tribe."

"Yeah, a tiny little tribe in Alaska which is far, far away from the rest of the world." He sighed. "But I'll tell you one thing about Cambridge, B? It's very much in the outside world. TV has started up again with news reports. There's still so much fighting goin' on, it's scary. Last week they even showed the news reporter getting shot when she was doing a story on organized crime."

"You're not in any danger, are you?" I asked concerned.

"Nah, not really." He tried to downplay it. "There are so many security guards, walking around campus that it some times feels like I'm in a prison instead of a University. I constantly hear sirens, with the police or ambulance always in motion. Sometimes it makes it hard to study, especially when our buildings are evacuated on a regular basis from bomb threats. It kinda makes me homesick..." his voice sounded wistful, "...but it's nice to get your emails, along with Rachel's and Mandy's."

"You get my emails?" I pondered. "You hardly ever reply so I did wonder."

"Gimme a break, B." He gave a sharp look. "I like reading about how your abilities as a Circulator are developing but when you talk about the Werewolf stuff? It only reminds me why you're not at Cambridge. I can tell you try to leave out a lot of stuff about Grant in your emails, but I can read between the lines. He's with you and I'm not, so I'm pissed off about that."

"OK here's something that should make you feel better." I said coolly. "Because I'm a Circulator, I can't give Grant children."

"Huh?" Derik suddenly stopped swinging to turn my way. "Whadya mean you can't have kids?!"

"My bio-electromagnetic field is in temporal flux and so is my womb apparently. My husband's sperm can't fertilize my eggs. So there you go Derik, you can feel lucky that you didn't get a rotten egg like me." I said bluntly.

"But you're a Werewolf..." he looked dumbfounded, "...I thought you guys were supernaturally sex charged! I thought it's what made you so fertile."

"Thanks a lot!" I laughingly kicked his leg.

"No, I mean all the other Werewolves in the pack like Uncle Fin or Harry or Ian, have at least three kids or more. So if you're a Werewolf and Grant is a Werewolf, I'm surprised you don't have a little Werewolf of your own running around. When I told Aunt Arabella I'd come back for your Great Grandma's funeral, I was even preparing myself to see you pregnant." He spoke openly.

"Nope." I sighed, whilst looking up at the stars that peeked through the silvery-blue sky. "You can blame the space time continuum coz when it made me the Last Circulator, it really did make me the LAST Circulator."

Derik's eyes narrowed, "Grant's not giving you a hard time because of it, is he?"

"No!" I laughingly kicked his leg again. "Aside from yourself, he must be one of the nicest guys in existence. I offered him a divorce so he could run off and impregnate a fully functioning female but he was pissed off by the very suggestion."

"Yeah well, so would have I." He kicked my leg back. "You don't like me putting myself down, huh? Have you looked in the mirror lately?"

"Shut up!" I giggled, kicking him harder.

"Oow! Your heel is higher than mine so that hurt!" He pushed my swing sideways.

"Don't be such a wimpy little human!" I taunted.

"Don't be such a bitch!" he pushed my swing away again.

As soon as those words left his mouth, we both fell into a fit of hysterics from the accuracy of his insult.

"Derik's a weak little human...!" I sung as I kicked him.

"Bianca is a bitch...!" he sung back, pushing my swing sideways.

This only made us laugh harder, as we got dirt all over our good clothes from our play fight.

*****

Not all of the members of the tribe came to the Wake at Gran and Grandfather's house, just the people who were the closest to Great Grandma. But still there were a lot of people sitting in fold-up chairs out the front of their house, which spoke very highly of her.

People had formed into separate groups, which was typical for tribal shindigs. However, it was still foremost in our minds the reason why we were here. The gathering wasn't as loud as our gatherings could be. Aunt Susan was sitting in one group, talking to Mum, Gran, Nana and a couple of other women. Grant was standing with Ian, Dad and the rest of the pack. However as I looked around, Declan was still absent.

I sat in a small circle with my oldest and dearest; Derik, Rachel and Mandy. We were sitting holding plastic plates laden with food as well as sipping on plastic cups filled with soda.

A lineup of fold-away tables by the veranda, were laden with dishes from each family who were attending. At the end of the tables, were several eskies holding bottles of Coca Cola, Fanta, Creaming Soda or Root Beer.

"Mmm, nice casserole." Derik nodded enthusiastically as he ate. "It sure beats frozen dinners any day."

"The casserole? Oh, you mean the rabbit stew." Mandy realized.

"Casserole?" Rachel laughed at Derik. "Is that the Cambridge way of saying stew?"

"Shut up." He laughingly rolled his eyes.

"So you're really loving it over there, huh?" Mandy asked.

"I'm not 'loving it', but it's a nice getaway." He shrugged.

Mandy and Rachel immediately knew what he meant by that so they quickly moved on.

"I wonder who brought the rabbit stew?" Rachel looked around at the other families. "It tastes familiar."

"It was Great Grandma's recipe." I informed.

"Oh, did your Gran and Grandfather make it?" Mandy wondered.

"Nope," I said simply, "Grant did." Derik's eyes widen as he stopped chewing, when I kicked his leg again. "Don't be stupid, now eat up."

"Oow! Would you stop frickin' kickin' me!" He poked me in the ribs.

I didn't have to turn my head to see, but I sensed this attracted Grant's attention. However he remained standing with Ian and Dad, half-heartedly participating in their conversation as his eyes were looking in another direction...mine.

"When Grant and I were married, Great Grandma gave us copies of her recipes. Yesterday when he came home from hunting, Grant skinned the rabbits, chopped them up and he cooked up the stew." I explained casually.

"Thanks B, I really needed to know that." Derik rolled his eyes.

"I thought I recognized the recipe." Rachel quickly moved the conversation along. "Your Great Grandma's cooking was famous."

"It still is." Mandy nodded in agreement. "Hey, do you guys remember the times Clara Riverclaw babysat us at her house?" When we all nodded she continued, "remember when she baked those cookies or cakes for us and how we all used to fight over the bowl or the beaters?"

"Derik and B had to share the bowl as Mandy and I got a beater each." Rachel recited off by heart.

"You once punched me in the stomach to steal my beater, because you had already licked yours clean!" Mandy glowered her way.

"Hey, it was raw chocolate cake mix! I saw you watching me eat mine as you nearly did the same to me!" She retorted. "Besides, Aunt Clara got me back as she made me wash up all those dishes, remember?"

Derik and I laughed at the two as our old jokes and taunts returned and we were probably the loudest group at the Wake. But I didn't care, we were remembering Great Grandma our way; with humor and fondness. We attracted many an amused glance from either our parents or our grandparents, but no-one shushed us.

After an hour, I excused myself to go use the bathroom. But on my way back from the house, I swung by the members of the pack as they stood together. I affectionately put my arm about Grant's waist as I rubbed my face against his arm as my 'hallo'.

"You do know that we're at a funeral, don't you B?" Ian jokingly scolded. "Even the people in Alma can hear you cackling away!"

"Shut up Ian." Grant rebuked as he put his arm about his wife.

"Mom always liked the sound of laughter," Grandfather smiled sadly, "just as she loved the sound of children playing. It's why she volunteered so much to mind her grandchildren and then her great grandchildren."

"Yep." Uncle Jules sighed. "Grandma was a special lady alright."

"If only Jess had Aunt Clara's quiet disposition." Ian continued to joke.

"Now where would be the fun in that?" Dad smirked, before casting an appreciative look Mum's way.

"With Jess' temper, we could put her on patrol and we'd never be bothered by outsiders again." Uncle Jules chuckled to Ian.

"Maybe we could make a recording of one of Jess' temper tantrums then we could set up loud speakers along the perimeter of Lokoti Land. Instead of us running around all night, we could just play Jess' shouting instead." Ian ribbed.

All of the male Lokoti Werewolves cracked up laughing including Dad, at Ian's 'cunning plan'.

"Hey Mum?" Suddenly I turned her way. She stopped talking with Aunt Susan to look back. "Can you come here for a minute? Ian needs your help with something."

"What? No!" Ian's eyes bulged. "Shut up, B! Don't make her come over here!"

Now the male Lokoti Werewolves all laughed harder at the worried look on his face. Mum's eyes narrowed as she sensed that something was afoot.

She gave Ian her best glare as she declared, "I'm not going to get out of my chair to help Ian Elm! He needs help with a LOT of things! I wouldn't know where to start!"

Aunt Susan, Gran, Nana and Ian's wife Rebecca, all burst into laughter!

"You know, I preferred it when we were an exclusively ALL MALE kind of club." He said sulkily.

"Nup, this is way more fun!" Uncle Jules gave him a playful elbow.

"Maybe we should roster you and Jess together on a patrol? The strangers wouldn't know what to think if they saw you two fighting." Uncle Harry threatened.

"You wouldn't...!" Ian's face fell.

"Now that's something I would love to see." Grant chuckled.

"Especially with a silver sword in Jess' hands." Dad guffawed along.

"You guys are just cruel and unusual. I think it's time for you to go hunting to release your bloodlust." He complained to further laughter.

~~~~~~

25th August 2085

I was sitting at the dining table with my books spread about and my laptop switched on. I was writing up an assignment which was typical for an afternoon's work.

"OK, I'm going to the store." Grant came up to kiss me on the cheek.

"Have you got the shopping list?" I queried, which he smilingly held up. "Cool bananas, have fun."

"Enjoy your studies." He stroked my hair before he turned to leave the house.

I watched him depart via the front door and then I listened as he started his jeep and reversed out.

As I returned to work, I happily highlighted sentences before I typed up the ideas that they gave. I was so involved that I didn't hear anybody approach the house. So when there was a knock on the door, it gave me a fright!

I stood up to answer it and when it swung open, so did my mouth in surprise. Declan was standing on my veranda, holding a basket full of fruit and vegetables from his family's greenhouse.

"Hi." He said stiffly.

"Hi." I gave a funny look.

"Here," he thrust the basket into my arms, "I'm sorry for your loss."

"Oh." I said startled at his offering.

"So, how are you?"

"I'm fine, how are you?"

"I'm dandy as my Great Grandma didn't just die." He said sarcastically.

"The funeral was two days ago."

"I know."
~~~~~~

"It was good to see your Mum and Derik there, but where were you?"

"I was working."

"You had to work?" I looked on in disbelief. "My Great Grandma's funeral was almost a state occasion as the whole tribe was there."

"I had to work." He repeated.

As I looked on, it occurred to me why he wasn't at the funeral; because Declan only showed up when Grant wasn't around.

If he ran into my husband and I shopping together at the store, he would immediately leave. He avoided the two of us during a hunt, by either running out in front or dropping right back. Declan avoided tribal functions where he might see Grant and I together, including Great Grandma's funeral yesterday. Now that my husband has gone to the store, Declan shows up to pay his respects.

"You look good in black." He said shortly. "Goodbye."

Then he turned around and left my veranda. He walked off down the driveway, over to his truck which was parked on the road.

He doesn't - nah, he can't have - Declan doesn't have feelings for me still, does he? I shook my head in disbelief before I went back inside, shutting my door behind.

~~~~~~
~~~~~~

~ **13** ~

2nd August 2086

LONELY...

...I woke up.

PAIN...

...I blinked.

ANGER... RESENTMENT... JEALOUSY.

I felt the full force of these feelings wash over my body, making me tense up and almost change.

LONELY.

This feeling weighed me down as if I were experiencing it myself. My chest hurt and the force of the emotion made my eyes sting. What the hell is going on here?!

PAIN.

I sat upright before looking on Grant's sleeping form beside. But my husband was the very picture of peaceful and as I concentrated, I felt this emotion emanate from him. Then where are these horrible feelings coming from?

ANGER... RESENTMENT... JEALOUSY.

My shoulders tensed up again, as a growl made its way up my throat. I closed my eyes and took several deep breaths to stop myself from changing with the onslaught of these negative feelings.

OK, if it's not Grant feeling this way then who in the pack was? I couldn't think of why another Lokoti Werewolf could possibly be feeling like this. Then why was I feeling these emotions? Hang on, I think I just answered my own question.

A Lokoti Werewolf wasn't feeling this way but a European Werewolf was, our honorary sixteenth member of the pack - Declan. Tears welled in my eyes at the prospect that he could be feeling this way, or even why.

LONELY.

I looked down on Grant who was sleeping soundly, with his arm resting over my waist as we both slept naked. I couldn't stand it as there was no way I could sleep feeling like this. There was no way in hell I could rest knowing that Declan was going through this either.

PAIN.

Carefully, I lifted off his arm and crept out of bed. Grabbing my clothes on the way, I departed the bedroom. Once I had dressed downstairs, quietly I opened the front door to slip unnoticed from the house. I bolted almost at the speed of light as I knew that I didn't have much time. Grant would eventually sense my absence, just as I knew he would come looking.

ANGER... RESENTMENT... JEALOUSY.

Instinctively, I bolted in a particular direction as I streaked through the trees along the river, past Sunset Point. I was running to a certain glade by the river bank, a place I had only been to once by accident, only this time I ran to it with purpose. Running almost in light speed, it didn't take me long to get there. I high jumped the log and landed on all fours in the glade, within a minute that I had left my house.

As I rose, I saw Declan turn to look my way, instantly hearing as well as smelling my arrival. He was standing in the glade as a naked human showing that he had come here in his Werewolf form.

His glowing green eyes met my glowing turquoise ones, as we stared at each other with our Werewolf sight enabling us to see through the darkness as clear as day. His eyes momentarily flashed as he looked me over and I felt his relief wash over him to see that I had come. He began to walk over to my position with his arms reaching out...

"Stop!" I put up my hand, which he did as he looked on in surprise. I warned, "Grant will smell you on me and if I become aroused? He'll sense it and wake up."

Declan growled in jealousy upon hearing Grant's name. If he couldn't physically touch me, he tried to have me another way; by drinking up the very sight of me as well as by sniffing my scent. He began to circle like the predator he was, as he hungrily looked me over whilst I overheard him inhale deeply.

"His scent hasn't overwhelmed your scent... good." He spoke satisfactorily as he came to stand before me again. I stood still as I tried to keep my heart from racing. "I've heard that you can't have his child and that's even better."

My cheeks warmed in a blush at how easily this news spread amongst the tribe. I opened my mouth to rebuke him, but nothing came out.

"Why doesn't he leave you?" Declan whined with longing. "Why doesn't he leave you for another woman who can? Why can't he leave you and then that would leave you with me."

I kept quiet which wasn't hard considering I didn't know what to say. Instead I looked on his strong human body which hinted at his supernatural strength.

"If you won't let me touch you then why are you here?" He asked in annoyance.

"I felt you." I confessed. "I felt your pain."

"Yeah, YOU'RE the one who's put me in pain." He said bitterly. "YOU'RE the one who's mated to another."

Suddenly he stepped up so close we were almost touching. I listened to him inhale deeper still as I felt his body's greater heat emanate outwards. I watched his muscles flex as they looked taught and I realized that he was restraining himself.

"B, do you have any idea of what I want to do to you right now?" He growled softly.

My heart hurt with a longing which was his. I don't know how or why, but I could feel his emotions even stronger than Grant's. I was even battling my own selfish desires which wanted to dig my claws into his skin and have him right then and there!

"I still want you Declan..." I whispered, "...but you know that we can't."

"Two years B, it's been two years since I had you, before you were married off to *Grant Elm*," he bit out my husband's name with disgust, "and as *Grant Elm* gets to have you every night, I have to go without! I can't touch you because Grant would find out just as I can't have anybody else in the tribe either."

He couldn't have a human woman without running the risk of changing her or killing her, I remembered this fact well.

"But what if..." I began, "...what if you found another female Werewolf? If I've been mated off, maybe so should you be?"

"Who the hell am I supposed to mate with?!" He snapped. "You're the only female Werewolf in a thousand mile radius!"

"Then go to Canada or the States, where there are North American Werewolves; or across the Bering Straight into Europe and find a female of your kind?" I tried to think. "What about Asia where there are female Asian Werewolves?"

Declan's eyes widened in pain. "You WANT me to leave?"

"I want you to find peace and be happy." I said sadly as a tear escaped.

"Running off and screwing some strange female Werewolf isn't going to make me find peace, B." He said hurt. "I already have a mate...here."

My eyes widened with fear, "no Declan, you can't think like that! You have to hate me and you have to move on. Remember how much we used to fight? Remember how much you used to hate me, growing up? Remember all the mean things you used to say to me? I want us to go back to that."

"I never hated you B." He stated. "I've always been attracted to you, but because you were my little brother's best friend and girl, I resented the fact that I couldn't have you."

My eyes widened even further, this time in surprise. Our glowing eyes met and held, even if our bodies couldn't.

Declan went on, "my body has always sensed that you were different to the other girls of the tribe. My body probably sensed you were a Werewolf for years before you changed. My body's always wanted you. My body knew you were mine the morning I drove you home in my truck and I put my hand over yours."

My heart almost stopped as I vividly recalled the sensation of his hand over mine and how his touch warmed me all over.

"Then you changed, confirming what my body suspected about yours was right and true. Suddenly I lived, breathed and thought of nothing but you. I lost control when I had to have you and you know what I regret about that afternoon in the woods, B? That I stopped myself too soon. When I relive that afternoon in my head, I never stop. I never stop holding you and touching you and being inside you, whilst you never stop moving your body with mine." His voice turned tight.

I ducked my head with my forehead almost touching his bare chest as I squeezed my eyes shut, reliving that afternoon in my head too.

He spoke again, "I'm a European Werewolf and Grant is a Lokoti Werewolf. You're a Lokoti Werewolf but you're also a Circulator. You and I will outlive Grant by at least a hundred years and then you'll be mine again."

"What, you're going to wait the next 150 years for me?" I looked on in disbelief.

"I guess I have to, don't I?" He said helplessly.

This scared me how I had affected him so. I had always reassured myself what was between Declan and I was just sex. This cheap thought helped me think of another man less when I was with my husband. I had to make this so again, as I couldn't have him mooning around for the next 150 years. I had to be a faithful wife to Grant so I decided to put a stop to this, even if it had to be for once and for all.

"No Declan," my voice took on a sharp edge, "you don't love me because you and I were just sex and that's it."

A flash of pain ran over his face before his expression turned into one of anger.

"Hey I never said I love you, I just said I wanted to screw you and that's it!" He snapped.

"Good, because I'll admit you were a good lay but that's it, Declan Sabre."

"Hey, I KNOW I was good, even better than the kind you're getting now." He scoffed.

"I wouldn't bet on that if I were you." I said cruelly. "Grant is my mate, not you."

Declan's eyes widened with the hurt I was causing, but his glare was quick to replace it.

"I never said I was your mate!" He retorted. "It's frickin' typical of a woman to start thinking long term after sex!"

"Long term? You're the one who's talking about waiting for 150 years!"

"You know what? I think I might move away from this frickin' tribe, away from you and your frickin' husband! I think I will go and find someone else to screw!"

"Good, now go do that! I hope she fucks your brains out!" I raised my voice.

"Trust me B, if I do find a female of my kind? She'd leave you for dead!" He said spitefully. "She'd be a better lay than you any day! Hell, a HUMAN would probably be better than you!"

"Why don't you go and find this female then and stop making a nuisance of yourself?" I rebuked.

"Fine!" He shouted in my face.

"Fine!" I yelled back.

"Whatever B." Declan turned to walk away...when suddenly he whirled around, this time standing even closer than before. He looked down on my face in complete and utter longing. "Nice try," he breathed, "and by the way, your bed-hair looks awful."

"You're the one who damn well woke me up." I glared.

Declan's head bent as his mouth opened and my head tilted upwards whilst my lips parted... We stopped short with our mouths just an inch apart and we could even feel the other's breath on our lips. We both started to pant as simultaneously we restrained ourselves. My teeth sharpened as I felt my claws appear on the ends of my fingers and toes whilst I sensed the same changes in him. He backed his head away as his eyes looked over in wanting.

"Your hair looks like a birds nest." He insulted, to make us hate each other again.

"Yeah well, at least I HAVE hair." I made a dig at his crew cut.

"And you stink like Grant now."

"That's because I'm his mate."

"You're such a little pleaser for going ahead with the ceremony just to placate the Tribal Elders and the pack." He said icily.

"Maybe I wanted to screw Grant Elm instead of you?" I hit back.

He spoke quickly, "I don't love you and I have never loved you and I want you to get the hell away from me."

"Your wish is my command." I sung.

Then I raised my hand and clicked my fingers as I instantaneously phased out of the glade in a bright flash of light.

I reappeared in another flash of light onto my veranda and I soon found, I got home just in time too. Abruptly the front door opened and Grant wearing a pair of jeans stepped out. He paused when he saw me standing there and he looked on suspiciously.

"I'm not hunting human!" I said gruffly. "I couldn't sleep that's all. I went for a walk to get some air."

Grant crossed over to my side to lean on the veranda railing and look up at the starry sky. I watched him frown, deep in thought. He doesn't smell Declan on me, does he? I tried so hard not to do the wrong thing...

"Did you sense my absence?" I guessed.

"Of course." He said simply, before he looked on. "Where did you go?"

"I ran down to the river and back." I half-lied.

"Hmm...I can smell the mud from the riverbank on your feet." He concurred.

He can? Man, this guy is good at this! I swallowed hard as I crossed my arms and stared out at the dark forest.

"Anyways, I think I'm tired enough to come back to bed." I said dismissively and turned towards the front door.

"Are you sure?" He asked knowingly. "Your heart is racing and your shoulders are tense."

"Maybe I'll have a hot shower." I decided. "The hot water always relaxes me and it will also take care of the problem of my muddy feet."

"Did you want to go hunting first?" My husband offered, which would explain why he was just wearing jeans. He thought I must have been feeling like this because of the bloodlust. "If you need to go hunting B, I can take you right now."

"No, I'm not hungry." I quickly shook my head then I disappeared inside.

~~~~~~

2nd September 2086

After I secretly slipped out to see Declan, my husband's previous concerns over my bloodlust returned. Although I was relieved Grant didn't suspect me of cheating, I became annoyed at his constant worrying. His overprotective Lokoti Werewolf instincts were in full-force, as he continually tried to talk about my behavior.

"You can talk to me about the bloodlust, B." He tried again as he was washing up whilst I dried and put away. "The most important reason the pack had for our coupling, was so you would have someone to take you hunting or talk to about it."

"Grant, please!" I moaned wearily. "For once and for all, I didn't sneak out of the house to go hunting without you."

"So you got out of bed at one in the morning, just to go for a run?" He tested.

"Yes!" I cried out in frustration. "I did not go on a feeding frenzy on any humans in Alma or on any animals in the National Park! I went for a run and that's it."

"I'm just saying B, if you ever needed to hunt in between full moons I'd understand." He continued. "The first couple of years are hardest for a new Werewolf. Nobody expects you to stop craving human overnight."
~~~~~~

"I'm fine thank you." I said breezily as I put away the coffee mugs into one of the upper cupboards.

"If you did need to go hunting when it's not a full moon, you don't have to sneak out of the house to do it. Don't be afraid to wake me as of course I'd want to come with you." My husband gallantly offered.

"OK."

"Or even if you need to go hunting during the day when I'm away working with Ian or your father, I'd rather you come and tell me." He ordered.

"Grant, come on!" I was reaching the end of my tether. "I'm a grown woman, let alone a grown Werewolf as I'm almost twenty! I'm certainly not going to go looking for my husband to ask for permission if I want to hunt animal, let alone go for a run in the woods."

"But what if you hunted grizzly by yourself and you were harmed in the process?" He fretted. "You're not as strong as a male Lokoti Werewolf and I'd rather be with you incase anything went wrong."

"Alright, you win!" I snapped. "I won't hunt without you in future."

"So you were hunting the night you went for your 'run'?"

My eyes squeezed shut as I growled under my breath and I even deliberately banged my head against the cupboard door a couple of times. My word, I felt like flat-out lying to him that I had sex with another man!

"No Grant, I actually went back in time to Ancient Greece and participated in a Dionysian festival which was basically an orgy with food and wine." I said sarcastically.

"Is that why you, your mother and your grandmother have picked Ancient Greece for your first expedition as a Circulator?" He asked in amusement. "If that's the case, I'll be sure to come with you. I think your father and your Grandfather could be lured into coming along too."

A giggle escaped when I looked back in his direction, "yep that's secretly the reason why we're going there the end of this week; to get into a drunken orgy."

Grant emitted a deep, rumbling growl as he pulled me close. His wet hands dampened my t-shirt, which went through the fabric. I think the very idea of his wife soon visiting the era where orgies were held, brought out the possessive side of his Lokoti Werewolf personality.

He growled even louder as I felt his sharp teeth graze the skin on my neck, whilst his hands made a move at tugging off my clothes.

"Down boy!" I laughingly pushed him off. "Dishes first then maul your wife second."

"Yes dear." He gave a cheeky grin as he obeyed.

*****

On Friday morning at 9 AM, not only did Mum and Gran report in, but Dad and Grandfather accompanied their wives. In the manner Grant greeted the older Werewolves, it made me wonder if he were expecting them?

"So what's the plan?" Grandfather asked his wife.

"First Jess, B and I will instantaneously phase to Circulate HQ to change into costume inside the Props Room. Then via the Gate with Vincent behind the controls, we'll phase through time to 449 BC as Vincent moves our light waves to a 'safe house' in Athens." Gran advised.

"And then what?" Dad frowned in consternation. "What will you three be doing in Athens?"

"Just touristy stuff." Mum shrugged. "Look around the city and do a little shopping. You know, the usual things visitors do."

"You're not going to be attending any Dionysian festivals, are you?" Grant joked.

"Huh?" Mum gave a peculiar look.

"Never mind." He smilingly shook his head before throwing me a wink.

"We haven't planned on going to the theatre, but if there's a production on I suppose we could?" She shrugged. "Dionysus was the god of drama."

"As well as wine." I pointed out. "And a couple of other things..."

"You know that you can't drink any wine, don't you B?" My father said seriously. "If you got drunk and then lost control of the bloodlust -"

"Yes Dad, I know." I interrupted. "Alcohol and/ or drugs are a big no-no for Werewolves."

"What time will you be home?" Grandfather asked his wife.

"I'm not sure." She speculated. "It could be late so don't wait to cook until I get home, please go ahead and fix yourself something."

"Could you give us a ball park figure when you might get back?" Dad asked concerned.

Then it clicked inside my mind Dad and Grandfather came over, because the two had come to wait with Grant until our return.

"If you're THAT worried about us venturing through time without you, why don't you come along?" I teased.

However my husband, father or grandfather didn't laugh but instead they looked pained.

"We wish we could B..." Dad began.

"...but we can't." Grandfather finished.

"Remember how Lokoti Werewolves are tied to their hunting grounds?" Grant explained. "Although we can leave Tribal Lands for a couple of hours, or perhaps for a day or two as your father and your grandfather have visited England or Australia in this time period? Traveling back through time thousands of years ago in another country, would be too much for us."

"We would wane being so far from home." Dad said unhappily.

"Oh." I looked on the male Lokoti Werewolves in sympathy.

I never realized how also being a Circulator, made me much freer to move around. So far during the times I have left Tribal Lands to visit bookstores in London or libraries at Cambridge University, I haven't felt the restrictive yoke of my genetic ties. I virtually came and went as I pleased, only keeping in mind that I had a husband waiting at home.

"But Arabella has promised you won't be in any danger." Grandfather gave a reassuring grin. "If we thought you three could be in jeopardy…"

"…then of course we would come with you." Grant declared.

"Or we would talk you out of going." Dad said firmly.

"So what are you guys going to be doing all day?" I queried as I looked on the three standing together.

"I don't know." My husband shrugged, before he glanced at the older men for ideas.

"You're not going to just hang around waiting for your wives to come home, will you?" Mum raised her eyebrows unimpressed. "That's just sad."

"Jess, I won't be able to concentrate on work let alone do any; whilst my mate and young are walking around a time period where people enslave other people and especially foreigners!" Dad said in annoyance.

"Hang on, they enslave foreigners in Ancient Greece?" My husband's eyes widened with worry.

"Nobody is enslaving us, Hunter." Mum rolled her eyes. "We're not even taking our swords on this trip as we don't anticipate any trouble."

"You're not?" Grant's eyes widened even further. "Are you sure that's a good idea to go unarmed especially where there's slavery?"

"We will be visiting a relatively peaceful era of Ancient Greek history." I shrugged.

"'Relatively peaceful'?" He echoed. "Er, B? I'm starting to not like the sound of this -"

"Relax men." Gran smiled on the worrying Werewolves. "We'll be home safe and sound before midnight."

"How about you make it 9 PM and we'll have dinner waiting for you?" Grandfather negotiated. "We'll make a roast dinner with my Mom's special gravy."

"Em, you don't fight fair." She smirked.

"I'll make creamy potato bake instead of roast potatoes." Dad offered.

"Come on Hunter, now you're really cheating." Mum giggled at his bait.

"Er…" Grant now tried to think of something to entice his mate, "…I'll make chocolate brownies for dessert?"

"Alright, 9 PM it is." I walked up to wrap my arms about his neck, as Dad and Grandfather made a move to kiss goodbye their wives.

"If I make the chocolate brownies with chocolate fudge on top, would you take your sword with you?" He thought he'd try.

"I can't take my sword as it would look strange being an armed woman in that era. But you can still put on top the chocolate fudge if you'd like?" I leaned in to rub my nose against his.

"Well since you asked so nicely." My husband chuckled before his mouth smothered my own.

*****

Half an hour later, three Circulators stood inside the Props Room, assisting the other in getting dressed.

I stood still as Mum and Gran did my chiton in the Ionic way. It was made of a rose coloured cotton material, which I wore a white himation over it, wrapped in an over-the-shoulder style. My hair was pulled up in the Classical fashion, with several gold diadem's holding it in place. On my feet I wore leather sandals.

Whilst I was being dressed, I studied the Props Room. The walls were lined with racks of clothes from different cultures and eras of Earth's past. I saw Ancient Egyptian jewelry, as well as Roman togas. I saw 18th Century ball gowns hanging next to similarly dated English Army Officer's uniforms. There were even futuristic one-piece suits that came from the 25th Century.

"It seems such a shame." I thought out loud.

"What does?" Mum asked as she hung dangly gold earrings on my ears and then hers.

"All of these clothes sitting here unused, it's like walking into a costume room for a play that's been cancelled." I sighed.

"They're not 'unused' as we're using them right now." Gran returned.

"But we're not using ALL of them, are we?" I pointed out. "Once upon a time the Circulate had 696 members who circulated through Earth's different time periods. Now all that's left are three Circulators and one Calculator."

"I've used a couple of the clothes in here." My mother shrugged. "I've visited Egypt during the New Kingdom, 19th Century England and 25th Century Paris."

"I've visited the places Jess just mentioned, as well as more." My grandmother added on. "I've worn many a costume in this room. Don't fret B, as I'm sure so will you."

"In fact, Vincent's made the request that we start transporting some of these costumes to the Circulate HQ on Taurus Six." Mum announced.

"Why?" I pondered. "Isn't there a Props Room there too?"

"The HQ on Taurus Six is identical to the one here on Mars." She nodded. "But there are a couple of relics or costumes here that Vincent's requested to be stored at Taurus Six instead."

"That's odd." Gran frowned. "Vincent's been making me move a number of other things to the HQ on Taurus Six too."

Mum paused in our dressing to look on, "what do you think he's planning? Do you think he 'sees' something coming up?"

"Calculators are always planning something, Jess." My grandmother reminded. "That's what Calculators do; they 'see', as they calculate and therefore they plan."

My mother rolled her eyes at her glib reply, before she turned me around to face the mirror. "There you go B, you're dressed to party like it's 449."

The sight of the three of us standing together made me pause. Thanks to my supernatural physique as a Lokoti Werewolf, I was taller, more broad-shouldered and stronger looking than the other two. But we still looked related with our twenty-something appearances, our brown or black hair and blue eyes, albeit mine were a darker shade than theirs. Now our similar hairstyles and costume designs actually made us look like three sisters instead of grandmother, mother and daughter.

"Ladies, let's go to Ancient Greece." My grandmother beamed on her female lineage via the mirror.

We three left the Props Room and as soon as we walked into the Gate Room, we found Vincent already standing behind the crystallized control panel.

"Nice timing." Mum tittered.

"I'm sending your light waves to the Aristides 'safe house'. It's in the middle of Athens, near the agora." He announced. "I've programmed the date of the location as the 1st September 449 BC so all you need to do now is phase there."

We stepped up onto the circular, mirrored platform of the Gate, directly underneath another huge, circular mirror above. At first the top mirror merely showed our reflections, but as Vincent programmed our destination into the Gate; the image changed to show the city of Athens during the Classical Period. The city was primarily made up of houses and temples with the Acropolis in the background, where the temple of Athena had started to be rebuilt.

"Now, have you got your purses?" Our Calculator did his last-minute check.

We three pulled out the leather pouches which were tied to our girdles, secured underneath our himations.

"Do you remember your alias?" He next asked.

"We are visitors from Attica, staying with our cousins the Aristides family." Gran recited.

"And who is Aristides?" Vincent quizzed.

"A politician in Athens." I answered. "Who is also on the Court of Justice."

"It looks like you're ready to go." He smiled on the sight of us standing there, in our chitons. "I assume you'll instantaneously phase home to Alaska when your daytrip is done?"

"And not back to Circulate HQ via the Gate?" Mum shook her head. "No, we'll instantaneously phase back to Alaska tonight."

"Then don't forget to return your chitons to the Props Room later, or even take them to the Props Room at Taurus Six instead?" He requested.

"Take them to Taurus Six? Why Taurus Six, Vincent? Why are you moving so many things to our backup Headquarters?" Gran asked puzzled.

"The Gate is in operation, you may go into phase when ready." He quickly looked down on the crystallized controls.

I caught Mum and Gran exchange suspicious glances, before we three dissolved our biological bodies into light.

Since I've never circulated using the Gate before, I didn't know what to expect. I was taken over by the warm, floating sensation created by being in phase. I looked down to see my normally solid body, look bright and see-through. Then I looked up at the picture of Athens in the mirror above as I concentrated hard on the date 1st September 449 BC.

Suddenly I felt a rush like I was flying through air, as if I was pushed through the mirror like light passing through glass. Now I wasn't just looking at Athens in 449 BC but I was in Athens 449 BC. The city very quickly looked much closer and in particular, did a certain house. The next thing I saw was a room via a peculiar elongated, circular doorway. Gran's bright, ghost-like image went through the doorway first, with Mum second and I was third.

As soon as we were in the new room, we reformed into our biological bodies. When I looked back, to my surprise I saw the peculiar elongated, circular doorway was not a doorway; it was a polished metal mirror. Oh yeah that would make sense, we passed through one mirror to arrive via another.

This room appeared to be a bedroom which was tidy but spartan. It had a wooden floor, a painted wooden chest sitting in the corner, with a wooden bed and thin mattress nearby. I also saw a couple of woven tapestries on the wall for decoration. However as my eyesight was still recovering from the bright glare that our mode of travel caused, I didn't immediately pick up that there were two other people in the room.

Damn it B, I should have smelled them even if I didn't see them. Declan was right, I really was the most pathetic Werewolf in the world!

"Aristides and Calliope." Gran stepped forward to shake the man and woman's hands. "Thank you...for your kindness at granting us...sanctuary in your home."

Gran fumbled out her Ancient Greek rather slowly, since it wasn't our first language. But our hosts didn't seem to mind as they spoke slowly back.

"It is always an honor...to have such wise and powerful travelers...deign us with their presence. Like the Gods...who grant their goodwill on the chosen...my family owes many thanks to you." Aristides smiled widely.

"We have organized...a feast...in your honor." Calliope spoke whilst illustrating with her hands to get her meaning across.

"Thank you...for your kindness...but we will be...walking the city...to behold the sights." She politely declined. When she saw our host's faces fall she decided to offer; "Aristides...in return for your kindness...I can tell you this. In four years time...Athens and Sparta...will declare 'peace' but be warned...in fourteen years time...there will be another war."

I watched their eyes widen at Gran's prophecy. Whereas Calliope looked frightened by her words, Aristides looked thankful. He gave a nod with his head before he called out something I didn't recognize. A slave came running into the room, to which Aristides gave an order and the slave nodded before scurrying off to obey.

"I have instructed...my slaves to accompany you...on your journey through the city. Should you require my help...the slaves will come and find me." Aristides told Gran.

"Thank you Aristides." She shook his hand once more, before giving a polite nod to his wife and then she motioned for Mum and I to follow.

Gran led the way out of the large house, walking through an open courtyard in the centre before departing via the front door. As we walked out onto a street made of a dirt road which was lined with more houses, three male slaves followed us out. They carried these odd kind of wooden, triangular, shade coverings which they tried to hold above our heads.

I must admit, the heat of the city felt much hotter than I expected. It instantly dried out my lips as it made me feel thirsty. On some level, I appreciated the discomfort in a small way as it saved me the trouble of pinching myself to prove that all of this was really happening.

After all the years of reading about the ancient times now I was in them! I was standing in a city which still existed in my era; two thousand and five hundred years earlier. I was standing amongst a culture which was not only ancient, but responsible for many traditions, like the Olympic Games for example.

"Wow Gran, this is so cool!" I cried out ecstatically as I gazed around.

The street we were standing on, the road lay in a straight line on which the houses and other buildings sat. They were primarily white, made from stone or brick with red tiles on the roof. The traffic on the street ranged from the odd horse and chariot, or oxen and cart but primarily people simply walked.

"Which way is the agora, Mum?" my mother asked my grandmother.

"I think it's this way." Gran began to walk down the street.

My mother followed my grandmother, with me behind her and then the three slaves trailed after us. We probably looked a little like 'follow the leader' however we passed several other processions like this, with more slaves following their mistresses or masters. This made me feel uncomfortable as occasionally I shot off an awkward glance at 'our' slaves.

"Er, Mum?" I walked up beside, with the slaves quickly following with the shades. "Can't we tell the slaves that they're in luck as it's their day off and they can go do something else?"

"I don't think so," she frowned, "they could be beaten or other punishment inflicted."

"Ouch!" I flinched.

"But what I want to know is why your Gran disclosed future events in the timeline to Aristides?" My mother asked loud enough for her mother to hear. "Aren't there rules set by the Circulate Council against this kinda thing?"

Gran stopped in her tracks to talk to us quietly, with the slaves obediently stopping in theirs.

"The Circulate has thousands of 'safe houses' scattered throughout Earth's history." She repeated a fact we already knew. "But how do you think these safe houses are created? Not everyone's hands are out for money."

"Oh." Mum looked surprised. "So it's not just money that buys allegiance but it's knowledge?"

"We trade in information and not just economics." I reasoned. "It makes sense, but shouldn't we be selective over which information we disclose?"

"Of course." Gran gave a mischievous grin. "Come along B, you're the Bachelor of Arts in Ancient History student here. I mentioned to Aristides that a war would occur, but I didn't tell him who would win now did I?"

"No, you didn't." I grinned. "You can be as cunning as a fox, Gran."

"I may look like I'm still in my twenties but trust me, I've been around the block a couple of times." She snickered before she turned to lead once more. "This way!"

Since we were speaking in English, we didn't have to worry about eavesdropping as nobody could understand us. Our foreign language did earn some peculiar looks, but I think what protected us was our clothing and the accompaniment of slaves. We looked well-to-do with our gold jewelry and nice garments and the fact that we had slaves, meant we had rich relatives in the city.

Gran was right again, as Mum and I found ourselves following her into the agora which was at the end of the street. The agora was huge, with temporary market stalls set up in the centre. It was surrounded on two sides by a building with colonnades called a stoa which housed permanent shops. Mum and I followed Gran into the market stalls first, to explore what was being sold.

We saw stalls selling eggs, hens, fish, meat, cheese, fruit, vegetables or even cooked food. The cooked food enticed me immediately. Mum and Gran didn't mind buying something to eat, however we surprised the slaves when we bought them food too.

At first when I held out the cooked chicken to the slaves, they wouldn't take it. They kept shaking their heads if I were doing something wrong. But after a little of encouragement, eventually they came forward and took the food whilst bowing and nodding out their thanks.

I happily ate some cooked pork which was seasoned with garlic and coriander, as I followed after Mum and Gran who were munching on some olives. Whilst we continued to 'window shop', we attracted many odd looks, especially by the poorer men and women. I remembered that well-to-do women would never go food shopping, as they would have slaves or servants to do it for them. Because of this, I also saw resentment in their eyes as everyone saw us as rich foreigners in their midst.

After looking over the temporary stalls, we headed towards the stoa to take a look. The shops inside the stoa were different rooms with wooden benches out the front, to show off their wares. We saw oil lamps or cooking accessories for sale, or even pottery, leather or wool merchants.

When we left the stoa, we headed inside a couple of craftsmen's houses which were on the other side of the agora. The craftsmen had varieties of iron or bronze items on offer, as well as gold or silver jewelry for the richer customers.

"Hey B." Gran waved me over, whilst Mum looked on some polished bronze plates. "What do you think?"

She was holding in her hands a beautiful gold bracelet which was curved around with two lion's heads on the ends.

"That's pretty!" I proclaimed. "Are you getting it as a present for someone back home?"

"No, I'm buying it for you B." She smiled as she put it on my arm. "It's to commemorate you circulating to Ancient Greece for your first time."

"Thanks Gran!" I gushed appreciatively before kissing her on the cheek.

She paid the jeweler with the coins from her purse, before we moved on again.

The afternoon was spent by looking around and purchasing a couple more things. The slaves that Aristides had assigned to us now not only carried our wooden shade covers but they insisted on carrying our purchases as well.

We walked into the centre of the agora once more. I requested a closer look at the statues on display as I wanted to see what kind of gods they were? However upon closer inspection, I learned that not all of the statues were of gods but some of them were of famous poets, politicians or even athletes.

I pulled out a small digital camera which I had been secretly carrying in my purse. When I thought nobody was looking, I took photos of the statues and of the agora, the stoa and even the Acropolis in the background of the city. I tried to be discreet with Mum and Gran carrying on as normal, but I wasn't discreet enough. I had caught the attention of a group of six men whom had been standing around one of the statues. They came over to see what we were doing.

"Good one, B." Mum rolled her eyes.

"Let's all remain calm, shall we?" Gran sung quietly.

"What is your family's name?" The man who walked in the lead, spoke first.

"Aristides." Gran answered. "We are his cousins visiting from Attica."

"Aristides, eh?" The second man looked impressed. "He's a popular politician in our city."

"Yes we know." Mum said curtly.

"We are loyal citizens who vote for Aristides." The first man said.

"Good for you." She muttered when Gran nudged her to mind her manners.

"You do not look or act like you come from Attica." The third man eyed us suspiciously. "I have cousins in Attica and they do not talk as you do."

My mother opened her mouth to say something else but my grandmother interjected; "there appears to be some confusion here. This can all be sorted out at my cousin Aristides house."

"Yes, you must come with us." The first man ordered.

Gran, Mum, myself and our slaves turned to head in the direction of the street which led to Aristides house, but the group of men cut us off.

"No, you come with us." The second man demanded as he pointed in another direction.

"That's not the way to Aristides house." Gran's eyes narrowed.

"You come with us this way." The first man grabbed hold of her arm.

"Hey!" I barked out as my overprotective Lokoti Werewolf instinct was ignited. "You let go of my grandmother NOW!"

The leader didn't let go, but now his friends came forwards in a threatening manner. I was just as tall as them, but the men weren't put off by my strong appearance. I even caught the one standing the closest to my position, inhale deeply with his eyes widening. Oh no, not another fish hooked by the bait of my frickin' annoying pheromones!

As I squared off against the men who were threatening my family, I saw two of the slaves put down our things. They looked scared that they might have to fight as well. The third slave bolted off as fast as he could through the agora, towards the street where Aristides' house was located to get help.

"You are threatening a noblewoman from a nobleman's family." Slave One nervously forced out. "Release my Master's cousin at once!"

"You will be arrested for this." Slave Two tried to warn off our attackers.

"No I won't be arrested, but instead I'll earn a profit when I sell you off one at time." The leader sneered. "The males will be sold to work in the fields and the women..." he paused to look over my grandmother in lust, "...I know exactly what kind of 'work' I will put you under."

Just as I was about to give this disgusting slave trader a going over with my claws; Gran beat me to it. BAM! She punched the leader in the nose so fast, not only didn't he see it coming but the inertia added extra force to the impact!

The leader yelled in anger as he stumbled backwards with his blood spurting everywhere, when I stopped the second man from hitting her in retaliation. I grabbed his hand in mid-air, snapped it back which also resulted in the sound of another 'snap' of his bone and as he cried out; I punched him in the abdomen, sending him reeling away.

I fought three men at once as I attempted to use my supernatural strength to take the brunt of the fight. I was trying to protect my weaker mother and grandmother but I soon saw that although they may not be physically as strong they proved they were just as fast. They skillfully ducked and dodged their opponents, whilst sending out their own punches and kicks so fast that the speed added to the force of their strikes. Circulators with their light speed reflexes could make self defense look like it was for kindergarteners!

Opponent number one I was fighting, was sent flying into a statue face-first; opponent number two down to the ground with a dislocated knee; then with opponent three I simply punched and punched and then I punched him again. Each time my supernaturally strong fist landed in his face, I heard the soft cracking noises of the front of his skull fracturing. Blood was streaming out all of the openings in his face, including his eyes...

"B, stop it!" Mum cried out frightenedly.

Huh, what was that? I turned to look her way to see that she and Gran were looking on in horror. When I looked back at our 'attacker' I found his face was worse than pulverized, but it looked like it had turned into red jelly.

Oh oh, don't tell me that the bloodlust which wasn't permitted to taste human flesh, still got the better of me by murder instead? In shock, I let go of the man's bloodied tunic and he instantly dropped to the ground half dead. Worse still, when I looked down at my clothes I saw blood splatter was all over them. I felt like I was in the OJ Simpson case, caught wearing with the bloodied glove.

"I'm sorry!" I pleaded for forgiveness, "I am so sorry! I didn't mean to! I don't know what happened, when the man grabbed you like that? I lost control...I'm sorry, I'm so sorry."

Suddenly Slave Two surprised us when he came forwards. By using one of the wooden shade coverings he'd been holding over our heads all afternoon, he drove the wooden edge right through my bloodied opponent's head! My injured attacker went from half dead to all the way there, in a single blow.

"What was THAT for?!" Mum squawked taken aback. "He would have lived!"

Slave Two calmly looked from his victim, to Mum and then out to the crowd which was quickly gathering. Isn't that just typical of human behavior? No one in the agora came forward to help when we were attacked, but they were willing to stare or talk about it afterwards.

"Our witnesses have seen a slave kill his Mistress' attacker, after being given orders by his Master to protect. My Master is a powerful politician in this city whereas you are not a citizen so if you were tried, you could be executed." Slave Two said quietly.

To protect me, 'my' slave thought he should finish the job so I couldn't be implicated. My mouth fell open at the cunning of this stranger who had waited on me all day. All I gave him was some cooked chicken for lunch and he was giving me in return was innocence in the eyes of the law.

"What's your name?" I asked.

"Styx, my Lady." He bowed his head.

"Thank you Styx." I said humbly.

After ten more minutes, Aristides arrived via chariot to see what had happened. Slave Three who had run for help, accompanied him. Aristides looked from my bloodied hands, to Styx's even bloodier ones, before facing the large crowd that had gathered.

"I ordered my slave to protect my cousins from Attica and my slave fought bravely. The Slave Trader was unlawful in kidnapping my cousins, even after being advised who they were. I declare that his death is just and from this moment on, the slave called Styx is free!" He declared.

The surrounding crowd all cheered and applauded, especially the poorer looking men and women who could have been slaves themselves. There was even revelry at how the death of one man liberated another.

In shock, I turned to look on Gran and Mum to see their reactions in all this and they appeared just as stunned as I was. Mum passed me a helpless shrug as if to say, 'just go with the flow'. Then I saw Gran begin to smile, as if she could have been amused at how things turned out. She would probably call it in her English accent, 'poetic justice'.

However I was feeling anything BUT amused, as I was horrified at my actions. I really wanted to talk about this to someone, or even to somebody who would understand how the bloodlust got the better of me...

...

...and Grant lay on his side, resting his head on his hand as he listened to my confession in bed that night.

"It was just like the expression, 'all I saw was red'. When that low-life grabbed Gran like that and I heard the disgusting things he planned? My blood began to boil and I almost changed! I wanted to paint the white columns of the stoa, red with his blood!" I said vehemently.

"Hmm." He frowned thoughtfully.

"Is that wrong of me? Well of course it's wrong of me, just as I know the bloodlust is what's wrong with me! But what do I do Grant? I feel so guilty and at the same time, there's still a small part inside that wishes I had ripped that human's heart out and eaten it." I confessed.

"Don't beat yourself up about it, B." He spoke softly. "Today you acted like a Lokoti Werewolf. We're overprotective of our mates and family and if I had seen a man grab you or my mother or even one of my sisters like that? I would have acted the same way."

"You would have?" I watched his face intently.

"Humans call it 'crime of passion' whereas we call it territorial behavior." He smirked.

"Are you serious, Grant?" I pondered on all of this. "What I did or felt was natural instead of supernatural?"

His dark eyes held my own, "why do you think the male Werewolves patrol the borders, B? We fight what's on the outside trying to get in, who would harm our mates, young and families. The Lokoti Werewolves cannot abide any threat to our loved ones. We drove out the hoodlums in Alma after the death of one of our own. We may not start a fight, but we'll damn well end it."

I turned quiet as I allowed his words to sink in whilst I looked on my 'Mr. Nice Guy' husband in new understanding. I reached my hand out to gently touch his face, before resting my fingertips over his mouth. Grant was lying in bed in his human form, but I wanted to touch a part of his body which could become one of his most dangerous assets in his Werewolf body, such as his elongated, sharp teeth.

Grant growled tenderly as he pulled me closer, so our bodies were pressed together. Then he rolled on top, whilst holding onto me tighter. I eagerly accepted his advances, as I allowed my teeth and nails to sharpen. I growled excitedly when I felt the same changes in him, with his sharp nails scraping over my strong muscles. That evening we made love in our Werewolf bodies, enjoying our supernatural qualities and the dark passion they could bring.

It was moments like this, or his understanding of what I was going through; which helped me to understand the Tribal Elders or the pack's reasoning for our marriage. As much as today was exciting traveling around the world let alone through time? It was all the better knowing I had an empathetic husband waiting upon my return.

~~~~~~

3rd October 2086

A couple of weeks later, I was invited to Gran's house for coffee along with Mum and Aunt Susan. As much as I felt honored at the invitation to join the older women for coffee and a 'chin wag'? I also felt a little nervous about the chance to talk to Aunt Susan properly since this hasn't happened from my wedding onwards.

I arrived at Gran's to find that Grandfather was absent and the three older women were already sitting at the dining table with their coffees and a plate of Anzac biscuits Gran had baked. Their catch-up was already underway, as I could hear their giggling even before I reached the veranda steps. But still I politely knocked before I carried in the plate of brownies Grant had helped me prepare the night before.

"Ooh, yum! Brownies!" Mum's eyes lit up as I sat down. "Are these the same kind that Grant made?"
~~~~~~

"Yup." I verified. "They're Aunt Julienne's recipe."

I caught Aunt Susan's eyebrows rise warily as her lips pursed together. Whereas Mum, Gran and I freely helped ourselves to both the biscuits and the brownies, Aunt Susan only ate the biscuits.

When Gran got up to make me a coffee as well, Mum inquired; "did you bring your laptop, B?"

"Uh huh." I pulled it out of my backpack which was sitting next to my chair. "The photos are downloaded and they're pretty clear too, even with me taking the pictures as quickly as possible."

"What photos are these?" Aunt Susan asked out of curiosity.

"B snuck her digital camera back in time to when we visited Ancient Greece." Mum smiled mischievously. "She took photos of the agora and the city to help with her assignments."

"What's an 'agora'?" She queried.

"The market place in Athens," Gran called back from the kitchen, "or in any Greek town or city in the ancient times."

Aunt Susan's eyes widened impressed as she leaned forward to look at the photos on screen. Gran returned with my coffee, putting the mug next to my computer and then she remained standing to look on. The three women all crowded around to see as I went through the photos one by one.

"What's that hill in the background which you've taken a few photos of?" Aunt Susan asked.

"It's the Acropolis." Mum smirked. "It looks different without that huge temple on top, doesn't it? When we visited they had just started to rebuild it."

"THAT'S the Acropolis?" Her mouth fell open. "But it looks like a plain ole, ordinary hill..."

"It did have another temple on top of it, but it was ruined in one of the many wars." Gran said simply as she sat down again. "The surviving temple today was the temple they were building when we were there."

"Ava Maria!" Aunt Susan sat back in her seat as if she was overwhelmed. "What is with time? It makes our little ones grow up and go to College, or if you're a Circulator you can simply just go back and relive events!"

"How is Derik?" Mum asked, as if she had sensed it was the question that I wanted to ask.

"He's well." She nodded. "He's started his third year in Medicine. He was invited to move off campus with a couple of friends, but he decided to remain in the Holy Spirit College Dorms."

"It was good seeing him about tribal lands during the summer." Gran said fondly. "Isn't he looking much older now! He was always tall growing up, but now he's filling out with maturity."

"You're not the only one who thinks so, Arabella." She giggled. "When he was home for the summer, he went out a lot with Rachel."

"Do you mean with Rachel and Mandy?" I thought I had misheard.

"No, just Rachel." Aunt Susan said breezily, whilst picking up another Anzac biscuit.

"Oh." I sat up straighter in surprise.

"So er, Derik and Rachel are an item now?" Mum thought she should clarify.

"Yes they are." She answered.

"Actually that would make sense." I rushed out. "They've always gotten along well and – and – and they would make the perfect couple since they're so nice. So together they can be nice and um, be together."

"That's what I'm hoping for." Aunt Susan raised her coffee mug to take a sip.

"I haven't seen Rachel and Mandy in a little while." Mum moved the conversation along again. "What are the girls up to these days?"

"Rachel is studying Naturopathy with Grandpa and Mandy helps teach with Aunt Susan and Mr. Lightfoot." I told her.

"Mandy's a good teacher and the kids love her." Gran grinned. "I'm only a substitute teacher now, since Mandy took over my classes."

"Man they grow up so fast!" Mum shook her head in disbelief. "I still remember like it was only yesterday when B, Derik, Rachel and Mandy used to play together all day, everyday."

"You either saw them in groups of two or four." Aunt Susan giggled in agreement. "You would see either B and Derik, or Rachel and Mandy. Or you would you see them all playing together."

"Now it's Derik and Rachel as a twosome, so it's fitting in a way." Gran mused. "Being Circulators we have to study temporal causalities but it's always fascinated me how relationships can be the very embodiment of this notion. A leads to B which results in C; Rachel and Derik grew up together and after a certain event, they end up together."

I caught Aunt Susan sneak a look my way in the corner of her eye, so I thought I should straighten things out once and for all.

"I'm sorry if my arranged marriage to Grant hurt your family." I began. "But Derik has always been my best friend and he always will be. I've never had romantic interest in the boy who was like my twin, which I said to him even before Grant and I came together. I'm pleased to hear that he and Rachel have found happiness with each other."

This made Aunt Susan pause and study me for a moment. Gran and Mum remained quiet as they watched and waited to see what would happen.

After a moment she let out a sigh; "you're right B. I'm sorry for taking my anger about your arranged marriage out on you. I guess in a way I had always hoped that you and Derik would end up together? But seeing how happy Derik is with Rachel instead, I can see what your Gran means with certain things or even with people working out for a reason."

"Besides if blame was to be allocated over B's arranged marriage? You can thank the Tribal Elders and the pack for that bright idea." Mum said dryly.

"C'mon Mum, I know you like Grant." I poked her in the side.

"He's Ian Elm's little brother and now Ian Elm is like a son-in-law being the brother of my daughter's husband. Oh yeah, I thrilled about this!" She said sarcastically which made us crack up laughing.

"Has Derik sent you any new photos of Cambridge lately?" Gran asked.

"Yes, he sent me a couple attached to his email last week. I printed them out and put them into the photo album and I thought I brought the album with me?" She next leaned over to check her large carry bag. "Nice one, Susan! I'd forget my head if it wasn't screwed on. What I wanted to show you was a photo that Derik took of these two trophies in his College Bar. He mentioned something about your ancestors on them or some such?"

"Oh yeah, Derik told me about them at Great Grandma's funeral." I recalled, before I turned to Mum and Gran. "He said in the Holy Spirit College Bar there is one trophy for darts with Vincent Moher's name on it and another for rowing with Jarrod Worthall's name."

"Really?" Mum asked impressed.

"Hmm, I remember." Gran gave a nod. "I read about them in my grandmother's diaries of her time at Cambridge."

Just then we all heard the sound of somebody's truck pulling up at the end of the driveway. Aunt Susan checked her watch, before frowning.

"Declan's twenty minutes early, he must have finished his shift at the Garage already." She mused.

"Why is he here?" Mum wondered.

"He's my ride home." She told her. "I told him I'd walk as I needed the exercise, but he growled at me."

Just then the women cracked up laughing at his typical behavior.

"Sounds like Declan alright." Gran finished off her coffee.

"Oh but he's a wonderful son." Aunt Susan smiled softly. "He's always helping around the house, especially in the kitchen. Mind you with his supernatural strength, he never runs out of energy."

"Is Declan dating anyone at the moment?" Mum inquired.

"No." She answered. "Whenever I've asked about it or suggested he ask a girl out? He always replies that he can't be with a human woman without harming her or risk changing her."

My eyes dropped as I began to drum my nails against the side of my mug. The topic of Declan dating disturbed me much more than the idea of Derik and Rachel getting together. I momentarily closed my eyes as I silently chastised myself since it was the very thing I had urged Declan to do; be with another woman.

"Hmm, I've heard that too." Gran frowned.

"Same here." Mum sighed. "But surely he can have dinner or watch a movie with a girl, or even hold her hand?"

"That's what I said!" Aunt Susan waved her hand in agreement. "But nope, he flatly denies he has interest in a particular girl. I mean, I've seen him check out girls so I know he's not the other way inclined. I've seen him watch them, sniff them or even once when he was sixteen; I caught him using his Werewolf eyes to peak through a girl's darkened bedroom window."

This made the mothers laugh and I must admit, a giggle did escape as I recalled seeing him do this myself – to mine.

"Men and Werewolves have something in common; they're both dogs." Mum expounded her opinion.

"That's not nice, Jess!" Gran lightly whacked her on the arm. "You're married to the tribe's 'quietest Werewolf' who probably feels bad if he steps on a blade of grass and breaks it."

This made Aunt Susan laugh even harder, before she turned my way; "B, would you be a dear and run and see if I left the photo album in the truck? I want to show you all the latest pictures Derik sent."

I stood up from the table and without another word, I walked out of the house and down the veranda steps. I spotted his light blue truck first and Declan whom was sitting inside second, at the bottom of the driveway.

At first my heart started to race by this chance to speak to him again. But then I wondered what to say? I couldn't think of anything deep and meaningful so maybe I shouldn't say anything.

As my feet crunched down the gravel drive, I heard Declan's truck's stereo system playing loudly. It sounded like he was listening to an old Bruce Springsteen album. He didn't see me coming because his eyes were squeezed shut as he was singing along.

"Hey little girl is your Daddy home? Or did he go and leave you all alone... Mmm, I've got a bad desire. Ooooh I'm on fire... Tell me now baby is he good to you, can he do to you the things that I can do, oh no? I can take you higher...ooooh I'm on fire."

I walked up to the passenger's side and leant on the open window. The music was playing pretty loudly, so Declan didn't hear my approach either. I stood there for about ten seconds unnoticed, smiling at the intense look on his face.

Declan continued to sing, still oblivious to my presence; "at night I wake up with the sheets soaking wet and a freight training running through the middle of my head, over you...you cool my desire. Oooh I'm on fire."

Next, I saw him sniff and then sniff again, when his eyes popped open. He was quick to turn his head in my direction before embarrassed, he leaned over to turn the volume down.

"What are you smirking about?" He asked gruffly but I didn't respond, all I could do was stand there and grin like an idiot. He noticed this, which started to make him smirk as well. "You look especially crappy today, B."

"I must have subconsciously dressed this way in the hope of seeing you."

"Did you come out to talk to me for a reason?" He arched his eyebrows.

"Your Mum sent me to fetch a photo album." I answered.

He immediately leaned over once more and rifled around for something under the seat. As he raised himself again, the said album was in his hand. He held it out whilst his bright blue eyes held onto my darker blue ones.

When he passed it over, he purposefully bumped his fingers into mine so he could brush them with his finger tips. His touch made my heart pound and my skin turn hot! Nervously, I lost my coordination and I almost dropped the album.

"Oh yeah, you're real cool, calm and collected. Is your self defense that bad, too?" He ribbed.

"Shut up." I felt my face flush.

"All the enemy has to do is hand you something and you go all spastic." He continued.

"Drop dead, Declan."

"This is the real reason why you're not allowed to patrol; as soon as you'd try to bitch-slap a stranger, you'd fall to pieces."

"Get lost!"

"I can't, I'm here to pick up my Mom."

"I'll let her know." I huffed before I started to walk away, when I changed my mind and returned. I caught his eyes widen when I reappeared at the passenger's window. "Why don't you come inside? You could be waiting a while, as your Mum, my Mum and Gran are doing their typical chin-wagging."

"You know why I can't, B." He said softly.

This made me pause as our eyes met and held once more...before Declan made himself look away first. He busied himself by changing songs on the truck's stereo as he turned the volume up again.

With the Bruce Springsteen song 'Hungry Heart' blaring out, I walked back up the driveway and then the veranda steps, as I reluctantly returned to the house.

~~~~~~
~~~~~~

~ 14 ~

2nd July 2088

It was a hot summer's day, so warm it was twenty-eight degrees Celsius in the sun. Grant was at work, building furniture in the large shed out the back of Ian's house and I felt too restless to sit indoors and write essays on Ancient History. Instead I went for a walk to the river to enjoy this glorious day.

As I sat on a large rock by the riverbank dangling my feet in the cool water, I looked on admiringly at the beauty in my surroundings. I was sitting in the shade as both the warm breeze and the coolness of the river improved my mood. I looked up at the clear blue skies above, then on the bright green, bushy leaves across the river and lastly, down at the sparkling dark blue waters which were steadily flowing past. I inhaled deeply the crisp, clean air as I said a quiet word of thanks to God or whatever deity existed for blessing us with such bounties.

Then I don't know why, maybe it was because I felt a rush of crazy inspiration from the nature about? But I threw back my head and I tried to howl!

"Aarrrooooo!" I cried out in a girlish voice.

OK that sounded so much better in my mind when I pictured it. I partially turned, so my dark blue eyes glowed turquoise. My teeth and nails grew slightly longer and I tried again in my deep, rumbling Werewolf voice;

"AAARRRRROOOOOOOO... er hm ergh!" I coughed and spluttered.

What the...? I'm a Werewolf, so why can't I howl like one? I've heard the male Werewolves howl plenty of times, so why can't I?

I threw back my head and gave it one more go; "aaaaAARROOOOOooooo!"

Nope, I still sounded weak and pathetic. I give up! As I returned to my human form, it was then I heard;

AAAAARRRRROOOOOOOOOOOWWWLLL!

What in the world...? Startled, I looked about when I saw something standing off in the distance, on the other side of the river.

A female Lokoti Wolf stood on all fours, looking at me with bright blue eyes coupled with her beautiful black, grey and white coat. Was that her? Maybe she was trying to help me in some way? For her, I'll give it one more shot;

"aaAAARrrrrrrooooOOOOooooo...!"

I felt my face burn in embarrassment for being so bad, especially around the animal who in legend, was responsible for my supernatural state.

The female Lokoti Wolf, nobly raised her head in the air and let her haunting cry permeate through the air.

AAAAAARRRRROOOOOOOOOOOOWWLLLL!

I looked on with admiration, when she looked back expectantly as if to say, 'well come on then, try again'. But I couldn't, I felt too ridiculous! So I did something else, I sang Iggy Pop's song 'Candy' to her;

"I've had a hole in my heart for so long; I've learned to fake it and just smile along. Down on the street the men are all the same; I need a love not games; not games…"

I sang out loud, putting as much emotion into the song as I could, when the female Lokoti Wolf raised her head and howled along with me!

AAAARRRRROOOOOOOOOOOOWWWLLLL.

"Candy, Candy, Candy I can't let you go! All my life you're haunting me; I love you so…" I sung away.

Suddenly I got fright when a male voice joined in!

"Beautiful, beautiful girl from the north; you've burned my heart with a flickering torch…"

My head whipped around to see it was Declan. He was dressed in his dirty work clothes which showed he had been at the Garage, but now he came out of the woods carrying a fishing rod and tackle box.

He continued to sing, "I had a dream that no-one else could see…you gave me love for free."

Declan was smiling in amusement at having 'sprung me' as such whilst he sang. He came to a stop in singing as well as walking, as he came to stand beside the rock I was sitting on. Then he looked over at the female Lokoti Wolf standing across, watching.

"You don't see that every day." He remarked.

"No, they don't usually come this close to the community centre of our Tribal Lands." I agreed.

"Maybe she felt sorry for you when she heard your pathetic excuse for a howl and thought you were begging for help." He smirked.

Typical, he HAD to have heard that, didn't he? I rolled my eyes as I looked away. "Maybe."

Just then the female was joined by a male Lokoti Wolf and beside him we saw three pups.

"Oh, would you look at that? It's her mate and family." He smiled on the sight.

The female turned her head to look at her mate and then the two Lokoti Wolves together looked back at Declan and I. Don't ask me how, but I had the distinct impression that the male and the female were looking on us the same way we were looking at them; they thought we were mates too. Then the parents and three kids turned and left the river bank, to disappear into the woods without throwing us another glance.

"Just like that they're gone." He sighed. "Oh well, I guess it was a treat for us to see them being so rare and all."

"Hmm." I frowned as I thought on something else. Why did the Lokoti Wolves think we were mates? Was it because we sung together? However I changed the subject by commenting, "I didn't know you liked 'Iggy Pop'."

"You didn't know?" He arched his eyebrows. "Frickin' Derik kept swiping my 'Iggy Pop' CD to take to your house!"

"That was YOUR 'Iggy Pop' album?" I gawked.

"No it was my Mom's." He said sarcastically.

Next, he further surprised me by coming to sit beside on the rock, but he kept a respectful distance. As I looked on, I wondered why after all of this time of working so hard to generally avoid me that he wasn't doing so now? The last time we spoke was nearly two years ago. I watched as he casually readied his fishing rod, by putting some bait from his tackle box on the end of his hook. Then with his supernatural strength, he easily flicked the line into the water a fair distance away.

"Have you finished work at the Garage?" I implied his grease-stained jeans and t-shirt.

"Yup." He answered whilst looking out at the river. "Fin gave me an early mark when I finished working on the Lightfoot's truck."

"So, how are you?"

Declan glared in my direction, "how do you think?"

My eyebrows rose at how fast his mood changed. When he saw my expression, his glare softened into a dissatisfied frown before he used this opportunity to look me over closely. His eyes freely ran over my tight t-shirt, especially with the v-neck which gave away a hint of cleavage. I felt myself begin to blush as I looked away uncomfortably.

Maybe I should leave? Hang on a sec, what's Declan doing here? Besides the obvious answer of fishing; I mean, why isn't he avoiding me?

"Why didn't you turn around and walk away again when you saw me, like you've been doing lately?" I referred to the past year or so.

"Grant's not here and neither is Derik, just as no-one else is either." He said coolly.

I tried not to smirk in amusement at his candor. His supernatural strength didn't just stop at his muscles, but even his language could have brute force.

"So you only talk to me when there's nobody else around?" I asked dryly.

"Yup."

"That doesn't happen very often, which means we may not talk much."

"It's probably for the best." He said simply.

Declan momentarily returned his attention back to his fishing rod as he jiggled it a couple of times before he started to reel it in. I watched as he pulled a 40 cm long Salmon from the water.

"Wow." I looked on impressed. "That didn't take you long to catch."

"It's a pity that my luck only extends to fish." He smirked.

I turned quiet as I watched him hold the flopping fish steady to remove the hook, then he sat it on the rock by his basket to put more bait on his line. He returned the line into the river, before he leant back on his other hand. We comfortably sat as we watched his fishing line be pulled along by the flow. We were silent for a good couple of minutes though, as I didn't know what to say.

"Thanks by the way." He suddenly said.

"For what?"

"For not going to Derik and Rachel's Housewarming, although I knew that you wanted to." He spoke plainly.

"I – I – I didn't go because I was scared that if I went with Grant then you wouldn't go."

"I know." He said curtly. "I wouldn't have."

I stared down at my feet which were submerged in the water, "how are they? How was the party?"

"Rachel and Derik are 'as happy as Larry'." He answered. "The Housewarming went as much as you'd expect. Nearly everyone from the Tribe came and gave their presents as they helped them set up their home."

"Did they like the dining table set?" I asked furtively.

Declan flashed a look of annoyance, "the one your *husband*," he said icily, "helped his brother make?" Then he looked back out to the river, "yeah they like it fine, it hasn't been chopped up into firewood."

That made me laugh as I couldn't imagine Derik taking an axe to it but the image of Declan smashing it possibly in his Werewolf form, came to mind.

He said bitterly, "everyone in this tribe gets a Housewarming but me."

"Then find a female Werewolf to marry and bring her back here then we'll throw you a Housewarming." I tried to joke.

"Oh yeah, now there's an idea." He said sarcastically. "So I'll just go to Europe and find some mutilated woman from her change into a European Werewolf to drag back here. But since I'm the only European Werewolf that's not a man-eater; as soon as the tribe throws us a Housewarming and maybe I get at least one night of jollies with her? I'll just stand back and let the Lokoti Werewolves or even the Circulators of this tribe kill her for trying to eat a human! Or worse, I'll kill her instead when she tries to eat my human brother or mother. Then the tribe can throw me a Funeral for her."

I held my tongue as I stared into the water, but Declan was on a roll with his temper ignited.

He continued on, "hang on, maybe I'll find myself a female Asian Werewolf instead? Oh darn it! They still eat human too, don't they? So what else does that leave me with, a female North American Werewolf? Oh dear, some North American Werewolves don't even know that they're Werewolves! They 'black out' every time they change and eat any human nearby. Or, maybe I'll find a female North American Werewolf who knows about her dangerous ways but still she's happy to snack on human every full moon."

I rubbed my face hard as I listened to his rant. I could understand his anger and frustration on the subject. I just wished I could have done something to help though.

His voice rose in fury, "the one female Werewolf in this world let alone this tribe that would have made my perfect mate as she DOESN'T eat human is married off to another.   The Lokoti Werewolf she's mated to could have married a human woman but no, he gets the tribe's first female Lokoti Werewolf instead.   Whereas I can't mate with a human woman without harming her and my one and only chance of happiness is taken away!"

He had worked himself up so much that he no longer could sit still. He whipped his line out of the water as he quickly reeled it in with his supernatural speed. He put the fish into his basket, before he stood up and picked up the basket and rod to carry.

"Declan, wait!"

He had just started to stalk off when he hesitated however he didn't turn around as he tried to keep his back to me.   To meet his angry gaze, I walked around to stand before him.   When our eyes met and held, I watched his widen as they took me in.

"It's not Grant's fault -" I began, but he cut me off.

"Not Grant's fault?" His blue eyes turned ice cold. "NOT Grant's fault?!"

"You and I hated each other for years..." I pointed out, "...you treated me like crap and I hated you for it."

"I told you, B." He rolled his eyes. "I couldn't do anything because you were Derik's girl."

"That's a load of shit because Derik and I were best friends all our lives before his intentions turned romantic!"

"Exactly!" Declan snapped. "You were always Derik's girl! The two of you played soccer together whereas I wasn't allowed to play because I could harm someone with my supernatural strength. The two of you would study together when you knew I hated schoolwork. You two were always doing things without me, so no wonder I got pissed off! You and Derik were the only kids in the tribe that weren't afraid of me but then you started excluding me. The only time you talked to me B, was when we fought!"

Now it was my eyes that widened...all those years I had hated him for his meanness? I was unaware that he was acting out because he saw me as starting it.

"Talk about miscommunication." I said apologetically. "But you can't hate Grant for my arranged marriage, Declan. With you and me, it was just the wrong place and the wrong time -"

"The wrong place?" He looked on like I was an idiot. "You're the first female Lokoti Werewolf who's practically the girl next door! That first night you changed and I stopped you on the border? I even thought that you could have changed just for me so I wouldn't be alone anymore! We grew up together in the same frickin' tribe! That's NOT the wrong place, B!"

"We were definitely the wrong time then, because growing up I hated you! You're constantly biting people's heads off! Do you remember what you said to me after we 'did it', Declan? You told me that it was a one-time thing and you wished it hadn't of been me but I was the only girl you could touch! Well, what would you have done if I did end up marrying Derik? He sure as hell treated me better than you! What would you have done then, as you would still be alone?"

Declan let out a bitter laugh as he momentarily looked away. I thought that my words had hit home, until he leaned forward to look me right in the eye to say;

"You would never have married Derik, even if you hadn't changed." I arched my left eyebrow warily as I wondered what his game was? "The night you changed and you were over at our place for dinner? When I walked in on you and Derik making out or I should say he was trying to make out; I saw the look on your face. You hated him kissing you and touching you like that."

My mouth fell open as I looked on, taken aback. His face wore a smug expression as he saw that his words made more of an effect than mine.

He continued, "the night Jack died when I drove you home in my truck and I put my hand over yours? I felt your heart race and your skin heat up. When I kissed you on the border, you kissed me back! I certainly wouldn't have pounced on you in the woods later if I saw the same look on your face when you were with Derik."

I felt so bad that I felt wretched and I had to look down at the ground.

"I – I – I tried to talk Derik into remaining friends, or best friends more like." I found myself confessing. "But -"

"But he was stubborn? I know all of this, B." Declan said softly. "You loved Derik as a best friend but he saw you more than that." I looked up into his waiting blue eyes when he gave a rueful look. "It's sad, isn't it? I definitely have way too much time on my hands, being the permanently single person of the tribe. I may appear that I don't care but it's just defense tactic. I may look like I don't see but I've been watching you for years, B. I watched you grow as I smelled your Lokoti Werewolf pheromones before you changed. I can even guess your emotions by your aura changing colours being a Circulator."

My voice broke, "if you...have been watching me for years...then what would you have done if I never...changed into a Werewolf?"

"You mean how would we be together without me turning you or harming you in the throws of passion?" He asked to which I gave a nod.

Just then he stepped up so close, we were only an inch apart so he could look hungrily into my eyes.

"Trust me B, I would have found a way. I would have moved heaven and earth to find it. Hell, it may have even been fun trying, as we could have got to experiment a little." Declan gave a brief mischievous smirk, but it was quick to fade. "But because you married Grant that has been taken away for good."

Then he side-stepped me in supernatural speed and just as I turned my head; I barely caught sight of his muscled back disappear through the trees as he stormed off. Just like that he was gone.

~~~~~~

20th July 2088

Last night my husband and I were invited to dine at Vine's house with the rest of the Elm clan.

On one end of the table sat Aunt Julienne as the matriarch of the family, as on the other sat Ian as the patriarch. At the 'kids table' sat the youngest generation of Elm's in the shapes of Ian's, Vine's and Hannah's children. However, the now older Leaf sat at the table with the grown-ups with his pregnant new wife.

He wasn't a Werewolf and the way things were going with the pack, it would appear that the Elm's were going to skip a generation by not activating Leaf but it was a sure fire guess that his first born would be a son. Then he would be activated instead.

Everyone fussed over Sonia, the whole night through. Throughout dinner they passed her dishes of food first as they kept cracking jokes how she 'was eating for two'. Four years ago, the same attention was lavished on me being the newest member of the Elm family. Then either Ian, his sisters or mother cracked jokes like; "no B you go first, as I'm sure we're going to hear the announcement soon on how busy you and Grant have been in the marriage."

Once upon a time the Elm family as did the whole tribe, saw our joining as the 'bees knees'. Our marriage was the 'best thing since sliced bread' because it was uniting three of the tribe's oldest families. Since it was two Lokoti Werewolves marrying, everybody thought that we would have a litter of kids by now, thanks to our virility as Werewolves.

Nope! It wasn't Grant's fault that our second bedroom was never turned into a nursery, it was mine. To his credit, he never said a bad thing nor did I sense any resentment about my condition.

I tried to keep my jealous thoughts from triggering my bloodlust at all the attention on Sonia tonight. It was then I felt Grant's hand take hold of mine under the table give it a supportive squeeze. Although I appreciated his sympathy, I couldn't stop my thoughts from turning towards another who didn't see my infertility as a disability but as a blessing instead.

"Why doesn't he leave you?" Declan whined with longing. "Why doesn't he leave you for another woman who can? Why can't he leave you and then that would leave you with me."
~~~~~~

As I sat quietly at the Elm family table with my husband beside, I watched Sonia bask in all of the attention because of her pregnant state. I even started to fantasize what it would be like at another family's table as I reminisced back to all the times I had eaten at the Sabre's growing up. I recalled the numerous times Declan and I would fight or how Derik and I would always team up.

Declan and I would fight over the last piece of garlic bread. We would fight over the last glass of soda. Hell, we even fought over where we wanted to sit at the frickin' table. I would be sitting down and minding the seat beside for Derik as places became scarce with so many guests which included my parents and grandparents. By the time Derik's bottom came even near the seat, he would get a surprise when he landed in Declan's lap instead!

"Nup, I'm sitting here." He would say smugly. "Go and find another seat."

"DECLAN!" My best friend would shout. "I was sitting here first!"

"Then why is it my ass in the seat and not yours?" He taunted. "Now shove off!"

However the only seat left at the table would be on a corner, far away from me. Instead of taking that seat, Derik walked off in a sulk to eat in the lounge room. Then I would always vacate my seat to go and eat with him.

"You are so mean that you're going to end up alone for the rest of your life!" I said coldly when I thought he was just being nasty.

Now being the older and wiser whist recalling scenes from my childhood, I remembered something else; Declan's face would fall when he saw me move away. My stomach dropped like it was made of cement as I felt riddled with guilt. In light of my recent conversation, what I said to him when I was a 13 year old, now sounded like the cruelest thing imaginable.

"B...?"

"Bianca?"

"B!"

Huh, what was that? I came back to the present to find the table of Elm's looking on like I was an idiot or even having some kind of seizure.

"Sorry, what?" I snapped out of it.

"Would you like another bread roll?" Ian waved the basket in front of my face.

My eyes fell on Sonia's plate and I found one already sitting next to her roast dinner. She had been offered a bread roll first...again.

"No thanks." I looked down at my empty plate.

I had been especially hungry tonight and although I could have eaten second helpings, I didn't because I was sulking. Ian shrugged and as he started to move the basket away, Grant snatched one up.

"Thanks for offering me one, bro." He rolled his eyes then he proceeded to break the bread roll open to butter both halves.

"Ladies first little brother! Didn't we teach you anything?" Ian teased, before he offered the basket to his mother and sisters.

Grant may have been a Werewolf but he was cunning like a fox; he inconspicuously put one half of his buttered bread roll onto my plate as he casually ate the other.

"Thank you." I breathed out so only he could hear then I felt him squeeze my hand again.

I know all of this could have made me sound like a spoilt brat but honestly, these feelings were a long time coming. Over the past three years since the news of my infertility came out, a series of small misgivings snowballed into my current jealousy.

Two and a half years ago when I was shopping by myself in the general store, Macy Hindbark was served first even though I was before her. She was three months pregnant with barely a bulge and there were much less things in her basket than there were in mine. But because she was pregnant, Mr. Barley asked me to stand aside. Six months after that, at a tribal function in the meeting hall when Grant and I were lined up at the drinks table to get some sodas? Jenny Bean was served before us because her 5 year old daughter was having a temper tantrum. Jenny Bean's obnoxious 5 year old scored the last can of Creaming Soda even though we were in the line ahead and we had waited for the longest. Last year when we had the Elm family over for dinner, Aunt Julienne made the remark to my husband;

"Oh Grant, I was storing your old crib in the garage for the day that you have kids? But since that's not going to happen now, I gave it to Harriet and Bobby Mason for their Housewarming. I didn't think that you'd mind as it was just sitting in the garage gathering dust."

Harriet and Bobby Mason's Housewarming had been the scandalous 'shotgun wedding' of the tribe, due to the fact that Harriet was four months pregnant and the couple were only 16 years old. The Tribal Elders had asked a couple of members of the pack such as Dad and Ian, to have words with Harriet's father. It was done to prevent him harming Bobby when he found out his daughter's condition. I think the Tribal Elders deliberately didn't ask Grant as if they thought he had enough on his plate with his wife's reproductive failure. The Elders as well as the pack treated the issue of me not being able to procreate like it was a taboo subject.

I still felt bad for Grant that he got lumped with a 'lemon' like me. If it wasn't for our arranged marriage, he could have fallen in love with a human woman with whom he could have had rug rats. Instead, he gets the first female Lokoti Werewolf who is also the first Lokoti Werewolf in the history of the pack who can't breed. Within the tribe there are two other women who are reputedly barren, but since they aren't Werewolves nor are married to Werewolves, I think they're less judged than I am.

I practically dropped my half eaten bread roll as I slumped back into my chair. No wonder Aunt Julienne has given up, as I'm not just letting down Grant but I've let down his family too.

*****

I was relieved when my husband came up with an excuse for us to leave the family gathering earlier than expected.

Quietly, he led me by the hand out to his jeep, opened the door for me and closed it too once I was inside. Then we drove out of the community centre towards the hill where our house was, with one hand on the wheel as the other rested on my leg. Neither of us said a thing and I noticed in the corner of my eye that he snuck numerous looks my way, but I deliberately kept my head turned.

As soon as he pulled up in our driveway, I was quick to open my door and I accidentally slammed it shut. Sometimes I was still getting used to my supernatural strength and I felt like the clumsiest let alone the strongest girl in the tribe. Immediately, I unlocked the front door of the house and I went inside as he was still climbing out.

However once I was inside, I didn't know what to do with myself! So I went into the kitchen where I proceeded to make myself a cup of chamomile tea. I heard Grant come inside and shut the front door which I had left open.

Out of politeness I offered, "would you like a cup of tea?"

"No thanks."

I vaguely became aware of my husband coming to stand in the entrance way of our kitchen. I deliberately avoided eye contact as I carried out my task. As soon as my cup of tea was made, I brushed past to carry it outside to drink on the veranda steps whilst gazing up at the stars.

I like looking up at the stars... I don't think it was because I was a Werewolf that I appreciated the night sky, but as a Circulator the great beyond comforted me. Every time I looked up at the thousands of celestial objects I thought to myself; "I have living relatives up there somewhere."

Next, I heard the front door open and close again as Grant came out to sit beside. He gave up on being polite or sympathetic, so instead he went straight to the punch line.

"B, you're still holding back." Grant said unhappily. "I can sense you're trying to hide something as it feels like there's a glass wall between our minds. I see your torment but I can't hear your thoughts. Since we're two Lokoti Werewolves, I should be able to hear you as you can hear me sometimes."

This annoyed me, because besides the obvious that I was trying to hide my residual feelings for Declan? I didn't want Grant snooping around my private thoughts! I had fallen in love with him, but he certainly pushed his own feelings and expectations hard enough.

"Grant, isn't it enough that you can feel my emotions? Isn't it enough that we're biologically joined together? Isn't it enough that we lie together, night after night, week after week, month after month? What more do you want from me?" I moaned, before I added on bitterly, "besides a child?"

My husband opened his mouth to respond but I stood up and went back inside before he could speak. However he dutifully followed me into the house where he found me in the living area.

"Can we please talk about this?" He asked tiredly as he shut the front door.

"Talk about what?" I quipped as I took one more mouthful of tea.

I left my mug sitting on the table to jog up the stairs and go into the bathroom. I had my evening shower before I reluctantly went into the bedroom and hopped into bed. Grant was lying on his side facing me, but I rolled onto mine so my back was to him.

"Why are you wearing pajamas?" He asked unhappily.

"Why wouldn't I be wearing pajamas?" I retorted. "It's what people customarily put on when they do go to bed."

"You hardly ever wear pajamas just as I haven't since we married." He said simply. "By you wearing the fabric, it's another wall you're putting up about yourself."

What I wanted to say was that I felt like I didn't have a choice on sleeping naked, especially with his consistency towards the marriage bed. But I bit my lower lip to prevent me from saying something that I might regret. Instead I sat up, pulled off the pajama shirt over my head before I kicked off my pajama pants. Then I lay back down as I returned to my side with my back facing him whilst I stared in annoyance at the wall.

"B, please." He spoke softly as I felt him wrap his arm about my waist. "Don't be angry about your condition."

"I'm the most useless woman out there." I said miserably. "Sonia is three years younger than I am but because she's pregnant, everyone thinks she's better than me."

"No they don't."

"Yes your family does, Grant."

"It's all in your head B, because you're hurting right now you can't see straight." He rolled me onto my back so he could meet my eyes. "But if you wanted to, we could try harder for pregnancy."

I looked on puzzled as I thought we had been 'trying' since the first day we were married?

He tried to hold my gaze as he moved closer. "I talked to Fern and he told me that there have been instances in the past where a Lokoti Werewolf had married a woman who was so-called 'infertile'. However the woman became pregnant for mating with the Werewolf."

"How?" I demanded. "You and I have been at it every day since we married so what are we doing wrong?"

"Think on your Nana for a moment, she and your Grandpa only had one child, your father. Didn't you ever wonder why?" He pointed out.

"I thought it was because Grandpa's body changed, like you said Lokoti Werewolves can. I thought his body suspected that it would be dangerous for her to have any more children, just like the reason why I'm an only child." I pondered.

"Ling was told when she was 16 years old that she wouldn't be able to conceive after she was treated for tumors on her ovaries. She told Fern before they were married but he didn't care, he loved the woman and not just what the marriage could produce. At the time, he was an apprentice Medicine Man and he knew there were certain things that he could try as a Lokoti Werewolf. Just as our bodies can stop our fertility, we can also increase it." He explained.

This gave me pause...Nana was supposedly infertile like I was? I never knew that Dad was a miracle baby for them! It explained a lot actually, in particular the way they would look on Dad with so much love, which filtered down to his only child.

Nana and Grandpa always acted like they couldn't do enough for my family when I was growing up. Both sets of grandparents would converge on my parent's house. The women would laugh altogether in the kitchen as the men would chuckle at their mates play fighting over how to decorate my birthday cake with candles. Grandpa held me in his arms as Grandfather laughed at my eagerness to attack the cake or even the bowl of icing.

"You'd better get a good grip there, Fern." Grandfather joked as he watched me squirm. "She's eyeing off the icing most of all."

"I've got her." Grandpa chuckled, before picking me up in his arms.

"Grandpa let go...!" I whinged.

"Nice try little one, but patience is a virtue!" Dad tweaked my nose.

"I'd listen to your father if I were you." Grandpa smiled. "Patience does pay off, B. Your Nana and I had to be patient and because of it, we were blessed with your father. Now you're just as special as he was, being an only child."

However Grant brought me back to the present with the feel of his hand running up and down my side.

"Your Nana became pregnant after being married for a year. It took a little work, but your Grandpa knew the medical alternatives as well as a couple of supernatural ones." He continued.

"But we've been married for four years and nothing's happened." I pointed out.

"Like I said B, there are certain things we could try."

My eyebrows arose in skepticism, "then why didn't you suggest this when I first told you that I was infertile three years ago?"

"Because we're already using one of the methods." He sighed.

"We are?"

Grant snickered, "didn't you wonder about the constancy of my affection?"

"Well, yeah..." I blushed as I momentarily looked down, "...I just thought it was because of my pheromones or something."

"They do help." He growled contentedly as he caressed my cheek with his nose.

"Then what else do you want to try?" I watched his face turn serious as he looked hesitant to say. "Grant, what is it?"

"I don't want to scare you..." he said carefully, "...but I could change into my Werewolf form and not hold back. With your Lokoti Werewolf strength, you would be able to handle mine. I've already noticed that I don't have to hold myself back as much with you as I've had to with a human woman. But we could go...a little wild."

"What do you mean?" I asked warily.

"Tonight I could have you in my Werewolf form then tomorrow night you could also revert to your Werewolf form. Like this for the next three weeks, we would alternate. I would always be in my Werewolf form but you would swap as we try to find your most susceptive form for fertilization." He thought aloud.

"Why wouldn't you be swapping like I would be?" I wondered.

"In our Werewolf form, a male Lokoti Werewolf is his most fertile."

"You mean we would 'do it' in our Werewolf form like on our wedding night and a couple of other times since then?"

"Yeah, but I would go even more wild than that."

"MORE wild?" I blanched. "You're not going to beat me up, are you?"

"Nooo!" He half laughed and half growled at the idea. "I would never put you at risk because remember, we're overprotective of our mates. However if we did this, you might experience some discomfort."

Oh oh... my heart skipped a beat from just hearing about it. I echoed nervously, "discomfort?"

"I could never knowingly harm you, B." He frowned. "But my actions would be made clear to your body by what I was trying to do. It would be less about pleasuring each other as I would become very driven."

"Oh." I looked away as I anxiously chewed on my lip.

I was starting to dislike the sound of this but after mulling it over, I changed my mind. I thought my families, the Riverclaw's, the Wisetail's or even the Elm's still expected a rug rat from me. I mean, if Grandpa and Grant have talked about this, maybe everyone was still waiting? Although no-one has said anything, I felt like my reproductive inadequacy was letting everyone down. I didn't want to be the childless wonder of this frickin' tribe anymore!

"OK." I took a deep breath. "Let's do this."

"Bianca." He spoke gravely. "We don't have to, but I thought you should know it was an option -"

"No!" I said firmly. "Let's just do this."

"B -"

"Grant, let's just get this over and done with."

He sighed sadly, almost chastising himself for mentioning it now. But my husband still did his 'manly duty' by rolling on top of his wife. As he moved into position, he frowned further when he felt me tense up.

"Just try to relax." He kissed my ear. "Remember, I could never knowingly hurt you and if I suspected I might be, my body would stop immediately."

~~~~~~

20th August 2088

Grant didn't injure me in anyway. His body expanded with his extra muscle, he bared his razor sharp teeth, his brown eyes turned their glowing silver and his claws appeared on his hands and feet.

He had his wife in his Werewolf form and growled a lot, whilst he panted hard as he moved hard. He took complete control over our movements in bed, moving me into different positions, some of them I liked and some of them I didn't. He was demanding almost to the point of pain, but he never crossed the line. It was like his body really did sense where my threshold was.

It wasn't just his prowess that was relentless, but during the whole time I felt his Werewolf will beat down on my reproductive organs rebelliousness. When I was also in my Werewolf form I heard, *BREED*; but when I was in my human form I only felt its effects. We had to change the sheets every morning during this baby making festival. Surely there was enough of Grant to populate five new tribes!

After the three weeks of this baby-making circus was up; on the last evening when Grant was winding down he was still constant with his show of love. He kissed me over and over again whilst breathing hard out of his nose. I felt his sharp teeth graze my lips but they didn't puncture. His heart pounded through his expanded chest before I felt him shrink back to his human form to go to sleep. Periodically through the night I felt him nuzzle affectionately as he held on tightly.

Yesterday morning as I was using the bathroom to brush my teeth, I had a realization. It occurred to me on this particular Tuesday morning that I was two days late which NEVER happens. My body was like a clock, as it kept perfect time just as did Mum and Gran's. I guess it was because we were time manipulators that our bodies kept their own chronometers. I felt goose bumps appear on my skin as I paused half-way through brushing my teeth...

... can I be? Could this be it? Can Bianca Elm really be pregnant?

Instantly I started imagining what it would be like if I had a baby boy or girl. If I had a boy, he could be a Werewolf when he grows up. If I had a girl, she probably wouldn't be a Circulator since I was called the last, but could she become a Werewolf instead? It would be nice no longer being the tribe's one and only female Werewolf and she could be a strong woman with her abilities. There was so much I could teach her as I would show her the best the world had to offer.

Gleefully, I rinsed my toothbrush and then I happily skipped down the stairs. Grant smiled as I passed him sitting at our dining table, eating his toast.
~~~~~~

I went into the kitchen to open the fridge and stared as I tried to decide what I wanted to eat?

"We don't have anymore eggs." I announced chirpily, shutting the fridge door again.

"I'll pick up some more on my way home." He stood up from the table to carry his plate and mug to the sink.

Next, he pulled me into his arms to bestow my goodbye kiss before he departed for the day to build furniture with his older brother.

"You smell different." He commented.

My heart leapt with joy! I've heard male Lokoti Werewolves can smell when their mates are carrying young, just as all Werewolves could smell when a female was pregnant. I think it was because of our predator inclinations coupled with our highly tuned sense of smell.

"Really?" My eyes widened.

"Uh huh." He pulled me closer to run his nose along my neck. "You smell even better than usual."

"Truly?"

Grant laughed as he pulled away slightly to look on. "B, you're glowing!"

"I'm late." I said proudly.

His eyes widened with my news before he looked from me to the calendar on our fridge. On different days we wrote down our appointments, events, due dates for my assignments or I even left little stars when I started and finished my period. I saw him quickly count the days since the last star and then he beamed.

"That's wonderful news!" He laughed and picked me up to spin me around.

"Do I really smell different?" I asked when he put me back down.

"Hell yeah," he said softly as he held me close, "you don't just smell like choc-chip cookies now, but you smell like choc-chip AND macadamia cookies."

"Are you kidding me?"

"I like choc-chip and macadamia cookies." He growled hungrily as he gently began to maul my neck with his mouth.

I laughed when I felt his teeth tickle and then I turned my head to kiss back. That morning in the kitchen, I kissed the father of my child in both relief and happiness at our condition.

*****

I floated around the house for the rest of the day in a dream like state. I felt like I had finally gained acceptance into an exclusive club that nearly all the tribe belonged to. The name of this club was parenthood and our membership packs were kids hanging from our arms.

Finally I felt just like everybody else in the tribe. I wasn't such an oddity now, being the first female Lokoti Werewolf as well as a barren one. I belonged...! I finally, completely belong! I was just like everybody else now!

I wanted to go to Mum's and Gran's houses and tell them. I wanted to jump on top of my roof and yell it out for the whole tribe to hear! Bianca Elm is PREGNANT! Bianca Elm is with child! Bianca Elm has a bun in the oven and can get pregnant just as everyone else can! My body was finally living up to the responsibility of my arranged marriage.

I was so excited that I couldn't concentrate on Uni work. Instead, I put on my MP3 player and I went out to the greenhouse to do some light work such as watering and pruning. After lunch, I had finally settled down enough to concentrate on an assignment which was due next week. I sat down at the dining table, with my laptop and my books open to type up my draft.

It was then I felt a twinge of pain in my abdomen - oh oh - that felt like period pain. No it can't be, it must be my imagination. I tried to refocus on the task at hand but I felt it again! Then I felt another cramp and another...

...no, please no! No, no, no! The familiar painful throbbing kicked-in, making my hips, lower back and even my legs ache.

"NO!" I whimpered as I bent over the table. "Please no...!"

After a couple of minutes of sitting still as if I could ignore it and it would go away; it didn't so I slowly raised myself to my feet. I made my way upstairs and went into the bathroom to check. Yep, I had it alright. I sunk onto the cold, tiled bathroom floor. The chill made the aching worse, but right then I felt I deserved the pain as I curled up into a ball and cried.

I hate my body! I HATE it! Why did it have to let me down this way? It's always letting me down! I HATE IT I HATE IT I HATE IT! I cried from both the emotional pain of this set back and from the physical pain as my cramps grew worse. I'm still a disappointment. I'm still a freak of nature. After all of Grant's hard work and how his eyes lit up this morning? I was NOT looking forward to seeing his disappointment.

Helplessly, I laid next to the bath tub as I cried. I don't want to be me anymore and five years ago the boys at Ben's party wanted THIS body? What a laugh!

But poor Grant...poor, poor Grant...he was forced into this marriage like I was. We both had tried to make the best of it, but I let him down again. No matter how hard I try to do the right thing, fate keeps kicking me in the teeth.

Out of the blue, I heard the sound of his jeep pull up out the front of the house. I caught a glimpse of my watch and saw it was only 2.03 PM in the afternoon so he was home early. He must have driven fast too because when he pulled up, I heard the sound of his wheels skidding to a halt on our gravel driveway. I listened to the front door open and close downstairs before he raced up the staircase.

He barged in through the bathroom doorway and I saw his eyes widen when they took me in.

"Grant...? I'm so sorry!"

"Shhh B, c'mon now." He knelt down to slide his arms underneath.

My husband picked up his wife to carry her out of the bathroom and into the bedroom where he laid her out on top of the bed.

Grant moved quickly as he grabbed the spare blanket that sat on the rocking chair, to lay it over me. Then he hurried back to the bathroom and I listened to him open up the mirror cabinet before he poured a glass of water. He returned to the bedroom and sat beside whilst holding out the small bottle of painkillers and the H2o.

"No," I tearfully shook my head, "I want to feel the cramps today."

"Don't be foolish." He said sternly as he held the glass and the tablets even closer.

I shook my head again before I looked away. Grant growled in annoyance as he put down the glass of water, opened up the small bottle, placed two tablets in his palm and then he sat me upright. He stubbornly placed the two tablets in my hand as he placed the glass of water in my other. He wasn't going to take no for an answer.

Tearfully, I put the drugs into my mouth and I swallowed them with the water before I lay back down again. Grant came to lie on my other side to spoon me from behind, as he massaged my aching hips.

"I was assembling the Mason's new tallboy when I felt you." He spoke with his mouth right over my ear. "I felt your pain first and your fear second. I surprised Ian when I bolted out of his shed and ran for my jeep."

His words reminded me of how Grandfather immediately came home from work when he felt Gran was in labor, or how Dad left a hunt on a full moon when he felt Mum was giving birth. It made me cry harder as I felt like even more of a failure.

"Shhh..." he murmured whilst rubbing my tummy, "...shhh."

"You're supposed to sense it when I go into labor, not when I get period pain!" I cried hard.

"B, I sense it when you're hungry." He chuckled in my ear. "I even sense what kind of food you crave."

I sobbed into my pillow as my husband's kindness made me feel more guilty!

"This isn't the end of the world, Bianca Grace Elm." He spoke firmly. "We can always adopt because of the war, there are plenty of orphaned or starving kids out there who need a good home. It's not the end B, it isn't. We have a roof over our heads and food in our greenhouse and kitchen. We have created a loving home that can provide well for an adopted child."

My heart hurt even more it turned into a black hole inside my chest, sucking in all signs of hope and light into the crushing abyss.

DON'T BE SAD B, PLEASE DON'T BE – he thought.

I said dismally, "I don't really smell different, do I?"

There was a pause before he sighed, "I thought that you did."

"How?"

"I don't know, but you did."

"But not anymore?"

Grant changed the subject as he held me tighter, "I'm serious B, there are a lot of homeless children whose parents have died. Last year some of the strangers whom we gave food to, were a couple with four children. Two of those kids weren't theirs, but they were looking after them after their parents passed away."

"Really?"

"Yep."

"Great, so the next time we have orphans turn up on our land then we'll adopt those." I said bitterly.

"Why not?" I felt him shrug.

Frickin' hell, I could just hear the tribe talking about that next; "Bianca Elm can't have kids so her husband brings home strays that he finds on patrol."

I burst into another round of tears as Grant patiently did his best to console.

~~~~~~

1st September 2088

As all of this was happening, the unusually warm weather kept up. It was another beautiful sunny day and with all that was going on in my life even if I wasn't producing any; I couldn't concentrate on Uni work. I had to get out of the house and my head.

For a little while I sat on the veranda steps, watching the wind blow through the trees of the surrounding forest. Then I decided that I should go for a walk. I stood up, checked to make sure I had my keys before I walked down the driveway and onto the dirt road.

I headed down the hill towards the community centre. I thought I might walk to the general store and get some ice cream which I thought would make me feel better. Sweet things always made me feel better...

As I walked with the sun warming my skin and the wind blowing through my hair, I did begin to feel better. I enjoyed the twenty-five minute trek and I could see the tribe's younger generation also thought this weather was too nice to stay indoors; a game of soccer had started with a couple of people sitting on the side to watch. It made me recall how I used to play soccer with Derik, as Mandy and Rachel would sit on the side cheering us on. I missed those days when life was so simple; schoolwork and soccer instead of arranged marriages and infertility.
~~~~~~

When I walked towards the general store with the petrol pump out the front and the garage beside, my heart raced. It usually did whenever I approached because I would wonder if Declan was working? As I came closer, I saw that Ben and Toby were repairing a motor on the back of a small boat but Declan was nowhere to be found.

Rock music blared out as they toiled away. It was 'The Cult' which the familiar tunes reminded me of the last time I heard this song; Declan was leaning over the motor of a truck in his dirty jeans and tight t-shirt. I became so caught up in my little reverie that I walked into a couple of people as they were leaving the store.

"B!"

I snapped out of it when I realized it was Mandy and Rachel. My face lit up when I saw my oldest friends and they looked equally pleased to see me. With everything that has been going on, they certainly were a sight for sore eyes! Although Rachel and Derik were newlyweds, neither of us sensed hostility about this in the other. I threw my arms about Rachel and hugged her tightly, before I hugged my other friend.

"How are you B?" Mandy asked. "Long time no see!"

"Yeah, it has been a while." I agreed. "How are you two?"

"Good." She shrugged. "My teaching job is keeping me busy."

"Yeah I was just saying to her how frightened I was at the prospect that she can now influence the minds of our younger generation." Rachel joked, making me laugh.

"Now you understand how worried I felt about the idea of you taking up naturopathy and providing many of the herbal remedies our Medicine Men use." Mandy rolled her eyes.

"How's your degree going, B?" Rachel queried.

"Good thanks." I nodded. "I'm doing my final year now. I had to do it over five years instead of three because I'm taught via correspondence."

"Then you'll have a Bachelor of Arts in Ancient History, huh?" Mandy grinned. "Good on you!"

"Are you going to do a Masters and then a PhD afterwards?" Rachel asked next.

"I don't know yet." I shrugged.

"If you do, you could teach academically." She went on.

"Just who is she supposed to teach academically, Rachel? She's a Lokoti Werewolf! B can't leave our land for extended periods of time and there aren't any open Universities in this state." Mandy reminded.

"She could do guest lecturing or something, OK?" She rolled her eyes. "Stop being so pedantic all the time, Mandy! You really do sound like a teacher!"

"Shouldn't you also be of a critical mind?" Mandy teased. "You're really making me nervous by the fact that your husband and our tribe's second Medicine Man is using what you make up."

I almost fell sideways from laughing so hard, making a couple of passersby look on strangely.

"Come on then," Rachel shook her head, "let's get you indoors before you're arrested for drunk and disorder."

They grabbed an arm each to lead me down the road, away from the store.

"Where are we going?" I asked once I was able to talk again.

"To my place." Rachel said simply.

"For coffee and a catch up." Mandy added on.

My eyebrows arose in surprise as I hadn't seen Rachel and Derik's place yet.

*****

Their 'new' house was on the other side of the community centre. It was small as most houses on tribal lands were, as well as constructed of wood. Inside was renovated, with new wooden floors and freshly painted walls.

"Declan, Ben and Toby helped Derik do up the house before we moved in." Rachel advised as we came in. "It still smells of paint and lacquer, I'm afraid."

I may not have attended Derik and Rachel's Housewarming, but my family did. I used the excuse that I had several assignments due so my husband wouldn't feel obligated into going. Although Derik and Grant were polite to each other now, I could still sense the underlying tension between the two whenever they saw each other. That was the reason I told the women anyways. The real reason was so Declan wouldn't have to boycott his own brother's Housewarming.

Their house was decorated as much as I expected it to be, with second hand furniture and tribal made decorations such as the woven rugs on the floor. I even recognized one of Mr. Lightfoot's landscape paintings on the wall of their living room. When Mandy and I followed Rachel into her kitchen – combined – dining area, I found Ian's and Grant's constructed pine dining table and chairs, along with a buffet unit.

"Oh good, you're using it!" I gushed as soon as I saw them.

"Of course we're using it." She laughed. "It's a nice present from the Elm family."

"I'm sorry that I didn't go to your Housewarming Rachel -" I began.

"B, I know it's also from you and Grant too." She said patiently. "Just as I know why you both didn't come, so sit down and shut up."

As Mandy and I pulled up a seat at the table, we watched Rachel switch on her kettle as she prepared our beverages.

"I know there's still some tension between Derik and Grant." She went on. "When you were first married, Derik was angry for months."

I looked on Mandy for her opinion and she said, "Rachel is giving you the politically correct version of Derik almost buying silver bullets and going gunning for Grant."

"After his first year at Cambridge, Derik asked me out when he was home for the summer. At first I wondered if I was the 'rebound girl'." Rachel continued.

"Oh." I sat up straighter. "But you know Derik's not like that, don't you? I mean, he wouldn't have asked you out if he didn't honestly like you."

"Of course I knew that!" She laughed again. "I married the male, didn't I?"

We laughed along with her, before I asked, "well can I hear all the goss, such as how the two of you got together?"

"It happened quite quickly." She admitted.

"And suddenly!" Mandy agreed. "Derik was home during the holidays two years ago when the two became inseparable. Whenever Derik was home for holidays, they were joined at the hip! I knew when he was back in the country because I wouldn't see Rachel except with him."

She gave her friend a withering look for her complaint before she poured the boiling water into the waiting mugs.

"First it's B who's married off." Mandy mockingly rolled her eyes. "Then it's Rachel and Derik going all goo-goo over each other. Meanwhile it's me who gets the shaft as all these weak women dump my company in preference to getting laid."

"I told you that you should go out with Toby and get some yourself." She shook her head.

"Yeah, like I'm going to date Toby all because the horny little toad wants to get in some action!" Mandy sneered.

"Does Toby like Mandy?" I looked at Rachel.

"But Mandy won't give the poor guy the time of day." She sighed as she carried our coffees over before she returned to the kitchen. She opened up the pantry again and pulled out the biscuit tin. "Toby's asked Mandy out *repeatedly*," she stressed the word, "but she refuses to go out with him."

I looked worriedly on Mandy, "it's not because you still like Declan, is it?"

"Declan? What the...? No way!" She cracked up laughing like it was the funniest thing she'd ever heard.

"Man you are behind B, as that craze passed two years ago." Rachel placed the biscuits in the centre of the table.

"More like three years ago, thank you very much!" She said indignantly.

"Oh?" I looked on.

"It was a no-win situation." Rachel sighed. "Derik told us that Declan said that he couldn't 'mate' with her because she was human."

"Apparently European Werewolves are different from Lokoti Werewolves." Mandy turned serious. "They can't mate with a human woman without accidentally killing her or worse, turning her."

As the three of us sat there and frowned, I half lied, "yeah I think I've heard that before."

"Poor Declan, he may never get some because of this big 'stop sign' in his face." Rachel said sympathetically. "I think he gets lonely. I mean, he has the company of his Mom and the two come around frequently to visit; but it's not the same thing."

"It's probably why the man is cranky all the time." Mandy winked.

"Apparently the European Werewolf lust is just as bad as the bloodlust." She informed.

"Did Derik tell you this too?" Mandy wondered.

"Derik worries about his older brother." She frowned. "As we all do. Derik thought that two years ago, Declan was considering traveling to Europe to look for a female of his own kind."

My heart sank as I recalled that two years ago, I yelled at him during a clandestine midnight meeting in the woods to go do this very thing. I quickly raised my coffee mug to hide behind.

"But I think Declan was worried about leaving his mother behind or how long it might take so he changed his mind." She ended.

Mandy looked my way in curiosity, "B you're one of the pack, what would they do if Declan did suddenly leave one day?"

"You mean would we try to stop him?" I asked.

"Yeah."

I shook my head, "I don't think so. I mean, we would miss him of course as he's one of us, but I don't think they'd stop him. Declan's got a good hold on the bloodlust and I think the pack trusts him."

"I don't think they could physically stop him if he did want to leave." Rachel blanched. "I've only seen him in his Werewolf form once, but I tell you now I'm glad he was weaned from eating human, because if he wasn't? There's not many who can stop him with his size, strength and speed."

"Not even the pack?" Mandy's eyes widened.

She shook her head, "maybe not even the pack."

The two turned silent as we sat back and sipped on our coffees.

"So, what does Declan look like in his Werewolf form?" Mandy wondered.

"You were over him three years ago, huh?" She teased.

"Excuse me for being curious about this supernatural creature living in our midst!" Mandy rolled her eyes.

Rachel looked to me to answer, I guess because she thought I regularly saw Declan in Werewolf form during hunting on a full moon.

"Well um," I stiffened, "he doubles in height as he triples in width. He looks like a huge, hulking, hairless wolf with four claws, sharp teeth inside of a short snout and glowing green eyes with his round pupils turning into long slits."

"Wacky-do." Mandy's eyes widened even further, as she looked at Rachel. "I've seen his European Werewolf eyes before, as has anyone who's made him angry. But if he's stronger and faster than the Lokoti Werewolves, you wouldn't want something like that hunting you."

As they shared a laugh, I looked away uncomfortably. My eyes settled on something brightly coloured, sitting on the buffet unit. I leaned over to look on closer.

"Is that a 'Big Bird' doll from the TV show that used to be on before the War, 'Sesame Street'?" I asked out of curiosity.

What were kids toys doing inside of Rachel's house? I thought she had recently babysat a young relative or something.

"Oh." Her mouth wavered before she and Mandy exchanged a long look.

I wondered at their hesitation. "What?"

"Go on, tell her." Mandy ordered. "B's our friend and she's going to find out sooner or later."

Rachel turned to face me to say, "I'm pregnant."

She and Derik had only been married for two months and already they're expecting their first child? Meanwhile Grant and I who've been married for four years struggle on? Now my husband has given up and is talking about adoption. As my heart split into two, one half crumbled into dust and the other continued to beat onwards for the sake of friendship.

When I caught their worried looks, it made me rush out, "congratulations Rachel, I'm really happy for you and Derik. I think the two of you were meant to end up together..." my voice broke as my eyes watered, but I continued on, "...don't worry about me, I'm not upset over you carrying Derik's child. It's just that recently Grant and I encountered another set back in the reproduction department."

Rachel tried to put her hand over mine, but I pulled back. She and Mandy exchanged another unhappy glance.

Tearfully, I laughed at myself, "look at how ridiculous I'm behaving! Don't worry about me, I've got my period and we all know how hormonal I can get when that happens."

"Did you know there are some herbs that you can try?" She began. "There are plants that act as an aphrodisiac, just as there are some plants which can -"

"Increase my ovulation? Change the lining of my uterus? Or even change my cycle?" I laughed bitterly. "Don't worry about it Rachel, really. We've even tried Lokoti Werewolf mating techniques but that didn't work either!"

I stood up angrily to carry my mug over to the sink, as they shared a glum look. This made me feel childish and stupid as it's not my friend's fault that there's something wrong with me.

"But you know what?" I forced myself to sound cheerful as I dried my face with my sleeves. "Rachel, you and Derik are going to make great parents. You have Derik with his good heart and we have you with your sense of humor. This baby is going to be well taken care of, as you'll have Aunt Susan who's a great teacher to be the kid's grandmother. We have Mandy who's smart and able to help the kid with their homework, like she helped us growing up. Then you'll have me, the tribe's first female Werewolf looking out for it. I may not be able to produce life but I'm frickin' good at taking it away. So if somebody even looks at your kid wrong? They'll have to answer to me."

Rachel stood up and walked over to where I was standing to hug me tightly.

"You're hired." She announced. "You're gonna be our kid's godmother as you guard our bundle of joy."

"For the rest of its life, I promise you." I held her back before I kissed her cheek, "and I have a damn long life span, I can promise you that."

"Is it true that Circulators can last in a mortal existence for a thousand years?" Mandy giggled. "You would outlive Rachel's baby's baby."

I pulled back when I saw her sitting there, watching. I didn't want the third person of our trio left out. I asked, "can Mandy be co-godmother with me?"

"She'll be the godmother of my next child." She said simply.

"Oh I will just?" Our friend raised her eyebrows. "B's not going to have to teach me sword fighting to become your second child's bodyguard too, will she?"

"What's wrong with sword fighting? It's fun! You can hack people's heads and arms off." I joked.

"Uh huh." My old friend pretended to look nervous. "B, have you ever heard of Darwin's theory of evolution? Maybe it's a good thing that you can't have kids, otherwise we would have sword waving, miniature Werewolves running around the tribe, unable to contain their bloodlust."

Just as we burst out laughing, at that moment Derik came home. He was carrying his 'medicine bundle' which was an old black, leather doctor's bag. As soon as he walked into the kitchen area and saw me, he beamed.

"B!" He greeted as he came over to kiss my cheek. "How are you?"

"Good thanks Derik. How's being a Medicine Man going?" I eyed off his 'medicine bundle'.

"An apprentice Medicine Man." He said modestly. "Yeah, it's going alright. I had to take Declan with me when I set Jonah Huntington's broken leg."

Right as he said that, Declan also appeared in the kitchen doorway. His eyes immediately widened as soon as he saw me. I had to force myself to quickly look away.

He told his wife, "Declan had to hold Jonah still as the pain was pretty bad, with the bone protruding through the skin."

"Eew!" Mandy cringed. "Derik, can't you see this coffee in my hands? Do you think I wanted to hear that as I enjoy my afternoon cup?"

The husband and wife laughed at our old friend and I think a few more jokes were thrown around the room but I didn't hear them. My eyes crept towards Declan once more, who stared back.

"Excuse me." He abruptly turned to leave.

Everybody looked on in surprise at his sudden departure. But I felt bad that I could be chasing him out of his own brother's house.

"No." I said firmly, causing Declan to look back. Quickly, I turned to Rachel and Derik and kissed both of their cheeks. "Congratulations on your news but I should be going now." I walked away as I went over to kiss Mandy's cheek next. "I'll catch up with you guys soon."

As I brushed past him, I breathed in his maple syrup scent whilst I overheard him do the same to me. I speedily walked up to the front door, opened it and then I shut it again on my way out. With my sensitive hearing, I managed to catch their words.

"What was that about?" Derik queried.

To which Rachel answered, "B's happy for us with our news, she's just sad at her own circumstance. Apparently she and Grant had another set back on the road to having their own family."

Hastily I walked out of the community centre and towards the hill. It was 4 PM and the day was changing colours with the onset of afternoon. I power walked as fast as I could all the way home. As I hurried, I felt my last remaining piece of heart stop beating and slowly turn to dust.

Why me why me why me why me why me why me why me why me why me why me why me why me...?

Why can't I get pregnant too? Rachel and Derik were only human, so why can't Grant and I have children considering we were both supposed to be the virile Werewolves? Or at least one of us was as I remained defective...

I hiked up the dirt road past Uncle Julian's and Aunt Danika's house, past Nana and Grandpa's house, past Gran and Grandfather's house, past Mum and Dad's house and eventually made it to the top of the hill where our house was. Although being a Werewolf kept me in good shape, I found myself gasping for breath not because I was unfit, but because I simply felt like I couldn't breathe.

As I walked up my gravel driveway towards the veranda steps, I slowed. There was something sitting on the top step. When I came closer, I saw it was a small posy of ferns with a single flower from somebody's greenhouse, tied together with a piece of red ribbon.

I came to a complete stop as I stared down...the flower was an orchid and I knew of only two families who grew orchids in their greenhouses and one of them was the Huntington family. Declan had been to the Huntington house that afternoon with Derik, to set Jonah's broken leg.

Quickly, I raised my head to scan the surrounding woods to try to see him. I sensed he was hidden just as I sensed he was watching me. He must have raced up through the woods, to deliver this before I arrived home.

Eventually I walked over to pick up my offering, before I sat down on the steps with it. I carefully held the fragile flower in my hands to examine. The orchid was peach coloured with a yellow centre and it looked truly and utterly beautiful, especially against the delicate green fronds of the ferns.

It was Declan's way of comforting me, I knew it. When I held it up to my nose, I smelled his maple syrup scent on the ribbon from where he had been holding it. It was a touching gesture and it did help me feel better, particularly for the fact that it was the very first time that I had ever received flowers.

~~~~~~
~~~~~~

~ 15 ~

13th July 2089

Not only being the tribe's first female Lokoti Werewolf let alone a barren one was a bitch; so were my mood swings. I was put on a medication by Vincent to increase my ovulation, which in turn also increased my hormone-induced temper. Then hewould harvest the eggs to work on outside my body.

My Calculator experimented with IVF, ICSI, Blastocyst Culture and Assisted Hatching, using the sophisticated 25th Century technology in the Medical Bay at Circulate Headquarters. However as he used medical ways of treating normal infertility, with my case he also had to treat this as paranormal infertility. Instead of simply introducing Grant's sperm to my eggs, he also hit the eggs with gamma rays, or dark matter, or photons or even different types of light frequencies which produced differing levels of radiation in several experiments.

"If you want to treat B's eggs with radiation, why don't we return them to our time frame and visit the worst-hit areas after the nuclear bombing?" Grant asked sourly.

"Because the residue of the plutonium based radiation isn't strong enough." Vincent replied.

Hell, my Calculator even took them into the Science Lab one day and put them inside of what looked like to be a futuristic microwave oven. I was advised that it was in fact a device which could create small, temporary quantum singularities. Or in layman's terms, he put my eggs down a black hole... we looked on like he was nuts!

"I'm trying to alter the temporal signature of the eggs to match Grant's sperm." He said coolly then he handed my husband another sample cup. "Now if you wouldn't mind going into the next room and do what I assume is one of the things a Werewolf can do best?"

I overheard the low, dangerous growl emitted between his clenched teeth as he glared. However without another word, he snatched the cup and quickly left the room.

At each of these sessions where I lay on the examination bench to undergo the uncomfortable procedure of Vincent removing my eggs; Grant dutifully stood beside, holding my hand in his role as the supportive spouse. But I could sense that by this stage, his saintly patience was starting to run thin.

To give credit where credit was due, Vincent was trying his best to solve a problem which was unsolvable. In the beginning he had advised that there was no man-made way to change living tissue's temporal signature, short of putting it into temporal flux which is how a Circulator is created. However he postured that astronomically, the temporal signature of matter is converted this way all the time in outer space; by time differentials in the gravity well of certain stars or even black holes. Vincent said it was worth a try to apply the same techniques to my harvested eggs.

However with all my domestic discontent? Our home on Tribal Lands was paradise when compared to the radiation sickness and pollution in the outside world. When we caught snippets of news reports on the old communication methods of AM or FM radio, what we heard was:

"The US Government refuses to confirm or deny that a mutated strain of Measles has taken over the southern states of Texas, Louisiana and Mississippi, however ..."

"Tentative talks have begun between the US Government and China to disarm the last of the nuclear missiles, however..."

"The Marines were called in to dispel the protest march which turned violent on Government controlled agricultural produce. The protest march was just outside of Minneapolis, however ..."

"Hospitals have reported a new height has been reached in the birth-defects poll. Not only deformities such as missing limbs are hampering our newest generation; but cancer has appeared in the newborns, however..."

Or my personal favourite was;

"New test results have concluded that radiation sickness has effected sperm production. Government-run medical clinics are now offering payment to healthy sperm donors, however..."

Grant and I were sitting in our lounge room sipping on home-made lemonade, as we listened. News reports were sketchy, but they were the only news we had on what was happening outside of Alaska. In the UK or in some other parts of the States there was limited TV. Although our isolation in Alaska may have protected us from fall out; it also isolated us from the burgeoning media which was reforming after the War.

When we heard the last report, I looked over to my husband, "it looks like Uncle Sam is signing you up. Your wife can't reproduce but who says you can't? Your country needs you, Grant."

"B that's just not funny." He grumbled as he stood up from the couch.

He got up to carry his empty glass into the kitchen as I sat by myself, leaning further into the couch.

"I thought it was." I said quietly. "I mean, just because our Tribal Elders tell you who to marry, who says that you still can't have kids?"

He walked back into the living room to snatch up my empty glass as well as give me a glare, before he returned to the kitchen with it.

I overheard him turn on the taps at the kitchen sink, as he began to wash up the glasses with our dinner mess. I stood up from the couch and dawdled in to help. My husband was quiet as he washed up whilst I dried and put away.

"Grant seriously," I frowned, "you're a fully-functioning male. You still have the option of taking another female and knocking her up."

It was this night that I realized I had reached the end of his infinite patience. He paused as he squeezed his eyes shut and I heard a dissatisfied growl come out. Next, I heard him mumble, "...she's only acting like this way because she's hormonal. It's the drug to increase her ovulation which has made her talk like that. B's just hormonal and drug induced, that's all."

Pursing my lips, I quietly watched him finish the washing up. He didn't say anything else especially to me, as he completed the dishes. Then he drained the sink, dried his hands on the spare tea towel hanging on the oven before he faced me again.

"B, I want you to listen to me and I want you to listen carefully." His voice was deep and growly, implying he wanted my attention.

"What?"

"I want you to stop the tablets."

"What?" I blinked.

"I want you to stop the artificial hormones or whatever Vincent has you on."

"Why?"

"Because they're not working."

"Huh?"

"The only thing that they produce is PMS − not babies! I don't want you to take another pill or undergo any further treatment for infertility."

"But Grant -"

He cupped my face in the both of his hands, "if my supernatural sperm can't impregnate you the natural way, then I doubt these scientific ways can either. Stop stressing B, please. Like I said, there's always adoption and after the War there would be plenty of children that need a good home."

"But there aren't plenty of children!" I objected. "Certainly not healthy ones! You heard the news reports, either men or women are becoming infertile, or babies are born mutated -"

Grant interrupted; "I've seen these sick children, B. They arrive on our borders with their desperate parents. They're either missing a hand or a foot, or both hands and feet. Sometimes what they're missing is even worse than that..." my mouth fell open in surprise, but he continued, "...the parents are sick with radiation sickness and they're also suffering from malnutrition. Hundreds of times, the parents have begged if they can't stay can their children instead? And each of these times, we've had to say no."

My husband's eyes watered with guilt over the things he's had to do on patrol in protecting his land and family. But I could understand the pack's and the Tribal Elders decision to move on the strangers; history was full of instances where people had lost their land, living and home from invasion. It would also be unfair in deciding the criteria for who could stay, so the Elders decided that nobody could. Another reason was to protect our natural resources against overpopulation.

"B," his eyes held my own, "what if this is fate's way of telling us that we should adopt? I could ask the Tribal Elders for permission in granting sanctuary for one of the orphans I would usually turn away."

Oh great, isn't this just peachy? I could just hear the rumors now, 'Bianca Wisetail can't have children, so her husband has to bring home mutants'. As if Grant telepathically overheard this, he disappointedly turned away and went upstairs.

Poor Grant, you try so hard to do the right thing but what do you get? An immature wife, who's barren and has a massive insecurity problem because of it. I groaned as I rubbed at my face. Is there a rule book somewhere, like a book of comportment and manners; a book which tells people how to act in arranged marriages, or how to cope with infertility gracefully? Because right now I would buy a hundred copies.

Eventually I turned off all of the lights downstairs before I meandered upstairs. I quickly stripped to have a brief shower before I gradually climbed into bed, cleansed of the day's dirt but not absolved from my sins. Grant was in bed before me, I noted. I turned off my lamp and we laid there in the darkness. This time, my husband kept to his side of the bed as we lay with our backs to the other.

I kept expecting him to suddenly roll over and wrap his arm about my waist, but tonight it didn't happen.   Maybe I should offer the reconciliatory gesture instead? But nope, my stubbornness made me remain where I was. Although I was consumed by self hatred, oddly enough I was fast to fall asleep...or I hoped that I had fallen asleep, because what I saw next? I prayed that they were nightmares.

I dreamt of a hospital or what I thought was a hospital. I had never seen one in real life, but only in the movies we watched. But it was big with lots of different rooms where people lay ill or dying. Only this hospital wasn't as white and clean as the hospitals I saw in movies, this one was dank and dirty. There weren't enough medical supplies and definitely not enough staff. People seemed to be either rushing around or lying in pain.

Floating along in my dream-like state, I moved through the overcrowded hallways, with sick or injured people lying in either beds in rooms or on stretchers in the hallways. I was drawn inside of a room with flickering lights where I saw a pregnant Caucasian woman scream in agony on an operating table. A young man of Asian descent appearance and a middle-aged African-American woman, stood in between her parted legs, looking anxious.

"She's hemorrhaging." The African-American woman frowned.

"And what do you want me to do about it?" The Asian descent man asked helplessly.

"You're the doctor!" The woman retorted, who must have been the nurse. "You think of something!"

"I haven't got a doctors license!" The man objected. "I did two years of biology at college, before the government officials slapped a doctor's coat on my back!"

"Then you're lucky." The nurse sneered. "The last 'doctor' I assisted, didn't even know what a doctor's license was. He was a First Aid Instructor who was shoved into an operating theatre."

The pregnant woman who was bleeding and in agony, looked over her huge stomach at her 'medical team'.

"Where's my husband?!" she screamed hysterically.

"Your husband?" the 'doctor' echoed.

"Alright so he's not my husband, he's just the guy who knocked me up! But where is he?" The frightened patient demanded.

"Er..." the nurse looked pained, "...you mean the man who dropped you off at the emergency ward?"

"Yes, that's him! That's Brian!" the Caucasian woman nodded her pale, pasty face.

"Um well, he must care for you because he rushed you here as quickly as he could." The nurse tried to console.

The 'doctor' passed the nurse a knowing look, "he did a runner, didn't he?"

"Before we could get him to sign the admissions papers." The nurse sighed sadly.

"What?!" The scared and bleeding patient screeched. "It was HIS idea that we fucking well have this thing! I wanted to take the abortion pill!"

"It was a good thing that he wanted to, because if your child is healthy? Then you'll be entitled to the Government's Living Assistance." The doctor said brightly.

Then the patient couldn't talk any longer as she screamed in agony and bled profusely.

"Oh look, I can see something! Nurse, can you see something? I think it's the baby coming!" the doctor cried out excitedly.

"I think you mean that the baby's crowning, doctor." The nurse tried to kick him with her hint.

"Push! Push! Push!" The doctor screamed at the woman giving birth.

"Wait!" The nurse objected. "The patient is bleeding too much! She could bleed to death!"

"But we have to get the baby out!" The doctor argued back. "Push Fiona! Push!"

"My name isn't Fiona, it's Felicity!" The patient yelled back.

"Whatever! Just push!" The doctor shouted.

After much more shouting and screaming, eventually a tiny thing with an odd shape and covered in blood, emerged from the patient. The 'doctor' and the nurse who had more experience, exchanged a grim look as he picked up the baby in his bloodied hands. After a moment I saw why...the baby wasn't just missing most of its limbs but its head was concaved.

"Is that it? Is that my baby?" The patient cried as she weakly tried to sit up to see.

"It's a beautifully baby er, boy." The nurse gave her patient a brave smile.

"Are you sure you wanna build her hopes up like that?" The doctor muttered to the nurse.

"Look at how much blood there is? The patient isn't going to live just like the baby isn't." The nurse sighed sadly.

Then I realized something else which was wrong with this scene; the doctor or nurse didn't bother inducing the child to breathe. The nurse instead took the newborn out of the doctor's hands to carry it over to the woman. The woman cried as she took her newborn into her arms and placed it over her breasts. She was so delirious with blood loss she didn't see her child's defections. The baby lay there like that, not moving and not breathing and the woman wasn't far behind from joining it.

"We'll just leave you to have these first few minutes with your child." The nurse patted the woman on the shoulder, before she shot off a pointed look to the doctor.

The medical team left the room and the woman for her last few moments of life left with the new life that she tried to create.

"I'll go sign the death certificates." The doctor sighed in defeat once they were out of the room.

"I'll go have a cigarette." The nurse said glumly in the style of 'another one bites the dust'.

The two curtailed off, walking in opposite directions of the overcrowded hallway.

I thought that sad scene was the end of this nightmare? But for some reason I floated behind the nurse as if I were being pulled after. That was until I happened to glance inside one of the rooms we passed by.

Through one of the many doorways in the busy corridor, I caught sight of a wounded man lying on a bed. Then as if my invisible handcuffs which were tying me to the nurse were released, I hovered into this particular room instead. This hospital room looked different to all the others, because it looked exactly like my bedroom. It had the same furniture in the same layout and had exactly the same rug on the floor.

However, I did notice that there was someone lying on top of the queen sized bed. It was a man with bronzed, smooth skin and long black hair, wearing just a pair of jeans. This man reminded me of someone, or maybe it was just because Lokoti Werewolves only wore a pair of jeans when they changed? But mind you, this man did have the same skin and hair colouring of a Native Alaskan. But if only I could see his face clearly, which was covered in blood.

Curiosity killed the cat, and it also made me hover closer in my non-corporeal form. I looked closely at the body to find more blood, which was coming from the multiple bullet holes which were all over the man's body. There were several in his legs, arms and even more so in his torso, including his heart. The reason why there was so much blood on his face was because there were three more bullet holes there too. The bullet holes were seeping blood yet there was something strangely familiar about his broken up face...then his eyes snapped open and they were glowing silver!

Oh my God, it's Grant! It's my husband Grant! He's been shot!

Finally the nightmare ended when I jolted awake. I was back in my actual bedroom in Alaska, shaking from such a horrible vision.

Oh no, was that a dream? The horrible feeling in the pit of my stomach said otherwise. Although I'd been asleep, I sensed it wasn't just a dream but it was an omen! Somewhere else in the States, a woman died from childbirth tonight. This meant that sometime in the near future my husband could die from being shot multiple times. I knew it was a vision, I just knew it!

My mate's biological bonding to his wife woke him up. As if he empathically sensed my distress, he rolled over and sleepily uttered out, "B?"

"It's nothing..." I managed out.

"Then why are you scared?" His head rose to look on in the darkness.

"Am I?" I tried to lie.

"Did you have a bad dream?" He rubbed his eyes.

"You could say that."

Grant's arm crept about my waist as he pulled me to him. Then he yawned out, "it was just a dream, B. Go back to sleep."

I wished it was, truly I did but the dread sitting in my stomach like a bowling ball said otherwise. The image of his punctured face was scalded into my brain.

"Get some sleep, B." He grazed his lips along my forehead. "In the morning you'll feel better, I promise."

I closed my eyes as I tried to concentrate on the sound of his breathing as his herb garden scent filled my senses. Our close contact did feel good with his heart beating hard in his chest and the feel of his warm body pressed against mine. He's alive – your mate is alive – my Lokoti Werewolf instincts tried to belay my fears.

However my all-knowing sense as a Circulator couldn't give in so easily.

*****

The next morning I awoke by the feel of the end of the bed sinking when Grant sat down to pull on his work boots. He had quietly dressed for work to allow his wife a sleep in. But instead of the extra sleep being appreciated, I sat up in alarm.

"What's the time?" I asked worriedly.

"It's 8.23 AM." He answered, briefly looking over his shoulder at his digital clock. "I thought after your nightmare last night, you'd need the extra sleep."

But I surprised him when I practically leapt out of bed to land in his lap! I flung my arms about his neck as I held onto him as if for dear life.

"I'm sorry for being such a bitch last night and for the past couple of weeks, Grant. I'm so, so sorry..." I rushed out, "...of course I'll stop those horrible tablets."

"I know you're sorry, B." He gave a patient smile. "I felt your regret last night."

"You did?"

"Uh huh."

The convenience of having a husband who was empathically attuned to his wife made me smile. "You're really handy to have around, you know that?"

"I do try." He chuckled. "So, what are you going to be doing today? Since you've finished your BA, you're a 'free agent' now."

"I was thinking of instantaneously phasing to London either today or sometime this week to buy some more books. I have an idea for my thesis when I start my Masters in Ancient History." I announced.

Whilst I was sitting in his lap with his arms about my waist, Grant listened. I sensed he appreciated my verbal apology as his hands ran up and down my back.

"If I sense your departure from tribal lands, then I won't feel worried that you've run away permanently." He joked.

Talking about departures, though...? The horrible feeling of dread reappeared in my stomach thanks to my 'dream' last night.

"Um, I may have to go to Circulate HQ to check something out." I added on lastly. "So if I'm not home when you come back, I'm either in London or on Mars."

"Ladies and Gentlemen that's my very own 'Light Person'; space and time are hers to command." He affectionately messed up my already messy hair before gently lifting me off his lap. "I have to go but I should be home before five."

Just as my husband stood up from the bed to leave, I jumped on him again! He laughed when he felt my legs wrap around his waist as my arms returned about his neck. Hell, I even dug my claws into his back in a possessive manner.

"Be late for work this morning, just this once?" My dark blue eyes met his dark brown ones. "Please...?"

"It wouldn't be 'just this once' because for my birthday, I was late for work too." Grant broke out in a grin. "As well as the time earlier this year, late last year and shall I go on?"

"You're complaining about 'getting some'?" My eyebrows rose in mock offence.

"I love my Werewolf wife!" He laughed out loud as he purposefully fell backwards onto the bed with me on top.

*****

Grant was only an hour late to build furniture. I dressed when he redressed and as soon as I heard his jeep reverse out of the driveway; I instantaneously phased to Circulate HQ. I disappeared from my bedroom in Alaska in a bright flash of light then in another, I arrived in the Medical Lab.

I was expecting to find my Calculator but he was nowhere to be seen. So I went to check the Science Lab but he wasn't there either.

"Where are you, Vincent?" I wondered out loud.

"Vincent Moher is in his personal quarters." The electronic female voice of the computer replied.

Oh, I wasn't talking to her but I guess the smart computer which was the Circulate Mainframe, thought I was.

"Thanks." I said in partial surprise.

"You are welcome, Bianca." The computer replied.

I turned around to walk in the other direction down the corridor towards the other hallway which led to the Personnel Quarters. As soon as I soon saw the familiar frosted-over, automatic glass door with Vincent's name on the lit up computer panel; my hand hit the 'doorbell' even before I came to a stop.

"Bianca Elm requesting entry." I heard the computer announce.

Within five seconds, the door slid open with my Calculator wearing a late 21st Century business suit. He was doing up a tie when he looked on in surprise.

"B, we don't have an appointment today." He said puzzled. "Your grandmother is taking me to the Hodge Endeavor Head Office in London shortly. I've got meetings all day with the Board of Directors as well as with the English Government."

"This isn't about knocking me up today, Vincent." I spoke bluntly. "In fact, Grant and I've decided not to try anymore medical procedures."

"Oh?" My Calculator nearly paused in surprise. "Very well, it's probably for the best anyways. But can we discuss this later? I haven't had breakfast yet and Arabella will be here in twenty minutes."

"Vincent please," I looked on desperately, "this is important and I really need your help with something."

He had just finished adjusting his tie, when he gazed on my face closely. "What's wrong, B?"

What I couldn't blurt out to my husband, I could to my Calculator; "I had a vision of Grant dying."

Now this really gave him pause, "when is this supposed to happen?"

"I don't know which is why I've come to you." My eyes watered. "Can you help me find out?"

He looked like he was deep in thought as his hand stroked his freshly-shaven chin. "I suppose we could go to the Viewing Room and look on Grant's timeline. We could fast forward through his life to find out when it ends?"

With a curt nod, I spun on my heel to immediately go there as my Calculator walked after.

The Viewing Room had a long circular, glass top desk which ran around in a ring. Spread about the desk were three crystallized computer controls where three Calculators used to sit to monitor Earth's timeline and the movement of its' Circulators. In the centre of the ring hung a huge, upside down, three-sided crystal pyramid which slowly turned. In the three sides of the pyramid, different eras and locations on Earth were shown or even scenes of outer space. The Circulate Mainframe now performed the task of monitoring human history as well as for any spatial disturbances which ruptured time could cause. When it detected an abnormality, it would report it immediately to the Last Calculator.

"Computer we need to perform a search." Vincent ordered as he sat down at one of the control panels.

"Please enter the search parameters." The computer replied politely.

He worked the crystallized computer controls, which lit up as they were being used. He worked swiftly, deftly typing in his commands onto the flat, touch screen crystallized interface. I watched him select the years to search through including the one I had just left; 2089 AD for the subject, Grant Elm.

"Using the parameters I just input, run a scan of the timeline of the Last Circulator's husband, Grant Elm." He gave the verbal command.

"Scanning now." The computer obeyed.

Next, I saw on the three sides of the huge, upside down, crystal pyramid scenes of Grant's and my life together.

The computer started from our Joining Ceremony where I saw we were wearing our traditional 'skins'. It felt surreal watching the computer fast forward through my marriage like this. I blushed when it momentarily showed our darkened bedroom of the wedding night before it moved on again. It even showed my training as both a Circulator and Werewolf and how Grant was present for both. It didn't stop fast forwarding until our fight last night, after washing the dishes...

...when suddenly there was a bright flash of light from the screen and all of the images abruptly stopped.

"Oh no, not again." He moaned.

"What is it? What's wrong?" I asked concerned.

"Remember after you first changed and you were brought to the Medical Lab to be examined?" He began. "I told you and your family how I didn't see your upcoming transformation because something was blocking my sight and Circulate systems?"

"Yes?"

"This is it." Vincent waved towards the pyramid. "Your timeline is fragmented with certain moments in time being 'blanked out'."

"What do you mean?" I shook my head in confusion.

Using the controls, he rewound the images so again we watched the fight in the kitchen last night but as soon as we saw me go upstairs to bed? Another bright flash of light erupted from the pyramid and all that was left was a blank, white screen.

"But what does this mean, Vincent? Is Grant is going to die by a white light? What's going on?" My voice turned shrill with fear.

"Of course Grant isn't going to die by a white light," he rolled his eyes, "but whenever I try to see certain parts of your life or even when I try to calculate your future? I can't see anything but this blank white screen! It's quite frustrating, really."

"You're telling me!" I huffed in annoyance. "Then can we fast forward through my life again and see if Grant's still in it?"

"Good idea." He pressed in the commands.

The white light on the three sides of the upside down crystal pyramid then changed to images of my bedroom. It looked to be daytime and I was lying in bed alone. The image of myself looked distraught and I was hugging onto Grant's pillow whilst crying.

"When is THIS going to happen?" I cried out in fear.

"The date is the 10th October 2089." He answered. "Your birthday, B."

"So Grant is going to die before my birthday?" My mouth fell open.

"Apparently so."

"But how is he going to die?" I demanded. "Can you rewind and find out?"

My Calculator obeyed as he rewound the image but all we saw was a white screen again. The crystal pyramid slowly turned, with all three sides were just a blank white.

"OK," I started to pace up and down to help me think, "in my vision, Grant was riddled with bullet holes. So obviously he dies this way but I have to find out when!"

"It would be logical to assume it may happen when he's on patrol." He postured. "You could keep an eye on him when it's his turn by patrolling with him?"

"Women aren't allowed to patrol," I said flatly, "especially first female Lokoti Werewolves."

"Typical." He sighed in dissatisfaction. "Seriously I don't know what you, Jess and Arabella see in these Neanderthals that you're married to."

"Shut up, Vincent." I seethed. "They do it for our protection!"

"I'm sure they do."

"You as a Calculator should know of the ramifications!" I snapped. "If they didn't patrol, then our Tribal Lands would be overrun, our homes could be taken away and even the natural resources in the National Park would be ruined! Hell, you should even 'see' that with female Werewolves being so rare, they're keeping me safe by protecting the secret of my existence!"

"Let's give them a medal, shall we?" He said snidely.

Just as I opened my mouth to really let him have it, I realized there wasn't any point. Vincent would never share my view since his mind was made up on the subject, as I knew he couldn't help any further on the matter.

Once more I spun on my heel to stalk off, but I disappeared in a bright flash of light before I even reached the door of the Viewing Room. I instantaneously phased back to Alaska to the time frame I had left, to think of something else.

*****

It was 4.55 PM when I heard the sound of Grant's jeep pull into the driveway. To his surprise, I walked out onto the veranda to meet him. He smiled at my eagerness and wider still when I welcomed him home with a passionate kiss.

"I should tell you to come off fertility drugs more often." He joked, before leading me back inside.

"How was your day?" I queried as I followed him into the kitchen.

"It was OK." He shrugged as he opened up the fridge. "We finished the Shallow Water's new bed and bedside tables. They'll be picking them up tomorrow."

I watched him pull out the ingredients to make himself a sandwich. When he grabbed the loaf of bread, I saw that he pulled out enough slices to make me one too.

"Man you're hungry." I observed. "You can't wait until dinner?"

"I don't have time for a proper dinner." He warned. "I have to start my patrol early tonight. When your Dad and Grandpa were doing their rounds last night, they had to move on a group of refugees but they didn't move very far. We think they're gonna come back tonight."

What the...? I froze in fear as my eyes bulged. Grant was on patrol TONIGHT?! How could I have forgotten this all important fact when trying to keep my husband safe?

"Can you pour the glasses of milk to go with our sandwiches?" He asked. "I have to eat and run, I'm afraid."

To his surprise, I grabbed hold of his arm as I said desperately; "not tonight, Grant! Please don't go out tonight?"

"B?" He gave a funny look.

"Please don't patrol tonight because I have a bad feeling! I'm worried for your safety!" I pleaded.

"C'mon B, we've been through this." He frowned. "It's my turn tonight and if I don't go then it's unfair for someone else in the pack who has to instead. Besides, I always come home."

"But what if this time you don't?" My eyes watered.

"Is this about your nightmare last night?" He guessed. "It was just a bad dream, B."

"But what if it wasn't?" I tried to reason. "Circulators have visions Grant, even in their sleep."

"How do you know when it's a vision or a dream though?" He teased. "Remember when you had the dream that the entire tribe turned into Muppets as our Tribal Lands turned into 'Sesame Street'?"

"Grant, this is different." I said dejectedly.

"That was funny." He chuckled. "Who did your Dad turn into again, 'Big Bird'? Now who did your Grandfather turn into, wasn't it 'Grover'?"

How can he laugh at a time like this? Why doesn't he believe me? Dad and Grandfather always believe Mum and Gran when they 'see' something if they're asleep or not.

"Grant please," I begged, "then at least let me come with you on patrol tonight."

"B." He loudly put down the knife he was using to slice the tomato. "You know the rules."

"But this is about life and death!"

"I know it is!" He raised his voice which rumbled out like thunder. "If you patrol and strangers saw you in your Werewolf form? Then you would be easily identified being the only female Lokoti Werewolf."

"I don't care if people know about me when your life is at risk!" I objected.

"What if you use your light speed as a Circulator? You'd also be putting your mother and grandmother at risk by giving away the existence of Circulators." He shook his head. "No, you are NOT coming on patrol with me."

"Look I understand the First and the pack's decision why normally I can't patrol..." I clung to the front of his shirt, "...I even defended you against Vincent today. But tonight and for the next couple of weeks or so, I'll come along and -"

"NO!" He roared with his brown eyes flashing their supernatural silver. "No stranger may know that my wife is a Werewolf!"

Then my husband used his greater strength to pull my hands off his shirt as his glowing silver eyes drilled into my dark blue ones. He held me at arms length as he silently fumed.

OBEY YOUR HUSBAND AND PACK, BIANCA ELM – His Werewolf will demanded.

My head drooped forward in defeat as my human eyes watered with hot, helpless tears. Grant pulled me closer to hold in an embrace, to dry my wet face with his shirt as he even tenderly began to stroke my hair.

"I'll come home to you, B." He murmured. "I always do. Remember, I have a bright future to look forward to, being the mate of the tribe's Last Light Person."

However today his usual promise he typically made before he went on patrol sounded empty and false, which only made me cry harder.

~~~~~~

30th September 2089

One of the most renowned eras of Ancient Greece was the Mycenaean period. Homer wrote of the Trojan War and the tragic characters Clytemnestra, Agamemnon, Helen, Paris and the 'seer' Cassandra. In legend, Cassandra was beautiful although perhaps not as gorgeous of Helen of Troy but enough to capture the attention of Apollo.

As a way to woo Cassandra, Apollo gave her the gift of prophecy but Cassandra tried to metaphorically take the money and run. To punish her, Apollo made it so nobody would believe her visions. When she tried to warn the Trojans about the large wooden horse they found on their doorstep? Nobody believed her and low and behold, the Mycenaean Greeks won the war.

However as nothing lasts forever, the Mycenaean period ended after a series of wars, famine, earthquakes and other misfortune. History records Ancient Greece's Dark Age beginning after the Mycenaean era ended. As was typical for human behavior in this period (or even after it); when the going gets tough, the tough go looting. Egyptian history records a battle with the 'Sea Peoples' who were in part Mycenaean, attacking the Mediterranean in battleships.

One of the things which attracted me to ancient history was the curious repetition throughout the human timeline. How many times has a civilization reached the pinnacle in power, glory and might before it topples? True to the saying, "power corrupts" and in hindsight we can sit back and say "I told you so", yet human nature will repeat the same mistake over and over again.

Three months ago on the 14th July, despite my own prophecy of doom my husband still went to 'war'. Grant left to patrol with his older brother to protect his land and family from our version of 'Sea Peoples'. From the radioactive fall out after World War Three, many Americans had to leave their
~~~~~~

homes to migrate north. For the last twenty or so years Canada has taken the brunt with the overflow spilling into Alaska.

Thanks to the foresight of my grandmother Arabella Riverclaw; she had the multinational corporation Hodge Endeavor sponsor the World Heritage Listed, National Park in Alaska before the War. By bureaucracy and a whopping great bank cheque, Hunter National Park was renamed the Lokoti National Park "in honor of its original landowners the Lokoti People"; as the Alaskan State Government signed off.

The land was held in great spiritual reverence by the tribe. It was the home of their spirit guide the Lokoti Wolf which was a rare subspecies of Grey Wolf. The land also provided for the Lokoti who lived in harmony with nature; never hunting to excess, replanting for every tree that was cut down, with stories of the tribe's connection to the mountains of the Alaska Range and the deep, dark blue river which was interconnected to the vast river system of Alaska as a whole.

In the aftermath of the War, the Lokoti Tribal Elders decided that no-one but Lokoti could live on the land. When outsiders would ask, "what gives you the right to say you own a National Park?" The members of the pack would reply, "actually the World Heritage Listed land is in our name and we have lived on it for thousands of years."

The borders of the National Park were fenceless as the land was so vast, it would be ridiculous to try to enclose it and it would also effect the migration of animals which would go against Lokoti ideology. There were however signposts every ten kilometers around the perimeter declaring the land as the 'World Heritage Listed Lokoti National Park'. The signposts had small electronic devices which acted like a homing device. When a marauder tried to knock down the sign so they could try to declare ignorance of trespassing, the disruption to the signal would be picked up.

However thanks to the Lokoti Werewolves supernatural sense of smell, the technology was hardly needed. In a dog eat dog world of looting where neighbor turned on each other; who better to protect than Werewolves? At first the members of the pack would meet the strangers in human form, who were usually refugees. The members of the pack would politely ask the strangers to move on, or even give out food and medical supplies to the sick and the desperate.

When the strangers turned violent, so did the Werewolves as they expanded into their supernaturally strong bodies. As the humans used guns, the Werewolves used lightening fast reflexes and claws. It was human monster verses paranormal monster, with the empathic members of the pack sensing when one of their kin were in trouble and run to their aid. In my five years of marriage, eight times had I heard the telepathic battle cry whereas my husband could answer; I wasn't permitted.

STRANGERS ON THE EASTERN BORDER IN THE VALLEY HAVE AUTOMATICS – I felt their will.

Grant would leap out of bed, grabbing his jeans on his way past whilst yelling; "go back to bed, B! You know you can't come."

July 14th was such a night. I was banished home because of my isolating role as the first female Lokoti Werewolf. However from my connection to the male Werewolves and hunting with my kin each and every full moon, I was on their wavelength. I heard the same thoughts as I felt the same will that the rest of the pack did.

THE STRANGERS FROM LAST NIGHT HAVE RETURNED – Ian telepathically declared – *AND THIS TIME THEY'RE ARMED.*

WHERE ARE YOU? – I heard Dad think.

GRANT AND I ARE ON THE SOUTH WESTERN BORDER IN THE RIVER VALLEY – Ian thought back.

I'M COMING TO YOU – Dad responded.

AS AM I – Grandpa joined in.

I'M ON MY WAY – Grandfather chimed.

TONIGHT WOLVES WE FIGHT – Harry's thoughts dominated the pack – *THE STRANGERS HAD BEEN WARNED WHEN THEY TOOK THE FOOD AND SUPPLIES WE OFFERED, BUT NOW THEY HAVE COME TO TAKE MORE*

I felt the bloodlust begin to boil in my kin as they ran to battle. I too felt the same murderous urges to harm the humans who would harm my mate. I paced the floorboards in the living room faster and faster as I felt my nails and teeth extend.

Screw this, Grant's in danger! I'll risk the wrath of going against the will of the pack but tonight I'm going to fight too...

Just as I was running up the stairs to get my sword out of my wardrobe; I felt a sudden, sharp pain in my right hip!

"Oow!" I fell face first on the wooden steps as my longer, sharper teeth punctured my bottom lip. "Damn...!" I raised my hand to feel my injured mouth to see blood on it.

Out of the blue, I felt several more sharp pains in my abdomen, my shoulders, my arms and even in my legs! I writhed on the wooden staircase. "Oow! Oow! Oow!"

The discomfort was so bad, they were like stabbing pains! Hang on, what I was feeling weren't stabbing pains but they were shooting pains. Maybe what I was feeling was like I was being shot? Or somebody else was...Grant.

"NOOOOOOOO!!" I howled in horror.

Although my body was hurting all over, I bolted up the rest of the steps in light speed! I zoomed into my bedroom and almost smashed through the wardrobe door to get my sword. Simultaneously as I strapped the sheath onto my back, I instantaneously phased out of my bedroom in a bright flash of light.

I reappeared in another bright flash of light in the river valley on the south western side of the border. I recognized the land from hunting here a couple of times. The landscape still looked bright and almost cheerful thanks to summer's extended daylight hours as the scenery looked deceptively serene.

BANG! BANG! BANG!

What was that? I quickly turned towards the part of the forest where the noises came from. I started to jog towards the ruckus when...

BANG! BANG! BANG!

...my head suddenly hurt with a blinding headache, making me stagger sideways! Grant! I made my body expand with Werewolf muscle as I changed into my supernaturally stronger shape to stop myself from collapsing to the ground.

"NNNOOOOOOOOOAAAAAAARRRWW!!" I heard Ian's roar.

In my Werewolf form with the sword strapped to my back, I ran through the trees towards the sound of gunfire. I was running blindly with my glowing turquoise eyes watering profusely. Every part of my being was hurting because Grant was hurting. I pushed myself onwards when I felt a debilitating sharp pain in my chest, which meant my husband had just been shot through the heart!

"Grant!" I screamed in my thunderous voice. "Grant!"

I leapt over a small embankment into the foray, where Werewolf was shredding human. The huge, hulking, hairless European Werewolf form of Declan overpowered four humans at once, as the rest of the Lokoti Werewolves pounced. Dad hit the rifle out of his opponent's hands before he hit the man in the face with his clawed fist, sending the man flying backwards. Grandpa was also fighting, as the fourteen male Werewolves bar Grant, all had their hands full.

BANG! BANG! BANG!

Several more shots were fired and I felt the whiz of one bullet just miss, but still I continued to run into the thick of the carnage.

"Oh my god there's even a female of those freaks!" I heard somebody shout. "Quick, shoot it!"

BANG! BANG! BANG! BANG!

I heard the shooting but I didn't feel the bullets, even though a primitive part of my brain knew I should have. I vaguely made out in the corner of my eye Declan with his muscle bulk and hardened hide, had leapt into the line of fire. With four new bullet holes in his torso, he pounced upon the two men and made mince meat of them with his large, canine jaws.

"Get out of here, B!" Grandfather roared in anger.

But I ignored his command as I ran past he and Uncle Harry, who were disarming and deposing their attackers with their claws. I bolted past Finn and Quinn who were ripping their opponents' throats out with their elongated, sharp teeth. I ran past Uncle Julian who was fighting another human behind one of the five large RV's that the strangers had arrived in. I saw in the back of the vehicles such a stash of weapons it could make the Army envious.

Eventually amongst all the greenery of leaf, moss and wood, I spotted Grant by the red colour of his blood seeping out of his multiple bullet wounds. He was sitting slumped against a tree trunk whilst struggling to keep his fading silver eyes open. There were three more bullet holes in his head, with one in his cheek and two in his forehead. I also saw a small part of the back of his skull was missing, from where the bullets exited.

"GRANT!" I skidded in the dirt to land on my knees by his side.

I cupped his bloodied face in my hands as I leaned in to sniff his injuries. The bullets weren't silver but there were enough of them inside to still do plenty of damage.

"B...?" he managed out.

As I smoothed back his long, black, bloodied hair from his face I desperately tried to soothe, "you're not as badly shot as you were in my dream."

"B..." his head began to drop forward as his eyes began to close.

"No Grant, please no!" I shook with sobs. "C'mon, you're not as shot as badly as you were in my dream! You can live through this!"

Suddenly we were joined by Ian in his Werewolf form, also skidding to a stop on his knees. With his lightening fast reflexes, he used his elongated teeth to put a gash on the inside of his wrist, before jamming it inside Grant's mouth.

"C'mon little brother, drink!" Ian growled out as his glowing pink eyes watered.

It looked like he was trying to share his blood with his kin, but Grant wasn't drinking. I recalled Werewolves healing each other or their mates in this fashion. I looked on helplessly as he pushed his bleeding wrist harder into Grant's hanging mouth.

"Drink Grant, drink!" Ian snarled stubbornly. "Drink damn it!"

Then I don't know how or why but like it was an instinct telling me what to do, I raised my left wrist to my sharp mouth to put a gash in it too. Then I turned my wrist over and tried to aim my dripping blood over my mate's worst injuries. I tried to bleed directly into the gaping hole in his chest which had ruptured his heart.

I saw my blood was going inside of his body just as Ian's was, but nothing was happening...am I doing this wrong?

"B?" Grandfather dropped to his knees by my side as Dad appeared beside Ian. He gently tried to pull my arm back. "B, I'm sorry but it's not going to work, he's gone."

"But am I doing it the right way?" I cried, moving my wound back over my husband's. "Am I doing this the right way?!"

"You're doing this the right way, B." Grandfather shrunk back into his human body to speak softly. "But it's not going to work because Grant's gone."

"No..." I tearfully shook my head as I trembled all over. My blood began to spill all over the place because my arm was shaking so badly. "...no!"

Dad was also pulling Ian's arm back before he slumped against his best friend in defeat. Grandfather tried to pull me into his arms but I refused to leave Grant's side.

"Nooooo!!!" I wailed whilst trying to wrap my arms about my mate's neck. "Grant? Please Grant! Nooooooo...!"

Dad held his best friend tighter as Ian shook hard with angry sobs. I barely made out the rest of the pack all come to stand around to look on sadly, with Declan in his great European Werewolf body towering over everyone.

I buried my wet face into my mate's bloodied chest, as if my tears might revive him instead? But nope! I couldn't hear his usually strong heart beat and his scent was fading fast. My empathic pain which had been my husband's was now replaced with the even greater ache of a Lokoti Werewolf who had lost their mate.

My God, I would have asked to have been shot instead! That kind of physical pain paled in comparison to the emotional trauma of your life now turning meaningless with the absence of your other half.

*****

~ 16 ~

The living room clock ticked; the living room clock tocked. Each second ticked by; each completed sixty seconds made up a new minute; each completed sixty minutes made a new hour.

Time kept onwards. I was supposed to keep onwards. But I couldn't move, I could barely breathe. I lay on top of my bed with my sword still strapped to my back.

I was a dismal failure as a wife as I couldn't give my husband a child. I was a dismal failure as a protector and one of the pack. I was a dismal failure as a Circulator as I just wasn't fast enough...

...and Grant paid for my failure, his life paid for it well.

I barely heard their voices as I clung to my pillow. My claws were piercing the fabric as I lay stiff and rock hard. My muscles were tense, my claws detracted and my teeth bared.

"First, let's get that sword off her back." I heard Grandfather's voice which sounded far away.

I felt someone tugging at the straps as they removed the sword in its sheath. However I didn't react as I didn't move. I didn't say a thing.

"How long has she been like this?" Uncle Harry asked.

Harry...he was here too?

"Since Hunter brought her home." He answered.

"That was three days ago." Uncle Quinn said sternly.

Uncle Quinn was here?

"She hasn't moved, she hasn't blinked, she hasn't spoken and she hasn't slept." Mum said unhappily.

"Let's get her out of those bloodied clothes and into a shower." Gran ordered.

I felt the hands try to sit me up to undress me but I snapped my sharp teeth at them!

"OK, bad idea." Mum said worriedly.

"B, we need to change you." Grandfather said seriously.

I growled out one of the longest, unhappiest, most dangerous sounding noises yet in my career as a Werewolf...

"Bianca Grace!" He growled back. "We need to get you out of those clothes."

"We need to put you in a shower and change you before Grant's funeral." Dad organized.

Grant's funeral...? Did he just say Grant's funeral? They were already holding his funeral? My glowing eyes watered as I whined in pain at the very idea of putting his body on top of a wooden pyre to burn...

"Come on B, let's get you ready." Dad sat me upright.

Suddenly my rock-hard body flopped like a stretched elastic band snapping loose. My glowing eyes faded... I faded.

They were going to burn Grant's body? They were really going to burn it? How could they?!

"You're not missing your own husband's funeral." Dad said firmly, before he heaved me to my feet.

*****

Don't ask how they undressed me. Don't ask how the cleaned me and don't ask how they dressed me in clean clothes. Don't even ask who damn well did all of these things, because I simply don't know.

I really didn't know as I was barely aware of any of it. I was barely aware of being led out of the house by Dad as he walked me over to his truck. I was barely aware of the fading afternoon's light as I was seated in between he and Mum as he drove us down to the Holy Grounds.   I was barely aware of being held up by my father and grandfather as they stood me before the funeral pyre which was constructed before the three Sacred Totems.

The late summer's sun sank that afternoon over a horizon which glowed a fiery orange with a purple hue. That would soon be the pyre when it burned...

I vaguely heard the drum beat as the whole of the Lokoti tribe stood about. I vaguely became aware of the Tribal Elders with their faces painted and wearing their customary 'skins', were singing the funeral chant. I saw a body wrapped in a traditional woven blanket of Lokoti design, carried up to the temporary square structure of wood.

Soon the square wooden structure was burning. The pyre was set alight as the flames began to burn the body on top of it. The burning flesh started to smell of an earthy herb garden of oregano, rosemary, thyme and even of coriander...

...oh my God, they're burning Grant! They're really burning Grant!

I jumped in fright! They're burning my husband, who laid there wrapped in the woven funeral shroud. No! I wanted to leap on top of that fire myself! I wanted to gather the body up in my arms and quickly extinguish the flames by jumping into the river with him!

"NO!" I cried out, but Dad and Grandfather held me steady.

I tried to go to him, to hold him, to nurse him back to health...!

"Bianca." Grandfather growled quietly. "Say goodbye to your mate."

"NO!" I cried out frightenedly as the flames completely engulfed Grant's body. "NO! NO! NO! You're burning him! Can't you smell him?! Can't you smell his scent?! This is Grant! NO, STOP THIS!"

Again I tried to run to him but their strong arms which held onto my weaker ones, refused to let go.

"We're freeing him, Bianca." Dad said sadly. "We're freeing his spirit from his earth-bound body so he can join our ancestors in the Holy Hunting Grounds."

But the smell of his scent which was released in the air from the flames was calling on me...they were calling on me...my mate was calling for me!

"No, you're killing him! NO! Let go of me, please! Let me go! Grant needs me! We can't do this to him! We can't!"

I blindly struggled against their grip as all I could see were the flames of the funeral pyre against the flaming sunset of the Alaskan summer.

"Let's get her out of here." Dad muttered.

The next thing I knew, I was being pulled backwards. Futilely I struggled against the arms which were pulling me away from the Holy Grounds.

"We're taking you home, B." I heard Mum's voice.

"Jess, you drive with your mother. Hunter and I will go with B, in Hunter's truck." Grandfather ordered.

"But I want to be with B...!" She objected.

"You will be, when we get her home." His voice softened.

I felt that I was sitting down again, as I heard two car doors close; closing me in. But all I could see were the large flames as they leapt into the oncoming night. The fire leapt higher and higher into the air, as if it were my husband himself reaching into the starry sky.

"Safe traveling Grant." Dad said softly.

*****

My father carried me into my bedroom. He tried to carefully lay me out on the bed but immediately I dove face first into my pillow. Somebody started to take off my shoes, but I didn't care about getting mud on the bed.

I just wanted to feel Grant lying beside. I just wanted to feel his body pressed up against mine. I just wanted to feel him once more, as he would kiss my ear and hold me in his strong arms. I would have killed somebody, just to feel him stroke my hair one more time...

...but this time it was Grandfather stroking my hair, as he sat beside instead. I rolled away unhappily, so my back was to him.

I don't want you, I want Grant! I want my mate to be comforting me. If Grant was doing this then I wouldn't have been so upset, would I?

"Give her two of these," now I heard Derik's voice, "they'll put her to sleep."

"Thanks." Dad said.

"Here's a glass of water." Mum walked into my room.

I felt somebody turn me over and sit me up as two white tablets sat on my father's palm.

"NO!" I snapped at the hand!

How dare they try to ease my grief by drugging me!

"B." My father's face appeared before mine. "You have to go to sleep. Your bloodlust is getting worse because you're over tired."

Don't they understand? Don't they see? My bloodlust was the only thing keeping my heart beating...

"It's time for you to sleep, B." Grandfather said in his deep, rumbling voice.

SLEEP - I could feel his Werewolf will battle my own.

"NO!" I snarled as my turquoise eyes glowed brightly.

Simultaneously, I felt my teeth and nails grow long and sharp. I locked my jaws together so nothing was going to be able to get past my elongated teeth. I felt Dad's hands try to pry apart my mouth. I growled viciously at his interference, as I tried to struggle out of Grandfather's hold.

"Hunter, don't!" Mum cried out.

"Jess, no!" Grandfather warned as he wrestled her daughter. "B's bloodlust is getting out of hand!"

"Come on Jess." I watched Gran take her arm to lead her from the room.

"No!" She hit her mother's hand away. She rushed up as she tried to pull Dad off. "You are NOT going to force tablets down my daughter's throat! We fucking forced this marriage onto her and now look what it's done!"

"I could give B a sedative by injection." Derik frowned.

"And how about one for Jess too?" I heard Uncle Jules ask dryly.

Uncle Julian was here as well? As I snarled at all of these interfering males, I finally took a good look around my room. I saw not only Grandfather, Gran, Mum, Dad and Derik here... but I saw Uncle Julian and Aunt Danika too. They all looked on like they were frightened of me.

"Do you hear that snarling, Jess?" My uncle frowned. "It's because the bloodlust has taken over!"

Dad tried one more time to put the tablets in my mouth, but I knocked them out of his hand and sent them flying to the floor!

"Derik, get the injection ready!" Grandfather ordered as he fought to keep his hold on my writhing body.

"Can't we just leave her alone? Can't we just leave her alone in her room to mourn and get it out of her system?" Mum cried.

"B hasn't slept since Grant's death three days ago. When a Werewolf loses their self control from either alcohol or sleep deprivation, they lose their control of the bloodlust. We have to sedate her!" Her brother said unhappily.

I saw Derik start to walk forwards with a syringe in his hand...

"NOOOO!!" I roared as I struggled harder.

Allow me my pain at least! I don't want to sleep! How dare you all interfere this way!   When Derik came closer, I kicked out at him! I nearly would have got him too but Dad caught my leg.

You're faster than them**,* the familiar cold voice goaded, ***you're a Circulator! Use your ability on them!

I tried to phase out of Grandfather and Dad's clutches but their will interfered with my concentration. Instead, I sped up my reflexes and it started to work too as I began to slip from their grasp...

"Hurry, Derik!" Grandfather growled as he used all of his might to keep his hold.

"I can't, you have to hold her still!" He objected.

My bedroom looked like a scene of domestic violence was playing out... A struggling female was fighting against two older males who were trying to hold her down. Gran's and Aunt Danika's faces paled as they looked on helplessly. Mum was yelling at both Dad and Grandfather to just leave me alone. Derik stood at the end of my bed, armed with a syringe which was pointed my way.

Things were looking grim to say the least until we heard;

AAAAAARRRRRRROOOOOOOOOOOOOOOOOOAAAAAWWWRRRRR!

Huh, what was that? That sounded like a howl...! It was so loud, as if it came from right outside my window.

AAAAAARRRRRRROOOOOOOOOOOOOOOOOOAAAAAWWWRRRRR!

There was pain in the voice, like the owner was crying out in anguish. It was loud as it was full of emotion and it mirrored exactly how I felt. It was like it was expressing my mourning for me, at the passing of my mate. Everyone paused by how haunting the sound was, as everybody's eyes crept towards the bedroom windows where the howling was the closest. The women shivered, looking unnerved by the noise.

If I could have howled, I would have howled like that. If I could have howled, I would have mourned the passing of my mate as such. But I couldn't howl like that and somebody who knew this, howled for me. This somebody was standing outside the front of my house now.

"It's Declan." Grandfather recognized.

AAAAAARRRRROOOOOOOOOOOOOOOOOOOOOAAAAAARRRRWWW!

I lay still as I listened. The noise permeated through my body and even my soul. Just like you hear a song come on the radio that mirrored exactly how you were feeling right then, it was the same way Declan's howl placated my bloodlust. It began to bubble back down from the sound which to me, was soulful and touching.

AAAAARRRRROOOOOOOOOOOOOOOOOOOOOAAAAARRRRWWW!

My glowing eyes started to fade and my sharp teeth began to retract, as did the claws on the ends of my hands and feet.

"Look." Uncle Julian spoke up. "Now Derik, now!"

He darted forwards and stabbed the syringe into my thigh whilst I was lying still, staring out the window. My eyes blazed as I snarled one last time from the pain the syringe caused! Then my already out of focus bedroom also turned dark...

...and then nothingness.

~~~~~~

30th October 2089

I slept a lot and it was almost like I slept constantly. Some days I couldn't keep my eyes open. I felt so tired, weary even. This wasn't caused from any further medication, it was caused from hopelessness.

The distress was like a thick, heavy blanket. When it covered my mind and heart, all I felt was a suffocating sadness that could even slow my heart beat from its oppressive weight.

I barely ate and I didn't leave my bed except to use the bathroom. I just slept...I slept and I slept, as I held Grant's pillow against my face. His scent was still on the pillowcase. I couldn't stand the thought of changing the sheets.

As I was lying in bed, sometimes I would stare at one of his shirts hanging in the wardrobe with the sleeve poking through the doors. Or, I would stare at a part of his boxer shorts that were sticking up from our underwear draw. Or, I would dismally stare down at the floor, at his workman's boots. They always sat in their usual spot, by the end of the bed.

Grant used sit on the bed to pull them on before he left for work. Then before his evening shower, he would sit down on the bed again to take them off and ready for the next morning. Sometimes in the mornings, especially around 8.23 AM; I would wake up from the feel of somebody sitting down at the end of the bed where he used to sit. My eyes would snap open, but nobody was there.

I'd turn tearful and disheartened, I'd glance at his digital clock on his bedside table. 8.23 AM was usually the time of the morning that he pulled on his boots before giving me my goodbye kiss. He would walk out the front door at 8.30 AM to go to work with either Dad or Ian or sometimes even both.

This morning I felt it again, I felt my mattress sink by somebody sitting on the end of my bed. My eyes snapped open from old habit, but instead of seeing Grant, I found Mandy sitting there.

"G'morning B!" She greeted brightly. "How are you on this fine fall day?"

"You're sitting in Grant's spot."
~~~~~~

She smirked at my flat response before she looked down to notice his boots on the floor near her feet. "That's a bit of hazard, having shoes lying around on the floor. Somebody could trip over them."

Then she picked up the boots and moved them...

"No!" I cried out in alarm. "No Mandy, don't!"

However it was too late, she had carried them over to the wardrobe, opened the doors, tossed them in and then shut the doors again. She had also disturbed the way Grant's shirt had been hanging, as it was no longer peeking through. The shoes were gone and now so was his shirt, from visibility anyways.

"Gees it stinks in here." She screwed up her face. She stood with her hands on her hips as she looked about. "Let's change the sheets and do some laundry, shall we?"

"NO!" I roared in anger and partially changed by the very suggestion. I pointed my clawed hand at her. "You will NOT touch anything!"

"Oh I get it." She rolled her eyes. "You're doing what the Ancient Egyptians did when somebody died, but instead of burying Grant with his possessions, you're burying yourself with his things."

"Mandy, go away." I growled unhappily as I lay back down.

"I brought you some caribou casserole." She walked over to her bag which I noticed was on the floor by the bedroom doorway.

Just then my stomach growled hungrily by the very mention of it. Drat! I was going to tell her that all I wanted was to be left alone. Frickin' hell, my constant hunger as a Werewolf always gives me away.

"Hungry?" She taunted, waving the plastic container filled with food.

It did smell good I had to admit, my eyes followed her movements and I couldn't look away from the container.

She went on, "I'm guessing you're hungry since the last time you ate was probably two days ago, on the pasta bake that Derik and Rachel brought over. So B, here's the deal. We're going to get you into a shower and I'm going to change the sheets on your bed. Then whilst the washing machine is on, we're going to eat."

My face fell at such a cruel request. "You know what, Mandy? I'm not that hungry anyway."

But my stomach growled even louder than last time! She smiled patiently as she tauntingly opened the lid. She used the smell of the food to bribe the starving person in the room.

"Mmm, smells good don't it? Oh well, more for me." She snapped the lid shut again, picked up her bag and prepared to leave.

"No, wait! Look, maybe we could come to some arrangement here..." I tried to think, "...if we change the sheets then at least allow me to keep this?" I snatched up Grant's pillow and held onto it protectively.

"Hey, whatever floats your boat." She shrugged as she put down her bag again. "I'm not one to judge."

Soon the bed was stripped as well as my pillowcase whilst Grant's pillow sat on top of the tallboy. Mandy carried the dirty linen and my numerous pairs of pajamas, down to the laundry as I went into the bathroom to shower. At the end, we met up again in the bedroom.

I must admit, it was nice lying in a fresh pair of pajamas with washed hair, amongst clean sheets. But I was still comforted by Grant's pillow, sitting beside my newer, clean one. Whilst I was in the shower, Mandy had also tidied up my bedroom. She had put up the blinds as well as opened the curtains and even opened the windows a crack to let some new air in, but not all of the cold.

My bedroom looked clean and fresh, I noted as I lay on my side on a full stomach thanks to the delicious casserole. I was starting to feel a little better as Mandy's temperament has always been one of humor and optimism, which suited perfectly my bright and tidy bedroom. She was sitting in the chair beside my bed, which Gran had placed there when she and Mum came to sit with me.

Mandy was still finishing up her bowl of casserole as I had devoured mine long ago. As she was eating, she was sitting back comfortably in the chair, with her feet up on the windowsill. We were both looking out at the grey sky as we talked speculatively.

"I think it's going to snow soon." She commented.

"Didn't it snow yesterday?"

"Yeah but not much." She sighed as she placed her empty bowl on the floor beside her chair. "B, I'm worried about you."

"Join the club." I gave my glib reply. "My family practically patrol me, like the Werewolves patrol the borders."

She continued, "I can see why people keep bringing over food, as there's hardly anything in your fridge and cupboards! When was the last time you went grocery shopping?"

"When Grant was alive."

"Four months ago? Please don't tell me the off-milk I tipped out while you were in the shower...?" She looked disgusted.

"No." I scowled. "Gran and Grandfather brought that over two weeks ago with some other groceries. But the food went off because I wasn't using it to prepare anything. So Mum and Dad came over and used some of it to cook for me. The leftovers ran out three days ago."

"Then why don't you get out of bed, go grocery shopping and cook up something to eat to last for the week?" She gave a pointed look.

"Because I don't want to."

"You're going to have to start living life eventually." She sung. "Especially with winter coming, otherwise your family are going to take you out of this house and put you into theirs, as they'll think that you can't look after yourself. Then you'll be away from Grant's things permanently."

"Shut up Mandy." I said darkly as I looked away.

"Speaking of life, it looks like somebody in the outside world is thinking about you." She leaned over in her chair again to reach for something inside her bag. "Here you go."

She handed over a large, white envelope which had the Cambridge University logo on the corner, as well as postage stamps from England. A renewed sense of purpose flooded my veins, as I sat up with a start whilst looking down on the mail with wide eyes.

"Mandy..." I uttered out, "...could this be?"

"What?" She turned in her chair to face me properly, as she eagerly waited. "What is it, B?"

I extended the claws on my right hand to neatly rip the envelope open, before retracting them to remove the documents. In my hand along with a list of grades earned for the classes I completed by correspondence; was my Bachelor of Arts in Ancient History. It was a thick piece of paper with cardboard-like qualities. The writing was embossed and golden as the edges of the document were decorated.

"Wow that looks just like Derik's 'piece of paper,' as Declan calls it." She joked.

"'Piece of paper'?" I arched my eyebrows.

"Yeah, you know Declan. If he can't kill it, eat it or work on it in a Garage then he's not interested. He's always ribbing Derik for living away in Cambridge those three years. He goads, 'you went away for three years just for this, a piece of paper?'" She mimed in a deep, gruff voice.

It was a pretty good impression too, as it made me laugh. I could picture Declan's scowl as she was saying it.

Mandy pondered, "I don't understand, B. You finished your degree almost six months ago. So why are you getting your Bachelor only now?"

"I dunno." I shrugged. "University bureaucracy or the way the postal service is? I suppose I should be happy that I received it at all and it didn't go missing like so many things do these days."

"Don't you just love the way our government services are still recovering after the War, twenty years on?" She rolled her eyes. "It doesn't leave one with much faith in how they were before the War, does it?"

~~~~~~

30th November 2089

After Mandy dropped off my mail with the included Bachelor of Arts, I felt a little different. I didn't feel as weary as before. When I lay in bed all day, my thoughts weren't just of Grant, but I began to think about my Masters again.

During one of Gran's visits, she said that she had advised Cambridge University I had deferred for a semester. So instead of commencing my Masters in the fall, I could start in winter. But I could tell both my
~~~~~~

grandmother and mother were hoping that 2090 wouldn't just bring in the New Year, it would also bring renewed hope.

Four days after Mandy's visit, I woke up at 8.23 AM like clockwork. However instead of immediately feeling Grant's absence like an abyss inside of my chest, my heart beat onwards. Rather than just looking at one of Grant's possessions lying around the bedroom and dissolving into another set of tears, I took a deep breath and I sat up.

Outside, the snow fell softly and so were my steps out of bed and out of the bedroom. I moved gently, taking things slowly as I gingerly went into the bathroom and next downstairs to the kitchen. I switched on the kettle and as the water boiled, I opened up the fridge to reach for the milk...when I remembered I didn't have any.

Oh, Mandy was right. I leaned over to take a long, hard look at my almost empty refrigerator. What looked back were a jar of almost expired olives, a half empty jar of Vegemite and a tub of butter which was borderline. Hmm, I think one of the first steps I'm gonna take with getting my life back on track, will be stocking up on food for this journey.

I didn't want to drink black coffee, so I returned upstairs to my bedroom where I got dressed. After fixing my hair, I pulled on my brown suede jacket and made sure my purse and passport were inside my bag.

In a bright flash of light, I instantaneously phased out of my bedroom in Alaska at 8.43 AM to reappear inside an unused office in the Hodge Endeavor building in London at 9 AM. So much for taking things slowly but what the hell? I left the office building and on my way to the Underground, I stopped in at a café and bought a takeaway Latte.

When I departed the Underground, I bought another Latte. Whilst sipping on my second caffeine fix, I went into my favourite bookstore which had the huge history section. The smell of the books as well as the thousands of decorated covers picked up my spirits like a kid in a candy store.

For two hours, I prowled around the history section looking for the books to use for my thesis. I also browsed through a couple other academics' work, kinda like I was checking out the competition. A couple of times I snickered at how a couple got things wrong, which I knew from my excursions back through time. There was one historian who was so off the mark, I decided to still buy their book anyways for a laugh!

I paid for all of the books and left the bookstore carrying four cotton carry bags away. I walked back down the busy London street but instead of heading for the Underground, I cheated. I spotted an alleyway which I turned down and when I was out of sight, in another bright flash of light I instantaneously phased home.

As soon as I placed the four heavy bags of books on top of my dining table, my stomach growled. Darn it, I should have had lunch in London! There's nothing in my house to eat except a jar of olives. Eugh, no thanks! I'm gonna need to eat some cheese or crackers with them if that's the case.

The clock on my living room wall read as nearly midday in Alaska. Man I love how being a time manipulator, I could bypass time zones and jet lag! Being the middle of the day on a Friday the general store would certainly be open. I emptied the carry bags of books so I could fill them with food instead. However as I left the house via the front door, I suddenly stopped just as my heart did.

Grant's black jeep sat on the snowy driveway, ready and waiting to be driven. It was in the exact same position he had parked it the last time he came home from work. I had a spare set of car keys in my bag, which jingled along with my house keys or even my old key for Mum and Dad's.

There was no way I could drive HIS jeep, no frickin' way in hell. It was too soon, it's still HIS jeep. HIS scent would still be strong in the car, which nobody had been in since HE had. Nah ah, I physically shook my head at the idea of using HIS pride and joy.

Now what? I still needed food! It's a twenty-five minute walk down the hill to the community centre and then it would be the same for the walk back, carrying the bags of food. I'm hungry right now, starving in fact. There was nothing for it, I was going to have to cheat again...

In a bright flash of light, I suddenly appeared inside the general store from instantaneously phasing there. I startled a couple of people who were shopping and Mrs. Lightfoot dropped the bottle of milk she was carrying!

"Bianca Wisetail Elm, do you mind?!" Mrs. Lightfoot exhorted in fright, as she placed her hand over her racing heart.

"I'm sorry!" I cried out apologetically. "I'm sorry, are you OK?"

"I'll give you my answer when my heart attack is over." She gave a glare.

In a huff, she walked off to grab another bottle of milk from the refrigerated section as Mr. Barley left the counter to fetch a mop and bucket. I felt so bad being the reason of the mess that I volunteered to mop up milk for him. As soon as I finished, I grabbed one of the baskets by the front door.

Good one, B! How about instantaneously phasing OUTSIDE of the store next time? Man I'm an idiot for a Circulator. I think everyone else thought so, as I received plenty of peculiar looks as I shopped.

I tried to keep my shopping as brief as possible although I had to restock an empty kitchen back home. I grabbed some milk, cheese, eggs, bacon, bread, juice and lots of tinned food, such as asparagus, creamed corn, spam, spaghetti or baked beans. I could easily live off meals on toast for the next week or so.

When it came to take my purchases to the 'check out', I put everything on the counter for Mr. Barley to mark in his book of accounts. As he was writing up the tally, I put my groceries into my cotton carry bags. I guess because I had just been shopping the 'normal' way in London, subconsciously I pulled my credit card out of my purse to pay for everything.

"Oh." He looked on the piece of plastic in surprise. "Er, it's not necessary thanks B, but you can pay with money if you really want to."

"Sorry!" I blushed a second time, now feeling like a bigger idiot.

Hang on, usually Mr. Barley would write up the things I was checking out under the 'Grant and Bianca Elm' account. Grant would usually settle the account by trade with his furniture construction. With his demise, I would have to use my Hodge Endeavor credit card or try to find something else to trade? I leaned closer, when I saw that he wasn't writing the things under the 'Grant and Bianca Elm' account; he made the list under the 'Hunter and Jessica Wisetail' account. I was back on my parents' account?

"What's this?" I wondered aloud. "Why are you writing my groceries under Mum and Dad's account?"

"Well..." He shifted uncomfortably, "...it's the custom, B."

"What's the custom?"

"When a woman's husband dies, she re-enters her father's protection. If the father is no longer alive, then the woman's brother or her brother-in-law looks after her." He explained patiently. "A couple of weeks after Grant's death when your parents were buying you some groceries, your father said to put it on his account again."

Like the elderly grocer had physically punched his fist through my rib cage and grabbed hold of my heart to squeeze; it gave a painful spasm. I even felt breathless as my emotional pain turned physical. Not only was the agony of Grant's absence upon me, but my Werewolf temper was ignited!

"What a primitive way of doing things!" I objected. "I DON'T need protection from my father or my brother-in-law! I can pay my own way!"

"OK B." He quickly nodded. "Then if you want to give me your credit card I'll put it through the old machine and see if it works. I've heard of some banks starting up in Alaska again -"

"It's Hodge Endeavor money!" I slapped my piece of plastic down onto the counter. "Trust me, the card works!"

"Alright then, I'll put it through for you now." He swiped the credit card and then turned the EFTPOS machine around for me to put in my PIN.

"I'm a Circulator! The Circulate owns Hodge Endeavor! Hodge Endeavor are paying for my living allowance whilst I study, as well as for my degree! I've got my BA and I'm about to start my Masters!" I seethed as I waited for the transaction to be approved.

"Right you are, B." He tried to placate as the receipt was printed. "There, you see? The transaction was approved and the groceries are yours."

"Take my name off Mum and Dad's account!" I growled out as I snatched my receipt.

"Sure, I'll do that for you now." The old man quickly scribbled out my name. Then I watched as he flicked through the pages back to the scribbled out 'Grant and Bianca Elm' account. Next to this scribble he wrote, 'Bianca Elm Only' as well as today's date, the dollar amount I just paid and the receipt number. "There we go B, it's all done."

However, seeing the line through Grant's name resulted in another painful throb in my chest. 'Bianca Elm Only' sat there alone and without my husband's... I gasped as I took an uneven step backwards. I literally felt like I couldn't breathe properly! I think the room started to spin a little too?

"How about you just sit down now B and take things easy?" Mr. Barley offered. "Your father is working nearby as he's repairing the Shallow Water's roof today with your brother-in-law. They can come pick you up and take you home."

Dazed, I looked away and noticed my little tantrum had attracted an audience. Everyone who was shopping in the store, had paused to watch. They were all staring at the crazy widow who yelled at the poor storekeeper over a tribal custom.

Just then my eyes met a familiar pair of bright blue ones and when my focus returned, I realized I was staring at Declan. He was standing by the entrance, wearing his usual dirty work clothes from the Garage which was next door. He didn't hear my rant and come to investigate, did he?

"You come and sit by the counter now B, while we fetch your father for you." Mr. Barley organized. "Chris? Go to the Shallow Water's and see if Hunter Wisetail is still there."

"No..." my eyes watered as my face burned, "...I can take myself home."

"I got it." Declan told the thirteen year old Chris Barley who had stopped stacking shelves, to obey his grandfather. Then he spoke to the older Mr. Barley, "I'll take her home."

"No!" I cried out embarrassed, "I'll go home now!"

Abruptly, I disappeared in another bright flash of light as I instantaneously phased home. Within one second I was standing in my living area once more, however I was empty-handed. Drat it! I had just left all of my food behind.

I landed on my ass as my legs gave away. I hugged my legs tightly as I rocked myself in a fetal position. I gasped again and I honestly thought I could have been having a heart attack, my chest was hurting that much.

Grant – Grant – Grant – I miss you! Grant – Grant – Grant – I can't do this without you! Grant – Grant – Grant – I wish I was with you!

I heaved hard to try to get enough oxygen to stave off the dizziness. If this was a heart attack, then I should probably be using First Aid techniques. So I lay on my side on the hard wooden floor and tilted my head upwards to clear the airways. This worked too, as I did start to breathe easier so maybe I really was having a heart attack?

Maybe this was waning without one's mate? Maybe I'm literally dying of a broken heart? Grant, I don't know if I can carry on without you. In fact I know I can't! I tried today, I really did but it was a fail.

Amidst all this wretchedness, I heard the sound of a pick up truck, pull up in the driveway. The engine sounded familiar, but it wasn't Dad's or Ian's. I lay there, trying to work it out when I heard a single door open and close. I heard the person stomp up the icy veranda steps and just as I expected them to knock and wait on the veranda? My front door opened as this person simply let himself in.

Declan casually walked into my kitchen whilst carrying my four bags of groceries. He stepped over me as cool as a cucumber, not even looking down. I heard him put the bags of groceries onto the kitchen counter before he came to lean on the kitchen entranceway. He looked on unimpressed at how I was lying on the floor.

"B, I don't know if anyone's ever explained the concept of 'shopping' to you? But traditionally after a person pays for something, they leave the store with what they purchased."

"Get out." I said flatly.

"You're welcome." He said sourly as he turned around and went back into the kitchen. I heard him turn on the kettle as he rifled amongst my new food.

"What are you doing?" I asked in annoyance.

"Making a coffee to go with a cheese and spam sandwich." He said coolly. "Since I'm playing the delivery guy on my lunch hour, I may as well get a feed."

I sat up indignantly, "you're eating my food that I just paid for?!"

"Hey, you wouldn't have any olives by any chance would you...?" I heard him open up the fridge. "Yes! Excellent! The olives will give our cheese and spam sandwiches some extra zest."

I stood up from the floor to go stand with my hands on my hips in the kitchen entranceway, "get the hell out of my kitchen and away from my food!"

"If you're gonna be like that, I won't make you a sandwich." He chuckled as he continued. "So, are you going to put your food away or are you waiting for Grant to come back from the dead to do it for you?"

"Get lost, Declan!"

"You see B, when a person comes home from grocery shopping, they put the food away into either the refrigerator or pantry. It's called storing your food, as it can help keep it as well as stop people from tripping over it."

"Shut up." I rolled my eyes.

"You could at least make yourself helpful by making the coffees while I make the sandwiches." He went on.

"If I make you a coffee and you make yourself a sandwich, then will you go away?"

"My lunch break ends in twenty-eight minutes if that answers your question?" He replied.

Declan's great height and his even greater build, took up more room in the kitchen than Grant did. I kept accidentally bumping into him as I put away the groceries and then I made the coffees. With his huge muscles, I was expecting him to cook in an oafish and clumsy manner, but his skill surprised me. He expertly sliced the spam and the cheese as well as the olives. Within ten minutes he'd made six sandwiches; four for him and two for me.

As we sat at the table to eat, Declan watched me tentatively take a bite and then my eyes widen.

"This actually tastes good...!" I said shocked.

"Thanks for not sounding so surprised about it." He rolled his eyes, before looking at the piles of new books. "What's all this?"

"Books to study for my Masters."

"What, you're gonna get another piece of paper?" He arched his eyebrows.

"Yes and then another." I retorted. "When I finish my Masters, I'm thinking of doing a PhD."

"What's that gonna get you?"

"A doctorate in Ancient History."

"A 'doctorate'? You mean you're gonna become a Medicine Woman and heal historical things?" He pondered. "What's the point in that?"

I started to laugh, thinking that he was being funny? But then I stopped when I saw his look of resentment that I was laughing at him. Oh my gosh, he was being serious?!

"Um, it means I'll be able to teach history." I said as I quickly continued to eat.

"Mandy and my Mom are teachers without doctorates." He said sullenly.

"But I'll be qualified to teach at University as well as publish academically." I added on.

"Are you saying my Mom isn't 'qualified' to teach at University?" His voice dropped dangerously. "She's been frickin' teaching this tribe for the past twenty years."

This made me pause from the icy look in his blue eyes which even began to look a little glowing green... Don't tell me I had accidentally insulted the most dangerous breed of Werewolf's mother? Then Declan who had already finished his sandwiches, reached across and snatched up my last triangle!

"Made you look." He teased and then he laughingly jumped backwards with my sandwich before I could retaliate.

~~~~~~

30th January 2090

Winter without Grant was the hardest. The shorter daylight or even the week where the sun didn't come up, made me feel like not leaving my bed at all. I dozed all day, occasionally waking up to lie on my back and stare despondently at the ceiling.

On one such dark afternoon when I was lying around, I noticed something. A small shadow of a water stain had darkened the paint. A water stain on the ceiling must mean that a couple of shingles on the roof were damaged. It was probably from the icy winter, which split the shingles.
~~~~~~

Damn it, with no husband to do the repairs and I didn't have a clue how to do it myself; I think I'll just leave it. Maybe I'll get lucky that the roof might buckle from the weight of the snow and ice and come crashing down on my head...

Thoughts of my self-destruction were momentarily interrupted when I heard the sound of Dad's pick up truck, parking on my snow-covered driveway.

I lay still, listening to the sound of two doors opening and closing. Eventually I heaved myself out of bed when I heard Mum and Dad knock, before helping themselves into the house. As I came down the stairs, I saw them carry bags of food into the kitchen.

"Hey B!" She sung cheerfully. "We've bought some more groceries for you."

"There's some caribou steaks as well as a couple of rabbits which I've skinned and gutted." He began to stack the wrapped up meat into my freezer.

When my parents had finished putting away their tokens of parental love, Mum switched on the kettle to make everyone a cup of coffee. Dad came to stand in the kitchen entranceway and he frowned when he saw that I was still in my pajamas.

"It's four o'clock in the afternoon, B. Don't tell me you were still in bed?" He asked unhappily.

"Er, yes I was." I admitted.

"Aren't you starting your Masters this year?" He guessed. "Your mother told me that you were and that you had the books to boot."

"Yes I am Dad and I do have the books I need." I answered as I came to sit at the table, as did he.

"Well, have you started your studies or what?" He looked around my spotless living area for any signs of academic work.

"The two subjects that I'm supposed to do for the first semester before I work on my thesis in the second semester; begin at the end of January." I told him.

"It IS the end of January, B."

This gave me pause, as I asked in disbelief, "it's the end of January?"

"Today's the 28th." Dad declared.

"I think we need to put a new calendar on your fridge, B." Mum called from the kitchen. "Then you can write up your assignment due dates again."

Then my father stood up and left the table to go into the kitchen. He helped his mate finish off the coffees and when the two returned, they also had a plate of freshly-baked Anzac biscuits. As soon as the plate was sitting on the table, the smell made me ravenously hungry. My parents watched as I jammed biscuit after biscuit into my mouth.

"When was the last time you ate?" He asked warily.

"Um, I think it was lunch time yesterday when I had some baked beans on toast." I shrugged.

My parents exchanged an unhappy look, before Dad turned back my way. "B, your mother and I have been talking -"

"Oh oh, that's never a good thing." I tried to joke.

"How about you come and stay with us for the rest of the winter?" Mum asked brightly. "Your old room is ready and waiting and you'll have two parents to cook for you again, like live-in chefs."

"No thanks, Mum." I shook my head.

"B, your mother tipped out the off milk that was in your fridge when she put away the new milk that we brought." Dad began to lecture. "We don't think that you're able to look after yourself. Winter is the most dangerous season in Alaska. Old people who can't provide for themselves anymore die the most this time of year."

"No thanks, Dad." I shook my head again.

"But B -" he began to argue when she interrupted.

"B's books for her course are all here, so that's probably why she wants to remain."

"Then she can bring her books when she comes home with us!" He said adamantly.

"I'm not starting my Masters this month." I suddenly announced.

"Huh?" Mum blinked. "Why not?"

"I've decided to defer a semester again." I said simply. "I'm not ready to return to my studies."

His eyes narrowed, "then you'll come and stay with us for the rest of winter and maybe for longer. That is until you're ready to return to studying or even return to living your life."

"No Dad, I won't." I said coolly.

"This isn't up for debate, Bianca!" He demanded.

"And this isn't the Stone Age, where a widow has to re-enter her father's protection!" I flared. "I'm turning 24 years old this year and I'm NOT going back home to live with my parents after they forced me to leave by shoving me into a fucking arranged marriage!"

I left this as my parting argument when in a fury, I stood up and left the table by marching back upstairs.

Just before I slammed my bedroom door behind, I overheard Mum retort; "she's got you there, Hunter."

~~~~~~
~~~~~~

~ 17 ~

20th May 2090

BANG! BANG! BANG!

I woke up with a start.

BANG! BANG! BANG!

What the hell is that?!

BANG! BANG! RIIIIIP! BANG!

What the...?! That sounds like it's coming from my roof? That was coming from directly above!

BAM! BAM! BAM!

I literally fell out of bed as I stumbled out of my bedroom...

BANG! BAM! CRASH!

...and I almost fell down my stairs...

BAM! BANG! RIIIIPPP!

...whilst in a daze, I walked out my front door. As soon as I stepped off my patio, I saw strange things on the ground that I think used to be shingles...

BAM! BANG! RRRIIIIIIPPP!

....I looked up at my roof and saw Declan – DECLAN?! – perched on top with a hammer and a crow bar. He was tossing away the rotten shingles as he was making a huge hole in my roof!

"What the hell are you doing?!" I yelled indignantly.

Declan looked down as his annoyingly familiar smirk appeared. He looked on me standing there in my flannel pajamas and bed-hair.

"Hey B." He gave a little wave, before he returned to jamming his crowbar in between the shingles.

"What the hell are you doing to my roof?!" I demanded.

"What does it look like I'm doing? I'm replacing the rotten shingles." He shrugged casually.

"Declan, do you know what time it is?!"

He looked at his watch, before he answered with, "9.13 AM." Then he tossed another shingle down to the ground.

"Get off my roof!"

"No."

"GET OFF MY ROOF RIGHT NOW!" I bellowed.

"If I got off your roof right now, you would have a hole the size of a Werewolf and it looks like it's going to rain again."

"What the hell do you think you're doing?!"

He gave a peculiar look, "what the hell do you think I'm doing? I'm replacing your rotten shingles."

"Nobody asked you do that!"

"I know." He shrugged.

"My Dad said he was going to do that!"

"I know, but it's supposed to rain heavily over the next few days and your roof is already leaking. I'm saving him the trouble."

"Get off my roof Declan! I'll frickin' well do it myself!" I huffed.

"Yeah right!" He scoffed. "You can't frickin' get out of bed let alone feed yourself these days, so how are you supposed to do it?"

"Get off my roof!"

"No." He tossed another rotten shingle onto the ground.

"GET THE HELL OFF MY ROOF RIGHT NOW!"

Declan continued hammering away as he said simply, "you could just say thanks."

"I didn't ask you to do that!"

"You could make me dinner to pay me back."

"No way in hell!"

He tossed down another rotten shingle which almost hit me!

"Bianca, go and get dressed will you? And brush your hair for Pete's sake! You are so NOT a morning person." He sneered.

Then he ignored me as he mutilated my roof... I don't believe this, I really don't believe this! Fine! I'm going to ignore him too! I didn't ask him to do this! Who the hell asked him to do this?!

I walked back inside, now with muddy feet which pissed me off even more. I went upstairs and my first point of call was the bathroom to wash my feet in the bath tub. Eventually I dressed to the sound of more banging, before I came back downstairs to make myself a coffee.

I didn't want to be up. I didn't want to be out of bed but I couldn't sleep with all the racket he was making. Now what do I do? I'll continue ignoring him, that's what! So I went and found my MP3 player. Next, I placed the earphones over my ears and went out to the greenhouse to catch up on my gardening.

*****

I stayed in the greenhouse all day, weeding, watering, fertilizing and pulling out the rotten vegetables which I had neglected to collect when they were ripe. I threw out a whole basketful of spoiled tomatoes, withered carrots, rotten radishes and wilted lettuce.

Damn it, it was a waste of food. I carried the basket of rotten produce out to the compost bin to dump it in there. Oh well, I might as well try and get some use out of it.

"That was a waste."

I looked up to find Declan was watching from the roof. I scowled as I returned to the greenhouse to try to save what plants I could. I stood and surveyed my former food-producing nursery which made me feel bad. Grant wouldn't have approved of my wasting food.

I heard his chirpy voice inside my head, "what we don't eat we can trade."

The picture of him with his dirty hands, working away to the music we used to play on his iPod and mini-speakers as we worked together, came to mind. My eyes watered for their millionth time and I almost left the greenhouse to escape his memory. But no, I forced myself to remain where I was. It was because I was avoiding his memory that got me into this mess in the first place.

I rubbed my eyes with the back of my hands, turned my music up louder and forced myself to continue.

*****

By the time I returned to the house with only a quarter of a basket of edible produce, it was 3 PM. I washed my hands in the kitchen sink before I started washing the vegetables I had brought in.

I had done a good days work, even if the work itself made me feel bad considering how neglectful I had been. I had torn out everything dead and rotting – oh if I could only do that to my heart – and replanted new seeds to start again. I had run out of tomato seeds though, I would have to go down to the store in the next couple of days and get some more.

BANG! BANG! BANG!

It sounds like the lunk head was still here, doing whatever it was that he was doing to my roof. Does he even know how to fix shingles? Has he even done this before? I thought his roof was made of aluminum, so how would he know how to replace shingles? I bet Dad will still have to fix the roof, to repair Declan's 'repairs'.

I shook my head as I took out a frozen rabbit from my freezer. I chucked it into the microwave to defrost as I proceeded to cut up the vegetables. Over the next half hour, I prepared a rabbit stew by memory from Great Grandma's recipe. As I cooked, I noticed outside my kitchen window that the weather turned dark. It had even started to drizzle.

Ha ha! Sucked in to Declan, it's raining on him! I paused as I stood still and listened.

BAM! BAM! BAM!

He continued to work away in the drizzle, which I found surprising. I was sure that he would quit with the rain as his excuse. I wonder why he's doing this?

Has he come to gloat? Has he come to see me mope in my mourning? Has he come to do a good deed by helping the widow?   I was sick of everybody's pity! Seeing my family's pitiful expressions, as they regarded me was infuriating! The way the whole tribe regarded me was a wretched experience.

"Look at poor Bianca Elm. She was married off and even though the union was arranged, she and Grant still fell in love. Then Grant dies in a skirmish on our border, dying defending the tribe. Bianca's all alone with no kids since she's barren." I imagined what they were saying. "Now she's going to be alone for the rest of her life..."

BAM! BANG! BAM!

Declan's hammering slowly brought me back to reality. It was just in time too, as the bile was seriously beginning to build up, almost making me nauseas. Once I had tipped in the chopped up vegetables along with the rabbit pieces, I lastly added the herbs. Then I left it to cook as I went to sit on the couch to read a book.

BANG! BANG! BANG!

I tried to ignore the noise and concentrate on the book I was reading. It was a collection of plays by Tenesee Williams which Gran had leant me. I was currently reading 'A Streetcar Named Desire' and to be honest, I wasn't particularly enjoying it as I didn't like any of the characters.

Stella pissed me off for being so stupid that she would marry a brute of a man like Stanley. It annoyed me in the beginning that she didn't tell her sister to go and take a hike. Blanche pissed me off for being so vacuous and yet conniving. Then I started to imagine what I would do if I came across Stanley. I knew exactly how I would introduce myself to him, by taking a swipe at him with my claws! I put down the book as I closed my eyes and I imagined him running away, screaming into the night...

Hmm, I think on this full moon I should go hunting with the pack again. I had put it off the last ten months, with my loss of appetite. I think Dad and Grandfather were right, it wasn't healthy and I could accidentally revert and hurt someone.

*****

After five o'clock I returned to the kitchen, turned off the stove and served myself. I carried the bowl of stew over to the table and sat down and slowly began to pick at it whilst I read the next play called 'The Glass

Menagerie'. As I ate, I eventually realized that a full twenty minutes had passed without any further construction noises coming from my roof.

Does this mean that he's finished? Does this mean that he's gone home? That's a bit rude, just leaving like that without saying goodbye. Then again this is Declan whom we were talking about, 'rude' was his middle name.

Abruptly, my front door opened and a damp Declan walked in.

"Hmm, rabbit stew." He saw what I was eating. "Your Great Grandma's recipe, I presume?"

I watched him walk into my kitchen, pull a bowl from the cupboard and help himself to serving some.

"What are you doing?" I asked indignantly. However he ignored me as he came to sit at the table. He picked up his spoon to begin eating as I said sarcastically, "please, help yourself."

"I just did." He spoke with his mouthful.

I rolled my eyes before I returned to my book, absentmindedly stirring my meal. He was pensive for a moment as he observed.

"The stew's good. You should eat it, not play with it." He bossed me around. I ignored and tried to concentrate on the play. "What's your book about?"

"It's not just a book, they're different plays." I said curtly.

"Plays?" He raised his eyebrows. "Sounds kind of artsy and boring." I definitely ignored that remark, as I tried to focus on the words. Declan kept talking, "what's it about? Is it a bunch of pansies wearing tights?"

"Huh?" I looked on like he was an idiot.

"My Mom tried to make me read some god-awful play called 'A Summer's Fantasy' or some crap like it? I swear they were all gay." He rolled his eyes.

"Do you mean, 'A Midsummer Night's Dream'?"

"Yeah, that's it."

"It's a play by William Shakespeare! It's a classic!" I stated.

"Full of fairies and lovey-dovey shit." He shook his head in disapproval before he nodded to my book. "What's that one about?"

"Well, in the last play I read, a man raped his wife's sister." I said flatly.

Declan raised his eyebrows in surprise. "You like reading stuff like that? I think the fact that you haven't gone hunting in a while is starting to bother your animal instincts."

"Oh, so your small town hick, uneducated, grease monkey brain immediately thinks that I want to run outside and rape somebody?" I put down my book.

"Hey, you said it not me."

"So no never mind that I'm fantasizing about what my claws could do to the rapist?"

He raised his eyebrows even higher, "definitely time to go hunting, I think."

I pushed away my bowl in disgust at his behavior as I sat back, crossing my arms. "Declan, why are you here making a nuisance of yourself?"

"A nuisance? I've just spent the last eight hours repairing your roof! And just in time too, have you noticed the weather outside?" He retorted.

"I was hoping you would fall off and break your neck."

"You're welcome." He said moodily as he continued to eat.

Within two minutes he had finished his bowl and now I watched him stand up to walk into the kitchen and serve himself another.

"Oh please, help yourself, Declan. Please help yourself to my food. Eat as much of the stew as you like, no never mind it's meant to last me the rest of the week!" I said in a surly voice.

"Thanks, I will." He gave himself a generous amount before he came back to the table and sat down again.

"Why are you here, Declan?" I demanded.

"No never mind me telling you twice what I've been doing all day, as I worked my ass off. But have you noticed your roof isn't leaking anymore?" He returned.

"But why did YOU do it? Why did the thought pop into your tiny brain that went, 'ding!' I'm going to fix the chick with the dead husband's roof!"

"Pity." He shrugged.

"Pity?"

"Yeah, pity."

Grrr! Now that WAS the wrong thing to say! My dark blue eyes burned turquoise in fury and I felt claws emerge...

"Here you are, ten months after your hubby biting the big one and you've fallen apart." He continued. "You're a mess, you can't look after yourself and you have everybody else providing for you. So I thought I'd do a good deed and help the useless chick with the dead husband."

"GET OUT OF MY HOUSE!" I roared as I jumped to my feet so fast, my chair fell over.

"I mean B, have you looked at yourself in the mirror lately? You used to be one hot female Werewolf, but now? Boy, you've gone down hill." He sighed as he continued eating.

"GET OUT OF MY HOUSE RIGHT NOW!"

"I thought with you being a Lokoti Werewolf and a Circulator, it would mean that you would keep your looks for longer? Nope! These past ten months, you've really been looking old." He scooped up the stew to put into his smug mouth.

"GET OUT DECLAN!"

"You've always been a bitch, but at least you had the pheromones and the pretty face. Now you don't even have that." He gobbled down my food.

"GET THE HELL OUT OF MY HOUSE YOU SON OF A BITCH!"

"Careful B, you might make me think I'm making a dent in your stone cold heart." He snickered.

I picked up his frickin' bowl of stew and threw it off the table! The bowl smashed onto the floor, smearing stew in a wide circle.

Declan coolly raised his eyebrows, "I'm not cleaning that up."

When he started to reach for my bowl to eat that instead, I picked it up first and threw that over my shoulder as well! The bowl hit the wall behind before it smashed on the floor, leaving a trail of rabbit stew going down the wall.

"Do you want me to go and fetch the saucepan of stew so you can throw that around too?" He sat back and laughed.

He laughed! The infuriating, smug, stuck-up bastard was laughing at me!

"Shut up!" I screeched.

"Well well, it looks like you're still alive after all." He arched an eyebrow.

"GET OUT GET OUT GET OUT!" I screamed enraged.

I felt my body completely change as my muscles bulked up and the nails on my hands and feet extended, as did my teeth.

"There's the girl we all know and love." He looked me up and down.

I lashed out and it happened so quickly, it was almost like I didn't have control over my arm! But the next thing I knew, Declan had four deep cuts on the right side of his face! As much as the fury and the bloodlust were eating me up inside...I froze as soon as I saw what I did to him.

In supernatural speed, Declan leapt to his feet and pulled me across the table! He gripped onto my arms hard, as his blue eyes burned bright green and his round pupils turned into narrow slits.

"Are you hungry yet?" He growled.

His European Werewolf eyes hypnotized me for what must have been a second, although it felt longer than that. What happened next, I lost track of all sense of time as Declan pulled me to him whilst simultaneously I pushed my mouth over his.

I grabbed onto the front of his shirt with my claws accidentally cutting the fabric. I felt myself pushed backwards onto the table's surface as we kissed, using our sharp teeth to scrape over each other's lips. He leaned over, letting go of my arms and the next thing I felt, was my jeans being undone. As he pushed them down, I squirmed underneath.

"My shoes...!" I snarled frustratedly as I tried to kick them off.

Declan whipped the shoes off my feet although they were still done up and then he completely pulled off my jeans which is what I wanted. I pulled him over me whilst unbuttoning his and he pushed them down without bothering to take them off. He gave a push with his hips and we instantly growled in a satisfied way the moment we came together.

He moved hard as he moved fast, with our mouths fighting over who would be the dominant. As we kissed using our tongues, our sharp teeth knocked into the other's as we growled, snarled and tried to bite each other. Next, his hands ripped open my shirt and went straight for my breasts. I felt his claws dig into the soft flesh, bringing both pleasure and pain. The food on the walls, floor or even in the pot was forgotten, as instead we feasted on each other.

After the first couple of times, it didn't placate my lust; it only made me want more. I started to notice it was the same for Declan. I grew tired of the same position on the table top, so I stopped him. We looked at each other for maybe a second, before we both said at the same time;

"Upstairs."

He picked me up, wrapping my strong legs about his waist. He stumbled blindly over to the staircase with his jeans hanging around his knees before he managed to carry me up the staircase. Our mouths couldn't bear to be apart which hindered his sight greatly, as I felt my back knock into the banister and then the walls but I didn't care. I would have been more annoyed if he had turned away to look where he was going.

Thirty seconds later, we were rolling naked between the sheets. This was my second time with Declan, but now our first time in an actual bed with the both of us naked this time.

I loved the feel of his skin touching mine. I loved the feel of his teeth biting into different parts of my body. I inhaled deeply, taking in his maple syrup scent. I loved rolling on top and sitting up, by the way his bright blue eyes widened as they took in the sight of my bare body. Then they changed back to his glowing green colour as he sat upright, enveloping me in his arms.

I cried out as I felt him bite deeply into the skin in between my neck and left shoulder. I got goose bumps when I felt him taste me, which roused my own yearning. I drove my teeth into his right shoulder, delighting in the sensation of my teeth piercing his tough epidermis, to reach the warm, red sweetness inside.

He grunted in both pain and satisfaction as this stirred our bloodlust and fueled our frenzy for another three hours...

...when it eventually ended, I lay on top of him with my face half hidden in his warm neck. My eyes closed contentedly, as I breathed in his scent coming off his sweaty skin. Our panting took nearly half an hour to subside. Neither of us spoke as neither of us said a thing.

We just laid there, listening to rain outside, breathing in the other. But his sharp nails did run lightly up and down my back...that felt nice.

*****

I don't remember falling asleep or even for how long, but I vaguely recalled opening my eyes at some stage to watch Declan dress. I think it was just before dawn, because it smelled early.

He looked down on the bed as he pulled on his ripped shirt, when he noticed me sleepily looking up. He half-smiled my way, giving me a small, secretive smile. I noticed where I scratched him on his face was completely healed over without any scars showing.

With that, Declan walked out of my bedroom. I listened to him go down the stairs, with the lose stair creaking loudly when he stepped on it. I was asleep again before he even closed the front door behind.

*****

The next time I opened my eyes, it was mid-morning. It was wet and grey outside and I could even hear the rain patter over the newly-repaired roof.

It felt strange waking up naked in bed again and still be alone. I hadn't slept naked since Grant was alive. When I was with him, I never woke up both naked and alone. The morning after a romantic night, he had always ensured that when my eyes opened, he was the first thing that I would see.

I rolled onto my back as I sighed and stared up at my ceiling. But I could understand why Declan didn't hang around though. I think I even knew the reasons why.

The first was so we wouldn't have to go through the awkward 'morning after' of not knowing what to say to the other. The second reason was to ensure secrecy. It would look strange that he went over to repair my roof but he didn't go home until the next morning. I knew he would have snuck back into his house and lied to his mother about either patrolling or hunting.

Our secrecy was because I was a Lokoti Werewolf who had lost her mate and I wasn't meant to take on another. Once we lose a mate that was it, we were meant to remain alone. From our biological asymmetry to the one we had lost, it supposedly prevented us from taking another.

Again, I seemed to be the aversion to tradition. I'm the first female Lokoti Werewolf as I'm the first Lokoti Werewolf to be barren. Now I'm the first Lokoti Werewolf to have sex again after their mate died.

It was good sex, although it was guilty sex. I moaned as I pulled my pillow over my face, as if I were trying to smother myself. Nup, damn it! I can still breathe.

*****

The day passed quietly, like the eerie calm in the eye of a hurricane. I got up and dressed and then I went downstairs. I picked up my jeans and shoes off the floor. When I threw the jeans into the dirty laundry basket, I saw how full it was, so I did my laundry.

I cleaned up the broken bowls and the spilt stew. I had to use my Werewolf muscle to scrub the congealed stew off. I put the left over stew from the pot, into tupperwear containers which I stacked into my freezer. Then I sat on the couch and finished the book of plays so I could give it back to Gran when I saw her next.

As it turned dark outside, I found myself staring out the window. My hand ran over the healed bite mark on my left shoulder which tingled strangely, from thinking about the person who had put it there. I could sense although don't ask me how, that Declan was thinking about me too.

I gave up trying to read and instead I went upstairs for a long, hot bubble bath before dinner.

~~~~~~

25th May 2090

BANG! BANG! BANG!

Huh?

BAM! BAM! BAM!

Sleepily I raised my head to listen.

BANG! BAM! RIIIPPP!

That wasn't coming from my roof this time, it was coming from inside of the house.

BANG! BAM! RRRIIIIPPP!

I stumbled out of bed to walk over to the top of the staircase. When I looked down, I found Declan was repairing the lose stair. After a second, he noticed me standing over and he chuckled as he shook his head.

"I love that bed-hair you've got goin' in the morning." He greeted.

Then I noticed two cups of coffees sitting on the step above him. He made me coffee?

"Are one of those for me?" I nodded to the beverages.

"No, I always make myself two cups of coffee." He said sarcastically.

"That wouldn't surprise me." I walked down part of the staircase before I stopped. I sat down two steps up from where he was working to pick up the cup on the right which was still full. I gingerly drank from it, when my eyebrows arose in surprise. "You got it right."

"Huh?"

"You made my coffee how I like it."
~~~~~~

"It's not hard, white and two is the standard for most people." Declan shrugged off my reluctant praise. "I drink my coffee that way."

I eyed him warily, "why are you here, repairing my lose stair and making me coffee in the morning?"

"Someone's gotta do it." He shrugged again.

Declan tore off the lose stair completely and dropped it loudly onto the living room floor. Next, he picked up a perfectly cut wooden board that was an exact match for the one he was replacing it with.

"There." He smiled smugly as he fit the new board over the space. "Am I good or am I good?"

"Where did this perfectly-cut board come from?" I asked knowingly.

"I cut it yesterday." He answered. "How good am I for memorizing the measurements even though I didn't take any?"

I smirked as I liked the idea that even when we were apart, he was thinking about me. Even if it came out as memorizing the shape of my stairs, I was still touched.

"Not bad for a grease monkey." I conceded.

"At least I'm more useful than you who just sits around reading books all day."

"It's called education, Declan. I know you're a little fuzzy with that concept since you quit school at the wise old age of thirteen? But doing a degree is appreciated by some people, like my parents or even the Tribal Elders."

"They're just humoring you."

I laughed! I liked fighting with him and at least he isn't turning all mushy or anything. I sighed as I sat back with my coffee and watched him start to nail down the new board.

"Can you go get dressed and do something about that hair?" He quipped.

"What's wrong with my flannel pajamas?"

"They're kids pajamas with those cartoon whatever's all over them."

"They're cows." I corrected.

"A grown woman shouldn't sleep in pajamas with cartoon cows all over them." He spouted off his opinion.

"Oh and what should I be sleeping in?"

"Negligee."

"Even in freezing Alaska where temperatures can drop to minus fifty degrees Celsius?"

"It's almost summer as it's an even fifteen degrees outside."

"And whereabouts am I supposed to buy this said negligee? From our little general store here on Tribal Lands?" I asked in amusement.

"You're the Circulator, I thought you could go anywhere you pleased."

"But why would it please me to circulate in time just so I can go negligee shopping?"

"Look lady," he paused in his hammering to frown my way, "I didn't spend all day Monday up on your roof, or half the day yesterday cutting this board; to rock up first thing in morning to repair your staircase for the hell of it! I'm paying for your services. If I'm going to get sex out of you, you can at least look sexy for me."

I cracked up laughing at the serious expression on his face, belying the joke.

"Well, I hope you can keep this little arrangement between us, Declan. Otherwise I would have all the boys in the tribe trying to repair my greenhouse next."

"What's wrong with your greenhouse?"

"One of the windows is cracked."

He sighed wearily, "I'll fix it on Friday."

"Declan that wasn't a hint – it was a joke!"

"Like I said, this is a business transaction." He pointed the hammer at me. "Just because you're the only girl around that I can have sex with, don't get this confused with love or anything like that. I'm paying for your services."

"Fine but just so you know, I'm a widower and the man that I loved is dead! I'm just using you too."

"Good."

"Good." I looked away in annoyance. "I DON'T want another mate."

"What?!" He blanched, before he laughed nervously. "Listen B, who said anything about mating? I'm just here for a good time."

"Likewise," I glared, "and if anybody should ever find out about us? I will refute it and say that I can't stand you."

"Trust me, nobody is going to find out." He said firmly.

"Good, so have we got that settled?"

"You're preaching to the choir." He returned to his hammering.

*****

It was 2.43 AM when I opened my eyes, catching Declan dress on his way out. Again he looked down to watch me sleep, with the sheet hanging loosely over my waist, exposing my skin.

"Forget about the negligee, just sleep like that from now on." He said simply. "I'll see you in a day's time to fix that greenhouse."

I didn't respond, I just watched him turn and leave the bedroom. Next, I heard him go down the stairs with the repaired staircase no longer squeaking, before I heard my front door open and shut. I fell back asleep to the sound of his truck starting up outside, without giving another thought.

*****

On Friday morning I awoke, got up and made the bed. I practically danced around upstairs as I energetically dressed in my bedroom before heading to the bathroom to brush my hair. Lastly, I skipped down the steps to go into the kitchen to switch on the kettle...

...when I found a cup of coffee already made which was waiting for me on the kitchen bench.

A grin spread across my face as I picked up the mug and carried it out the back door and down the path to the greenhouse. I went inside and found Declan removing the broken glass panel, with a new one waiting to be installed. As I approached, I noticed another half-drunk cup of coffee sitting on the cement floor for himself.

"Did you cut that yesterday?" I greeted as I sat up on the work bench whilst looking down at the new glass.

"Yup."

"From memory again?"

"Yep."

I sipped my coffee as I watched him work. He carefully unscrewed the broken glass panel from the frame, before gently placing the broken pieces onto the ground. He gingerly picked up the new glass panel minding his supernatural strength, as he placed it over the fittings on the wooden frame.

"Ah ha!" He looked over his shoulder my way to smile smugly. He was showing off how the new panel was a perfect fit.

"Yeah yeah." I rolled my eyes. "Well done."

"What did you do without me?" He joked as he screwed in the new piece.

"I led a peaceful life."

"With a leaking roof, a broken stair and a smashed greenhouse?"

"I would have fixed them eventually."

"Sure!"

"Well, my Dad and my Grandfather would have fixed my roof." I shrugged. "I could have done the rest."

"Maybe you should take your nose out of the books and learn from everyday life for a change. Then you can fix your own roof." He said. "Your Dad and your Grandfather aren't going to be around all the time."

What the...?! His latest barb really cut, even worse than the broken glass could have.

"What's that supposed to mean?" I slammed down my coffee onto the bench.

"Huh?" He looked back in surprise.

"What do you mean by that?!"

"I mean that eventually they're gonna die of old age in a hundred years time, then what are you gonna do? Live under a leaking roof with your vegetables wilting in a broken greenhouse in the middle of a hard winter?"

"Oh sure..." I hopped off the bench angrily, "...because EVERYBODY dies right? Especially the people around me? Because I can't reproduce, my barrenness has turned into 'deathness' and that's why Grant's dead!"

He stood up so he could turn my way, "what the hell are you going on about now?"

"Go home!"

"No."

"Go home Declan!" I yelled in his face. "Get out of here!"

"I'm not finished." He spoke calmly.

"I don't care about the frickin' window! Just get out!" I pointed towards the door.

"Nope." He turned back around to continue with what he was doing.

Fine, I don't care what he does! But I certainly am not letting him use my 'services' tonight! I turned around and stormed back into the house. However once I was inside, I was so angry I couldn't remain still.

I paced around the living room a couple of times, unable to sit down because of how angry I felt. Declan calls it as it is, he's a loud-mouthed idiot but at least he's honest. What if he was voicing how the whole tribe sees me, as a Black Widow? I can't have young and I can't keep a mate either. But I've always had a green thumb and when I didn't neglect my plants, they thrived. I'm not THAT bad, am I? I had to get out of here...

My front door was left open as I stomped off the veranda, pouted past Declan's truck parked out front and I stormed into the woods with the proverbial steam whistling out of my ears.

As I power walked through the trees towards the river, I noticed I was growling under my breath. I also noticed that the nails on my feet and hands were starting to get a little long...which I had to stop otherwise risk ruining another pair of shoes. The noises of the forest turned silent, as the crickets stopped singing, the birds stopped chirping and nearly all the wildlife hid from me, this predator in their midst.

Great, that's just wonderful! So not only can I NOT produce new life, I kill off my mate and even the woods cringe from me. I marched down the muddy path, growling even louder. I was so angry that I didn't hear the footsteps behind until it was too late.

"Grraaawwwwlll!!!"

Next, I found myself being tackled from behind as I went flying into the ferns!

"Oomph!" I landed on my back with Declan laughing on top!

"Some Werewolf you are, you didn't even hear me coming!"

"Get off me!" I tried to shove him aside but he pinned me down.

"Jinx." He smiled teasingly.

Frickin' hell, so not only am I a Black Widow but now I'm a jinx?

"Thank god we're not mates otherwise I'd kill you!" I growled threateningly.

I tried snapping at him, but he easily held me down whilst holding himself up out of harms way.

"Look at where we are, B." He momentarily looked about. "This is where we did it the first time, six years ago."

Huh? I raised my head to glance around. Oh, he was right. We were in the exact spot in the woods, near the path going down to the river.

"Jinx." He repeated.

Oh that's why he was saying 'jinx', he wasn't calling me a jinx but he was implying the coincidence that we're back here.

Declan laid himself over my body, smothering my mouth with his. I felt his hands scurry down to each of our pants to undo them. We got pretty wet, especially me since I was underneath as he insisted on claiming the dominant position. I felt the cold, wet earth seep through my clothes, giving me goose-bumps, but at least he worked up quite a grass stain on his knees.

I had to admit, being here did bring it all back; as our passion heated us up, keeping away the cold. I even found myself looking up at the canopy of trees again, just as I did then.

Being outside in the woods and 'back to nature'; seemed to inspire Declan as he behaved insatiable. He held onto my thighs so tightly, he squeezed them against his waist. He dug his sharp nails into my skin as he pushed himself harder, grunting audibly. It almost seemed like he was trying to hurt which he didn't, instead it pushed my pleasure even higher. When I was on the brink of losing control, I dug my claws into his back as a release which in turn, excited him even more.

This went for nearly an hour, I could tell by the change of position of the sun through the branches of the trees.

"Oh hell yes, hell yes, oh hell yeah!" He gasped as he wound down. He went kerplunk! as he collapsed onto my softer body. "Oh yeah that was good."

He tried to catch his breath but then I caught sight of an odd expression on his face. I didn't like it, it made me nervous.

"Declan...?"

"You can't have kids, right?" He looked back down as he even looked a little fearful.

"You know I can't! The whole frickin' tribe does." I said narkily.

"Still, I'd rather be safe than sorry...!" He started to move his head downwards.

"Declan!" Indignantly I grabbed hold of his hair to stop him. "What the hell?!"

"Look, do you want to be the pregnant widow? You wanna be known as the Lokoti Werewolf who's mated a second time?" He forcibly removed my hand.

"No but -"

"Then shut up and stay still."

"Declan!" I sat upright. "Don't be stupid! Anyways, why are you worried about THAT now? You weren't so concerned the last two times."

"B, can't you feel it?" He looked on, anxiously. "Today was different because today my body acted of its own accord, like it was deliberately trying to plant my seed. I lost control of myself."

This only made me angrier! Instead I completely pushed him off so I could stand up. He landed face-first into the wet ferns, but he was quick to roll onto his back to look up.

"I'm going home." I said coldly as I redressed.

"B -"

"Shut up, Declan."

"B!"

He tried to stop me again but I pushed his hands off! Next, I marched through the ferns, over to the muddy path and back up to my house. I didn't even wait for him.

"What the hell is wrong with you today?!" He complained as he fell into step beside whilst buttoning up his jeans.

I hurried up the hill as my answer, but Declan refused to be put off.

"You've got a bee under your bonnet about something, now what is it? Why did you get all angry in the greenhouse?"

I didn't reply, I simply walked faster. I charged through the woods and onto my property once more.

He growled out, "man you are one frustrating bird! Thankfully this isn't a REAL relationship, as you are the most infuriating woman that anybody could ever go out with!"

I ran up the veranda steps and into the house via the front door which I slammed in his face before he could follow after. Unfortunately it didn't stop him though, he simply opened it again and ignored my blatant hint. I didn't hesitate but instead I bolted up my staircase.

Whilst stripping off my wet clothes, I walked into the bathroom to have a long, hot shower. I was expecting that by the time the shower was finished, Declan would have gone home. However after five minutes, he came into the bathroom naked, as he joined me.

"What are you doing?" I glared.

"You ask a lot of stupid questions for a University educated snob." He directed the shower head his way to wash himself down.

"Where are your clothes?"

"In your washing machine." He answered casually.

Declan started to wash his hair, using my shampoo. As he lathered up he directed the shower head back on me. I washed the conditioner out of my hair before I grabbed my loofa and shower gel. Just as I began to use it over my body, he snatched it off me.

"Turn around." He barked before he began to massage the soapy sponge into my back.

Oh that felt good and he wasn't stingy on rushing either. Declan lifted up my long, wet hair as he massaged the sponge over my shoulders and then down my spine. He turned me around again when he knelt down to rub my legs before he worked his way up.

"My go." He handed the loofa over after the leisurely massage he gave.

He turned around so I was facing his back. I sponged him down next, taking as long as he did. I paused when he turned back around so I could do his chest next, as his physique still left me breathless. Declan sensed this as his eyes glowed green in excitement. He stepped up closer with his mouth parting and I dropped the sponge as I practically leapt upon him!

****

Two hours later, I was lying on my back in bed, with Declan resting his head on my abdomen whilst looking up into my face.

We were winding down, with the afternoon sun making the bedroom look extra bright. My hair was still damp from not drying it properly however when I ran my hand through Declan's shorter, blonde hair I felt that it was completely dry.

"So," he began, "let's indulge in the human habit of the 'deep and meaningful' after sex, shall we? Are you going to tell me what was biting your ass this morning?"

"No."

"Why not?"

"Why do you want to know?" I asked coolly. "This isn't a relationship so I don't have to tell you anything."

"Good point." He arched his eyebrows before he passed a cheeky grin, "but it's kinda helpful just the same, to know when I say something wrong incase I wanna say it again."

I sighed as I stared up at the water stain on the ceiling, from when the roof used to leak. "I'm a Black Widow."

"You're a what? You're a spider?" He gave a peculiar look.

"In a sense, I create death."

"Huh?" Then he prodded, "you care to elaborate on that?"

"I end life."

"So do I, big deal! I have to battle myself every full moon as sometimes it's like I'm literally fighting the bloodlust." Declan admitted. "You and the other Lokoti Werewolves have successfully placated it by hunting animal? When I eat animal, for me it's like constantly eating an entree with no main course afterwards. It's frickin' frustrating, that's what it is!

I looked on in surprise, "I thought you were cured."

"Are you kidding me?" He raised his eyebrows. "The bloodlust never goes away, it's occasionally our control of it does."

I sat up in shock, "do you mean that you've -"

"Once." He confessed. "A few years ago when you were married to Grant, I snuck off tribal lands when I stalked a human's house on the outskirts of Alma."

"And?"

"And I managed to get control of myself again so I came home." He shrugged.

"So you've actually made it across the border when you were hunting human?"

"Hunt yes, but thank god I regained control of myself just in time. I nearly smashed through the window and ate the young family inside; man, woman and baby." He looked away guiltily. "I nearly became the monster that killed my father and nearly killed me, when I was three."

I swallowed hard, as I could picture the carnage of what nearly happened.

"Did the townspeople see you?" I asked as I ran my hand through his short, thick hair.

"No." He sighed, before he looked back. "B, you don't think you're a Black Widow because you can't have kids and you think that's somehow related to Grant dying, do you?"   I looked on taken aback at this sudden perceptiveness, before I have a nod. He chuckled, "man, you are one melodramatic chick!"

Just as I started to remove my hand from his hair, he quickly grabbed it to put it back on his head.

"That's nice, don't stop." He looked on pleadingly.

I returned to running my fingers through his short hair, as he sighed contentedly whilst resting his head on my muscle-toned stomach.

"B." He spoke again as he turned his head to look me in the eye when he said this. "Besides the fact that you're the only woman not just in the tribe but in a thousand mile radius that I can screw without killing or turning you; besides the fact that you just happen to be somebody I grew up with; besides the fact that I was in love with you before you changed; besides the fact that you are the first female Lokoti Werewolf in history which works out to my advantage? You are my perfect mate because you can't have kids."

Huh, what was that? My eyes widened as I looked on in surprise. Did I just hear correctly that the tribe's bad-ass made a confession of love?

Declan sniffed me and then he said seriously, "you're not pregnant, I can't get you pregnant and that works out fine with me. I have a hard enough time controlling my own bloodlust that I don't think I'd cope if I created offspring which had it too." Then he sighed in resignation, "and the pack and the Tribal Elders think so as well."

"Why do you say that?"

"There were two unmarried males in the pack, me and Grant. They married you off to Grant because they see me as a liability." Declan said in annoyance.

I felt sorry for him as I tenderly ran my fingers over his crew cut. I said after a moment, "I don't think it was quite like that."

"Oh and how do you see it as?" He asked sulkily. "I would have been a better mate for you than Grant! My breed of Werewolf is supposed to live for 300 years instead of the Lokoti Werewolf lifespan of 200 years, which would suit your longevity as a Circulator. I was the one who caught up to you on the border and stopped you from reaching town the first night you changed. I was the one closer in age to you than Grant was."

"Declan..." I began, "...the day I came home and I overheard my parents arguing about the idea of an arranged marriage? They told Mum why they chose Grant to become my mate instead of you."

"They did?" He asked in surprise. "What did 'they' say about me?"

"Grandpa said, *'she can't consider Declan as a mate for two very obvious reasons. One, it would cause a rift in his family between he and his brother Derik. Two, is because Declan isn't a Lokoti Werewolf, he's a European Werewolf. Declan is still battling to keep his bloodlust under control and we aren't sure of the mating habits of his breed. As far as we know, his species isn't designed for long-term mating. His breed of Werewolf doesn't live in packs and his species has never been sighted with a long-term mate. His Werewolf gene may or may not be passed genetically from him to his children? But more importantly, he could harm the woman who is not of his breed when he mates with her'.*"

"Harm the woman? Did you just say HARM the woman? What the...!" He sat up, furious. "What, they think I would harm you?!"

I shrugged back, "I dunno."

"I take care of you, don't I?" He said indignantly. "I fixed your house, didn't I? HARM my woman? They think I'd harm my B...? I'll frickin' harm them in a minute!"

I accidentally let out a snicker at his quick temper, which immediately attracted his attention.

"What are you laughing at?" He snapped.

"You!" I laughingly pointed at his head.

"Oh yeah?" He grouchily hit my hand away, but I returned it to wave it in his face. "You're not afraid that I'm gonna HARM you?" He playfully tried to bite my finger.

"What are you going to do, insult me to death?" I smirked.

"True." He smirked back, before he settled over me once more. We both appreciated the feel of our warm, strong bodies pressed together. His face was right above mine so he could say this next bit, "I take care of my mother, don't I? I patrol for her, don't I? I didn't abandon her to look for a female European Werewolf when you were married, did I? I don't hunt human because my Mom's human and I don't hunt human because of you, B."

"Me?" I gave him a funny look. "What have I got to do with the price of fish?"

Declan rolled his eyes, "don't play dumb with me, you know I'm frickin' in love with you."

"Oh bestill my beating heart! When you say it romantically like that, I go into a swoon!" I gave an unimpressed look.

"Well if you want lovey-dovey bullshit then you're with the wrong breed." He chuckled, pushing apart my legs to settle in between.

"What, I get this instead? Wham-bam-but-NO-thank-yous-ma'am?" I asked sourly.

"Nope, you get the best sex in the tribe." He leaned in to graze my neck with his sharp teeth. He muttered as he licked and chewed his way over my skin, "there's a reason why I'm stronger, faster and downright better than the Lokoti Werewolves..."

"...and you have a bigger ego than the Lokoti Werewolves too."

I have to admit that when he kissed me like that? It could turn my skin hot as well as make my heart pound! Like we were two magnets drawn to each other, I gave up trying to stay away. I felt my body soften as it welcomed his.

"I felt that." He gloatingly sung.

"Declan." I grabbed hold of his head by his hair, to force him to look upwards again. "What are we going to do?"

"Do? Do about what?" He shook my hand off. "Oh, you mean about us and the 'mate once for life' rule?" Then he added on cheekily, "typical of a woman to start thinking long-term after frickin' sex!"

He laughed out loud when I slapped him on the ass!

"You're not going to get any sex in a minute if you don't behave!" I threatened.

"I can't believe that you remembered all of what was said, five years ago!" He continued to chuckle.

"I think I have a photographic memory because I remember conversations. I think it could be a Circulator thing, because so does my Mum and my Gran. If you ever read our diaries, you would see different conversations we've had with people." I shrugged.

"You write down your conversations?" Declan gave a peculiar look again. "Why?"

I shrugged once more, "I don't know, but we who have descended from Elisha have always kept diaries to log our lives. I guess because when we leave for the space time continuum, it's the last thing of us that remains."

"So right now my words are being recorded?" His smug grin returned, "cool, I'm being immortalized in the Circulate's Hall of Fame!"

"I think that's already happened because you're screwing the very last Circulator in existence." I joked along.

"Heh heh!" He chuckled cheekily. "So I am and you have to admit, I'm pretty good, aren't I?"

"What?!" I grabbed my pillow to smother his smirking face with it!

He laughingly tossed the pillow aside as he rolled over whilst pulling me on top. As I sat upright over his crotch, my dark blue eyes watched his bright blue ones widen. Simultaneously as I took him inside, he gave an eager thrust. I rested my hands on his strong chest which turned hot.

We both watched the other's faces change from expressions of helpless yearning to pure delight as our ecstasy took over...

...

...until I woke up at midnight to see Declan dressing in my dark bedroom.

"Do you need anything else fixed that I can use on the pretense of seeing you?" He joked. When I sleepily shook my head, he sighed out, "OK I'll sneak over tomorrow night then."

He leaned over to leave a kiss on my shoulder with his departure.

~ **18** ~

15th August 2090

Declan did sneak over to see me the next night, and the next and then the next after it. I began to establish a routine where I would go to bed early like 9 PM and remain until 9 AM the next morning.

I would lightly doze until midnight as it would be about this time that I would be woken from the sound of my backdoor downstairs, opening. I would lie still as I listened to the intruder come inside, walk through the living area and come up the stairs. By this stage, his maple syrup scent would be as clear as day.

He would walk naked into my bedroom, indicating that he had made his way here as a Werewolf either on the pretense of patrolling or hunting. Then as he pulled down my covers, I immediately welcomed him with open arms. He would settle over me, pressing his eager body against mine as our lips molded together.

We would remain together until 5 AM when Declan would growl in annoyance at the time glowing on Grant's digital clock. Reluctantly, he would leave my queen size bed to return to his single one, inside his mother's house. I listened to him leave via the back door as his scent would start to fade with his departure. Then from 5.30 AM to 9.30 AM, I would catch up on the rest of my sleep.

However on Wednesday nights when he patrolled, our pattern was different. I would sleep until 5 AM when the sound of the backdoor opening, woke me. Declan would hastily come in, jump into bed for an hour and then he would hastily depart. On these particular early mornings he growled even louder, further annoyed at our circumstance which made him do this.

And so it continued this way, with our affair secret and hidden under the cover of darkness... As I understood it, Declan never came via the roads but he ran up through the woods. Using his predatory skills, he was careful to cover his tracks and avoid open spaces, using the trees to hide his massive, dangerous shape. It was also why he used my backdoor, as it was closer to the tree line than the front.

Two weeks later when it was a full moon, I finally rejoined the pack to hunt but Declan and I were careful to avoid the other.

I liked to run at the front of the pack, as it allowed me to 'stretch my legs' and show off my greater speed. But when we caught the scent of a family of mountain lions whom had strayed into our territory, I dropped back. Declan next ran out in front to take on the strongest and feast alone. Then at dawn when we ran home, he dropped to the back once more as I ran out in front. However, I felt his glowing green eyes on my back the whole night through.

I sensed the pack's relief when I came out with them. I think they were worried that if I held out any longer, I might have reverted by accident and attacked a human. On the hunt, the Lokoti Werewolves dropped back to allow me to chase down the female Mountain Lion. Once I had stopped her heart Dad, Grandpa, Grandfather and Uncle Jules came forwards to share my kill.

Two days after the full moon, both Dad and Grandfather came to my house. They arrived in Grandfather's truck, which pulled up out the front. From the living room window, I watched them retrieve their tool kits from the back of the truck before approaching my veranda.

Frantically, I raced upstairs to my bedroom to rip the sheets off my bed! I just managed to race back downstairs by running in light speed to cram the sheets into the washing machine, before they knocked on my front door. I couldn't risk them catching Declan's scent in the sheets, which would expose us. Grandfather knocked a second time as I dropped in the laundry powder and turned on the machine.

I took a deep breath just before I opened the door to let them in, as I tried to slow my racing heart.

"Hi guys!" I beamed as I put on a false bravado. "What brings you two to my neck of the woods today?"

"Does a grandfather need an excuse to visit his granddaughter?" He smiled.

He came in first, with Dad walking in after. My grandfather kissed me on the right side of my face as my father kissed me on the left.

"How are you, B?" He enquired whilst Grandfather looked around.

"I'm fine thanks, Dad. How are you?"

"Fine thanks, yeah. Your mother is also well." He said amiably.

"So is your Gran." Grandfather added on. "She and I would like to have you over for dinner tomorrow night."

"Er yeah, sounds great." I quickly nodded.

Then both men stood back as they openly looked me over.

"You seem to be doing much better, B." He smiled in relief.

"I am doing much better, thanks." I gave a nod.

"It was good to see you hunting again." Dad commented. "To be honest, we were getting worried about you."

"Why, did you think I was secretly sneaking off the tribal lands and snacking on human?" I raised my eyebrows. Both men exchanged concerned glances before looking back my way. "Have you heard of any murders in Alma that sounds like a Werewolf could have done it?" I put my hands on my hips.

"Don't get all defensive B, we have to ask." He said gently. "Just as we would check on any other member of the pack who went for ten months without hunting."

"Well you don't have to worry, I used the bloodlust for other things." I half lied.

"Like what?" Grandfather asked.

I looked down at the tool kits that they were carrying before I answered, "I fixed the roof."

"You fixed the roof?" Dad echoed in disbelief.

"Yep, I replaced the damaged shingles so my roof doesn't leak anymore. I also repaired the lose stair and I even replaced the broken glass pane in the greenhouse." I lied through my teeth.

"You did ALL of that?" My father's eyes almost popped out of his head.

"That's impressive, B." Grandfather beamed.

"You did ALL of that by yourself?" He looked on skeptically.

Pause...come on B, careful now. Declan did drive here in his truck during his day visits, so someone could have seen him. It could have even been them, as he would have had to drive past their houses, coming up the hill.

"Well alright," I pretended to confess, "Declan gave me the wooden shingles, the new piece of board for the stair and the new glass pane but I did the installation myself."

"Declan gave you these things?" Grandfather asked in partial surprise. Then they looked about my house before exchanging another look. "That's why I can smell his scent here." He said half to me and half to Dad, who nodded in agreement.

Damn! Just remain calm, B. I tried hard to keep both my breathing and my gaze steady.

"Yeah, he wasn't here for long though." I laughed nervously. "I took what I wanted and then I kicked him out."

"When did all this happen?" Dad gave a funny look.

"Er, last month...?" I half-lied.

"That's strange," Grandfather frowned, "his scent is pretty strong, like he was here only recently."

Double damn! Triple damn! Man, I was tempted to just instantaneously phase away from them and their questions.

"Oh, he was here yesterday when I gave him some vegetables to pay for the materials." I rushed out before I turned to walk into the kitchen. "Would you two like a cup of coffee?"

"Yeah, sure." My father agreed.

"Yes please, B." My grandfather answered.

The two men put their tool kits on top of the dining table and sat down.

"If you've repaired the shingles; how about the water damage to the ceiling in your bedroom?" Dad asked next.

"Oh um no, I haven't." I struggled to keep my voice calm.

"We could do that today?" My father looked to his father-in-law, who nodded in agreement.

Frickin' hell! Now what do I do? If they can smell Declan in my living area, they would sure as hell detect that his scent was stronger in my bedroom!

"Um actually, guys?" I turned back around to make my excuse. "Thanks so much for the offer but um, I was planning on going down to the store today. Um, I mean this morning, to get some groceries, er to get some groceries because um, I'm out of food at the moment."

I can't lie to save my life! How dodgy did that just sound then?

Dad started to laugh for some reason. "You can still do that, B."

"We'll even mind the house for you, while you're away." Grandfather chuckled.

"You don't need to stand around babysitting us while we work on the bedroom ceiling." My father smiled in amusement.

Frickin' hell, lying was hard work! Now what do I do? So I tried an approach I've seen Mum use a couple of times. Whenever she really wanted something, she used her whiney voice as she pouted and she even batted her eyelashes. Dad ALWAYS turned into putty in her hands, when she used her secret weapon. I've even witnessed Vincent give in the couple of times she used it on him.

"Yes but I have to make my bed and I don't want you guys standing on it, when you work on the ceiling." I whined. "What if you drop plasterboard everywhere? I just vacuumed yesterday! It will leave such a mess -"

"Hunter." Grandfather interrupted. "I think we'll leave the bedroom ceiling because can you see how territorial she's behaving?"

"Uh huh." Dad snickered.

"It's alright B, you can relax. I acknowledge your independence and I can see that you prefer to do your own repair work. You could have just said so, instead getting all hot and bothered." He said patiently.

Phew! I was saved by the bell, or feminism or equality or whatever you want to call it. I think I'll leave Mum's secret weapon with her and take the high road.

"Thanks guys." I let out a sigh of relief. "I'll keep that in mind for next time."

"So, does this mean no coffee either?" Dad smirked.

"Huh?" I looked on blankly. "Oh right, coffee!"

I used that excuse to escape back into the kitchen to calm my nerves.

*****

I lay awake in bed that night as I waited for Declan to make his appearance. I was still anxious after my father and grandfather's visit that I didn't nap before my nocturnal tryst with my supernatural lover. Instead, I lay listening to my MP3 player.

The 'Smashing Pumpkins' played on full volume, blasting my ears with the grunge music. I let the rhythm wash over me to loosen my tense shoulders, but tonight the loud music didn't soothe. As much as I was looking forward to my visit with my secret lover, I was also scared of somebody finding out.

The time ticked past midnight and then onwards to one o'clock, as I watched the glowing digits on Grant's digital clock change.

Grant's clock? I was lying in my former marriage bed waiting for my secret lover, beside my late husband's alarm clock. The clock which kept track of my stolen time with Declan; my stomach knotted with guilt...

Quickly, I pulled off my earphones then I got up to rip the power chord from the wall! I picked up the clock and marched it over to the closet. I tossed his clock onto the top shelf, before I slammed the door shut and I quickly climbed back into bed. It's alright, I still have my clock on my bedside table. Albeit it's just an old battery-operated travel alarm clock but still, I can do without.

I turned my MP3 player back on but the deafening music brought little comfort. The music was so loud that I didn't hear my backdoor downstairs open and close. I didn't hear the footsteps going up my staircase just as I didn't hear the person come into my bedroom. I lay in bed with my eyes squeezed shut and the music taking up my concentration so I got quite the fright, when the person hopped into bed with me.

My eyes flashed turquoise, as I grabbed this person about the throat and I growled threateningly!

"What the hell?!" Declan ripped my hand away from his neck. "B, what the hell is wrong with you?!" Next, he bad-temperedly tossed my MP3 player off the bed, flinging my earphones along with it.

"Sorry." I said shortly.

I lay back down as I took several deep breaths to calm my racing heart and my urge to kill something...

"Sorry I'm late, I had to take a detour." He stretched out onto his back, beside. "I ran into Harry while he was on patrol."

"Harry?!" I echoed in alarm.

"I told him I was hunting, so I had to take off in the opposite direction of your house before doubling back." He huffed in annoyance. "I had to make sure he didn't catch my scent heading up the hill."

We laid in bed side by side, quiet in thought for a couple of moments.

"Dad and Grandfather came by today." I broke the silence.

"Oh yeah?"

"They smelled your scent inside the house and I lied, saying that you gave me the materials, but I fixed the house myself." I said unhappily.

"Being a Werewolf among a pack of Werewolves is a bitch."

"You're telling me."

"If we were human, nobody would give a hoot if we were doing it or not."

"Hmm." I frowned in agreement.

Declan looked my way in disbelief, "your grandfather and father actually bought the lie that you did the repairs yourself?"

"They were surprised but they believed me."

Then we turned quiet again until after a minute, he rolled my way. I felt his hands begin to remove my pajamas as his lips smothered the left side of my neck...

"Declan!" I pushed him off.

"What?!" He exclaimed.

"I don't think we should do it, tonight. I think we should take a break from each other, or in the least see each other less." I reluctantly straightened out my clothes.

"What?!" He sat upright in indignation.

I pursed my lips together determinedly, which made Declan glare down not just angry, but also hurt.

"B, I'm doing EVERYTHING in my power to make sure that we don't get caught!" He cried out infuriated. "You think this just affects you? Well wake up and smell the coffee! I could have fourteen Lokoti Werewolves after my skin if they found out about us! Plus two of these Werewolves are married to Circulators who each own a silver-coated, sharp, one meter long sword!"

His words made me laugh, "Mum and Gran AREN'T going to kill you over this!"

"No maybe not, but if we were found out I could be run out of town! How do you think that would affect my Mom?" He asked in a hurt voice. "I'm not just dangerous for you, but you're probably more dangerous for me! If we were found out, I could be run out of the tribe! My little brother is married and is a practicing Medicine Man now, an upstanding man of the tribe. I still live at home with my Mom and take care of her. If I get run out of here, how do you think that's going to affect them?"

Oh yeah, I could see his point of view. I felt bad because Declan was right, he was risking more than I was by our dangerous liaison.

"Then maybe that's reason enough to end this now, before anybody finds out." I said quietly.

Declan growled loudly and abruptly pulled me closer. His eyes flashed glowing green in the darkness and he even bared his teeth, like he was preparing for battle!

"There's no way in hell that I'm going to give you up! Not after all of the waiting. Not now and not ever." He spoke in a low voice.

Suddenly he ripped open my pajama shirt, which made two of the buttons come flying off! He bent over as he went straight for my breasts. His sharpening teeth bit into the tender skin which excited me! Soon I was kicking off my pajama pants myself however I must have taken too long as he ripped these off too, snapping the elastic at the top.

I had to admit, if the sex wasn't thrilling enough between two Werewolves? The danger of being discovered made it all the more tantalizing...

"This ain't over until the fat lady sings or turns into a Werewolf, whatever comes first." He growled in my ear, before our glowing eyes met and held.

Declan pushed me into the mattress as his lips smothered mine. Then his mouth traveled over my chin, down my neck, past my collar bone, over my breasts, past my belly button and even further south. My back arched in utter delight, as I felt my nails turn into claws in excitement. My teeth grew sharp as my body began to bulk up and turn strong. I growled as I writhed, unable to contain the bloodlust let alone the lust, he brought out.

His hands which were holding me down were firm as his grip was strong. As much as I growled and panted, he showed no sign of relenting. After a hypnotizing twenty minutes, I slowly reverted back to my human form. I lay there almost helplessly, as my glowing turquoise eyes dulled to their human dark blue colour.

I lay there a widow, being pleasured by another man in a secret affair. By my mate dying, this bed was supposed to become a chastity icon, like a patron saint of celibacy or some sort; a landmark of faithfulness to a dead person.

Don't hate me Grant, please don't! What I have with Declan? It was a long time coming - six years too long.

*****

Normally, we might make love for a couple of hours and then rest by lying in each other's arms? But last night we never stopped moving, not once. It's curious about the aphrodisiac effect of impending doom can have over a relationship. It wasn't until the big hand was on the twelve and the little hand was on the five, that Declan reluctantly released his hold to sit on the side of the bed.

"Don't go yet." I reached out to place my hand on his back.

"You know I have to, B." He growled in annoyance. "I have to get home before Mom wakes up and the older she gets, the earlier she rises."

I moaned as I rubbed my face in frustration, "this is ridiculous! I'm a grown woman who's almost 24 years old. You're a grown man who's turning 27 years old. We shouldn't have to sneak around like this!"

He turned to give a rueful grin, "but you gotta admit, it certainly adds to the sex, all this secrecy."

I smiled sadly, "maybe we wouldn't be interested in each other if we didn't have to sneak around?"

He sighed again as he temporarily lay back down to scoop me into his arms.

"I thought about that, but nup! It still doesn't change the fact that you're the only girl around that I can be doing this with." He teased.

"Thanks a lot!" I playfully pulled on his hair.

Declan chuckled as he shook my hand off, "I was going mad with frustration when you were married! I wanted to risk another episode in the woods with you, or challenge Grant to a fight where the victor got to have you."

This wiped the grin off my face, "THAT isn't funny."

The idea of Grant getting hurt over this was too painful to consider...

"I know," he sighed apologetically, "which only left me with plan C."

"What was plan C?"

"Getting the hell out of here and moving to either Canada or Russia." He said unhappily. "But wherever it was, it had to be at least a thousand miles away from you and your husband."

When he rolled out of bed once more, I missed his body's warmth immediately.

"Declan?"

Quickly I stood up on my knees, so when he turned around, my mouth could instantly smother his. We kissed longingly over and over again, as the both of us were reluctant to let the other go.

"You know I have to go now, B." He said in a pained voice whilst running his sharp nails lightly over my back. "I'll see you before dawn tomorrow morning."

"Why so late?"

"Today's Wednesday, I'm on patrol tonight." He reminded.

"Oh." I realized, but then I remembered something else, "that might be a good thing anyway. I have to go to dinner at Gran and Grandfather's."

He gave one last squeeze, "just make sure you shower properly before you go. We don't want your Grandfather smelling me on you."

Then he playfully tickled me and darted out of my bedroom laughing, before I could hit back!

"I'll see you before dawn tomorrow." Declan called out from downstairs then I heard my backdoor close, signaling his departure.

*****

The next evening when I turned on my porch light on my way out the door, I paused. There was something waiting for me on the veranda steps. I pulled on my coat and walked over to pick it up.

It was a white orchid, with flecks of pink near the soft centre. The delicate flower was contrasted against a couple of dark green fern fronds, tied together with a pink ribbon. It was beautiful, my heart leapt as my eyes widened at such a gift.

Then I heard something which made my head shoot upwards as my eyes narrowed. I used my Werewolf eyes to see into the surrounding dark woods. It didn't take me long to spot him, with my night-vision. His glowing green eyes stood out against the blackness. He knew that I could see him, just as I knew that he was watching for my reaction.

I raised the orchid to my face whilst looking his way. When I gently ran the soft flower across my lips, I picked up with my supernatural hearing that he whined. I caressed the flower across my cheek, hearing him whine again. I threw him a teasing smile before I went down the veranda steps. I unlocked Grant's jeep and climbed in, whilst putting my offering on the passenger's seat beside.

The delicate fragrance of the orchid, coupled with Declan's maple syrup scent which was on the ribbon; made it easier sitting in Grant's old jeep. His herb garden odor had almost completely faded from the upholstery.

As I reversed out, I caught Declan's glowing green eyes follow me through the woods. He more than easily jogged along beside the road, as I drove two minutes down the hill to Gran and Grandfather's house. When I climbed out of the jeep again, I saw his glowing green eyes in the woods across the driveway. I left my offering inside the car, as I climbed up the veranda steps to the front door.

Before I went in, I turned and looked back out. I stared at the glowing green eyes which were watching my every movement. I blew a kiss to him and then I disappeared inside.

*****

Dinner with my parents, grandparents and other relatives was mostly an enjoyable evening, although it did have its scary moments.

Gran and Grandfather served up roast caribou with Great Grandma's special gravy. An 18 year old Phoebe and a 20 year old Phoenix set the table, before helping their grandparents in the kitchen. I sat in the living room with theirs and my parents.

"Your father is right," my mother smilingly looked me over, "you are looking much better."

"Her light has returned." Uncle Julian agreed.

I blushed as I looked downwards. I fidgeted with my glass of juice when Aunt Danika I guess being a telepath, looked on knowingly.

Please don't say anything, please don't! I threw her a pleading look.

She raised her eyebrows in surprise before she looked away. She stroked her husband's hand which was resting on her lap, careful not act suspiciously in front of my parents.

Thank you! I mentally gushed in relief.

"What are you doing with yourself these days, B?" Her husband asked. "Did you decide to do a Masters?"

"Um, I'll start my Masters in September." I answered. "I just took some time off from my studies."

"That's a good idea." Uncle Julian said understandingly. "A lot's happened these past twelve months, it's best to start afresh."

I cleared my throat as I shifted in my seat and I redirected the conversation, "Phoenix must be getting close to changing soon, especially with Uncle Graeme's great age. Then Phoenix's Lokoti Werewolf genes will be activated to become one of the pack."

"Hmm." He frowned thoughtfully, before he looked up to catch his son whack his sister on the arm. "Hey, Phoenix! What did I tell you about hitting your sister?!"

"Ha ha!" Phoebe stuck her tongue out at her old brother.

"Then tell her to shut up! She keeps blurting out my private thoughts!" Phoenix complained.

"Phoebe, what did I tell you about that?" Aunt Danika sung warningly.

"Yes Mum." She sung back.

I smirked as I watched the 20 year old and the 18 year old brother and sister get 'roused' on, just as they used to when they were children.

"They still fight like cat and dog, huh?" I snickered.

"Always!" Uncle Julian rolled his eyes, before he looked to Mum. "They're worse than what you and I used to be like."

Dad laughed out loud, "Er, Julian? You and Jess still fight like that and you're both 43 years old!"

"Yeah, but I quit bashing up my sister when we were 18 years old." Uncle Julian argued.

"You didn't bash me up, I bashed you up!" Mum retorted.

"Julian, the last time you hit your twin sister on the arm? I warned that if you did that again I would give you what for, so you stopped." Dad growled at his fellow Werewolf.

"That was around the time that I started sword fighting too, which was probably the real reason why you stopped." Mum glared at her brother.

"Sorry Jess, but your Werewolf husband is way scarier than you are as a Circulator." Uncle Julian laughed.

"OK kids, dinner's ready!" Gran called out, which was quite funny to hear from my grandmother who still had the appearance of a woman in her twenties.

However during family gatherings, she and Grandfather still called their children and grandchildren, 'kids'. What was more peculiar was that she looked the same age as her son and daughter or even me, her granddaughter. Grandfather looked like a man in his early forties and he was the same age as Gran. He certainly didn't mind this fact, as his face would light up whenever she entered the room.

Phoebe and Phoenix sat at the table first as the rest of us left our seats in the lounge room to join them.

"Come on, little wolf." Dad grabbed my hand and pulled me up too.

We all took our seats as Gran and Grandfather carried out the gravy boat as well as the dishes of roast caribou, mashed potato, roast pumpkin, roast sweet potato, peas and corn. The food hardly had the chance to hit the table, before Phoenix attacked it. He was simultaneously helping himself to the roast caribou as he was pouring the gravy. I could literally see his mouth water with anticipation!

"Hungry, Phoenix?" Grandfather observed.

"Famished actually." He replied, now eagerly spooning the vegetables onto his plate.

The male Werewolves exchanged knowing looks, as I picked up their mental exchange and so did Aunt Danika.

SOON PHOENIX WILL BE JOINING THE RANKS – was their consensus.

"What's this?" Gran noticed something was afoot, with the men at the table all looking on Uncle Jules' eldest.

"They think Phoenix is going to turn into a Werewolf soon." Phoebe brought her up to speed, from telepathically listening in.

"Huh?" Phoenix looked up in surprise.

"Eat your dinner, kids." Uncle Jules ordered, now serving himself as well as his wife who was sitting beside.

As he did so, the parents exchanged a sad smile, as if they had already discussed this.

"So Phoenix," I picked up the butter to spread on my bread roll, "are you interested in any particular girl at the moment? I thought I saw you talking to Rainbow Shallow Water after your soccer game yesterday."

"She's OK." My cousin shrugged back. "But if I'm really going to turn into a Werewolf? There's no way that I'm gonna take a mate yet."

"Oh?" Dad looked on in amusement. "Why not? I took a mate at your age."

"From what happened to B, that's why. If my mate dies when I'm still young? Then I'm screwed because it means I'm not gonna get laid for the rest of my life!" He blurted out.

Silence...everybody looked on in shock at his lack of tact.

"Phoenix!" Uncle Jules punched him on the arm, embarrassed. "How about filling that big mouth of yours with food?"

However I wasn't offended, especially not with the secret that I was carrying around inside...which Phoebe immediately picked up. Her head snapped around in my direction so fast, it almost fell off!

Damn it! I'm hopeless at this, I really am! I don't have a poker face nor can I keep a secret; which is detrimental when one is having a secret affair.

I shot off my scariest look I could muster towards Phoebe, along with the thought; *breathe one word and you'll limp for the rest of your life!*

Her eyes bulged as if she also saw the violent image that was playing in my mind, when she heard the thoughts.

"Phoebe?" Grandfather noticed her fearful expression. "B? What are you girls talking about?"

"Nothing." We sung automatically as we returned to our meals.

"Those two are always conspiring about something." Uncle Jules chuckled. "Do you remember when B used to get Phoebe to help her spy on people?"

"Yep," Dad shook his head at the memory, "I remember well, when B used to have Phoebe eavesdrop on the pack's conversations about patrolling."

"Now you're one of the pack." Mum smiled my way, before she frowned. "Although I still think it's sexist that B isn't allowed to patrol like the male Werewolves can. Or what about the tribe's Circulators? We can certainly help keep our land safe."

All of the male Lokoti Werewolves at the table groaned tiredly at the same time. It was an old argument of Mum bickering about her feminist beliefs where the pack was concerned.

"Jess, don't start." Her father ordered.

"Yeah Jess, just eat your dinner." Her brother chimed.

"Jules, would you like me to instantaneously phase home to get my silver sword to help you cut that meat up?" She asked coolly.

Now it was his turn for his eyes to bulge as he hastily changed tact, "actually Jess, I love hearing your thoughts on how women should be allowed to patrol."

Phoenix and Phoebe laughed at how their father's twin sister could still make him nervous.

"Can I have a silver sword too?" Phoebe looked to Gran.

"Of course you can sweetheart." She answered in good humor, before she gave Grandfather a wink.

*****

When I pulled up in my driveway, I gently picked up my flowery offering from the passenger's seat to take inside.

My first stop was the kitchen and since I didn't have any small vases, I grabbed a glass out of the cupboard and half filled it with water. Next, I carried the glass and the flower upstairs to my bedroom to place on my bedside table. Lastly, I untied the ribbon and then I placed the flower and ferns into the water.

As I sat on the side of my bed to look on my beautiful present, I smiled like the cat that stole the cream. That was until it reminded me of something else and I left the bedroom to head back downstairs again.

I walked over to my copy of 'The Encyclopedia of Mythology', a huge heavy book that was sitting on the bottom shelf. I pulled it out to open it up. Inside, pressed between the pages was the first orchid that I had received from Declan.

It was still tied together with the red ribbon and ferns. It was the very first flower I had ever received, let alone from the man whose presence made my world spin. The afternoon I got my gift, I took it inside and after looking at it longingly, I put it inside the book to hide from Grant.

The yellow orchid had shriveled from time as they weren't the best flower to be preserved. But I liked the shape of it against the now pale green fern fronds. I took it out of the book to carry upstairs and I placed my first gift on the bedside table beside the newer present.

When Declan comes over tonight, he would see it and know. Reluctantly, I parted from my gifts as I prepared for bed.

*****

I have to admit, I didn't sleep well that night. Maybe it was from eating dinner with two telepaths who now knew my secret, even if they were good enough to keep it. Maybe it was because I had sat with three Lokoti Werewolves in the shapes of my Grandfather, Uncle Jules and Dad who wouldn't understand. Maybe I was scared of being judged for being the first Lokoti Werewolf to enter a second romantic relationship after their first mate died.

I tossed and turned as I slept fitfully. My heart raced as my sleep was filled with unpleasant dreams. Or, I hoped that they were dreams...

I was in the woods on the southern border between Lokoti land and Alma. It was a cold, wet night and being outside in my pajamas? I became wet through as my feet turned muddy. I dreamt of gunfire with the sounds of shouting and of the Werewolves roaring. I dreamt of seeing a man's naked body lying a short distance away, in the mud.

I couldn't see him clearly as he was covered in mud and because he was lying with his back to me. But I knew he must have been a Werewolf for the lack of clothing. I smelled that this Werewolf was dead from several gun shot wounds.

Oh no Grant, not again! I felt horror as at first I thought I was reliving a scene from the past? I ran up to the body that was lying in the mud however the closer I came, I realized that this Werewolf in human form wasn't a Lokoti Werewolf. This Werewolf had short blonde hair in a crew cut...

...Declan? It's Declan! Oh no, please no, please not Declan!

I landed on my knees in the mud, to roll the limp body over. His blue eyes were open as they stared vacantly. Above his eyes, I saw a bullet hole on the left side of his forehead as I saw another in his chest where his heart was. I could smell the bitter, metallic scent of silver in the wounds, indicating that he had been shot with silver bullets. Not only was there blood seeping out of the wounds, but so was a small stream of red smoke from the chemical reaction of his Shape Shifter flesh to the silver.

"Not again! Not Declan!" I cried as I moved his head into my lap. Declan simply stared past with his empty eyes. "DECLAN!" I roared in pain as I nursed his usually strong body.

No Declan no! You are my true love, just as you are my true mate! I wanted to tell you this and I wouldn't be able to bear it if you left me! Grant's death almost killed me but losing you would finish the job.

"DECLAN!" I shook him. "Don't leave me! You're supposed to be the strongest and live the longest of all the breeds! So what do you call this? Now heal!"

However his response to my desperation was his head rolling to the side as his vacant eyes stared off into another direction.

"NO!" I threw back my head and howled. "NOOOOOOOO!!!"

And then I woke up...my eyes snapped open as my body gave a jolt.

My chest physically hurt as my eyes stung with tears. Hell, even my pillow felt wet from crying in my sleep. I rolled onto my side as I hugged my damp pillow with my shaking arms. I lay on my side whilst taking deep breaths to calm my aching heart. As I did so, I noticed on my bedside table the orchids sitting on top.

Alive flowers, dead flowers. Dead flowers, alive flowers. The shriveled orchid sat next to the vibrant one in the glass of water. How apt of my circumstance I thought, with one dead husband and one living lover...

Did my subconscious transpose what happened to Grant onto my new relationship with Declan? But how come I was in my pajamas? How come Declan died from being shot with silver bullets and Grant didn't? Sure, both scenes of death occurred in the woods but I knew that it wasn't just some flashback of Grant's death. It even took place in different locations, this dream was on the border between Lokoti land and Alma whereas Grant had died on the south eastern border, in the river valley.

I started to cry, as I had to release the pain like a pressure valve and I felt the trauma was crushing my heart.

"I love you, Declan." I sobbed. "I'm sorry Grant, but I love Declan and I always have." I confessed as if my husband could hear wherever he was. "I'm sorry Grant, I'm so sorry. If you were still alive, I would never have acted on my feelings, I promise. I would have remained loyal to you. You made me happy and you were a good husband but now you're gone. So please let me have Declan?"

Not surprisingly, my dark bedroom nor my quiet house, didn't respond. I lay still, using my sensitive ears to pick up some kind of noise? But all that came back was the hum of the refrigerator or the sound of the clock ticking.

"Please let me keep Declan, please...?" I whimpered frightenedly. "Please don't let anything happen to him, please?"

In the silence, I vividly recalled what happened last month on top of my dining table with my new lover. We threw aside caution as well as our clothes, in turn breaking the tradition that Lokoti Werewolves mate once for life. But maybe that tradition was still intact? I knew in my heart where this tradition came from. When a Lokoti Werewolf mates, we become so biologically and empathically connected to this one person that it becomes impossible to move on after our mate dies. Our bodies, minds and hearts are tied to the one person, even after death.

I think Declan must have inadvertently become my mate before I married Grant. It would explain how I could return to him after my husband's death. Otherwise, how could I have sensed Declan's pain that night, when his loneliness woke me up? None of the other Lokoti Werewolves sensed it.

If Declan did die, I knew for a stone cold, hard fact that I would remain alone for the rest of my existence. I may be a Circulator which promised eternity if I evolved, but I'm also Lokoti Werewolf. I was biologically, empathically and emotionally bound to the European Werewolf...damn it.

I used the sheet to dry my face as I took a deep breath. What would Declan say if I told him? I thought back on all our barbs, insults, glares and growls at each other over the years. Surely this wasn't just sex? When I looked back at the orchids, I saw it was something else.

He could have gone away during my married years. He could have left Lokoti land on search for a female of his breed. He could have easily sought solace in the arms of another. I sighed again as I reached out to gingerly touched the soft texture of the petals on my gift.

For sickness and in health, for better or for worse, Declan and I were in this together whether we liked it or not.

*****

The clock read as 4.44 AM and I was still awake when I heard my back door downstairs open. I listened to the heavy footsteps cross my wooden floor and come up my wooden staircase, which creaked under his weight. When he came into my room I heard his panting as well as the odd growl under his breath.

I rolled onto my back to look up at a huge, hulking, hairless European Werewolf. He was standing so tall, that he had to bend his head since it kept knocking the ceiling.

The monster's eyes were glowing green with the black slits for pupils were trained my way. He had a short stubby snout over his open jaws, showing rows of razor sharp teeth. His pale-tanned hide was hardened which rippled with supernatural muscle bulk. Standing upright on his hind legs, his dangerous claws were making scratching noises on the wooden floor. He flexed his front claws as he hungrily looked down.

Declan had come from patrolling our lands to keep his loved ones safe. In his monstrous body he ran up to speeds reaching 300 km/h, he sniffed out trespassers and he scared away looters by bounding onto the scene.

I kicked off my covers as I held out my arms to him. He whined softly as he bent over and his snout tenderly touched my face. Soon I felt his large tongue dart out to lap at mine. Eagerly, I lapped back when I heard him whine again. Then he opened his large jaws and settled them over the bottom half of my face in a passionate kiss.

Whilst moaning, I tried to hold onto his huge, hulking, hairless frame. Declan released my face from his jaws as he moved his snout down my body, sniffing as he went. Using his teeth to tear off my pajamas, the fabric didn't last long from their razor sharp quality. I felt his huge, hot tongue move over my skin as it became exposed, making me moan even louder.

Finally, he shrunk back into his human body so he could lie himself on top. Immediately, I wrapped my arms about his neck as my legs did the same to his waist. His human mouth smothered my own, as his tongue moved with mine.

Tonight we kissed continually as our mouths never left the other's. We moved quickly, since we knew we didn't have much time. We knew this had to be fast so we moved fast. We both groaned as we came, before we pushed onwards. We moved at a rushed pace, as if we were trying to scoff down a six course banquet in the space of a three course menu.

I was pushed further up against the head board as he panted loudly. I saw the expression on his red, sweaty face which reminded me of the first time we 'did it'. He looked like he was either in pain, or that the pain was leaving somehow. He acted insatiable, like I was part of the bloodlust that he experienced being a Werewolf. Instead of gorging on flesh, he acted like had to gorge himself on me. He even whimpered helplessly as he pushed harder.

Suddenly I surprised him when I cupped his face to make him look my way.

"I love you Declan." I uttered out as my dark blue eyes met his bright blue ones. "I always have and I always will...but don't tell anyone."

He stopped moving as he looked on with a shocked expression. His eyes were wide and even his mouth hung open in surprise.

"I should bring you flowers more often." He grinned and I smiled back as my heart felt like it expanded to take over my entire chest. "You were always my mate B and you always will be." He declared before his mouth reclaimed mine.

At 5.44 AM the already bright sky thanks to summer's longer daylight hours, forced our tryst to end. Declan reluctantly hauled himself out of my bed and he sat on the side for a moment, perhaps to get his bearings? I curled up behind to caress the skin on his muscled back.

"Hmm, that feels good." He sighed. "Well, I guess I'll see you tonight."

I watched him slowly stand up and walk over to my bedroom doorway, before he paused to look back. Our eyes met and held for a moment, before his ran over my naked form once more.

"Get some sleep." He gave a wink with his departure.

I listened to him go down the stairs, cross to my back door, open it and then shut it behind himself.

An hour passed until I decided to get up and begin my day. There was no way that I could go back to sleep. The fuzzy feelings I felt with Declan when he was here, dissipated fast. The previous sense of foreboding I felt from my 'nightmare' had returned.

Once I was dressed, I stood in my kitchen to make myself a coffee. Apart from the sound of the water boiling, my house was achingly silent.

Sometimes the silence comforts me, or it did when I was in mourning. The house was so quiet that I felt like it could have been my fault. It only came back to life in the night when there were two people here.

This house needs more than one person and I wanted the second person to be Declan. I think the house likes him, as he did fix the roof, the lose stair and the greenhouse. He certainly did fill the house with life and noise through argument and passion. This house and he belonged together, or so I thought.

I carried my coffee over to the dining table where yesterday's books sat next to my laptop. I had begun my research on comparative world mythology although I hadn't officially started my Masters yet. I liked academic work, it kept me interested as it kept me occupied.

*****

That evening as I lay awake in bed, staring up at the stars via my bedroom window? I heard my back door downstairs open and close. I looked at my clock and saw the time was only 10.38 PM, he was early.

Declan soon appeared in my bedroom doorway and I smiled as I lifted the covers to allow him to quickly leap into bed.

"Well hello there." His grin was immediate when he realized I wasn't wearing any clothes.

"I've had to throw out two sets of pajamas since our little adventure began; including the pair I was wearing last night." I pretended to be cross.

"Yeah, but you love it when I tear your clothes off, admit it." He chuckled as he held me close.

"That's why I'm not charging you to buy me a new pair." I smirked.

"You know the obvious answer to this problem then don't you?" He smirked back. "Don't wear any clothes to bed."

"Yeah but I'm a widow." I frowned. "It might look funny if something happens and I'm sleeping naked when I'm meant to be home alone."

"So your argument is single people or widows don't sleep naked?" He arched his eyebrows.

"Precisely."

"What a load of codswallop!" He retorted. "Before I started doing you, I slept naked. When I came home from patrolling or hunting and I went straight to sleep? There was no point in dressing for bed."

"Yeah, but that's your excuse. I'm not a European Werewolf and if I turn, I wear those elastic gym clothes."

"Then run through the woods naked." He shrugged, before he gave me a mischievous grin, "you might like it."

"Oh sure! I bet my Dad or my Grandpa would be impressed with that!"

"Who cares? I would be impressed with that." He chuckled as he rolled on top.

I giggled back before his mouth settled over mine and then the rest of us came together. However tonight was different than last night. We were both tired, Declan from patrolling the night before and I was tired from the bad dreams. We made love just the once and then we did something that we hadn't done since our affair began…we slept together.

To ensure he wouldn't oversleep, I set my alarm to go off at 4 AM so he could skulk home whilst the tribe was still asleep. Then we settled down as we slept side by side, with Declan on his back and I was on my side. My back was tucked up against him as my cheek rested on his arm which acted as my pillow.

When I lifted up my head for a moment, I found him asleep before I was! His face was turned in my direction as he was breathing deeply, like he was inhaling my scent as he slumbered. I smilingly put my head back down on his large arm as I closed my eyes. I easily fell asleep, comforted by his warm body next to mine. His maple syrup smell filled my senses completely…

…until the odor of rain overtook this.

I found myself bare foot, in my pajamas and in the woods again. The cold mud squished between my toes, so I noted as I heard the shouting of strangers. I heard the roars of the pack who were fighting them. I heard the sound of gunfire as I smelled the gun powder and silver bullets.

Then I saw him again, lying naked in his human form in the mud. I smelled his bloody bullet holes, as well as the red smoke snaking into the air. His maple syrup scent was fading just like he was.

It felt like my heart had stopped as I stood still, looking on his lifeless form. I knew that my blood wouldn't be able to regenerate him so I didn't know what to do? As the icy rain splashed on my face, I looked about with stinging eyes to try to learn when this could happen.

Think B, think! Try to learn more about this dream incase it is a vision of what's to come. I turned my head to see the Lokoti Werewolves fight five strangers whom were all men. They were firing off all kinds of guns loaded with silver bullets.

I saw two more Werewolves fall from the dangerous ammunition, as they bled and more red smoke seeped out of their wounds. The strangers knew to use silver bullets, but how is this so? I turned and walked away from Declan's body towards the strangers. The five strange men didn't shoot at me because they like the Werewolves, didn't see me. It was like I was invisible, as what can happen when you dream.

The strangers continued to fire on, as three more members of the pack fell. The strangers advanced on the Lokoti Werewolves, empowered by the weapons in their hands.

"You're not so powerful now, are ya? Werewolf freaks! Dirty muts!" One of the strangers laughed maddeningly as he fired off several rounds at Dad.

My father managed to leap to the side, away from the gun fire but then the stranger hit Uncle Quinn who didn't duck as fast.

The strangers made no sign of getting away, as they kept firing at the Werewolves. When one gun ran out of silver ammunition, they simply dropped it and used another. They were carrying numerous weapons on their backs or on their belts or more which were in holsters that were strapped to their legs. The strangers seemed to have come here to deliberately shoot the Werewolves! I smelled silver ammunition in every gun they used.

I tried to snatch a rifle off one of the men whose bullets were chasing Grandfather, but my hands went through the gun. I tried to punch the man instead, but my hand sailed through his head. I couldn't touch anything because I'm not really here, this was only a premonition of what was to come. All I could do was stand there, feeling cold and wet and horror, whilst watching my pack fight and fall.

Nine of the fifteen male Werewolves were down but Dad, Grandpa, Grandfather, Uncle Jules, Ian and Harry fought on.

Dad leapt high into the air to land on the stranger in the middle! As soon as he landed on top, he whipped out his claws and took down the other two men on either side. This distracted the last two strangers on the ends that gave the remaining Werewolves their chance to pounce...

...and pounce they did! Dad killed the human he had leapt on top of, by his elongated teeth ripping out the man's throat! Grandpa, Grandfather, Uncle Jules, Ian and Harry did the same to the other four.

My mouth watered at the human flesh my kin were tasting, as my bloodlust was stirred. They used their teeth and claws to ravage the humans! When the strangers were dead, with their throats or hearts eaten out; the remaining Werewolves stood tall and victorious as well as covered in blood. Their glowing eyes burned in anger at the strangers that lay on their land.

"We should have done this a long time ago, when we first removed them from Alma." Uncle Harry said unhappily.

"But if we had killed the first time, it would have made the people in Alma distrust us." Grandfather growled back.

Then the uninjured Werewolves split up to see to their wounded kin.

"We have to get the injured back to my house. I have to remove the silver bullets before we can share our blood to regenerate them." Grandpa instructed.

Everyone nodded as they began to tend to the fallen. Grandfather checked to make sure Uncle Quinn was still breathing which thankfully he was, before he got up to walk over to Declan.

The pack's Second stood still as he looked down on the young man who was staring emptily into the great beyond. He knew there was no way to save Declan with a silver bullet to his heart and brain. He remained there for a minute or two, looking downward with glowing, tearful eyes.

Our Medicine Man walked past to kneel by Declan's side and he sniffed at his injuries before he looked up to say, "he's gone."

Grandfather hung his head, "I know and I'm not looking forward to telling Susan. First her husband and now her eldest?"

This made Grandpa's glowing orange eyes soften as he gave a nod of understanding. He said as he stood up, "you take Declan home to his mother and stay with her. I'll see to the rest of the pack."

Our Second nodded back before he turned his head to watch the walking Werewolves pick up the wounded. They slung them over their backs to carry one on each shoulder. I watched Grandfather stoop down, pick up Declan's limp body and sling him over his muscled back. Like that, he proceeded to carry him home.

He was carrying the fallen son home to his mother. I remember how scared Aunt Susan was the night Jack died when Declan was on patrol and now her worst nightmare has come true. But I didn't want to see this, it wasn't helpful. I needed more information!

It appeared that the five strangers knew of the pack and the pack knew them? Uncle Harry said that the Werewolves had made them leave Alma. Were these strangers the 'bad element' that the people of Alma asked the Lokoti Werewolves to remove six years ago?   The humans held a grudge enough to come back with silver bullets. But why was Declan the first to be shot? Does this mean he was patrolling? I need to find out more, I have to know what to do.

Just then something strange happened as everything around me started to rewind like I was in a movie.

Grandfather walked backwards and returned Declan to the ground... the other Lokoti Werewolves returned with the injured and put them back... then the Werewolves attacked the strangers who came back to life... Dad went flying backwards through the air off the stranger in the middle... the strangers fired as the silver bullets were sucked back into the guns... and the injured Werewolves all got up from the ground uninjured... and then several of them started to disappear through the trees instead of appear... Declan fell upright into the air from the ground... instantly expanding back into his huge, hulking, hairless European Werewolf form... and the silver bullets were sucked out of his heart and his head as they flew through the air back into one particular gun; the shotgun of the stranger standing in the middle.

OK B, remember that - it's the stranger in the middle's gun.

I saw Declan disappear through the trees and it left only the strangers standing there in the small clearing of woods. I also saw the strangers more clearly now. The man in the middle had a grey, bushy moustache and was missing quite a lot of teeth. The other men's hair was thinning like it was falling out and two of them had weird blotches on their skin.

Stop, now play forwards! I closed my eyes and took a deep breath as I issued these commands. When I opened my eyes again, I saw that it had worked. The five strangers were standing altogether, readying their weapons.

"Where are they?" One asked another.

"They'll smell us soon enough and then they'll come." The stranger in the middle replied, as he loaded his shotgun with silver bullets.

Then I heard the deafening noise of Declan roaring! His roar reverberated through the forest, to instill fear upon his approach. Four of the strangers blanched, but the one in the middle who appeared to be the leader, was calm.

"OK, lock and load!" The stranger in the middle ordered. "Now let's give these supernatural bastards a taste of their own medicine. They moved us on? It's time to return the favour."

The other four flanked the one in the middle as they stood ready...

"Declan, no!" I yelled out as I heard him bound through the trees in this direction. "No Declan, turn around!"

However he didn't hear as he leapt out of the tree line and landed in the small clearing the strangers were standing in. Four of the strangers looked visibly frightened when they saw his monstrous form. All but the leader, looked like they wanted to run away! Declan saw this as he roared out his warning at the men to leave. But the leader sneered back as he raised his shotgun. The European Werewolf roared out his warning again as he stalked in front of the strangers on all fours, but the strangers remained.

"Tonight is our turn to make you leave you bastard!" The leader spat.

He started to rise onto his hind legs so he could use his greater height to intimidate them; when the lead stranger fired off the first bullet which hit Declan right in the heart! I stood there and uselessly cried as he roared in pain. Then the leader fired his next shot and the second bullet pierced his forehead...

The European Werewolf started to fall sideways in the air, killed immediately from the silver bullet to the brain. As he fell, his huge, hulking body shrunk back into his human form. He landed in the mud as a naked man, with his supernatural glowing green eyes fading to their natural blue colour.

"They're not so scary now, are they?" the leader smirked to his men, as they chuckled along with their momentary hero.

Then the other male Werewolves began to arrive, as they ran to Declan's aid albeit too late. I had seen enough, I know what happens now. I turned away from the bloodshed to walk towards my lover lying in the mud. Tearfully, I collapsed before him.

"Declan, we trained you not to kill and instead you yourself are killed?"

My chest felt like it had been hacked open as my heart split apart from the amount of pain I was experiencing. I lay in the mud beside as I tried to lie against his chest, which was no longer moving. The rain drenched my pajamas as I was trying to hold him, to desperately be with him...

Beep beep! Beep beep! Beep beep!

Huh, what was that?

Beep beep! Beep beep! Beep beep!

That sounds like my alarm clock...? Abruptly, I found myself no longer lying in the mud beside a dead Declan; but I was lying in the arms of my lover who was warm, safe and dry.

He reached over me to turn off the alarm clock before he yawned. He sat upright whereas I felt like I couldn't move. My eyes were watering and I felt like I couldn't breathe properly, because of how much my heart was hurting! All I could do was lie there and stare up at him.

"Go back to sleep." He sighed as he gave my back an affectionate rub. "I'll see you tonight."

He started to climb out of bed but in a lightening fast move, I grabbed hold and pulled him back down again!

"B!" He started to laugh but then he frowned. "B, your heart's racing and you're shaking. What's wrong?" I couldn't answer, all I could do was stare tearfully back. "B, what is it?" He cupped my face as he looked on worriedly. "Why are you scared?"

"It's not a bad dream Declan, it's a vision!" I uttered out frightenedly.

"You had a vision?" His eyes immediately widened. "What did you see?"

But I didn't know what to tell him, because I didn't know the exact night this would happen. What was I supposed to say, that I know you're going to die?!

"B, come on! You've got a mouth, now use it! Just frickin' tell me what's wrong?" He persisted.

I buried my wet face in his neck and I guess he thought the only thing he could do right now, was to hold me. So he did, as he rubbed my back in a soothing manner.

"Shhh, I'm sure it was just a bad dream." He said helplessly. "I mean, how often is it that you have these visions?"

I swallowed hard, "the last time I had a vision was of the night Grant died."

After a moment, he pulled away to look on in horror.

"You didn't - you didn't - you didn't see somebody else die?" He managed out to which I nodded. He asked in alarm, "who B? It wasn't my Mom, was it? Or Derik? Who was it?"

I looked on helplessly, unable to say that it was him, it was he who died...

"B, tell me! Was it any of my family?" He demanded when I closed my eyes to shake my head. He asked next, "it wasn't your Grandfather was it?"

I shook my head once more as it was like I had turned into a mute. I couldn't talk nor could I move properly from my petrified state. I think this is what they meant by the expression, 'scared stiff'.

Declan rolled his eyes in frustration; "OK, enough with the 'Twenty Questions' and just tell me what you frickin' saw!"

I gulped, "strangers with silver bullets who knew about us. They came here for some kind of revenge."

His eyes almost popped out of his head, "they had silver bullets?!"

I nodded back, before we both noticed the sky outside lighten with the onset of dawn.

"Frickin' hell, talk about the worst frickin' timing!" He glared out the window as he sat upright whilst still holding me. "Look, I'll run home and I'll get dressed. I'll tell my Mom that I have to do something and then I'll drive back here, OK? I'll be as fast as humanly possible without giving us away."

He growled out the last part, showing his annoyance at our predicament. Then he planted a kiss on my forehead before he released his hold and he climbed out of bed. He almost bounded out of the bedroom before he paused in the doorway to look back.

"I'll be right back, OK?" He promised with wide eyes.

I nodded for the last time, before he turned and I heard him hurry out of the house.

*****

~ 19 ~

Twenty minutes later, I was dressed in a pair of jeans and a white woolen jumper whilst sitting at the dining table, sipping on a cup of coffee.

It was light outside when I heard Declan's pick up truck pull into the driveway. As soon as the engine turned off, I heard his door open and slam shut as almost simultaneously, my front door opened. He was dressed in his typical jeans, grey t-shirt and flannel shirt, as he rushed over to where I was sitting.

I pointed at the second mug I had made, at the chair opposite to mine and he reluctantly sat across. He tossed down a small packet onto the table.

"What's that?" I looked on.

"Cherry tomato seeds." He declared. "So if anyone wonders why my truck's in your driveway? We can say my Mom gave me these to give to you."

"Oh, I like cherry tomatoes." I said congenially as I picked up the small envelope.

He growled gruffly, "alright I'm here, now spill it!"

I looked him in the eye, "you die."

Silence... Declan looked on hurt like I might have been instigating this myself.

"And – and – and you had a vision of Grant dying?" He swallowed hard. I gave a nod as his eyes watered. "But I can't die, B! Who will look after my Mom when I'm gone?"

Frickin' hell, those words stung just as his hurt expression did! I tell him he's going to die and his first concern is the welfare of others?! I jumped out of my chair to whip around the table and land in his lap.

I hugged him tightly as I spoke in his ear, "I think this happens on a night that you're on patrol? So next Wednesday, take me with you. I'll patrol with you every Wednesday night, no matter how long it takes. I can move faster than bullets and I can instantaneously phase you out of danger. I won't let anything happen to you!"

Declan's arms slowly wrapped about my waist to firmly hold on. He chuckled back, "this should be interesting trying to explain to the pack why I have a bodyguard with me."

"I'll say I'm stalking you if you like." I tried to joke. "I'll let it be known that you have a female Werewolf with a stupid crush on you or something."

He pushed me away slightly so he could look me in the eyes when he said this next part, "it would serve me right for stalking you."

"When did you stalk me?" I started to smile as I thought he was still joking.

"After you changed and I kissed you on the border, when you were in lock down."

"Oh THAT!" I giggled out, "I remember."

He turned serious, "every night I wasn't on patrol, I sat in the woods outside your house to watch your window. You saw me just a couple of times? But when your Dad nearly sprung me, I had to leave. When I wasn't at the Garage or helping my Mom with something, I circled your house. Didn't you wonder about my sudden appearance in the woods that afternoon?"

My eyes widened in surprise as it did explain a lot, actually.

He carried on bitterly, "after you married Grant, sometimes I still prowled past your place. I'd see you standing on your porch, looking up at the stars and then I'd see Grant pull you inside. I had to restrain myself from mauling him! I wanted so bad to sling you over my shoulder and run off into the night."

Oh, I didn't like that part. I looked on speechless, as I didn't know he stalked me during my married years...

"B, if you only knew how strong the bloodlust burns inside when I crave human? My lust feels just as bad when I crave you." He wore his helpless expression once more. "If the pack knew how close I came to killing Grant, I would have been destroyed. It was my lucky day when those strangers took him out instead and saved me the trouble. I know as a cold, hard fact that I couldn't have waited a hundred years until you were mine again."

This stopped being sweet as this was very quickly turning sour! I tried to get up and move away, but Declan was quick to hold me down. He wouldn't let me leave him.

"So there you go B, I'm not such an uncaring bastard as you first thought, huh? I'm not uncaring but I'm still a bastard, as you're so fond of calling me. You're probably thinking now that I deserve my fate and that my oncoming death is justified, right?" He said coldly. "I wished Grant dead and now I'm about to join him?"

"Stop it Declan!" I cried out in alarm.

I forced his hands off so I could stand up and walk away. I stood at the bottom of the staircase as I took several deep breaths to calm my racing heart. I battled to get a grip on my overprotective nature. Declan's threatening words about Grant stirred my overriding urge to protect – my husband. The memory of my marriage and of a husband who was always there for me, was still vivid in my recollection.

"OK." He called this meeting back to hand. "Strangers are going to show up with silver bullets and you have the impression they've come for revenge? This means we should know who they are."

I sat down on the staircase as I nodded back. Although I was sulking about his threats, I tried to refocus on the pressing issue.

He frowned as he thought on who it could be. "We've sent away hundreds of strangers over the years."

"How many of those times did you do this in your Werewolf form?" I asked.

"That halves it." He rubbed his chin thoughtfully. "On half of these occasions does it escalate and we have to frighten them off. Then halve that again if things turn violent."

I closed my eyes as I tried to recall the exact words the strangers said in my dream;

""Where are they?" One asked another. "They'll smell us soon enough and then they'll come." The stranger in the middle replied, as he loaded his shotgun with silver bullets. "OK, lock and load!" The stranger in the middle ordered. "Now let's give these supernatural bastards a taste of their own medicine. They moved us on? It's time to return the favour.""

Declan frowned as he listened to me regurgitate the words from my subconscious. He stood up from his seat as he began to pace whilst he chewed this over.

"The leader, was he a man?" He guessed.

"They were all male." I answered.

"What did the leader look like?"

"Three of them were tall, as two of them looked to be in their forties. The leader looked like he was missing some teeth and he had a grey moustache. He had a slight accent and he spoke like he was trying to be a cowboy or something."

He snapped his fingers as he looked on excitedly, "I know who it is! These 'strangers', they're not strangers at all!"

"They're not?"

"The lead guy, I think his name is Darr. He was the one who reopened the bar in Alma seven years ago and served the moonshine he made. He was also the ring leader of the organized crime, as his friends looted the small town and gave him a percentage. They were the 'bad element' that we ran out of Alma after Jack was killed. That's how they know how we work and how they know we can smell them on our land!"

"We should tell Dad and Grandfather." I stood up again.

Here he faltered, "er no B, we can't do that."

"What? Why not?" I looked on as if he were crazy.

"How would we explain that you're having visions about me? I mean, the last time you had visions about somebody dying, it was about your mate!"

"Oh...!" My face fell as I sunk back onto the step.

"Look B," he came over to kneel before me, "consider me warned. Now I know what to expect, I'll be alright. We don't have to risk exposing us. Don't tell your Dad or your Grandfather and don't come with me when I patrol. Now I know who it is and that they have silver bullets, I'll know what to do."

I looked on in disbelief, "Declan, you're not faster than a speeding bullet!"

"B," he cupped my face, "I don't want to risk losing you."

"And I don't want you dying on me!" I cried indignantly.

"Listen to me for a minute," he tried to hold my gaze with his own, "let's just review the facts here. To go back to a prior discussion, if anybody found out about us, we could be separated. I could be run off the tribal lands. It could affect Mom and it could affect Derik and I don't want to risk that or being separated from you." His words started to soften my heart until he added on, "so far you're my only option of getting regular sex and I'm not about to give that up after five years of abstaining."

What the...! In a tempter I shoved him backwards as Declan laughingly fell onto his back. After a minute of further laughter, he moved to sit beside me on the step. Playfully, he used his stronger ass to shove mine across before he took hold of my hands.

He spoke seriously with his deep voice, "so like this relationship, we'll keep your vision just between you and me. Now I know what will happen, I'll be ready. There's too much at stake to tell people about what you've seen."

I looked on as if he really had gone completely nuts, "you want to risk a silver bullet to your heart and head, than risk the possibility of anybody finding out about us?!"

"That's what I just said, isn't it?"

"No!" I stood up so I could glare down. "I'm not going to risk that!"

"B, it's not your decision." He glared back.

"Not MY decision?!" I raised my voice. "These are MY visions!"

"Yeah, about me!"

"What, so if I had a vision of Grandfather getting shot and he pleaded with me not to tell Gran, he can claim ownership over that too?!"

"Exactly!" He stood up to stare me down.

"That is the stupidest thing that I've ever heard!"

"I don't care what you think! This is about me and this is MY life that's on the line! You've done your duty as you've warned me about what you've seen so good job and thank you! Now leave it to me."

"Get bent!" I fired back before I turned to run up the stairs.

I ran into my bedroom as I slammed my bedroom door shut behind. I hurried over to my wardrobe to pull out my silver sword. I wasn't in my room for long, before Declan burst through my door as he charged in after. His face was contorted in anger and he looked like he was going to yell at me some more, but as soon as he sniffed the silver on the blade he immediately stopped.

"What, are you going to kill me instead?" He blanched.

"No, but as much as I'm tempted to?" I replied sarcastically. "I'm going to go to the Viewing Room at Circulate HQ. This time I'll find out the exact night this happens, then I'm going to instantaneously phase there and end this myself!"

In a lightening fast move, he snatched the sword off me!

"Like hell you are!" He roared. "You're just as allergic to silver as I am! You're not going anywhere near those silver bullets!"

"I am, am I?" I raised my eyebrows, before I held out my hand. "Give it to me."

"No!"

"Give me back my sword so I can frickin' show you something!"

"No!"

I moved in the speed of light to snatch my sword back! Before he could stop me, I unsheathed it which made him take a step backwards away from the silver. His eyes widened with worry as I held the sword in my right hand and I raised my left arm.

"B, no! What the hell are you doing?!" He cried out fearfully as he watched me purposefully nick my arm.

I grimaced from the sting, but then I lowered the sword to hold up my wound, "look."

Declan stared in surprise at the ordinary looking cut. It bled, but what surprised him was that there was no red smoke which was customary when a Werewolf was injured by silver. He even grabbed hold of my injured arm to sniff it.

"What, you're not allergic to silver?" He asked in amazement.

"A silver bullet can still do more damage than an ordinary bullet, but I'm not as allergic to it as the rest of our kind are. Gran thinks it's because of some kind of harmonization of my Werewolf regenerative ability and my bio-electromagnetic frequency as a Circulator." I explained.

"So you're faster than a speeding bullet and you're almost silver bullet proof." He gave a small smile.

"Almost." I smirked.

He took a step closer as he warily pulled the sword out of my hand to put it safely aside. Then he turned my way to raise my injured arm to his mouth. I watched him duck his head to smother the wound with his parted lips, which made my stomach melt. At first I felt him suck on it as if he enjoyed the taste of my blood, before I felt him run his tongue over the cut, sending it numb. I recognized what he was doing, he was using his saliva to heal my injury faster.

After a minute or so, he released me and when I looked at it again, I found that the cut was completely healed and I couldn't even see where it used to be! I looked on impressed at how his European Werewolf regenerative ability was much stronger than a Lokoti Werewolf. If I or my kin had done that, there would still be a small, pink line on the surface.

"Come here." Declan said softly as he pulled me into a passionate embrace.

*****

It was midday when it was over and I lay on top of him. Our hearts were still pounding which we felt in the other with our close contact. The drumming noise also reverberated in our sensitive ears.

I smiled knowingly upon him, "nice try."

"Huh?"

"Trying to make me forget that I was going to instantaneously phase to Circulate HQ by sweeping me off my feet? Nice try."

"Yeah well, it did make you forget for the last six hours, didn't it?"

"What are you going to do to stop me in future, THIS all day?"

"It's a hard life, but somebody's got to do it." He chuckled.

"I think people might notice if that's the case and then we'll be found out."

Declan rolled his eyes in annoyance at the mention of the world outside the bedroom. As if to console himself, he ran his right hand through my long, dark hair before capturing a wisp of it. He let go when he used the both of his hands to cup my face as he drilled his eyes into mine.

"Leave this to me, B. You may be faster as a Circulator and you may be less allergic to silver than I am? But it's still your weakness. I have far more experience in fighting than you do and I'm a damn sight stronger than you."

I pulled my head out of his hands to scowling look away. "Yes, it's a tad convenient that you have more experience at fighting than I do; particularly when I'm not allowed to patrol."

"You know the reason, B." He sighed as he stretched out before resting his hands behind his head. "You're the tribe's first female Lokoti Werewolf and as there's only one female so far, that makes you rare. Plus you're not as strong as the male Werewolves, even if you are faster. Call us a bunch of sexist bastards, but when the male is stronger than the female? It does make us want to protect."

"Alright then…" I looked back, "…I will call you a sexist bastard."

Declan chuckled in good humor, "I would no more let you fight than I would my own mother. You haven't seen these strangers that turn up on our borders, B. They may be human but they're the real monsters."

"I vaguely recall these monsters pumping something like thirty bullets into my husband, when he asked them to leave." I said coolly.

"You see, you're not missing much. Trust me, if I didn't have to patrol once a week, I wouldn't miss it. But when I think about either you or my Mom fighting what's on the outside trying to get in? I'd patrol every night if I had to."

"The humans I saw in my vision, some had these weird marks on their skin and others were missing teeth or hair."

"It's called radiation sickness, B." He said flatly. "Where we live is paradise when compared to the devastated areas of this continent. All thanks to humans and their penchant to press red buttons."

I sighed even heavier this time as I rested my cheek on Declan's sweaty chest. I could tell he appreciated our closeness when he used his fingertips to trace up and down my spine. Then he gave up trying to be tender, to swamp me in a huge hug.

"You wanna know the reason why this place is so good, B? Besides unpolluted land, water and air, it's because of love." He growled affectionately.

"All you need is love...!" I jokingly sung the Beatles song.

He chuckled again as he continued; "the love the Lokoti have for the land they've lived on for generation upon generation in harmony with nature. The love a Lokoti Werewolf feels for its mate, family and its tribe. The way a human Lokoti looks up to the Werewolf and their Elders, which ensures law and respect. I can't imagine what it would have been like not growing up here. My Dad may still be alive or he may not be. Instead of getting killed by a European Werewolf, he could have been killed by looters. Derik and I could have grown up fighting on the streets of a decaying city, for our lives as well as for food. However my mother was able to raise us in safety, here on tribal lands. My mother is respected for starting up the school as my little brother is respected for being the tribe's second Medicine Man."

Lastly, he lifted my head using his forefinger under my chin to hold my gaze. "It's not just us that I'm scared for B, but it's my Mom and Derik too. So leave this with me."

I felt torn, as half of me wished he could make this better but the other half knew better. The ominous feeling in the pit of my stomach was like a warning bell. As I looked on Declan's concerned face, I saw his love for me and the love for his family. But I loved him too and I didn't want to lose him.

Our eye contact ended when I looked away first. Using my fingertips, I traced over the claw mark which was on the left side of his chest. Then I grazed my fingers over the scar of the teeth marks on his left shoulder.

"I suppose if you weren't a European Werewolf, we may not be together." I said vaguely. "You would be a human and then you could marry any girl that you choose."

He grinned as he pulled me closer, "I don't know about that. You'd still have your alluring pheromones and I remember chasing away the other men in the tribe, like what happened at Ben's party." But his smile faded as he returned to being serious, "nice try by the way, with changing the subject."

"Declan -"

"No."

"Declan, please -"

"No!"

"Declan!"

"B, if you utter one word of this to a person in the tribe, let alone to a Werewolf? So help me I will pick you up, run you to the river and throw you in!"

"You've already done that so think of something else!"

"I'd be forced to leave the tribal lands and you as a Lokoti Werewolf would have to stay here, on your hunting grounds! We could be separated for good and you may never see me again!"

That did it, my heart emitted a painful spasm just by the very thought of this.

"Fine!" I huffed. "I won't tell anybody about my vision."

"Good."

"But I'm still gonna try to find out when this happens."

His eyes glowed green in anger. Next, he flipped me onto my back and pinned me underneath. As he held me down, he bared his sharpening teeth whilst snarling ferociously. I could tell this impressive display was to intimidate but he didn't scare me, he only made me laugh.

"If you do anything stupid so help me I will maul you!" He roared.

"Promises promises." I giggled back.

I could tell my laughter startled him, as he didn't know what to do next. Declan released me as he fell onto his back and I curled up on top once more. He rolled his eyes as he shook his head at either me or himself, before a smile escaped.

"I'm not sure if I'm relieved or worried that my woman's not scared of me anymore." He said dryly. "But then again, you were always the one kid in the tribe who would stand up to me and my temper."

"You scared me when I was little." I admitted. "But with my change, it made me understand you better."

"Yeah?" His eyes widened. "The bloodlust, the lust and the constant hunger for flesh, food or sex? The urge to kill to feast on fresh kill?"

"Actually it helped me understand why you were such an asshole growing up." I stated.

"Say what?" He blinked.

Then I squealed with laughter when I was flipped over and pinned once more. He playfully bit into my stomach and tickled with his tongue. Helplessly, I writhed unable to break his hold however I soon stopped trying when his licking turned slow and sensuous.

~~~~~~
~~~~~~

17th August 2090

Since Declan and I saw each other at night, he wouldn't know what I did during the day. The following morning after our conversation when he was working at the Garage, I instantaneously phased to Circulate HQ. However I still maintained our secrecy, because I knew Vincent would be away in England and therefore the Viewing Room would be all mine.

"Welcome to the Viewing Room, Circulate member Bianca Elm." The electronic female voice of the smart computer greeted.

The Circulate Mainframe immediately picked up my arrival as soon as I instantaneously phased inside.

"Hi." I sat down at one of the three control panels on the glass top desk which ran around in a ring. "Computer, I need you to help me perform a search."

"Please enter the search parameters." The computer politely requested.

"Um," I looked on helplessly at the unfamiliar interface, "I don't know how."

"You may begin by entering the years that you would like to search as well as the name of the subject." The computer instructed.

I pressed into the crystallized touch screen computer interface the name DECLAN SABRE as well as the year 2090 AD.

"Would you like me to fast forward through Declan Sabre's timeline in this twelve month period?" The computer offered.

"Yes please." I gave a nod before I added on, "or there's something specific that you could search for."

"What would you like me to target in the subject's timeline?" The computer asked.

"Um, I'll be completely honest with you," I confessed, "I think he's going to die this year and I have to know when. So if you could look from the month of August onwards? I'd really appreciate it."

"Scanning now." The computer obeyed.

I looked up at the huge, hanging upside down, crystal pyramid in the centre of the room. As it slowly turned, I saw in the three sides Declan's life play out in the month of August.

Scenes from his work at the Garage, or coming home to help his mother with dinner were put on display. Then in the evenings once Aunt Susan had gone to bed, he snuck out of the house without any clothes on to expand into his huge, hulking, hairless European Werewolf body. He ran in supernatural speed through the woods, up the hill to my house before returning to his human shape as he approached my backdoor. He would look around the woods with his glowing green eyes and even sniff the air to ensure he wasn't followed, before going inside. In my bedroom I watched myself welcome him to my bed with open arms and how eagerly he pressed his body against mine.

"OK!" I felt my face burn as embarrassed, I averted my eyes.

The computer continued to fast forward through the month, also showing Declan on patrol. He bounded along the borders of the National Park on all fours in his European Werewolf shape. The majestic mountain peaks of the Alaska Range, was his backdrop. He ran in supernatural speed, only stopping occasionally to sniff the air and listen to the noises of the night before breaking into another run.

All of a sudden there was a bright flash of light and the three sides of crystal pyramid turned a blank white...

"Oh no, not again!" I felt my heart stop. "Computer, is this the same interference that happens with me?"

"Correct." The computer reported. "We are currently experiencing the same interference when either Circulate systems or the Last Calculator Vincent Moher attempts to calculate your future."

"But why is it happening to Declan?" I pondered.

"From the evidence available Bianca, I can conjecture that the night Declan Sabre is on patrol, you will appear. As Circulate systems are blocked from seeing certain points in your timeline; the same interference carries over to the people or places you come into contact with." The computer postulated.

"Then what's the date of this night that Declan's on patrol and I show up to 'block'?" I demanded.

"The date that the interference occurred is the 20th August 2090 at 2333 hours." The Circulate Mainframe reported.

"Thanks!" I jumped up out of my seat.

"You are welcome." The computer chirped.

I instantaneously phased home with at least some kind of idea of a date that Declan's demise occurred on. Although I was happy with this heads up, he wasn't when I told him.

"B, you promised you wouldn't say anything!" He growled.

"Ah but I didn't say anything to anybody or any Werewolf, did I?" I wrapped my arms about his neck as we lay in bed. "I spoke to a computer."

"Stop twisting the words around, B!" He snapped. "Now I don't want you to do anything else."

"But Declan -"

"No!"

"Declan, if you would just listen to me -"

"Shut up, B!" He snarled in bad temper. "Man, you are one frustrating woman to be with! You're like some spoilt princess, as you do whatever you feel like, no never mind the consequences!"

He was so angry that he rolled off me to sit on the side of the bed to sulk.

"Declan after what happened to Grant, why can't you understand the reason why I'm doing all of this?!" I complained.

I moved to sit beside him, before gently turning his face my way so our eyes could meet and hold.

"Declan Sabre, you are my mate. I couldn't bare to lose you just as I would do anything to keep you safe and by my side." I said strongly. "Even if it means calling a meeting with the pack and Tribal Elders to publicly declare this."

"Go out and buy a clue, B!" He pushed my hands away. "You really think that people are going to accept the fact that you're mated to me? Then you really do live in dreamland."

"What's that supposed to mean?" I asked hurt.

"Your father doesn't trust me because of the breed of Werewolf I am. He would no sooner approve of our coupling if hell froze over!" He said vehemently. "If he found out that his daughter and only child was MATED to a European Werewolf? He'd lead the lynch squad to tear my hide."

Oh, Declan's picked up Dad's distrust then. I recalled all of the things Dad has ever said about him or how he put down European Werewolves in general.

He continued to vent, "then what about Ian Elm? He's your father's best friend and the brother of your late husband. Do you think he's going to be happy that you've returned to the Werewolf that you were secretly involved with before your marriage? He'd frickin' hold me down as your father tore strips off me!"

Disheartened I looked away, as I felt confused what to do next. Declan was right, we were in a situation that looked like there were no happy endings. We were damned if we do and damned if we don't.

"But you don't deserve to die, Declan." I said tearfully.

I think my pain made him pause, as he slipped from anger to regret.

"Come here." He pulled me into his lap to hold me tightly. "I suppose I should just be happy that I got to have you at all."

"What are you talking about?" I sniffed.

He cupped my face to hold it an inch away from his, "because I'm a Werewolf I see your aura as a Circulator but because Derik was just plain human, he couldn't. When you were human I couldn't be with you without harming you but then you changed so I could. I still think fate turned you because it felt sorry for me. If it means that I have to sneak around to be with you, or risk my life on patrol? It's worth it."

I half cried and half laughed out, "that's the cheesiest load of crap that I've ever heard or I never expected to hear you say, Declan Sabre!"

"It's your fault, B." He chuckled back. "I'm supposed to have the reputation of the tribe's most dangerous Werewolf, but you've turned into my weakness."

"Oh yay." I said dead pan. "I don't want to be your downfall, Declan."

My lover lowered my head to allow me to tuck my wet face into his hot, strong neck and then we simply sat there like that, in each other's arms.

~~~~~~

<div align="right">25th August 2090</div>

The following diary entry starts off from my point of view, but after what happened on August 20th, it changes perspective. Declan is still fuming about what I did, but ironically I would call it one of the most profound experiences of my life. It wasn't all bad, although I guess the people around would disagree as it's their perspective that the entry changes to.

However my actions did alter irrevocably our lives the night of August 20th. New understandings were made as life took on new meaning. Peoples' views were changed as they reassessed their lives and what they held important.

To start with, at 10.30 PM I instantaneously phased into the woods that were on the border between Lokoti land and Alma. I was dressed in my stretchy gym clothes to handle my Lokoti Werewolf muscle bulk with my silver sword strapped to my back. In short, I was reporting in for battle.

Funnily enough the small clearing I was standing in, was deceptively calm and quiet before the strangers arrival. I was going to wait for them to come and frighten them off myself. To do this, I looked around for a good tree to hide behind. I left the clearing to stand behind a large fur which was both wide as it was tall.

As I stood barefoot on the moist earth, it began to rain. My heart began to pound as already this night was following the order of events in my vision. When I saw how muddied my feet became, my heart raced in fear. I looked around the tree trunk back into the clearing. Nup, still no strangers but when I turned back around again? I jumped in fright!

Declan in his monstrous European Werewolf shape was standing right behind!

MAN YOU REALLY ARE A PATHETIC WEREWOLF NOT TO SMELL MY APPROACH EVEN IF I WAS SILENTLY STALKING YOU – he shook his beastly head.

"Get lost!" I growled in my deep, rumbling Werewolf voice. "Go away and patrol, would you?"

YEAH IT'S MY TURN TO PATROL AND YOU SHOW UP, SO WHY AREN'T I SURPRISED? – he thought sarcastically.

"This is where the strangers come to attack." I said curtly.

YEP I FIGURED AS MUCH BUT YOU DO KNOW WITH YOU BEING HERE WILL GIVE THE WHOLE THING AWAY? – he mentally retorted.

"I don't care, just as long as you live." I growled softly.

IF YOU DON'T GO HOME RIGHT NOW I'LL FRICKIN' CARRY YOU HOME – he threatened.

"If you do, I'll just instantaneously phase back here." I smirked with my elongated teeth jutting out.
~~~~~~

GO HOME B – Declan demanded – *NOW I KNOW THE TIME AND PLACE I'LL BE READY FOR THEM.*

"So will I, as I fight beside you." I rumbled adamantly.

He emitted a vicious snarl as he lowered his dangerous jaws right in front of my face, his hot breath scalded.

GET HOME NOW! – he warned – *I WON'T TELL YOU AGAIN!*

"Yes you will." I tittered which came out as an odd kind of growl.

I heard him emit a helpless whine in frustration and roll his glowing green eyes.

OF ALL THE FEMALE WEREWOLVES IN THE WORLD I COULD MATE WITH, I GET THE SCREWBALL WHO'S AS STUBBORN AS SHE IS STUPID – he complained.

"Hey, who's the one with the BA and the upcoming Masters?" I put my clawed hands on my hips.

RIGHT THAT'S IT! – Declan decided as he abruptly bent forwards.

"What the...?" I suddenly found myself slung over his hardened back!

Then I saw the ground which was upside down, quickly rush by as he bolted off towards the hill that my house sat on top of. He ran in supernatural speed and didn't slow down until I saw the tree line of the woods behind. When he lowered me to my feet once more? I found myself standing on my front veranda.

"Declan!" I stomped my clawed foot. "What's this going to prove? I can always instantaneously phase back to the clearing! Are we going to do this all night?!"

STAY! – he pointed his front right claw my way, before he added on jokingly – *OR IT'S BACK TO OBEDIENCE TRAINING FOR YOU.*

Next, I watched him turn around and bolt off on all fours from my property. I flexed my claw-like hands anxiously as I watched him disappear. Declan was right, my presence would not only give our relationship away but if he's running me home all night because he refuses to let me fight; what will happen to the rest of the pack when the strangers are shooting at them with silver bullets? They would need all of their attention to duck and dodge the silver bullets coming their way.

Disgruntled, I turned and headed inside. I would simply have to stay home until I hear the pack's battle cry. But as soon as I walked into the living room, I realized I was leaving behind a muddy trail with even more mud on my gym clothes. Damn it, I'm gonna have to shower and change.

I quickly showered before I hurriedly redressed in my bedroom. I caught the time on my small travel alarm clock which read 10.59 PM. It felt like time was getting away and just as I was about to put my sword back on, I paused. I realized I had just put on my pajamas instead of a new pair of gym clothes! Truly I was a creature of habit because I shower in the evening, I subconsciously dressed for bed.

Just before I could take off my flannel pajama shirt, I heard it.

ARMED STRANGERS ARE ON THE BORDER BETWEEN LOKOTI LAND AND ALMA! THEY HAVE SILVER BULLETS AND THEY'RE THE 'BAD ELEMENT' WE SENT AWAY SIX YEARS AGO – Grandfather called on the pack.

Oh my god, the strangers are here! They arrived with the rain and I'm in my pajamas! Everything is happening just as I saw it would. Then that means Declan was in danger...

My sword which was still in its sheath, dropped to the bedroom floor as I instantaneously phased into the dark, wet woods outside.

I barely felt the cold mud squish between my toes or the icy rain drench my pajamas, with all the loud gunfire. I was standing unseen in the far corner of the clearing, with the five strangers all shooting at Declan and the Lokoti Werewolf who was on patrol with him, which was Grandfather.

They leapt behind the trees to use as cover, whilst the silver bullets which were meant for them, embedded in the bark. Time seemed to slow as I watched in horror, the leader who was standing in the middle of his men, aim his shotgun at the tree Declan was behind. He knew just as I did that my mate would leap out the first chance he had.

The strangers had them pinned. Grandfather sensed as I did, that the rest of the pack were on their way and they were about to run into a line of fire. To protect his men, he tried to draw the gunfire unto himself by leaping behind tree to tree. This started to work too, as I recognized several members of the pack arrive on the scene but they were able to take cover. However when Declan saw that his father figure was in danger, he made his move and it was then that the stranger in the middle pulled the trigger.

This was the last thing I remember of the gunfight, as I felt a strange kind of pull which physically moved me.

I was barely aware that my body acted of its own accord, as I lurched forwards in light speed to get between Declan and the silver bullet. As it was sailing through the air towards his heart, I only just felt the impact in the back of my head. The force of the bullet entering my cranium felt like getting hit with a baseball bat that had a nail sticking out of it...and then darkness.

I definitely didn't feel the rain or the mud after that. I didn't feel much at all as all I saw was blackness...

...

...or at first it was just blackness, but I began to make out small dots of light. The small dots of lights seemed to be moving past me, or I was moving past them. I felt a like I was floating, which was the same kind of feeling I experienced when I went into phase and I was a bodiless mass of light.

The small dots of light began to stream past, or I was streaking past them. I sensed I was flying fast somewhere and I know this is going to sound strange, but I got the impression I was flying through outer space. Those white dots were in fact distant stars I was passing.

Then I saw where I was being pulled to, as on the horizon I made out some kind of line of white light.

The closer I was pulled towards it, the brighter the light became. It wasn't a tunnel of light you sometimes hear about, but it looked like a white line that stretched far and wide. It was almost like on the edge of outer space where the darkness ended, the light began. Although I was flying through space as a bodiless mass, I couldn't escape from it. I sensed that this white light which held up all of existence, was pulling me in...

Abruptly the white light changed to a softer yellow one, when oddly a set of doors opened to allow me entrance into an ornate, candle-lit room.

"My Lords, Ladies and Gentlemen, I present to you Lady Bianca Elm."

As I walked into a gilt ballroom which was full of people wearing period costume, I realized I had a body again. In fact, on my body was the same kind of clothing everyone else was wearing. I was wearing a long, sea green silk dress with these weird wide hoops on the side. I think I was wearing an 18th Century ball gown?

What the...? What's going on here? One minute I'm flying through outer space and the next I'm at a ball? But what happened to the woods I was just in? I had no idea where I was or what was happening.

Worriedly, I did a little turn as I further examined myself. I also noticed that my body looked different. When I changed into a Lokoti Werewolf, my height increased as my shoulders became broader and even in human form, I looked a little muscled with an athletic physique. But right now, my body looked smaller and felt weaker as I appeared completely human.

My heart raced as I glanced upwards from my strange appearance to the rest of the well dressed humans in the room. Not only did I look like them, but it was like I WAS them. Where exactly was I?

Just then a tall man with short dark hair and dark brown eyes, wearing an 18th Century English Army uniform of a Captain, broke off from talking to two other people, to walk my way. He had been talking to a man who had dark brown eyes and longer, curly dark hair tied back in a small pony tail. The man was wearing an 18th Century English Naval uniform also of the rank of Captain. The woman standing beside him was wearing an ornate, beaded white dress also of 18th Century standard. The couple toasted their wine glasses to me, as they watched their friend cross the room to come to my side.

"Dear girl." The Army Captain greeted as he stopped short to give a small bow. "It's good to see you've arrived."

"Um, do you know me?" I asked shyly. "Er, where am I?"

"Know you, my dear?" The man grinned mischievously. "Oh yes, we 'know' each other quite well."

"How do you know me?" I queried. "I've never seen you before just as I've never seen this place until now."

"Oh?" He looked on in good humor. "No you haven't, but we thought it would be appropriate to make you, us and your surroundings appear as such."

"You did?" I looked around with wide eyes. "Um, why?"

"Because we decided we should show you your beginnings." He spoke in an English accent.

"What, has this got something to do with the Worthall's and Blythe Castle?" I frowned in confusion. "I mean, I haven't been to Blythe in a few years to visit my English relatives but their ballroom looks completely different to this."

"You are at the Fox's Ball at Holland House." The strange man proclaimed.

"Hang on that sounds familiar..." I tried to think, then his grin widened when he saw my eyes did in recognition, "...this is where my great, great grandmother came for her first time travel trip as a Circulator!"

"Well done, my dear." The man took my hand to kiss it.

I removed my hand from his, "erm, so why do you think you know me?"

"Come now, Bianca." The man chuckled. "You're a Circulator, you've studied temporal causalities with your mother and your grandmother. You've read the information on reincarnation on the Circulate Mainframe."

"Because you know Elisha Worthall, you think you know me?" I pondered.

"I met your grandmother Elisha Baker at this Ball." The man nodded back to his friends across the room, who raised their wine glasses to toast us again. "But I didn't meet you here."

"Then where did you?" I demanded.

I probably sounded a little rude, but I had to know what was going on.

"The last time I was in my mortal form, I knew you when we lived on Lokoti tribal lands." The man answered congenially. "Elisha Baker met me as Captain Greyson, but you know me by another name."

Right at that moment a servant in a white wig and livery walked past, carrying a tray of wine glasses. Captain Greyson lifted two glasses and handed me one.

"Um, I don't drink alcohol." I looked into the red liquid. "I can't, because I'm a Werewolf."

If this guy knew me from living on tribal lands, he should know I'm a Lokoti Werewolf. He should know that we can't drink lest risk losing control of the bloodlust.

"Not here you're not." He chuckled. "Just as I'm not one either."

I blinked in disbelief at his words, "you were a Lokoti Werewolf?"

"No, but I was a Werewolf in one of my past lives." Captain Greyson chuckled. "Otherwise when I was human, people still called me a dog by my misbehavior."

I saw that he found my confusion of who he was and what was happening to me quite amusing.

"You're enjoying this, aren't you?" I glared.

"Quite." He chinked his glass with mine before he drank a couple of mouthfuls.

I watched how easily this previous Werewolf and now human, drank up before I looked back down into my glass. Warily, I raised it to my lips and tentatively took a small sip. The wine tasted nice actually, or I think humans like wine connoisseurs would say it had a nice 'palate'.

"So why aren't I a Werewolf here and where is here exactly?" I lowered my glass as I took another look around.

"I'm surprised that you cannot guess." Captain Greyson said.

I took another look around the gilt ballroom which had hundreds of candles lit that cast a flattering, soft glow on the people in their silk, velvet, jewels and gold trim. I caught sight of some windows across the room, which I began to walk towards.

However what was on the other side of the windows, made me look on in shock. Instead of seeing the outside of a house or even a garden; I was looking on what felt like all existence, with different shaped galaxies which were slowly moving. The spiral galaxies slowly spun like wheels, as the cluster galaxies moved past and two spiral galaxies even slowly collided to look like an odd shaped cross.

My heart began to pound as my eyes watered whilst I looked at the spiral galaxies and in particular, I tried to find mine. Which one was the Milky Way? Where was Earth, where my tribal lands, family and mate were? I instantly felt homesick by how far away everything was.

Captain Greyson came to stand beside, as he sipped his wine whilst looking out at the surreal view.

"Astounding, isn't it?" He observed. "No matter how many times I come back between life cycles, the view always impresses."

"Where's home?" I asked in a small voice.

"The Milky Way galaxy is that one over there." Greyson pointed. "But I'm afraid I can't show you Earth, it's too small to see."

"I feel so lost." I admitted as I blinked back my tears.

"But why?" He gave a funny look. "You are home."

"I'm not when I don't have my family, friends or loved ones with me." I said sulkily.

"Dear girl, look about you for heaven's sake!" He laughed out loud. "We've brought you back to your beginnings, remember?"

This time when I looked around, I found that everybody had stopped mingling and were all staring my way. In particular the pretty girl in the white gown with the Navy Captain, who seemed to have been watching the whole time. She did look familiar, but I couldn't place where although I sensed she was waiting for me to recognize her.

"Wake up and smell the coffee B, and stop acting like such a princess." Greyson said softly as he stepped up close.

What the...? My heart stopped as my mouth fell open. I looked up into the waiting eyes of this unfamiliar stranger.

"Declan?!" I gaped. "Is that you?"

The English Army Captain smirked, "it took you long enough."

"But are you...does that mean...did you die?" I uttered out afraid.

"I've died plenty of times, B." Greyson/ Declan said in good humor.

"Then that means what happened with the strangers -"

"No, I lived that night." He reassured as he took hold of my hand again.

"Then if I'm here..." my eyes watered once more, "...I didn't?"

"This place," he waved his arm, "is just a waiting room."

"A waiting room?"

"Think of it as a preview of what's to come." His dark brown eyes sparkled. "This is just the outside of eternity, as you're not there yet. You're not meant to remain but the next time you come, you shall."

"So I died but I'm not going to stay dead?" I wondered.

"It's very hard for a Circulator to stay dead, B." He gave my cheek a tender caress. "Your light is ongoing just as it is attractive."

I clutched onto his hand which held mine back just as strongly, "so I'm going to see you again?"

"Of course." He chuckled again. "I have your scent, B. I'll dig my claws in if I have to, but you're in my clutches now."

As if perfectly timed, we were interrupted when the large double doors that I had come in, opened again.

The people who came through made me blink in disbelief. A youthful Great Grandma walked in beside a handsome Lokoti male. They were dressed in traditional 'skins' complete with a bow and quiver full of arrows on the man's back. The couple walked calmly through the throng of English Aristocrats, who nodded their heads respectfully.

"Elisha." Great Grandma smiled at the pretty woman in the white gown, with the Navy Captain. "Hello Guy."

Say what? That pretty woman in the white dress was the Elisha Worthall whom was my great, great grandmother?! She was my foremother and the Circulator who made Circulate history by passing on her ability down her female lineage! Then that also means that the Navy Captain was Guy Robertson/ Mike Sabre.

"B." Great Grandma and the Lokoti man who looked an awful lot alike Grandfather joined us. "You have to go back now."

"Great Grandma?" I stared at the youthful woman who was short and stout, just like the elderly woman I knew had been, before I looked at the man beside. "Who's this?"

"Hello Bianca." He smiled warmly. "I'm your Great Grandfather, David Riverclaw."

"Did you just get here too?" I pondered at their sudden appearance.

"No." Great Grandma tried not to laugh. "We were in the Holy Hunting Grounds when your Grandpa called on us."

"He called on you?" I shook my head in confusion. "What, did he call you on a walky-talky or some kind of supernatural telephone?"

The dead/ reincarnated people exchanged amused glances.

"The Tribal Elders asked their spirit guide the Lokoti Wolf to bring you back." Great Grandfather explained patiently. "Your body is waiting for you at your grandparent's house."

"But I just got here!" I objected and then I looked over at my great, great grandmother. "I haven't met everybody yet."

"You will meet Elisha, but not now." Great Grandma promised. "You're just visiting this time but you'll come back for good."

"That's what he said." I nodded towards Greyson/ Declan. "But tell me Great Grandma, he also told me that this is the place of my beginnings. Besides my great, great grandmother, who are all these people?"

"A curious little thing, isn't she?" He chuckled to Great Grandfather who laughed along.

"Family of course." Great Grandma smiled. "They came to see you and to make sure you wouldn't be alone."

"Family?" I looked around once more. "Besides Greyson/ Declan and Elisha with Guy/ Mike, who else is here that I would know?"

"Your family of the past and future, B." She took hold of my arm to lead me through the populated room back towards the doors.

I craned my neck to stare at the sea of faces. "Like who else? Tell me Great Grandma, please! Don't send me back yet."

"You're the kind of girl who likes to read the end of the book before she buys it, aren't you?" Great Grandfather smilingly shook his head as he and Greyson/ Declan walked behind.

"Impatient as well as impetuous," my mate mused, "but in the bedroom it can be quite an alluring trait."

We four stopped before the closed double doors as my great grandfather and my mate walked around to open them.

"Drink up, B." Great Grandma looked down at the wine glass still in my hand. "You need to drink now."

I looked puzzled into the red wine, to see it mysteriously look a lot thicker. In fact, it smelled like blood as I'd know that smell anywhere.

"You need to drink the blood of your mate to return to him." Great Grandfather instructed.

"You want me to what?" I looked on like they had gone mad.

Greyson/ Declan put his hands over mine to raise the glass to my mouth. I tried to push them away but I ended up holding onto his arm. He tenderly but firmly pressed the glass against my lips and tilted it. As I drank the red liquid, his eyes held mine as I watched their unfamiliar dark brown colour begin to look a familiar glowing green.

"I'll see you soon dear girl," Greyson's English accent slipped to an American one, "now come back to me, B."

Great Grandma took away the wine glass just as Great Grandfather opened the double doors. All of the candles in the ballroom went out as if a gust of wind had just blown through. But in the darkness, I could still feel my hands holding onto Declan's arm as the taste of his blood filled my mouth...

*****

~ **20** ~

"Noooooooooooo!!"

To me time seemed to move in slow motion, whereas to everyone else it all happened so fast.

From my perspective, I instantaneously phased out of my bedroom, in my pajamas to reappear in the rain. I found myself standing in the section of woods that was on the border between Alma and Lokoti land. I saw the five strangers standing in the small clearing. I heard the roar of Declan in his European Werewolf form, readying to leap out to maul the threat to his land and loved ones. I heard the growls of the Lokoti Werewolves running to his aid. I heard the 'click' of the shotgun barrel being readied as I saw the leader take aim at Declan.

"No!" I leapt forwards in the speed of light, although I don't recall my cry but I've been informed I made it.

The shotgun went off and then blackness... I don't remember anything else as I didn't feel anything else. I was mid-air when everything went black. I don't even remember falling to the ground as I don't think I would have landed correctly.

Nothing. Nada. Zip. Zilch. Zero; so long, farewell, auf weidersen and good night, as the song goes.

I didn't particularly mind, because as I said, I don't know what happened. However after this moment, the following that is transcribed here are all third person accounts from the different people who told later me their version of events.

Declan and Grandfather watched as I fell face first in the mud. I guess it must have looked kinda funny in a perverse way; leaping into the air and then doing a frontal swan dive into the muddy ground.

Silence...the Werewolves paused and even the strangers halted. I hadn't been in my Werewolf form, so the Strangers thought that they had just shot a normal woman, an 'innocent bystander' although I came out of nowhere.

"Noooooooooooo!!"

The first cry came from Grandfather when he saw his granddaughter appear in the middle of a gunfight. Whereas the second cry, came from Declan when he saw his one and only avenue of 'getting any' take a bullet to the head.

My lover instantly fell to his knees as a naked human in the cold rain. Although it was I who was shot, my European Werewolf mate completed deflated into his smaller body. Declan picked me up and turned me over in his arms, nursing my head in his right hand.

"B – B – B – B c'mon, please!" He tearfully called.

Grandfather, Dad and Ian fell to their knees on the ground around, as they too reverted to human form. Grandfather grabbed hold of Declan's right hand that had been nursing my head, to look at the blood on it - my blood. The four men all exchanged sickened looks, which they then turned my way as they looked on my limp form.

"Her heart's stopped." Ian said.

As they knelt there in the mud in human form and in terror, the rest of the pack took out the strangers.

Harry led the other Werewolves as they used the strangers surprise at my sudden appearance against them.   In the human's hesitation, the Lokoti Werewolves pounced in lightening fast speed! The guns containing the silver bullets were destroyed in the Werewolves supernaturally strong hands, as the strangers were knocked out and ultimate contained. Ironically all of this happened without further fatality to either party as within a minute the battle was over, with just one casualty...me.

"No, this isn't possible because she's a Circulator!" Grandfather shook his head in disbelief.

"She's also Lokoti Werewolf and there's a silver bullet in her brain." Ian said flatly.

"Bianca...?" Dad reached out.

His hands tenderly wiped at my muddy face as his brown, human eyes overflowed with hot tears. Declan sat there crying in the mud, as he carefully held me in his arms like I was a piece of broken glass.

"We can do something, right? We can fix her, can't we?" He tearfully looked from my father to my grandfather.

"Bianca..." Dad crumpled into tears, "...my baby B? That's my baby B!"

Ian put his hand on Dad's shoulder, but he shook it off. He moved closer to where I was lying as he began to smooth away my wet hair as if cleaning me up would help somehow.

"This is my little girl! This is my baby B! This is Bianca...!" My father whimpered in agony.

When he pulled back his hand, he saw it was stained with my blood.

"NOOOOO!!"   He   threw   back   his   head   and   howled! "NOOOOAAAARRRW!!!"

He leapt to his feet to turn on the unconscious humans that the pack were grouping together. He morphed into his larger, more dangerous form as his body bulked up and his eyes glowed red. His claws extended from the end of his fingers and toes.

"Hunter, no!" Ian sprang up, just as Dad was about to leap onto the strangers. He held back his best friend. "Hunter no! The code, man! You have to control it man, now control it!"

Dad shook with helpless rage as Ian held onto him tightly. In his human form, he squeezed my father with his larger Lokoti Werewolf shape, against his chest.

"I know, buddy." Ian said tearfully. "She was your baby B, your daughter and your only flesh and blood. I know man, I know! I felt the same way when they killed my little brother Grant."

As Declan rocked my lifeless form against his chest, he openly cried in front of the other Werewolves. His pained noises sounded like a mournful howling, as he gripped onto me harder. Grandfather saw the agony on his face as he saw through our secret.

"She was your mate, wasn't she." He stated rather than asked. "That's why she came, that's why she's here. She felt that you were in danger and she came to you."

Declan simply looked back through his tears as he rocked my lifeless body. Then Grandfather's face changed from one of shock and sadness, to resolution and determination.

"We have to get her home." He told him. "She may have been Lokoti Werewolf, but she's still a Circulator. We have to take her to the other Circulators."

My lover looked on in hope at his words. My grandfather stood up first with my lover second, whilst lifting me up into his strong arms.

"Hunter." Grandfather called his son-in-law. "We have to take B to her mother and her grandmother."

Dad pulled out of his best friend's hold to see the determined look on his face before he gave a single nod. However the Werewolves didn't have to run me home to the Circulators, instead a Circulator instantaneously phased to their position.

Suddenly Mum appeared beside Dad in a bright flash of light, in her pajamas too. It was as if she had a vision herself which also made her come running, or phasing to our location. Right away she saw Declan carrying her dead daughter which made her eyes widen.

"Oh shit!" She bit out. "So it WAS a vision and not just a dream!"

Next, she rushed forward to examine my injuries as Dad and the other Werewolves eagerly watched.

"Aunt Jess, you can do something right?" Declan pleaded. "Can't you?"

Mum turned my head around to see the gunshot hole, as her eyes watered.

"Jess?" My father walked up to try to hug her.

"No!" My mother shook him off, as she seemed both angry yet determined. "We have to take her to her Mum! She will know what to do." Then she looked to Dad, Grandfather and Ian. "Put your hands on my shoulders."

As soon as they did so, Mum placed hers on Declan's shoulder and the small group disappeared in another flash of light.

When they reappeared in the living area of my grandparents' house, Gran rushed over also in her pajamas. Whilst Declan held me up, she closed her eyes as she put her hand over my head. Then she moved her hand over my face and over my chest, before opening her eyes to give her diagnosis.

"There's no brain activity and the electrical impulses along her central nerve system are fading." She said unhappily. "Take her upstairs."

Declan rushed me up the staircase, running two to three steps at a time. He carried me down the hallway and into the first bedroom he saw. As he carefully laid me out onto a bed, everybody filed in after. Once he stepped back, Ian handed him a bathrobe which he saw was hanging behind the door. He absent-mindedly pulled the robe on as he never took his eyes off me. He watched Gran move to sit beside on the bed, as she worriedly looked over her dead granddaughter.

"You can do something, right Mum?" My mother asked tearfully as she stood with her husband.

"First, I'll remove the bullet from her brain." She announced as she took a deep breath.

Everyone watched hopeful, as she placed her hands on my arm before she closed her eyes and concentrated. Gran went into phase before she put me into phase with her. We both turned see-through and bright as we looked like two ghosts. After a full minute, she returned us to our corporeal bodies. She put her hand behind my head and when she removed it, she had a bloodied silver bullet sitting on her palm.

"Yes!" Ian breathed as his eyes widened impressed.

Declan cried out worriedly, "but her heart's not beating!"

"I only removed the bullet, I haven't tried healing her other injuries yet." Gran said curtly. "One step at a time, Declan."

"Well, why aren't you? Can't you do it? Come on, do it!" My mate demanded.

"Declan." Grandfather said softly as he put his hand on his shoulder.

My grandmother looked up at her husband, before she looked on her daughter and son-in-law next.

"Jess, I'm going to need your help." Gran told her. "I'm going to need you to go into phase with me. You and I will have to go into perfect sync with each other. Healing the wounded tissue isn't the problem but I've never reinitiated somebody's electrical impulses before."

"What do we have to do?" She asked, taken aback.

"Not only do we have to phase together her wounded tissue, but we have to try to restore her electrical impulses in her brain, heart and central nerve system." Gran said grimly.

"But I've never done something like this before." Her face fell. "I've removed bullets or healed cuts, but I've never dealt with the brain."

"But you can do it, can't you?" Declan goaded. "I mean you guys are supposed to be some kind of time and space manipulators! You guys are supposed to be all powerful and shit! The Lokoti call you Light People!"

The Werewolves looked on the Circulators expectantly, which made Mum and Gran exchange raised eyebrows.

Gran instructed, "whilst we're in phase together, we'll be able to hear each other's thoughts and I'll guide you through the process. When I go into phase I will put Bianca into phase and then you'll join us. What we need to do must be in perfect harmony, as we increase our power output to reinitiate Bianca's as well."

Mum blanched, "increase our power output? You mean raise our bio-electromagnetic frequency on purpose! But what if that destabilizes our wavelength and we continue to rise in energy output? What if that makes us evolve? What if you go back to the space time continuum?"

"Jess!" She said firmly. "To reinstate Bianca's electrical impulses we have to raise our power levels. Now are you ready?"

Mum paused, however she was keenly aware that all eyes in the room were on her. After an uncomfortable moment, she nodded back her consent. She came to sit on the other side of the bed with her dead daughter lying between her and her mother.

The three topless men in muddy jeans and the fourth in a bathrobe, all watched in silence. Declan nervously twitched as he tried not to growl under his breath, as he was just aching to help somehow. Dad, Grandfather and Ian stood as still as statues, as they watched the Circulators work.

Gran closed her eyes again as she went into phase. She turned bright and see-through before she turned my body the same and then Mum joined us. We looked like three ghosts on the bed as we three steadily turned brighter and brighter. However the brighter our luminescence, the less human we looked as our formations blurred. Our human shapes began to alter as we looked like instead, three circles of blinding white light.

The Werewolves could no longer look without hurting their eyes, as the light we produced poured out of the window which even lit up the forest encrusted hill!

"Arabella?" Grandfather called worriedly.

"Jess?" Dad blindly tried to take a step forward.

"Come on girls, you can do it...!" Declan chanted softly.

"Woah, did the sun crash on earth or something?" Ian complained.

Suddenly there was a blinding flash of light! The men flinched as they had to turn their heads away. However when they opened their eyes again, they saw we had returned to normal. Gran, Mum and I had returned to our biological bodies, as we appeared solid once more.

Silence...as for a second, everybody seemed scared to speak. Gran watched my mother as she leaned over my face to listen.

"I can hear her breathing! Mum, I can hear her breathing!" She let out a joyful laugh. "It worked, she's alive!"

"I can hear her heart beating!" Dad moved forwards to pull Mum into his arms for a celebratory hug.

Declan's eyes watered, as he looked on his mate lying on the bed. Although he was happy that he hadn't lost me, he was still scared how close the threat had come.

"When will she open her eyes?" Grandfather asked Gran.

"I don't know..." she faltered, "...I've never done this before, Em. I don't know what's supposed to happen."

He walked over to place a supportive hand on his wife's shoulders, then together they looked on their granddaughter.

"What do you mean you don't know when her eyes will open?" Declan demanded.

Gran closed her eyes and held her hand over my head once more to declare, "The electrical impulses in her brain; they're there but they're dull."

Mum frowned as she pulled away from Dad to come back over to investigate. She copied off Gran by moving her hand over my head. To an ordinary human this would look unusual, but to the Werewolves who could see a Circulator's aura; the space where they ran their hands was where the Werewolves saw the auras around our bodies, which was produced from our higher bio-electromagnetic fields.

"Yes, they're there but they're weak, because B's weak. Now what do we do?" Mum asked helplessly.

"I don't know what else I can do to help her." Gran turned tearful.

"You did all you could, Arabella." Grandfather said as he stroked her hair. "You did good."

"What happens now?" Declan asked fearfully.

"We wait." Ian answered.

"We wait?" He echoed impatiently. "For how long?"

"For as long as it takes." Dad said stubbornly as he gazed on his only child.

Everybody turned quiet again as they looked frightenedly on my muddy face.

*****

As Mum and Gran cleaned me up and put me into some new pajamas, the men also cleaned up in another part of the house. Grandfather leant his spare clothes to the male Werewolves. Once dressed in Grandfather's jeans and flannel shirt, Declan came to sit on the bed beside my unconscious form.

He stroked my hair whilst staring down expectantly into my face, as if I could wake up at any moment. Or he would pick up my cold hands in his hot ones, as if to warm them. His behavior was observed by my family who stood in the room to look over their wounded daughter/ granddaughter.

Gran exchanged a 'let's talk' look with Grandfather and the two left to go downstairs. Ian had helped himself to my grandparents' kitchen as he proceeded to make coffees for everyone for the long wait ahead, which Gran saw. So she pulled her husband outside to talk privately on the veranda.

As soon as she shut the door, she asked quietly, "what's with Declan and Bianca?"

Grandfather shrugged, "this is the first I've seen confirmation of it."

"Confirmation?"

He looked out at the rainy night, "I had my suspicions."

"You did?"

"Yeah, for a while now."

"A while?"

"Yeah, when Bianca married Grant, I noticed a change in Declan's behavior."

"You did?"

"Yeah."

Gran groaned in frustration before she whacked Grandfather on the arm! She cried out, "Em, would you stop doing that!"

"Doing what?" He looked on in surprise.

"You do this – this – this short answers or deliberate obtuseness or whatever you want to call it!" She said annoyed. "Now can you please tell me what you know?!"

He chuckled as he pulled his mate closely to him. "You're still beautiful when you're angry and what about those sparks!"

"Thanks Em, but it's time for the exchange of information now."

"Alright so," he began, "I noticed Declan started to avoid Bianca when she was with Grant. During a hunt he would run at the back of the pack, away from the two. Declan stopped attending tribal functions where the two would be. He didn't come to Mom's funeral, but Grant told me later that he came by the house when he was out to give B a basketful of fruit and vegetables. He didn't go to Grant's funeral either, remember? But he was there when B lost control after his death, by howling for her. When I went to visit her a month or so ago with her father, I smelled Declan's scent was strong inside her house. Mysteriously, I also noticed that her roof was suddenly repaired as well as a couple of other things around her house."

Gran looked in through the lounge room window at Ian finishing off the cups of coffees. She asked in concern, "do you think Ian will mind?"

"I don't know." He sighed. "It's been a year since Grant's death. Not only would Bianca would be the first female Lokoti Werewolf, but she will also be the first Lokoti Werewolf to mate a second time after the death of her first."

She walked over to lean on the balcony railing, "Em, I would have been more surprised if she didn't take another mate. Circulators can live a long time and she was widowed when she was only 23 years old."

He also came to lean on the railing beside as he frowned thoughtfully. He asked, whilst keeping his voice neutral, "does this mean that you would take a mate after me?"

"No." She smiled softly. "I can't stand the thought of losing you at all. I would want you to come with me."

Grandfather looked back in surprise, "go with you?"

"Come with me to the space time continuum." She looked on in hope.

This made him beam, "you really want me to come with you? To be with you forever and ever?"

"You would come with me?"

"Well hell yeah!"

"Really?" Gran wrapped her arms about his waist.

"I'd be there with bells on." Grandfather affirmed.

She kissed him in relief, to which her husband eagerly responded.

*****

Mum did her customary pacing up and down in the bedroom as Dad leant against the wall with his arms folded, frowning deeply. He wasn't happy about his only child being shot and he wasn't exactly thrilled to see Declan so emotionally attached to me either. He wanted to throw off his hand which was stroking my hair.

'It's only been a year since Grant's death,' he thought unhappily. Then something else occurred to him and he pushed himself off the wall to walk up to the bed. He barked out at the younger European Werewolf. "Did you repair her broken roof a couple of months ago?"

Mum paused in surprise, before she looked wonderingly from Dad to Declan.

My lover took a deep breath as he squared his shoulders and then he looked both of my parents in the eye. "Yeah I did fix her broken shingles and I repaired the broken step and I fixed the broken window in her greenhouse."

"Oh." Mum looked startled to her husband.

Dad didn't look happy, he did NOT look happy at all. He abruptly turned around to walk out of the room and into the bathroom and Mum followed after. He leant forwards on the bathroom sink to take several deep breaths to calm himself.

"Hunter, what is it?" She walked up behind.

"He's mated with Bianca!" He growled whilst gripping onto the sink hard.

"What? Who? Declan?" She uttered in surprise.

"A Lokoti Werewolf mates ONCE in their life time! Bianca is a Lokoti Werewolf! It's only been twelve months since Grant's death!" He shouted in a whisper.

"Why are we whispering?" She wondered.

"So Ian downstairs doesn't hear!" He hissed.

"Oh." Mum gave a nod before she closed the bathroom door to give them privacy. "Look Hunter, I don't see what the big deal is -"

"WHAT?!" Dad bellowed under his breath. "Grant has only been dead for a year and Declan just swoops in!"

"Look." She put out her hand to steady him. "Maybe we should just get the facts first before we do or say anything -"

"She just appeared like that in her pajamas, as if she sensed he was in trouble. She put herself in the line of fire for him! I think she's - she's - she's in love with him." His eyes watered with helpless anger as she stood back and listened.

"Actually, it makes sense." She sighed. "I suspected she might have liked someone before she got married, I just thought it might have been Derik."

He looked back guiltily, "then Jess, what if this is my fault? I mean, I was one of the people who thought she should marry Grant. What if she and Declan had feelings for each other all the way back then?"

"Maybe." She shrugged. "But six years ago she and Declan were still fighting like cat and dog."

"I noticed changes in Declan after Grant and Bianca were married. At first I thought it was because he was angry for his brother. But then I couldn't figure out why he was still avoiding them even after Bianca became friends with Derik again." He leant further forwards on the vanity.

"Hmm," she frowned, "I noticed Declan never came to tribal gatherings or celebrations. Derik and Susan would be there, but Declan wasn't." Then she crossed her arms as she thought about this. "Bianca never asked where he was. I mean, they started fighting when she was 7 years old and used to throw insults at each other. But after her marriage, they completely stopped talking."

"Yeah, when she was with Grant." He put his hands on his hips.

"Shit!" She suddenly kicked the bathtub! "What if she DID have feelings for Declan before she married Grant? She behaved really secretive after her change. I wondered why she didn't seem to miss Derik that much when she was in lock down."

"Derik was her best friend, but he was in the way of his brother." He moaned as he inwardly kicked himself for not picking this up sooner.

She agreed, "I always thought that B and Declan fought a little too much or a little too hard. They seemed to delight in rubbing each other the wrong way."

"Sexual tension?" He guessed what she meant.

"Gees I'm an idiot!" Mum kicked the bathtub again. "And I'm supposed to be a Circulator so I'm supposed to 'see'!"

"Now Derik is married to Rachel and Grant is dead? Declan probably thought that he finally had his chance to be with Bianca." He sighed heavily. "But what are we going to do about Ian?"

"What do you mean?" She gave a funny look.

"Ian is the head of his family and Grant was his younger brother. Bianca entered his family when she married Grant. He was Lokoti Werewolf, just as Ian is and Lokoti Werewolves are meant to mate once for life. He might object to B moving on with Declan." Dad spoke plainly.

"Really?" Mum's eyes widened. "Would Ian really do that?"

"I don't know, but he has the right to."

"No way!" She gaped.

"I'm afraid so."

"I'll go talk to him." She turned towards the bathroom door, but he reached out to stop her.

"No, not tonight Jess." He shook his head. "We'll cross that bridge when we come to it."

Out of the blue, Mum started sobbing! This took Dad by surprise, before he pulled her to him as he hated seeing her upset. He tried to comfort the love of his life as he held her closely.

"Our little girl was shot in the head tonight...!" She cried. "I don't like this Werewolf business anymore! B shouldn't be a Werewolf, she's still our little girl!"

"Our baby B." He agreed as he kissed her on the forehead.

Tearfully, she gazed into his face, "she really appeared out of nowhere and jumped in front of the bullet like that? The bullet that was meant for Declan?"

He nodded before he spoke, "as soon as the bullet entered her head, Declan collapsed. He deflated back to human to pick her up and cry over her. He completely forgot about the battle and he NEVER walks away from a fight."

Mum pulled away to say sadly, "let's go back and be with our baby girl."

Dad opened the door for her and then together they left the bathroom.

*****

Grandpa arrived shortly after with his 'medicine bundle', which was an old fashioned, black leather doctor's case like Derik's. Everyone stood around, sipping the coffees that Ian had made whilst watching the Medicine Man examine me. Declan refused to leave my side however, which Ian noted.

"Her heart beat is strong and her breathing is regular." Grandpa listened to my chest before he checked my eyes, "but her pupils are dilated."

"And?" My mate looked on expectantly.

"It's not a good sign, Declan." Grandpa said unhappily. "It means that although her biological injuries have been healed, her neural pathways have been disrupted. There could be brain damage and I think she's in a coma."

"A coma?" He sat up straighter with a start.

"I'm afraid so." Grandpa said sadly before he looked on the Circulators. "You both did a good job of bringing her back from the dead, but I'm afraid it's a waiting game to see if she truly does come back to life."

My grandfather and father both put their arms about their mates to comfort them as everyone looked on my vegetative state.

"How long do we have to wait?" Declan demanded.

"I don't know as it could be hours, days, or even weeks." Grandpa sighed in resignation. "Her spirit isn't in this room with us as it's floating somewhere far away. She could be trapped between life and the afterlife."

"If we were able to return her spirit, would she wake up?" Grandfather asked.

"Maybe." He shrugged as he began to put away his medical instruments inside his medicine bundle. "I'm going to call an emergency meeting of the Elders. We will hold a prayer vigil and contact our spirit guides. We'll ask the Lokoti Wolf to guide her back."

"Thank you Fern." Grandfather nodded in appreciation.

Our Medicine Man started to leave as Grandfather released Gran to show him out, when he stopped. Before he passed through the bedroom door, he turned and looked on Declan sitting on the bed with his arm about my unconscious form.

"Keep her mate close." Grandpa said matter-of-factly. "If her will is strong enough to lead her to death because of him, her will should lead her back to him in life."

Then he turned and left the bedroom as well as the house, with Grandfather showing him out. Everybody and especially Ian, looked surprised at his words. He folded his arms as he glared on my dangerous liaison.

"I think that you and I need to have a 'talk', don't you?" Ian spoke coldly.

Declan sighed in resignation, "I'm sure we will."

*****

Night turned into day as dawn broke and the rain eased. Inside things were unchanged as I lay dead to the world, with my mate remaining by my side. I hadn't moved and I didn't even twitch.

"B?" He opened my eyes to check the pupils himself. "Come on B, wake up. Insult me or something. I'll even let you slap me around again."

He gently shook my body, but I didn't stir. Mum and Gran were sitting in chairs by my bed that Grandfather had brought in, with my mother dozing as my grandmother caught up on some sewing.

She laughed softly at his words, "you two certainly have that fiery chemistry."

He sighed as he purposefully hit the back of his head on the head board. "This girl has been nothing but trouble in my life, but I don't want it to end."

"A typical love/ hate relationship then." She smiled as she used her sewing scissors to cut a piece of cotton before threading it though a sewing needle.

The morning sun poured onto the bedroom floor and Declan looked on the light in sadness. He murmured, "come on B, come back towards the light; the morning light that is."

Mum shifted uncomfortably in her seat before she opened her eyes and immediately looked my way.

"Anything?" She checked.

"No." Gran answered.

She stood up to stretch, before she walked over and kissed my cheek. Then she turned around to head for the door as she offered. "I feel like a bacon and egg sandwich, any takers?"

"That sounds lovely Jess, with cheese on mine please." Gran smiled.

When Mum looked to Declan, he answered dismally; "nothing for me, I'm not hungry."

She went downstairs where Grandfather, Dad and Ian were drinking more coffee whilst sitting at the dining table to talk. As Mum walked into the kitchen and opened the fridge, she listened in to the men's conversation. The Lokoti Werewolves were talking about our relationship.

"If B wakes up, I'm not going to make a fuss about her and Declan." Ian sighed. "But I am going to have a talk with him."

"Listen Ian, all we're saying is we understand if you're angry. Because before B turned into a Werewolf, our pack had been the same for thousands of years." Dad said sympathetically.

"But by B becoming the first female Lokoti Werewolf, the guidelines for our breed of Werewolf have been thrown out of whack." Grandfather acknowledged.

"Before it was simple, there were fifteen Lokoti Werewolves who were all males, as it was passed down the blood line from father to son. But with B becoming the first female Lokoti Werewolf, plus the fact that she's barren and now she's the first Lokoti Werewolf to mate a second time?" Dad rubbed his face tiredly.

"But she brings a lot to the pack just as Arabella has done for our tribe." Grandfather tried to put a positive spin on things.

"Look fellas," Ian looked at the two, "I'm NOT going to cause a scene, I promise."

"I just want you to know Ian that it's come as a surprise to all of us." Dad said unhappily.

"You're telling me." He smirked.

"What are you going to talk to Declan about?" Grandfather inquired.

His jaw set, "I'm going to talk to him about protocol and tradition. I'm gonna tell the European Werewolf that when a member of the pack dies, you don't swoop in like a vulture on the fallen Lokoti Werewolf's widow!"

"Listen Ian, I've gotta talk to you about that." Dad sighed guiltily. "This could partially be my fault."

"Your fault, Hunter?" He looked on in surprise.

"Declan and Bianca may have had feelings for each other for some time. But because of Derik and then Grant, they didn't do anything about it until now." Dad confessed. "It could be my fault for pushing B into marrying Grant."

He turned quiet as he rubbed his jaw in contemplation, which Grandfather observed.

"No Hunter, it wouldn't be your fault." Ian finally spoke again. "I went along with the marriage idea just as you, the pack and the Tribal Elders did. At the time it seemed like the best thing to do about B's transformation and I know that she made him happy. He didn't regret marrying her."

"B did fall in love with Grant." Grandfather promised. "The change that came over her during her marriage, we all saw her find peace."

"Yeah I know." He let out a loud sigh. "I'm not doubting her feelings for Grant or the type of mate she made him. I'm just reeling in surprise, that's all."

"Aren't we all." Dad rubbed his tired eyes.

"But the way she just ran like that, without a moment's hesitation in front of the bullet?" Ian shook his head in wonder. "In my talk to Declan I'm going to make damn sure that he lives up to the standard of the Lokoti Werewolf mating procedure! That girl is still in my family until I formally acknowledge him as her mate."

Grandfather nodded, "we know Declan comes from a good home, as we admire Susan with all the work she's done as a teacher. I'm sure he'll honor his obligations and his family."

By this time, Mum had already begun frying the bacon and the eggs. As they were sizzling away, the men all sniffed at the delicious smell and they turned to watch her work.

"That smells good, Jess." Dad remarked.

"Don't worry, I'm already making you some." She sung back.

"That's my mate for you." My father said proudly as he stood up to go into the kitchen to help.

"And that's my daughter." Grandfather joked, as he joined them.

"That's my best friend's girl and...my mother-in-law?" Ian said bemused and then the three men laughed.

"Ian, do you want to eat the eggs or wear them?" She threatened.

*****

At ten o'clock in the morning the tribe's second Medicine Man in the shape of Derik showed up. My best friend arrived with his 'medicine bundle' as he gravely walked into the room. However he froze upon the sight of my unconscious form and of his older brother sitting loyally by my side.

"Derik." His brother said shortly. "You can punch me out later but just check on B, would you?"

"Where's Fern?" Gran enquired.

"He's with the Tribal Elders in prayer on the Holy Grounds." Derik answered.

Then he stiffly moved forwards to sit on the side of the bed as he opened up his 'medicine bundle'. Declan watched his little brother take out his stethoscope which he placed over my chest to listen to my heartbeat. My family stood around to watch Derik work.

"Her heart beat is strong." He sounded surprised as he removed the stethoscope. "Fern says she was shot in the head?"

"Uh huh." Declan answered.

"Where?" He turned my head to examine it next.

"Here, at the back." Declan showed him.

His eyes widened in surprise as his felt around my healed over skull before he looked in closer to see my scalp was completely healed too.

"She's not even missing any hair." Derik commented.

"We were able to heal her biological injuries as well as reinstate the electrical impulses in her central nerve system." Gran advised. "But the electrical impulses in her brain are very weak. Fern said that she could have brain damage."

Derik shone a small torch into my eyes to check my pupils. He said unhappily as he moved the torch away, "no response."

"But you can do something, can't you?" Declan asked desperately. "C'mon bro, you're the tribe's second Medicine Man! I've helped you set broken legs for pete's sake!"

He frowned as he looked upon my face. Next, Declan watched him pick up one of Gran's sewing needles from the bedside table and prick my fingers with it before he did the same to the big toes on each of my feet. When there was still no response, his frown turned deeper still.

"Derik?" His older brother watched anxiously.

"She's completely unresponsive to external stimuli." He sighed in defeat as he sat back. "I think she's in a coma."

Grandfather squeezed Gran's hand but then he had to leave the room as he could feel his rage building up. He was scared of turning and accidentally hurting someone. Declan knew exactly how he felt, as he growled under his breath.

"And how long is her coma going to last for?" My mate demanded.

"I don't know..." His little brother helplessly shook his head, "...comas can last for hours, or they can last for years."

"YEARS?!" Declan roared in fury as his hand flew across to grab hold of his shirt. "Can't you do something?! Can't you wake her?!"

"Well..." Derik glared as removed his older brother's hand, "...at the beginning of this century, there were these experiments performed by a German Neurologist. He was able to wake up five different coma patients by introducing an electromagnetic frequency into their brains, which changed their brain waves -"

"A German Neurologist?" Mum interrupted before she looked on Gran in hope.

"Was this German Neurologist, a Dr. Dystar by any chance?" She guessed.

"Um yeah, I think it was." He turned to give her a funny look.

"Dr. Dystar!" Mum let out a gleeful laugh. "I'll go -"

"No, I will." She stopped her. "He's never met you before Jess, so he may not want to help. But he should remember me from the time Belle introduced us."

In a bright flash of light, she instantaneously phased out of the room let alone the decade, to a different time period. Grandfather whom immediately sensed the departure of his mate, walked back into the bedroom to look on questioningly.

"Where's Arabella?" He wondered.

"She's gone to Germany about fifty years ago, to find a German Neurologist by the name of Dystar." Mum beamed. "Derik you're brilliant! You do know that don't you?"

"Dystar?" Grandfather's eyes widened in recognition. "As in the name of the drug, DYSTAR?"

"Mum's gone to get the inventor himself." My mother grinned. "The inventor who aside from studying Circulators, psychics, stigmatics and telepaths; also invented a medical procedure to wake up coma patients."

"Really?" His eyes widened impressed.

"You see B?" My mate caressed my cheek. "We've got your back. You'll be fighting with me again before you know it."

Derik's eyes narrowed as he regarded his older brother. He asked coldly, "so how long has this been going on for?"

My lover warily looked from his little brother to my brother-in-law who was also listening in.

"We'll talk about this later. But first, we bring back B and then you can kick the shit out of me." He said flatly.

Just then they were interrupted by my mother who clapped her hands as she gave a little jump.

"What am I doing?!" She prattled off. "I'm an idiot! Dr. Dystar may not be the only one who can help her! Vincent would know if 25th Century Medicine also has a way to treat coma patients!"

Then she too disappeared in another flash of light as she instantaneously phased to Mars to retrieve our Calculator. Dad and Grandfather exchanged surprised looks, now with the both of them missing a mate.

"It's a good idea." Derik conceded as he stood up. "In this case, I wouldn't say too many cooks would spoil the broth. Right now, I'd be happy to have a second opinion. I'd appreciate two other physician's advice."

Grandfather looked kindly on the younger man, "you're doing well Derik. Fern told us how you saved Missy Hindbark during her delivery last week. He says you've got the nose and intuition of a Werewolf."

"Thanks." Our Medicine Man said modestly. "When I'm not treating a head injury, I'm fine. But because the brain is so hard to treat without state-of-the-art computer equipment, I'm completely in the dark."

"It's not just the brain that's the problem." Ian sighed as he leant on the back of the bed to look on. "Fern said that her soul wasn't here, that it's trapped somewhere between life and the afterlife."

"Yeah, that's what the Tribal Elders prayer meeting is about; to guide her soul home." Derik concurred. "Five years ago, I wouldn't have believed it. But after the Tribal Elders contacted their spirit guides; Frank Brown woke up from the week-long coma his stroke put him in. If anybody can guide her back, it's the Elders' spirit guides."

*****

Half an hour later, Gran returned with an elderly man with silvery grey hair, dark blue eyes and pale skin; along with several cases of medical equipment. At the same time, Mum returned with a younger man, in the familiar form of my Calculator Vincent; carrying a 25th Century medical kit.

"Oh, of course!" Gran's eyes widened when she saw him. "How are you Vincent?"

"You could have come to me first!" Our Calculator barked in his usual unfriendly manner whilst looking insulted on the German doctor.

Dr. Dystar looked on Gran puzzled, as he waited for the introductions.

"Wil, this is Vincent who is our Calculator and our physician." Gran waved her hand. "Vincent, this is -"

"Dr. Frederik Wilhelm Dystar, born on the 2nd of April, 1970. He became Germany's top Neurosurgeon, until his fascination with the paranormal took over. He began interviewing psychics, telepaths, telekinetics and stigmatics in the year 2004 for his upcoming medical trials on their differing brain activity. Hodge Endeavor sponsored his work which led to him in the year 2015, inventing the drug DYSTAR, along with it RYPWYN." Vincent spouted off.

"I prefer Wil for short." Dr. Dystar smiled in good humor before he looked at Mum.

"Wil, this is my daughter Jessica, who is also a Circulator." Gran informed.

"Sorry, Vincent is very much a Calculator; all work and no play." She joked as she shook Wil's hand. "Who probably spends a little too much time alone at Circulate HQ on Mars, with his constant calculating."

"I don't hear you complain when you want something!" He said curtly.

"So the ability to circulate has been passed on to the women of your family?" Wil queried. "Just as the ability to calculate has ended up in a male with Vincent?"

"Yes." Gran confirmed. "Although Bianca is the last on the line because she is the last Circulator to be born."

"Fascinating!" Wil beamed as he looked from Mum, to me and then back to Gran. Then he walked over to Vincent to give him a good stare. "Your great, great, great, great grandmother met me shortly before she traveled back in time to meet your forefather, Vincent Worthall; whom you look very much like by the way. I assisted her and Herr Xavier Bell on the SSIT investigations into ESP and reincarnation."

"Yes, I've read them. The SSIT reports are stored in the Circulate Mainframe." Vincent said very nonplussed.

"Along with the reports on Vampires, Werewolves, Voodoo, Zombies, Time Warps, Time Recordings, Hauntings and other elements of the supernatural." Mum listed off. "It makes for some pretty interesting reading, actually."

Just then Derik returned to the room, followed by Dad, Grandfather and Ian.

"Wil, this is my husband Emanuel Riverclaw, my son-in-law Hunter Wisetail, our tribe's second Medicine Man, Derik Sabre and another Lokoti Werewolf in the pack, Ian Elm." Gran introduced.

"Sabre?" Wil recognized the name, as he looked closely on Derik's face. "Are you a relation of Mike Sabre? You look a lot like him."

"Yeah he does, doesn't he." Gran smiled. "It seems with genetics that Derik doesn't just look like Mike, but he's also in the field of Medicine."

Derik gave her a funny look to be discussed so, as Dad, Grandfather and Ian exchanged looks of amusement.

Wil now looked over the strong appearances of the Lokoti Werewolves in the room. "Werewolves, hmm?"

"Yep, they're Lokoti Werewolves. They're not like their European, North American or Asian cousins, as they look different when they turn and they don't eat human." She told him.

"There aren't any Werewolves in Africa, South America or Australia?" He asked curiously.

"No, Vampires are more world wide than Werewolves and there's more of a variety of those. Indeed, Elisha and Xavier discovered a common genetic trait in Werewolves and Vampires; that they're in the Shape Shifter family."

The Lokoti Werewolves all exchanged raised eyebrows at how easily Gran discussed them with the stranger, like they were at a scientific conference or some such. Wil's eyes widened worriedly as he looked on the three predators in human form.

"Oh don't worry, they don't eat human." Mum reminded. "The Lokoti Werewolves have curbed their bloodlust to crave animal instead."

"Ah." Wil looked instantly relieved.

"Nor do we eat guests in our houses either." My former brother-in-law smirked at the German doctor's concern.

"Listen ladies, with all due respect," Declan called over, "it's all very fascinating I'm sure. But can we get the doctors to look at the patient now please?"

"Here here." Vincent agreed as he opened up his medical kit.

Wil walked over to my side to lean over and briefly open my eyelids, before he checked my pulse.

"The patient is completely unresponsive to external stimuli." Derik advised.

"And how are her brain waves?" Wil inquired.

"Er, I wouldn't know. Do you see any computers around to monitor this?" He retorted.

"The electrical impulses in her brain are very weak." Gran added on.

"Who's this?" Wil looked on Declan who sat with his arm protectively about his mate.

"Oh that's Declan Sabre, Derik's older brother. He's the European Werewolf that was raised by the pack and trained not to eat human. He was turned when he was 3 years old, in the attack which killed his father." Mum informed.

My mate raised his eyebrows in annoyance having his dossier spouted off.

"Declan, I need you to move please." Wil told him.

He growled dangerously as his blue eyes turned glowing green, to show the strange doctor there was no way he was going to leave my side. It made Wil take a wary step backwards from the territorial European Werewolf.

"Our tribe's other Medicine Man recommended that Declan stay put." Dad said unhappily.

"The chora between Werewolf and mate can actually affect the mate's vital signs." Vincent told him as he took out his 25th Century medical scanner to wave over my head. "There have been cases where Werewolves can control their mate's heart beat, respiration and blood pressure."

"Hmm, interesting." Wil's eyebrows arose impressed.

"Her electrical impulses are faint." Our Calculator reported the scanner's readings. "Her brain waves are hardly registering at all."

Wil frowned at this piece of news, "of all the brain waves present, which is the strongest?"

"The Alpha Wave." He reported whilst looking on the scanner.

"The Alpha Wave is the strongest when a human is either asleep or deep in thought. When I ran the tests on Elisha, I found that her Alpha Wave was the dominant 24 hours a day. Being a Circulator, her Alpha Waves were in constant use, moving between the conscious and the subconscious mind. It's what we can try to use to our advantage, by increasing Bianca's Alpha Waves." Wil thought aloud.

"In your report, you conjectured that it wasn't an individual part of the brain that was responsible for a Circulator's ability to see through time or to put themselves into phase." Vincent looked back. "You said it was the increased electrical activity of the brain as a whole."

"Then I will introduce EM waves into her entire brain, to hyper stimulate the Alpha Waves." The German doctor decided, as he began to organize the medical equipment he and Gran brought with them.

"It's not going to work." Our Calculator announced.

This made Wil pause to back in surprise.

"What's not going to work?" Derik asked.

"It's not going to work, what Wil wants to do." He said adamantly.

"Why not?" Gran wondered.

"Basically what he will be doing, is what you and Jess have already done; when you put her into phase and increased her bio-electromagnetic frequency. You already did what Wil is about to do. Your EM waves fused with Bianca's when you resuscitated her. Although you returned the electrical impulses to her central nerve system again, it didn't bring back her consciousness." Vincent explained.

"Oh." Gran's face fell.

"But I mean, can't we at least try?" Derik stepped forwards. "The guy has brought five other patients around by this technique -"

"Yes five HUMAN patients." Our Calculator rebuked. "Bianca is a Circulator! A Circulator's and a Calculator's brains function differently! Their different bio-electromagnetic fields which gives them the ability to phase and to 'see' is directly linked to the electrical impulses in their brains!"

"But -" Derik began to argue.

"No, Herr Sabre." Wil said. "Vincent is right. It's how DYSTAR is able to stop a Circulator temporarily going into phase, by affecting their brain's electrical impulses and not the chemistry. It's also how RYPWYN is able to affect their ability to see, as it does in a human psychic, by also affecting their brain's electrical impulses."

The German doctor walked around in what little space there was left in the crowded bedroom. The Medicine Man and Calculator joined him in thought, as they began to walk around in a circle too. Everyone in the room seemed to deflate in defeat.

"Well this is frickin' helpful." My lover rolled his eyes.

"Declan." Grandfather growled quietly to let the doctors think.

But my mate couldn't keep quiet, "come on Derik! You've always been the brains of our family, like I've been the brawn. You're the golden child who got to study Medicine at Cambridge. Now think!"

Derik paused to glare back at his brother, but to his surprise he saw Declan turn tearful. Indeed it gave everyone pause. They weren't used to seeing the tribe's most sarcastic and dangerous Werewolf, show such emotion.

"Come on man, do something! You have Rachel and baby Michael, let me at least have B? Bring her back to me, Derik. I know you can do it, bro. Think of something! Bring her back to me, please?" The European Werewolf openly cried.

Ian couldn't stand this anymore as he turned and left the room. He didn't stop walking until he came to stand on the gravel drive. As much as Ian was angry about our coupling; he could understand his pain.

Along with the rest of the pack, Ian had 'the talk' with him when he was 14 years old. It was when Declan's lust for the opposite sex began to develop along with his impending manhood. It worried the pack just how strong it was, as his bloodlust was still being controlled by the will of the pack. Declan as a young European Werewolf in the midst of the Lokoti Werewolf pack, his difference was a constant cause for concern. His continued cravings for human instead of animal was an ongoing worry. As the other Lokoti Werewolves were able to curve theirs, Declan was in constant war with his. He was faster and stronger than the Lokoti Werewolves, which made them exercise their will over him double time, especially at the age of fourteen he outmatched their physical abilities.

Ian remembered clearly the particular morning after a hunt, they pulled the 14 year old European Werewolf aside for 'the talk'. He felt guilt over the hurt look on his youthful face when the pack told him that he could never take a human woman for a mate, as he could risk killing her with his overpowering strength; or he could accidentally turn her by biting in the heat of passion. The pack told him that any kind of sexual relations was a risk with a female who was not of his breed.

He thought, "with Jack's death six years later, along came Bianca the tribe's first female Lokoti Werewolf." With her being both Circulator and Lokoti Werewolf, her abilities also outmatched the pack. Only Declan was able to stop her on the border that fateful night she first changed. Ian vividly recalled Declan carrying her unconscious body back after he subdued her. With reverence, he laid her out on her parent's front veranda, looking on her unconscious form in utter longing before he pulled himself back and bounded away.

"Bianca is Declan's chance at happiness, of ending his loneliness and frustration. Then what happens? The Tribal Elders recommended that Grant should marry Bianca, to help her control her bloodlust. By mating her to another Lokoti Werewolf, they reasoned it would help curb her bloodlust from human to animal." Although Grant was at first surprised by the suggestion, he sensed they were all in agreement, which made him acquiesce. Ian saw in the first month of marriage, his little brother fall for his mate as he completely doted on her. He also recalled how Bianca's face lit up when his brother walked into the room, "indicating her feelings begin to develop for Grant as well...which left Declan alone and still different."

The pack worried over the European Werewolf's growing resentment as they sensed his jealousy whenever he saw Grant and Bianca together. The pack began to realize that Declan was avoiding tribal gatherings or places where Grant and Bianca would be, started to stem from his longing for Bianca himself. It was probably out of respect for Derik, that he stayed away from her in the beginning...or so Ian thought, but now he wondered?

This realization hit him hard, as he recalled one evening three years ago a conversation he had with his little brother, as the two worked together on repairing Ian's pick up truck. He was under the vehicle, working on the starter motor as Grant sat to the side, handing him what tools he asked for.

"Hand me the socket wrench, would you?" He held out his hand and his brother complied. As he tightened the tiny bolts, he asked, "so do you feel gypped that you were married off to the tribe's first female Werewolf, who ironically unlike her male associates, isn't fertile in the least?"

Grant chuckled as he kicked his older brother's leg. "I don't know how Bec puts up with that blunt tongue of yours."

"Bec quite likes that blunt tongue of mine, especially with what it can do to her body." Ian laughed and then he laughed harder when his little brother kicked him a second time.

He sighed, "I'm a little disappointed sure, as I always imagined that one day I would have kids. But I'm certainly not disappointed in B, I'm just disappointed in our circumstances." Then he paused for a moment before he went on, "do you remember when she offered dissolution to our marriage, so I could mate with someone else who could give me kids?"

"Yeah I remember."

"I put that idea out of her head quick smart." He stated. "We had our first ever fight regarding the issue."

"That was your FIRST fight?" Ian echoed in surprise. "You had been married for nearly a year when it came out that B couldn't conceive and that was your FIRST fight? That girl is the second most fiery, argumentative, stubborn woman I have encountered that comes in a close second to her fiery, argumentative, stubborn mother!"

"Yep, Jess certainly gives Hunter a run for his money alright." He laughed.

"But the guy loves every minute of it. Do you see it, when those Circulators get angry and how their aura's change colour and sparks literally fly off them?"

"Do I see it?" Grant scoffed. "It's a huge turn on! Sometimes I'll deliberately do something that I know will annoy B, because when she yells, her pheromones increase along with the sparks."

"Do you think humans can see their auras?" Ian wondered.

"You mean their auras as Circulators?" He mused. "I don't think so, not most humans anyway. I think some humans with ESP might. I think it's more appreciated by our kind."

He picked up his can of soda to take a long drink. Ian rolled out from under the truck to sit up to drink from his soda too.

"So," he winked at his little brother cheekily, "those sparks turn you on, huh?"

"Everything about that female is a turn on..." Grant grinned, "...her light, her smell, her temper, her thoughtful expression when she's reading or studying. I still feel like the luckiest bastard to be chosen to marry her."

"Really?" He asked in partial surprise. "Even with this 'no kids' issue?"

"Trust me, there's a lot of activity without the actual procreation going on." My husband chuckled smugly. "It's no wonder Derik and Declan hate me for it."

"They don't 'hate' you for it." Ian tried to find the right words. "They're just...sulking."

"Derik and B talked for the first time since we were married, when he and Susan came to Clara Riverclaw's funeral. But I still had to make myself scarce from the daggers Derik was throwing my way."

"Declan wasn't at the funeral." Ian noted.

"Last Monday when B and I were getting some groceries? He walked into the store and when he saw us together, he turned around and walked out again." Grant frowned. "That was the fifth time he's done that. I don't think his resentment is just his loyalty for his little brother losing B."

He kept quiet for a moment, but he had sensed the same thing too as the whole pack had.

"Yeah well, the guy isn't even allowed to have sex! He's just jealous that you're getting some and he isn't." He tried to joke as he rolled back under the truck to continue working. "Pass me the WD40 and the rag, would you?"

Grant passed him those next as he changed the conversation slightly, "I wasn't a virgin when I married B and neither was she. But I probably had more experience than she had, because she was so nervous on our wedding night that she was shaking."

This made him stop what he was doing, as he rolled back out to look at his little brother inquiringly, "was B mated to Derik?"

"What? No!" My husband's eyes widened in horror. "I certainly wouldn't have gone ahead with the wedding if she was! That first day she found out about our arranged marriage and I followed her up to Sunset Point? She blurted out she wasn't a virgin, thinking that she could turn me off the idea. When I smelled her, I couldn't smell Derik or anyone else on her so I knew she wasn't mated."

"Thank heavens for that! I didn't want to be known as the guy with the brother whose wife has two mates!" Ian joked, which earned another kick.

As he remembered this night of long ago, something went 'click' in his mind; "what if B had sex with Declan and not Derik before she married Grant? It would explain his ongoing resentment, even after his brother moved on and married. They eventually became friends again, but Declan still avoided B and Grant like they were the plague."

It all made sense to him now as like a game of 'Tetris,' all the pieces fell to fit in perfectly together...

"That sneaky bastard!" Ian growled furious at the idea of Declan and I together before my marriage. "He was told he couldn't have sex because of the risks involved!"

"Ah yes, sex with a human woman right?" The other side of Ian's brain debated. "But B wasn't a human woman which meant she would be able to take on his supernatural strength and she wouldn't be turned by his bite. In this regard, she was his perfect mate. But from seeing Declan cry back there, I know it wasn't just about sex either." The European Werewolf didn't want to spend the next 250 years of his existence alone, without her and he couldn't resent him because of that.

Just then he was joined by my grandfather and father who came out of the house. They found him pacing up and down the driveway, with his hands shoved deep in his pockets. He looked like he was restraining himself.

"Ian, are you OK?" Dad looked on his best friend.

"Yeah Hunter, I'll live!" He growled as he rolled his eyes.

Suddenly he kicked a rock so hard off the gravel driveway, it became imbedded in the bark of the tree it hit in the surrounding woods.

"Nice shot." Grandfather raised his eyebrows impressed.

"Look, I won't kill Declan I promise." Ian huffed. "I can understand that until B turned, he was alone because he couldn't mate with a human woman. It just gets to me, you know? When I look at B, I still see Grant beside her.”

Dad sighed unhappily, “yeah, I know. So do I, as a matter of fact.”

The three Werewolves turned quiet for a moment, as Ian continued to pace with his hands in his pockets.

“Ian.” Grandfather began. “As much as my loyalties lie with the pack; I also feel protective over my mate Arabella, our daughter Jess and my granddaughter Bianca.”

“I know, Em.” He frowned as he moodily looked away.

“When I saw B’s pain after Grant’s death and those days where she couldn’t get out of bed? I almost cut open my wrist to jam into her mouth to force my will to live on her! She worried me Ian, she really, really worried me.” Grandfather continued.

“She worried Jess and me too.” Dad agreed. “B’s light faded until it almost disappeared.”

“Two months ago, when Hunter and I went to repair the broken shingles on her roof; she looked different as her light had returned. She lied to us about fixing the roof herself and although I knew she was lying, I didn’t care. I let it go because she was well again. I didn’t know it was because she had mated again, but I felt relieved as all hell that she looked like her vibrant self.” Grandfather went on.

“We even let her lie to us about why we could smell Declan’s scent in her house.” Dad said guiltily.

When Ian looked more unhappy by this, it made Grandfather stick up for his comatose granddaughter.

“Bianca is my responsibility.” He announced, causing the men to look on in surprise. “I married Arabella and brought her here to live with me, my family and the tribe. Together we created Jessica and Julian,. I knew by mating with Arabella since she was a Circulator, it could affect our traditions. Lokoti Werewolves are of the past and Circulators are very much of the future. I knew the risks involved so if there is going to be any blame, I want you to blame me. I will also tell this to the Elder’s and the rest of the pack. Bianca is every bit a Circulator as she is a Lokoti Werewolf and thankfully as we witnessed last night, Circulator’s are ongoing.”

“Em, I’m not looking to crucify anybody over this.” Ian smirked.

“It was my decision to save Declan’s life when Arabella acknowledged the Sabre’s as kin as it was my blood that I gave him to drink.” He went on. “I also accept the responsibility over his actions as well.”

“No Em.” My father spoke up. “We can no more blame Arabella, Jess and B for being Circulators and changing history than we can blame ourselves for being Lokoti Werewolves, steeped in history. Arabella helped our tribe prepare for life after the War. Jess saved our tribe against the Invaders. We wouldn’t be alive, let alone living on our land if it wasn’t for my mate and yours. Although I’m worried about what kind of mate a European Werewolf will make for my daughter? I saw what B did for him last night.”

"OK guys." Ian rubbed his face as he sighed wearily. "Enough with the self-blame and the 'pick me' attitudes, OK?   Like I said, I'm not looking to crucify somebody over this."

Grandfather's eyes watered momentarily, "I just don't want B to think that she can't come back because of what will happen to her if she does."

"No, nor do I." Dad said worriedly.

Just then the Werewolves exchange was interrupted by the arrival of Uncle Julian, Aunt Danika and Phoebe. Their red four-wheel-drive pulled up on the driveway before them.

"How is she?" Uncle Julian asked as he hopped out first with his family a close second.

"She's in a coma?" Aunt Danika read the men's minds.

"A coma?" He looked from his wife to the men in concern.

"Arabella and Jess have brought Dr. Dystar and Vincent here, to help Derik treat her." Grandfather told them.

"Dr. Dystar?" Aunt Danika's eyes widened in recognition of the name.

"Who's Dr. Dystar?" Uncle Julian looked to his mate.

"He's the man that introduced your great grandmother Elisha Worthall to my great grandmother, Belle Dupont when SSIT investigated ESP." She advised before she looked at the three men standing on the driveway. "Take Phoebe and I to Bianca."

The Werewolves eyes widened at the telepath's determined expression, before they acquiesced to her command.

*****

They all streamed into the bedroom in which I was lying down. Uncle Julian's eyes widened in surprise to see how Declan was sitting so closely, but Aunt Danika and Phoebe didn't seem perturbed.

"That cat's out of the bag." Phoebe smirked to her mother.

"You KNEW about this?" His eyes widened at their secrecy.

"Julian, we're telepaths." Aunt Danika reminded as if he should have known better.

"We found out the night before B's Joining Ceremony to Grant." She shrugged.

"WHAT?" Ian roared. "What happened between Declan and B before she married Grant?!"

"We'll talk about it later." Aunt Danika said calmly as she and Phoebe came to stand by my bedside.

The German doctor's eyes widened as he watched the two women close their eyes and concentrate.

"No, we'll talk about this right now!" Ian became enraged, as if it were the last straw.

"Nothing happened, OK?" Declan rolled his eyes. "We had a fight. B told me she was marrying your brother and that was that!"

"So this has been going on for six years, when she was still MY girlfriend?" Derik looked on in fury.

"Was this the night she 'accidentally fell' into the river?" Dad's eyes narrowed.

Declan let out a frustrated sigh, "yeah alright, so I pushed her in."

"You pushed her into the river?" Grandfather glared warningly.

"I'll frickin' push YOU into the river!" Derik spat out.

"And I'll make sure that you don't come out!" Ian growled as his eyes glowed pink in anger.

"Yeah yeah." My lover sighed again in defeat. "You can all hang, draw and quarter me later but can we please at least make sure B wakes up first?"

Gran, who had been watching Aunt Danika and Phoebe as was Dr. Dystar, saw the two women frown in consternation. She held up her hand to silence the room, to help the mind readers concentrate. "Guys, shut up!"

"What are they doing?" Dr. Dystar asked.

"Danika and Phoebe are telepaths. They're descendants of Belle's." She told him. "They're trying to wake B up."

The whole room turned silent as they watched the two women work.

"I can't sense her!" Phoebe cried out in frustration, opening her eyes to look at her mother. "Mum, can you sense her?"

"She's not here." Aunt Danika announced.

"Not this again!" Declan rolled his eyes. "Come on girls, you're telepaths! Can't you mentally call her back?"

"If Bianca was simply asleep, we could." My Aunt said unhappily. "But I don't think this is an ordinary coma, she's long gone."

"Don't say that!" My lover's eyes watered once more. "I mean, can't you sense where she is? Can't you find her?"

"My telepathic range is a five kilometer radius and Phoebe's is two." Aunt Danika said crisply. "Where ever Bianca is, I don't think she's even on the planet anymore."

"You mean the afterlife?" Derik's eyes widened.

"Or the space time continuum." Gran said.

"I don't know where she is." Aunt Danika shrugged before she declared in her English accent, "but Elvis has left the building."

"But it can't be the space time continuum." Phoebe looked to Gran. "She has to evolve to go there."

"Not necessarily." My grandmother said grimly, before the whole room looked on her to continue. "The space time continuum is what upholds the timeline and it's the very fabric of what existence is made from."

"Ja?" Dr. Dystar listened with interest.

"Circulators can 'evolve' to become pure light to join with the energy of the space time continuum. But humans and everything else, when their energy signatures 'die' in the corporeal world, their energy signatures change to match the frequency of the space time continuum. Remember, energy doesn't cease to exist but it changes form. I've met deceased humans in the space time continuum, who go there between corporeal existences before they return to the timeline as reincarnated souls." She explained.

"Then Bianca could be there now? Not as an evolved Circulator, but her energy is in the space time continuum like a deceased human's in the afterlife?" Dr. Dystar clarified.

"The space time continuum isn't just the afterlife, but it's another plane of existence. It is existence. It's responsible for the Big Bang and the Big Crunch, the continual cycle and recycle of life. It's the undiminished light in the dark nothingness." Gran's eyes watered with emotion, which gave away her attachment. "Science calls it the space time continuum, Christians call it Heaven and the Lokoti Tribal Elders call it the Holy Hunting Grounds."

"But Arabella? If you want me to come with you to the space time continuum, maybe you won't have to turn me into a Circulator after all. Wouldn't I just end up there with you when I die?" Grandfather wondered.

"I asked you to come with me as a Circulator because this way you could stay with me forever in the continuum. We wouldn't be separated when you're later reincarnated into the timeline. Circulators can't be reincarnated, because their energy is in temporal flux." She said tearfully. "I'm selfish, I know. I don't want to lose you, Em. By coming with me, you would give up reincarnation by staying with me always."

"That's not selfish." He smiled softly. "I knew you were a Circulator from the very first moment we met. I knew my path would become your path which would become our path. Of course I'll remain as your mate in the next life, as you are my mate in this one."

The room watched the two hug tightly, when Dad turned towards Mum.

"Yes." He said.

"Yes?" She gave a funny look.

"When the time comes, I want you to turn me into a Circulator and take me with you to the space time continuum too." Dad announced.

Mum's eyes widened in shock, "you WANT me to change you? You WANT to leave your mortality behind to never be reincarnated into the timeline?"

"Yes." He said simply.

"Oh." She looked away, troubled.

"Jess?" Now he looked troubled too, "you don't want me to come with you?"

"Um, I've never thought about it to be honest. I've always been so busy, especially when my daughter turned into a Werewolf! Next, she's forced into a primitive arranged marriage when she's just eighteen? Then I have to help train her ability as a Circulator? Then finding out she can't conceive when Grandma died? Then there's the skirmishes on the border with looters and Grant dying, resulting in us looking after Bianca again? Now my daughter is shot in the head and we may not be able to bring her back?" Mum rattled off. "Trust me Hunter, the space time continuum is the last thing on my mind!"

"Well, now you know." Dad said patiently to the love of his life.

"Thanks, it's a good thing to know." Mum gave a small smile back.

Ian snickered, "Jess would probably argue all the way to eternity and back."

"Yes, but there's nobody that I'd rather argue with." My mother walked up to hug her husband.

"Elisha's light lives on." Dr. Dystar looked on Mum and Gran, before he looked at the two telepaths. "Belle's unique gift continues." Lastly, he looked on the Werewolves in the room. "It's fitting that the different supernatural elements you bring, should all combine so well. I'm sure this is what Elisha and Xavier hoped for when they worked on SSIT."

However by this stage, Declan was seriously getting fed up. His bloodlust fueled temper was teetering on the edge.

"Frickin' hell!" He cried out exasperated. "What do I have to do around here to get somebody to make B wake up?"

"Right." Gran said determinedly as she looked my way. "I could go to the space time continuum to try to bring her back."

"But Arabella," Grandfather said worriedly, "what if you get stuck there again? I want you to take me with you, incase we can't return."

"But Em," she looked on her husband, "you're only 67 years old! You've got another hundred years at least as a Lokoti Werewolf."

The German doctor's eyes widened once more when he heard how old my youthful my grandfather was, or how long his longevity could be.

"I know, Arabella," Grandfather took hold of her hand, "but I can't risk being separated from you again."

Just then Phoebe turned to look on Dr. Dystar, who was walking around in a small circle again, deep in thought.

"We could try it." She shrugged as she read the older man's mind.

He looked back in partial surprise, before he frowned contemplatively.

"Try what?" Uncle Jules looked from his daughter to the older doctor.

"It makes sense." Aunt Danika agreed, reading their minds.

"All this talk about Circulator's brain patterns and the space time continuum, has triggered something in his memory." Phoebe announced.

Dr. Dystar looked quizzically at the telepaths, as the three engaged in a silent conversation.

"I think it's a risk worth taking." Aunt Danika said seriously.

Declan sat up straighter, "what risk?"

"What's going on here?" Our Medicine Man looked at the older physician.

"There is another procedure I could try on Bianca." Dr. Dystar said reluctantly.

"Yes?" My mate prompted.

"But it is extremely risky, because I haven't put it through any medical trials yet." He warned.

"Consider this your first one." Phoebe shrugged.

"You are aware of how DYSTAR and RYPWYN work?" Dr. Dystar looked on Vincent.

My Calculator answered, "they work by targeting the electrical impulses in the brain. The RYPWYN stops Circulators, Calculators and psychics from 'seeing' through time. The DYSTAR inhibits a Circulator from going into phase by inhibiting the brain's electrical impulses, which triggers their higher bio-electromagnetic fields from changing their biological bodies into one of light."

"Last year, I created a third drug called AMBROSIA." Dr. Dystar announced. "It is the antithesis to DYSTAR and RYPWYN."

Vincent's mouth fell open in surprise, "you did what?"

"What does it do?" Gran asked.

"When I met your grandmother Elisha Worthall and she told me how she temporarily lost the ability to phase from my future invention DYSTAR? I couldn't get it out of my mind. If I could create a drug that affects the electrical impulses of the brain by stopping visions or the ability to phase; then it should be possible to create a drug which can return them." The German physician explained.

"But there's nothing recorded in time about you creating a drug called AMBROSIA." Our Calculator said perturbed.

"One of the reasons why I haven't put it under clinical trial yet, was because I didn't want the Circulate to know." Dr. Dystar glared at him. "The Circulate is behind Hodge Endeavor who is in control of my funding, which gives the organization complete access to my notes. I worked on AMBROSIA in secret, spending many a late night in my lab without any of my Hodge Endeavor paid lab assistants. I didn't put the chemical composition on my work computer, but I kept it hidden behind passwords on my personal laptop."

"You created this drug in secret?" Vincent asked suspiciously. "Why didn't you want the Circulate to know?"

The German doctor suddenly went quiet as he glared at my Calculator in distrust.

"Oh don't worry, the Circulate don't exist anymore; not as humans anyway. Elisha took them with her into the space time continuum." Aunt Danika hastily spoke after reading Dr. Dystar's mind. "Vincent is the last Calculator, as Arabella, Jessica and Bianca are the last three Circulators in human history."

Dr. Dystar looked from Aunt Danika to Vincent before he warily spoke again.

"I wanted to create a cure after what happened to Elisha when she was drugged with DYSTAR by the Circulate without her consent. Although she got her ability back as she told me that she can self regenerate? In a way she blamed me for inventing the drug in the first place, although I certainly didn't know that it would be used in such a fashion. I invented AMBROSIA so it would be on hand if she should ever need it."

"What does AMBROSIA do?" Vincent's eyes narrowed further.

"As DYSTAR decreases the electrical impulses in a Circulator's brain, AMBROSIA will increase them." Dr. Dystar informed.

"Increase them how?" Mum asked in fascination.

"In my studies of ESP with several subjects allowing me to take brain tissue samples? I found a unique chemical which I called Zemyr inside Circulators, Calculators and other humans with ESP. Zemyr causes a chemical reaction, which quadruples their electrical impulses." Dr. Dystar explained.

"But you're playing God!" Vincent objected loudly. "Arabella and Jessica! By Wil here inventing AMBROSIA? If he injected it into a normal human being, it could turn them into a psychic!"

"Can it also turn them into Calculators and Circulators?" Grandfather asked.

"Nein." The German doctor shook his head.

"No," Our Calculator began to pace as he lectured, "because Circulator's and Calculator's bio-electromagnetic fields are still higher. Our higher bio-electromagnetic fields aren't just a result of our brains, but our brains emit more Alpha Waves as we use both our conscious and subconscious as a whole. It's how we have visions awake or asleep. Calculators are able to calculate by having higher brain activity than a Circulator. A Circulator's brain controls their bio-electromagnetic fields which is even higher than a Calculator's, to put their bodies into phase. When Elisha turned the ordinary human Mike Sabre into a Circulator, she put his bio-electromagnetic frequency into temporal flux as well as hyper stimulating his brain."

"So AMBROSIA would hyper stimulate a normal human's brain, by giving them psychic abilities; but they can't calculate or circulate through time because their bio-electromagnetic frequencies are still too low?" Derik clarified.

"Correct." Vincent answered, before he glared at Dr. Dystar. "I cannot allow your plans for the AMBROSIA to go ahead."

The room turned into a stand off, with young doctor challenging old, as each folded their arms and glared at the other.

"Why not?" Mum wondered at his adamant behavior.

"Because he would be changing history you idiot!" Vincent yelled, causing Dad to growl warningly. He ignored him as he carried on, "everything happens for a reason, which is why being your Calculator I have to monitor any changes you make to the timeline to ensure that you don't create any temporal paradoxes! Elisha was meant to temporarily lose her ability! She was meant to leave Cambridge and return to Sydney! She was meant to meet Dr. Mike Sabre at the Royal Prince Alfred hospital! Mike was meant to fall in love with Elisha, to risk his life for her when she was nearly raped!"

Here the Lokoti Werewolves all growled unhappily upon hearing that word, as they were sensitive to this type of crime from another event that happened in the tribe's history.

He ignored the dangerous sound effects as he ranted, "Elisha was meant to accidentally change Mike into a Circulator when she healed him after the attack. Right now, Elisha and Mike are together with the rest of the Circulate inside of the space time continuum. If Elisha is given AMBROSIA as soon as she's drugged with DYSTAR, she may never meet Mike. He'll never be turned into a Circulator and since he's already inside the continuum? If you change the timeline now, you're not just changing history, but you could destabilize the actual space time continuum! That's a threat I cannot let you make."

The room had turned deathly silent as everyone processed Vincent's words, including Dr. Dystar. Our Calculator's words clearly affected him.

The German doctor sighed ruefully, "so if I give the AMBROSIA to Elisha, I could very well be destabilizing the entire fabric of existence?"

All eyes turned to Vincent who answered in a low voice, "yes."

As if this was a tennis match, all eyes now turned back to Dr. Dystar. The German doctor backed down, as I guess he didn't want to be responsible for the destruction of not just the timeline but the space time continuum.

"Then you have my word that I will not carry out my plan." The elderly physician promised.

Again it was Declan who called back everyone's attention. He later told me that the 'science mumbo jumbo' was lost on him, but everyone soon found out he also lost the last of his patience.

"Great, so we all get to live today and we won't all be annihilated from the end of existence? That's great news!" He said with false bravado. "But as the Englishman says, everything happens for a reason. I think this German was meant to invent AMBROSIA so he can give it to my woman, activate her whatever you call it inside her brain and she'll wake up from her coma! Yay! Excellent! Progress! BUT CAN WE JUST PUMP THE DRUG INTO B NOW PLEASE?!"

Declan's roar was so loud, the windows actually rattled. Dr. Dystar took a wary step backwards, as did Vincent. But Gran and Mum exchanged small smiles, approving of my mate's one-track-minded pursuit of my return to health.

"Where's the AMBROSIA now?" Derik asked.

The German doctor opened his coat and pulled out from an inside pocket a small medical vial. Inside was a bright white liquid that looked luminescent. It was mostly an opal-white with different colours sparkling inside of it. Everybody's eyes widened at the magical looking liquid.

"That's not the only sample you have, is it?" Vincent stared.

"It is so far," Dr. Dystar held it in his hand, "it's the first sample which I secretly produced."

Vincent's eyes widened as he eyed the vial in wonder, as everyone did.

"How does it glow like that?" Mum stared at the vial transfixed.

"How come it has different colours sparkling inside?" Dad stared too.

"It looks just like Arabella's, Jessica's and Bianca's auras." Grandfather observed.

"Hmm," all of the Werewolves in the room nodded in agreement, including Declan.

"How did you create it?" Our Calculator looked on amazed.

"I created it exactly opposite to how I created DYSTAR." The physician informed. "Both DYSTAR's and AMBROSIA's primary ingredient is the chemical called Zemyr. When I created DYSTAR I reversed the electrical charge in Zemyr from positive to negative. The negative composition in DYSTAR inhibits the Circulator's brain by decreasing their electrical activity. With AMBROSIA, I empowered the positive particles instead, so theoretically it will increase the electrons firing."

"Theoretically?" Declan raised his eyebrows. "What does that mean?"

"As I said," The German doctor looked on, "in keeping AMBROSIA secret from Hodge Endeavor and the Circulate, I have not yet put the drug under any clinical trials."

The room then watched Dr. Dystar hand Vincent the small, glowing vial and take out a sterilized packet containing a syringe from one of his medical cases.

"This in no way will hurt her or further injure B, right?" My mate's eyes narrowed as he watched the elderly physician take the lid off the syringe.

"There is a 75% chance it will not cause further harm to the patient." Dr. Dystar answered as he retook the vial of AMBROSIA back from Vincent.

"Not a 100% chance?" Declan asked unhappily.

"Bianca will be my first test subject." Dr. Dystar stated as he filled the syringe from the vial.

The European Werewolf's eyes narrowed as he watched the German doctor suck up the glowing liquid via the needle.

"Wait." Vincent licked his lips nervously. "Just explain to me how you positively charged the Zemyr?"

"I cannot explain accurately," Dr. Dystar said simply, "because Zemyr isn't supposed to exist as it is a non-carbon based substance. It isn't meant to exist inside of Calculators, Circulators or humans with ESP, as we are carbon based life forms. But the Gamma Rays accelerated the positive particles in Zemyr into the liquid you see now."

The elderly physician carefully handed the syringe to the younger physician to hold, before he opened a small packet of alcohol swabs. Next, he sat on the bed as he picked up my arm and raised the sleeve of my pajamas. Then he ran the alcohol swab over the inside of my elbow where he was going to inject the drug.

"Vincent, turn on the bedside light so I can find her vein." Dr. Dystar instructed.

My Calculator obeyed before he handed the syringe back. Then he quickly grabbed his medical scanner and turned it on. He held it over my form so he could monitor the effects of the drug.

Just as Dr. Dystar held the syringe over my skin, Declan's arm jutted out to stop him.

"Please tell me there's a 100% chance that B won't be harmed by this." He looked on fearfully.

"I cannot." Dr. Dystar stated.

"Declan, you wanted results? It's this or nothing." Vincent said seriously.

My mate gulped as he looked from the elderly physician to his brother, another Medicine Man for some kind of reassurance. "Derik?"

My best friend shrugged helplessly, "I don't know Declan, they're the ones with the experience of treating Circulators."

"Declan," Grandfather growled softly, "let them try."

My mate's blue eyes filled with tears as he looked from Grandfather down to me, whilst removing his arm from Dr. Dystar's.

"Come on baby, we've made it this far and I only just got you back." Declan whispered as he leaned in to kiss my forehead. "I won't lose you to another or by another way again."

Dr. Dystar slid the syringe into the vein in my arm and he slowly injected the glowing liquid inside...when everything happened suddenly! Just as Dr. Dystar was removing the emptied syringe, I convulsed.

"What?" Declan looked on in alarm.

I convulsed again and again like I was having a seizure, as my skin turned bright and several ripples of light emanated outwards!

"What's happening to her?!" He cried out worriedly.

I kept convulsing as the ripples of light turned brighter and brighter...

"She's evolving!" Gran cried out in alarm.

"WHAT THE HELL HAVE YOU DONE TO HER?!?" The European Werewolf roared as his eyes glowed green in anger.

When my mate reached across to throttle the German doctor, in lightening fast speed my brother-in-law and father pushed him up against the wall to restrain him!

"The electrical impulses in her brain have turned hyperactive!" Vincent barked as he read off the scanner. "Bianca's having a seizure, it was too high a dose!"

Dr. Dystar quickly stood up to look down at the readings on the scanner Vincent was holding.

"If this keeps up, she'll have a stroke and go into cardiac arrest...!" The German doctor paled. "I'll prepare some DYSTAR to give to her."

"DON'T YOU FRICKIN' TOUCH HER!" Declan snarled menacingly.

Dad and Ian slammed the almost morphing male back against the wall, using all of their strength to hold him still. Grandfather and Uncle Julian had to come forwards to help keep a hold on the stronger European Werewolf. But my mate wasn't just stronger than the Lokoti Werewolves, he was faster than them too.

Declan knocked the four Lokoti Werewolves backwards onto the floor! Before they could get up again, he leapt across the bed in a single bound. He also knocked over Vincent and Dr. Dystar, by almost landing right on top of them! Growling loudly, he snatched up Gran's sewing scissors that were sitting on the bedside table as he looked down on the German doctor menacingly...

"DECLAN NO!" Grandfather leapt to his feet, along with Dad, Ian and Uncle Julian.

The four scrambled on my mate's position as he raised the sewing scissors precariously over the German doctor. But when he brought the scissors down, he stabbed himself in his wrist! He grunted in pain as he left a jagged, deep gash in his skin.

"Wait!" Gran cried out, as she and Mum rushed forwards in light speed to stop the Lokoti Werewolves from taking Declan out.

Before anyone could stop him, he shoved his bleeding arm into my mouth. Declan crouched by my side whilst he bled into me...

... when my hands flew up and grabbed onto his arm! My glowing turquoise eyes snapped opened as I began to drink. Immediately I stopped convulsing, and even the ripples of light started to fade.

I clung onto my mate's arm as I drank down his regenerative blood. I could feel my Lokoti Werewolf strength return as my own regenerative ability took control of my rising bio-electromagnetic frequency, which started to lower again. The more I drank, the more I felt myself slowly return to normal.

"Hey B." Declan smiled in relief and I caught his glowing green eyes look a little teary.

"Bianca?" My best friend came closer to look on in concern.

"So, do you still want to throw me into the river?" My mate glanced over his shoulder at his little brother.

Derik tried not to smile, "nah I'll keep you around just a little bit longer."

*****

~ 21 ~

Everyone in the room visibly let out a sigh of relief, or a laugh. My Calculator stood up from the floor first and helped the older physician to his feet, before he looked on my mate sharing his blood.

"Good save, Declan." Vincent said flatly. "Not bad for one as untrained in Circulator lore as a European Werewolf."

"Yeah well, you SUCK as a frickin' Calculator if you didn't see all of THAT happening." He returned.

"Whinge whinge whinge." Vincent picked up his scanner from the floor and proceeded to pack it into his medical kit.

Dr. Dystar watched with interest as I drank down Declan's blood whilst holding onto his arm. My turquoise eyes glowed brighter by the second, as my supernatural strength returned.

"Fascinating." The German doctor shook his head in bewilderment, before he turned to Gran. "Arabella, may I read the SSIT notes made on Werewolves?"

"Sure." She shrugged. "There are several though, as the different reports were made on the several different breeds of Werewolf."

"Did Elisha and Xavier meet all of these breeds?" He marveled.

"Well," she frowned, "I think my grandmother may have met several by herself and then showed Xavier her findings. Lokoti Werewolves are the only species in the world that no longer feeds on human. Several times Elisha did her own investigating without Xavier as she didn't want to put him at risk."

Dr. Dystar looked on Grandfather in admiration, "I greatly respect the traditions of your people. When I first began to investigate ESP, I found many cases of psychics in the U.S. were often Native Americans. I would appreciate finding out more about your species, such as when in your history did you change your diet from human to animal?"

His eyes widened as he laughed awkwardly, "er it's a long story doctor."

"Come along, Wil." Gran took Dr. Dystar's arm to lead him out of the room. "Before you go chasing Werewolves, maybe you'd like to read the SSIT case files?"

"Ja." The elderly physician willingly agreed. As the two disappeared downstairs, we heard him ask, "I noticed that Declan Sabre's eyes looked different from your husband, son-in-law and his friend. Do the different species all have unique physical characteristics as well as dietary requirements?"

Mum snickered as she walked over to hug Dad, to which he tenderly held her back whilst they looked upon my revival in relief.

"Er, Declan?" Ian spoke up. "She's been drinking for a little while now, are you alright?"

"I'm OK." My mate said shortly as he held his arm steady.

"Declan, you're skin is starting to turn a little white." Derik said in concern. "Maybe you should stop and build up your strength again."

It occurred to me that maybe I was being a little too greedy and that my bloodlust was what made me so thirsty, not my injuries? I released his arm as I fell back into the pillow panting hard whilst I tried to take control over my dangerous craving.

"If she needs more blood...?" Grandfather came forward as he rolled up his sleeve.

"NO!" I growled as I closed my eyes to concentrate.

"B, you were shot in the head last night." Grandfather frowned. "You're probably still healing."

Huh, what was that? I sat up to look on in surprise. "I was?"

Everyone in the room now gave a peculiar look at my question.

"You don't remember?" Declan frowned, before he put his wrist in his mouth to use his saliva to speed up his healing.

I stared up at the ceiling, trying to recall everything that had happened in the last day or so.

"What do you remember, B?" Derik asked as the medical professional.

"I don't know..." I closed my eyes as I pieced together the disjointed images, "I was in bedroom after my evening shower... I felt the word *STRANGERS* and I realized Declan was in danger... I instantaneously phased out of the house... I was getting wet in the woods in the rain... I saw the stranger from my dream aim his shotgun at Declan...and then that's it, that's all that I remember."

"You jumped in front of the bullet meant for him, you got shot in the head and you landed face first in the mud, dead." Dad finished with a frown.

"Is that what happened?" I asked taken aback. "I really was shot?"

"What, you didn't mean to save my life?" My lover raised his eyebrows.

"Oh no, I meant to do that..." I shook my head confused, "...but I don't remember getting shot."

"Because you died." Ian said flatly.

"I did?" I echoed. "I really did?"

"You were dead as a door nail." Uncle Julian confirmed.

"Really?" I looked on everybody's faces in disbelief.

"Really." Dad returned flatly.

"What, have you turned deaf as well as dead?!" Declan retorted. "You frickin' carked it, OK?!"

"Yes!" I let out a small cheer to everyone's surprise. "It means I didn't imagine the whole thing then."

Phoebe saw what I was thinking as she sat on the end of the bed. She asked interested, "what did you see?"

"What did I see?" I looked back in a daze.

"Yeah, you saw something, didn't you? Like an OBE." She nodded.

"An OBE?" Declan gave a funny look.

"Outer Body Experience." Vincent translated.

"What did you see, B?" Phoebe pressed. "Were you in the space time continuum?"

"I don't know." I stared down at the quilt.

"Where did you go, B?" Grandfather asked gently.

The room turned quiet as it became apparent that everybody was waiting for my answer.

"I went to the Fox's Ball." I proclaimed.

"You went to a Ball?" Derik's eyebrows rose.

"Yeah, I went to the Fox's Ball."

"Who are the Fox's?" Dad looked around for an answer.

"Lady Caroline Lennox whom was Charles the Second's great granddaughter, married a politician called Henry Fox. Their son Charles James Fox became the Prime Minister of England during King George the Third's reign." Vincent educated. "Elisha went to the Fox's Ball for her first excursion through time in 1755 AD."

"I was wearing a long, sea-green silk dress and I even drank wine." I nodded.

"You drank wine at the Ball?" Declan looked on like I was delirious or something. "You know we can't drink alcohol."

"But I wasn't a Werewolf in the space time continuum, so I didn't have to worry about the bloodlust." I shrugged before my eyes widened which I turned his way. "You're Greyson!"

"I'm who?" He raised his eyebrows.

"When Elisha first met you in 1755 at the Fox's Ball, your name was Greyson." I spoke quickly. "Except in that life you had brown hair and brown eyes. You tried to hit on Elisha because you thought she was a wealthy heiress? But then you stepped aside when you saw your best friend Guy Robertson fall for her. You helped Elisha save Guy's life in India, after the Battle of Plassey!"

"Declan is Captain Greyson, the youngest son of Earl Greyson who then became the next Earl upon the death of his father and older brother?" Vincent scoffed. "Declan is English Aristocracy? Hardly!"

"I'm Aristocratic, cool." My mate sat upright impressed before he asked, "so does that mean I'm rich?"

"Not quite." My Calculator smirked. "Your family sold the family estate at the beginning of the 20th Century to cover the then Earl Greyson's gambling debts."

"Oh." His face fell.

"It was also to pay off the three different women who had the Earl's illegitimate children, which were named in his scandalous public divorce." Vincent said smugly as he crossed his arms.

"Bummer." Declan said before he gave me a wink. "It's a good thing that you can't have kids, as I don't seem to have much luck with 'em."

"One could even argue that your designs on Bianca could be you trying to get your dirty claws on Blythe Castle and the Worthall fortune." Vincent teased.

"Am I that transparent?" My mate joked along, before he looked my way in absolute adoration.

When the tribe's most dangerous Werewolf reached out to gently caress my cheek; it took me by surprise his public display of affection, as it made the other people in the room ill-at-ease.

"I'll be downstairs." Ian quickly left the room.

"Me too." Derik also decided to depart.

Grandfather, Dad and Uncle Julian exchanged worried looks before they too decided to head downstairs.

"It's good to see you better, B." Grandfather left a parting kiss on the forehead.

"Get some rest, I'll be right back." Dad affectionately tweaked my nose, also on his way out.

However when Dad pulled away, I caught the glare he flashed Declan's way before he left the room. But so did Mum and she whacked Dad on the arm on their way out. Declan let out a sigh of resignation, as if he wasn't surprised.

Uncle Julian simply winked my way on his departure, before throwing a parting look towards his mate. Aunt Danika caught this before she exchanged a knowing look with her daughter. The telepathic family was well practiced in silently communicating with the other.

"OK." Phoebe shrugged as she acquiesced to her parent's command. "Good to see you're no longer a vegetable, B." She kissed my cheek before she jumped up from the bed.

"Actually, I could do with a cup of tea." Vincent used as his excuse as he too left the room.

Suddenly, Declan and I found ourselves alone which was in direct contrast to how exposed we felt.

"That was fast." I raised my eyebrows in surprise.

"As Phoebe so succinctly put it, 'that cat's out of the bag'." Declan gave a rueful smile. "I think your 'Superwoman' impersonation of flying in the air to cop a bullet in your brain to spare me, also gave us away."

He caressed my cheek again as he sat there looking on with a soft smile on his face...but his smile was quick to disappear.

"And if you ever do anything so stupid again such as getting yourself killed, I will hunt you down in the afterlife and maul you!" He growled with his blue eyes momentarily glowing green again.

"I didn't do it on purpose!" I exclaimed. "It was an accident!"

"Obviously!" He rebuked. "Do you know how selfish that was, getting yourself killed and nearly leaving me alone for the next 250 years?!"

"Oh, I'm sorry!" I said sarcastically. "Is it nearly as selfish as you almost dying instead of me?!"

"Hey, I would rather die any day than spend the next 250 years alone and without sex!"

"Oh yeah and what about me? I'll be known as the chick with the two dead mates! I'll be known as a walking Bermuda Triangle! I'll be seen as a Black Widow by killing any Werewolf who mates with me!"

"Ain't that the truth!" Declan shouted. "So help me, if you even scrape your toe or break a fingernail, I will give you what for!"

"Don't even think about carrying on like my mate, because you're not!"

"Hell yeah, I am!"

"The hell you're not! You're not my mate, you're just some guy I'm shagging!"

"Like you're just some girl I pay for sex by repairing her house!"

Then I don't know who grabbed who first? But our lips slammed against each other's as our hands almost turned claw-like as we clung to the front of the other's clothes.

*****

Downstairs, everyone had reconvened around the dining table. Gran and Grandfather were making tea and coffee for everyone in the kitchen. However everyone momentarily quietened when they noticed our shouting upstairs.

When they heard the last sentence that Declan angrily yelled out, Derik's face flushed with embarrassment as Ian growled unhappily under his breath.

"Is my equipment safe that's still upstairs?" Dr. Dystar smirked.

My forther brother-in-law wearily shook his head as he turned and headed towards the front door.

"Ian?" Dad watched him go.

As he opened the door, he looked back on the Lokoti Werewolves. "I officially acknowledge them as mates and may heaven help us." Then as he closed the front door behind, they caught him mutter, "that girl's even worse than her mother!"

Grandfather, Uncle Julian and Dad all exchanged surprised glances.

"What, that's it?" My uncle joked. "I was expecting a flogging or something like it."

"Oh, I think Declan's going to get that from B for the rest of his life." Dad snuck a cheeky look to Mum.

"Our daughter's temper is my fault, is it?" She asked indignantly as she put her hands on her hips.

"Technically since B's a Werewolf and you're a Circulator, we can blame her homicidal tendencies on her father." Our Calculator sided with her.

"Thanks Vincent for all your help, just make sure the door doesn't hit you on the way out." Dad said grumpily as he went to sit on one of the couches in the lounge area.

*****

The Englishman ended up putting Dad's words into effect; he was tired and he needed to distance himself from Dr. Dystar's onslaught of questions. So he took his cup of tea to drink on the veranda whilst looking up at the stars.

The German Neurologist was putting Dad, Grandfather and Uncle Jules through a round of 'Twenty Questions' by asking them about the differences of the Lokoti Werewolves to the other breeds. However Vincent had enough of Werewolves. He never approved of the way the pack handled my change. He resented their way of coping was to marry me off to another member. This was the real reason why he didn't go to my Joining Ceremony instead of the other that I suspected; that he foresaw something in Grant's and my future.

"There's so much B can do, as a Werewolf and a Circulator. She's strong as she's fast and she's curious about the world. But what do the male Werewolves do? They mate her off! Bloody brilliant planning, that is." He thought sarcastically. "Grant's death should have let B off a leash and enable to do more traveling through time. But now THAT European Werewolf has got its claws into her and I know what THEY'RE like from the SSIT Report. European Werewolves are bigger monsters than Lokoti Werewolves. She's bloody tied to the kitchen sink yet again, thanks to Declan's Neanderthal tendencies."

"They're not as bad as you think." A female voice spoke chirpily from behind.

Startled, Vincent turned to see Phoebe standing in the doorway as she telepathically eavesdropped.

"Can't you get into trouble for doing that?" He asked defensively.

"Don't try to change the subject. You're busted, so we might as well talk about it." She laughed as she came to sit beside.

Vincent politely moved over to give her room, but he was surprised again when Phoebe acted like she didn't want more room. Instead, she closely sat beside to share his body heat as she nursed her cup of tea in her hands.

"Would you like my coat?" He started to take it off.

"No." She answered. He raised his eyebrows in surprise at her advances, but he kept quiet as he pulled his jacket back on. She smirked, "you don't have to do that. I hear your words whether you physically say them or not."

"I wish you wouldn't do that."

"No you don't, you like it." She giggled. "Mum told me when you lived with her at Blythe, you were put her through ESP tests. She said you thought she was the best thing since sliced bread being a telepath, until you met Jess who was a Circulator."

"Yes, about that." Vincent cleared his throat. "Your mother and yourself have an amazing ability being telepaths. Arabella, Jess and B have an extraordinary ability being Circulators. They could go anywhere in time and space, but what do they do? They let these Werewolves get their claws into them."

"We're not prisoners." Phoebe said patiently. "Lokoti Werewolves are just overprotective of their mates and young."

"So I hear." Vincent rolled his eyes.

"I'm going to Cambridge next year." She announced.

"Really?" His eyes widened in surprise. "I thought your father and the other Werewolves wouldn't allow it."

"My father loves me so of course he's concerned for my safety. Before he agreed, he found out about campus security. Plus the Worthall's promised to keep any eye on me, so I'll be staying with them at Blythe often. Gran has also agreed to use her ability as a Circulator to take me home to Alaska at least four times a year. So her ability as a Circulator is not going to waste, Vincent." She gave a playful nudge. "But Dad knows I enjoy architecture and because he loves me, he wants to help me reach my goal."

"Wonderful," He said sarcastically, "the female telepath is allowed to go to University but the female Werewolf wasn't?"

"B is a Lokoti Werewolf and numerous instances have shown that they wane when they're away from their hunting grounds. Nobody stopped her from completing her BA, instead they helped her achieve it by other means. She's starting her Masters next." She spoke casually.

"That's a small concession, Phoebe." He debated. "B has to study at home because she's not permitted to go to class, like you are. She was married off to Grant and now Declan's got his claws into her. Isn't she allowed to be independent and NOT be mated off to a Werewolf?"

"Obviously you weren't paying attention, or you didn't calculate properly." Phoebe teased. "Declan and B were together before B and Grant were."

"Pardon?" He blinked at her frankness.

"Yep," She verified, "but because Declan is a European Werewolf, they had to keep it secret because they were worried it wouldn't be allowed."

"Well it shouldn't be allowed!" He raised his voice. "Have you read the SSIT Report on European Werewolves, Phoebe? They're monsters!"

"Exactly." She smiled patiently. "That's what they were worried about; unfair prejudice by lumping one good apple among a barrel full of bad ones."

"Phoebe!" He argued. "You saw what happened upstairs! We all thought Declan was going to KILL Dr. Dystar! He has a supernatural temper and he's genetically designed thanks to his Werewolf DNA, to harm others!"

"I saw a Werewolf fight for his mate." She said simply. "I saw a Werewolf save his mate when a human doctor and a Calculator almost failed."

That shut Vincent up on the subject.

He grumbled whilst looking out into the night, "bloody hell, we're back to Calculators supposedly knowing the winning lottery numbers again."

"Vincent," She began, "did you avoid B's Joining Ceremony because you knew what was going to happen to Grant? I asked Mum after Grant died and she said she didn't know."

He looked back in astonishment, "I'm surprised that you're even asking that question."

Phoebe paused as she read his mind and saw that the answer was a firm 'no'.

"Mum and I can only read your mind, if you're within a couple of kilometers from us." She smiled again. "We don't know what you're thinking when you're all the way on Mars, in a different era."

"Maybe with further training, one day you could?" He shrugged.

"Where is Mars?" Phoebe looked up into the night sky.

"There." Vincent leaned in to point upwards, so he could align his hand with her sight.

"Oh, there it is." She gazed. "I've only been there twice with Gran. But you do spend a lot of time there alone, Vincent."

He lowered his arm as he pulled away, but to his surprise she followed him by leaning against his side.

"When I'm not on Mars, I'm at Blythe Castle. When I'm not at Blythe, I'm sitting in a board room at the Hodge Endeavor Head Office in London. When I'm on Earth, I'm surrounded by people and their constant chatter. I like the quiet of Circulate Headquarters." He said softly as her ear was a lot closer now.

"That's because you're the only person there."

"Not when Arabella, Jess and B train there, or pester me with questions about the timeline."

"But they don't go there more than once a week." She pointed out.

"Sometimes it's even twice a week." He joked.

"But you prefer to live alone, in a deserted place like the Headquarters?"

"It doesn't feel 'deserted', Phoebe." He argued. "It's clean and quiet as there are no people around, so there's no fighting. The technology is futuristic and it's RELIABLE, which is more than you can say about human beings at the moment. The country side of Mars is healthy and unpolluted, with no fall out. I don't see myself as alone, being one Calculator to three Circulators. I enjoy the peace when I have the Headquarters to myself."

She listened with interest before she smiled, "so you think that I'm making an unfair assessment about your lifestyle or an incorrect judgment about why you choose to live there?"

"Precisely." He smiled back.

"Just like you're making an unfair assessment about the lifestyle of Arabella, Jess and B, being the mates of Werewolves?" She grinned. "Or perhaps an incorrect judgment about Declan, because he's a European Werewolf?"

His face turned into a mask of bewilderment at her cunning and charm. Phoebe had just completely blind-sided him with her point. Vincent was so used to making calculations of the future that he wasn't used to being surprised.

"Thanks for the chat, Vincent." She now stood up. "Excuse me as I go to help with dinner, which I hope you'll stay for."

Next, Phoebe picked up his empty tea cup to take inside with her. All he could do was sit there gob smacked, as she gave him a wink and then she went inside via the front door.

Vincent laughed quietly to himself as he looked back up into the night sky, "when did she suddenly grow up?"

*****

That evening I spent the night in the spare bedroom at Gran and Grandfather's. Although I was healed thanks to Dr. Dystar's secret formula and Declan's blood; when I tried to go home I was stopped before I even left the bed.

"Where do you think you're going?" My mate growled.

"Home." I said simply.

"I don't think so!" He returned the covers over my form. "Last night you were shot in the head with a silver bullet, so you're not just going to go home!"

However I felt awkward, with Declan sitting beside on the bed when my family were just downstairs.

"Here we go, B." Mum walked into the room carrying a cold meat and salad sandwich, with a glass of milk. "Declan, would you like something?"

"Yes please Aunt Jess." He was quick to agree as he eyed off my food.

"You must be starving, you poor thing as you haven't eaten all day." Mum said sympathetically.

She went back downstairs to procure him a sandwich too. When she returned ten minutes later with Declan's dinner, she sat at the end of my bed to eat hers with us. After another minute, Gran came and joined us with a sandwich for herself. But I wondered where everyone else was?

"So, what's the vibe downstairs?" I asked the two.

"They're talking." Mum shrugged.

"Your father and grandfather are being very patient in answering Dr. Dystar's questions. Your uncle thinks he's hilarious, like he's a 'David Attenborough' of the supernatural." Gran giggled. "After I've eaten, I'll take him back to the Germany of his era."

"No." I swallowed hard. "I mean, what's the reaction to...?" But I couldn't say it so I nodded towards Declan instead.

"Real smooth, B." He rolled his eyes.

"Oh." Mum looked at Gran as she wondered what to say? "Um well, Ian has given his permission."

"He has?" I stared in surprise. "So soon?"

"Whadya mean, so soon?! We've been sneaking around for months!" Declan gave a funny look. "I haven't had a proper night's sleep in that long!"

"It's been longer than that apparently..." she smirked, "...if the two of you were secretly seeing each other before B's marriage."

Gran lowered her plate so she could give Declan and I an incredulous look, "why didn't the two of you say something? We certainly wouldn't have arranged B's marriage to Grant if we knew -"

"Oh, you wouldn't have?" He gave them a pointed glare. "It didn't stop you from bypassing Derik's feelings and Derik isn't the most hated breed of Werewolf!"

Mum and Gran instantly looked guilty, before they exchanged sad expressions.

"I went along with the marriage to another Werewolf idea, because I was told it was the best thing to do for B." Mum explained. "But what we're saying Declan, is that if we knew that you and B had feelings for each other? Then we wouldn't have pushed her onto yet another Werewolf in the shape of Grant."

My mate stood up from the bed with his plate of sandwiches to eat while he glared out the window.

"What's done is done," we heard him mutter, "it's not honorable snaking your brother's girl. Grant had to break B and Derik up."

I looked Mum's way again, "what's the consensus of the pack? Am I going to get a bitch-slap? Is Declan going to be run out of the tribe? What's going on?"

"I don't think so, since Ian was talked around." Gran shook her head.

Mum snickered, "I don't think you'll be kicked out of the tribe or pack."

"Then why are Dad and Grandfather downstairs, avoiding us?" I asked anxiously.

"Because they're answering Dr. Dystar's questions." She shrugged.

Just then another family member appeared in the doorway in the shape of my best friend.

"Derik!" I smiled in relief. "I thought you had left."

Declan turned to look at his younger brother, but he made it obvious that he was ignoring him.

"I'm going to take off now." Derik announced. "Thanks for the sandwiches Aunt Arabella, but I'll check on B's vital signs and then head off home to Rachel and the baby."

I put aside my plate and sat still for him to do this. He checked my eyes, listened to my heart, checked my blood pressure and he even took my temperature.

"Wow, it's like you're completely healed." He said impressed as he stepped back from the bed. "Nobody would know that 24 hours ago, you died by a bullet to the head."

"So I can go home then?" I started to pull back the covers.

"Woah woah woah!" Declan came forward. "Not so fast!"

"You're sleeping here tonight, B." Gran advised.

"Just to make sure nothing else goes wrong." Mum said in concern.

"I've never healed a person who's been shot in the head before." She frowned. "If this was a hospital, we'd keep you in for observation."

"Head injuries are the riskiest to treat." Derik nodded in agreement.

Then we watched him pack up his medical equipment into his 'medicine bundle' as he prepared to leave. Next, we saw Dad and Grandfather come to stand in the doorway.

"All good?" Grandfather asked my physician.

"Too good." He joked.

"Thanks Derik." Grandfather shook his hand and then so did Dad. "Now go home and rest with Rachel and the baby."

"With a toddler, I don't know how much rest I'm going to get." He chuckled.

"True, I still remember all the trouble you and B got into at that age." Dad smiled on him. "You two were always crawling under furniture."

Declan looked away uncomfortably and I sensed he felt left out.

"See ya, B." He threw a wave but he still didn't look his brother's way.

"Bye Derik and thanks again." I called after.

"B will be sleeping here tonight so we can keep an eye on her recovery." Gran told her mate.

"Good idea." Grandfather nodded in agreement before he looked at the European Werewolf. "You're welcome to stay with her, Declan."

Dad didn't look thrilled by this as his face hardened and he pursed his lips together. However, he went along with Grandfather because he was his father-in-law let alone Second in the pack.

Declan looked on in appreciation. He and Grandfather have always been the closest, with all the time he spent training him. He regarded our elder with deep love and respect.

"Thanks Uncle Em." My mate said gratefully.

Grandfather gave him a nod back, before he left the room with Dad right behind. My father made a point to throw another glare Declan's way before he disappeared. I was starting to feel sorry for him, as this was almost as bad as the ramifications we used to fear.

"Well, I have to return a German Neurosurgeon to his era." Gran stood up, before collecting everybody's plates.

"I'll give you a hand, as there's a lot of equipment." Mum looked about at all the medical cases. "Then I'll take Vincent back to Circulate HQ."

Declan and I were left alone again as everybody went about their tasks. I gave him a brave smile and held out my hand to him. My mate was quick to come over to take and kiss it. Next, he lay on the bed beside, on top of the covers as I lay underneath.

"I'm exhausted!" He proclaimed as he snuggled down whilst closing his eyes.

"Really?"

"Well I haven't slept for days. I saved my girl's life by letting her nearly drain me dry..." he opened his eyes momentarily to give a wink, "...and I just ate for the first time in 48 hours."

I asked anxiously, "but seriously Declan, what was it like when everybody found out?"

Instead he yawned back, "c'mon B, let's crash."

That was his way of saying, 'I don't want to talk about it.' I sighed in defeat as I stared up at the ceiling because I was too worried to sleep properly.

*****

The next morning was an unusual experience breakfasting at Gran and Grandfather's table, with Mum and Dad present as well as my lover. Dad and Declan were the quietest, occasionally shooting a glare the other's way. Mum kicked Dad's leg under the table to make him behave, before Grandfather sparked up a conversation.

"Declan can borrow my vehicle to drive B home this morning." He offered.

"Why?" I shrugged. "It's a nice morning, I'll just walk home."

"In your pajamas?" Declan arched his eyebrows.

"Then I'll instantaneously phase home." I thought up next.

"No B." Gran frowned as she finished off her pancakes with maple syrup. "You shouldn't use your ability for at least a week, to make sure you don't almost evolve again."

"Your bio-electromagnetic field is really high at the moment." Mum warned.

"Could B have really evolved last night?" Dad asked Gran. "If a Circulator doesn't evolve when their body's electrical field escalates, how can they have a stroke and a heart attack?"

"Our bio-electromagnetic frequencies become so high, that it affects the electrical impulses in our brain and along our central nerve system. With the brain it can cause a stroke and with the central nerve system? Your heart is an important part of that system." She explained as she stood up to collect everyone's dirty dishes.

Grandfather quickly stood up to help, before the two carried them into the kitchen to start the washing up.

"Oh yeah." Mum agreed. "That makes sense, I mean in the movie 'The Matrix' it compared the human body to a battery, so just imagine if we overcharged a battery? We were only starting learning about these kinda things in High School, which stopped because of the War. Otherwise we'd know."

"I know them." Dad shrugged.

"How do you know?" She asked skeptically. "You didn't finish High School either because of the War."

"I know how the body works." He said simply.

"How?"

"Because we're Werewolves." Grandfather said from the kitchen.

"So?" Mum queried.

"We know because it affects our food supply, in humans or animals. We can smell it, hear it and see it, in our food." My mate spoke plainly. "We can tell if our prey is sick or not by our senses. It affects our longevity, if we eat bad meat."

"Oh." She looked taken aback.

"Thanks Declan." Dad said annoyed, as now he left the table to carry the remaining cups into the kitchen. Then he volunteered, "I'll wash up. Arabella, you and Jess cooked up a great breakfast this morning. Let me at least wash up to say thanks."

"It's alright Hunter, I've started now." She replied.

"I'll wash up faster than you." Dad taunted.

"You're challenging a Circulator on speed?" She giggled.

Just then Gran squealed in further laughter when he gently picked her up and carried her out of the kitchen before taking her place at the sink.

"Arabella, how many years have we been married?" Grandfather asked humorously. "You should know by now how stubborn a Lokoti Werewolf can be."

"Tell me about it." Declan snuck a small smile in my direction.

*****

When it was time to leave, I was bundled up in a spare pair of slippers and robe from Gran's wardrobe over one of her nightgowns I was already wearing. Then Declan carried me out of the house and over to Grandfather's pick up truck which was waiting on the driveway. My parents as well as my grandparents watched us depart from the front veranda.

"I can walk you know." I snickered.

"Shut up." Declan smirked.

Grandfather came over to open the door on the passenger's side as Declan carefully placed me on the seat.

"I'll drop off the vehicle in half an hour." He promised when Grandfather handed him the keys.

"There's no rush." He gave him a pat on the shoulder.

Grandfather carefully shut my door as I was buckling myself in. I wound down the window so I could say goodbye to him and everyone else who stood watching. I thought it was a little strange, how everyone came out to see Declan drive me home. It was almost like a 'handing over' was going on.

"Take care of yourself, kiddo." Dad waved first.

Mum also waved as she leaned into his side and he was quick to put his arm about her, as always.

"We'll come by and check up on you tonight." She called out.

"OK." I waved back.

"Get some sleep and take things easy, OK?" Grandfather reached through the open window to smooth my hair back.

"I will." I promised.

Gran seemed extra thoughtful, as she regarded Declan and I together. When Grandfather went to stand beside her, he too pulled her close. Together they watched my mate climb into the driver's seat and shut the door.

"Are you buckled in?" Declan double checked as he started up the truck.

"Yeah, like we're really going to have a car accident during the whole two minutes we're driving." I gave a funny look.

"Shut up." He rolled his eyes before he turned his head to reverse out of the driveway.

My parents and grandparents all watched the truck disappear up the road. The last thing I saw was Grandfather leading Gran back inside the house, as Dad escorted Mum to their truck to leave too. I guess I was paying extra attention to the way my family were behaving this morning, as I was trying to gage their reaction to my new relationship.

When Declan pulled up in my driveway, he ensured my door was right in front of the veranda steps. Once the motor had turned off, I started to unbuckle myself and open the passenger door when he stopped me again.

"Don't even think about it!" He barked out.

"What?" I looked on like he was mad.

"Stay right where you are."

He jumped out and accidentally slammed the door with his supernatural strength, before he hurried around to come and open my door for me. Then he gathered me up into his arms and proceeded to carry me up the steps and across the threshold.

"This is getting ridiculous!" I started to blush. "I'm not an invalid!"

"Shut up." He said flatly as he back-kicked my front door shut.

Declan even carried me up the staircase and into my bedroom.

"This is getting beyond a joke." My feet jiggled in annoyance.

"You're telling me! Chicks are supposed to dig the guy acting all chivalrous and crap. But you've bitched and moaned the whole way here." He grouched.

Then he carried me over to my bed and where upon he dropped me!

"Hey!" I complained. "That's not romantic!"

"Shut up." He chuckled as he proceeded to take off my slippers and robe before he pulled the covers down.

As he tucked me in, I looked on him closely. "Declan, are you feeling alright?"

"Shut up."

Then he left my bedroom as I heard him go into the bathroom and turn on the tap for a moment. When he returned to my room, he was carrying a glass of water.

"What's that for?" I looked at it.

"To grow Sea Monkeys, what do you frickin' think? For you to drink when you get thirsty!"

"Then I'll get out of bed to get myself a drink, thank you very much!"

"You're not leaving this bed until your parents come over, later on tonight." Declan waved his finger warningly.

Hang on a minute, it sounded like he wasn't sticking around?

"Where are you gonna be?" I frowned.

"I gotta go home." He said unhappily. "I gotta talk to my Mom and tell her about us, if she hasn't heard already from Derik or somebody else."

"Oh." My face fell.

"Yeah, oh." He said sarcastically.

"Well um, will I see you later on tonight?"

"Er," he frowned, "I'm not sure B."

"Oh." I faltered. He's not chickening out, is he?

"Wow." Declan started to smile. "You actually look disappointed by this."

"No I'm not!" I quickly tried to cover it up.

"B," He sat on the side of my bed whilst grinning like an idiot, "you've got the worst poker face, you know that?"

"Go away Declan." I gave him a shove.

"Heh heh!" He gloated. "You're not gonna wane with me away, are you?"

"Get lost!" I shoved him again.

"I've got my very own Lokoti Werewolf as a mate, so does this mean you can empathically sense what I'm feeling?" He pulled me close.

"No way!" I tried to lie.

He laughingly gave a sloppy kiss and then he jumped away before I could whack him!

"I'll see you soon, 'wild thing'." He gave a wink and then he disappeared.

As I lay down in the bed, I listened to the front door shut with his departure and then Grandfather's truck start up.

I DID miss his presence, how sad was that? I rolled my eyes at my pathetic behavior as I also rolled onto my side to allow myself to fall asleep. I tried not to worry what Aunt Susan's reaction would be, to our relationship. I tried not to fret if she would order her grown son not to see the tribe's 'tramp' of a female Lokoti Werewolf who has taken a second mate.

I slept solidly through the day, right up until the evening when Mum and Dad came over with a casserole for dinner. They stayed for two hours, fussing about until they saw my eyes start to droop. Then they put me back to bed, just like they used to when I was a little girl. The only thing that was missing was the bedtime story.

Surprisingly, Dad didn't say a thing about my relationship with Declan. He tried very hard to talk about anything else but the topic which was obviously on his mind. He was quieter than usual though, which gave away his dissatisfaction whereas Mum was her usual loud self, as she bossed us about.

The last thing I heard as I fell back asleep was Dad's truck reversing out of the driveway. It was like my body still needed to recuperate after my recent brush with death. I slept so soundly into the next morning, that I didn't hear another two pick up trucks pull into my driveway and their engines turn off.

I was sleeping so peacefully, that I didn't hear their voices as they climbed out. I was in such a deep sleep, that I didn't hear my backdoor open as somebody came in, walk through the house to unlock my front door. I was so imbedded in dreamland that I didn't hear the two people talking downstairs or the sound of things being carried inside.

I didn't wake up until the noise of something heavy being dropped on the floor of my bedroom startled me! I jumped, as my eyes flew open and I saw Declan standing beside a large cardboard box.

"G'mornin' B." He chuckled, showing that he had deliberately dropped it to wake me. I raised my head as I looked from Declan to the box, wondering what was going on? He chuckled, "I sure do love that bed-hair thing you've got goin' in the morning. I guess that's just one of the many delights that I'm going to have to get used to."

Declan continued to chuckle as he walked out of the bedroom. Huh, what's he going on about? I watched him go before I stared at the cardboard box that looked like there were clothes poking out from the top of it... Clothes? I sat up, just as he came back whilst carrying another large box which he also dropped loudly. There were more clothes sticking out of the top and this time I recognized one of his shirts hanging out.

"So, you wanna get dressed and give us a hand?" He asked casually, as he walked out of my bedroom again.

What the hell is going on here?! I remained sitting upright in bed as Declan came back a third time, carrying another large box. This time with the rattling noise coming from it, it didn't sound like there were any clothes in there.

"I'm going to need you to move some of your stuff and tell me what draws I can use." He pointed at the closet and tallboy.

"Why?" I looked on as if he had gone mad.

"Why? Why do you think?" He returned the look. "What, are you going to make me live out of these boxes?"

"Declan, is B awake?" I heard Aunt Susan call out from downstairs.

"Yeah!" He called back.

"Ask her if she would like a cup of coffee before we get started." She requested.

He looked my way questioningly. "Well, do you?" When I didn't answer, he turned to shout back, "white and two please!"

"OK, I am going to remain calm." I stumbled out of bed as I took a deep breath. "Um, do you care to tell me what you're doing?"

"What does it look like I'm doing?" He retorted. "I'm moving in."

"You're MOVING IN?!" I exclaimed. "No!"

"What do you mean, no?" He asked indignantly.

"NO!" I yelled in horror.

"Oh great." He scratched the back of his head. "Of all the chicks in this tribe, I get landed with the screwball who wants to try 'long distance mating'."

"So your Mum knows about us then?" I blanched.

"The whole frickin' tribe knows about us!" He looked on like I was an idiot.

"OK, this is not good. This is so NOT good this is worse than bad!" I started to pace up and down. "I'm officially the first Lokoti Werewolf who's taken on a second mate! Everybody who knows this will talk about me! What do we do?"

"Get dressed, drink coffee and help me unpack!" He said in annoyance before he turned around to walk out again.

Oh no! The WHOLE TRIBE knows about us? Now Declan is moving in? This is bad...! Reluctantly I dressed in jeans and a jumper, pulled my hair into a ponytail and then I warily came downstairs.

"Good morning, B." Aunt Susan smirked when I joined her in the kitchen and she handed me the coffee she had made. "Declan is right, you're not a morning person. You look like you're still asleep!"

"Huh?" I looked at her in surprise that they had talked about me as such? Then I gawked in further surprise at what she was doing, she was re-organizing my freezer by stocking it with extra tupperwear containers of food she had brought.

"I've made lasagna for you both. Also there's a large pre-made salad that you can just dip into during the week. Plus here is the toss salad dressing." She held up a bottle of homemade dressing. "These are Declan's favourite foods in the whole world. I've made copies of the recipes of lasagna and a couple more of his favourite dishes, like spaghetti bolognaise, tuna bake, carbonara and caneloni. I also threw in the famous Sabre recipe for tiramisu."

I tried not to frown at how Aunt Susan made it sound like I was going to turn into some housewife who does all of the cooking?

"Actually, I don't do that much cooking..." I laughed nervously, "...I usually make up a big batch of stew or something and eat that through the week."

"That's what we do." She shrugged. "Pasta dishes are exceptionally handy for that."

"Pasta dishes?" My eyebrows rose. "Um, where do I get the pasta from?"

"Declan knows how to make it." She said proudly, before she dropped her voice. "The man may be 27 years old and is only moving out of home now? But he's in no way useless or a 'Momma's Boy,' I can assure you. He's part Italian, so he's a good cook. Plus he's a clean freak, so watch out. You'll put something down and then turn around to pick it up again and you'll find it's been put away. He likes to keep busy, so he's always on the move."

My eyes bulged as I gulped some coffee to swallow down the lump in my throat. I'm getting tips from Aunt Susan on Declan's living habits? However she thought our being alone in the kitchen must have been a good time for a heart to heart. As she worked, she deigned to share her private thoughts. What came out both surprised and touched me, as it also made me wonder if her speculating was sometimes a chastisement?

"You and Derik grew up together and were such close friends, you were almost in each other's pockets. When Derik first told me that he was in love with you, I was pleased. I liked seeing the two of you sit at the table and plan to go to Cambridge together." She began which made me duck my head, thinking that this was a dig.

"You see B," Aunt Susan paused to look my way, "I believe in Karma. I believe what goes around, comes around. I believe that things happen for a reason. When you first changed into a Lokoti Werewolf and were married off to Grant Elm, I didn't understand. I thought you and Derik belonged together but I was happy when he started to date Rachel when he was home for the holidays, because I saw he was moving on. I was happy when he told me he had proposed to Rachel and within their first month of marriage they told me she was expecting. But I still worried about Declan because although Derik could move on after your marriage, my eldest couldn't."

She had an angry look on her face when she said this next part, "when Declan cried to me when he was 14 years old over what the pack had told him; that he could never mate with a human woman because he could either kill or turn her? I was so angry at the pack for hurting him like that! But with his supernatural strength and the amount of times he accidentally broke something, or how his eyes would glow green when he constantly lost his temper? I understood why the pack said what they did. I worried about his loneliness and sense of isolation. He was constantly angry and withdrawn, being the only member of the tribe who was unable to have a romantic relationship."

Aunt Susan shut the freezer door to pick up her coffee, "so when you turned and the pack decided to marry you off to Grant Elm? Although I love Derik, I was annoyed at the pack for ostracizing Declan again for not even considering him to be your mate. So was he but I didn't know then that he had feelings for you too, I just thought he was hurt that the Lokoti Werewolves wouldn't allow him any kind of chance at happiness at all, with human or with a rarity such as yourself, a female Werewolf."

It could still make me blush by the way people said 'female Werewolf,' like I was the 'Tooth Fairy'.

She sighed sadly, "during those five years you were married to Grant; I saw Declan get angrier and angrier. I felt his pain and it worried me how much time he spent hunting alone, without the pack. But after Grant's death, I noticed another change come over him. He started to act hopeful about something, cheerful even. Two months ago when the two of you started secretly seeing each other? I had my suspicions, but I didn't say anything because something miraculous started to happen; his anger went away. He started whistling as he worked and he seemed almost peaceful."

"Peaceful?!" I cracked up laughing! "Declan, peaceful? No way!"

"Exactly!" She laughed along. "That was my reaction too! My oldest, anger-ball for a son, was starting to find peace? I nearly became a born-again Christian from the amount of times my eyes raised to the heavens to thank God!"

We both laughed so hard that we had to put down our coffees so not to spill them! Declan walked past the entrance to the kitchen, carrying another cardboard box, when he stopped. Aunt Susan and I saw Declan standing there, looking on like we had lost our minds or something; it only made us laugh harder.

"Shoo!" She waved her arm at her eldest. "Go and unpack or something, would you?"

"Women!" He shook his head as he turned away to carry his load upstairs.

"So you see B?" She sighed as she wiped her eyes from laughing so hard. "Things do happen for a reason. Grant Elm was meant to split you and Derik up, just as you and Declan were meant to come together. Because you changed into a Werewolf, my eldest is no longer alone. You have no idea what kind of satisfaction that gives a mother, knowing that a son supernatural or not, isn't going to spend his life alone and miserable."

I think I blushed at her honesty, as I ducked my head again and I picked up my coffee to continue drinking.

"Come on." She changed the subject. "Let's get this son of mine settled in."

I gave a nod before I followed her out of the kitchen.

After I showed Declan the draws in the tall boy he could use which used to be Grant's, and the side of the closet which also used to be Grant's; I had to leave the bedroom. It made me feel uneasy when I saw him use my prior mate's previous space. Instead I worked downstairs with Aunt Susan to unpack Declan's boxes of CD's, DVD's and books.

However when I saw the types of books I was putting away, I must admit seeing his reading pattern surprised me again.

"'Dracula'?" I held up the novels in disbelief. "'Lair of the White Worm', 'Lady Chatterley's Lover', 'Works of Byron', 'Mansfield Park', 'Brideshead Revisited', 'Works of the Bronte Sisters', 'The Lover' and 'Henry & June'? Declan's READ all these?"

"He certainly has." She confirmed. "Look at how creased 'Lady Chatterley's Lover' and 'The Lover' is. I think he's read those at least fifty times."

She was right, the books certainly looked 'worn in' with their wrinkles and creased pages.

Aunt Susan smirked, "well he IS a Werewolf who's been single for most of his life. Romances interested him, since he couldn't have a relationship in real life so he had to experience it in the books instead. I offered to borrow old Mrs. Huntington's 'Mills & Boon' novels, on the pretext that it was me reading them so he wouldn't get embarrassed? But he said he wouldn't be caught dead with those books. So I had to stick to giving him the Classics, so he could pretend he was reading the books for the historical value and not for the romance."

I had to laugh at that, as I put the books on the shelf in alphabetical order. I had to admit, this day was just full of surprises especially about Declan.

*****

After lunch Aunt Susan decided that it would be a good time to 'bow out' and make herself scarce.

Declan and I walked her out to her truck, as I watched the love and respect he treated his mother with. He opened her door for her and then shut it for her too. He even poked his head through the window to give her a goodbye kiss on the cheek.

"I want you two to come to dinner this Sunday night." She ordered.

"OK." He agreed as he stepped back from the vehicle.

"I'll also have Derik, Rachel and little Michael over." She organized.

Oh oh...this gave me pause.

"Um," I frowned, "are you sure that's a good idea?"

Declan nudged me sharply to shut up before he promised, "we'll be there."

"We're family." Aunt Susan declared. "So we're going to act like one."

Next, we watched her reverse out of the driveway, wave and disappear down the hill.

"'Are you sure that's a good idea'?" He mimed in a whiny voice.

"What?" I asked defensively.

He shook his head as he turned and went back inside. Instead of following after, I went and sat on the veranda steps to think.

Declan has moved in and it was only days ago that I was shot and everybody found out about us. It felt too soon. I mean, it was nice about how supportive Aunt Susan was and I could understand why she was happy for her son? But how about the rest of the tribe, how were they going to behave?

After another five minutes he came back out to sit beside whilst carrying two coffees. He handed me a mug before he drank his quietly. The two of us sat there, not saying a thing for five minutes.

"What do you want me to say, B?" He broke the silence. "Do you want me to promise you that everything will be alright and we'll live happily ever after? Or that nobody in the tribe will ever say a bad thing about us?"

My eyes narrowed as I stared at a particular tree across the driveway. Ironically it was an elm, whose leaves swayed gently in the breeze.

"I can't do that." He said crankily. "Our circumstance won't allow it. I'm not exactly thrilled that I'll be living inside the house that your husband bought you as a wedding present, just as I'm not happy about seeing his belongings up the top of the closet. I can still smell him on his things, which means every time I open the closet, I'm going to smell your dead husband."

I took a deep breath as I spoke reluctantly, "I'll take his stuff out of the closet and put it somewhere else, like the attic or something."

"It's a start." He said flatly. "But don't you think that I would have liked a Joining Ceremony? Wouldn't it be nice if the whole tribe threw us a Housewarming too? But instead, we have our one-person celebration squad, of only my Mom supporting our relationship."

His words not only surprised me that Declan could be mushy that way; but I also felt sad for him. I thought I had it bad as the first Lokoti Werewolf known to take another mate? He had to go through the stigma of being the guy who moved in to take the place of the deceased.

Suddenly I stood up and pulled him up too. I grinned, "I have an idea."

"Hey, I'm resting here!" He complained.

"Come on you slack-ass!" I laughed. "We'll have a two-person Housewarming. We'll put on some loud music like 'Nirvana' or something as I put the last of Grant's stuff into the attic and we'll finish getting you settled in."

"I'd rather 'Pearl Jam'." He smirked but he let me pull him back inside.

As we cranked up the music, I used the cardboard boxes that Declan brought to put in the last of Grant's things that sat on the top shelf of the wardrobe. After I carried the box up into the attic, I returned to the bedroom. I found him wiping over the top shelf of the wardrobe with multi-purpose spray. He even wiped down all of the surfaces in the bedroom, as if he was trying to wipe away all traces of Grant.

I sat on the bed to watch him put his digital clock on the bedside table, before turning it on and programming the time into it. Funnily enough, the song 'Alive' came on at that moment.

"Heeeyyy I'm still aliiiiive...!" He sung, as he scattered his personal effects around the bedroom.

I had to laugh, when I noticed how particular he was with where he put his things. It reminded me of the habit that all Werewolves must possess;

territorial behavior. He treated with reverence the old family photo of his Mum and Dad holding him when he was a baby, which he put on the tall boy.

"Heeeeeyy I'm still alive!" I sung as I jumped on top of the bed.

When I began to 'head bang' to the music, Declan jumped up onto the bed to do a wicked 'air guitar' during the instrumental bit, making me cheer him on! When the song came to a close, he flipped me over onto my back as he fell on top. This is the hopeless romantic who's read Anais Nin?

"I think you need to read 'The Lover' a couple more times." I criticized his technique.

"Oh yeah?" He arched his eyebrows before he bent his head to run his sharpening teeth down my neck. I heard him chuckle smugly when my eyes closed and my head went backwards.

"You know two can play at that game." I growled out as I allowed my claws to detract so I could run them down his torso. I smirked back when I felt his arousal.

"Oh, you want to turn this into a competition, do you?" He taunted. "OK then, whoever breaks first by ripping the other's clothes off has to do the dishes for a week."

"Fine." I agreed as next I ran my claws down his back under his clothes.

His response was immediate. "Oh shit that's not fair!" He gasped. "But like you said, two can play at that game...!"

He pulled on the neckline of my jumper to run his sharpening teeth across my left shoulder. He snickered as he watched me start to turn my head from side to side. My heart pounded as I heard his did too. Our breaths came out faster as our skin heated up under the other's touch.

"You look like you're about to turn." He tried to goad.

"So do you." I panted.

"You're looking a little hot and flustered there, B."

"So do you."

"You know there's no shame in giving in to your lust and ravaging me."

"Keep dreaming."

He gasped when I dug my claws deeper into his skin! I watched him squeeze his eyes shut and the veins pop out in his thick neck as he tried to restrain himself.

"Screw this!" He snarled in frustratration. He ripped off his shirt then t-shirt over his head, as I gleefully laughed. "I don't trust your washing up skills anyway! Your mugs still have coffee stains in them!"

He tried to talk indignantly but it didn't work because he said it as he was hurriedly undressing the both of us.

*****

Two hours later I lay on my side, smiling like the cat that stole the cream. Declan also lay on his side facing my direction with his arms and legs resting over mine. His eyes were closed and he looked like he was asleep.

"Oh come on!" I suddenly poked him in the ribs with my finger, startling him. "It's only 2.30 in the afternoon! Don't you dare fall asleep!"

"Oow!" He crankily hit my hand away before he tried to close his eyes again.

"Declan!" I tickled him. "Don't you dare!"

"B!" He growled warningly as he rolled onto his back.

I moved to sit on top of him. "You're the European Werewolf who visited me for over two months, shagged me all night and then ran home again!"

"No wonder I'm frickin' tired!" He laughed.

"So you cannot be sleepy now, after only two hours of misbehaving and doing things to me that could get us arrested in certain countries!" I tickled him again.

"Get lost!" Declan rolled me off so we were lying on our sides facing the other again, "ever thought that perhaps that I'm just satisfied?"

"No."

"I'm a Werewolf, which means we're ten times worse than the Average Joe. The human male may roll over and go to sleep after maybe twenty minutes of foolin' around, thinking he's some kind of god or something? But I deserve the rest after making you come something like twenty times over two hours."

"And you're so modest too...!" I poked him again.

"B." He slapped my hand away once more.

"Where have the nights gone where we wouldn't stop for six hours straight?" I gave him another poke.

"B!" He frowned with his eyes closed.

"Hmm? Where Mr. Sabre, where?" I poked him over and over again.

Declan grabbed my finger and started to put it into his mouth to bite, but I whipped it out of his grasp.

"Frickin' hell!" He snarled as he rolled onto his back again. "This is the first time we have sex in OUR home where I'm now ALLOWED to fall asleep afterwards without worrying I could be punished for it; and you're not even letting me rest?!"

"Now you know the real reason why Grant died; because of exhaustion!" I joked.

"Yeah well, he was just a Lokoti Werewolf so he wasn't the right breed for you." He gave a teasing smile.

"Now I'm with a European Werewolf who can't keep up with me either!" I sat upright. "Maybe I should go back in time and find myself a Circulator instead?"

"Don't even think about it!" Declan pulled me back down to hold me in his arms.

He snuggled down as he held me tighter and after a minute or two, I heard his tell-tale deep breathing indicating that he really had fallen asleep! I sighed as I stared up at the ceiling, but I was smiling to myself.

Aunt Susan was right, Declan WAS at peace. Was it really because of me? Nah, it's just his satiated body now he's regularly 'getting some'.

*****

It felt strange seeing him around the house. The next morning I woke up, I gave myself a fright and Declan too. When my eyes opened, they immediately settled on the digits on his digital alarm clock... 7.53 AM.

Hmm, there was nothing unusual about this as I often woke up at this time to begin my day. Hang on, why are the digits a lime green colour? Grant's clock has red digits. Oh oh, why is there a muscled arm, draped over my waist? I could smell maple syrup, which is Declan's scent...

I rolled onto my back to look on my lover who was fast asleep, which I could see as clear as day in the morning light. Oh shit! He's slept in, past dawn! Now when he runs home, people could see him! People would find out!

"Declan, wake up!" I shook him in alarm.

"Hmm, what?" He opened his sleepy eyes. "What is it?"

"You slept in!"

"Nah, it's cool B." He tried to pull me back into his arms. "Finn gave me this week off, so I don't have to go into work."

Huh, what has his job at the Garage got to do with it?

"Declan!" I shook him again. "Get up!"

"Aw, get lost B!" He growled out as he rolled over in annoyance to face the other direction.

I was about to extend my claws to scratch him and make him get up and go home, when I caught sight of his family photo on top of the tallboy. Next, I noticed his watch sitting on the bedside table, as well as his other items. Hell, I even saw one of his flannel shirts were peaking out from the wardrobe.

Oh yeah, Declan IS home. What the hell is WRONG with me?! Maybe I do have brain damage?

"Declan." I said quietly.

"What?"

"I think I do have brain damage from being shot in the head."

"You got that right." He said grouchily.

I looked over at a pair of his work boots sitting on the floor, next to the tallboy. Far out, I really DO have another mate and everyone knows this. Derik knows, Aunt Susan knows, Mum and Dad know, Gran and Grandfather know, Ian knows which means the rest of Grant's family would. It made me wonder what the fall out would be?

The world was still recovering from World War Three so how will the tribe recover from the bomb we dropped with our relationship? Declan and I saw it as my returning to my first mate, but would other people see it that way?

"B." He said crossly as he rolled onto his back. "Did you wake up and panic over seeing me still in your bed after dawn?"

"Yes." I admitted and then I flinched as I expected to be yelled at, or some kind of insult to come my way.

"Do you know why I'm tired this morning?"

"Er, because you had a big day yesterday?"

"I didn't sleep much last night because I kept waking up." He said gruffly. "I woke up because I wasn't used to this house's smell. I woke up because I couldn't hear my Mom snoring in her bedroom and I went into a panic, thinking that something had happened to her. I woke up when you elbowed me in your sleep. Then I woke up at dawn, thinking it was time to go home when I realized that this was my home."

My eyes widened at his words, before I gave him a silly smile. "You too?"

"Yup." He pulled me close. "Me too."

I rolled on top of him to nestle my face into his neck, as his scent filled my senses completely. I could also feel his strong, steady pulse with my nose pressed into his skin. I think he liked it when I did this, as his hold tightened. We both let out a contented sigh.

"This is it, B." He said happily. "It's just you and me baby."

A giggle escaped as I raised my head to look down into his face. I echoed in amusement. "Baby?"

"Sweetie Pie?"

"No."

"Sugar?"

"Nup."

"Um I don't like 'dear'. Every time an elderly person calls me 'dear' I have to hold myself back from mauling them." Declan frowned.

"I don't mind an older person calling me dear, but if a husband ever did it? I'd scratch him senseless for being so sexist." I threatened.

"Promises promises." He laughed. "You know what, B? You don't really seem the type to be called pet names."

"I should hope not!"

"How about Baby B?"

"How about I remove one of your kidneys?"

"Just one?"

"Well I need some life left in you as I'm not done with you yet." I tittered.

"Who said you could remove your head from my neck?" Declan pushed my head back down. I heard him emit a low, contented growl as I nuzzled into his skin.

"Declan?"

"B?"

"I wonder what would happen if we did remove a Werewolf's kidney, do you think they could regenerate and grow back a new one?"

"I guess." I felt him shrug. "I know from experience that European Werewolves are better healers than Lokoti Werewolves. From the amount of times I've been shot over the years and even once in the heart? I was completely regenerated in 48 hours."

My head arose in shock. "You were shot in the heart?!"

"Yup."

"When did THIS happen?"

"When I was 18 years old, but it wasn't a silver bullet so it was OK."

"No it's not OK!" I flared. "Your mother must have had a fit when it happened!"

Declan sighed out, "I hid it from her."

I asked in disbelief, "how the hell did you do THAT?! Wouldn't she notice the hole in your chest?!"

"I was on patrol with Finn when it happened." He recanted. "The gun was aimed at him, but I arrived just in time. I knew I was stronger so I purposefully jumped in the way. It hurt but it would have hurt Finn a hell of a lot more."

When he saw my worried expression, he quickly moved on, "after the rest of the pack took care of the strangers, I went back to Finn's house. Your Grandpa removed the bullet and I slept for a couple of hours. I told them not to tell my mother otherwise she'd freak out, so they told her instead that I was having a late breakfast at Finn's. In six hours the flesh had healed, but my blood pressure and pulse were still out of whack. Finn cooked me up some brunch when I woke up hungry around four o'clock in the afternoon, then he gave me a lift home. I told my Mom I was still tired and went to bed, to sleep off the rest of my regeneration. The next morning I was right as rain."

The look on my face still mustn't have been a good one, so Declan tried to say casually, "you see B? It's no big deal. European Werewolves are as tough as nails; we take a lickin' and keep on tickin'!"

But it didn't make me laugh, it made me mad. I asked indignantly, "the pack just took you home afterwards?!"

"Your Grandpa stayed with me at Finn's, to oversee my recovery. Then he came by the next morning, to see how I was holding up. But he brought along some knitting magazines to lend to Mom, to pass it off as a social visit." When I opened my mouth to argue further, he interrupted, "it's no big deal B, really. I only brought it up as an example to the kidney question."

"But – but – but why didn't you ever tell me?"

"You were 15 years old at the time. Every time I opened my mouth, you would bite my head off! You may have only been human then, but you could act pretty bitchy."

"That's because you were a bastard! You kept making nasty comments or you talked to me sarcastically."

"Of course I did, I had to! I wouldn't have been allowed to sniff in your direction let alone ask you out. The pack would have come down on me like a ton of bricks." He retorted.

"Well you did a VERY good job of hiding your true feelings."

"Thank you!"

I opened my mouth to yell at him some more as he watched intently, waiting for what else I could fire at him? But instead my voice turned sad.

"So you had the pack to talk to about patrolling, but you had to hide your feelings for me? Your mother sympathized with you for not dating, but you couldn't talk to her about patrolling? Was there one person in your life that you could talk freely to, Declan?"

"Aw, B..." he shifted awkwardly, "...stop making me sound like some sad case that used to go on those talk shows like 'Dr Phil'!"

"Declan," I cupped his face to make him look me in the eye, "I want you to tell me EVERYTHING, do you understand me? I mean ANYTHING! I may not like hearing it, but I would get angrier if I found out you kept something from me."

A silly grin spread across his face, "you already are there for me, just as you always have been."

"Huh?"

"You heard me."

"But how?" I wondered.

"Don't make me get all mushy, it's too early in the day for that crap."

"Declan!" My hand was quick to grab his short hair and pull it.

"Oow!" He laughingly tried to remove my hand, but I wouldn't let go.

"Spill it, you uneducated, grease monkey!"

"See, right there!" Declan guffawed.

"WHAT?!" I lost my patience and pulled harder.

"Yes!" He cried out, like he liked the pain. Eew! I let go of his hair as I tried to roll away, but he was quick to pull me back. He grinned like an idiot, "I like this. I don't want touchy-feely, expressing your feelings crap. If I'm angry and you're a stranger, you'll know it when you find a bloodied claw mark across your skin. I'm a European Werewolf, I don't want cuddles and sweet-nothings, I want someone to vent to. I treated my Mom and my kid brother carefully but at least with you, I could be myself."

"When were you ever honest with me?" I objected. "You were downright abusive!"

"That WAS being honest, B." He rolled his eyes. "When you were a baby, I was in awe of the little glow-in-the-dark girl who was the only baby in the tribe who had an aura, because she was a Circulator. When you got older and we started to fight? I liked how your aura changed when you got angry. I liked how you always stood up to me."

I gave him a funny look, "but your eyes glowed green as your face turned red and you looked like you were about to maul me."

"I wouldn't have mauled to kill, I would have mauled like a play fight." He shrugged again. "I liked it when you and Derik studied at the table and I'd walk past to insult you and you'd throw your pen at me. I liked it when you threw wet flour on me. I liked it when you shouted in my face and told me to drop dead, because every mean thing we said and did to each other? I could vent my bloodlust without causing grievous harm."

Oh, I saw his point as I confessed, "I always wondered why I seemed to be the person you were the rudest to."

"It's because you could handle me." He grinned. "I also liked to watch the sparks fly off your aura when I made you furious."

"Yeah right!"

"Why do you think the three Circulators of the tribe all happen to be mated to Werewolves?" He arched his eyebrows. "It's because we can see a Circulator's aura when most humans can't so we appreciate it."

"How can you see it?"

"I dunno, maybe it's something to do with our night vision or whatever."

"But I'm a Werewolf and I can't see auras."

"Say what?" He looked on in surprise. "You can't see yours, or your mother's, or your grandmother's auras?"

"No."

"But you can see better in the dark as a Werewolf, right?"

"Yeah."

"Then how do humans look in the dark?"

"I dunno, like humans?" I gave a funny look.

He paused for a moment before he asked, "do humans look the same, or does everything look the same when you're in Werewolf form?"

"Yeah, pretty much. In my Werewolf form, I just see better in the dark." I shrugged.

This surprised him so much so, he partially sat up to give a long, hard look.

"B," he began, "when I'm in Werewolf form, I can basically see infrared. I spot humans and animals by their heat signatures. Werewolves have a different heat signature because we emit greater body heat. When I see you or another Circulator with my Werewolf eyes? You look like a human torch because there's so much light coming off you."

"Why, because of my aura as a Circulator?" I asked curiously.

"Yup."

"Then maybe it's just like that for European Werewolves." I pondered.

"Nope." He corrected. "It's the same with the other Lokoti Werewolves."

"What? No way!" I said in disbelief. "So they can see infrared too?"

"Yep." He verified. "It's how we hunt and it's one of the ways we know if our prey is healthy or not, by the colours they emit so we don't eat bad meat."

"But I thought it was just because of how our prey smelled."

Declan regarded me closely, "maybe it's got to do with something with you being both Werewolf and Circulator."

"Maybe." I shrugged. "Can you see time warps?"

"No." He looked on like I was mad.

"Can you see the past or the future?"

"Nope."

"I can." I smiled. "You have your vision and I have mine."

This made him smile back, "you know what, B?"

"What Declan?"

"This is going to be an interesting 250 years together."

As I gazed back into his bright blue eyes, I felt excitement. Some people may be intimidated by such a long time to be attached to the one person but we were more afraid of facing the years without the other. However he was right though, I could tell just how interesting our lives would be from how our first day turned out.

By the time we hauled ourselves out of bed, dressed and went downstairs to start our day, our further differences became evident. My first stop was switching on the kettle and Declan's was raiding the fridge. As I reached for the coffee; he was pulling out the milk, eggs, cheese, butter and bread.

"You want some scrambled eggs?" He offered.

I shook my head, "no, do you want some coffee?"

"Yup." He answered so I grabbed an extra mug to make his too. As he watched me procure our caffeine fix he inquired, "what do you usually have for breakfast? You better not say muesli, coz that's just glorified rabbit food!"

"Most of the time I don't have breakfast." I shrugged. "I might on a weekend but not usually."

"Say what?" He paused to look on in surprise. "Your breakfast is a cup of coffee?"

"Several cups of coffee, all morning until lunch time when I make myself a sandwich."

"B," He cried indignantly, "you're a frickin' Werewolf! A WEREWOLF! We're hungry all the time!"

"Not ALL of the time." I corrected.

"Uh huh," he put an extra two slices of bread into the toaster for me, "ALL of the time."

I opened my mouth to dispute this but then I recalled how Dad or Grandfather would never skip a meal. When I grew up, Dad would always ask Mum what time dinner would be if it was her turn to cook and if he couldn't wait, he'd make himself a snack.

"I mean, I do eat more than Mum." I turned thoughtful as I leant back on the bench. "My appetite has increased with my change but I'm not perpetually hungry," then I gave him a cheeky smile, "for food anyways."

Declan gave a wink, "welcome to my world."

*****

I happily guzzled down the scrambled eggs on toast that my new mate procured, impressed with his culinary skills. Apparently Declan doesn't just know how to make pasta; but his scrambled eggs were utterly delicious. After breakfast, I sat up on the bench and teased him as he had to wash up, whilst I finished my cup of coffee.

"Laugh it up, B." He said coolly. "The next time you WILL lose the bet, I guarantee."

For the rest of the day, I started to see what Aunt Susan meant by him constantly moving around. His domineering behavior, coupled with his supernatural strength, made it hard for him to remain still for long periods of time. Declan cleaned the outside of the house by sweeping the veranda and then the greenhouse. If I had a lawn or flower beds, he probably would have done the gardening. Next, he tidied up the greenhouse supplies, before planting a new crop of vegetables and herbs he needed for his recipes.

For lunch I made us a couple of toasted cheese and tomato sandwiches, when Declan asked expectantly, "OK, that's the first two now where's the others?"

"What others?" I replied.

His eyebrows rose unimpressed, "you think TWO sandwiches are enough?" Next, he went into the kitchen and made himself FOUR more! Altogether he ate six sandwiches! Then straight after lunch, I found him by the sink washing up again.

"Leave it, Declan." I tried to stop him. "I usually wash up the lunch things with the dinner mess."

"Nope." He said simply. "I'll wash up when I want to, thanks very much!"

I shrugged as I left him to it, to sit at the dining table to catch up on my studies. I was researching the importance of religion on Ancient Greek life when I noticed in the corner of my eye, Declan went outside again. After twenty minutes, I was disturbed by a strange noise which sounded like an engine running. What the hell was he doing now? I couldn't concentrate, so I bad-temperedly pushed my chair from the table and flung open the front door.

I stood on the veranda with my hands on my hips to find Declan leaning over the black jeep with the hood propped up, while its engine was on. A tool kit was sitting open on the driveway beside.

"What are you doing?" I demanded.

"Your fan belt is loose." He reported. "I noticed it was making a funny noise last week."

"Oh." I said impressed at his skills as a mechanic to pick that up. "So why is the motor running?"

"I'm checking the engine's noises." He straightened as he wiped his dirty hands on his t-shirt. "I think your carburetor is clogged, as it sounds like its choking."

"Oh." I tried to hide my admiration for my own personal, muscled mechanic.

"Plus your engine needs a tune up." He frowned. "Gees, B! When was the last time you had this vehicle looked on?"

My heart skipped a beat, before I eventually managed out, "Grant and Ian used to work on it together." Then I turned around and went inside again.

*****

For the rest of the day, I worked inside as Declan worked outside. I finished typing up my notes before I put my laptop and books away. Just as I went into the kitchen to start preparing dinner, I heard the front door open and he came into the kitchen. He washed his hands at the sink, as he peered over his shoulder at the things I was taking out of the fridge.

"Are we having lasagna and salad for dinner?" He guessed.

"Yes."

He wiped his hands dry on a tea towel as I took two portions of lasagna out of the baking dish to put onto a plate. Just as I was about to put the plate into the microwave, he stopped me by taking it away.

"Nah ah." He objected. "The microwave turns the pasta hard, so you need to slowly heat it up in the oven."

I ended up standing back as he took over. Declan put the lasagna portions on a tray, which he put inside the oven and then he turned the heat on low. Next, he scooped up some salad out of the larger bowl by putting some into a smaller bowl along with some dressing, drizzled over the top. I crossed my arms and frowned as he mixed the dressing through.

Declan was certainly making my home into his, as he rearranged my house, my car and now he was taking over my kitchen! I suppressed a growl because the Werewolf inside recognized what it was he was doing; he was claiming this house as his territory.

He noticed my mood but he didn't look my way as he continued working. He asked shortly, "do you wanna talk about it?"

"No."

"Thank God for that." He muttered. "I was scared you were going to get all touchy-feely on me, by communicating your emotions on the subject of your dead husband."

I saw that this was a sore point for the European Werewolf as he was still jealous of the guy. He pushed aside the finished salad to turn his attention to setting the table as I stood and stared out the kitchen window.

"Well, your jeep is all fixed." He moved the conversation along. "I don't have all my tools with me though, just the ones in the truck. I accidentally left them back at Mom's which I'll pick up tomorrow."

"OK."

"I don't think I forgot anything else, just my tools. It was probably because they're in the garage and not in the house with the majority of my stuff."

"Uh huh."

"We should build a garage, to protect our vehicles so they're not just sitting outside in the elements all of the time, especially in winter."

"Alright."

"I mean, doesn't that get annoying for you, B? In the middle of winter when we've had heavy snow fall, you have to knock the snow off the car?"

I shrugged, as I didn't really care. Grant used to put tarpaulin over it, so when he wanted to use the jeep, he just took off the cover and all the snow came off with it. But I couldn't say this right now to the jealous European Werewolf.

"The black paint is holding up well. I thought it would look faded or cracked but it's not." He remarked as he grabbed the cutlery out of the draw.

Grant would spend hours washing and polishing the jeep, which kept the paint job in good condition. I could picture him now, out on the driveway with the rag and turtle wax.

"Aside from the carburetor, the fan belt and a few other bits and pieces, the jeep has kept well." He admitted. "Grant did a good job looking after it, like he did with you, I'll give him that."

Huh, what did he just say? I looked back in surprise, but he had already moved on. I watched him carry the salad bowl over to the table.

He returned to the kitchen to stand before me. "You know what, B?"

"What, Declan?"

"I feel like some garlic bread with dinner tonight."

"Huh?" My head spun at how quickly he changed the subject. "But we don't have any garlic bread."

"Watch and learn baby." He gave a wink.

Declan grabbed the butter, two cloves of garlic, a small bottle of dried parsley along with two frozen bread rolls. I ended up sitting on the kitchen bench, watching him prepare homemade garlic bread.

When the garlic bread was warming under the grill, he gave a mischievous grin, "you see, B? I didn't need a BA to do that."

I kicked out which he laughingly dodged with his supernatural reflexes.

*****

It was getting late but I was nearly at the end of my book and I didn't want to put it down. I was lying on the couch when I looked at the time on the display of the DVD player and saw it was 10.53 PM. My eyes were stinging, but I pushed onwards whilst blinking repeatedly to refocus my tired eyes.

Declan came down the stairs in a clean t-shirt and boxer shorts, smelling soapy from his recent shower. He moaned tiredly as he pushed me sideways on the couch to make room for himself. After he lay down beside, he rested his head on my breasts as he wrapped his arms and legs about my body.

I smiled to myself, appreciating this contact as I continued with my reading. After a minute, I felt his hands slip under my jumper to begin to stroke my skin.

"This is nice." He sighed contentedly. "No more secrecy and no more sneaking around. Now I can actually sleep the whole night through in your arms. You should get shot in the head more often."

I laughed out, "you said if I did anything like that again, you'd maul me."

"I WILL maul you if you ever try to leave." He said staunchly. "You're officially mine for the next 250 years."

"I am, am I?" I giggled.

"Hell yeah!" He exclaimed before he raised his head to look me in the eye. "We're officially recognized as mates. Ian handed you to me on a gold platter."

"He did not!"

"Well alright, I was threatened with drowning at one stage. But I told everyone very bravely I might add, 'do what you want with me, just make sure my only avenue of sex survives'."

"That was very brave of you." I snickered.

"I know, so you owe me." Declan grabbed hold of my book and tossed it onto the floor.

"Hey!" I objected as I started to roll across him to retrieve it when he held me down to kiss passionately. His ardor ignited my own desires, especially since he was holding my groin against his hardening one.

"We've been at it like rabbits since you moved in..." I giggled as I moved my face away so he would move his mouth down my neck, "...haven't you had enough?"

"Nuh uh." He uttered with his mouthful. He licked and chewed his way down my neck to my collar bone, when he stopped. He whipped off my jumper over my head which was acting as his barrier so his mouth could continue to my breasts. Next, I felt his hands undo my jeans as he growled out, "you weren't the one who had to be frickin' celibate for 27 years of their life!"

"What, you wanted to have sex when you were a one year old?" I snickered.

"Alright, let me rephrase that. You weren't the one who had to be celibate for the last 13 years and trust me, the lust is just as bad as the bloodlust." He tossed away my pants.

"Oh poor Declan..." I started to taunt but then I gasped when I felt his hand slide over my crotch.

"You were saying?" He smirked as his fingers parted my moist folds to tantalize further.

"... you weren't exactly celibate that afternoon in the woods when I was 18 years old..." I uttered out in my escalating pleasure.

"You didn't exactly complain." He hastily removed his boxers so he could push inside. We both moaned at the same time with our fingernails almost turning into claws as we gripped onto the other. He panted out, "and we haven't been at it like rabbits; we've been at it like Werewolves."

Declan rolled us off the couch and onto the hard, wooden floor with himself landing on top.

"Oomph! Oow, that hurt!" I scratched his back.

"So sue me!" He kissed hard as he moved hard.

"No wonder... you were told... to not... have sex... as a human woman wouldn't live through... the experience!" I growled as I wrapped my legs tightly about his waist.

"Oh shut up." He purposefully bit my lower lip which made me grunt in pain. Then he moaned in further delight as he ran his tongue over my wound, tasting my blood as he simultaneously began to heal it. "Besides, you wouldn't like it if I did try to be 'gentle'."

I pulled back to look on challengingly. "Oh yeah?"

We glared at each other for a moment, before Declan changed position. He used his greater strength to unclamp my thighs which were so taught, if he was human I probably would have broken his back. He raised himself higher above, so our bodies no longer had the friction of rubbing against each other then he slowly began to move.

"Is this gentle enough for you?" He arched his eyebrows.

I lay there for nearly a minute, bored out of my brain and starting to feel extremely frustrated...!

"Grrrraaaawwwwll!" I growled ferociously as I knocked him sideways!

He landed on his back with our coffee table almost breaking from the force he banged into it when I pounced on him.

"Now that's what I'm talking about!" He laughed out loud, before he was silenced when I bit him on his top lip to taste his blood back.

~~~~~~
~~~~~~

~ 22 ~

27th August 2090

I tried to keep my mind off ramifications and family feuds, by cleaning the house nearly all of Sunday. I vacuumed, mopped, cleaned the oven and the stove top, did the bathroom, dusted and I even reorganized my side of the wardrobe.

Declan spent the first half of the day sitting at the dining table making pesto, preserving sun-dried tomatoes and marinating olives in jars of olive oil and herbs. He had found where Grant used to store our empty jars and other items to reuse or recycle and he decided to put them to use. As he worked, he dutifully lifted up his feet when I vacuumed and then I mopped around him.

However he arched his eyebrows at my cleaning frenzy, before he shrugged and returned to work. I paused to watch him chop up pine nuts for the pesto.

"What's that for?" I asked as took off my earphones to point at what he was doing.

"What, the pesto?"

"Yeah."

"You can use pesto for lots of things; stir it through pasta or put it on sandwiches. Since it's made with olive oil, it's actually healthier than butter."

I said warily, "usually when somebody says something's healthy it doesn't taste very nice."

He raised his eyebrows, "oh really?"

I returned the earphones as well as to my mopping. I was listening to one of Declan's CD's as I worked, which I had downloaded onto my laptop to put on my MP3 player. It was another late 20th Century band called 'Death In Vegas'. Although I was enjoying the music, I didn't tell Declan so he could gloat about it.

When I stopped to take a breather, I sat outside on the veranda steps to cool down before making some lunch. However I received a nice surprise when Declan carried out plates of salad sandwiches for the both of us. I was touched that he had thought of me, but then I wondered why he was watching intently as I munched away.

"Hmm, this is good." I commented. "Is there salad dressing or something on the salad?"

"Nup." He started to smirk.

I looked on in disbelief, "but it tastes like garlic and herbs."

"It ain't salad dressing."

I still didn't believe him, so I pulled apart my sandwich when I found this funny green stuff smeared on the bread.

"What's this?" I frowned.

"Pesto."

"What, instead of butter?"

"You like it, don't you?" He gloated. "It's healthy B, maybe you shouldn't eat it anymore."

I looked away and ate the rest of my sandwich in silence, as did he.

After lunch, Declan decided to spend the rest of his Sunday afternoon relaxing. He lay on one of the couches reading a book as he listened to one of his The Tea Party CD's. He looked up to watch me walk through the living area from the laundry as I carried the cleaning products to do the bathroom.

"Why don't you spend your Sunday afternoon like a normal person by taking it easy?" He called out.

"Huh?" I paused at the bottom of the staircase to remove my earphones. "What did you say?"

"You're a frickin' Werewolf with supersensitive hearing, don't you think that music is a bit too loud?" He glared.

"Shut up." I replaced the earphones as I turned the music up louder. As I went up the stairs I muttered, "you're so bossy!"

"I heard that."

After attacking the bathroom, I reorganized my wardrobe. When my wardrobe was completed, I did the task that I liked the least and therefore left for last; the dusting. Listening to 'Death In Vegas' helped, as I danced whilst I dusted and I turned the music up to full volume. I got so carried away that I didn't hear Declan call out my name before he stood up from the couch to walk over.

"Frickin' hell!" He yanked my earphones off. "If you didn't look so hot, dancing around like that I would have thrown you over my shoulder, bolted down to the river and thrown you in again!" I tried to ignore him and retake my earphones but he held them away as he said stroppily, "it's 4.30 PM."

"Thanks for the time Mr. Wolf." I said coolly.

"We're leaving at 5.30 to go to Mom's for dinner." He ordered.

"Oh are we just?"

"I did tell you what time we had to leave, but you had your frickin' earphones on and you probably didn't hear."

"Oh really?"

Declan glared, "seriously B that music is too loud. I could hear the music blasting from the earphones when you were cleaning upstairs!"

"So, you're a Werewolf and you're supposed to have supersensitive hearing."

"And so are you!" He snapped as he shoved the earphones back into my hands. Then he turned around to head upstairs. "If you're not going to shower first then I will, but we're walking out that door at 5.30 on the dot!"

I muttered to myself, "so frickin' bossy!"

"I heard that!" He called back before he went into the bathroom.

I shook my head as I returned the music to my ears. I tried to use the loud noise to blast away my anxiety about going to Aunt Susan's tonight. I was in no rush to sit awkwardly at a table with Derik glaring at his brother and I sitting together, as their mother tried to force us into one big, happy family.

I was finishing up the dusting, when Declan jogged back down the stairs showered and changed. I saw his mouth move as he walked towards me, but I had no idea what he was saying.

"What?!" I bad-temperedly removed the earphones before he could rip them off himself.

"It's 4.55 PM," He still snatched up my MP3 player as well as the duster, "time for your shower."

"Don't tell me what to do!"

"I know what you chicks are like getting ready for something, now scram!"

"How the hell would you know what I'm like when I get ready to go out?" I put my hands on my hips.

"When you were 15 years old, you rocked up late to our house for dinner with your parents. I overheard your father tell Uncle Em it was because you took so long in the shower." He retorted.

"That wasn't my fault as I had to wash my hair!"

"And the time you were 16 years old and you were late to Ben's birthday party?"

"That wasn't my fault either, the button on my favourite jeans broke and Dad had to sew it up."

"When you were 17 years old and you were late for Toby's barbecue?"

"I couldn't find the shoes I wanted to wear." I said stubbornly.

Declan looked at his watch again, "it's now 4.59 PM and you just wasted four minutes standing around and arguing with me. Now get your butt upstairs and into that shower, but I won't let you make me late."

I swore under my breath as I headed for the stairs when he sung out yet again, "I heard that."

*****

I shaved my legs whilst simultaneously washing my hair as fast as humanly possible. I had learnt the hard way previously where a razor was concerned, you can't shave in light speed. I came out of the shower and towel dried my hair before I brushed it back into a bun. In the bedroom when I put on a long, black cotton dress which had purple roses printed over it; I caught the time on Declan's digital clock as 5.27 PM.

"Three minutes, B!" He called from downstairs.

I sat on the side of the bed to pull on my black strappy high heels. However when I stood up to look at myself analytically in the mirror, I frowned. Because the dress was cotton, the high heels looked too dressy. I walked over to my wardrobe to look for my black flat sandals instead.

"Thirty seconds, B!" He called out again.

I tried to ignore him as I searched for the other pair of shoes. Frickin' hell, where are they? I messed up my newly organized wardrobe by rummaging for them, but they were nowhere to be found.

"10...9...8...7...6...5...4...3...2...1... ready or not, here I come!"

I heard Declan jog up the stairs and barge into the bedroom when he froze with his eyes widening. I was bending over in the high heels with my legs inadvertently on display by the slit up the back of the dress, as I rummaged for the flat sandals.

"I can't find the right shoes!" I growled dangerously. "So don't start!"

"You're wearing shoes!"

"They're not the right ones, I want to wear the flat ones."

"Don't you dare." He growled whilst looking me up and down. "Your legs look frickin' hot in that dress and those shoes."

"I look too dressed up for a family dinner!" I complained.

"Nah ah." He walked up to pull me away from the wardrobe. He grabbed my brown suede jacket as he started pushing me towards the bedroom door.

"Declan, stop it!" I snarled as I reached the end of my tether.

"It's time to go." He tried to push me through the bedroom doorway.

I grabbed onto the door frame when he pried my hands off and suddenly bent over to sling me over his shoulder!

"DECLAN PUT ME DOWN!"

"Nope," he chuckled as he jogged down the stairs. He headed straight out the front door whilst locking it behind.

"DECLAN SABRE PUT ME DOWN RIGHT NOW YOU SEXIST BASTARD!"

He laughed as he carried me down the veranda steps and over to the passengers' side of his truck. He opened the door, lowered me onto the seat before shutting the door behind. I watched him guffaw as he walked around to the drivers' seat, climbed in and put his key into the ignition.

"You think you're so good don't you?" I spoke icily. "But have you forgotten that I'm a Circulator and I can instantaneously phase back inside?"

In a flash, Declan grabbed onto my arm as his eyes glowed green, "don't you DARE!"

"Let go of my arm!" I growled back.

"B, would you just chill out?!" He snapped whist his eyes returned to their human colour. "Just admit it, the shoes aren't the problem. Your clothes aren't the problem. Washing your hair isn't the problem. Cleaning the house like a mad woman today wasn't the problem, but I knew what you were doing. You were trying to put off tonight!"

"I was not!"

"Oh yeah?" He returned knowingly. "Then how come I had to force you to start getting ready? How come you tried to play ignorant when I told you what time we had to leave?"

I glaringly looked out the windscreen ahead as he started to reverse out of the driveway and onto the dirt road.

Declan ranted, "I'm the one who has more to lose than you but as usual, you're only thinking about yourself! I haven't spoken to Derik since you were shot. If anyone's gonna be nervous, it should be me!"

"Then maybe we shouldn't go tonight." I said quietly.

"Yeah right!" He rolled his eyes. "I told Mom we'd be there so we'll be there."

The truck lurched forwards down the road, as we left the hill to turn into the community centre.

*****

Declan pulled up in the driveway of his old house, beside Derik and Rachel's four wheel drive. He jumped out of the truck and slammed his door shut, before he walked around whilst I was slowly climbing out. He firmly took hold of my hand as he slammed my door shut too and then he proceeded to lead us to the front door.

I looked about to see if there was anybody around as I had to admit, I felt nervous even being seen together in the community centre where his mother's house was. As we approached the front door I slowed down to knock, but Declan gave a funny look as he simply opened it and walked right in.

He pulled me inside before he closed the front door behind. I heard more voices here than I thought I would, as the warmth of the house hit me as did the delicious smell of dinner cooking.

"Declan, is that you?" Aunt Susan called out.

"Yeah Mom, it's us." He called back as he proceeded to pull me away from the front door and into the living area.

Aunt Susan walked out of the kitchen first with Mandy next, then Rachel as she carried little Michael before an unhappy looking Derik, walked out last.

"Hi Dec." She walked over to her eldest.

He released his hold of my hand to hug and kiss his mother on the cheek. I saw how his mother looked like she relished his signs of affection, which made me think she must miss not seeing him everyday.

"B." She smiled my way next before she kissed me on the cheek. "You look very nice this evening."

I blushed, "I couldn't find my flat sandals."

Mandy snickered to Rachel, "yeah that's the only reason why she looks nice."

"I would compliment her on the dress she's wearing," she joked back, "but since it's a rarity that B even wears dresses, she might retort that her jeans were in the wash."

Just then I smelled something else other than dinner cooking and I think it was coming from Rachel. She smelled different, I mean she still smelled like Rachel of course, but her smell was slightly off. But I ignored my Werewolf instincts as I tried to carry on as normal.

"Hi guys." I laughed at my old friends' sense of humor.

"Maybe we could use reverse psychology on her?" Mandy continued to joke.

"B that's a terrible dress you're wearing, don't ever wear it again." Rachel pretended to say crossly.

"That's an even crappier red blouse you're wearing Rachel, don't ever wear that color again." I smirked.

"Mandy, why aren't you married yet?" She next hit up our old friend.

"Why are men throw backs from the dinosaur era?" Mandy replied.

Derik snickered at our typical banter as Aunt Susan smilingly shook her head.

"On that note, I better go check on the carbonara sauce." Aunt Susan brushed past on her way back to the kitchen. "Derik, can you see to Declan's and B's drinks?"

My best friend frowned again, but he quietly obeyed his mother's command as he followed her into the other room. I left Declan's side as I walked forwards to kiss Mandy and Rachel on their cheeks before I pulled Michael out of Rachel's arms for a hold.

"How's my favourite godson going?" I cooed as I tickled him.

"Be careful with the tickling." His mother warned. "He has an upset stomach at the moment and we don't want your hideous dress to look even more disgusting."

"Well then," I looked from her back to Declan, "if that happened, I would have to instantaneously phase back home to change now wouldn't I?"

"Don't even think about it!" He quickly walked forwards to hold his nephew instead.

"How's your head?" Mandy suddenly asked.

"My head?" I echoed.

"Er yeah, I heard you were shot in the head...?" She gave a funny look.

"Oh THAT!" I laughed it off. "It's fine, I'm fine and everything's fine."

"She died and had an OBE." Declan said unhappily.

"An OBE?" Rachel queried.

"Out of Body Experience." The school teacher clued her in.

"Oh," her eyes widened, "and what did you see, B?"

"I went to an 18th Century English Ball with a bunch of past life and future souls." I shrugged.

"As you do when you're dead." Mandy shrugged.

"I mean, that's what I want to do when I die; hang around a bunch of powdered stiffs tied up in corsets with wigs on top of their heads." She mused.

"Damn it, Rachel!" Mandy pretended to get annoyed. "That was MY idea!"

"Oh well, maybe you can still do that and end up with a European Werewolf afterwards." She patted her on the arm.

"What's the point in dying from a bullet to the head and going to an English Ball if you're not going to end up with a European Werewolf afterwards? It's just a pity they don't have any English Werewolves then it would really authenticate the experience." Mandy made us laugh as Declan rolled his eyes.

"Sorry ladies, there's just one of me to go around." He said dryly.

"I don't know if I'd want to go through the experience of getting shot in the head and going to a Ball because of it; if I can't end the excitement with a European Werewolf afterwards." Rachel mockingly shook her head.

Just as she said that, Derik had returned carrying our glasses of soda and he did NOT look amused by our subject one bit.

"Well, you ended up with the European Werewolf's brother. How's that for a trade off?" Mandy asked her.

"Yes, I suppose Derik will have to do." She took the drinks out of her husband's stiff hands to pass them on to Declan and I.

"Oh well, Derik is a doctor now. Maybe after dinner tonight you could put on a nurse's uniform and play 'doctors and nurses' with him?" I joked.

"I don't need to dress up to do that, thanks B." She giggled as her husband blushed.

"I'm not married, so maybe that where the confusion lies?" Mandy pretended to look puzzled. "But I always thought that the occasion would involve taking off clothes instead of putting clothes on."

"You may not be married Mandy, but you've got the right idea." Declan smirked.

"What have you been up to when you've been going on all these dates but you keep refusing the poor boys' marriage proposals?" I made a dig at her.

"In a word? Scrabble." She said simply. "I'm not kidding, they cook me dinner and I test their IQ over a game of Scrabble. If they can't spell correctly 'celibacy', they have to damn well live it out instead!"

We erupted into loud laughter and even little Michael giggled as he didn't want to feel left out. He was tucked into Declan's large arms safe and sound, as he periodically looked up at his supernaturally strong uncle with wide eyes.

"What was that?" Aunt Susan called out from the kitchen.

"Nothing Mom." Derik's response was automatic.

"We're not being treated to another one of Mandy's 'Single Life' philosophies, are we?" She asked knowingly.

"We're learning the importance of spelling." Declan promised.

"That's what I like to hear!" Their mother sung back.

*****

Dinner was served at 6.30 PM and we all sat down at the Sabre table to eat. We ate fettuccine carbonara with garlic bread and the food was so delicious, it could almost serve as an excuse for the quietness that settled over the family meal. On one side sat Derik and Rachel with Michael in his high chair between them; as on the other sat Declan and I. Then at either of the ends of the table were Aunt Susan and Mandy.

Derik passed many a look of death his brother's way, which my mate noted as he glared down at his plate and continued eating. I marveled at his stolid stomach as it appeared nothing could interrupt his eating pattern. But then I felt his free hand move to sit on top of my leg under the table. I tried to inconspicuously place my hand over his which Declan squeezed back appreciatively.

"So," Aunt Susan decided to break the uncomfortable silence, "Mandy and I were hoping to ask B something tonight."

I looked up from my plate in surprise with my mouthful of pasta.

"B, when you start your Masters in Ancient History, you'll be doing that via correspondence again won't you?" Mandy guessed.

"Er, yeah?" I swallowed.

"But it's not like you're going to be at home studying all day, every day though?" She continued.

"Probably not." I wondered where she was going with this.

"I showed Susan your papers on mythology and life in ancient times and she agreed." She declared.

"She did?" I looked from her to Aunt Susan.

"The kids really enjoyed the morning you came to school and taught them about the Greek Gods as they talked about it for weeks. Mandy and I were thinking that instead of borrowing your books or papers on the subject; what if you taught one morning a week?" My aunt announced.

"Teach? Me? Once a week?" I echoed in shock.

"It would just be for an hour on Friday mornings." She shrugged. "But when you showed those pictures that went along with your papers? The kids thought they were the best thing since sliced bread."

"Ancient History is your specialty." Mandy went on. "I think the kids and even their parents would appreciate it."

"I can vouch for that." Rachel looked on hopeful. "If we had a Circulator teaching Ancient History when Michael goes to school that would be awesome!"

"But – but – but I don't know if I have enough material to teach with." I said nervously.

"Go on, B." Declan gave a nudge. "What have you got to lose? I work at the Garage four to five days a week, it'd be nice to have another 'income' in the house."

"Hodge Endeavor pays for my education and for my living expenses." I said in annoyance. "When this tribe uses money in dealings with outsiders, the money usually comes from Hodge Endeavor thanks to Gran. I am in no way financially reliant on you Declan."

He dropped his fork loudly to glare my way, "that wasn't what I meant."

"No? But it sure sounded like it." Derik gave him another dirty look. When his brother seethed back at his interference, he went on, "who sat at this table six years ago and tried to tell me that I couldn't go to Cambridge because this family couldn't afford it? But Hodge Endeavor paid for my education as they paid me a living allowance while I was at Cambridge, just like they're doing for B."

"Oh that's right," Declan said sarcastically, "they paid for you because of who our great, great grand uncle was or something like it."

"Gran and Grandfather have a photo of Mike Sabre here on Lokoti land when he came to a tribal gathering once." I spoke up. "Mum met him when she was 13 years old or something."

"He must have been pretty old then." He remarked.

"In the photo he has the appearance of a man in his twenties." I coolly replied. "He's posing beside my Great, Great Gran who has the appearance of a girl in her late teens."

Declan looked on askance and even his fork hung in midair.

"Your Great, Great Gran looked like a teenaged girl?!" Mandy blanched before she looked in disbelief at Aunt Susan. "And B's 62 year old Gran still looks like a woman in her twenties!"

Rachel shook her head. "So when Declan starts to look elderly after 200 years, you're still going to look as you do right now?"

I shrugged as I returned to my eating whilst I tried not to blush.

"B," Aunt Susan pondered, "have you done much more time traveling as a Circulator?"

"Well." I finished my mouthful before talking again. "Every time I go to Mars, I travel through time because Circulate Headquarters is 250,000 years in the past, when Mars had vegetation and an oxygen atmosphere. But as to traveling around Earth, I've been to Athens in the Classical Age, Thebes during the New Kingdom and Babylon when Alexander the Great was alive. I usually travel when I need to do some extra research for an assignment."

"You cheat." Derik smilingly shook his head.

"I usually get a HD out of it." I giggled back.

"A HD?" Declan queried.

"A High Distinction is the highest mark you can receive at University. I only got one of those on a paper I handed in on red blood cells." He sighed.

"But you got a hell of a lot of Distinctions for your other work and Medicine is one of the hardest courses a person can do." Their mother looked on proudly.

"OK...!" Declan's eyebrows rose, before he looked my way again. "Look B, you're smart and you're financially independent so yeah, I get that. But what I meant to say is, I think you spend a little too much time alone, with your nose constantly in books or with those damned earphones on! I think this teaching job would be good to get you out of the house on a regular basis."

"I think teaching while you do your Masters and then your PhD would be excellent practice for the day you teach academically." Mandy pointed out.

"Hold on a minute here, first things first. Take small steps, baby steps of getting you out of the house and around tribal lands again. Then if you decide to teach at University one day," he flashed her a look of annoyance, "we'll consider our options if we have to move or whatever."

"Move?" Rachel echoed unhappily. "Mandy, don't tell my other best friend she has to move!"

"B's a Lokoti Werewolf so won't she wane if she moved away?" Derik frowned.

"Dad and Grandfather get antsy if they're away in England or Australia for more than a day, but I'm fine." I shrugged. "I think it's because I'm a Circulator as well."

Aunt Susan looked on her eldest concerned, "but what about Declan? There aren't many places in the world where he can change and hunt like he can here."

"Declan's a European Werewolf and there's still a lot of untouched forest in Russia." Mandy shrugged. "I'm sure that's what the other European Werewolves must be doing."

He cracked up laughing, "great! Then I can be with my 'own kind' as B teaches at a Russian University. Is there anything else you would like us to do while we're at it, Mandy?"

"Look, I'm just pointing out your options that's all." She rolled her eyes.

"Mandy, although I'm not thrilled about the idea my older brother is 'mated' to my ex-girlfriend?" Derik passed yet another glare, "I don't want to see them move either. B's still our friend and that lunk head sitting across is still my brother."

"Lunk head?" Declan smirked. "Who are you calling a 'lunk head' you pencil neck?"

"I'd rather be a 'pencil neck' than a lunk head that breaks everything he touches." He smirked back.

His older brother sat up straighter, "who helped Mom with most of the cooking? Who cooked half of your meals when you were growing up?"

"Declan, when you crush garlic you don't even use a garlic crusher like a normal person does!" Derik hit back.

"I didn't see you complain about my strength when you asked me to remove lids from jars for you. Or, what about the time when I walked up behind that kid you nearly got into a fight with? He took one look at me and ran for the hills!"

"I can fight my own battles!" He fired up.

"I don't break EVERYTHING I touch." My mate sulked. "I mean, B's still alive isn't she? It was MY blood that helped bring her back, wasn't it?"

"It's a good thing B was always as strong or as fast as a boy growing up." Mandy gave a wry grin.

"Also when her strength quadrupled the night she changed." Rachel agreed.

The European Werewolf taunted his human brother, "you probably only hung around B so if it wasn't me protecting your smartass, it was her."

"Remember the time you were given detention for punching Timothy when he was picking on us?" Mandy snickered my way.

"I remember Aunt Susan making me write a hundred lines, 'violence doesn't solve anything'." I looked sideways at the matriarch of this family.

"Well you learned your lesson as you didn't do it again, did you?" She tried not to laugh.

"You got detention from punching somebody?" My mate looked on impressed.

"Declan, don't encourage her!" Aunt Susan rolled her eyes. "Oh, I can see what a fine pair you will make as godparents to little Michael! Declan the boy who all the kids were afraid of and B as the girl who went around punching people!"

"Remember the time Declan chased down that older kid Daniel and he pushed him off Derik's bike?" Mandy giggled to Rachel who laughed along.

"The poor boy had a huge graze going all the way up his leg because you pushed him over whilst riding!" Aunt Susan said indignantly.

"Hey, he deserved it!" My mate retorted. "It was Derik's new bike that he was riding when he frickin' tried to steal it."

"Then you were meant to find me or another adult and tell them! Not chase the kid down and push him off the bike!" Their mother snapped.

"Well he learned his lesson as he didn't do it again, did he?" Declan repeated, to much laughter.

"And I hope so did you young man, when I put you on cleaning duty for the next month!" She glared on her eldest.

Her youngest snickered, "I helped Declan clean up that month to say thanks for getting my bike back."

"Derik!" Their mother exhorted. "That was Declan's lesson to be learned!"

"Yeah the lesson was not to get caught." My mate grinned mischievously, making his little brother laugh.

Our reminiscing and laughter seemed to seal the peace between the brothers, for when Derik looked at Declan now, it wasn't in anger.

"The school 'riff raff' who pushed people off bikes or punched people are now your godmother and godfather to your son?" Mandy joked to Rachel.

"I told you we were making the right decision in making two Werewolves as godparents for Michael. Nobody in school will ever bother him because of it!" She tittered to her husband who laughingly put his arm about her.

"Speaking of which..." he smiled tenderly on his wife, "...should we?"

"Since we're talking about kids and godparents, I think we should." She smiled back.

"You should what?" Aunt Susan looked on the pair.

"Rachel's pregnant." I blurted out.

Silence...although it wasn't the news that Rachel was pregnant that shocked people, but it was the fact that I knew about it.

Declan chortled as he proudly put his arm about his mate, "did you smell it as soon as you came into the house too?"

"Pretty much." I leaned into his side.

"You can smell that my wife is pregnant?" Derik looked on in surprise.

"Well we ARE Werewolves!" I laughingly rolled my eyes.

"Fern could smell I was pregnant." Rachel pointed out.

"Yeah, but he's the tribe's Medicine Man, he's supposed to pick up things like that. This is my brother we're talking about here. I feel more than a little uncomfortable with the fact that he can smell when my wife's pregnant!" Derik said indignantly.

"My best friend who is also a Werewolf can smell it." She shrugged.

Mandy asked curiously, "did you smell the first time Rachel was pregnant, B?"

"No, I didn't. Maybe I would have if I didn't have a lot on my mind that day. But as Declan is so fond of pointing out, sometimes I can't see outside of my own problems." I said flatly.

This made him frown as he remembered why I was upset when he next rubbed the back of my neck sympathetically.

"So I'm going to be a grandmother again?" Aunt Susan asked brightly. "How far along are you? Do you know if it's a boy or a girl yet?"

"It's a girl." Declan stated.

Everyone looked on in surprise again, everyone but me that is.

"You can smell THAT too?" Derik asked in further shock.

"Can you?" My mate looked my way.

"Yep." I gave a small smile as he continued to rub my neck.

"OK then." Aunt Susan looked from the two Werewolves to the human couple in question. "Let's test how good B and Declan are. How far along is Rachel?"

"Six weeks." Declan answered.

"Six weeks, five days, twelve hours and thirty minutes." I said next.

My mate looked on in disbelief, "yeah right! There is no way you can sniff that out!"

"I cheated, I just saw Blanche's timeline using my vision as a Circulator." I giggled.

"Aw what?!" He tickled me. "No fair! I demand a rematch!"

"You cheat!" Derik laughed as he picked up a slice of garlic bread to throw playfully at my head.

"Wait a minute!" Aunt Susan called for silence. "Everybody hold up for a moment please... B, what did you call their little girl?"

Oh oh, my eyes widened as I realized the monumental mistake I made.

"Um I forgot." I tried to lie.

"She called her Blanche." Mandy remembered.

"Blanche?" Rachel echoed in surprise. "That was my Granny's name."

"I know." I said.

"Blanche?" Derik looked on his wife as he played with the sound of it. "That's not a bad name actually. Michael and Blanche...?"

"So can you 'see' how many more kids Derik and Rachel have, B?" Mandy asked in fascination.

When I thought this should be safe to answer, I told the table; "Blanche is the youngest."

Derik and Rachel exchanged a knowing grin, I guess from a similar discussion.

Aunt Susan looked on askance, "B do you know everybody's future?"

"No." I quickly shook my head.

"How do you 'see'?" Rachel wondered. "Do you have visions when you're awake or asleep?"

"Pretty much both." I shrugged as I picked up the piece of garlic bread.

"OK, then tell me something." Mandy looked on with a deadly serious expression on her face.

"This isn't a question about if you're going to die soon, is it?" Declan frowned as he replaced his arm about my shoulders. "Trust me, we're over that topic."

"Shut up Sabre, this is very important and I HAVE to know!" She snapped before she asked earnestly, "tell me B, do you see in my future any hot women who look like Angelina Jolie, or even with the intelligence or charm of Elizabeth Bennett?"

Nearly everyone's eyes popped out of their heads at her words, everyone's but Rachel's and mine.

"Er no, sorry Mandy." I smiled apologetically. "I can see a couple of relationships in your future but no Angelina Jolie look-a-likes."

"You're GAY?!" Declan gaped.

"I'm bisexual!" She corrected. "If I were gay, I wouldn't have liked you once in a passing craze, would I?"

He laughed out his surprise as our other friends exchanged small smiles.

"It would explain why she can't commit to one guy." Derik shrugged.

"No, I can't commit to one guy because all the guys around here are useless!" She huffed. "I go on a date which starts out as a bit of fun, then the male starts telling me how many kids they want! Er, I'm around kids all day at school, you think I want to come home to more?!"

Aunt Susan laughed the loudest on this wisecrack, which made her sons exchange worried looks.

"Not ALL guys are useless..." I thought on her words, "...just the ones that happen to have testosterone inside them."

"What?!" Declan turned around to tickle me again.

When my mate pulled me into his arms to playfully bite my neck whilst growling, he accidentally frightened little Michael. The two year old blanched upon the sight of his big, strong uncle 'maul' his aunt and he even started to cry.

"Do you mind not scaring my kids?" His father shook his head as he picked up his son to soothe.

"Well, we have Werewolves as godparents for Michael and now we have a bisexual school teacher as our godmother for Blanche. This is a pretty productive evening so far." Rachel giggled to her husband.

"Productive for you maybe, but I don't score with any good looking Angelina Jolie types." Mandy rolled her eyes.

"I'm going to have a grandson and a granddaughter." My aunt beamed.

"And I'm married to another school bully." Declan smiled softly my way.

"To bring our conversation back to our original subject," Mandy clapped her hands together, "B are you going to be our Ancient History teacher or what?"

I looked from her to Aunt Susan before I smilingly shrugged, "if you want a former troublemaker teaching the impressionable, young minds of this tribe? Yeah sure, why not."

"Don't worry B, we'll keep you in line." My aunt smirked. "I had 27 years of practice on Declan, didn't I?"

"Yeah, my brother could tempt St. Theresa into picking up a gun that was loaded with silver bullets and aim it his way!" Derik snorted.

"Hey!" He objected. "If some kid tries to steal your bike again, I'm just going to sit back and let him!"

*****

After we finished eating the pasta, the matriarch of the family surprised us by bringing out tiramisu for dessert. This earned a round of applause as well as enthusiastic cheering from the table.

"OH YUM!" Rachel, Mandy and I cheered. "Thanks Aunt Susan!"

"Go Mom!" Derik and Declan clapped and whooped.

She jokingly took a bow before returning to her seat. But the fanfare got Michael intrigued, as he wondered for what all the fuss was about? His little head turned as he watched with wide eyes as the slices of tiramisu were handed around. Once Rachel's bowl sat in front of her, he excitedly kicked his legs as he looked eagerly at his mother's piece.

"Look at the kid go!" My mate laughed. "He knows the good stuff alright."

"This kid takes after his Uncle by how excited he gets around food." Derik jested.

"The kid's no idiot, he knows what's good for him." Declan winked at the toddler whom giggled back.

I smilingly sat back to watch Derik and Rachel together and how they were as parents. They both took turns sharing their pieces of tiramisu with little Michael, as they individually fed him tiny bits from their spoons. They looked like a proper family unit, as they also took turns to wipe their youngster's face.

Just then I felt Declan's hot hand squeeze my thigh under the table. I looked back to see he had noticed what I was watching. He gave a wink as he continued to squeeze my leg whilst he finished up dessert. With his European Werewolf appetite he was the first to finish with my Lokoti Werewolf appetite coming in a close second. As we put down our spoons, we saw that everyone else were only half way through! They cracked up laughing at the two Werewolves at the table.

"Declan, I think you may have met your match," Aunt Susan smiled wryly, "a life partner who can keep up with your appetite."

"Trust me Mom, B's tame when it comes to my ferocious stomach." He sat back to boast.

"He's right." I agreed with my mate. "When Declan makes us sandwiches for lunch, he makes me two and himself six."

"Six?!" Mandy blinked. "You eat six sandwiches?"

"That sounds familiar." His mother grinned in good humor.

"Growing up, I used to be woken up during the night by this one's abnormal nocturnal habits." My best friend nodded at the European Werewolf for his older brother. "He would be constantly sneaking into the kitchen to steal food from the fridge. When Mom would ask the next day where had the leftovers had disappeared to? A couple of times Declan tried to make out it was ME who ate them!"

Rachel laughed the loudest over that one, "is that why you got so defensive yesterday when I asked you what happened to the cold meat in the fridge?"

"It wasn't me!" He cried out.

"If it wasn't Derik and it wasn't Rachel, then who was it?" Mandy snickered.

For some reason all eyes but mine, turned towards Declan.

"Aw, come off it!" He objected as he looked to his little brother, "dude, I did NOT leave my house on top of the hill, to sneak into yours to raid your fridge!"

My heart warmed at how he called my house his, as I squeezed his hand once more.

"B," Mandy looked my way, "has Declan had any unexplained absences during the night?"

All eyes at the table now turned in my direction.

"Nope, he's out like a light." I answered. "He's a deep sleeper."

For some reason this statement stunned his mother and brother.

"Declan's a deep sleeper?" Derik reiterated in disbelief.

"Er, yeah?" I wondered what all the fuss was about.

They exchanged shocked expressions which they turned on Declan.

"This is new for you." His little brother said skeptically.

"Yeah well I'm a married man now, whose wife is another Werewolf." The older brother shrugged. "I'm a lot more tired these days."

Mandy and Rachel instantly snickered at his words.

"I see." Derik cleared his throat.

"What's going on?" I looked around inquiringly. "What's the big deal about Declan's sleeping habits?"

"He used to be a light sleeper." His mother informed. "Perhaps it's because European Werewolves are meant to hunt at night? But he would sleep no more than four hours before he'd get up. Derik and I would be woken in the wee hours of the morning by Declan tidying the house or his room or when he organized his books, CD or DVD collections. It was also this time when he read the most. Sometimes at 2 AM he would cook up meals for the next day or even for the entire week."

Now it was my turn to look on my mate in surprise, "even when it wasn't a full moon you were restless?"

"Yeah well like I said, thing's have changed. I sleep the whole night through now." He said dismissively.

"B, how about Declan hunting once a week, do you join him for those?" Derik wondered. "Or do you only hunt with the pack?"

"What hunting once a week?" I looked from younger to older brother. "It's a full moon next week so I guess we'll be hunting with the pack then."

"You haven't gone hunting by yourself?" Aunt Susan looked on her eldest in further surprise.

"Er no, I haven't needed to." He busied himself by sweeping up the crumbs into his hand which he emptied into his bowl.

"Say what?" Derik stared. "When was the last time that you hunted without the pack, Declan?"

"What is this, a frickin' inquisition?!" He asked defensively. "Since B and I started seeing each other, I haven't needed to hunt when it's not a full moon and I sleep the night through. That's the current affairs done with, do you wanna check the 'weather channel' now?"

Everyone wore these amused expressions on their faces as they nodded diplomatically. I felt my face heat up as embarrassedly, I snuck a sideways glace at my mate whose face was looking just as flushed.

"You've always slept fine from what I've seen." I said awkwardly.

"So is there anymore tiramisu?" Declan changed the subject by looking into the empty dessert dish before looking inquiringly at his mother.

"No, that was it." She answered.

"OK then, I'll start on the dishes." He quickly stood up as he began to round up the plates and cutlery.

"I'll help." I jumped up to follow him out of the room.

*****

Declan washed up as Mandy and I dried and put away. With so much of our childhoods spent inside this house, we certainly knew where everything went. Once the dishes were finished, we returned to the lounge room with coffees for everyone.

As we sipped on our beverages, I shared a couch with Declan as Aunt Susan and Rachel sat on another. I snuggled into his side for warmth as we smilingly watched. His mother was holding her grandson in her lap whilst reading to him a story from a book of Fairy Tales. Derik helped by kneeling beside on the floor and pointing out the different pictures to his little boy. As this was happening, Mandy sat on the arm rest beside Rachel as the two looked on.

My best friend was a wonderful father as he was patient, attentive and generous, just like his mother was. As Aunt Susan read to her grandson, Derik put in the sound effects which kept his young amused. She finished reading out 'Hansel & Grettel' before she started on 'Little Red Riding Hood'.

"Here we go," Declan complained, "the wolf is made out to be the baddie."

"Well the wolf DID eat Grandma as it tried to eat Little Red." Derik pointed out.

"In THAT story sure, but as Michael grows up safe and sound on tribal lands, it's partly thanks to wolves." He retorted.

"How are wolves helping Michael grow up safe and sound on tribal lands?" Derik gave a funny look.

My mate immediately looked to me to fill him in as the whole room waited.

"The Lokoti Wolf shared his blood as his spirit merged with the dying warrior Aru, which created the first Lokoti Werewolf." I recited.

"Aaahhh...!" Everyone nodded as they remembered the story of old.

"Oh dear." Aunt Susan paused as she looked down on her grandson. "Michael, I don't think it's a good idea that I read you a story that has negative propaganda about wolves, as we're offending your Aunt and Uncle. How about 'Snow White' instead?"

Hang on a sec, did she just call us, 'your Aunt and Uncle' like we were married? Does Aunt Susan see us as husband and wife? Declan did call himself a married man at the table. Whether we had a Joining Ceremony/ Housewarming or not, I guess it was how the Sabre family saw it.

*****

The evening ended around 10 PM when Derik and Rachel with a sleepy one year old were the first to call it quits.

"Can I get a lift home with you guys?" Mandy asked the parents as they headed out.

"Sure." She readily agreed.

Declan and I stood by the front door with Aunt Susan, as we saw them off.

"Let me give my grandson one last kiss goodnight." His grandmother bent her head over the toddler's drooping one, whilst his father held onto him securely.

"G'night Mom, thanks for an awesome dinner." Derik smiled warmly.

"I'll see you at work on Monday." Mandy kissed her cheek before she threw me a wave on her way out the door. "B, I'll come over during the week to talk more about your classes."

"Cool." I waved back.

"G'night B and Declan." Rachel gave a cheeky smile on her exit. "Happy 'deep sleeping' tonight."

"If you prefer, I'll come by your house tonight at 2 AM and clean it for you?" He joked back.

"Just as long as you don't clean out our fridge too." Derik shook his head.

"Get lost you little pipsqueak, you can't use my constant hunger as your alibi anymore." He scoffed.

"Oh you two!" Their mother rolled her eyes at their brotherly banter. "You're both married and starting families of your own and you still carry on like this?"

"Yep." Declan chuckled.

"Always Mom, that's something time cannot change." Derik said as he and his older brother broke into cheeky grins. Then he gently raised his son's little hand to wave as he put on a fake toddler's voice; "g'night Aunt B."

"G'night godson." I planted a kiss on Michael's forehead before I placed another on his father's cheek, "g'night best friend."

"Don't you mean, 'g'night nephew'?" He smilingly corrected. "Because you had the poor taste to shack up with my older brother, you're like Michael's aunt or somethin'."

Oh wow, I hadn't considered that before. My eyebrows arose in surprise as my mate put a possessive arm about my shoulders.

"Poor taste?" He refuted. "Don't you mean that like a fine wine, B's taste improved with age?"

"Yeah keep telling yourself that Declan." My best friend rolled his eyes as he departed via the front door.

"Drive safely." Aunt Susan waved him off.

We watched him carefully place his sleeping son in the child safety seat in the back where Mandy was sitting. Next, he climbed into the passenger's seat as Rachel was in the driver's. We all exchanged one last wave as she started the engine and then we watched them reverse out before driving away.

"Well," my mate turned to his mother, "nobody died of food poisoning so I guess it was a successful evening."

"He always says that at the end of an evening's entertainment." Aunt Susan's eyes sparkled with affection.

"How about I wash up the coffee mugs and then B and I might have to head off home as well." Declan told her.

"No." She said.

"No?" He echoed in surprise.

"I am quite capable of washing up a couple of coffee mugs." She told her eldest. "You can take B home right now."

"Are you sure?" He offered. "It won't take me long -"

"Declan go home." She ordered.

Then I caught the long look which passed between mother and son who had been each other's company for the last 27 years. Aunt Susan never remarried after the death of her husband and I'm not sure if she ever dated? But Declan had assumed the role of 'man of the house' from an early age as he helped his mother raise Derik as well as with the cooking and the cleaning.

She reached out her hand to lovingly caress her eldest's cheek as he caught it to hold in his larger one. She smiled softly, "go home my son. At last it's your turn to be with a family of your own."

"OK." He left his mother with a parting kiss on the forehead.

He took hold of my hand and led me out of the house towards his truck. Aunt Susan stood in the doorway to watch her son unlock the passenger's door first to open it for me, before he closed it once I was inside. Declan threw her a wave as he walked around to the driver's seat and then he climbed in. He started the ignition as he pulled on his seat belt. We waved again as we reversed out before she closed her front door.

We drove home in a comfortable silence as it felt right that I was going home with him in his old truck that chugged loudly up the steep hill. It reminded me of another occasion when he drove me home, the night Uncle Jack died. I guess Declan was thinking the same thing, as I felt his hand rest over mine. Our fingers entwined very similar to the way he held my hand way back when. He didn't look my way but he kept his eyes on the road ahead.

Declan expertly drove with one hand on the wheel, as his grip on my hand was iron-clad. He didn't even let go, when he pulled into the driveway and he turned off the engine. Still holding my hand, he walked us up the veranda steps and to the front door which he automatically opened with his keys in hand. Then he led us inside whilst swinging the door shut on our way through.

The house wasn't dark since I had left the kitchen light on. I guess I got the habit from my parents, as they always left the kitchen light on when we went out of an evening. Funnily enough, a lot of our evenings were spent at the Sabre house or with the Sabre's at Gran and Grandfather's. In the middle of our living room, Declan turned around to pull me into his arms.

"We're home Mrs. Sabre." He smiled.

"Mrs. Sabre?"

"Frickin' hell, now what?" He was quick to roll his eyes in annoyance. "Not only do I get the screwball of the tribe who wants to try long-distance mating but long-distance marriage as well?"

"Very funny."

"Yes MRS. DECLAN SABRE." He deliberately said the words slowly. "You see B, there's a social status that the Lokoti as well as outsiders call marriage. It's where a male and female shack-up in an arrangement that's supposed to be for life, perhaps you've heard of it?"

"Real amusing." I folded my arms in front.

"Mrs. B-i-a-n-c-a S-a-b-r-e," he spelt out, "would you like me to write it down for you?"

"Declan, frickin' shut up!"

I lost patience with his sarcastic attitude when I grabbed hold of his shirt to kiss the life out of him! It effectively shut him up for a good minute or so.

"Mmmm..." he happily held me close, "...whenever I want a kiss, now I know what to do. I'll just make you lose your temper."

"If you want me to scratch and bite too." I breathed in his maple syrup scent as I hungrily began to maul his neck with my mouth.

"Oh yeah that's definitely what I'll do then!" He laughed out loud before his mouth reclaimed mine.

Slowly he lifted me up so my feet were no longer touching the floor. With his assistance, I hoisted up my dress so I could wrap my legs about his waist. Then like this, he carried me up the stairs.

~~~~~~
~~~~~~

~ 23 ~

30th August 2090

After breakfast, I went outside to work in the greenhouse. I wanted to check on my previous crops as well as water the new vegetables and herbs Declan had planted. I was harvesting some ripe radishes, lettuce and cucumber when my new mate found me.

"I'm going down to the store. Aside from a few odds and ends, I'll get some stuff to make spaghetti bolognaise for dinner. You want anything?" He offered.

"Um yeah, I think we need some more milk." I said but then he held up the shopping list in his hand and I saw that milk was already on it. I squinted as I quickly read the list. When I noticed there was something missing I asked, "oh can you get some more choc-chip cookies?"

"Choc-chip cookies?" He arched his eyebrows.

"Yeah, I like to eat something sweet after dinner." I shrugged. "If they don't have any cookies, then get some cake."

"Cake, what kind of cake?"

"Chocolate."

"And if they don't have chocolate cake?"

"Um…" I thought for a moment, "…I don't know, then get something else that's sweet. Oh, but don't get fruit cake."

"No fruit cake?"

"I hate fruit cake!" I scrunched up my face in distaste.

"That's right, you don't like plum pudding or hot cross buns or raisin toast either." I raised my eyebrows, impressed how he remembered that when he rolled his eyes, "well I DID grow up with you and I saw how finicky you were at the dinner table."

"Oh and Declan, sometimes Mandy's Mum trades in home-made ice cream, so see if there's any. If there is, get some chocolate ice cream. If there's no chocolate, then get the vanilla. Don't get strawberry though, I don't like it. Mandy's Mum puts actual strawberries in so there are seeds through it. Eugh!"

"Look," he lost his patience, "just come and pick what you want yourself!"

My stomach sank…we had been living together for just over a week which meant it had been nine days since I was shot and the tribe found out about us. If I went to the Store with Declan now, it might be too soon for us to be seen together.

"What?" He gave a funny look, but then he must have guessed my thoughts. "Come on B, we can't hide up here forever."

I sighed as I reluctantly pulled my gardening gloves off. I threw Declan an unhappy look as if he were asking for a lot, which he returned with a typical glare. He held the door open for me as I left the greenhouse with him...

...

... then he opened the door for the store for me and walked in behind. Old Mr. Barley turned away from serving to stare in surprise. Old Mrs. Huntington also turned to look on the sight of us shopping together.

They're actually staring at us? My heart raced as I felt my face burn. Declan ignored them as he picked up a plastic shopping basket by the door to carry for us.

"Here." He handed me the list. Then he walked over and grabbed a loaf of bread before he moved on to grab a two litre bottle of milk from the fridge.

A couple of people in the same aisle as us, also stared as we passed by. Again he pretended he didn't see them, but I felt him briefly squeeze my hand supportively. I tried to breathe normally as I kept my eyes peeled to the list.

"Ketchup?" I read next when I gave him a funny look. "You're using ketchup in the bolognaise?"

"The recipe calls for tomato paste, but the store never stocks any so Mom had to improvise." He shrugged as he grabbed a bottle to put into the basket.

"I like your Mum's spaghetti bolognaise." I frowned. "But I don't like ketchup."

"Yes B, you've actually been eating ketchup all the years you ate spaghetti bolognaise at our house." He chuckled at the expression on my face.

"Are you for real?" I looked on in surprise.

"When it's cooked with the garlic and the other herbs, you don't notice it do you?" He pointed out.

"Oh." I shrugged as I saw his point. "I guess not."

"I have to make the spaghetti tonight so the pasta will be ready when I make the bolognaise tomorrow." He organized as he grabbed a bottle of olive oil from the shelf. "I'll teach you, it's pretty easy."

"Do I have to?" I whined. "Can't I just watch or something?"

"Fine." Declan rolled his eyes again. "I'll teach you while you watch."

"I don't like to cook." I grumbled as I watched him examine the packets of dried herbs.

"That's because you're lazy."

"I am not!" I whacked him on the arm which made him laugh. "I just don't like to cook."

"Whatever." He chuckled whilst shaking his head. "Then I'll do most of the cooking and you can do most of the cleaning."

"Fine." I agreed. "But it's still your turn to wash up coz you lost the bet."

"Yeah well..." he snuck a small smile my way, "...it was worth it."

I ducked my head to hide my blush but as I did so, I managed to pass him a small smile back.

"Hey, is oregano on the list?" He returned to the task at hand.

"Um, no."

"I don't think I saw any in the pantry so I'd better get some. The crop I planted won't be ready for weeks." He thought out loud as he pulled a bottle of the dried herb from the shelf.

Suddenly we were interrupted by a loud voice; "you two should be ashamed of yourselves!"

Declan and I quickly turned to see Hannah standing at the end of the aisle glaring tearfully. Oh shit this just had to happen, didn't it? We were haunted not by Grant but by his family.

"Is it true?" She demanded. "That you two are actually living together now?"

My mouth turned dry as I didn't know what to say to her, or how to appease her pain.

"You've moved in on my little brother's widow?" Hannah yelled at Declan. "You've moved into my little brother's house?"

My mate didn't answer as instead his eyes narrowed into a glare.

This infuriated Hannah all the more, "you're living in my brother's house with the furniture that Grant and B got when they married? Tell me Declan, do you like her curtains? My sister, mother and I made those curtains for their Housewarming. Then you just swoop in and move into the home that the whole tribe helped Grant create for B!"

I saw how Declan tensed up as he restrained himself to keep quiet.

"I should have expected something as such from a non-Lokoti Werewolf, Declan! Your breed has no honor!" She spat out, before she seethed at me. "And you B, you ARE Lokoti Werewolf! So what's your excuse?"

The European Werewolf came to stand protectively in front to take the brunt of her fury, which further angered her.

"Look at you two! Grant's gone for barely a year and you take ANOTHER mate, just like that? Where's your respect for my brother who DIED protecting his land and family!" She shouted tearfully.

My eyes stung as I quickly blinked so I wouldn't cry in public and make this scene any worse.

"Grant wasn't dead for twelve months before you two secretly started to see each other!" She ranted. "There are even rumors that the two of you were secretly seeing each other while my brother was alive!"

That was the last straw for Declan, as he couldn't take anymore of this.

"That's a crock of shit and you know it, Hannah!" He shouted back. "B was a loyal wife to your brother! Which is more than fair considering how she was forced upon him with a frickin' arranged marriage!"

"But she doesn't make him a loyal widow, does she?!" Hannah retorted. "Nor does it make you loyal to the pack either, Declan! The pack helped raise you! Grant was your brother in arms! Hell, B was involved with your actual brother Derik, wasn't she? What does he think of you two?!"

"Get a life lady and mind your own frickin' business!" He growled warningly. "My family supports the idea of B and I together, including my little brother who's happily married with a wife and kids of his own!"

"Yes, well." She scoffed. "At least that's something isn't it, that B can't have kids? I bet you wouldn't be so interested if she had given Grant children! You wouldn't be so eager to move in and play house then, would you Declan?"

"HEY!" He roared, startling her when his eyes glowed green. "That's a low blow and you know it!"

I quickly grabbed hold of my mate's arm as I was scared he was about to change in anger! Then that would really make people stare with a huge, hulking, hairless European Werewolf growling in the aisles of a grocery store.

"Declan no, let's go home." I pleaded. "Let's just go home, please? Declan, please take me home."

He grabbed hold of my hand to storm past Hannah with everybody watching our departure. He dumped our shopping basket on the counter in front of Mr. Barley and loudly opened the door to pull me towards his truck. I climbed in beside him as I tearfully stared out the window. He started the engine and drove us away from the community centre.

In the privacy of the truck I allowed my tears to escape, but I kept my face turned so Declan wouldn't see. Neither of us said a word as we drove up the hill and then he pulled into our driveway. He turned off the ignition as he let out a low growl.

My face was bright red. I felt mortified as I was truly and utterly humiliated. My face felt so hot that even my tears were hot too. Hannah was Grant's older sister, so she did have a right to say those things. I sat as still as a statue whilst I stared out my window.

"B, you haven't done anything wrong, you know that don't you?" He finally spoke but I remained quiet. He barked out his annoyance, "you mourned Grant for ten months, in the outside world that's the appropriate time to mourn. Forget about these stupid Lokoti customs. They're just small town folk with nothing better to do than to gossip and poke their noses into other peoples' business!"

I couldn't speak as I kept my face turned away. I trembled as my hot tears soaked my skin. I felt like I had been degraded before the whole tribe...

"Screw this!" Declan snarled. "I'm sick of these hypocritical double standards! At first they didn't trust me so they pushed you onto Grant. I waited five frickin' years for you! Now that we're finally together, there's no way in the hell I'm going to let them make my wife feel bad for being married to me!"

With that, he hopped out of his truck, slammed his door shut and then he marched around to open my door and pull me out.

"We're packing!" He looked on with fury in his eyes.

"Packing...?"

The enraged European Werewolf in human form, pulled me up the veranda steps to the front door which he opened and then he ushered us inside. Holding onto my hand so tightly he almost crushed it, he pulled me upstairs.

"Right." He walked us into the bedroom. "I think I once saw a suitcase under your bed?"

Declan knelt on the floor beside and pulled out two suitcases which he tossed them open on top of the mattress.

He was SERIOUS? I asked numbly, "but where are we going to move to?"

"Canada!" He declared as he opened his draws in the tallboy first. "I've heard there's still some unpolluted land in the Northwest Territories. There we should be safe away from fall out or marauders."

"But where are we going to live?"

"I'll build a log cabin." He shrugged. "With your help and our Werewolf strength, it won't take us long."

I suddenly felt lost at the idea of leaving this hill I grew up on, with its woods and the river, along with my parents and my grandparents living nearby. What if this was what I had to do? Maybe this was my punishment for mating a second time.

"We'll pack food and tools." He went on. "We'll be fine!"

I leaned against the bedroom door as I slowly slid to the floor. Declan paused in the middle of packing when he saw me sitting there, staring tearfully at the wall. He came over to crouch before me to cup my face in his larger hands as he made me look into his eyes.

"B, you're my mate." He said seriously. "I'm not going to let anyone put you down because of it."

I cried harder as I looked on frightened, "I don't know how to build a log cabin."

Declan gently banged his forehead against mine, "actually, neither do I."

We both let out a rueful laugh, as I put my trembling hands over his stronger ones.

"I'm a Circulator." I tried to give to give a brave smile through the tears. "We could always go back in time before the War and that way we could live anywhere we like."

This made him smile lovingly, "you see? It won't be so bad."

"But I guess it would still have to be somewhere with woods for us to hunt and change in privacy." I took a deep breath.

"There's plenty of woods to try in Canada before the War." He grinned encouragingly.

"We could move to the 19th Century." I continued. "Then we wouldn't have to worry about the nuclear war for 300 years, which is your life span."

"Canada was out of the way during World War One and World War Two so we should be safe." He agreed. "You see B? We'll be OK as we set up for ourselves. It'll be just you and me, away from everybody else."

"But even if we live in the 19th Century; just because women did all the cooking and cleaning back then, I still don't want to cook." I frowned.

"I'll make a deal with you, I'll do all of the cooking and you do all of the cleaning?" He held out his hand and I shook on it. Then he stood up as he pulled me to my feet, "now that we have that settled, let's pack."

I looked on the suitcases as I frowned thoughtfully, "if we're going to move to the 19th Century then we can't take 21st Century clothing with us."

"We can't?" He realized. "Oh yeah."

"Let's just pack sentimental things, like photos or keepsakes that we can hide under the bed and pull out to look at now and then." I thought up.

"OK." He put his clothes back into the draws and grabbed his old family photo from the tall boy instead.

"Plus we'll only take one suitcase." I continued to think.

"OK." He nodded in agreement. "One will be easier to hide than two."

I grabbed my MP3 player from the bedside table as I gave a helpless look, "but we're going to need 'Pearl Jam' and our other favourite bands to listen to, because music back then really sucked."

Declan laughed out loud as he waved his hand towards the suitcase, "throw it in."

I did so before I found my small portable speakers as well as my earphones and I packed these as well.

*****

We packed slowly as we went through our personal keepsakes whilst we carefully deliberated on what to bring. An hour passed as our one suitcase eventually filled up with photos, my MP3 player, my laptop, a watch Declan told me used to belong to his father or even his mother's recipe book she made for us.

"So how are we going to do this?" He asked as we worked. "Just pop into Canada in the 19th Century and live there?"

"I was thinking that we could live at Circulate Headquarters while we prepare." I thought out loud. "This way we'll have food and shelter while we buy a house and land, along with furniture and everything. Plus at Circulate Headquarters there's the 'Props Room' where we can find some clothes for the era."

"It sounds like a plan." He nodded as he sorted through his belongings.

Just then we heard the familiar sound of my grandparent's truck pulling into our driveway. We paused in our packing to share a surprised look, when we heard the sound of two more vehicles pull up. At the same time, we both headed over to the window to look out and see what was going on.

We saw Gran and Grandfather get out of their truck and each grab a bag full of groceries from the back. We saw Mum and Dad also get out of theirs. Then to our surprise, we watched Ian climb out of his vehicle. All five people next headed for our veranda to knock on the front door.

"Oh oh." My stomach sank as I passed Declan a worried look. "What's the bet this is about what happened in the store?"

He growled under his breath as he pulled his shoulders back and his eyes narrowed. He marched out of the bedroom and headed downstairs as if he was readying for battle. I sighed as I reluctantly followed after, whilst I mentally prepared myself for another emotional beating.

As I slowly traipsed down the stairs Gran, Grandfather, Mum, Dad and Ian were coming into the house as my mate held open the front door.

"Hi Sweetie." Mum beamed. But she instantly stopped smiling when she saw the look on my face. "Oh oh."

"My word B, you look pale." Gran stopped short as she too stared.

My mate came to stand at the bottom of the stairs after closing the front door. I stopped beside to take hold of his hand. Next, we watched my Grandfather take the bag of groceries from my Gran to carry it into the kitchen where he had put his.

"Mr. Barley said these were the things in your shopping basket when you suddenly left the store." He said congenially, as he came to stand beside Gran.

Declan's hand squeezed mine as he looked from Grandfather to Dad and then at Ian. I moved closer, to show not only my allegiance to my new mate but I guess I was also hoping to absorb some of his strength. He was fearless as he squared off against my family. I sensed his European Werewolf temper was still burning and he would fight tooth and claw the whole tribe if he had to.

"Thanks but I don't think we'll be needing it anymore." He said coolly.

"Why?" Dad asked warily.

"Because we're leaving town today." He declared.

"You're leaving?" Mum cried out as her eyes instantly widened.

"And where are you going to live?" Grandfather asked calmly.

"Canada in the 1800's." He stated. "Well away from this time and place."

Grandfather exchanged a long look with Dad and Ian, before the three Lokoti Werewolves turned back our way.

"Look Declan, we heard what happened at the store today -" Dad began.

"Oh yeah? You and the whole tribe unsurprisingly!" He quipped.

Ian stepped forwards, "Hannah shouldn't have said what she did."

"No..." I swallowed hard, "...she's entitled to feel angry."

"B." My new mate was quick to frown.

"I let your family down," I spoke to Ian, "and for that I'm truly sorry. Grant was a good husband and a good man."

"B." He said softly. "Please don't."

"But so is Declan," I continued, "and he didn't just 'swoop in' like a vulture nor is he stealing Grant's 'nest'. So we're leaving to start a new life together."

"How about you both start a new life here?" Gran asked brightly.

"How?" I retorted. "The tribe doesn't know the truth about us, but they're still willing to judge. No Gran, we're leaving."

"But you won't like the 19th Century!" Mum tried to discourage. "Sure it's fun to visit once in a while, but to live? Do you know what women living in that era had to endure? It's not just corsets which can choke you, but you can't have a career, you can't vote and..." she dropped her voice, "...every time your monthly blues comes along? There are no proper pads or decent painkillers!"

Dad and Grandfather quickly ducked their heads to snicker at her way of coaxing us not to leave.

"Yep, those are important reasons why not to leave home, Jess." Ian laughingly shook his head.

"If that happens Mum, I'll phase to Circulate Headquarters and use the supplies in the Medical Lab." I said calmly.

Then to Declan's and my surprise, Ian walked over to the front door to open it and wave somebody in. We heard somebody else climb out of his truck when next Hannah walked in our front door.

"With the death of our father, I became the head of the Elm family." He said seriously. "When I make a decision, my family is supposed to fall in line behind me. I made the decision to acknowledge you two as mates, so my family should respect this decision."

He glared demandingly at his younger sister, who now looked as embarrassed as I had an hour ago. I even felt sorry for her by being made to do this.

"I'm sorry for what I said in the store today." She managed out with a red face whilst staring at the floor.

However, her apology or her embarrassed state didn't make Declan feel better.

"No deal." He fumed. "We're still leaving."

This made Hannah look up in surprise as Declan glared from her to Ian. He passed his furious look to Dad and then my Grandfather, before he spoke.

"Hannah has a right to her opinion, although she didn't have to scream it out like that." He seethed before he looked at Ian again. "Your brother got to marry the girl that I loved. The pack decided that I wasn't good enough for Emanuel Riverclaw's granddaughter and Hunter Wisetail's only child. I was trained by the pack not to hunt human and our family was accepted because Aunt Arabella knew my Great, Great Grand Uncle. But I have always been made to feel different, like an outsider."

The male Lokoti Werewolves frowned but they remained respectfully quiet as they listened.

Declan went on, "you guys told me that I'd never be able to take a mate because it could harm a human woman. But when a female Lokoti Werewolf was created, somebody whom I already had feelings for? You pushed her onto Grant! You knowingly ostracized me by forcing me to remain alone!"

Grandfather looked on guiltily as I saw that he felt truly sorry over what the European Werewolf ranted about.

"Uncle Em, I respected you." He said hurt as he looked on. "You, who gave your blood to save my life, because you called us family. You, who worked with me the hardest, spending night after night training me to control the bloodlust. But then you won't even consider me for your granddaughter? That's hypocritical hogwash! How can you call me family but you don't see me as good enough to marry your own?!"

"No." Dad suddenly spoke up. "It's not Em's fault. If you're going to start throwing around the blame why you weren't considered to become B's mate? Then you can put all the blame on me, Declan."

"I know the role you played, Hunter." He said hatefully. "You always liked Derik better than me. You treated us differently from the moment my little brother was born."

"That's because Derik didn't have the bloodlust of a European Werewolf." My father put his hands on his hips as he met my mate's angry gaze with his own. "I felt you nearly lose control through out your childhood and right up into your adult life. Of course I didn't want to risk B with that! How could you help her control the bloodlust when you were still struggling with your own?"

"I was the one who stopped her that night she changed!" He raised his voice. "I was the one who was stronger and fast enough to catch her! I was the one who brought her home to you!"

"Consider this," Dad spoke coldly, "you are the first European Werewolf EVER to turn away from human flesh. You're the first European Werewolf to live in a pack. European Werewolves have never been seen with a long-term mate. Of course we took all of these facts into consideration!"

"Hey!" Mum interrupted. "Can we please stop focusing on the past and just concentrate on the future?"

"Jess is right." Gran said. "The past is just that, the past. Now it's time to discuss B and Declan's life ahead."

"There's nothing to discuss." My mate said adamantly. "B and I are getting out of this place. There's no way in hell that a wife of mine will be made to feel bad for being married to me!"

Hannah was looking really guilty now. She anxiously looked from Ian to Declan and then she tried to hold my gaze with her own to silently say sorry. I don't think she had planned instigating our departure.

"Alright!" Dad put up his hands to calm him down. "Let's just talk this through, OK?"

"B is Lokoti Werewolf, our people are tied to this land." Ian said flatly. "If you take her away, she'll wane."

"She's a hell of a lot more resilient than you think." Declan disagreed. "She's also a Circulator and they have an in-built drive to move around as they're time travelers."

"True." Gran said to Grandfather's surprise. "Well, it is."

"I wish I could do more traveling." Mum said as she moved to sit down at the dining table.

"I miss it." Her mother agreed as she went to sit down beside her. "Oh well, if B is absolutely sure she wants to move away? Then at least we'll get to travel when we visit her."

"Yeah." She sighed wistfully, before she looked back my way. "But not the 19th Century, please B? I really don't want to wear a corset when I come to visit."

Dad's face coloured angrily, "B's not going anywhere!"

"The hell she isn't!" My mate took a threatening step forwards.

"Hey hey hey! Men, please!" Grandfather quickly jumped in the middle.

"B is Lokoti!" My father proclaimed. "She belongs on Lokoti land!"

"Yeah and I noticed that you didn't say that I was Lokoti and I belong here too!" Declan bellowed.

"Of course you belong here!" Grandfather faced the enraged European Werewolf. "You have Lokoti blood inside of you, MY blood! You ARE family Declan. You, your mother and your brother are family! That's why I helped raised you, because you are a part of my family. With you becoming B's mate, this makes it doubly so."

"You're a Sabre who ended up with a Baker, who had married a Worthall, who married a Carmichael and then who married a Riverclaw." Gran said softly.

My grandfather placed his hands on my mate's shoulders, "my father died in protecting me when I was 12 years old. Your father died protecting you when you were 3 years old. Our families are connected by Mike Sabre and Elisha Worthall. Your great, great grand uncle was turned into a Circulator when Elisha healed him after he nearly lost his life trying to protect her. My granddaughter took a silver bullet to the brain to save you. You ARE family and you two ARE mates and you two belong here with your family, on the land you both grew up on. Declan, you are almost as much as a Riverclaw as you are a Sabre. You belong here with your family, just as much as B does."

I saw Declan's tense shoulders start to lower as his words clearly affected him. When Grandfather released him to take a step back, he swallowed hard before he turned to look my way questioningly. It was as if he was silently asking me what to do? I shrugged back, unsure now.

"Declan." My father took a step forwards. "I admit that I don't trust you with my daughter. I've always felt uneasy around you, because of your breed. But because Em is the head of the family I married into and he declared that you were a part of that family? I fell in line and kept my mouth shut. When the Elders and the pack decided to marry off B, I was with the majority that said it should be Grant. Lokoti Werewolves are fiercely protective over their mates and their young and I was scared B could be harmed if she mated with you."

"But Dad -" I began to object simultaneously as Mum did.

"Hunter!" She snapped. "You really are a judgmental so and so, you know that?"

The European Werewolf's face remained impassive as he fixed my father with his icy-cold gaze. Dad didn't flinch from Declan's temper, as he carried on with abandon. They stood face to face, with my mate slightly taller let alone stronger. However this didn't effect my father's decision to finally speak his mind.

"I truly wish that Grant was alive right now but not just for my best friend Ian's sake. I wish he was still alive because I trusted him with my beloved only child. Now to see B end up with you, it's like acid eating me inside out. My daughter mates with a European Werewolf, the strongest as well as the most violent of all the breeds of Werewolf out there. I would sooner challenge your breed to a fight then let one near my daughter. However B sees something inside you that I don't. Circulators have a unique vision which we Werewolves still struggle to comprehend sometimes. If I refused to allow B to be with you, I can see that it would wound her. As much as the darkness inside of you Declan, scares me? There's something supernatural about your mating considering how you're responsible for bringing her light back."

I squeezed his hand as I looked on my mate with love. He momentarily looked away from his foe which was my father, to turn my way. I watched the coldness in his eyes immediately disappear before they widened at my show of affection. He squeezed my hand back as if it were always going to stay this way. Like this, he looked back at the other Werewolves.

"If B and I consider staying here, there are going to have to be some changes." He began.

"Understandably." Grandfather gave a nod.

"The first..." he nodded towards the windows, "...is give Hannah her curtains back."

There was a pause as everyone but Hannah pondered this in confusion.

She turned an even brighter red, "the curtains were just a metaphor!"

"I don't care." Declan said moodily. "I don't like them anyways, the pattern or the meaning that comes with it."

I couldn't help but to snicker at my mate's sharp tongue which for a change wasn't directed at me.

"Didn't you and Vine make the curtains?" Mum asked her.

"As well as Mom, for Grant and B's Housewarming." She said indignantly.

"I can understand that B would like to continue living in this house because it's on the same hill where her parents and grandparents live? But I don't want to live in a dead guy's shadow, or simply take over the nest." He glared again. "I've fixed this roof, the lose stair and the broken window in the greenhouse so I think I've earned the right to say no to the curtains."

"OK." Grandfather saw his point of view.

"I know I can't expect everyone to turn lovey-dovey and throw B and I a Housewarming? But we're going to replace the curtains and the furniture in the main bedroom." He said determinedly.

"We are?" I looked back in surprise.

"I'm not sleeping in some dead guy's bed just because I worship the ground my woman walks on! I can take a lot B, but we need a new bed." He looked on unhappily.

Hannah's face changed as she looked on Declan in a new light. "Fine, he does have a point. I'd personally feel better if they had a different marriage bed."

The male Lokoti Werewolves looked back at Hannah in surprise.

"I'll buy you guys a new bed as a wedding present." Gran was quick to put up her hand.

"Then I'll buy you guy's new curtains." Mum agreed.

"And buy them new sheets." Hannah looked over at the women. "They would be on par with the new bed."

"OK." My grandmother shrugged to my mother. "We could go to New York and have a shopping day at 'Bloomingdales'."

"What era?" She asked back.

"How about just before the War?" Gran suggested. "Then the styles won't be too outdated."

"How about the future?" She recommended instead. "Like in 2120? It's not too far ahead."

"Good idea." Gran nodded. "Then all we'll have to do is get Credit Cards from the Hodge Endeavor in that era."

I was starting to like the sound of this! A shopping spree in the future? It sounds like fun.

"Can I come?" I moved away from my mate to sit with them.

"Sure." Mum shrugged.

"Can we do some clothes shopping as well as for homewares?" I asked hopeful.

"Hmm, we'll see." Gran frowned. "You would have to buy classic styles in cotton or wool, so you don't look odd walking around in futuristic clothes."

Hannah walked over to where we were sitting to ask stiffly, "if I gave you a list, could you pick up a few things for me too?"

"Why don't you come with us?" Mum invited.

"Really?" She asked in surprise.

"As long as you don't scream at me while I'm shopping, sure." I said wryly.

Hannah sat down at the table with us, "I won't."

Pause...then she started to snicker, which made me laugh and then it made Mum and Gran giggle too.

"Were you really considering the 19th Century to live in?" My mother looked on like I was nuts.

"We were packing and everything." I told her. "I don't mind the idea of the corsets, but I was going to take my MP3 player with me."

"I couldn't live in that era." She shook her head. "No electricity, no showers, no freedom for women."

"Jess if you lived in that era, you would have become the first feminist terrorist!" Gran guffawed and so did Hannah.

The men stood there, watching in amusement.

"I don't believe this!" My mate looked on with an incredulous expression.

"Peace is formed over shopping?" Ian speculated. "Maybe if the world's leaders had been women, we could have avoided World War Three by them shopping together."

"I can see it now, Jess arguing over the price of clothes as well as trade agreements between countries." Dad smilingly watched his mate.

"Women!" Declan rolled his eyes.

"Hey, you were the one who wanted new curtains and furniture." Ian returned.

"You try living in a dead guy's scent!" He retorted, but then he looked apologetic. "No offence to your brother."

"No, it's understandable." Ian sighed reluctantly. "It must be a Werewolf thing by another man's scent bothering us. Once, Bec came home smelling like Gavin. Although nothing happened but she accidentally walked into him; I nearly punched the guy."

"Yeah, I would punch Gavin if Jess came home smelling like him." Dad's eyebrows rose unimpressed.

Grandfather laughingly shook his head at the younger Werewolves' territorial behavior.

~~~~~~

1ˢᵗ September 2090

Although Declan said that he didn't expect a Housewarming, an unofficial celebration presented itself in the forms of our families. Even the Elm's joined in the festivities.

Bright and early on Saturday morning as I was getting ready to go shopping, I heard the sound of Aunt Susan's truck park in the driveway. I was in the bathroom upstairs, pulling my hair into a pony tail as I listened to Declan open the front door and greet her with a kiss on the cheek.

Aunt Susan had come over to make pasta with him. I think they were going to spend the majority of the day, sitting at the table doing this. I think they were planning on making an extra large batch for their entire family. As I brushed my teeth, I listened to them walk into the kitchen as Declan proceeded to make coffee first of all.

"B, you wanna coffee?" He called out.

After I spat out the toothpaste and rinsed my mouth, I called back; "no thanks, I don't think I have time!"

I was right, because as soon as I said this, I heard the sound of two more vehicles pull up out the front. As I went downstairs to greet the arrivals, not only did I see Mum and Gran walk through my front door but to my surprise, I saw Vine arrive with Hannah. Declan and Aunt Susan welcomed the new arrivals.

"Hi B." Vine smiled warmly.

"Is it OK if she comes too? I told her about our shopping expedition and she decided to invite herself along." Hannah flashed a look of annoyance at her older sister.

"Cool." I smilingly shrugged.

"The more the merrier." Mum agreed.

"I'll be right back, I'll just get a couple more Credit Cards from Vincent." Gran organized before she instantaneously phased out of the room in a bright flash of light.

I looked at my watch as I wondered when two more of our party were going to make their appearance? My question was answered by the sound of another four-wheel-drive, pulling up in the crowded driveway.

"Rachel and Mandy are here." I sung as I went over to the door to wave them in.

"They're coming along too?" Declan's eyes widened, before they almost popped out when he saw Derik walk in with his wife and friend.
~~~~~~

"Hi guys!" Mandy greeted enthusiastically. "I couldn't wait for today, it's going to be so much fun!"

"I've never gone shopping off tribal lands before." Rachel excitedly agreed. "Let alone in New York!"

"Bro, you're going SHOPPING?!" He looked on his little brother in shock.

"No." Derik instantly frowned upon the idea. "But I thought I'd come and learn how to make pasta while Rachel's away."

Aunt Susan beamed and I saw his words even touched Declan, at how his little brother was finally showing interest in the family 'business'.

"Pull up a chair." He invited him to the table. "You want a coffee?"

"Yeah that would be great, thanks." Derik agreed as he sat down.

"Aunt Susan, would you like to come shopping with us?" I offered.

"Oh no but thank you for the kind offer, B. Today is pasta day with my boys." She smilingly reached out to run her hand through Derik's hair. Then she pulled out a shopping list from her pocket, "but if you could possibly pick up a couple of things for me? It would sure be appreciated."

"No problem." I immediately agreed by taking her list to scan over with my eyes. I frowned in confusion at one of the items. "Chanel No. 5? Um, what's that?"

"It's perfume, B." Mum snickered at my obtuseness.

"But if it's too expensive...?" My aunt looked guilty.

"Don't be silly, Susan!" She scoffed. "We're shopping on the Hodge Endeavor account in one of New York's most expensive department stores. Trust me, I don't think a bottle of perfume will be the straw that breaks the camel's back!"

Just then in another bright flash of light, Gran instantaneously phased back into the room. In her hands she was holding a thick, white envelope.

"Alright girls." She proceeded to hand out small plastic cards from the envelope. "The PIN is 13061984. When you pay for your shopping, you have to put in this PIN every time you use the credit card."

"How much is the credit limit on each card?" Mum enquired.

"Credit limit?" She echoed in surprise. "Oh, I don't know."

"You don't know?" My mother echoed back. "Mum, you didn't think that this piece of knowledge might have been helpful?"

"What I mean to say, is I don't think there is a limit." She mused.

All eyes in the room widened as we stared at my grandmother in shock.

"We're shopping with limitless funds?!" Hannah cried out in disbelief.

"Not LIMITLESS funds no." She laughed. "If we tried to buy the city of New York as a whole, we might encounter a problem. But I think each card might have a limit of a million credits or some such."

"A million credits?!" Derik blanched, before he looked to Declan. "Bro, you've married into some SERIOUS money!"

"It sounds like it!" My mate chuckled. "Plus my woman's a hot, rich chick! How much do you hate me?"

My face flushed as my hand swung out and I whacked him on the arm!

"Oow!" He laughingly flinched.

"Dude, you just got bitch-slapped by the hot, rich chick!" My best friend laughingly pointed at his older brother.

"I'll do more than bitch-slap you in a minute, Derik Sabre!" Rachel whacked her husband's arm next.

"Ha ha!" Declan pointed back at his little brother.

"Girls, please!" Aunt Susan smilingly scolded. "What did I tell you in school about beating up your male classmates?"

"Violence doesn't solve anything but witty come backs make the world go around." Mandy recited.

"Where's Michael?" She looked to the young parents to see her grandson.

"My Mom's minding him for the day." Rachel told her.

"Very well, I guess it's time for us to depart." Gran looked at her watch before she looked to Mum and I. "I was thinking that we could instantaneously phase into the empty Ladies bathroom on the ground floor in 'Bloomingdales' right on 9 AM, when the store has just opened. We shouldn't have any witnesses then."

"And the date?" Mum prepared herself by doing a little stretch.

"Um, the date will be..." she checked something scribbled on the outside of the envelope, "...the 13th June, 2120. That's the date Vincent advised so Hodge Endeavor will be expecting the withdrawal of funds from the company account."

"Cool." I nodded as I moved to go stand with my mother and grandmother. "Vine and Hannah, can you put your hands on my shoulders? Rachel and Mandy, you can put yours on Mum and Gran's."

"Hey hey hey! Wait a minute here!" Declan objected and we all turned in surprise. He stood there with his hands on his hips as he looked on demandingly, "where's my kiss goodbye?"

"And mine?" Derik agreed as he shot off a look to Rachel.

"Men!" Mandy rolled her eyes. "They always find something to complain about!"

"Is that why you're not married, Mandy?" Vine smirked at the younger woman.

"You think I'm going to tie myself down to something with the maturity level of a gnat?" She retorted.

"Oh, you've met my husband then." Hannah joked.

Rachel and I giggled as we momentarily left our positions to give the boys their requested signs of affection. Declan wrapped his arms about my waist as his face softened. I heard him inhale my scent as he bent his head to tenderly cover my mouth with his own.

When he eventually he pulled his lips away, he asked; "how long will you be away?"

"Um, I'm not sure but probably all day."

"If you're not home by six, I'll call your Dad and Grandfather and arrange a search party." He growled playfully.

I giggled again as I turned around and went to stand with the shopping party.

"Have fun." Derik affectionately rubbed Rachel's back before he released her.

"If you're good, I'll even bring you back a present." She gave her husband one last kiss before she returned to stand beside my grandmother.

The Sabre family then watched the seven of us disappear in a bigger and brighter flash of light.

*****

"OK." Gran took charge as the seven of us walked out of the Ladies bathroom on the ground floor of the department store. "Jess and I will first of all, take B to the furniture section and then the homewares."

"Don't forget I have to get new curtains and bed linen too, Gran." I reminded.

"I think haberdashery is in the homewares department, B." Mum advised.

"I want to go to the children's department and buy baby clothes and toys." Rachel announced.

"I'll come with you." Mandy volunteered. "I'll buy some educational toys for school as well as some new books to use as teaching aids."

"I want to check out the food hall." Vine spoke up.

"I'll come with you and then we'll check out homewares too." Hannah agreed with her sister.

"Right." Gran looked at her watch. "The time is now 9.05 AM. Let's all meet up at the main entrance of the store at 12 PM for lunch."

"Why the main entrance?" Mum queried. "Doesn't this department store have a restaurant too?"

"It does." She nodded. "But I've planned something special for lunch."

"Oooh!" Hannah giggled excitedly. "Are we going to go out of the store for lunch to see New York City?"

"That we are." She smiled. "OK ladies, let the games begin!"

We all split up to walk off in different directions. Rachel and Mandy went one way as Vine and Hannah went in another. I departed with Mum and Gran as we headed towards the escalators.

We were so excited about our day that we didn't notice that we had attracted the attention of two store employees. The man and woman dressed in 'Bloomingdales' uniforms, exchanged a surprised look when they saw six Native Alaskan women and one young looking Englishwoman, suddenly walk out of the Ladies room since they didn't see us walk in there in the beginning.

The employees wondered at my Gran's accent and what an Englishwoman was doing, bossing around the Native Alaskan women. They pondered over our antiquated country appearance as we were all dressed in boots, jeans, shirts and suede jackets, some in Lokoti design of beads and leather tassels.

"Did that young Native Alaskan woman call the young Englishwoman, 'Gran'?" The male employee questioned the female employee.

"Yeah, I think she did." She watched us walk away in curiousity.

However throughout the day, I began to notice that we attracted a lot of curious looks. During our first hour in the furniture department, I decided on which bedroom suite and mattress I wanted. I chose an antique style wooden 'sleigh' bed with matching bedside tables and tall boy. When it came time to pay for it, Gran insisted that she put it on her credit card.

"It is yours and Declan's Housewarming present, B." Mum smirked. "So let your grandmother pay for it."

I huffed as I stood in between the two at the counter. A young African-American who was serving us, smiled at our bickering.

"A housewarming present, huh?" The man smiled. "Congratulations."

"Thanks." I smiled back.

"You've just moved out of home for your first time?" The employee asked as he processed the transaction in his computer.

"Er, no." I laughed uneasily, as I didn't know how to explain my situation so I didn't say anything else.

The man continued to look upon my appearance as I caught him take a deep breath, as if he could smell my Lokoti Werewolf pheromones.

"You know, although our sale on Bedding finished last week..." the man began, "...I think I could still knock 10% off the price for you."

"Really?" My mother's eyebrows arose before she exchanged an amused look with her mother.

"Sure." The employee agreed as he hit a command into his computer console. "I'll just put it in the computer that the bed has a scratch in the wooden frame or something."

"That's very nice of you." Gran smiled on him.

The young man nervously laughed, as I guess he liked the look of all three of us as he obviously thought we were all in our twenties like he was.

"You know what? I'll put in the computer that there was a scratch on the tallboy too, so it will knock another 5% off the price." The young man now winked at Gran.

She gloatingly swiped her credit card and put in her PIN to pay for the cheaper furniture.

"So, are you ladies visiting New York on a holiday or something?" He looked over our 'country' appearance.

"Yep." Mum answered.

"Say, if you need a tour guide? I'd be more than happy to show you three the Big Apple." The young man offered. "Give me a call."

When he handed Gran her receipt, there was a number scribbled down on the back of it. She looked amused by this, as Mum laughed and I blushed!

"Thank you very much...Todd." My grandmother caught the name on his badge. "But we're only in New York for the day."

"Oh." His face fell in disappointment. "Well, the next time you're in the city, look me up."

"Careful, we just might do that." Mum teased. "Then what will you do with all three of us?"

"Mum!" I turned an even brighter red as I nudged her!

Todd looked surprised when I called her 'Mum', before his eyes widened further when he remembered that I called the Englishwoman 'Gran'. He watched us walk away in complete befuddlement.

*****

When we left the furniture department, we went to the floor for homewares next. I picked which sheet sets I wanted and I even chose a couple new quilt covers as well. Mum paid for these on her credit card and then afterwards the older women took me to look at curtains.

I bought several sets of pre-made curtains where all you had to do was thread the fabric onto curtain rods, which I already had at home.

As we shopped throughout the day, we handed our purchases over to a kind of valet that was located on each floor of the store. The valet would put aside our shopping in a back room with a ticket given, so all we had to do at the end of the day was just present our tickets to pick them up.

At 12 PM we met up with the others by the doors to the main entrance. We all followed Gran out of the department store to a luxury mini-bus we found was waiting outside.

"Is this for us?" Mandy looked on the fancy futuristic vehicle in surprise.

"It certainly is." She led the way on board, as the female driver in a smart uniform stood by to greet us.

We were driven through some of the scenic parts of the city as we all looked out the windows in further excitement.

The mini-bus dropped us off out the front of the restored Empire State Building. We went to eat lunch in a fancy restaurant located on the top floor. When we stepped out of the elevator, we were immediately inside the restaurant.

Gran greeted the Hostess, "table for Riverclaw."

"Right this way." The smartly-dressed restaurant employee showed us the way.

We were seated at a long table by the windows overlooking Central Park. Once we were seated, a waiter came over to hand out the menus. Rachel, Mandy, Vine and Hannah's eyes widened as they looked on the range of gourmet dishes and the expensive prices next to them.

"Ladies, lunch is on me." Gran announced to the table. "To celebrate Declan and B's Housewarming."

"To Declan and B's Housewarming." Mum raised her glass of champagne.

"To Declan and B's Housewarming." Everyone else followed suit before we all chinked glasses.

Everybody but Rachel and I, drank champagne where instead we drank de-alcoholized wine. Rachel had to because she was pregnant and I had to because I was the Werewolf in the party. I had a good hold of the bloodlust, but it was a firm rule that no Lokoti Werewolf imbibed alcohol. I hardly felt left out, especially when I ordered Lobster Mornay for lunch.

"I'm going to miss not having a Circulator in the family anymore." Vine sighed to her sister.

"It certainly was handy." Hannah agreed.

"What are you two talking about?" Gran gave a funny look. "We're still family but you're also related to the Sabre's now."

"Mum's right." My mother nodded. "Your little brother Grant became a Riverclaw and a Wisetail on the day he married B, just as much as B became an Elm. Now that B is mated to Declan, you're also in the Sabre family."

Vine and Hannah exchanged looks of amusement at their logic.

"Here's to family." Rachel raised her glass again.

"And here's to tribe." Mandy joined her.

"To family and to tribe." We all chinked glasses a second time.

Rachel gave me a wink over her glass, as we sipped on our de-alcoholized drinks.

*****

After lunch we were driven back to Bloomingdales in the mini-bus to continue with our shopping. This time we shopped altogether in a large group. We hit the menswear floor and bought new clothing for the men in our lives. Then we hit the womens clothing and shopped for ourselves. We ended the day by visiting the cosmetics section where we bought perfume, make-up and other accessories.

At 7 PM New York time, we instantaneously phased back to Alaska to the day we left; arriving at 7 PM tribal lands time. Gran, Mum and I had to do several trips to bring back all of our shopping. Then the they had to help me instantaneously phase the large furniture boxes back.

When we arrived, we found all of our husbands in the living room waiting, including Vine and Hannah's. I also found Ian as well as Nana and Grandpa were here.

"What time do you call this?!" Declan tapped on his watch in annoyance.

"It was late night shopping." I shrugged back.

"Um guys, did you leave anything left in the store?" Ian stared at all of our shopping bags and boxes which filled up the entire living room.

"Shut up Ian." Mum rolled her eyes.

"Keep talking like that and you won't get your present." Hannah glared at her older brother.

"I got a present?" He smiled upon the sound of that.

"Aunt Susan." I handed over the shopping bag full of the items she requested.

"B!" Her eyes lit up as she pulled out the bottles of perfume and cosmetic packages. "Thank you!"

"So, what's the special occasion for you all to be here?" I looked on the large assembly in surprise, before I turned back to Declan, "I'm one hour late! You weren't seriously organizing a search party, were you?"

"Hey, don't look at me!" He retorted. "They showed up by their own accord half an hour ago."

I looked inquiringly back at Ian, wondering at his unforeseen appearance?

"Who builds furniture for a living? Me." He folded his arms like I should have known better. He indicated my new bedroom furniture that was in several different boxes. "Somebody's going to have to help you assemble your new bedroom set."

"I'll go and get the tools from the truck." Vine's husband momentarily left the house.

"Who made your curtains when you moved in here?" Vine agreed with her brother. "Hannah and I did. Somebody's going to have to help you take down the old curtains to put up the new."

"Where are the curtains, B?" Hannah started hunting around the different bags on the floor to find them.

"Wait just a darn minute here, everybody!" Aunt Susan called out. We all paused to look back in surprise. "It's 7 o'clock! Before we all start building bedroom suites and redecorating the house tonight, we're going to eat dinner first. I can't have you all working up a sweat and then keeling over sideways from starvation. Now, Derik and Declan; help your mother serve, would you?"

"I'll get the bottles of soda from the truck." Hannah's husband next left the house.

As Derik made a move through the sea of shopping bags to go into the kitchen with his mother, Declan and I exchanged a look of wonder.

I think this really was our Housewarming today and I could tell this touched him. His face turned pink as he passed me a small smile before he ducked into the kitchen to help out.

Vine and Hannah's husbands returned from their respective trucks, carrying either tool kits or several large bottles of sodas. Next, Hannah organized cups for everyone by helping herself to my kitchen as she and her husband worked on doling out the drinks. Derik and Declan helped Aunt Susan serve up and in ten minutes everybody had a plate of spaghetti bolognaise with a serving of garlic bread. As there weren't enough seats especially with shopping bags everywhere, we all remained standing as we ate and drank.

"If I could get everybody's attention." Dad interrupted just as we all started to tuck into our meals. The room turned quiet to look his way, as my father picked up his cup of soda indicating a toast was coming up. He wore a composed expression as he looked on the European Werewolf standing beside his daughter. "I would just like to officially welcome Declan into the Wisetail family."

"Welcome Declan." Grandpa saluted with his soda.

"The Sabre's were acknowledged as family by the Riverclaw's 24 years ago when they arrived that fateful September night, the night we lost Uncle Yule." Dad looked on the Elm family whose eyes turned misty by their father's name. "Uncle Yule fought bravely for his tribe against the man-eating monster which turned Declan. Now for the past 11 years Declan has also fought for this tribe as one of the pack. I now formally acknowledge him as part of the Wisetail family."

"Welcome Declan." Mum and Nana raised their cups.

We all drank to his toast, whilst my lover and father exchanged wary looks over their drinks.

"And on that note," Ian spoke up, "just as my father died protecting his family and tribe, so did my little brother Grant. Six years ago we assembled on the Holy Grounds before the three Sacred Totems and I formally welcomed B into the Elm family. Now as the head of that family, I formally acknowledge B and Declan as mates. Bianca Grace Wisetail Elm, may you be known from this day forward as Bianca Grace Wisetail Elm Sabre."

Everyone laughed as my name seemed to grow longer by the minute!

"Man that's a mouthful!" He chuckled. "Declan, I'm relieved that as a European Werewolf you have a longer life span than a Lokoti Werewolf.

Because if B should mate again? I am NOT looking forward to trying to say out her next name in a single breath!"

"Ian!" I turned bright red from everyone laughing again. Even Declan chuckled as he put his arm about my shoulders.

"I guess it's my turn." Aunt Susan spoke up. "Since I'm the head of the Sabre family with my husband who was Derik's and Declan's father, Anthony Sabre is gone. Anthony also died the same night and in the same manner as Yule Elm. With our arrival, not just the Riverclaw's but the Lokoti Tribe as a whole, took us in. They provided a house for me and my children and I was pleased to be able to start teaching to show my thanks for everything the tribe has done for us. Em and Arabella as well as Jess and Hunter, helped me raise my two boys who became playmates for B. The pack trained Declan and now Derik is the tribe's second Medicine Man, under the tutelage of Fern Wisetail."

Everyone nodded as they looked on Declan standing beside me as well as at Derik standing with Rachel.

She finished, "with our connection, I almost feel like I don't have to welcome B into the Sabre clan as she's always been family. So I guess I should just wish Declan and B a long and happy life together because when you have somebody to share it with? The years will pass in busy happiness."

"To Declan and Bianca." Derik raised his cup.

"To Declan and Bianca." Everybody toasted.

My European Werewolf mate and I exchanged small smiles before I gave him a hug. As I tucked my face into his warm neck and inhaled his maple syrup scent, he affectionately rubbed my back.

"This certainly beats the plan to move to Canada." He joked in my ear which made me giggle.

~~~~~~
~~~~~~

~ 24 ~

3rd June 2145

I woke up weakened from how much pain I was in. The bedroom was still dark and I caught the time on Declan's digital clock as 1.09 AM. I was in agony as my hips ached, my legs throbbed, my knees were locked and even my feet felt sore. I could barely raise my head let alone get out of bed, so I turned to look on the person who would have to get out of bed for me.

My mate was slumbering away with his mouth wide open whilst he quietly snored, when I reached out to rest my hand on his muscled chest.

"Declan." I gently shook him. "Declan?"

His snoring stopped for about five seconds and I thought he was waking up? But nope, it started up again.

"Declan!" I detracted my claws to dig in.

"OOW!" His blue eyes snapped open as he was quick to swipe my hand off. "That frickin' HURT!"

"Declan…!" I whimpered as my eyes watered.

He heard the agony in my voice immediately which made him quickly sit up to look down in concern.

"B, what is it?" He asked worriedly as he sniffed me. I didn't have say anything else when he moved out of bed fast. "I'll get the painkillers."

I watched him disappear from the bedroom in his silk boxer shorts. I listened to him go into the bathroom, open up the mirrored cabinet as well as fill up a glass of water. He quickly returned to the bedroom to sit on my side of the bed whilst holding out the small jar of tablets and the H2o. He frowned as he watched me struggle to sit up, then further still when he watched me take four painkillers out of the jar. I threw them down with the water.

Fifty-five years of marriage had trained him well as he knew exactly what to do. When I had finished, Declan placed the now empty glass and the small jar onto my bedside table before he climbed over and back under the sheet. He pulled me into his strong arms whilst resting his leg over mine to warm them, as he started to rub my lower back.

"Why didn't you wake me sooner?" He gently scolded. "If you woke me before the pain got too bad, you wouldn't need to take so many tablets."

"I only just woke up…!" I answered as my voice cracked from emotional upheaval. "I hate this, Declan. I really, really hate this…!"

"Shhhh." He murmured into my ear. "Shhhh."

"It's a cruel fucking joke that's what it is!" I growled tearfully. "I can't have kids but I still get the curse of what comes from being a woman?!"

"Shhhh." He kissed my ear next.

"I'm frickin' 78 years old and I still have to put up with this shit?!"

"Shhhh."

"Rachel stopped going through this twenty years ago!"

"Shhhh."

"If I were human instead of a Circulator, I would have stopped this twenty years ago."

"Shhhh."

"If I had the body of a 78 year old human woman, I wouldn't be going through this!"

"Hey!" He said grouchily. "You have the body of a frickin' hot twenty-something year old. Leave your body out of it! I quite like your body."

I was a 78 year old Circulator and Lokoti Werewolf, who was married to an 81 year old European Werewolf and the neither of us looked past our twenties.

"I want to go through menopause...!" I began to cry as Declan rubbed my back harder.

"No you don't, nobody does." He refuted. "The humans hate us because we're still strong and the pack thinks it's funny that we don't look like we're in our thirties yet."

"Yes I do!" I sniffed. "I'm tired of this pain! Month after month, year after year, it's pushing me to breaking point."

"It's just a sign that you're still young and gorgeous." Declan kissed my cheek.

"I don't care about looking young and gorgeous anymore...!" I wailed.

"Yes you do." He rolled his eyes.

"No I don't!"

"Come on B, at least your bones will never become brittle as your skin will never sag. You'll never get dementia or Alzheimer's nor will the cold kill you like it could if you were frail. Besides if you were old, you wouldn't be able to do your favourite thing in the whole wide world anymore, like beating me up." He sadly jested.

I knew where this was coming from, since his mother passed away ten years ago. Aunt Susan's death affected Declan deeply. Then my 71 year old husband with his appearance of a 29 year old, stood beside his younger brother Derik whom was a 68 year old and who looked like a 68 year old, as did his human wife Rachel. The two brothers, one European Werewolf and the other human, sent off their 92 year old human mother with the help of the tribe who treated Aunt Susan's passing like a state funeral.

As time marched on, it started to become more evident in this tribe who was human and who wasn't.

My grandmother, mother and I remained eternally youthful as Circulators because our bio-electromagnetic frequencies were in temporal flux. All three of us looked like women in our twenties when our actual ages were 116 years old, 97 years old and 78 years old.

Grandfather was the same age as Gran and as a Lokoti Werewolf he had the appearance of a man in his late fifties. Mum was married to another Lokoti Werewolf and Dad looked like a man in his late forties. Uncle Julian who was another Lokoti Werewolf and Mum's twin, also looked to be in his late forties.

Uncle Jules had been married to the telepathic Aunt Danika who was four years younger than he was and unfortunately she died four years ago at the age of 90 years. Nana died many years previously at the age of 91 years old, leaving Grandpa widowed and in mourning for the remaining years of his life. Even Ian's mate, Bec died last year at the age of 96.

Time marched on like an army as it collected numbers willing or not and unfortunately it was a war the Lokoti Werewolves just could not win. They could protect their mates against natural opponents like looters as they could protect them from supernatural threats such as other breeds of Werewolves. However they couldn't stop Time itself from staking its claim on our human beloved.

I could understand Declan's optimistic view of my monthly blues, because I was experiencing the bad side of a young body? It meant that he wouldn't go through the trauma of losing his mate to old age. He patiently rubbed my lower back for a full ten minutes as the painkillers slowly took effect. Although he felt the tension in my muscles loosen in relief with the lessening of the pain, he didn't stop.

"Get some rest, B." He murmured as his lips tenderly grazed my forehead. "Go back to sleep, as we have a big day tomorrow."

I yawned as I moved into my customary position of slinging my leg over his hip, snuggling against his hot chest as well as burying my face in his warm neck. I used his body's heat like a security blanket whilst inhaling his maple syrup scent. This felt so nice I growled softly in contentment. I felt Declan chuckle quietly as he never stopped rubbing my back although the pain was long gone.

*****

My mate's digital alarm clock woke us up at 9 AM with the Internet Radio coming on.

"G'morning my fellow Alaskans!" The DJ greeted chirpily. "It's a beautiful summer's day outside, with the sky expected to remain clear and temperatures are meant to hit 21 degrees Celsius in Fairbanks and 18 degrees in Anchorage. For those of you who've been up since 2 AM like our sun has? Let's see if you can last as long as our summer's light as sunset tonight will reportedly be around 10.45 PM. But while you're still rubbing the sleep out of your eyes, here's a classic that should help put the spring back into your step!

It's an oldie but a goodie, here's The Verve and their song, 'Bittersweet Symphony'."

The song began to play and I reached over to turn it up. I yawned as I hauled myself upright and I sat there for a minute or two, listening to the music and getting my bearings. Declan hadn't moved yet, as he lay still with his eyes closed. He only opened them when my mobile phone rang, which made me turn the music back down to answer.

"Hi Gran." I greeted from reading off her name on caller ID.

"B," she rushed out, "how far away are you guys?"

Declan and I exchanged a funny look, as he overheard the question with his sensitive hearing.

"Um, in bed." I answered.

"In BED?!" She squawked. "You're supposed to be here in half an hour!"

"We will be there in half an hour." I yawned a second time as I stood up. "All we have to do is dress since we won't be needing breakfast because we'll be eating all day at the festivities."

"Look, I need you two to drive into town and buy twelve more two litre bottles of soda from the supermarket." She instructed. "The general store is shut today so you won't be able to buy them there."

"But why?" I frowned. "I thought the Elm's were bringing more soda."

"Hannah is in pretty bad shape as the influenza has turned in pneumonia." Gran said sadly. "Ian won't be coming today as he wants to stay by her side."

"Oh." I turned to look at Declan who frowned back. "OK, we'll leave in twenty minutes for Alma to get the soda."

"Thanks B, you're a sweetie! I'll tell everyone why you're delayed." She said appreciatively.

We hung up and I put my phone back on the bedside table before I hesitated as the bad news settled in.

"Hannah's not doing so good, huh?" Declan raised his eyebrows from listening in. I shook my head as he looked sympathetic. "Poor Ian, first his sister Vine kicks the bucket, then his wife Bec and now Hannah's knocking on heaven's door."

Of course he left out that Ian's youngest sibling Grant died 56 years ago.

We both started to get dressed in our smart casual clothes. I put on a long, navy cotton dress and high-heeled sandals. Declan pulled on his 'good' jeans, which were the dark blue pair which weren't torn or stained; as well as a black shirt and a red silk tie Gran had bought him several Christmases ago.

I frowned as I watched him struggle to put it on as he didn't seem like a tie person, it was just wrong somehow. He was glaring at it in the mirror as he fumbled, when I walked over to start fiddling. He smiled appreciatively when he thought I was helping, which switched to an annoyed look when I took it off instead.

"What are you doing?!" He objected.

"Lose it." I ordered and tossed it over to the other side of the room before he could stop me. "It's not you."

"Hey!" Declan started to go and get it, but I grabbed his arm and pulled him into the bathroom to brush his teeth with me instead.

*****

Ten minutes later, we left the house dressed with our teeth and hair brushed. I followed him out to his new pick up truck parked in the garage. He hit his remote control to open the doors and then he stood by my door to close it for me.

"Declan, are you feeling alright?" I teased.

"You should wear dresses more often." He growled in approval as he looked me over.

I laughed as I climbed in and once he shut my door behind, he walked around and climbed into the driver's seat.

"Now, have you got everything?" He checked as he punched in the ignition code and the vehicle instantly purred to life.

"Yes."

"Got your keys?"

"Yes."

"Got your purse?"

"Yes."

"Is your Credit Card in your purse?" He arched his eyebrows.

"Declan that happened ONCE!" I rolled my eyes. "It wasn't my fault, Honey Dew was the one who took it out when she was playing with it!"

He was referring to the episode last year when Blanche's daughter Honey Dew was playing with my purse and by playing with it, she completely emptied it but didn't remember to put everything back in. So when I went shopping at the supermarket and it came to paying for it all at the self checkout; I had no Credit Card. Embarrassedly, I called Declan at the Garage. My bad-tempered mate wasn't happy when he had rush into town to pay instead.

"Got a spare pad?" He next quizzed.

"Yes!" I rolled my eyes at his referring to another incident during another tribal gathering when I found I had run out at a most inconvenient time. Declan had to rush to the 24 hour supermarket to procure a packet for me when the store on tribal lands was closed.

"Got your painkillers?" He asked lastly which made me pause. He rolled his eyes, "oh come on!"

I quickly jumped out of the truck and instantaneously phased into my bedroom. There, I grabbed the small jar of pills from my bedside table, put them in my purse and I instantaneously phased back outside. I hopped into the truck with Declan growling impatiently.

"Frickin' hell woman, you'll be the death of me." He shook his head whilst making sure I had my seat belt on before he reversed out of the driveway. "What's the bet that you would have needed them halfway through the day and sent ME home to get them?"

"Oh shut up!" I rolled my eyes. "If that DID happen I could instantaneously phase home myself."

"Yeah right!" He scoffed as he rested his free hand on my lap whilst we drove down the hill. "I think you purposefully forget these things because you like working my ass off."

"Since you no longer have to patrol the borders with the Sheriff's Station opening in Alma, how else are you going to get regular exercise?" I joked back as I rested my hand over his.

"That's rich coming from you." He taunted. "Who slaves away at the Garage while you sit on your ass, working on your history papers?"

"Who gets paid handsomely, to give guest lectures in different universities?" I boasted.

Since completing my PhD via correspondence thirty years ago, I had been invited to be a guest lecturer now and then because of my unique 'insight' with my work. Of course, I could never be long in these strange cities nor be away overnight. Declan and I could wane if we were away from each other for extended periods of time. It's why I never flew, I just pretended I did as I instantaneously phased inside of airports where I had drivers waiting to pick me up. Thanks to Vincent's control of the corporate conglomeration that was Hodge Endeavor; its large legal department updated my passport with the required customs stamps or visas.

*****

We drove off tribal lands and into the township of Alma in Declan's pride and joy; his metallic black, plasma-powered, pick up truck. It still had 'new car' smell and compared to his first truck, which had been second hand (and third and fourth) since it originated from the late 20th Century; it almost seemed like a luxury vehicle.

Alma was a bustling town again, even busier before the war according to my parents and grandparents. Before the war, the population was just over 1,000 and now according to the 'Welcome to Alma' sign, there were just under 5,000 people living here.

When the Sheriff's Station opened in 2103 AD, the pack no longer had to patrol the borders of the Lokoti National Park. The small number of original townspeople before the resurgence, kept the secret of the Werewolves existence as a gesture of thanks to their protection over the years. The townspeople however never knew of the existence of a female Lokoti Werewolf though, because I wasn't allowed to patrol. But along with the return of law to the majority of the United States, was a return to order.

Alma had a bustling Main Street with two hotels, four bars, several cafés and restaurants, a cinema and many stores. There was a gigantic supermarket which the Lokoti frequented and Lokoti kids also attended the Elementary School as well as the High School which had reopened. In 2103 when the Sheriff Station first opened, so did the schools and the supermarket. Alma attracted its population because it promised stability as well as opportunity to grow and yet it was still small enough to be called quiet living.

In the year 2101 AD the reformed United Nations had every country sign the 'Apology Admission' to relinquish the last of the blame for World War Three. The last of the nuclear weapons were dismantled and used for energy purposes instead.   Poverty was annihilated as the entire world tentatively began the 'Third Renaissance' with countries sharing in each other's advancement in medicine and science. There were major breakthroughs in space exploration and plasma power replacing electricity, which was a higher form of power more environmentally friendly to produce. Technology such as TV or Radio was run off the Internet which was everywhere and information was accessible in nearly every form imaginable.

What was kept out of the World Wide Media, was the Circulate's crucial assistance with the 'Apology Admission'. Hodge Endeavor as one of the few remaining multinational companies that survived the War, its finances grew in leaps and bounds. This was helped by having a Calculator as the Head Chairman on the Company Board of Directors who never made a bad investment. Gran, Mum and I had several meetings with Vincent at Circulate HQ to discuss Hodge Endeavor's involvement in world wide politics. We ultimately decided to use the company's financial success to float the previous Third World economies which eradicated the last of poverty. This in turn, lead to several meetings of the world's leaders who eventually agreed to sign the 'Apology Admission'. With the world's governments no longer worrying what their neighbor was doing, they could concentrate on radiation clean up. Science invented new ways at treating radiation poisoning or even harnessing it for other uses. Looting and plundering finally ceased as permanent police forces returned.

I enjoyed visiting Alma over the years because to me, this small town outside of our tribal lands represented the world's reformation. Food was readily accessible and no longer fought over, which the 24 hour supermarket represented. The latest technology was sold in specialty stores on the Main Street. People no longer felt unsafe and capitalism thrived.

Declan parked the truck in the supermarket's busy car park and next we walked in hand-in-hand through the automatic doors. He pushed the hover-trolley as he led the way straight to the aisle where sodas were kept. He was a lot more perfunctory than I was.

"Oh look, there's caramel mudcake for sale!" I pointed at the bakery section as we passed.

"Don't even think about it!" He growled as he pulled me along. "We don't have time to window shop."

We loaded up the trolley with twelve bottles of two litre sodas before Declan lead us to an available self check-out. I helped him scan all of the bottles in the trolley before I swiped my Credit Card to pay. Next, we walked past the security sensors as we left the supermarket. Declan pushed the hover-trolley back to his truck where we put the bottles of soda in the back, before he returned the hover-trolley to the trolley bay.

I must admit, since Credits had taken over as the world's currency, it made life much more simple. I never have to worry about changing money when I travel to different countries now. All I had to do is swipe my Credit Card and key in the PIN which used the credit sitting in my bank account. No-one handled cash anymore as it simply ceased to exist.

We drove the seven kilometers back to Lokoti land. Declan pulled up outside of the meeting hall where Uncle Harry's 175th Birthday Celebration was held. Lastly, we carried the cotton shopping bags full of soda inside.

"Over here!" Gran waved us over to the drinks table. The other sodas sat in tubs full of ice that my grandparents and several other families provided.

"Hi Gran." I kissed her cheek and so did Declan.

"Where do you want this?" He asked.

"In there please." She pointed at the ice-filled tubs.

We knelt down and began to put our additions into the already large collection. Hardly anybody in the tribe let alone a Werewolf, drank alcohol so sodas were the most popular drink.

"Thank you guys." Gran said appreciatively as she unpacked all of the bio-degradable disposable cups.

"How is Hannah?" Declan asked as he worked.

"Not good." She said sadly. "Fern doesn't think she'll make it to the end of the week."

We exchanged concerned glances as we finished putting the drinks away before we stood up again.

"Do you need a hand with anything else?" I offered.

"Um, I don't think so." Gran frowned thoughtfully as she looked over the hall. "I think everything's been done."

Several fold away tables and chairs had been set up, which took up the most space. There was a separate dance area near the stage where a DJ would be playing music. Everything looked ready, with more members of the tribe bringing in food to sit on the long tables buffet style, which ran along the side of the hall.

Just then Grandfather walked in whilst carrying a 13 year old Honey Dew on his back. He walked with Uncle Julian, Phoenix and his teenaged son Chiron and lastly, the elderly Derik. I wondered where Honey Dew's parents were?

"Hi Derik." I kissed his cheek as he and his 'posse' arrived at the drinks table.

"Hey bro." Declan shook his hand. "How are you?"

He coughed which showed he was still getting over the flu. I noticed this caused my mate concern and he frowned on this old man for a younger brother.

"Not bad for an ordinary human." Derik joked in a husky voice.

"Hi B." Grandfather kissed my cheek, then so did Uncle Julian and Phoenix.

"Shivers! B is wearing a dress." My cousin teased, looking me up and down. "Should we run out and buy a lottery ticket?"

Uncle Julian laughed with his son and his grandson Chiron.

"Are you feeling OK, B?" Derik ribbed in his role as Medicine Man, which made his brother chuckle.

"Shut up Phoenix!" I whacked him on the arm. "Now look at what you've started."

Honey Dew laughed and pointed at her Uncle Phoenix for getting smacked.

"Hey monkey." Declan pulled her from her Uncle Em's back to hold up his giggling 13 year old Grand Niece in the air. "Look at how big you are now!"

Then Honey Dew's mother, Blanche came in with her husband, her brother Michael and his wife and their two kids, as well as with an elderly Rachel.

"Michael!" I beamed and instantly bestowed a kiss on his cheek. "How is my favourite godson?"

"Since I'm your only godson, I'm not sure how special that makes me feel." He joked.

I rolled my eyes as I shook my head at his sarcastic sense of humor which took after his uncle.

When Declan put Honey Dew down to greet the other arrivals, she immediately ran back to Grandfather. He easily picked her up to put her on his back again. Grandfather had this effect on the girls in our family, where we all wanted to be picked up by him. I remember doing the same thing when I was little and then so did Phoebe and then Blanche and now Honey Dew does it. Grandfather never complained, rather he smiled instead. I think it was because he gave off the vibe as being the 'Big Papa Bear' of our family, with infinite patience and kindness. This was his real strength, let alone his Werewolf muscle.

"Honey Dew." Derik frowned on his granddaughter. "Give your Uncle Em a break, you're 13 years old now. From the amount of kids that have climbed on him over the years, I'm surprised he's still walking."

"It's fine, Derik." My grandfather as a 117 year old Lokoti Werewolf, promised the frailer 78 year old human Medicine Man. "Besides, I still give Arabella piggy-back rides now and then."

"Em!" Gran blushed as she poked him in the side. Grandfather chuckled whilst he leaned in to kiss his wife on the cheek.

"Eew!" Honey Dew complained at their affection.

"Good." Declan said firmly as he wagged his finger in her face. "I want to hear the same reaction in another five years when you have Lokoti boys and the boys in Alma start asking you out on dates!"

"Hey, she won't even be allowed to date!" Derik jested.

"Dad and Uncle Declan, really!" Blanche snickered. "You're going to give my daughter a complex!"

"Excuse me, but I recall hearing the same thing from you once upon a time about boys. Don't think that with the passing of time that I forget things like that." My mate teased his niece whom looked older than him. "It's not just my body that's strong, but it's my memory as well. Just because I've kept my good looks, I'm still older than your father."

"Good looks? Ha!" His brother scoffed. "Who started dating first? You're just lucky that my looks have faded now."

I laughingly shook my head along with Blanche and Rachel at their brotherly banter.

"You're just jealous that I've always been stronger than you." Declan hit back.

"Me, jealous of you? Yeah, right! Growing up with you as my older brother was like growing up with the Incredible Hulk!" He teased. "With your temper and strength, I'm surprised the house we lived in is still standing!"

"Ha ha!" Honey Dew laughed at Declan. "You're the Incredible Hulk!"

"Right, that's it. Come here you!" He pulled her off Grandfather's back once again to tickle her mercilessly as she squealed with laughter.

With Honey Dew momentarily distracted, Grandfather used this chance to pull Gran into his arms. I watched my him lovingly look into his mate's youthful face as he kissed her softly. My grandparents may have known each other since they were 14 years old; but they looked on the other like the first day they met, as they neared their centennial wedding anniversary.

Now Mum and Dad arrived and I immediately waved them over to join us.

"Hi everyone." She greeted cheerfully.

Once they reached our position, she kissed everybody's cheeks as he shook their hands, except mine of course.

"Hi B." He gave a warm hug. "How are you?"

"Good thanks Dad." I smiled back.

"How is your lecturing going?" He enquired.

"Good." I nodded. "Last week I taught at Sydney Uni."

"That's right." He remembered. "Did you drop in on your Australian relatives?"

"Yeah, I had lunch with the Baker's." I nodded.

"And how are they?" Grandfather asked, overhearing our discussion.

"They're good." I promised. "They say hi of course and want you and Gran to come to dinner soon."

"Yeah, we should." Gran looked to her husband. "We haven't been to Sydney in ages."

"How about you call them this week and set something up?" He smiled as he never could say no to her.

"We should have a barbecue and invite the Baker's, the Bernard's and include the Worthall's to do a proper catch up that way." Mum suggested as she looked to Dad.

"Sure." He shrugged amiably.

Speaking of catch-ups with overseas relatives, at that moment Vincent arrived with Phoebe and their 40 year old daughter, Penelope.

Uncle Julian was quick to call them over. As soon as they joined us, he kissed his elderly daughter's cheek before he shook Vincent's hand. Although Penelope was a grown woman, she still giggled girlishly when Uncle Julian swamped her in a bear hug and spun her around.

"Did you have a good flight?" He asked the international family after he replaced his granddaughter to the ground.

"It was good thanks, Dad." The 73 year old Phoebe answered as she held her husband's hand.

"Thank goodness the Circulate still run Hodge Endeavor, so we can afford to travel First Class with all the globe-trotting we do." Penelope smirked.

Vincent may have been 102 years old, but being a Calculator he aged at slower rate, similar to the Werewolves. He had the appearance of somebody in their thirties but like the Werewolves, it in no way lessened his love for his younger wife who looked older than him.

As I looked on my cousin, I sighed sadly at seeing her age so. Since she's younger, it felt strange to see her look much older than I did. Of course being a telepath, she was unique in her own way. But her older brother Phoenix being one of the pack, also appeared younger than her. Their Lokoti Werewolf father even looked younger than his human daughter.

Phoebe whom overheard my thoughts, turned and pulled a face back which made me laugh.

Oh well, at least you don't get woken up in the middle of the night anymore from painful cramps – I thought her way.

"True." She agreed out loud. "THAT I don't miss."

"What?" Vincent looked on.

"Oh nothing." Phoebe smirked. Next, she heard my mother's thoughts. "Aunt Jess wants to ask you a question."

"What news on the Circulate front?" She asked as he turned her way.

He shrugged, "the Board of Hodge Endeavor are behaving themselves. Oh and the Worthall's send their regards and are going to arrange dinner next month to have you all over."

"We were just thinking of something similar, with the Baker's and the Bernard's." She laughed.

"If the Circulators don't mind circulating all the family to Blythe, the Worthall's would be happy to accommodate." He agreed.

"It was good staying at Blythe for a couple of days before we toured the continent." Mum sighed and Dad nodded in agreement about their recent trip to Europe. "The four weeks we were away passed so quickly."

"Where did you go again?" Blanche tried to recall.

"We started in London and then we did Paris, Lyon, Nice, Florence, Rome, Venice, Vienna, Munich, Frankfurt, Cologne, Amsterdam and then back to London." She recited off by heart. "I swear the trip just wasn't long enough."

"It WAS long enough." Dad disagreed. "It was a relief coming back and smelling home soil again."

The members of the pack all nodded in understanding, as Lokoti Werewolves they too waned if they were away from their home territory. I guess since I was also a Circulator, I didn't feel it as much as my male kin. I felt sorry for Mum, as she clearly wanted to have more international holidays but because of Dad, she didn't get much of a chance to do so. However she still did regular day trips through time as a Circulator, with Dad anxiously waiting at home.

Vincent frowned in annoyance at her biological ties to her husband. Our Calculator could still be vocal with his opinion that Mum's marriage was holding her back. It would turn into Calculator verses Lokoti Werewolf, as Dad and Vincent often butted heads. As Vincent urged Mum to travel through time to taste the delights human history had to offer? Dad stayed home and missed her terribly. This meant she couldn't be away for twelve hours at a time otherwise my parents could wane being apart.

"I would like to have a European holiday." I sighed to her.

"You would?" Declan looked on in surprise.

"Yeah! Although I'm a Circulator, I hardly circulate off Lokoti land!" I scoffed.

"That's because you're also a Lokoti Werewolf." Dad said adamantly. "You could wane if you're away for too long."

"But since B's never been away for longer than twelve hours," Vincent made reference to my guest lectures, "how would you know that this could happen?"

Now it wasn't just my father who looked on my Calculator in annoyance, it was my husband too.

"Twelve hours is long enough, thank you!" Declan said narkily, as he put his arm possessively about my waist.

"Sweetheart," Phoebe patted her husband on the chest, "you're about to get ripped apart by a Lokoti Werewolf and a European Werewolf."

"And if you calculated the odds of your survival if this happened? I don't think you'd like the answer." Grandfather chuckled in good humor.

*****

After lunch when the speeches were over, the music started up and several couples moved to the dance floor. I watched from my seat at the table I was sharing with Declan, Derik, Rachel and the vacant seats Michael, Blanche and their families previously habited. Their grown children were now mingling with other members of the tribe, as their grandchildren were running around the hall, playing one game or another.

"Let's dance!" I said brightly to my mate.

"Dance?" He looked on like I was nuts. "Since when have you ever seen me dance?"

"Exactly!" I whacked him on the arm. "It's time you took me dancing, Declan Sabre."

"As if!" He scoffed as he looked away.

I rolled my eyes as I next looked to Derik and Rachel, "you two should dance."

She snickered, "because your husband is a dismal failure on the dance floor, you want to reenact through us?"

"Yes, now go and dance!"

"I can't." She sighed in resignation.

"Rachel's hip is playing up again." Derik explained.

"Oh." My face fell as I felt like an idiot.

Mandy had passed away last year from cancer, leaving just Derik and Rachel and I, from our old circle of friends. Out of the remaining three, I was the only one whom had kept her vitality. I guess I'd forget that not everyone was as strong or youthful as the Werewolves or Circulators in the tribe.

Just then an old favourite song came on, Lou Bega and his 'Mambo Number 5'.

"Oh I love this song!" I gave a little jump as I clapped my hands. I looked imploringly to Declan. "Pleeeaaassee?"

"Nah ah." He firmly shook his head.

"Oooh!" I looked on with longing at the dance floor.

Derik shook his head at his older brother before he exchanged a look with his wife, who guessed his thoughts and smiled encouragingly.

"Shall we?" He turned my way.

"Really?" I looked to Rachel to make sure that she didn't mind.

"Just be gentle with him." She smirked.

I jumped to my feet as I pulled him out of his seat and onto the dance floor. Declan and Rachel laughed at my eagerness, at how it looked like I was dragging this 'older man' to dance with me. Derik graciously swung away to the Latin music, spinning me in his arms and then I swayed my body next to his.

"I bet you didn't see us doing this when we were 18 years old." He joked.

"Maybe I did, but just not in the way that you were imagining things would turn out." I gave a small smile back.

"True." He spun me around on the end of his arm again. "Then again you've always been my best friend. We grew up together then we grew old together, or I did anyways."

"I always will be your best friend, Derik." I smiled warmly.

I wasn't sure if it was the lighting of the room, but I could have sworn he turned a little misty eyed. As I swayed closer, I kissed his cheek before he spun me outwards again. We both laughed when I almost hit another couple dancing nearby.

Rachel smilingly watched as she joked; "she's still got the moves."

Declan observed his little brother keep up, "and so has he."

Next, she sighed wistfully, "if only all of us could remain young and stay together." My mate raised his eyebrows as he waited for her to finish, "I still remember going to school with Mandy, B and Derik like it was only yesterday."

"I remember the four of you hanging out when you were kids." My youthful husband smiled on the elderly woman, "and I remember yelling at you to turn your music down when I was trying to sleep after a hunt or a patrol."

"We used to be so afraid of you when we were little." She giggled back. "But B always stood up to you, when you used to shout at us to shut up? B would yell right back at you to shut up instead."

"Yeah..." he chuckled, "...she still does that."

Then she turned serious as she said gravely, "I'm glad that the two of you have each other, Declan. I really am. Mandy died alone last year. Although she was surrounded by friends, she died without a family of her own. I'm glad that that will never happen to you."

"So am I Rachel," his smile faded as he clearly looked perturbed by the idea, "so am I."

Derik remained on the dance floor with me for the next song. We waltzed along to U2's 'With or Without You' and then we laughed when he tried to dip me backwards.

When best friend caught a couple of teenaged boys watching me dance, he protectively put his arm about my waist as he mockingly growled, "alright small fry, the lady's taken. Skedaddle!"

I cracked up laughing when I saw the boys' eyes widen from their 'telling off' from the tribe's Medicine Man and they quite literally did! Declan had said this very thing sixty years ago at Ben's End of Summer Bonfire, when in those days, he was protecting Derik's interests. I didn't know that he had witnessed his older brother do this?

"How's teaching going?" He asked as we danced.

"It's not really teaching, it's just a guest lecture here and there." I said modestly.

"Declan's said that you've done quite a few at different Universities around the world." He grinned proudly.

It sounds like my husband's been boasting about his wife, which came as a pleasant surprise. Instead I shrugged modestly, "yeah, it's nice to be invited."

"I remember planning with you to study at University like it was only yesterday." Derik sighed.

"Same here." I agreed. "Do you notice that the older we get, the faster time speeds up? And yet sometimes it's like we're the ones moving in slow motion, recalling events like they were only yesterday."

He let out a laugh as he looked me up and down. "B, I don't think you're exactly in a position where you can talk about old age. It makes you sound pretentious."

"Shut up!" I playfully punched him on the arm.

"Youch!" He laughingly rubbed the spot where I hit him. "Careful, you've still got a mean right hook and my body isn't what it used to be."

"Don't worry Derik, if you fall I'll catch you again." I brought up a certain evening walk home.

He sighed ruefully as he danced with me in his arms. "I know B, besides the time you married another man and then you 'ran off' with my brother? Your loyalty has been unswerving."

Blushing, I punched him on the arm again as he chuckled in good humor. Uncle Julian who'd been watching from his seat, must have thought he should rescue Derik from his 'beating' as he stepped in to take his place.

"She's all yours!" He smiled in relief upon the older Lokoti Werewolf before he returned to his wife's side.

"B," my uncle jokingly chastised, "what have we told you about controlling the bloodlust? You're not allowed to beat up the old people in this tribe."

"Then I promise to be gentle with you, Uncle." I taunted, which made him laugh.

We danced slowly to a romantic song that came on when I heard him sigh sadly. I guess the music must have reminded him of his mate. I looked up into his face in concern.

"So, how are you Uncle Jules?"

"Yeah, I'm OK thanks B. It gets a little easier and yet harder with each day that passes." I heard the underlying loneliness in his voice. We were quiet for a moment or two before I saw him looking over at his table where Phoenix and Phoebe were sitting with their spouses and children, "having kids helps. It's nice to see Danika live on in the family we created."

I could see his point. With his beloved mate, they created a telepathic daughter who gave him a telepathic granddaughter. The Riverclaw Lokoti Werewolf genes continued on in his son and now his grandson.

My heart skipped a beat as I looked over to Declan, who was laughing with Derik, Rachel and their two grown children who had returned to sit with them. My husband was giving up procreation to be with me, so what if he was also giving up something which could later bring comfort and support?

After I danced with Uncle Jules, Dad took his place and I danced with him. Next, I danced with Grandfather before I danced with Phoenix and lastly, I danced with Chiron.

"How are you getting used to your new status as one of the pack?" I asked my younger relation.

The 18 year old Chiron changed two months ago when Uncle Quinn passed away. Chiron had to delay finishing High School as he learned to control his changes. He couldn't leave tribal lands as any human who weren't Lokoti, were a dangerous temptation to the bloodlust.

"It's nice to get out of the house and be in company again." He confessed as he looked about the crowded meeting hall.

However, I noticed that he gazed the longest on a pretty Lokoti girl standing just off to the side, talking to her friends as he said this.

"Yeah, I'll bet!" I laughed at his obvious attraction.

"Aw, come off it Aunt B!" He tried not to blush. "Besides, why would Rain Lightfoot even know who I am? She's that pretty, all the guys in school want to ask her out."

Just then, I caught her pass a small smile his way.

"I wouldn't be so sure, if I were you." I smirked. "Maybe you should ask her to dance?"

"Nup." He quickly shook his head.

"Chiron Riverclaw, you're now a Lokoti Werewolf which means you've got the Lokoti Werewolf pheromone thing going on. Now use it!" I ordered.

The young man paused for a moment as he looked on hopeful to which I nodded encouragingly.

"OK, here goes..." He muttered as he released me to walk towards Rain.

Suddenly I found myself without a dance partner. "You could have waited at least until the song had ended." I shook my head as I left the dance floor to rejoin Declan.

He, Derik and Rachel had just observed what took place and were chuckling. I sat down with them as we all watched Chiron struggle with a pink face to talk to Rain. She in turn blushed back, but eventually she nodded. He took hold of her hand to escort her out onto the dance floor before he held her closely.

"That was fast." Rachel snickered. "Look how close he's holding her and it's only their first dance!"

"The boy's got the moves alright." Derik chuckled in agreement.

"Yep, I taught him everything he knows." Declan gloatingly sat back into his seat.

"Yeah right!" I rolled my eyes, as did his brother and sister-in-law.

Just then Phoenix came over to sit in the vacated seat beside Declan, which had been Honey Dew's chair.

"Well I'll be! Chiron finally got the nerve to talk to Rain." He chuckled as he watched his son. "That boy's had a crush on her the last eighteen months but he's been too chicken to ask her out."

"Now that he's a Werewolf, I guess he's got the guts." Declan winked.

"Plus he's got the Lokoti Werewolf pheromones to use on her." Derik shook his head at his brother. "It's a good thing you're a European Werewolf as you didn't have that growing up."

"What do you mean that I don't have pheromones to attract the opposite sex?" He asked indignantly. "I've had LOTS of girls like me!"

"You wish!" Derik scoffed.

"What about your friend Mandy?" My mate reminded.

"Yeah but Mandy said so herself it was just a passing craze." His little brother rebuked.

"It wasn't your pheromones that had attracted her, it was your physique." Rachel told him.

"B, back me up here," my mate looked my way, "tell them I smell good!"

"Declan smells like maple syrup." I said simply.

As soon as I said that, the whole table burst into laughter!

"Thanks B." Declan rolled his eyes.

"What's wrong with that?" I shrugged. "I like maple syrup."

This only made Phoenix, Derik and Rachel laugh harder. Declan shook his head at the lot of us as next he looked out at the dance floor and then so did I.

'God Only Knows' by The Beach Boys started to play and many couples got out of their seats to dance. I saw Grandfather dancing with Gran, as well as Dad with Mum, Vincent with Phoebe, and Chiron still danced with Rain.

"Excuse me, I'm going to ask my beautiful wife for a dance." Phoenix stood up.

I watched him walk over to his middle-aged wife, murmur into her ear and I saw how quickly she giggled in agreement. He pulled out her chair for her before she took his hand as he led her out onto the dance floor.

"It's a slow song, you wanna risk it?" Derik smiled lovingly on Rachel.

"Why not?" She beamed back.

He stood up to pull out her chair for her, before he helped her up. But before he walked her out onto the dance floor, he whacked his older brother on the arm, "have a dance with your wife you wuss!"

Declan growled back and then he watched his elderly brother slowly sway to the music with his elderly wife in his arms.

"OK then." He looked my way as if I had just asked him to donate a kidney or some such. "Let's get this over with."

"Excuse me?" I raised my eyebrows unimpressed.

My European Werewolf mate stood up, pulled out my chair and then he roughly pulled me to my feet.

"Man, you really suck at this romantic stuff!" I said in annoyance as I was dragged out onto the dance floor.

"Yeah yeah." He growled in irritation as he began to move awkwardly.

I looked him over as it occurred to me, "you don't know how to dance."

"Of course I don't know how to dance!" He huffed. "I'm a frickin' European Werewolf, not a ballerina!"

"Right." I stopped us to teach him how to waltz. "Put your right hand on my waist and then hold up your left hand like this. Now, watch my feet."

Declan's face turned pink but he had to take my orders or look like a fool. We both kept our eyes downcast for the first minute or so, as we concentrated on him not stepping on my toes. Eventually, he started to get the gist of it.

"You see B?" He looked up proudly. "It's a piece of cake."

"But can you twirl her?" Chiron asked as he danced past. To boast, he spun Rain around in his arms before pulling her back to him.

"Show off!" He snarled bad-temperedly at the younger Werewolf.

This frightened Rain as she clearly blanched but Chiron laughed as he danced her away to another part of the floor.

"Declan, you're not frightening off my Great Grandson's dance partner, are you?" Grandfather smirked as he and Gran waltzed by.

She tittered at his words before her husband spun her away too.

I tenderly caressed my mate's face as I joked softly, "I really can't take you anywhere."

He looked on my gesture almost breathless. I could feel his heart pound inside of his strong chest, before he ducked his head to rest his lips on my forehead. Like this, we slow danced amongst our loved ones.

*****

Uncle Harry's Birthday Party disbanded around 6 PM and the families with small children left even earlier. Tiredly, I walked hand-in-hand with my husband, back to his truck when he used his remote to open the doors before he closed my door for me again.

I was quiet for the five minute drive home, as I stared out the window at the woods which surrounded our community centre. Being a Lokoti Werewolf, I felt an affinity to this land since it was ingrained in my very DNA to protect my home. To me, the National Park served as a reminder of the cycle of life, especially how it changed with the seasons.

In winter, life was in hibernation from the snow and the below freezing temperatures. Then in spring, the deciduous trees grew new leaves and seeds which had dropped, began to sprout new vegetation. Amongst the rebirth of flora, there was the birth of new fauna. The young were found beside their parents, who taught them how to find food and fend for themselves.

Both the woods and animals provided for the Lokoti. We hunted for meat and pelts, but never to excess. This included the pack who never hunted an animal into extinction. We hunted bear, bison, caribou, moose and other large quarry, but an instinct inside of us which was just as strong as the bloodlust, told us when to switch to new prey.

Seeing my family today was another example of the cycle of life. There were those who were in the winter of their lives, and those that were in the spring. There were those that were reaching the end of their timelines and those that were only beginning. Just as the space time continuum ensured the continuation of existence with the Big Bang, the Big Crunch and another Big Bang; so too did the woods with the change of seasons. It was the same with the continuation of family and tribe; Humans, Werewolves and Circulators alike...everyone except me, that is.

I was the last Circulator and the first female Lokoti Werewolf. I was both Yin and Yang. I was tied to the past, by my Lokoti Werewolf heritage just as I was tied to the future, with my bio-electromagnetic frequency in temporal flux. With the fact I couldn't create new life, made me question my existence such as why am I so far, the only female Lokoti Werewolf? Why am I not as supernaturally fertile as my male counterparts? As a Circulator I had the freedom of moving through time and space by will alone, but because I was called the last I couldn't reproduce.

Declan and I stood out with our youthful appearances although officially we could be called 'old'. We were in a miniscule minority of 'old people' who didn't have kids or grandkids. In a tribe of almost 500 members, those who chose to never marry nor procreate were less than twenty.

Just then a painful cramp made me squeeze my eyes shut, right as he pulled into our driveway. He turned off the engine before he turned to look my way in concern. "Are you OK?"

I opened my eyes whilst I opened my door and forced myself to climb out. Declan walked ahead to unlock the front door and let us into the house. The quietness of our clean abode was in direct contrast to the family-orientated celebration where we had spent all day. As I looked around our spotless living area, there was no sign of any kids created mess or kids created noise.

I walked into the kitchen to grab the water jug out of the fridge. I poured myself a glass before I pulled my pain killers out of my purse. He frowned as he watched me gulp down four more tablets.

534

"Maybe you should go and lie down." He suggested.

I shook my head as I walked past to go sit in the lounge room. However I didn't pick up my book I was in the middle of reading, just as I didn't reach for the remotes for the Internet TV or music system. I tucked my legs underneath to curl up on the couch. My ears were still ringing from the crowded meeting hall with everybody who attended including their children.

My husband opened up the fridge again to grab some soda. I knew it was a fizzy drink because of the hiss it made when he opened the bottle to pour himself a glass. He carried it into the lounge room as he came to sit beside and put his feet up on the coffee table.

We sat there quietly, in the silence that was our house. I stared at the 24 hour time on the digital display of the Internet TV, whilst he sipped on his soda. Neither of us said a thing for over five minutes, as we just sat there in the solitary silence of only the two of us...

Declan and B, the union of two different breeds of Werewolves with not a 'rug rat' between us; since nothing was produced from our constant procreational activities except placating the bloodlust.

I enquired, "do you wish that we had kids to fill our quiet house with noise?"

"Oh God, here we go again." He abruptly moaned. When I gave a funny look, he cried out exasperated, "every time, B! Every single frickin' time! Whenever we come back from a tribal gathering, I hear this!"

I looked on hurt at his reaction, but my husband continued to rant.

"I can't have kids, there's something wrong with me. Maybe you should leave me for someone who can give you kids?" He mimed in a whiny voice. "Frickin' hell! Have you ever stopped to consider what comes out of your mouth sometimes?!"

Seething, I looked away as I felt my face burn in anger but he wouldn't shut up.

"I don't want kids!" He snapped. "B, just admit that neither do you! You only mention them after a tribal gathering, because you feel left out. When there isn't a tribal gathering, you're quite happy to write your essays and lecture just as I'm happy with the Garage. I like having you whenever I want, where ever I want without worrying about if kids are asleep or not! We don't want kids!"

"How would you know if I want kids or not, Declan?" I asked in annoyance.

"Because I know you, B!" He faced me. "You're like a kid yourself, you see the children at tribal gatherings and you feel left out because you don't have one. But a day or two afterwards, you're fine again. You work on your research or in the greenhouse or at Circulate Headquarters. Whenever we have to babysit, I see that you're just as eager as I am to hand the kids back over to their parents!"

"I am not!"

"If you really wanted to have kids, you would talk about them all the time instead of just after a tribal gathering. Then I would take you seriously and consider adoption with you. But you don't want kids anymore than I do!" He looked away again.

"Well there's no point in considering adoption if you don't want kids."

He sighed loudly in annoyance before he spoke again. "OK, so for the sake of argument if we did adopt, what would you want? A boy or girl?"

"A girl...no a boy. Hang on, a girl. Oh, I don't know!" I huffed. "Maybe we're not meant to know, maybe we're supposed to end up with whoever needs parents the most?"

"Alright then," he continued, "at what age would we adopt? A newborn or older?"

"I don't know, I had always thought when it was still a baby. But maybe we should consider one who was older?"

"So we don't have to change any diapers or potty train them?" He guessed.

"Yeah but then if we adopted a 5 year old who saw us as Werewolves for the first time; we would probably traumatize the poor thing." I frowned as he snickered. "So maybe we should get an orphan who's a baby so it will grow up thinking it's normal having parents who were Werewolves."

"It sounds more logical." He nodded.

"But you're going to have to keep your temper in check." I sung warningly.

"MY temper?" Declan raised his eyebrows. "Well if this isn't the stove calling the kettle black! As soon as you raise your voice, sparks come flying off you!"

"Yeah right!"

"You think my European Werewolf temper is scary? Have you looked in the mirror lately? Every time you, your Mom or your Gran get angry; sometimes the air turns cold or lights flicker as your bio-electromagnetic frequencies go higher!"

"Oh yeah?" I rolled my eyes. "Somehow I don't think a human child is going to be able to see my aura. They'd be more worried about getting eaten by you when you change especially when you get angry."

"Unless the kid is psychic." He pointed out.

"Yeah alright, but what are the chances of us getting a psychic kid?"

"What are the chances of a European Werewolf mating with the first female Lokoti Werewolf in existence?" He smirked.

I moaned dejectedly, "the first Lokoti Werewolf to be barren in the history of the pack, what are the chances of that?" Then I looked on anxiously, "but don't you ever wonder what it would be like to have a child of your own?"

"And here we go again!" He slammed his glass down onto the coffee table so hard he put a crack in it! "Sometimes B, I think you only remember something that's convenient for you!"

"What's that supposed to mean?!"

"I can't have a human woman without either killing her or turning her, so what is so hard about that, you can't understand?!" He rebuked. "You're my perfect mate because you're not just stronger than a human woman, being a Lokoti Werewolf? But while everyone is dropping around us like flies, with you also being a Circulator I'll never have to worry about losing you! Not until I'm the one who dies first!"

Declan rose to his feet, picked up the broken glass and he stomped into the kitchen to drop it into the bin. Then I watched him storm up our staircase to have his evening shower.

*****

We didn't talk again for the rest of the night. He made some toasted cheese, tomato and onion sandwiches for a light dinner, but he left my plate he had prepared sitting on the kitchen counter instead of bringing out. He perfunctory ate his at the table as I ate mine on the couch, whilst reading a book.

When I came to bed, I walked into a dark bedroom with my husband already lying down. He lay on his side, facing the wall as I stripped out of my clothes to toddle off to the bathroom for my shower. Twenty minutes later when I climbed into bed, I settled onto my side facing away from him. We lay uncharacteristically not touching each other, whilst looking in opposite directions.

Five minutes passed and then ten minutes ticked by. But when we were coming up to fifteen minutes, Declan broke the stale mate by turning over and rolling me onto my back. I could tell he was still angry though, as his eyes were glowing green.

"Frickin' hell woman, you drive me mental." He growled in frustration. "I'm going to show you for once and for all, a big benefit to not having kids in the house!"

He roared loudly as he dove his sharp teeth into my left breast which made me squeal in laughter! Our growls could probably be heard from outside of the house if you had been standing outside on the driveway. My snarling matched his, as we passionately mauled the other, for almost all of the night. Our pajamas were shredded first with our sheets a close second, as yet another set were thrown to the wind.

Yep, I saw his point alright, as nights like this certainly turned our house into an 'Adults Only' zone.

~~~~~~
~~~~~~

6th June 2145

Declan acted suspiciously over the next couple of days. The following afternoon when he came home from work, I found him pacing up and down our driveway as he talked on his mobile phone. The next evening when his phone rang during dinner, he quickly got rid of the call.

"I can't talk now, as I'm eating dinner. Email me the documents at the Garage." He said shortly before he hung up. When he caught my peculiar look, he tried to play the innocent, "what?"

"What was that all about?"

"Oh um, it's work related." He tried to lie.

"Yeah right!"

"Oh, so you're the only one who can be all-important with work?" He asked coolly. "I suppose the fact that I'm now running the Garage is no never mind to you!"

"Your work at the Garage has never called you at night before."

"Overseas work contacts." He shrugged as he shoveled a huge forkful of lasagna into his mouth.

"Overseas work contacts?" I echoed in skepticism.

"Yeah, overseas contacts whom I have to buy parts from. Now do you mind? Quit with the third degree, woman!"

On the third night, whilst he was cooking in the kitchen, I overheard him make a secret call. I was sitting at the coffee table in our lounge area working on my laptop, when I heard him speak quietly as he was frying up some caribou steaks in garlic butter.

"No, the itinerary you sent was too long as it can't be longer than six weeks. Even six weeks is pushing it, because I don't want to be away for two full moons. Yep. Uh huh. Right. OK, I'll expect the updated version emailed to me tomorrow. Bye."

I tried to concentrate on my research, but what the hell was Declan doing?

When dinner was ready and I came to sit across from him at the table, I looked suspiciously across my rare steak, baked potato with sour cream and toss salad. He tried to look innocently back.

"Are you secretly adopting a baby?" I asked bluntly.

"Nah ah." He casually shook his head as he ate some potato with the sour cream. "Not unless you want to do all the diaper changing yourself?"

The fourth evening, I sat at the dining table typing my upcoming presentation on 'Gods of Love and War of the Ancient World', when I looked up at the clock. It was nearing 8 PM and my husband hadn't come home from work yet. Where was he? His suspicious behavior was really starting to unnerve me.

I started to let my eyes glaze over, so I could use my ability to 'see' where he was and what he was doing? But then I didn't need to, when I heard his truck pull into the driveway. I waited impatiently as I listened to him open his door and climb out before shutting the door behind. He engaged the remote central locking before he walked up the veranda steps and then opened the front door.

As soon as he came into the house, he found my eyes trained his way. This made him grin as he carried some papers under his arm.

"Hi honey I'm home, did you miss me?"

"Are you having an affair?" My eyes narrowed and I sniffed to see if I could smell female pheromones on him.

"That's rich coming from you. I wasn't the one who was married to someone else for five years." He said coolly as he walked over to where I was sitting.

He tossed down the papers onto the table before me and then he stood back and waited as I perused through them.

I sat up straighter with a start, when I realized what I was looking at. It was a travel itinerary complete with flights, hotel accommodation, car hire and different city tours for a six week long, European holiday!

"DECLAN NO WAY!" I leapt to my feet so suddenly it knocked my chair over, as I clutched onto the papers like they were the Holy Grail.

"Way," he smiled smugly at my reaction, "I can tell that you like getting away with your lecturing, even if it is for one day at a time. I know you wished you could be away for longer to look around the different cities you visit. B, this is what comes from not having kids, by being able to go on holidays like this."

"Paris, Lyon, Nice, Milan, Florence, Rome, Naples, Corfu, Athens, Venice, Munich, Vienna, Prague, Warsaw, Vilnius, Riga, St. Petersburg, Helsinki, Stockholm, Oslo, Hamburg, Berlin, Cologne, Amsterdam, Brussels and then back to Paris..." I read off the itinerary.

"Six weeks of Europe." He gloated. "This can be the honeymoon we never got to have. Tell me, how much do you love me?"

I leapt upon him! My arms flew about his neck as my legs wrapped around his waist. Declan laughed as he easily caught me in his strong arms to spin me around.

"Who's your daddy?" He laughingly held me close.

I laughed back as I almost squeezed the life out of him with the amount of gratitude I felt.

"How did you arrange all of this?" I pulled away slightly so I could see his face.

"I have my ways." He chuckled, but when he saw my eyes narrow again he answered, "I called your Gran and Grandfather and they put me in contact with their person in Hodge Endeavor. Apparently this 'contact' which is like a PA for your Gran, has ways of making things happen. She emailed me travel brochures and drafted together different itineraries for me to choose from. Apparently Hodge Endeavor will be paying for all of this. I think we're going to have the cushiest six weeks of our lives, with all the five-star hotels and luxury cars on this trip."

I squealed again as I hugged him once more and he did another little turn, whilst holding me back just as tightly.

He added on lastly, "I thought six weeks should be long enough to have a good look around, but it's not too long that we'll wane being away from our hunting grounds."

My eyes widened in worry as I pulled away to look on my mate, "but your bloodlust is worse than mine, Declan. I can control my bloodlust for six weeks while I'm away but what about you? You need to hunt in between full moons, so how are you going to cope?"

I watched my mate's eyes soften first before the rest of his face did; "B, I've got you. I could be put under any kind of endurance test but with you beside me, I wouldn't even blink because you sustain me."

That did the trick, my mouth molded to his as the travel itinerary slipped to the floor. Declan soon followed, as he sunk to his knees to lay me out beside the documents to celebrate our holiday and love in our typical style...

~~~~~~
~~~~~~

~ **25** ~

20th August 2145

I could tell my husband was getting bored because I had accidentally filled a quarter of our 'honeymoon' with shopping. We were half way through our stay in St. Petersburg and whereas I saw the night markets as an interesting cultural event? My husband saw it as more shopping.

We weren't just traveling with our own credit cards, but we were also using those that came with our five-star European holiday courtesy of Hodge Endeavor. It was times like these, made me awestruck at Gran's or Vincent's influence over one of the world's top ten companies. During our stay in Paris, I put aside a day to buy haute couture suits for my lecturing. However as we traveled, I saw more things that I liked either for myself or a loved one back at home. The next thing he knew, he was yanked off the street and through a shop door.

With balalaika music filling the air courtesy of local musicians, I was basking in the Russian atmosphere. I enjoyed the smell of local cuisine cooking from several stalls, as did the locals since there were many in the crowded market place. I loved listening to the Russian language and when I conscientiously tried to speak it, I could the locals appreciated the gesture and were helpful.

Declan was still restless although the full moon had passed. To give credit where credit was due, I thought he was handling the bloodlust admirably. As we walked hand-in-hand through the markets, I was starting to get the impression that he would have been happy to do just that; a walk through. But I was enjoying the sights, sounds and smells of the place. I pulled him over to a stall that was selling beautiful brocade bags, when I picked up a stifled growl.

"Alright, fine." I released his hand. "You go on."

"What?" He feigned innocence.

"Go on." I urged.

"Go where?"

"Go and do whatever it is that you would prefer to be doing, and I'll meet you back at the hotel."

"What is it that you think I want to do, B?" He arched his eyebrows.

"I don't know, but it's obviously NOT this."

"I didn't say a thing!"

"You didn't have to, I've heard you growl for the past hour."

"I have not!" He tried to protest when I looked on in disbelief. He sighed as he scratched the back of his head. "Well alright, so maybe the odd growl did escape."

Then his apologetic demeanor changed as he looked distractedly about the market place with his eyes narrowing.

"Declan, go and do whatever it is that you would prefer to be doing right now." I ordered.

"But there isn't anything that I want do in St. Petersburg." He shrugged before he looked about again whilst sniffing. "B, can you smell THAT?"

"Smell what?" I asked dismissively as I thought he was putting it on. "You obviously don't want to be here, so go and do something else."

"Like what?"

"I don't know, just something!" I gave him a playful push.

My mate walked a little away, before he turned around to stand closely, "what I'd rather be doing, is ravishing you in our hotel room."

"Wow, what a surprise. You haven't kept your teeth or claws to yourself since we got here." I smirked.

"What can I say? I'm obviously not a city dweller. I miss the Alaska Range and I miss not being able to change."

I looked on sympathetically, "I sense that." We exchanged a long gaze before I said quietly, "I'll meet you back at the hotel in exactly two hours and then you'll feast."

"No." He looked away with a frown.

"No?"

"No, I've tasted too much already and I don't want to weaken you." He said uneasily.

"Do I look weak to you?" I gave a small smile. "I'm fine, Declan. You go off and do whatever it is you want to do and I'll see you soon."

"B -"

"Declan, I'll be fine I promise. I'm enjoying this time away and I appreciate that I'm sharing this experience with you."

"Really?"

"Really." I reached out to take hold of his hand.

My mate stepped up closer to inhale my scent as I caught him mutter, "damn woman, you're irresistible." With that he turned to walk away, glancing back over his shoulder as he went.

I smilingly watched him depart and I was still grinning when I turned back to examine the brocade bags. I bought a handbag for me as well as several more for my loved ones back home. Then I moved on to the next stall which was a bookstall.

I admired the many books, some of which were very old. Although the language was Russian, I found their antique value impressive. I managed to interpret some of the titles and I picked up an old book which was on the Communist era. I tried to read and perhaps understood every second or third word? But I don't know why, Communism has always fascinated me. It's probably because my tribe had similar ways, or the very least we could be called Socialist. The Lokoti had a 'share and share alike' philosophy as we traded food or goods with each other, rather than money.

For a good ten minutes, I stood there reading in Russian. I became so wrapped up in the language, I almost didn't notice that I was being watched...almost.   I think it was my Werewolf instincts which made me momentarily look up.

I don't know if it was my imagination or not, but I thought I saw somebody standing at the stall opposite, watching? However within a second, this person vanished. I shrugged as I returned to the book on which I was concentrating so hard, my Werewolf senses didn't pick up that the somebody was now standing beside.

"You are interested in communist history, Gaspahszjah?" A deep, male Russian accent asked.

With a start, I turned to see a thin, pale man with blonde hair, faded blue eyes and a forty-something appearance standing on my right.   That's strange, as I didn't hear his approach.

"Er, yeah?" I took a wary step back.

He gave a winning smile, "forgive me, as I did not mean to startle you."

"No problem."

"You are American, da?"

"Yes."

"But you are also something else..." he looked on which made me pause, "...you seem very international, almost transcendental."

Transcendental? I suppose that was one way to look at a Circulator. I laughed back, "you could say that."

When he grinned, I noticed that this man's teeth were very white with receding gums which made them look long and sharp, especially his canine teeth.

"You are visiting Mother Russia on a honeymoon, da?" He guessed.

"Um, yeah." I gave a peculiar look as I wondered how he knew this?

"You are a traveler, but you haven't been able to travel as much as you would like?"

"Erm, actually no."

"But the desire has always been there."

"I guess."

"Your husband, he is your second husband as your first husband died, da?" The stranger went on.

How the hell does this guy know all of this?! I eyed him suspiciously, "er yeah."

"Your second marriage will be a success." The man picked up my hand to turn it over so he could see my palm. "Hmm..."

"What?" I looked on curiously.

Was this guy a palm reader and I'm about to hear my future? Although I was a Circulator complete with a Calculator, I was still curious to hear what he could come up with.

"You cannot bear children." He said sadly which made me withdraw my hand with a start. He peered into my eyes, "but you don't need children, Gaspahszjah. Other people have children to gain a sense of eternity, to see themselves as everlasting; but you ARE everlasting."

I looked on transfixed as his pale blue eyes pierced my dark blue ones.

"You are Native Alaskan, yes?" He changed the subject.

"Um, yes."

"But you are also something else, is it part Chinese? Or part English, or is it part Australian?"

"How about all of the above?" I beamed truly impressed. I have all of these nationalities in my blood!

"Your grandmother on your father's side is Chinese background and your grandmother on your mother's side has English blood." He reclaimed my hand.

"Yes."

"The women in your family..." he caressed the top of my hand, "...they're the ones who are transcendental. But the men in your family, they're something else are they not?"

Yes, yes and yes! My father, grandfather and grandpa are certainly something else, being Lokoti Werewolves! This guy must be psychic or something.

"Will you buy that book?" The owner of the bookstall interrupted.

Before I could look away, the stranger passed the stall owner his Credit Card to pay for me.

"Hey -" I began to object.

The stranger smiled once more, "please allow me, as I am not a fortune teller trying to sell you your fortune. But I am like a traveler through the long years and I see someone similar to me."

My lips parted in surprise as I looked on feeling almost hypnotized. However, the stranger carried on as normal as he took back his Credit Card as well as the book, to put it in my bag for me. Next, we walked away from the stall as I blushed from struggling how to ask my next question.

"Please forgive my naivety, but are you psychic?"

The stranger laughed back, "no."

"But..." I stopped walking, "...you've got everything right so far."

"As I said Gaspahszjah, I recognize someone similar to me."

"Then what are you?"

"Someone who is different to every person here." He looked about sadly before his gaze settled on my face once more.

"Do you have dreams of events in time?" I tested.

He led me by the hand though the market, "I dream of things past, da."

"What kind of things do you dream about?"

"Ah Gaspahszjah, that is a complicated question that deserves a long answer," he sighed, "and one that cannot be answered here in this market place. Come and drink with me."

He rested my hand on his arm as he began to lead me away from the market place, which made me pause a second time. B, snap out of it! You're leaving this public place with a stranger?

"Oh um," I shook my head as if I were shaking myself out of a reverie, "I'm sorry, but my husband is expecting me."

"Your husband," he gave a nod, "the handsome young man who was escorting you earlier?"

This comment made my predatory instinct growl warningly about the stranger who must have seen Declan and I together, but he waited until we were apart to approach.

The stranger gave a wry grin, "the handsome young man with the beautiful young woman. You may be celebrating your honeymoon, but there is something supernatural about your marriage, da?"

"Excuse me?" I pulled my hand back from his arm.

"You and the young man, there is more than meets the eye about your marriage. The young man loves you very much. He loved you before you married your first husband."

I looked on flabbergasted, how the hell does he know so much?!

"The young man whom is protective over his territory, his transcendental wife. But the same man who could not stand by you?"

Warily, I took a step away, "what's that supposed to mean?"

"Why is he not here right now?"

"He had to do something." I said uneasily.

"The young man who is possessive of you, because he hungers for what only you can give." The stranger raised my hand to his lips to kiss it deeply. "The young man that you fought for; the young man that you sacrificed everything for; the young man that you died for."

The stranger's cold lips on my skin made my heart quicken and my stomach jolt! I felt like I couldn't look away as my skin prickled with goose bumps.

He went on in his husky Russian accent, "you have an independent spirit, Gaspahszjah. You thirst for knowledge, as you thirst for passion. You find culture fulfilling but your young man is impatient with learning."

My hand was securely in his own as he began walking us away again. All this time the stranger continued to hold my gaze with his own. His piercing, pale eyes seemed to see so much! I gaped as I walked, no longer noticing the market place or the people.

"I want to introduce you to authentic Russian vodka." He led me down a small alleyway with poor lighting. "Come and bask in the real Russia with me tonight Gaspahszjah, before I return you to your brash young man. There is a tavern that I will take you to that has Russian delicacies that you will die for."

"Um, I don't know…" I faltered as I looked down the dark road ahead.

"It is not far from here and in two hours I will return you to your husband whom awaits you in your hotel room." I giggled at his mischievous grin when he said that. "I want to learn all about you, the transcendental beauty who I believe is older than she looks, da?"

B, what the HELL are you doing with this man?! Why the HELL are you going ANYWHERE with him?! The sudden internal roar of my enraged Lokoti Werewolf instincts, snapped me back to reality.

"Er," I stopped us in our tracks, "thank you very much for your kind offer, but I should go back to my hotel. No offence, but I only just met you -"

When I didn't have the chance to finish what I was saying, because we were interrupted by Declan appearing out of nowhere to ram the stranger up against the wall!

WHOOMP!

My mate pinned the stranger against the side of the building with his eyes glowing green whilst he snarled ferociously!

"Declan, what the hell are you doing?!" I screeched, embarrassed.

"B get out of here, NOW!" He roared, as his teeth and nails grew longer.

"Declan, we were just talking!" I tried to pull him off the stranger.

However he wouldn't budge as next I heard the sound of his clothes tear when he expanded into his gigantic European Werewolf body. Oh no, Declan's flipped! He's reverting against his control.

"DECLAN, NO!" I screamed as I desperately tried to pull him off the stranger. "Fight it! C'mon Dec, you have to fight it!"

I changed too, as I needed my Lokoti Werewolf muscle to try to pry him off the stranger! Just as I managed to loosen one of his claw-like hands with my increased strength, he knocked me backwards! He easily elbowed me off whilst never letting the stranger go.

I hit the wall behind, but I was quick to jump to my feet uninjured. However as I was about to take him on again, I froze… my mate in full European Werewolf regalia wasn't holding a human against the wall, but the stranger's pale blue eyes had turned completely white! Jutting from his mouth were two long, sharp fangs as he hissed at him, just like a snake.

What the hell is that man? Just who needs protection from whom? What the HELL was going on here?!

My European Werewolf mate let out a deafening roar as the stranger merely hissed back. My husband's larger jaws snapped at the stranger, but the stranger in supernatural speed moved his head away from his dangerous mouth. The stranger's head moved side to side so quickly, he looked like a blur! He was faster although Declan was clearly stronger.

As I stared in shock, I picked up that we were no longer alone... I heard the footsteps first and then a scream second, of a human howling in terror. I turned to see an elderly man, carrying a bag of food he had bought at the markets. He had just begun to walk down the alleyway, when he saw what was before him.

The elderly man saw me in Lokoti Werewolf form, with my glowing turquoise eyes, my bulked up body, my elongated teeth and the claws on my hands and feet. Then he saw Declan in his huge, hulking, hairless European Werewolf form, with glowing green eyes and razor sharp jaws. Lastly, he saw the hissing stranger with the glowing white eyes and the long, sharp fangs...? No wonder we put the poor man off his dinner!

Declan hesitated for barely half a second, which gave the stranger his chance to escape. He slipped out of his grasp and took off down the alleyway so fast, it was a case of blink and you'll miss. In a single leap, the stranger jumped from the alleyway onto the rooftop and just like that, he was gone.

The elderly man followed suit by turning around still screaming and running for his life back out to the market place.

Shit, we had a witness whom saw us in our supernatural forms! But my mate didn't seem to care about being seen, as he tried to chase after the stranger. He bounded off on all-fours, down the alleyway.

"Declan!" I boomed out in my thunderous Werewolf voice.

I rolled my glowing turquoise eyes as I picked up my fallen backpack and shopping bags. I also had to pick up his torn clothes, before I took off down the alleyway after them. With my speed as a Circulator, I easily caught up and just in time too.

When the end of the alleyway came out onto a busy street, my mate leapt over the road entirely! The sight of a huge, hulking, hairless European Werewolf leaping through the air caused one car to drive into another! The screech and ultimate crunch of metal from the vehicles made me cringe.

He disappeared down another alleyway on the other side of the street, still chasing after the stranger. I can't believe he would be so stupid to expose himself in public like this! He's running around in Werewolf form, in a frickin' foreign city! His bloodlust was well and truly ignited.

I instantaneously phased from the dark alleyway I was currently in, into the next on the other side of the road. Unseen by the public, I took off after my crazed European Werewolf mate. I caught sight of his huge form as I heard his claws scratch the cobbled alleyway he ran down.

We must have run through St. Petersburg's CBD within five minutes in supernatural speed. I ran right on Declan's tail as he stuck to the dark alleyways to hide his frightening form. I overheard him sniff the air as he bounded after the stranger. He seemed to be running in a particular direction as if tracking the stranger by his scent.

But what WAS that stranger? He wasn't another Werewolf, I was sure of it. How come I didn't smell his supernatural nature when he first approached in the market place? More importantly, how the hell am I going to stop Declan from killing it?! My husband seemed to be out of control as he went gunning for this slippery, sleazy stranger. I would have to jump on his back and instantaneously phase him back to Alaska, that was all there was to it.

Just then his huge form stopped so suddenly, I almost ran right into him! He growled unhappily with his head upwards, craning to see the rooftops. It looks like he's lost the stranger, thank goodness.

Finally he shrunk from his huge, hulking, four-legged European Werewolf shape, back into his bipedal human body. He stood naked in the shadows away from the streetlights, whilst sniffing the night air. I too reverted into my human form to look on unimpressed.

"Let's get out of here." I said flatly.

"No, I might catch his scent again." He said coldly.

"Declan, what the hell is the matter with you?!" I whacked him on the arm. "You changed in a foreign city and you caused a car accident back there! We have witnesses and you want to do it all over again?!"

"He's a vampire, B!" He yelled in my face. "Do you understand? A VAMPIRE!"

My mouth fell open as I looked back in shock, "that was a real live vampire?"

"No, he was just some whacko with glowing white eyes and poisonous fangs. Of course he was a frickin' vampire and YOU almost became his dinner!"

"But I'm a Werewolf..." I shook my head confused, "...why would a vampire want to eat me?"

"Because you're a female Werewolf and do you know how rare that is? Besides being the only female Lokoti Werewolf, there are hardly any female Werewolves left in the world so that makes you a frickin' delicacy!" He shouted, infuriated. "And you just frickin' left the markets with him? What the hell is wrong with you?!"

I stood there stunned as this slowly sunk in...

"But..." I began, "... why does he want to eat me? I thought Vampires like certain Werewolves, feed on human."

"They do! But they hunt Werewolves for our regenerative ability and strength which exceeds their own. Plus with your Lokoti Werewolf pheromones, they lured him in like you were a roast dinner! Now he's got YOUR scent so he'll be able to hunt you down."

I had wondered how the stranger seemed to know so much about me, but how does Declan know so much about IT? Before today, neither of us had seen a Vampire before.

I demanded, "how do you know all of this?"

"What do you mean, how do I know all of this? Why don't YOU know this, B? Can't you sense this about IT?" He asked incredulous.

"You mean all of this is coming to you now?"

"It's instinct B, it's ingrained in us! It's encoded in our very Werewolf DNA. Vampires aren't just our enemies, but they're our predators!"

I looked on dumfounded, "how can they be our predators if you're stronger than it?"

"I'M stronger because European Werewolves are built like tanks! A male Lokoti Werewolf should be stronger but I'm not sure about you. European Vampires are faster, as you saw how it got away from me. Plus they're poisonous which can paralyze Werewolves and kill humans. At least being Shape Shifters like we are, they're allergic to silver so that's one good thing."

I stood still as I felt cold all over which I think was from shock. For some reason, I even had trouble moving my legs which made me wonder if I had used my Circulator ability to excess?

Bad-temperedly, Declan walked around and back down the alleyway as he muttered unhappily, "come on, we've gotta get back to the hotel to pack. I doubt he lives in this city alone and I'm sure he's telling the other fang heads about you even as we speak. I doubt they're going to let a treat like you get away."

However I couldn't move as I began to shiver because I felt chilled to the bone. I asked in a small voice, "what makes you think he's got my scent?"

He whirled around to grab my arm and he held up the back of my hand. Where the stranger had kissed me, were two small puncture marks. My eyes widened in horror as I blanched at how I didn't feel that?!

"What the hell is wrong with you?" Declan looked on in a combination of hurt and disgust. "You're a Werewolf so you should have sniffed him out!"

He was right, what the hell IS wrong with me? I can't believe I nearly became a vampire's prey! Suddenly I dropped everything I had been carrying as my arms turned limp.

"What are you doing?" He rolled his eyes. "We don't have time for you to act like a shocked little princess right now...hang on B, are you feeling alright?"

I just stood there, feeling unbelievably cold and numb as my mouth wavered helplessly...

"B?" My mate picked up my hand with the puncture marks again to sniff it. "Shit, there's poison in there. He's frickin' poisoned you!"

Declan sprang into action by quickly picking up everything I had dropped and then he caught me, just as my legs started to give away.

"B!" He cried out in alarm. "I've got you B, I've got you. Now listen, we have to take you back to the hotel. I could carry you back, but it would take me longer as I'd have to use the alleyways and that may be too late. I need you to instantaneously phase us there, B. Can you do that for me? Can you concentrate and instantaneously phase us back?"

All I could do was stare as I lost all feeling in my body. Even my mind started to turn foggy and I knew that I had to do this quickly, before I lost all control.

I closed my eyes and instead of trying to use my muscles, I engaged my ability as a Circulator. Luckily my body turning into light to pass through time and space, didn't require any physical activity. I managed to instantaneously phase us out of the dark, dirty alleyway to reappear in our luxurious hotel room. It wasn't a minute too soon, as my eyesight started to blur next.

He dropped everything that he had been carrying except me, to rush us into the large, marble bathroom.

There, he sat me on the side of the bathtub whilst holding onto my arms to ensure that I didn't topple over. Next, he placed my wounded hand into his mouth. I felt his sharp teeth bite into the puncture marks, widening them which hurt. If my body wasn't paralyzed I would have recoiled. I couldn't even complain as only a whimper came out whilst my eyes watered.

My mate began to suck hard on my hand to draw the poison out, which he proceeded to spit into the tub beside. Suck – spit – suck – spit – suck – spit, over and over again. The blood and venom looked like a 'Pro Hart' painting against the white tub as my eyes roll backwards into my head. I literally thought I was about to pass out from blood loss!

Lastly, Declan grabbed my toiletries bag off the vanity to drop onto the floor beside. He purposefully tipped it over as he emptied it out all over the floor. What was he doing, looking for a band-aid?

"Finally!" He declared as he snatched up my manicure scissors. After lowering me to the floor so my back was propped up against the side of the tub, I watched him use the scissors to cut into his right wrist. He raised the wound to my mouth which he gently pushed inside. "Here."

I couldn't drink properly because I wasn't able to move my mouth, so he had to let his blood pool inside, before my automatic swallowing response did the rest. It was a slow process but after the fourth mouthful, I started to feel something when I could move my jaw again. As I began to drink faster, I could move my head as well as my hands. The more I drank, the stronger I became as Declan closed his eyes and exhaled. He was holding himself still as he let this happen.

As soon as I had control of my body again, I moved my head away. My heart raced as I struggled to contain my bloodlust from going overboard and draining my mate dry. He momentarily put his wrist inside his mouth to speed up his healing, before he turned my face his way to look on closely.

"Are you OK, B?" He asked as he stroked my hair.

My eyes watered, not from physical pain but because of the emotional pain I had caused.

"I'm sorry Declan that I didn't smell he was a Vampire. He was so charming and he even talked about you." I apologized.

"I know, B." My husband pulled me to him to hold on tightly. "I know."

"I'm such an idiot!" I pulled away to bang my head against the side of the tub as a form of punishment. "He just seemed to say all of the right things, it was like he was reading my mind."

"He read your mind?" His eyebrows rose. "What did he say?"

"He said some crap about me being transcendental."

"He said that?" His eyes widened. "Shit, he saw the Circulator in you straight away! You're more than smoked salmon to this guy, instead you're a gourmet hamper complete with French champagne!"

"Declan, what's wrong?" I asked.

My usually implacable mate quickly stood up in a panic, as he pulled me to my feet. "Are you right to pack? We're leaving, now!"

I followed him out of the bathroom to watch as he rushed over to his suitcase to put some clothes on. He dressed whilst simultaneously gathering up his things. His movements even looked a little frantic.

"We're instantaneously phasing back to Lokoti lands tonight." He barked out. "Now get packed!"

"We have two weeks of our holiday left..." I objected, "...can't we just move on to the next destination?"

"B," he looked on like I was nuts, "it has your scent!"

"But we've been planning this belated honeymoon for months..." I walked over, "...it seems unfair to just quit and go home."

"He's NOT alone!" Declan raised his voice. "If he came after us which I know he will, who knows how many there are? I can fight maybe two of them at a time, but I doubt you could handle just one!"

"Then how far can he track us?"

He unhappily jammed his things into his case. "He could probably track you all the way back to Alaska!"

"Then what's the point in going home?"

"Because we'll have fourteen other Werewolves as back up!"

"Hey, I'm trained in self defense as well as fencing!" I fired up. "I can fight too you know, I'm not completely useless."

"Ha!" He scoffed. "This is coming from the person who just landed us in this mess, in the first place?"

"Who me?"

"If you hadn't of pulled me off the fang head, he wouldn't be alive right now!"

"Next you're going to say it's my fault for even being a female Werewolf in the first place!" I walked away angrily.

He emitted a growl in frustration before he walked after to turn me around to face him again.

"Hey, it's not your fault you're like a perfect plum in a bowl full of rotten apples." He sighed. "Besides, if we're going to be throwing blame around, we could say it's my fault for leaving you alone."

"Declan you're my mate, not my babysitter!"

"Yeah, I'm your mate and I thought I could smell that something was wrong before I left you. But because I've never encountered a Vampire before, I didn't know what the stench was until it was too late." He held me closely.

"Look, it's neither of our fault." I looked up into his face. "He'd been watching us because he waited until you left before he moved in. But I swear, there was something else going on as he was TOO charming. It was like being under hypnosis or something."

He walked back over to his suitcase to continue packing. "I wouldn't be surprised, who knows just how poisonous those fang heads are?"

I frowned as I chewed thoughtfully on my lower lip, as an idea began to form.

"B, are you going to pack or what?" He tried to hurry me along.

I ignored his request as I began to pace, whilst I thought this over. My arms were crossed in front with my right hand moving to my mouth, which usually happened when I went into deep contemplation.

"Oh oh," My husband moaned, "I hate it when you do that. You're brewing something inside that head of yours and usually it means trouble."

"It does not!"

"In the last 55 years we've been together, an argument's usually followed one of these pacing sessions." He said flatly.

"Oh you poor thing," I said sarcastically, "and to think you have another 200 years of being married to me?"

"True." He gave a mischievous grin. "I'd leave you if the make-up sex wasn't so damn hot after these said arguments."

"I'll be sure to pass your feedback on to my next husband." I said in a surly voice.

That wiped the grin off his face, "yep this is some honeymoon we're having."

Just then my mobile phone rang which interrupted our bickering. I walked over to pull it out of my backpack, which was sitting on the floor amongst our things from the marketplace.

"Hallo?" I answered.

"Hi sweetheart." My mother greeted. "How's your holiday going?"

"Er, interesting thanks Mum." I said uneasily.

"Tell her we're coming home tonight," Declan ordered, "and why, so she can warn the Werewolves."

I turned to walk away, but Mum had overheard what he had said. She queried, "why do I have to warn the pack that you're coming home tonight?"

I glared his way as I sighed out, "it's nothing."

"It's nothing?" He looked incredulous. "I had to suck Vampire venom out of you not ten minutes ago!"

"Did Declan just say he sucked Vampire venom out of you ten minutes ago?" She echoed in surprise.

"Vampire venom?!" Now I heard Dad cry out when he overheard her. "A Vampire bit B?"

"Vampire venom?" Next, I heard Grandfather echo.

Oh no, my grandparents are with my parents? Great, this just had to happen, didn't it!

"Did you just say Vampire venom?" Gran sounded shocked in the background.

"Um, was there a reason why you rang, Mum?" I tried to move the conversation along.

"Yeah, I just had a bad feeling, that's all. Now I see my instincts were right again!" She said unhappily.

"Mum, I'm fine." I promised.

"Where was this Vampire? Is B in Russia? Was it a European Vampire that bit her?" I heard Grandfather prattle off worriedly. "Put her on speaker phone."

I heard Mum press something, then I heard all of them speak at the same time.

"You're in St. Petersburg, right?" She guessed.

"Yeah but look guys, it's fine…I'll sort this out." I said.

"Is Declan there?" Dad asked.

"Yes."

"Put us on speaker phone so he hears this too." Grandfather ordered.

I pressed the speaker-phone option on my phone as I put it on the bed and growled at my mate, "thanks a lot!"

"Declan?" Dad sounded.

"Yeah?" My mate replied.

"Get B home right now!" He barked.

"I'm trying to!" He glared my way.

"Was B poisoned by a European Vampire?" Grandfather asked my mate.

"I managed to suck out the poison and share my blood with her so she's alright now." He promised his in-laws.

"Bring her back immediately so we can get her checked out." Dad fretted.

"Look, if this thing can track me back to Alaska, I'm not leading it back home!" I said adamantly.

"How many were there?" Grandfather asked.

"So far, there's just the one." He answered.

"But I doubt it would be alone." My grandfather said unhappily.

I looked on Declan curiously, as I pondered how the hell does everyone seem to know more about them than I do?

"Since it bit her, it has her scent. But what is said to her, I don't think it will let her get away easily." My husband spoke to the other male Werewolves, with my mother and grandmother listening in.

"What did it say?" Dad demanded.

"It said that she's transcendental." He said unhappily.

I heard both Dad and Grandfather suck in their breath from further surprise.

"It can smell she's a Werewolf as well as see her aura as a Circulator." Grandfather said grimly. "Pack your things and instantaneously phase home NOW. I'll mobilize the pack."

"Hang on Em, what's wrong?" Gran spoke up.

"B's not just appealing as a female Werewolf, but he's also attracted to her light as a Circulator." Grandfather warned.

"Attracted to her light?" Mum repeated for further clarification.

There was a moment's pause, before my grandfather explained, "you're both Circulators and you know that Werewolves can see your auras which are a result of your high bio-electromagnetic frequencies."

"And B." Dad added on.

"All three of you are Circulators." He began again. "The Vampire is another creature in the supernatural world which can see your aura. He would want to feed on B not just because of her Werewolf regenerative capabilities, but for her being a Circulator as well. With her light and pheromones, to the Vampire it's like waving a bottle of vintage wine under an alcoholic's nose."

"But what's the appeal of drinking a Circulator?" Gran debated. "The vampire isn't going to be able to phase simply by drinking her blood!"

"You know that and I know that, but does IT know that?" Dad pointed out.

"Vampires take on certain characteristics of their victims, which is why they're choosy who they feed on." Grandfather continued. "They hunt Werewolves for their strength and the regenerative capabilities. They hunt psychics for their abilities. This Vampire thinks it can also assimilate B's ability as a Circulator."

"Did you say Vampires can become psychic by eating a psychic?" I clarified.

"Yes." He answered.

I looked up at Declan, "that would explain why it felt like it was reading my mind."

"What?" I could hear Dad gape via the phone.

"B told me that it said all of the right things as it seemed to hypnotize her." My husband said in annoyance.

"Right, I want the pair of you standing in this lounge room in two minutes!" Grandfather declared.

My mate recommenced his packing. "Copy that."

"It read B's mind?" Mum echoed again.

"Then it could know of another two Circulators and fourteen other Werewolves to snack on." Gran said grimly.

"Hang on a sec." I stopped everyone. "How do you all seem to know so much about Vampires? Up until tonight, I didn't know that they still existed!"

"We know from Elisha Worthall's SSIT Reports, as well as from two battles the Lokoti Werewolves have engaged in with Vampires." Grandfather announced. "But we can talk about this when you arrive."

I crossed my arms. "No, tell me now."

"B, we don't have time for this." Dad said in annoyance.

"You have one minute and thirty seconds to be standing in front of me." Grandfather said firmly.

"No."

My husband looked on as if I really had lost my marbles. "What?"

"B this isn't a debate, this is a direct order from the pack!" Dad demanded.

"It's for the pack and the tribe that I'm not coming home yet." I said coolly.

Next, my mate pulled out my suitcase as he began to shove my things into it. "Oh yes we are!"

"Declan said the Vampire is allergic to silver like we are, is that true?" I asked.

"He's right." Grandfather verified. "Vampires are Shape Shifters, just like we are. All Shape Shifters are allergic to silver."

"Does it need to be impaled through the heart or head by silver, the same as killing a Werewolf?" I guessed.

"It does." Grandfather stated. "That or decapitation."

"Then that's what I'll do." I said simply.

This made the European Werewolf pause in his packing, to stare in horror.

"There's no frickin' way you are going up against that THING again!" He cried out and he even threw one of his shirts into the suitcase in a bad temper. "B, you're going home to Alaska tonight even if I have to drag you back myself!"

Then I watched him march over to the shopping from the marketplace, pick up the cotton carry bags and then dump them in their entirety into my suitcase.

"Declan, how did you know about the Vampire's allergy to silver?" Mum wondered.

"I don't know..." he paused for a moment, "...I suddenly knew a lot today about Vampires when before I hadn't even considered them."

"It's ingrained in his European Werewolf DNA." Grandfather told her. "European Werewolves share the same geography as the European Vampires, it would be part of his survival instincts from eons of conflict between the predators."

"It's probably why European Werewolves are the strongest of all the breeds, so they wouldn't be hunted out by the European Vampires." My father thought out loud.

"Declan, did you fight this Vampire?" My mother asked interestedly.

"I did."

"Were you injured?" She asked out of concern.

I could see his mother-in-law's worry over his welfare touched my husband, before he admitted, "I'm fine Aunt Jess. I was stronger than it, but it was faster. It gave me the slip."

"How much faster was it?" She enquired.

"No Jess." Her mate said uneasily, as if he recognized that she was contemplating something.

"When it got away from Declan, it looked like it moved in the speed of sound." I told the other Circulators as I guessed their thoughts.

"It may be able to move at the speed of sound, but we can move at the speed of light." Gran proclaimed.

"Arabella, no." Her husband said firmly. "You would be giving it exactly what it wants; the blood of three Circulators."

"Please Arabella, Jess and B." My father pleaded. "Let the male Werewolves handle this because we're stronger than the Vampires."

Gran said matter-of-factly, "Circulators fight faster and the tribe's three 'Light People' all possess silver-coated swords."

Declan frowned down at the phone, "with all due respect Aunt Arabella, I don't want any of my women near these creatures. They're slippery and cunning bastards with poisonous fangs. That cretin paralyzed my Werewolf wife tonight and since you're not Werewolves, that bite can kill you. There's no way that I'm letting you, Aunt Jess or B anywhere near those things again."

"He's right." My grandfather agreed. "This is a matter for the male members of the pack."

"What's the pack's experience fighting these things, Grandfather?" I asked as I sat on the bed beside the phone.

"B, we'll talk about it when you get home." My father tried.

"Dad, I'm not coming home yet." I said stubbornly.

"What?" Declan objected. "The hell you are!"

"Grandfather." I ignored him. "Please tell me what happened when the pack engaged the Vampires in battle."

He sighed reluctantly. "I suppose if I tell you what happened, you'll come home when you hear what you're up against."

"Em?" I heard Gran prompt him.

I was sitting on the bed, as I listened to my family's voices via the technology. I briefly looked up to meet my mate's wide blue eyes and saw he was waiting to hear the story as well. We overheard my grandfather take in a deep breath as he began.

"The first battle occurred around six hundred years ago when a coven of three South American Vampires came to Alaska. They were once Aztec Priests, but they left after the fall of their civilization from the Spanish Conquistadores. They traveled up through the States feeding on the Native American tribes they encountered, before they came up via Canada. They had heard about the legend of the Lokoti Werewolf from the Native Alaskans they attacked and came to investigate. The three South American Vampires killed thirty of our human family members and seven Lokoti Werewolves, before the pack were able to destroy them. The South American Vampires were different to the European Vampire as they had speed, but they weren't poisonous."

I curled up by tucking my legs underneath as I listened intently, whilst Declan stood with his hands on his hips, frowning deeply.

"Two hundred years later, four European Vampires came across the Bering Sea from Russia to specifically hunt Werewolves. They came looking for North American Werewolves, but after feeding on other Native Alaskan's they heard of us again. The European Vampires held a third of the tribe hostage, to force the Lokoti Werewolves into submission. They tortured our mates and our children to try to make the pack surrender." He went on.

"The women and children?" My eyes widened in fear.

"They fed on them one at a time, to try to break the Lokoti Werewolf's will." He said hatefully.

I looked up in disgust at what I was hearing, as my mate's eyes narrowed showing his own displeasure.

"Then what happened, Em?" Gran urged him on.

"The pack very nearly surrendered, but the Tribal Elders reasoned that after the Vampires feasted on the Werewolves, what guarantee did we have that they wouldn't harm any more of the tribe? The Tribal Elders calmed the pack down, who were suffering as their mates and children were being harmed." His voice wavered. "Oh Arabella, if you only knew how it feels for a Lokoti Werewolf if our mates or children are in danger? You would not be volunteering for this fight."

"I have a fair idea." She said softly. "I feel it when I think you're in trouble."

There was a pause, which indicated that my grandparents were doing one of their typical long looks.

"And then what happened, Dad?" My mother prompted impatiently.

"The Lokoti Werewolves went into battle and eleven out of our fifteen members died, as did their human families." Grandfather claimed. "The European Vampires were faster than the pack. Their venom paralyzed the Werewolves which enabled them to feed and the same venom killed the humans."

My eyes bulged in horror, as I recalled how easily the European Vampire gave my European Werewolf mate the slip tonight. There is no way I could put my kin up against that!

"Because we've got Declan on our side, our chances have increased." Dad tried to say optimistically.

"Damn straight." My husband said adamantly. "I'm looking forward to seeing what Vampire flesh tastes like."

Casually, I stood up from the bed as I said, "then I'll cut off an arm and bring back to you."

"Say what? Bianca you are NOT going anywhere near those things!" He flared. "I'm putting my foot down!   Although the amount times I've seen you in a dress I can count on one hand; I still wear the pants in this family!   If you even... what? No! Get back here! B!!"

"What's going on?" Dad cried out anxiously over the phone.

"What happened?" Grandfather too sounded worried.

"B just instantly phased out of here!" My mate kicked the bed bad-temperedly.

"DECLAN!" Dad roared. "FIND HER!"

"I will!" He growled in frustration.

"She's probably gone to Circulate HQ first to find the European Vampire's coven in the Viewing Room." Gran thought out loud. "Jess and I can meet her there."

"What?" My father objected. "Don't just go and meet her there, drag her back here!"

"Hunter." My mother said sternly. "The Circulators can handle this."

"This is a Werewolf matter." My grandfather said sternly. "Vampires have always been the enemy of our kind. I don't want either of you two anywhere near this."

"Em," my grandmother said in concern, "the Vampires are faster than you but we're faster than them."

"Haven't you heard what we've been saying? They're poisonous! Their poison can temporarily paralyze us but it can kill you! Plus they hypnotized B so you three could be walking into a trap!" Dad lost his patience.

"And so could you!" Mum said indignantly. "Hunter, I love you but sometimes your chauvinism drives me up the wall!"

"Jess!" Grandfather growled at his daughter.

"Dad relax, Mum and I can handle this." My mother said stubbornly.

"You don't even know how many there are!" My father snapped.

"Well I doubt there'd be five hundred of them." She said dryly.

"Em, from what you told us in your history with these guys? Jess, Bianca and I would have a much better chance fighting them than the pack would." Gran reasoned.

"Arabella -" Grandfather tried to argue.

"We won't take any risks. We'll lop off a few Vampire heads with our silver-coated swords then we'll come straight home." She promised.

"NO!" Dad cried out.

My husband was still listening in. "What? What is it? What happened?"

"Arabella and Jess just instantaneously phased out of here!" Grandfather snarled in fury.

"Declan!" My father yelled. "Start scouring the city to find the Vampires' nest! While you're sniffing around, you should pick up Bianca's scent as soon as she returns to St. Petersburg."

"Right." He patted over his pockets to make sure he had his hotel security card and wallet on him.

"Declan?" Grandfather spoke lastly.

"Yeah?" He picked up my phone from the bed.

"Hunter and I along with a few of the pack will be there as soon as possible." His voice lowered. "But it could take us a couple of hours to reach you though."

He paused when he realized what Grandfather was non-verbally asking of him; *FIND OUR MATES AND ENSURE THEIR SAFETY AT ALL COST.*

"Understood." He hung up before he raced out the door.

It was what my father and my grandfather didn't say though, which was scorched into his brain.

PROVE YOURSELF TO THE PACK AND THE TRIBE WHY WE LET YOU LIVE TO BECOME THE MONSTER YOU ARE. THIS IS YOUR DAY TO PROVE WHY YOU ARE BIGGER, STRONGER AND MORE DANGEROUS AS THE BLOODLUST BURNS THE HOTTEST INSIDE OF YOU.

Although Grandfather probably wasn't thinking this; Declan still felt the words as if they came directly from the will of the Lokoti Werewolves themselves.

*****

~ **26** ~

My husband raced out of the lift and through the grand foyer, when he became aware of somebody calling out his name. He stopped short of the front doors of the hotel, to turn to see the concierge rush after him.

"Mr Sabre? Mr Sabre!" The uniformed woman puffed as she came to a stop.

"Yeah?" He looked on impatiently.

"This came for you while you were out." The employee spoke primly in her Russian accent as she handed him an envelope. "I'm sorry I didn't give it to you sooner, but I didn't see you return."

Declan snatched it from her as he was half expecting it to be from me. He ripped it open to take out a piece of paper scrawled in an unfamiliar hand.

MEET ME AT THE SMILINSK TAVERN AT MIDNIGHT IF YOU WANT YOUR MATE TO LIVE.

That was all it said and it wasn't signed. He knew the writing not to be my own so he raised the paper to sniff it. It didn't smell like the Vampire we had come up against tonight, but it didn't smell human either. He recognized the scent because he had smelled it everyday since he was three; it reeked of European Werewolf.

His eyes widened in fear, before he looked on the human woman in the hotel uniform before him.

"Who the hell gave this to you?!" He demanded.

The concierge's eyes widened at his fury, "a man came in and told me to give it to you. Why, is there a problem, Mr. Sabre?"

"What did this man look like?" He asked accusatorily as he loomed over the woman.

"He – he – he looked tall, black hair, green eyes, black leather jacket, unshaven, handsome but rough looking." The concierge answered nervously. "Please Mr. Sabe, is there something wrong?"

My husband didn't answer as he whirled around and burst out of the hotel via the front door, leaving the shocked hotel employee staring after.

"Great that's all I need, more man-eaters on our tail!" He grumbled. He looked at his watch and saw the time was 10.59 PM. "Right, first I'll sniff around for fifty minutes for the Vampires' nest, before I go to this tavern and kill something that I do know their whereabouts is."

In human form, the European Werewolf ran down the street whilst sniffing the air and looking about constantly. Like this, he scoured a small part of the foreign city. This caused passersby to regard him curiously, as they wondered why he was running in jeans and not work-out clothes?

"At least my sense of smell works in human form as well as in Werewolf", he conceded. "I could run a hell of a lot faster in my Werewolf body, but then I'd have to stick to the alleyways and side streets to hide myself."

For the next fifty minutes, Declan ran as fast as humanly possible. Not once did he lose breath, as he inhaled through his nose and out of his mouth which enabled him to track as he went. But the business centre of the old city was so large he only managed to cover half.

My mate didn't smell a thing, not supernatural anyway, in St Petersburg's CBD. No European Vampires, no European Werewolves and no me. He looked at his watch, saw the time and then he waved down a taxi.

"Smilinsk Tavern." He barked at the taxi driver as soon as he got in.

Luckily the taxi driver had heard of it, so he knew the way. Without a word, the driver switched on his meter and pulled out onto the road. He observed him change lanes to turn at the next intersection, as he made mental note of the directions.

*****

As soon as the taxi pulled up on the side of the street, Declan had his credit card ready to pay for his fare. He barely waited for the transaction to finish when he leapt out of the vehicle and across the pavement. He jogged down the stairs that led the way to the underground tavern, which was almost hidden but for the small, neon sign above the stairwell.

He only slowed once he reached the bar area, as he looked about unimpressed. To say the establishment wasn't fancy, would have been a compliment! The carpet underneath his shoes stunk not only of alcohol, but of mildew. He saw patches of mould on the ceiling and on the torn wallpaper-covered walls.

The tavern was almost empty, but for a couple of occupied tables in the corners of the room. He openly examined the groups of two or three people, sitting at the tables. Then he paused, as another scent hit him aside from decrepit dampness. It was a very familiar scent, as he smelled his own kind here.

My mate walked past the bar as he craned his neck to get a good look at the customers, whilst trying to pin point the scent.

"Bingo!" his mind sung when he caught sight of one of the tables where three people were watching him. There sat a man with black hair, green eyes and was wearing a black leather jacket, "the one who delivered the note no doubt", he thought.

The black leather jacket guy appeared to be in his twenties, but he smelled older. He was sitting opposite to an older man wearing a brown leather jacket, and an older woman wearing a red leather jacket. To say this older man and woman looked 'rough' would have been an understatement. The older man had brown hair, looked like he was in his forties and was missing an eye. The woman who looked to be in her late thirties, had dark blonde hair. She looked like she used to be attractive once, but for the hideous scarring over the left side of her mouth and cheek.

The three appeared to be drinking vodka from the smell, when the older man stood up. He took a step towards Declan as he gave a curt nod. My mate's eyes narrowed as he looked this older man up and down. He noted that the man had a limp as he and the woman looked like they had been through the wars, literally. However he smelled the older man's underlying strength and knew that he was in no way weakened, especially if it came to fighting.

"Comrade," the older man greeted in a Russian accent.

"I'm NOT your Comrade." Declan said stroppily as he held up the note. "I got your love letter. Now tell me, do you want me to kill you here or outside, for threatening my wife?"

The black leather jacket guy growled, but the woman put a restraining hand on his arm.

"The threat isn't from us, Comrade." The older man shrugged off his displeasure. "Smell us, we're your kind."

"Then what do you want?" My mate's voice dropped dangerously.

"Look at us, Comrade." The older man spoke calmly. "Including yourself, we are the last four European Werewolves in existence."

That caught his attention as his eyes widened. He knew this wasn't a lie as he had always sensed there weren't many of his kind left. The monster who turned him, had to migrate to find an uncontaminated food source; humans who didn't have radiation sickness. This made Declan grow up wondering how his other supernatural relations were faring.

The older man continued, "my name is Leo and that is my mate, Michelle. The young one is Marcus. I'm Russian, Michelle is Swiss and Marcus is Italian. We have migrated all over the continent, to stay ahead of the Vampires."

Declan's eyes widened as soon as he heard the word 'Vampires'.

"What do you know about them?" He demanded as he stepped forwards.

"They're old, they're fast and they're cunning." Leo declared. "I'm 197 years old, Michelle is 128 years old and Marcus is 46 years old. The Vampire you met tonight is Mikhail and he is 356 years old. Marcus lost his mate to him ten years ago."

"I thought our kind didn't have mates." He scoffed.

"Then what do you call that other species of Werewolf you are traveling with?" Michelle arched her eyebrows.

"He called her his wife." Marcus remembered his earlier threat.

"Yeah but I don't ally myself with other European Werewolves." Declan's top lip curled in disgust. "I was raised better than that."

Marcus growled even louder which made a nearby table of humans look their way.

"We hide our mates just as we hide our bloodlust to the public." Leo carried on as if nothing was amiss. "We can only mate with our own kind as we can kill a human woman by our physical strength alone. With our bloodlust it's hard to change a human woman into one of us, as quite often we lose control and they die from the process. Michelle is the last female of our kind, which is why the Vampires have been hunting us for the past fifty years."

"Why are the three of you together, like a pack?" He asked next. "I heard that our kind didn't have mates just as they didn't live in packs."

"Safety in numbers." Marcus said in a glib manner.

"Michelle and I saved Marcus when he tried to avenge his mate and he has traveled with us ever since. He in turn, fights with Michelle and I." Leo answered.

Declan sensed they were telling the truth but he also sensed that they didn't contact him for a 'family catch up' either. He knew the three were untrustworthy and dangerous, just as the knowledge about the Vampires came to him.

"Alright, enough with the 'welcome to the family' crap." He scrunched up the note and tossed it into a nearby ashtray. "Now what do you want?"

"To help you keep your mate safe from the Vampires." Leo shrugged.

"Yeah right! Out of the goodness of your hearts? I don't think so." Declan almost laughed.

"We'll help you and in return, you'll help us." Marcus spoke up.

"Figures," my husband rolled his eyes, "and what do you want?"

"One million credits." Leo said plainly.

"Say what?!" This time Declan did laugh. "Yeah, like I'm really rolling in that much dough!"

"You're mate has access to Hodge Endeavor funds." Michelle shrugged.

That wiped the sarcastic smile off his face, as his voice lowered threateningly, "how the hell would you know that?"

"One of the things which makes Michelle so appealing to the Vampires, is she's psychic. It used to be quite common in females of our kind." Leo said dryly.

"Forget it." He turned to leave.

"The Vampire coven which is lead by Mikhail, is twelve members big." Michelle spoke up.

"We know where it is and can help you fight them." Marcus added on.

"For a price of course," Leo said evenly, "or you can think of it as a donation to our cause which is your cause. Not all of us have been as lucky, being adopted by another species of Werewolf and growing up away from the radiation poisoning after the war. You grew up with abundant hunting, clean water and a warm bed. We have been running for years where sometimes we have to sleep on the streets."

"The good thing about constantly moving, is not being caught when we feed." Marcus said flatly.

"I don't eat human," he seethed, "and I would do ANYTHING to protect my mate, her family and our tribe. You hear me? MY tribe! Don't think I'm not as strong as you either, or that I've gone soft from 'easy' living."

Just then Michelle spoke to Leo in Russian, which Marcus also understood and the three exchanged a nod.

Leo turned back, "Michelle says you're right, you do know how to fight. You are used to protecting your home with the Indian Werewolves."

"Then you'll know to never to contact me again, or come anywhere near my mate. Don't even think about coming onto our territory!" He growled out as he turned to leave again.

"Do you know where the Vampire's nest is?" Marcus called.

"I don't need your help!" Declan retorted. "Now I know what they smell like, it won't be hard to find them."

"I wouldn't be so sure, Comrade." Leo smirked. "We searched for years to find their nest here in Russia. You certainly won't find it overnight!"

"You need Marcus and Leo's help as you cannot fight twelve of them yourself." Michelle quipped.

"I don't care. You really are a couple of dogs, you know that?" My husband said in disgust which made Marcus growl again, but he continued to ignore his threatening noises; "instead of just helping me when it would get them off your back as well as ensure Michelle's safety? You want to charge me. I don't trust the three of you as far as I could throw you! You'd lead me into a trap if it means saving your own skins."

Marcus stood up to look Declan in the eye, as his human green colour momentarily glowed their supernatural brightness. He was as tall and wide as my husband to show his rival that he was just as strong if not stronger.

"Si, you're right." Marcus said coolly. "By assisting you it would benefit us as well as yourself. But we need the money and since there's twelve of them, you need our help. We're stronger than your Indian Werewolves and you don't know how a Vampire fights. They can move at the speed of sound."

"I know how they move as I saw it for myself tonight." He rebuked.

"Do you know what the Vampires will do to your mate?" Marcus glared. "It's not a quick death. They torture their victims as they have perfected methods to drain every last drop from their meals."

"At least when we feed, it's usually a quick death for our prey. We make sure the humans are dead first to feast on fresh kill." Leo justified.

"Oh, that's real good of you." My husband said icily. "No never mind that you could be chowing down on a human's husband or wife or son or daughter!"

"This isn't up for moral debate!" Marcus barked out. "When you're paralyzed from a Vampire's bite, you can't move but you can still feel everything. Whilst your mate is still alive, they will cut her open and pulverize her flesh, like they were juicing an orange! She'll still be alive when they do this, as they need to keep her brain untouched to take what they want from her memories."

Declan almost leapt upon him enraged for putting this horrible picture inside his head, but Leo's eye glowed green as he growled, "I'm just as strong as you comrade and I have more fighting experience."

Michelle didn't seem perturbed by the supernatural testosterone flying around the room, as she kept this meeting business like. She walked forwards to hold out a piece of paper with banking details.

"One million credits will be transferred into our account within the next hour." She quipped.

"How am I supposed to scrape up that much credit, now after midnight?" He snatched the piece of paper off her.

"You have a contact in Hodge Endeavor whom you can call 24 hours a day. She will follow your orders because of who your mate is." She said knowingly. "Marcus and Leo will meet you in the lobby of your hotel once the money is in our account. They will take you to the Vampire's nest and fight with you. Then we part, never to bother each other again."

"I'm expecting back up -" my husband began.

"Your mate's family of Indian Werewolves are still in Alaska." She said snidely. "Your mate will arrive at the Vampire's nest while her pack will be on a plane, just entering Russian airspace."

"If Michelle knows this, don't you think the Vampires know this too?" Leo arched his eyebrow knowingly. "Their psychic abilities are more than a match."

Declan eyed them distrustfully, as they eyed him back. Marcus looked on in equal displeasure and perhaps with a little jealousy? Leo smiled like a con man and Michelle looked completely disinterested.

"You don't like us and we don't like you, but this is business. We need your money and you need our help." Marcus said gruffly.

"There are only three female Werewolves left in the world, including Michelle and your mate. If you lose your wife I don't think you'll fancy the last one, who's an elderly Asian Werewolf. Asian Werewolves don't smell as nice as your Indian Werewolves with their pheromones." Leo said cruelly.

Declan started walking backwards whilst eyeing off his kin hatefully, "you may be older and THINK you have more experience than me. But trust me, my mate has powerful friends. My mate's grandmother killed the Werewolf that turned me with two silver coated swords; the same swords which will also be here shortly."

Upon his last words, he noticed Leo's eyebrows arose before he left the tavern via the steps again. He walked quickly in the direction of our hotel whilst recommencing his sniffing as he walked. He knew it was a long shot, but he tried to pick up mine or the Vampires' scent. As he hurriedly walked whilst breathing in through his nose and out of his mouth, he made a call on his mobile phone.

"Uncle Em," he greeted, "where are you?"

"We're in a helicopter approaching Anchorage airport. Hunter, Fern, Julian and I will be on a private jet within half an hour." Grandfather told him. "Have you tracked down Bianca or found the Vampire coven?"

"No," he said unhappily, "something else tracked me down instead."

He told him about the note and then the meeting he was coming from. Grandfather was quiet for nearly a minute after he had finished speaking. Declan knew he was still on the phone, but he was pondering the risks of trusting the European Werewolves.

"I think we're going to have to pay for their help." Grandfather said eventually.

"Say what?" He uttered back in shock.

"Text message me the bank account number and I'll arrange the transfer." Grandfather instructed. "I've already been in touch with Arabella's contact at Hodge Endeavor. Her PA is the one who organized this helicopter and the private jet."

"Uncle Em, are you serious?" My husband stopped walking from surprise. "I mean, I know my own kind. Just as my instincts warned me about the Vampires, the same instincts are telling me not to trust them!"

Grandfather sighed in resignation, "under normal circumstances Declan, I would agree with you. One of the reasons why our pack doesn't mix with other Werewolves aside from keeping man-eaters away from the tribe, we know how unreliable the other breeds can be. Any Shape Shifter who continues to eat human is as it's part of their dangerous nature. Now I want you to meet this Leo and Marcus in the hotel foyer as I see to the transfer of credits. If they don't show, what we can hold over them is that our contact at Hodge Endeavor can also pull the credit out again."

"That's not what I'm worried about." He frowned as he kicked at the curb in frustration. "I don't know, but they seemed a bit too willing to help. I wouldn't be surprised if they lead me into a trap where they tried to take the money as well as B."

"That wouldn't surprise me either." Grandfather's frown was in his voice.

"Leo did say how hard it is to change a human female into one of their kind and that there are only three female Werewolves left in the world." He continued. "Marcus' mate died ten years ago and I don't think he's had another since."

"That's why you've got to go with them to find the coven." Grandfather ordered. "Keep an eye on the European Werewolves and on the European Vampires."

Declan wearily rubbed his face, "understood."

"Call me again when you know the location of the Vampires' nest." He signed off.

"Will do." My mate hung up before he took off down the street again. He cursed under his breath as he hurried, "some frickin' honeymoon this is! Why the hell do people keep trying to take B away from me? Damn that woman for having those damn pheromones! Get your own frickin' female, you losers!"

*****

It was nearing 1.30 AM as Declan paced impatiently in the luxurious lobby of the hotel. He paced around and around a lounge instead of sitting on it, whilst looking at the front doors and then his watch before pacing onwards. The night staff at check-in watched curiously, wondering why he was in the lobby instead of his expensive suite? Then he smelled THEM before he saw THEM.

He looked up just as Leo and Marcus walked in via the main door to wave him over. Next, the three European Werewolves left the hotel together. This made the hotel staff exchange wary looks at how three tall, strong men left together in the middle of the night.

"So where's the nest?" He demanded as soon as they were outside.

"In a townhouse on the outskirts of the city." Leo answered.

"Give me the specifics!" He barked.

Marcus growled unhappily at being talked to as such, but Leo put up his hand to stop him from taking him out.

"Nabezezhnaya 13, in Verpaknovskaya." Leo pronounced the Russian address.

His instincts told him that they were telling the truth. A truth bought for one million credits, but the truth nevertheless. As the three of them walked down the street, he called Grandfather.

"Uncle Em? The address is Nabezezhnaya 13, in Verpaknovskaya. It's a townhouse on the outskirts of the city."

"Are you with the European Werewolves now?" Grandfather guessed.

"Yep."

"Just remember what we talked about." He said gravely. "Hunter, Fern, Julian and I are on the plane now. We'll arrive in St. Petersburg in an hour."

"Copy that." My mate hung up.

Marcus looked on in amusement at Declan 'reporting in' to my family, as did Leo.

"You're bigger and stronger than them, but you take their orders?" He taunted.

"They're my pack as well as my in-laws." My mate said gruffly.

"Michelle ate her family the first night she changed." Leo chuckled. "It was by accident, as she couldn't control the bloodlust. She was depressed about it afterwards, but it liberated her from the last of her human concerns."

"Oh yeah, you guys are real reliable." Declan rolled his eyes.

"If you've never eaten human, I wouldn't judge if I were you." Marcus sneered. "You don't know the exquisite taste or the euphoria of satiating the never ending hunger."

"I know exactly what you're talking about." He glared at his rival. "I may not eat human but I have my mate and she satiates the bloodlust."

"I'm sure she does." Marcus quickly looked away.

"Michelle told us that the Vampires are after her for something else besides being a Werewolf. What's so special about your mate?" Leo asked.

"Wouldn't you like to know." Declan clammed up.

Marcus and Leo exchanged a secretive look, before the younger European Werewolf waved down a taxi.

*****

The taxi drove them to an up market area near the outskirts of St. Petersburg. It surprised Declan by how closely together the old houses were, which didn't seem to promise much in the way of privacy, especially for man-eaters.

When the taxi dropped them off, Leo and Marcus hopped out of the cab first to leave him with the fare. This didn't surprise Declan, as next he warily followed the other two down a quiet street to a back alleyway. He thought he was being taken directly to the Vampire's abode, but instead he found himself climbing up a fire escape and onto a roof.

The European Werewolves kept low so their figures wouldn't be seen against the skyline. The three eventually came to a stop to lie on their stomachs by the side of a roof. They looked out over a sleepy street which was lined with expensive cars and more expensive looking, renovated townhouses.

"OK then, where are they?" Declan asked skeptically.

Marcus silently pointed out a large, dark red painted townhouse with gold trim, which was two houses down across the road.

"Say what?" He raised his eyebrows in disbelief. "Are you kidding me? It's a bit ostentatious isn't it, even for them!"

"Keep your voice down, Comrade." Leo growled quietly. "Their hearing is almost as good as ours."

"If you don't believe us, smell it for yourself." Marcus scoffed. "Or has your easy living in your Indian Werewolf paradise made your senses go soft?"

Declan glared back before he closed his eyes and sniffed several times whilst concentrating hard.

"Ah yes that dead, decrepit, dank smell. It's them alright." He thought to himself before he asked quietly, "so twelve of them live in that mansion?"

"They live well, don't they?" Marcus spoke bitterly. "They have many expensive houses like this, across Europe. They don't just hunt Werewolves and psychics, but they feed off the rich to pay their way."

"Maybe we should let a Vampire live tonight, or just long enough to tell its secret on how it coerces the humans into giving away their money." Leo chuckled to his cohort.

"They hypnotize their victims." Declan said unhappily. "B told me they can be very persuasive."

The other two European Werewolves exchanged raised eyebrows at this piece of information.

"Poisonous words as well as poisonous fangs." Marcus glared upon the Vampires' house.

My husband saw the look of pure hatred on his face which prompted him to ask, "so what happened to your mate?"

The younger European Werewolf took a while to answer, as if he didn't want to discuss it let alone with him. Eventually he spoke, "Roberta was 93 years old, who looked like she was in her twenties with no scarring on the obvious parts of her body. She approached me in a nightclub in Florence. She lured me away to have sex and then feed but she changed her mind and let me live. From her bite, I changed on the next full moon and she taught me how to hunt and clean up the mess. After ten years of running, the Vampires found us. I tried to fight them off, but they bit me. Before I became completely paralyzed, I managed to escape. I fell out of a window and landed in the back of a passing garbage truck."

"You ABANDONED your mate?" My husband stared in disgust.

Before Leo could stop Marcus, he reached over in a lightening fast move to grab hold of Declan's coat in his fist.

"I saw them torture her and mutilate her as I lost all feeling in my legs." His green eyes glowed in anger. "How do you think I know what they'll do to your mate?"

Leo pulled Marcus' hand off Declan's coat as he growled at the pair of them, "do you two want to get caught by the Vampires?"

They exchanged dangerous looks however they did behave.

"So," the smartarse in my husband couldn't resist, "does this mean you haven't had sex in ten years?"

Marcus and Leo gave him an incredulous look before Leo asked unimpressed, "do you think our kind can go that long without?"

He almost blurted out that he nearly did when I was married to Grant, but he changed tact, "you said human females don't survive the experience."

"They don't." Marcus said simply.

"But why waste the meat?" Leo shrugged.

My husband's mouth fell open in shock and right at that moment, he had to use all of his willpower not to toss them over the side of the roof. He wanted to take his wife as far away from these two as possible! But the thought that stayed him, was he had to remove me from the Vampire threat first of all.

What my European Werewolf mate told me later, was from that night on he saw the Lokoti Werewolf willpower in a new light. He already respected the pack for being the protectors over their people. However, now he admired the Lokoti Werewolves for differentiating themselves from the other breeds. They honored the human traditions of family and tribal laws, which Declan's European Werewolf bloodlust used to challenge. That night he finally felt a sense of belonging to the Lokoti whom he saw as his people and his home. He didn't see Marcus, Leo or Michelle as 'his kind' at all, he saw them as a threat to what he held dear.

Reluctant but ready, my husband laid on the roof with his enemy waiting for the sign of when they could attack.

*****

The three European Werewolves lay on their stomachs on top of the cold, hard roof for over twenty minutes, whilst watching the Vampire house intently.

"We should attack now," Declan said uneasily, "before B gets here."

"No," Leo decided, "we wait until she arrives. We need her to distract the Vampires and then we pounce."

"You're using her as bait?" My mate growled unhappily.

"We're using her as a distraction." Marcus said simply.

"Tell me Marcus, is that what you did with your mate to save your own ass?" He asked coldly.

Marcus growled in displeasure but he couldn't make a move on him since Leo was in his way, lying in between the two.

"Your mate will live, Comrade." Leo promised. "We know that you can pull your money back out of our account just as easily as you put it in."

He rolled his eyes as he thought this 'guarantee' gave little comfort.

"Look." Marcus raised himself as he was looking at the house across the street.

My husband saw our arrival before he smelled it, from a bright flash of light which erupted from the front windows of an upstairs room. He recognized it was from the electrostatic charge of three Circulators instantaneously phasing into the Vampire house. He smelled my scent first then Mum and Gran's second.

"It's them." He quickly stood up, as did Leo.

The European Werewolves leapt across two houses which were side by side, until they were standing on the roof top of the house which was directly opposite.

"It's time!" Leo barked as he quickly stripped with Marcus following suit.

He didn't care about tearing his clothes as all he wanted was to see me again. But it didn't take the European Werewolves long to remove their garments since they were well practiced. The three piles of shoes and fabric were left on somebody's roof.

Marcus was the first to change as the younger male doubled in size and turned into a black coloured, huge, hulking hairless beast. His human green eyes glowed as his circular pupils turned into narrow slits over his razor sharp jaws. Leo was the second to change, as the limping man expanded into a brown coloured, huge, hulking hairless monster with one glowing green eye. His human mouth grew into a short, stubby snout with teeth and claws just as sharp.

Declan was a close third, matching the other two European Werewolves in both size and mass. He grew into a light-tanned coloured, huge, hulking, hairless wolf-beast. His human blue eyes turned glowing green with his round pupils turning into slits. He bared his teeth as he flexed his claws which could cut through metal.

Marcus, Leo and then Declan, all leapt from the roof to sail over the street below. They crashed through three windows on the top floor of the Vampires' townhouse. Declan landed on all-fours unharmed, but his heart lurched when he found me already engaged in a sword fight. I was wearing my gym clothes with my sword belt on my back. Gran, Mum and I were fighting in the thick of a snake's nest, surrounded by white-eyed and long fanged, hissing Vampires.

We were in antique style sitting room, with polished wooden floors, Persian rugs and Louis XIV chaises. He roared in anger when he saw me duck from the Vampire's silver blade and then that was it... I had to jump aside or be knocked over, when Declan leapt on top of the surprised Vampire. His large, dangerous jaws chomped off the Vampire's entire face!

The horror of this actually made me pause, which was a mistake because another Vampire leapt on me from behind. But before it could pierce my skin with its poisonous fangs, I instantaneously phased out of its grasp to reappear right behind. I swung my sword around when I heard the 'clunk' of its decapitated head falling to the floor and rolling a little away.

I battled a third Vampire as Mum and Gran polished off their two. The three Circulators in the room looked bright as we fought with our greater speed whilst the Vampires endeavored to keep up. It was light speed verses the speed of sound, as we crossed silver blades.

As I was sword fighting, I tried not to gawk at the two strange European Werewolves which had arrived with Declan, fight a Vampire each. Who were they and why were they helping us? But before I could contemplate on this any further, I was distracted by two more Vampires appearing on either side.

I had to defend myself against two Vampires at once. I swung my blade madly about as I blocked and parried. I may have been faster but they clearly had more experience than I did. As they swung their blades, they were closing in by deliberately making me lose my footing. My sword clanged against theirs whilst they started to drive me backwards.

Oh oh...I can fight one at a time, but two at a time? I was about to instantaneously phase away to find new footing, when my mate leapt on one of my attackers. Yes, go Declan! I almost cheered, but instead I cringed when I heard him yelp in pain as the Vampire's silver sword punctured his ribs.

"NO!" I cried out as I almost changed in anger, but this would have given my opponents their chance. Just from flinching with the empathic pain of my mate's injury, I very nearly gave the Vampires their window to win the fight.

"B look behind you!" Gran called out.

My senses picked up the close proximity of a third Vampire sneaking up behind to bite and paralyze. I instantaneously phased to change positions, now fighting the second Vampire again who hurt Declan. My mate lay wounded on the floor in his European Werewolf form whilst panting hard. His blood as well as a red smoke, poured out of his punctured side. He watched helplessly as I now fought the Vampire that did this to him.

Oh oh again, now I was fighting three Vampires at once! The other two joined the third as the three surrounded us. I battled onwards, trying to lead them away from my wounded husband. However the third Vampire used the other two as a distraction, when it was about to leap onto my back to bite...but suddenly a silver sword was thrown through the air, lopping off its poisonous head!

It was Mum! My own mother had done that! Next, she instantaneously phased to the fallen Vampires' side to retrieve her weapon when she had to quickly duck. The second Vampire tried to bite her but as she was bending over, she back-kicked the female Vampire in the face! It sent the Vampire staggering backwards with a bleeding nose, as the red blood looked a spooky contrast against her white eyes.

My mother and I fought side by side, as we repelled a Vampire each. Her presence seemed to inspire me to move faster and within seconds we each delivered another two headless Vampires to the floor.

Now there were four Vampires left, including the one I had met in the marketplace. He remained along with another male and two females. The other male and a female Vampire were fighting the two European Werewolves which had arrived with Declan. They swung their silver swords at their larger opponents, who dodged the blades. The Werewolves sent out swings of their own, with their strong, sharp claws. This left Gran, Mum and I to face off the Vampire from the marketplace and his female companion.

Out of the blue, the male Vampire I later learned its name was Mikhail, reverted to his human appearance as he sheathed his sword. His white eyes returned to their pale blue colour, as his long fangs retreated into his mouth. Like this, he smiled with his human teeth again.

"Well done Ladies." He commended in his Russian accent. "You fought as true English nobility."

"Huh?" Mum gave a funny look.

"Your Aristocratic blood as the Ladies of Blythe Castle is evident in the way you carry yourselves." He turned on the charm. "I do not want to destroy such beautiful English roses, I want you to join me."

As Mikhail was talking, I watched in the corner of my eye the other two European Werewolves fight onwards. The black beast's claws staggered his female Vampire opponent, which gave the monster its chance. It leapt upon the female Vampire to chew through her face!

"Misha!" The male Vampire hissed in fury to see his female companion killed in such a way. When he turned his sword on the black European Werewolf, it gave the brown European Werewolf its opportunity to leap on him! Soon the second Vampire laid waste on the floor as well.

The two human looking Vampires whom the Circulators were faced off against, continued to weave their magic.

"Arabella, I don't want to harm you or your daughter nor granddaughter. I know how precious you three are, as the last of the Circulators. I too, feel old and alone. I wanted to bring Bianca to meet my kin, for her to join with us then through her to meet you and Jessica. Vampires and Circulators are a lot alike, are we not?" Mikhail spoke.

"How does it know my name?" Gran a funny look, as she kept her sword trained on the Vampires.

"Maybe it's the psychic thing that we were talking about?" Mum wondered.

"Yep," I said coolly, "next thing we know, it'll start going on about how transcendental we are."

"Jessica, please." Mikhail spoke softly to my mother. "You always wanted to travel and see the world. You know that there's more to life than marriage. I can help all three of you to realize your potential."

She looked on in surprise at how he knew this, which almost made her lower her weapon.

Mikhail continued to speak almost tenderly, "Jessica, I can fill your life with art and literature. I can show you the wonders you have always craved. Join with me and by mixing our blood together, we will evolve to the space time continuum with you. Since you three can show us the wonders of the universe, allow us to repay you by showing what this planet has to offer first."

From the corner of my eye again, I watched the strange European Werewolves stalk towards Declan. They sniffed his wound and I thought that they were seeing to him but my mate growled warningly at the two to stay away. Why would he do that to his own kin, didn't they just help us?

"Bianca." Mikhail called back my attention. "I apologize for biting you. I didn't want to feed off you, I simply wanted to bring you here to meet my family. We weren't going to harm you, as we would have tended to you until the poison wore off. I was afraid that as soon as you found out we were Vampire, you wouldn't trust us."

The female Vampire joined in, "Mikhail was so excited when he came home to tell us about finding Circulators, as we haven't seen your kind in over a century. We wanted to meet you to exchange information. We are old and as we represent the past, you three represent the future. We admire your auras as you are beautiful to us."

"Oh, is that why you fought us tonight?" Mum asked sarcastically.

"Please, be reasonable Jessica." He looked on pleadingly. "You three attacked first by suddenly appearing inside our home."

"You brought that filth in with you!" The female European Vampire spat at the three European Werewolves, making the black one growl threateningly. "European Werewolves are our enemies as they have killed many of our kind."

"That 'filth' is my mate." I said icily as I pointed my sword in her direction.

Mikhail tried to put his spell over Gran, "please consider our request, Arabella. You three no longer have to be the last of your kind if you join with us. We can help you rebuild the Circulate and make it a wondrous place not just for Circulators and Calculators, but for all supernatural beings. We can start a council of Circulators, Calculators, Vampires and Werewolves. Your grandmother Elisha would have wanted that, as it's why she started SSIT to meet other supernatural beings like her."

The female Vampire spoke in a lilting manner, "we've heard how enlightened the Lokoti Werewolves are by no longer hunting human. We would be interested in learning from them to change our ways. We want to move out of the past and into the future with you. Become one with us and we can show you such delights that you have only dreamed about."

"Your auras are beautiful us," he sung, "we don't want to diminish your light, we want to bask in it beside you, as one of you."

The female Vampire continued, "we gladly surrender as we wish to peacefully co-exist with you."

"Arabella, you know it's what your grandmother Elisha would have wanted, for all of the supernatural to unite together. We can become one so let us fight no further." Mikhail crooned.

Declan growled helplessly as he watched the Circulators fall under the Vampires charm. He tried to stand up to come to our aid, but he collapsed weakly to the floor again. The other two European Werewolves simply hung back to watch and see what we would do.

NO B! YOU'RE IN DANGER! FIGHT THEM! YOU MUST FIGHT! - I felt Declan's desperation - *FIGHT OR RUN AS THEIR WORDS ARE POISON!*

I knew he was right, but for some odd reason my arms were starting to feel heavier and heavier. I noticed Mum and Gran's swords were also starting to lower.

FIGHT B! YOU HAVE TO CHANGE! - I felt my mate's anger - *CHANGE TO WOLF AND SEE THE SNAKES FOR WHAT THEY ARE!*

My husband wanted me to change into my Lokoti Werewolf form, but why? I didn't understand what it was going to prove. He growled in frustration as he struggled to raise himself only to collapse heavily to the wooden floor.

YOU ARE LOKOTI WEREWOLF! VAMPIRES ARE YOUR ENEMY! CHANGE TO WOLF AND SEE THE SNAKE! – He ordered.

That's your mate speaking to you, a new voice growled deep inside. ***You are not only Circulator, you are Lokoti Werewolf***. This new voice felt like it came from my chest, as it radiated outwards through my very being. ***You have my blood and strength inside you – now use it first female.***

The new voice triggered something else as I felt my body expand with my Lokoti Werewolf muscle. My clothes bulged as my dark blue eyes glowed turquoise. Claws appeared on the end of my fingers where my nails used to be, as I felt my teeth turn elongated and sharp. Then I saw the Vampires for what they were...

...I saw two snake-like humanoids who were hissing as they tried to coil about us. Their mouths were open with their two, long poisonous fangs ready to strike! I growled protectively as I leapt in front of my mother and grandmother, whilst swiping at the snakes with my sword.

Unfortunately these two Vampires seemed to be faster than the others, as they easily leapt backwards whilst unsheathing their own weapons. They were able to block everything I threw their way. However this time I fought as both Lokoti Werewolf and Circulator; with both speed and strength.

I fought faster as I pushed myself harder. My body strained as I sped up my reflexes until I looked like a bright whir, whilst using my Werewolf muscle to add extra force to my blows. Finally it began to work, as I drove them backwards away from Mum and Gran who stood still in their hypnotized states.

Just then I managed to swing my sword around so fast, it surprised the female Vampire. In a single blow, I lopped off her head! A bloodied stump of a neck remained, as her body crumpled to the floor.

"No!" Mikhail cried out angrily. "You BITCH!"

Out of vengeance, he tried to run me through with his sword but I went into phase so it merely sailed through air. When Mikhail pulled back, he tried again to run me through. However I kept my body in phase, as I swung my sword around which remained in corporeal form.

Mikhail didn't see my weapon coming and I must admit, it felt surreal the sensation of my blade cutting through his neck like I was carving up a roast. The silver on the blade burned his flesh, as it sliced through his weaker muscle. I cut until I felt my sword break the spine before the bloodied blade came out on the other side.

His sword dropped to the floor before he did. I watched Mikhail fall forwards with his head toppling off his shoulders, before the rest of him hit his Persian rug. I came out of phase to sheath my sword as I stood over my fallen enemy. I stood victorious as a Lokoti Werewolf who had removed the threat from her family. Gran and Mum were still standing there transfixed, but after a minute they blinked and then they blinked again.

Mum shook herself out of her reverie. "What?"

"That was an interesting experience." Gran frowned. "I can't say I've been hypnotized before."

"Were we hypnotized?" She looked on in surprise.

"We must have been..." my grandmother muttered, "...er, where did all the Vampires go?"

I walked past the two women and patted them on their shoulders as I went. I headed over to Declan as the other two European Werewolves watched with interest. I dropped to my mate's side to sniff his gaping wound.

Oh no, aside from the allergic reaction of his flesh to the silver, I could also smell Vampire poison in his injury. This meant the Vampires coated their weapons with the same poison which was excreted from their fangs. No wonder one single blow took him down. He futilely tried to sit up, but he could barely raise his head from the floor.

"I've got you." I growled softly in my deep Werewolf voice, as I rested his monstrous head against my chest.

Mum and Gran walked over to our position as they regarded the other two European Werewolves with suspicion. They held their swords ready for any further trouble from these new man-eaters. The two in turn kept their distance whilst eying off the silver on their sharp blades.

I lifted up my left wrist and used the claws on my right hand to put a deep gash in it. Then I gently placed the wound inside of Declan's open mouth which was ready and waiting. I closed my eyes as I felt him drink greedily to heal. Slowly his strength started to return as mine started to falter. But as the room came to realize, this was exactly what the other two European Werewolves had been waiting for.

Right at that moment, the brown Werewolf growled at the black Werewolf and everything happened at once!

The brown Werewolf swung out its claw, sending both Mum and Gran to the floor to duck its blow! Simultaneously, the black Werewolf locked its jaws on the back of my neck which is what Declan did to knock me out, the first night I changed. Before I could instantaneously phase out of its grasp...I blacked out. One minute I was sitting on the floor, nursing my mate back to health then the next I was unconscious. Just like that - goodnight!

Declan was still too weak to stop his double-crossing species. His head fell backwards onto the floor as I was ripped away from him. He barely managed to look up in time to see Marcus leap out of one of the broken windows with me slung across his back.

"B?" My mother cried out as she scrambled to her feet to run after. "B!!"

"Jess, watch out!" Her mother too, leapt to her feet.

The older Circulator swung around her sword to stop the older Werewolf's attack on her daughter. Gran's weapon completely cut off Leo's right claw! The brown European Werewolf roared in pain before he snapped his jaws at Gran. However she slipped into phase so his dangerous jaws simply went through her.

"What the hell did you do with my daughter you bastard?!" Mum screeched as she swung her sword around to strike him directly in the back!

Leo roared again from the agony of his flesh being singed by the silver. Then he turned around to leap out of another broken window.

"I'll follow them, stay with Declan until your father gets here!" My grandmother barked at my mother.

Then she too jumped out of the window. Mum ran over to the window sill to catch sight of her fall through the air in phase, so she would land uninjured. She watched as Gran landed lightly in her ghost-like form, when next she streaked off down the street which made her look like a bright blur.

"Damn those dogs to hell!" She swore as she kicked a nearby Vampire head as if it were a soccer ball. When she caught Declan watching in surprise, she muttered, "no offense."

He whimpered in pain as he rolled his glowing green eyes as if to say, 'don't mention it'.

*****

Within ten minutes of drinking my blood, my European Werewolf mate could now sit up. However he still panted in pain and Mum saw his wound look infected. She anxiously paced up and down whilst looking worriedly out the window her daughter had disappeared from, as well as to her son-in-law. He struggled to climb onto his four claws, before he collapsed again.

"Woah, take it easy Declan." She knelt by his side to steady him as she saw he was still very weak.

He growled stubbornly as he shook his large canine head whilst he struggled onto all-fours. She tried to help him up as best she could, which was difficult considering how big and heavy he was. Declan gently nudged her hands away as he panted loudly whilst limping over to the broken window Marcus had jumped from.

He sniffed the air as he vaguely caught my scent, but what worried him was how weak it was. He knew he would have to move fast to catch my trail, so he made a move to jump out the window too.

"No Declan!" She tried to block his way. "You're still too weak."

My mate growled softly as he moved his head to the left, which was his way of politely asking his mother-in-law to stand aside.

"Listen, I know that Dad, Julian, Hunter and Fern will be here soon." My mother tried to reassure. "Plus Mum is following the bastards. She can run faster than them, so they WON'T get away. When Dad arrives, he'll be able to track Mum by her scent. Don't worry, we won't lose Bianca."

He hung his head in guilt as he felt responsible for this happening. He had been afraid of this, as he had suspected Marcus' true motivation all along. He shuddered as the image replayed itself of Marcus' ripping his mate away. He was bigger and stronger than his Lokoti Werewolf wife, so he felt like he had let me down by saving me from one threat to deliver me into the claws of another.

'That's it' – he thought – 'I'm going after her!'

My husband firmly moved my mother aside with his huge head, before he limped out of the window. He landed with a heavy and painful thud onto the road, which made him fall onto his side again. However he heaved himself onto all-fours, to limp off down the street. In a bright flash of light, Mum instantaneously phased to the road beside, before the two of them jogged down the quiet street.

He rasped in pain and she hated hearing how bad he was, "perhaps we should slow down?"

He growled in annoyance at her fussing as he sped up, forcing himself to go faster. Mum easily kept pace as she jogged beside his huge form. Traffic was non-existent in the residential area since it was nearly three in the morning, but in the silence a new sound came to their ears.

At first it took the two a second to realize what that noise was, which sounded like it was getting louder the closer it came. Then he nodded his monstrous head towards a corner which they ducked around. It was just in time too, when a police car with its siren and lights blaring pulled into the street behind.

Mum's eyes widened as she peered around the corner to see two police officers emerge from the vehicle. Firstly they inspected the glass on the street from the broken windows, before investigating inside the house. She figured that they must have been called to the scene by the neighbors who objected to the fighting.

Just then her mobile phone rang which she quickly answered.

"Jess?" Dad greeted. "Where are you?"

"I have no idea, but somewhere in St. Petersburg." She said vaguely.

My mate gently nudged her with his snout to return to tracking. After taking one last look at the police car, she followed him down another quiet road.

"Are you running?" He guessed.

"Yep."

"Are you at the Vampire's nest?" He asked next.

"Nope, we've left there. They're all dead but now we're running after B."

"You're running after B?" He echoed in confusion.

"Two European Werewolves have kidnapped her."

"WHAT?!" His overprotective tendencies were ignited. Next, she overheard him say to somebody, "the European Werewolves have got B!" She heard growling in the background before he spoke to her again, "our plane has just landed and I'll track you by your scent. Your Dad, brother and my Dad are with me."

"OK then, you can tell Dad he can track Mum down by her scent too, as she went after them. Declan and I were slowed up because he's injured." She looked over her son-in-law in concern.

"Declan's injured?" He asked in alarm. "How bad is he?"

"He's slowly healing, but he's in pretty bad shape. The European Werewolves nabbed B when she was sharing her blood with him." She huffed in annoyance.

Next, she heard Dad relay this to the others, "the bastards grabbed B when she was sharing her blood with her injured mate." Mum heard more angry growling in the background before he spoke again. "Right, we should be there in fifteen minutes."

"I'll see you soon." She hung up and then she puffed to Declan as they ran, "they'll be here in fifteen minutes."

He rolled his eyes and if he could talk in Werewolf form he would have said dryly, "yeah thanks, I heard".

After another two minutes of jogging, the two had to hide around another corner when they came to a busy intersection which had heavy traffic.

"There's traffic at three in the morning?" Mum moaned. "Why the hell is there traffic at three in the morning?!"

He growled in agreement as he looked about the street and saw that weren't any alleyways to duck down either. He would have to bolt down the busy street, it was that or lose my trail which he wasn't willing to do.

Just then my European Werewolf mate shrunk back into his human form, so he could talk to her. He stood naked and weak beside her. Mum noticed in his human body, his injury looked much worse which caused her greater worry.

"Declan!" She caught him when he wavered on his two feet.

"There aren't any alleyways for me to go down, so I'll have to bolt down the street." He gasped as he leaned against the wall.

"But you can hardly stand let alone run!" Mum objected.

"We don't have a frickin' choice!" He snapped but immediately he pulled himself up for it. "Sorry Aunt Jess."

Mum gave a small smile to show she wasn't offended.

Declan rasped out, "look, I can run fast and I can leap over the traffic, but I'm worried about you navigating past the cars. So I want to carry you on my back."

"Don't worry about me, I can keep up -" she started to argue.

"I know you're faster than me, but I'd rather you were on my back so I don't have to worry about you getting hit." He frowned. "The trail goes through several busy intersections, because they're deliberately trying to throw us off their scent."

"Then I'll instantaneously phase from one side of the road to the other." She shrugged.

"Aunt Jess, please don't argue about this! We're going to have witnesses and I would rather you were on my back, so I don't have to keep looking behind to see what you're doing!" He growled impatiently.

"But you're injured." She fretted.

"Trust me, we're tougher than we look especially in Werewolf form. How the hell do you think I've been able to remain married to your daughter for the last 55 years?" He joked. When she snickered, he looked on expectantly, "have we got a deal?"

Mum saw his determination which made her sigh in defeat, "alright."

Declan expanded again into his huge, hulking, hairless European Werewolf body before he lowered his large back to let her climb up. He had to help her as she struggled to wrap her legs about his wide waist. It also took her a minute to get a good hold of his muscle-bulked shoulders.

"Just don't tell Hunter about this." She added on lastly, as he rose to his four feet again. "Or I'll never hear the end of it."

She felt him shake with inward laughter, before he took off! He bounded around the corner and down a footpath as she struggled to keep her hold. A couple of cars beeped in alarm at seeing such a large animal on their city streets. This made him speed up to make the drivers catching sight of him harder.

Then she gasped as he without warning, leapt over the four-lane street in a single bound!

They arrived safely on the other side as Declan landed running, racing after my scent. Mum's heart was beating probably just as fast. She later told me how she prayed as she held on for dear life! She wondered how the hell she had been talked into this? However she was impressed by how he seemed to know exactly what it was he was doing. She even started to feel less afraid as he jumped over busy street after busy street.

Mum cringed when she heard the loud crunch of metal behind. When Declan's monstrous form leapt over a car, the driver slammed on his breaks. Next, another vehicle hit that driver from behind! A small pile up eventuated from the sight of a huge, hulking, hairless European Werewolf bounding through the streets of St. Petersburg.

Declan didn't stop out of guilt for causing the car accident, but he kept running. In just over ten minutes, he had run in supernatural speed from one side of city to the next. He had bounded through the busiest parts and what next surprised her was the sight of four tall, strong looking, topless men in jeans, run after.

The four men had different coloured glowing eyes as two of them had long black hair flying behind, whilst the other two had shorter dark hair. She recognized the long haired ones first in the shapes of Grandpa and Uncle Julian. She made out Grandfather and Dad with their shorter hair, thanks to their glowing blue or red eyes.

The Lokoti Werewolves ran upright behind Declan, who bounded along on all-fours in his European Werewolf shape. Mum felt a surge of pride to see her father, father-in-law, husband and twin brother appear as a little piece of home in this foreign city. It wasn't until they reached the outskirts that everyone slowed.

My mate tore around a corner, before he slowed to a trot and eventually came to a complete stop, next to a tall brick wall. She found that they had arrived in an industrial area on the outskirts of the city, full of factories and warehouses. As soon as he stopped, he gently removed her from his back and then he collapsed to the ground. He was wheezing in pain from pushing himself so hard whilst injured.

"Declan!" Grandfather growled in concern as he dropped beside.

Grandpa also knelt down on the other side, to examine his wound. He sniffed the infected cut, before he growled out unhappily, "Vampire poison."

Dad put his arm about Mum, as they looked down in concern on their daughter's mate. Uncle Julian too, dropped to his knees by Declan's side, as he looked on worriedly at the honorary member of his pack.

"He needs our blood to heal." Grandpa advised.

My grandfather immediately raised his right wrist as he used the claws on his left hand, to break open the skin. Then he shoved the cut into my mate's open mouth. The European Werewolf looked up grateful as he drank. Then to Declan's surprise, Uncle Julian also opened up his wrist to replace Grandfathers. When Uncle Julian moved away, Grandpa shared his blood too.

Lastly, my father placed his bleeding wrist into the European Werewolf's mouth and held it steady. By doing so, my healing mate became strong again. My mother looked on pleasantly surprised, since she knew that her husband and son-in-law couldn't be called 'close'. It was a personal gesture, sharing blood to regenerate one's kin.

This Werewolf healing ritual certainly was effective, for when Dad removed his wrist and stood up, so did Declan. He stood on his hind legs, towering over the small group. The huge, hulking, hairless European Werewolf looked down on the smaller humanoid Lokoti Werewolves appreciatively, as the wound in his side was now just a small pink scar.

Next, he turned to jump over the high, brick wall with the Lokoti Werewolves following after. Dad put Mum on his back as he jumped over the wall last. Once he landed soundlessly in the dirt on the other side, he gently returned his beloved mate to her own two feet.

Now she found herself inside of a junk yard, which she looked about in the poor light. Walls of crushed cars surrounded them. Holding onto her husband's hand, they followed the group. The six silently stalked towards the large warehouse in the center and as they came closer, they saw Gran hiding by a pair of locked up metal doors.

My grandmother waved them over to her position and as soon as they reached her, she and her husband hugged.

"Right." She released her mate to whisper to everyone. "They're inside and there's three of them, two males and one female. B's unconscious and they've tied her to a chair." Both Declan and Dad growled dangerously upon this last part. She frowned, "I've been listening to them argue. They seem to think that B will become the black Werewolf's mate."

This time all of the Werewolves growled quietly but then everyone turned silent when they heard me speak and just like she said, I came to tied to a chair.

I'm tied to a chair?! How stupid is that, don't these people know what I am? Like being tied to a chair is frickin' going to hold me!

"What the hell is going on...?" I moaned woozily.

"She's awake." A woman in a red leather jacket spoke in a Swiss accent as she nodded my way. She had a horrible scar on the left side of her face that partially covered her mouth.

I blinked repeatedly as my focus returned. I looked from her towards a man who appeared to be in his forties, but he smelled older. He wore a brown leather jacket and he was missing an eye, with an ugly pit in his face which was an eye-socket. He looked angry and I could smell that he was wounded. Then I saw why, he was missing his right hand as his arm bled profusely.

"Look at what your grandmother did to me!" The older man shouted in a Russian accent, waving the bloody stump my way.

Just then a younger man with black hair, green eyes and was unshaven, walked towards me. He was wearing a black leather jacket over his bare chest along with a pair of dirty jeans. He reached out to caress my cheek, which made me move my head away as I glared back. What was the bet this guy was the black Werewolf who knocked me out?

"I won't kill you." The younger guy spoke in an Italian accent. "I'm Marcus and that's Leo and Michelle. You are Bianca, si?"

"I'm pissed off, that's what I am!" I cried out angrily. "Why the hell am I here?!"

"You're going to be his mate." Michelle pointed at Marcus.

"I'm going to be his WHAT?!" I spat out in disgust. "Go jump! I'm already taken."

"Not anymore you're not." Leo smiled evilly. "Your mate is going to die from his wound. We took you away before he had enough of your blood to regenerate."

My eyes widened fearfully, as my heart raced. Declan was in trouble? Right, that's it, I'm outta here! I went into phase which made the ropes fall through as I stood up from the chair.

"She's getting away, you have to knock her out!" Michelle barked out.

As soon as I started to reform back into my solid form, Marcus' followed her instruction. His fist sent me flying backwards over five meters away! I landed flat on my back with my head knocking hard against the concrete floor.

Oow that hurt! My head spun as I almost passed out again...almost.

"You are MY mate now!" He roared as he walked over to lift up my dazed body from the ground. Whilst holding me up, he shook me as if he were trying to scramble my senses. "You will obey ME!"

"Get real, loser!" My fist lashed out to punch him on the nose!

Marcus dropped me from the impact as I guess I was stronger than he had anticipated. I landed on my feet and just as I was about to instantaneously phase out of there, Michelle cried out again, "she's going to get away! You'll have to keep her unconscious!"

That was it for Declan and my family, who were listening in from outside...

BAM!

...my mate smashed through the locked metal doors in his towering, strong European Werewolf form. The locks and alloy were no match to his fury. Dad ran in right behind as did Mum, Grandfather, Gran, Uncle Jules and Grandpa. My husband snarled viciously at the younger European Werewolf for trying to claim what was already his.

"Declan!" I cried out in relief to see he was healed.

However Marcus' fist connected with my chin, sending me flying back to the floor! His punch didn't knock me out, but it did make me dazed. Woah...the room was spinning around as if I were tumbling down a steep hill.

Next, the younger European Werewolf threw off his black leather jacket to expand into his supernatural shape. Marcus' green eyes began to glow, with his circular pupils turning into long, thin slits which were trained Declan's way. On his hind legs which his torn jeans slipped off, he stalked towards Declan as my mate rose to his back legs to meet his challenger.

The Lokoti Werewolves in the forms of Dad, Grandfather, Grandpa and Uncle Julian, ran in front of Leo and Michelle. The other two European Werewolves in human form, looked on the Lokoti Werewolves nonplussed as they didn't seem threatened by my kin.

"You don't scare us, Indian breed." Leo scoffed.

Then everyone's attention was directed towards Declan and Marcus as they began to fight. Their deafening roars filled the entire warehouse as they stood on their hind legs and circled the other, swiping with their claws. Declan seemed to have an edge over Marcus, as his blows made a greater impact. He repeatedly knocked his rival to the ground leaving deep, bloodied gashes in his hide.

"That's Lokoti Werewolf blood inside of him." Grandfather rumbled proudly to a now worried looking Leo.

"But he didn't drink enough of her blood to heal." He said in disbelief.

"Who said it's just her blood inside of him?" Grandpa arched his eyebrows.

My mother ran over to where I was lying on the ground along with my grandmother. She put my head in her lap as she tried to soothe in a motherly voice, "It's alright, B. Everything's going to be OK."

Gran watched fearfully the two huge, hulking, hairless, male European Werewolves fight, as it was truly a sight to be seen... They looked like powerful giants with deadly claws, as their hardened hides rippled with supernaturally inflated muscles. Their razor sharp teeth could even make a shark swim away in fright! Declan's and Marcus' snarls could curdle the blood as they directed their bloodlust onto each other.

Marcus raised himself from being knocked down yet again. He emitted a deadly growl, showing his bad temper at how this battle was turning out. Then he tried the direct approach, by tackling Declan and engaging in a dog fight! The two huge European Werewolves made the earth quake from their fall, as we all felt the vibrations in the concrete. Soon they were rolling around biting, snapping, clawing and snarling at each other. I could see what they were doing, they were trying to go for the other's throat!

"Declan!" I sat up in alarm.

I morphed into my Lokoti Werewolf body, incase I had to come to my mate's aid. However, this was what Leo and Michelle were thinking too, except with an unfair edge. Leo threw off his coat, as did Michelle and the two expanded into their European Werewolf bodies to finish off Declan once and for all.

As quick as lightening, Grandfather and Uncle Julian tackled over Leo, as Grandpa and Dad took on Michelle. The four Lokoti Werewolves knew they had no hope in winning their fight against their larger and stronger opponents, but they fought to buy Declan time.

My grandmother, mother and I looked on worriedly as we saw the Lokoti Werewolves take a beating. But they fought on, to keep Leo and Michelle away from Declan's fight. When Leo swatted Grandfather like he was no more than an annoying insect, he was quick to leap back, albeit with a bloodied claw mark across his torso. Both father and son teams in the forms of Grandfather and Uncle Julian, then Grandpa and Dad, fought together.

I stood up from the ground and unsheathed Mum's silver coated sword from her back, since mine was mysteriously missing thanks to my kidnappers. I walked towards Michelle who was mauling Dad and Grandpa. The other Circulators stood back to watch, however Gran also unsheathed her blade in preparation.

"Help Grandfather and Uncle Julian." I growled to my father and my grandpa as I approached.

They looked on the weapon in my hand, before they backed away. I faced off Michelle who sniffed at the silver coated sword and growled threateningly. Then to try to intimidate, she stood up on her hind legs to tower over.

"Let's do this bitch." I went into my attack posture as I held the sword high.

Michelle lashed out with her claws to which I easily weaved between using my light speed reflexes. Next, she tried to attack by going directly for my head with her large jaws. I ducked as I simultaneously swung the sword around, cutting her right across the chest!

She howled in pain and immediately backed off...well, that wasn't much of a fight. As I faced off a retreating Michelle, Gran advanced upon Leo. He was practically shredding her family, but still the Lokoti Werewolves fought on.

"Gentlemen," Gran called them away, "it's my turn."

The men moved back, but they stood ready to come to her aid should she need it. As I kept my sword trained on Michelle; I was half watching Declan's fight with Marcus and now Gran's fight with Leo.

The older European Werewolf tried to leap on her, but she instantaneously phased so he missed. She reformed right behind as she swung her sword around and hit him squarely in the back! It was a second time he had been hit with a silver sword there tonight. He roared in pain as he tried to turn on her, but she was too fast for him. Every time he tried to claw or bite or pounce, she kept disappearing and then reappearing in a bright flash of light to deliver her own blows. After several strikes, Leo collapsed. He bled profusely, with a red smoke seeping out of his deep cuts.

Gran calmly handed her sword to Grandfather, who readily took the blade by the hilt. He held it over the European Werewolf's strong chest plate which protected its vital organ. Using his Lokoti Werewolf strength, he brought the sword down as it smashed through bone and ruptured its heart! Michelle howled a second time, as if she physically felt the loss of her mate.

It was around this time that Declan finished his fight with Marcus. His strong, sharp jaws had got hold of his throat which he ripped apart! The black European Werewolf collapsed dead with his canine head hanging loosely on hardly anything left of a neck.

My mate arose from the ground, with his scratches and bite marks already healed. He stood tall on his hind legs victorious, as he looked on Marcus' lifeless form as if he had been a nuisance and nothing more. Mum came to take her sword back which she kept trained on Michelle, to allow my reunion with my husband.

"Declan!" I cried out as I rushed into his awaiting claws.

He shrunk back into his human body as he held me tightly. One minute my face was pressed against hardened hide, the next against his softer skin. I too reverted into my human form so Declan's lips could momentarily smother mine. He held me firm for a long time, as I heard him inhale my scent deeply. Eventually he pulled away slightly to look on tenderly, until his soft expression turned hard and angry.

"B, if you ever run off on me again, I will hunt you down and give you what for!" He yelled in my face but I didn't care, I stood there grinning like an idiot as he ranted. "Do you know how sick you made me with worry? You also made your Grandfather, Dad, Grandpa and Uncle hop on a plane and fly here in the middle of the night. We could have just phased back to the tribal lands which would have saved all the hassle!"

Then he picked me up to almost squeeze the life out of me in another embrace! If I had been human, he certainly would have cracked a few ribs. However I appreciated the desperation, as it showed that he needed me just as much as I needed him. That was until he released his hold again to yell some more.

"AND you nearly got eaten by Vampires AGAIN! You, your Mom and your Gran! Don't you think we ordered you to stay away for a reason? We told you that we'd handle it because we're impervious to their mind games!" He pulled me to him for a third time as he laughed ruefully into my hair. "So help me woman, you'll be the death of me."

The Lokoti Werewolves exchanged humorous looks at our reunion, before Grandfather gave Gran her sword back. Then she started to fuss over her husband and son's claw marks, but they showed her they were healing. Dad and Grandpa had already regenerated as they reverted to their human forms first, with Grandfather and Uncle Jules a close second.

"What are we going to do about this one?" Mum called them over as she guarded Michelle.

My family crossed over to her position, with Gran in tow as she held Grandfather's hand. Declan held my hand too as we joined them. We looked warily on the female European Werewolf, all but my mate whom looked on in loathing.

Michelle howled mournfully as she looked on Leo's lifeless form, until she saw the dangerous looks in the male Werewolves eyes. She shrunk from her huge European Werewolf physique into her smaller human body, as she crouched naked on the floor. In this form, she looked at the males for pity. But Declan didn't buy it, as tonight had taught him an important lesson about his kind.

"Take B outside," he said in a cold and detached voice, "I'll do this."

My head turned sharply in surprise, as did Mum and Gran's.

"You'll do what?" My mother demanded.

"Come on, Jess." My father turned her around.

"Hunter, stop it! He's not talking about KILLING her, is he?!" She objected.

However Dad firmly marched her onwards, without casting another look Michelle's way.

"But she's surrendered." Gran disagreed.

"Come on, Arabella." Grandfather gently tried to pull her away.

"Em!" She refused to leave. "We can't kill a prisoner like this!"

"A prisoner...?" Grandpa looked on askance. "How are we going to hold her? We certainly can't put her inside of a human prison!"

"You'll be killing the last female of your kind." Michelle glared tearfully at Declan. "You could still mate with me, I can breed for you."

"Thanks, but I'm taken." His face turned to stone.

"But can she breed for you?" She asked knowingly. "You need me to help you repopulate our species."

This forced my eyes downwards over my reproductive failure.

"I certainly don't want anymore of our kind running around in this world." He said staunchly.

"If you kill me, you'll be alone until you turn somebody else." She said hatefully. "But after the War, no other women have been turned into our kind as they all die from the process."

Declan turned the male Lokoti Werewolves, "take them outside, now!"

Grandfather escorted Gran out of the warehouse whilst Grandpa and Uncle Julian took hold of my arms to do the same thing.

"No, wait!" I pulled out of their grasp so I could look searchingly into my husband's eyes. "Are you absolutely sure that don't you want to have kids? What if this is your last chance, Declan?"

He looked on unimpressed, "B are you for real? YOU'RE my mate!"

"But if she dies, are you really going to be the last European Werewolf?" I asked fearfully.

Then he squared off his shoulders to say firmly, "I'm not a European Werewolf, I'm Lokoti."

Grandpa's and Uncle Julian's chests rose with pride as they gave a nod as their affirmation.

"You're married to a murderer who is wiping out his own kind." Michelle tried to needle me.

"If I let you live, how many humans will die because of that decision?" My husband asked icily.

She tried to change tact, "then I won't hunt human any longer, I'll eat animal flesh instead." But she said that with the same amount of believability as she did with honesty – zilch.

"B, go outside now!" He yelled.

My grandpa and uncle grabbed hold of my arms again as they pulled me from the warehouse. As I was led outside, I was pulled past a dead Leo lying on the concrete floor in human form with a gaping, bloodied hole in his chest. I also passed another dead human male in the form of Marcus, with hardly anything left of a neck, showing his spine had been snapped into two. I was literally leaving a murder scene which was about to turn into a triple homicide.

I threw a last look over my shoulder before I was pulled through the broken door. I saw Declan morph into his huge European Werewolf shape and like this he towered over Michelle who cringed on the floor. I saw her start to cry as she whimpered pathetically.

Once outside, I found myself in a junk yard as the sky lightened with dawn breaking. I stared vacantly at the wrecks of cars, motorbikes and even a broken down boat sat on top of a pile of wreckage. How fitting to find myself in a place such as this, after all I had seen and done tonight.

I had killed a Vampire who was older than any Werewolf in existence. Just as I had helped eliminate a European Vampire coven, I also battled an endangered breed of Werewolf tonight. Now my mate was about to annihilate the last female and become the last of his kind.

Right at that moment, I heard Declan's roar and Michelle's screams of agony! Her cries abruptly ended and then I didn't hear anything else after it. What came to us in the junk yard was deathly silence. My stomach churned as my mouth turned sickeningly salty whilst I trembled in horror. My mate had just killed a woman who had begged for her life...

I started walking away from the warehouse as I felt like I had to get away from all this violence. I vaguely saw Grandfather hold Gran closely whilst murmuring reassurances in her ear. Dad too tried to hold an arguing Mum but I kept on walking. I had to move past all of this, but Grandpa fell into step beside.

"Declan saved numerous of lives today." He spoke as he walked. "There are now less supernatural predators in the world to prey on humans."

"He just made his own species practically extinct!" I said angrily. "When Declan dies, he will end the European Werewolf."

"Declan isn't a European Werewolf, he's Lokoti. He made his first steps to becoming a Lokoti Werewolf when he was first trained to hunt animal. He made his last steps tonight." Grandpa declared.

I didn't reply to that as I didn't see the point. My lingering doubts were, but at what cost? I was called the Last Circulator and the first female Lokoti Werewolf and for the fact that I couldn't breed? I had a very different appreciation of the term, 'last of their kind'.

*****

~ 27 ~

A couple of minutes later, my naked mate in human form walked out of the warehouse with fresh blood on his hands and mouth. The male Lokoti Werewolves all stood around topless in jeans. Grandfather was still holding Gran in his arms and Mum's arguments had died down thanks to Dad's calming effect.

Grandpa and Uncle Julian crossed over to Declan first to have a quiet word, as I stood well away. I was still unhappy with what had happened. I couldn't hear what they were saying, but I imagined it was along the lines of, "ding dong the bitch is dead."

I walked further away from the scene of the crime. As I began to march off through the junk yard, my husband fell into step beside. He recognized my unhappy look by the way my arms were crossed in a defensive position, so he didn't try to take hold of my hand. He didn't speak nor did I.

"Right," Grandpa organized as he walked behind, "now to find Declan some clothes so we can get out of here."

"B, Jess and I could instantaneously phase everyone back to their hotel room." Gran suggested.

Grandfather chuckled at having a Circulator for a mate, as he proudly kept his arm about her.

"Maybe we could get some breakfast there? I'm starving!" Mum readily agreed, "B?"

"Huh?" I vaguely looked back.

"We're instantaneously phasing back to your hotel room now." She gave a funny look.

"Oh yeah." I instantly walked away from my mate which he frowned upon, to cross over to my mother and grandmother.

The three Circulators stood together in the shape of a triangle as the Werewolves came to stand around. The men placed their hands on our shoulders as they knew the procedure off by heart.

"One." Gran began.

"Two." Mum said next.

"Three." I said lastly.

In a bright flash of light, the eight of us disappeared from the junk yard to reappear in the hotel room. We left behind dirt, wrecks and the smell of grease for a plush setting of carpet, soft couches and a King-sized bed.

"Wow, would you look at this!" My mother admired our suite. She did a little spin as she looked about the luxury and spaciousness. "This is awesome!"

"Yeah, this Hodge Endeavor group who arranged our holiday and expenses don't do things by halves." My husband conceded.

He and the other male Werewolves headed into the large, marble bathroom to clean up. They washed off the blood from their prior injuries as well as their enemies. Afterwards, Declan walked over to his suitcase on top of the bed to put some clothes on. Mum and Gran busied themselves with looking out the windows at the city, instead of my naked, muscled husband.

Declan also pulled out of his suitcase some new shirts which he had bought on one of our shopping trips. He distributed them out to Grandfather, Grandpa, Uncle Jules and Dad to put on. Whilst the males were dressing, I followed suit by changing in the bathroom out of my work-out clothes and into a pair of jeans and a jumper.

"Thanks." Uncle Julian said appreciatively.

My mate dressed in boxer shorts, jeans, t-shirt and a shirt, but he didn't bother with shoes since his feet were already dirty. I emerged from the bathroom as Mum started arguing with Dad about something new. My family laughed at her behavior.

"She's tired and hungry which is why she's grouchy." Dad apologized.

"The Circulators would have used their abilities tonight to the point of excess. Their vitamin, mineral and energy levels will be low." Grandpa spoke as the Medicine Man. "When we have breakfast, they should drink lots of fresh juice."

"I'm fine!" Mum snapped as she shrugged Dad's arm off. "Stop fussing so much, Hunter."

"Yeah, my sister is just naturally mean and nasty." Uncle Jules snickered.

"Shut up Julian!" She retorted. "At least *I* killed three Vampires tonight. How many did you take out?"

"Hey, I would have had my share if SOMEBODY didn't start the fight before we got there!" He returned. "You hogged all of the Vampires!"

"Excuses excuses! Keep telling yourself that, Julian." She rolled her eyes.

"You two are just as bad as when you were little and fought over your Grandma's gravy." Grandfather shook his head at his children.

My grandmother giggled to her mate as she comfortably leaned into him, "at least there's some things that time can't change."

He chuckled in agreement as he kissed the top of her head. Then the women left their swords sitting against the coffee table in our suite. With everybody cleaned up, we left the room to catch the elevator downstairs to the hotel's restaurant.

*****

When we walked out into the lobby, the staff and guests turned in surprise at our appearance. They gawked at the foreigners in their midst, as my Lokoti kin walked bare foot with new shirts over their dirty jeans. They looked from my family to my husband who was just as tall but stronger looking, wearing what looked to be new clothes but he also had dirty feet.

Gran was blissfully unaware of their stares as she walked with Grandfather's arm about her waist. Dad escorted Mum, resting a protective hand on her lower back. I led the way out in front with Declan to the hotel restaurant.   Uncle Jules and Grandpa who walked last, stared back at the expensively dressed guests.

"Do you ever get that feeling you're gate crashing a party you weren't invited to?" Uncle Jules chuckled.

"I've got that distinct impression right now, as a matter of fact." Grandpa laughed back.

The two Lokoti tossed back their long, black hair as they walked confidently.   After fighting European Werewolves whose strength was a hundred times that of a human; the snobby attitude of the guests in the posh hotel amused them.

At the entrance of the restaurant, I approached the host who stood behind his tall desk where a small computer sat.

"We would like a table for eight please." I requested.

"Do you have a reservation?" He asked.

"No, I didn't know we'd need one for breakfast." I replied.

"Reservations are required at all times of the day." He quipped.

"Well I can see lots of available tables, surely you can squeeze us in?" I looked towards the half empty restaurant.

"I'm afraid that this restaurant has a dress code -" the host looked down his nose at the men's dirty feet or even my Lokoti kin's dirty jeans.

"Look you idiot," Declan cut him off with a glare, "my wife and I are staying in this hotels' most expensive suite and paying top credit for it. If you don't skedaddle and get us a table; I'm going to ring up our PA at Hodge Endeavor and tell them to buy this stupid hotel just so I can see to you being fired!"

The host's eyes widened in recognition of the name 'Hodge Endeavor'. He quickly picked up his phone and spoke to someone quietly in Russian. As he talked, I watched his eyes bulge as I think he found out what my husband said was true.

"My apologies, Mr. Sabre." The host put down his phone. "Please allow me to escort you to your table."

Now the host did indeed 'skedaddle' as he led us through the restaurant.

"Not bad Declan," Grandfather chuckled as we walked behind, "you got the gist of the rich man's way of arguing, by using money as his means."

As we walked through the restaurant, we received more stares from the other patrons. The host escorted us to one of the best tables by a window with a magnificent view of the city. Grandfather pulled out Gran's chair for her, as Dad did the same for Mum and then Declan did the same for me. Once the women were seated, all the men sat down. The host snapped his fingers and instantly two waiters appeared to fill our water glasses, as a waitress carried over the menus.

"I hope you enjoy your breakfast this morning and if you should require anything else, please do not hesitate to ask for me." The host told our table and then he left us with the wait staff.

"Actually, I already know what I want." Mum handed her menu back to the girl. "I'll have bacon, scrambled eggs, grilled tomato, grilled mushrooms, buttered toast and orange juice please."

"Same for me thanks." Dad handed his menu back as well.

The waitress quickly typed their orders into her PDA as she moved on to take Grandpa's, Uncle Julian's, Gran's and Grandfather's requests. She came to Declan and I last of all.

"I'll have the strawberry crepe, as well as the banana pancakes and maple syrup. On the side, throw in some fried eggs, sausages and toast." Declan ordered.

I had to smirk as I caught the waitress try to cover her surprised expression at my mate's large appetite. Then she looked my way with her PDA ready.

"I'll just have a glass of orange juice and a Latte please." I said.

"B," he immediately frowned, "you've got to eat something! You've worked yourself hard all night."

Then the table burst into laughter at the waitress' shocked look on his choice of words.

"He means that we had a big night out on the town." Uncle Julian snickered.

The waitress ducked her head as she blushed, before she looked back my way to see if I would change my mind.

"That's it, thanks." I reassured and then I watched her leave.

"B," my mate lectured, "you need to build up your strength again."

"I'll be fine." I said flatly.

"Yeah right! I don't care what you say, but you're gonna eat something from my plate when the food arrives." He said firmly.

I looked away to stare despondently at the flower arrangement in the centre of our table. I felt Grandpa's concerned look, but I didn't want to acknowledge it.

"She'll probably be hungry by lunch time." My father told my husband. "She just needs to unwind from all the fighting."

Right as he said that, Mum tiredly leaned into Dad's side and sighed appreciatively when he was quick to put his arm about her.

Uncle Julian cautiously looked about before he leaned over to ask quietly, "so what do the fang heads look like? Do they slip from human to other like we do?"

"They look weird." His mother answered. "They reminded me of a snake and they hissed a lot too."

"Their eyes turn completely white." His sister added on. "It was spooky, seeing these long fangs with the white eyes and having these poisonous things hiss at you."

"They don't bulk up like you do when you change." Gran continued. "I don't think they're as strong as you, but they are faster though."

"They sure are." Declan said bitterly. "When that fang head stuck me with its poison-coated silver sword? It moved so fast I didn't see the weapon until I felt it sticking through me."

"So the next question is," Grandpa said seriously, "were the white-eyed ones you fought tonight the entire European species?"

"No, they wouldn't be." He said unhappily. "There would be more out there."

Grandpa exchanged a long look with Grandfather, which gave away their mental communication.

"I'm sorry to have to do this, but you both should still come home today." My grandfather ordered.

"But why?" Mum instantly argued. "They're out of danger and they still have two weeks left of their holiday."

"Because if there are more fang heads out there? They'll see that B is one of the Light People as well as a Lokoti you-know-what." Dad said softly.

"When you and I went on our holiday, we didn't have any problems." She said sulkily.

"We didn't visit as many places as Declan and B have, including Russia." He pointed out.

"The white-eyed ones will be drawn to her pheromones and her light, it's just too dangerous." Grandpa backed up Grandfather's decision.

"But there's still so much for them to do and see!" She disagreed. "Why should they be chased home, just because of a couple of white-eyed things?"

"Jess, please don't." Her husband looked uncomfortable.

"No, Jess is right." Gran spoke up. "B can't hide on Lokoti land forever, scared to leave home and see the world. Besides, who knows when the next danger will come to Alaska and seek her out?"

"Yeah!" Mum backed her. "We didn't raise her to hide from the world! She's loves traveling, being a 'Light Person'. If trouble has to happen then trouble will happen, no matter where she is. B knows how to fight and can take care of herself. Besides, she was in less danger tonight than she was when she was shot in the head by humans!"

"Shhh." Grandfather noticed a couple at another table look our way from overhearing her.

"I hate to agree with Jess." Uncle Julian joked to which she stuck out her tongue. "But I think my sister and my mother are right. B shouldn't be punished for being who she is. Remember the stories of the fang heads also coming to Alaska to hunt us? The world is a dangerous place, period. She hasn't just got Mum and Jess looking after her, but she's got me too. I don't want my niece to feel like she has to hide because of who she is."

Then he ended his argument with a wink my way. The debate made Grandpa sigh heavily, before he looked at Grandfather. The older men, one as a Tribal Elder and the other who was Second of the pack, exchanged another long look. My mate respectfully waited to hear his orders from his superiors.

After a long moment, Grandfather emitted a small smile. "I hope that you two enjoy the rest of your holiday."

"Yes!" Mum gave a gleeful clap of her hands which made Dad chuckle.

Declan turned to pass me a smile, thinking that this would have made me happy? But his smile faded when he caught me staring at the flower arrangement again.

*****

Our family breakfast went for over an hour. Everybody happily chatted or laughed away as they enjoyed the fine food in the five-star restaurant. Everybody except me, that is...

I smiled a couple of times out of politeness, but I was in no way inclined to share in the celebration. My shoulders were still tense, as a dark pit formed where my stomach used to be.   I was even distracted by a peculiar ringing in my ears, which oddly sounded like a woman screaming.

At the end of the meal, Declan and I escorted everybody back to our suite. The plan was everybody was going to instantaneously phase back to Tribal Lands from the privacy of our hotel room.

Grandpa caught the tension between my husband and I, as he noted how we were standing apart from each other. He frowned when he saw my defensive posture of my arms folded in front. He frowned further still, when he noted Declan's hands were shoved so deep into his pockets, like he was restraining himself.

"Alright everyone," he cleared his throat, "let's leave B and Declan to continue with their belated honeymoon in privacy."

"OK sweetie, have fun!" My mother walked up to give a warm hug, before she bestowed a kiss on my husband's cheek, "thanks for the piggy-back ride, Declan. It was actually a lot of fun."

"What?" My father looked on in surprise. "You hardly ever let me take you for rides on my back."

"That's a surprise, because I thought Jess would be an expert on riding people with her constant complaining." Uncle Jules goaded, before he laughingly dodged Mum's next whack.

As I left farewell kisses on their cheeks, Declan shook everyone's hand.

Grandpa said his goodbyes lastly, as he looked on with a somber expression which almost matched my own, "just remember what I told you earlier, B."

I forced a nod back before I watched my relatives enter a new formation. Both Grandpa and Dad rested their hands on Mum's shoulders, as Uncle Julian and Grandfather placed their hands on Gran's.

"Bye." I gave a little wave.

"Enjoy yourselves!" Mum winked, before she instantaneously phased herself, Dad and Grandpa out of our room in a bright flash of light.

"Bon voyage!" Gran grinned before she too disappeared in further brilliance, taking Uncle Jules and Grandfather with her.

Then my husband and I were left in an uncomfortable silence as my family's cheerful noise and bustle left with them.

"I'm gonna have a shower to wash off the city's pollution." He grumbled as he headed towards the marble bathroom.

I heard him start the shower as he stripped off his clothes. Next, I tiredly walked over to the soft couch in the centre of our suite whereupon I wearily fell backwards. I stared up at the high, decorated ceiling before I closed my eyes...and I saw it again.

I saw Declan's huge, hulking, hairless European Werewolf body tower over the woman in human form who cowered on the cold cement floor before him. His dangerous roar and the woman's screams rebounded in my ears. It made my eyes snapped open in repeat horror as the dark pit inside grew worse.

When I looked down at my hands, I found dried blood under my nails. I'm a killer who's married to another killer. I battled monsters tonight and became a monster myself, by allowing my mate kill a female who begged for her life.

I allowed myself to cry for the first time in years, as I mourned the last female European Werewolf. I wondered if that would be me one day, would a human deem me too dangerous to live and destroy me?

You are a human protector, not a human predator. You are one of the fifteen protectors of your tribe, Lokoti Werewolf - the strange growl rumbled from deep inside again.

After one last sniffle, I moved off the couch and started to undress. I thought a shower right now sounded like a good idea, as I wanted to wash off all traces of blood. Just as Declan turned off the shower and stepped out, I brushed past to turn the water back on.

He looked on with longing at my naked, wet body. Then he frowned when he watched me scrub hard at skin and nails as I stood under the scalding hot water. I continued to scrub even after the blood had been washed away. He unhappily walked out of the ensuite to dress in the bedroom.

*****

When I eventually emerged from the bathroom, I caught Declan's unimpressed look as he sat on the couch reading a magazine. I overheard him mutter under his breath as I passed, "out damn spot, out."

"I thought you didn't like all that airy-fairy, artsy, nonsense such as Shakespeare." I said dryly as I dressed by the bed.

"Some of his stuff was OK." He said casually. "Hamlet was downright annoying as he kept whining all the time but reading Macbeth was cool."

He looked up from the magazine to watch me pull on pressed black pants and a white silk blouse over my expensive lingerie, all of which came courtesy from a shopping trip in Paris.

"Whoops, you missed a spot." He quipped.

"Huh?" I gave a funny look.

"I saw a patch of healthy skin which wasn't rubbed raw, on your back." He said sarcastically as he looked back at the magazine. "You wanna go back under the hot water and attack it with steel wool or somethin'?"

I tried to ignore him as I finished getting dressed. But when I looked in the mirror on the dressing table as I brushed my hair, I caught him watching again.

"You've never looked at me like that before." Declan began as I remained quiet. "This is the part where you say, 'like what' and then I say in a hurt voice, 'you looked at me today like I was a monster'." He mimed although I knew he was being serious. "I think dearest that you're supposed to say, 'but you're not a monster, you're a hero'; or some such wishy-washy nonsense." He snapped the page of the magazine loudly as he turned it over, "then I take you into my big, strong arms and you're supposed to melt like butter as you give me one of your doe-eyed looks."

My hand holding the hairbrush started to tremble and I accidentally dropped it. I decided to leave it on the carpet as I began to twist my hair up into a French Roll. I tried very hard to carry on as normal in front of my husband.

"OK," he stood up as he tossed the magazine aside, "let's get this fight out of the way."

I pursed my lips shut as I pinned my hair in place. Although I kept my back to him, I tracked his movements via the mirror.

"Is this your new tactic, the silent treatment?" He walked up to stand directly behind. "That's unusual for you."

I blinked quickly to try to stop my eyes welling with hot, angry tears as I next put on a set of pearl earrings.

"OK then, I can fight for you as well as me. I did so last night as I fought the European Vampires and the European Werewolves for you." He came to lean against the dressing table as he sighed out, "you know B, I'm pretty strong and I can take a lot. I can recover from poisoned silver swords run through my lung and I can run wounded across the city with your Mom on my back. I can fight off kidnappers who try to take my mate away from me. But I can't take you, the woman I love, who can no longer look at me for doing the things I did for her safety."

I quickly turned away as I crossed back to the bed to slip on a pair of black shoes. Declan remained at the dressing table as he continued to watch before he spoke again.

"You can dress up as smartly as you like, to go out and absorb more 'culture' in museums and art galleries. You can even attract more suitors as you go, with your long, black hair, dark blue eyes and pheromones. But I'll still love you B and I'll always love you the same."

I almost hit back with, "do you know what love is, being a killer?" But I bit it back in time. However Declan's eyes widened with hurt, as if he did hear.

"Go on, say it." He raised his voice in anger. "Say it, B! Say it!"

"You were twice her size and you killed her like that!" I snapped my fingers before I ranted tearfully. "You just snuffed her out! You towered over her and I heard your roar and her scream and you killed her just like that!"

"B, she wasn't human and she was in no way helpless!" He flared. "I killed her for you! I killed her for the tribe! I killed her to stop killing other humans!"

I could sense him restrain himself as he shouted, before he whirled around to go stand by the window. I felt his helpless anger build up from the hurt I was causing, but the dark pit inside wouldn't let this rest.

"Leo, Marcus and Michelle all deserved their fates." He said bitterly. "Your Gran didn't hesitate when she brought the monster Leo down. Marcus would have forced himself on you with out any hesitation and Michelle? She ate her own family the first night she changed, but did her remorse stop her from feeding on other humans? No!"

I sank onto the bed, with my legs almost giving out as his words hit me like a sledge hammer.

He spoke as he stared out the window, "if I had let Michelle live, she would have turned a human male to become her next mate. Then together they could have rocked up to Alaska to exact her revenge. Two European Werewolves could easily wipe out the fourteen male Lokoti Werewolves! People think I was too young to remember the night I was changed, but I remember it well."

It started to rain and I heard the water hit the glass panes, before coursing down. We both watched the rain drench the city from our view before Declan went on.

"Tonight I met my own kind and they reconfirmed my low opinion of my breed and myself. I remember like it was only yesterday, the creature which killed my father before his family and then the agony of its claws trying to pry me out of my pregnant mother's arms. That one European Werewolf would have finished off my family AND the Lokoti Werewolves battling it. It took both a Circulator and a Lokoti Werewolf together to bring the beast down. Your Gran swung her silver swords in the speed of light, then it took your Grandfather's Lokoti Werewolf strength to pierce her sword through its protective chest plate. The same chest plate coincidentally which appears to reinforce my heart when I change."

Our argument turned into Declan's confessional, as he stared out at the rain. If he couldn't be absolved for his sins, he at least tried to explain why he committed them. I took a deep breath as I listened to him continue talking in a flat voice.

"I was near death as I heard the Lokoti Werewolves talk over me. At first they didn't want to save my life, as they told my Mom that that if they saved me, I would become the killer who attacked our family. But your Gran declared me and my Mom kin, because of who my great, great grand uncle was and your Grandfather out of love for his mate, gave his blood to revive me. When he adopted me into the pack, I could feel the Lokoti Werewolves disapproval when the bloodlust made me crave human flesh. It took the entire will of the pack to teach me to hunt animal instead, but by the Christian God in heaven, I tried. I lived by their rules to protect my mother and my little brother."

He looked my way tearfully, "when you changed, I thought 'thank God I'm not alone anymore'. But because of Derik's feelings, I had to be careful. Not only did I have to fight my bloodlust, but my lust for you as well. Then the pack and the Elders married you off to Grant Elm instead of me, because they didn't trust a European Werewolf."

Here I finally spoke, "tonight Grandpa told me that you were a full Lokoti Werewolf and not just a honorary member of the pack."

"Yeah now he says that!" He scoffed as he rolled his eyes. "But it only took me eighty years to earn their trust! Do you know why this is so? Because of you B. They say, the love of a good woman can create a good man? You calm my bloodlust as you strengthen my instinct to protect instead of to kill. When Leo and Marcus told me what I was missing because I didn't give in to the bloodlust to hunt human, do you know what I told them? That I didn't have to taste human flesh because my mate satiates me."

My husband's words not only touched my heart, but they began to fill up the dark pit inside which slowly extinguished it. I didn't like how it made me feel, scared and hopeless.

Declan walked over to where I was sitting on the bed and he knelt down on the floor before me. "Please don't turn away from me now B, because I couldn't stand it. I'd probably be the first European Werewolf to die of a broken heart, not one that was pierced with silver."

His eyes watered profusely as his voice broke. My mate's pain became my pain and I quickly pulled him to me, to end his suffering. He held me back tightly whilst burying his wet face in my lap. I bent over him to rest my cheek on his strong back.

"You may scare me sometimes Declan, but I've never stopped loving you." I murmured.

My husband cried in my lap as his tears wetted the front of my haute couture clothes, but I didn't care. I've never seen my mate cry like this before; I've seen him yell tearfully, but never sob. My clothes were scrunched in his tight fists, as I heard him rasp. He sounded like he could have been in physical agony.

"I'm here, Declan." I ran my hands up and down his back. "I'm here and I'm never going to leave you."

He raised his head to look up with his watery blue eyes as I cupped his face tenderly.

"I couldn't care less if that female European Werewolf could give me an entire litter! I don't care for my species nor do I care for continuing on a breed of beasts. I'm Lokoti Werewolf, just as my mate is." He proclaimed.

He cupped my face too so he could pull me in for a kiss. We made out with our wet faces rubbing against the others, before I felt his hands begin to tug off my clothes. We were undressing each other as he slowly began to push me backwards onto the bed.

*****

Afterwards we lay on our sides facing the other, with the sheet covering our lower halves. Today we looked on each other with new eyes. We had been mates for the past fifty-five years but no matter how strong Declan looked, I saw his vulnerable side. I sighed as I smiled dreamily upon him.

"What?" He smiled back.

"Just think, we're stuck with each other for another two hundred years."

"It doesn't sound so bad, does it?"

"No," I agreed, "it doesn't."

Declan reached out his muscled arm to use his thumb to caress my lips.

"Are you always going to remain this young and gorgeous?" He joked. "After my 200th Birthday when I start to grow old and ugly, are you going to look the same?"

"I guess." I shrugged.

"Good." He chuckled. "I like the idea of being a dirty old man with you by my side."

"So..." I slid my body up against his, "...are you going to become my sugar daddy?"

His response was automatic, "why, what do you want?"

"Well, sugar daddies take their bit of stuff shopping, you know." I teased.

"You want to do MORE shopping?" He blanched.

"You ripped two buttons from my blouse." I nodded to the discarded garment on the floor.

"Then I'll sew it back up."

"Of course you're going to sew it back up, but I want another one."

"No!"

"Come on Dec," I began to chew on his ear, "I know you enjoyed sitting in the shop, whilst I did my little fashion show by trying on all the clothes!"

"No B," he tried to remain steadfast although my show affection distracted him, "no more shopping."

"Yes!" I declared as I pushed him onto his back so I could sit on top. "We have two more weeks of sightseeing and shopping."

"For crying out loud!" He growled in frustration. He literally winced at the idea of shopping like it was some kind of torture. "Give me the woods, give me the river, give me the quiet glade, give me hunting on a full moon night... Just get me out of this frickin' city!"

"I hope you're not going to be like this for the next two hundred years." I bent my head to playfully bite him on the nipple.

"Oow!" He cried out. "That HURT!"

"You whinge a lot, you know that?"

"You cause pain, did you know that?" He rebuked.

"Would you like me to go and find someone else to torture?"

"Life without you would be torture." He cupped my face again. "Now say you'll always be here, by my side, every step of the way...?"

"I'll be right by your side every step of the way."

"Now say it like you mean it!" He tickled.

"No!" I squealed. "Stop it Declan!"

When he kept tickling, I bit him hard on the chest!

"Aagh!" He cried out before he held me at arms length in his stronger grip. "You are one vicious female, you know that?"

"You can call me a bitch."

"Nah ah." He frowned. "I'd kill the man who calls you that so I don't fancy taking a swan dive off the Eiffel Tower to kill myself either."

"The sweetest things you say..." I sung as I moved my crotch over his.

I smiled smugly as he immediately groaned from the effects of my actions. His hands holding my arms tightened as his head fell backwards into the pillows. I watched his eyes flutter closed as he began to move his hips with mine.

"Don't you realize it, woman?" He sighed weakly as he reopened his eyes. "You've got yourself your very own European Werewolf bodyguard and love slave for the rest of its life."

"Hmm, I'm starting to like that sound of that." I took him in deeper which made him exhale heavily. "So you know what this mean mistress is going to make you do, don't you? Take...me...shopping."

When he released my arms, I bent my head to chew on his neck with my sharpening teeth. I felt the nails on his hands dig into my skin as he lost his self-control. I picked up in speed as he picked up in strength as he pushed to his heart's delight. The mattress began to shudder from our strong movements as our breathing sped up into panting.

"Oh, you're cruel..." Declan groaned, "... and you don't fight fair."

"Say it."

"No!"

I licked his ear. "Say it."

"OK! Alright! We're going shopping!" He gave in to both my demands and his passion.

~~~~~~

10th September 2145

The last two weeks of our 'belated honeymoon' were wonderful. We drove our luxury rental car to the different cities, where we stayed in more five-star hotels. I didn't really do that much shopping, it was only two more times did I visit the haute couture houses. But I justified the spending to both Declan and my conscience; it was to buy more clothes for my role as Dr. Bianca Sabre, Ancient History Professor extraordinaire.

We walked around the different cities during the day, sightseeing in jeans and sneakers. Then in the evening we dressed formally to eat in expensive restaurants as we enjoyed the 'night life'. When we went out to dinner, Declan would put on a black suit and a pale blue shirt which suited his bright blue eyes perfectly, but I still wouldn't let him wear a tie.

"And you call me bossy?" He complained.

"It's not you." I said staunchly as I walked off with it before he could catch me.

The nights where he would wear a suit with his top button on his shirt undone, he looked very handsome. From catching the looks of other women around, I saw that I wasn't the only one who thought so. Even a gay usher at the opera seemed to agree.

We took in a show whilst we were in Brussels. Declan's well built frame filled out his suit nicely and made quite the impression. The usher was more than happy to personally escort us to our seats in the balcony of the theatre. Hell, he even gave us a free copy of the program instead of charging us.
~~~~~~

"Er, thanks." He blushed at the usher's attention as he handed me the program instead.

"Enjoy the show." The usher winked before he walked some other well dressed people to their seats.

I ducked my head to snicker when my husband embarrassed, put his arm about to hold me close, to show his attachment.

"I told you that you look good with out a tie." I tittered.

"Shut up." He rolled his eyes.

The theatre darkened and we began to watch the production of 'Madame Butterfly'. Then during intermission we each drank a glass of orange juice and shared some complimentary hors d'ouvres. Lastly, we returned to our seats to watch the second half of the show.

The story of 'Madame Butterfly' had a sad ending which made my eyes water to see the character's fate. To my surprise, I too saw Declan's eyes looking a little misty. When he caught me staring, he quickly blinked whilst straightening in his seat.

"Shut up." He growled quietly.

When the show came to a close, we applauded enthusiastically along with the rest of the audience as the cast did several curtain calls. Once the theatre's lights were back on, we stood up and slowly followed the crowd outside. As we left the opera house, I walked hand-in-hand beside my mate.

"That was cool." I sighed. "We should go to the opera more often."

"Yeah, it wasn't boring like the other Classical crap." He conceded.

"High praise indeed." I giggled as I playfully poked him.

He smilingly caught my hand which he raised to his lips to place a kiss. Next, he paused to wave down a taxi to take us back to our hotel.

"No." I stopped him. "It's a nice evening, let's walk."

My husband gave an approving look at his wife in her long, black, velvet evening dress with a white silk shawl about her bare shoulders.

"The high heels aren't hurting your feet?" He checked.

"Not much." I promised. "So let's walk."

I watched him turn away for a moment to sniff the air, as if he wanted to make sure we wouldn't come across any danger in our evening wear. Then he smiled softly my way, "let's walk then."

He squeezed my hand in his as we proceeded to stroll down the footpath.

It was a beautiful evening and it was a beautiful city to be walking in. It was just a beautiful moment, period. We walked past the old, restored buildings that were lit up to show their grandeur to the night. We passed other couples walking hand-in-hand and I caught him look twice at a lesbian couple we passed, at first in surprise and then in curiosity. I laughed at my husband as I pulled him along.

When we passed a busker playing an accordion, I made us stop to listen to the man play. I smiled contentedly as I felt his warm hand caress the bare skin on my back which the dress showed off. Another couple who were already standing there listening, next began to waltz to the music. As if he were worried I would try to make us dance too, my husband gently pulled me away.

It was a forty minute walk back to our hotel and twenty minutes into our stroll, I had to take off my shoes and walk bare foot, as the discomfort was too distracting. Declan gallantly carried my shoes for me, along with the program in one hand as his other held mine. We walked the majority of the way in a comfortable silence, before I caught the smug smirk on his face.

"What are you grinning about?" I poked him in the side again.

"Everything."

"Do you care to elaborate?" I enquired.

"Look at us B and look at where we are right now after all we've been through. Then how you look tonight and I have the beautiful girl hanging off my arm? I managed to get the girl in the end and more importantly, I got to keep the girl."

"You know what Declan? You're right." I began. "You have gone through a lot and because of it, I think you might have brain damage."

My mate laughingly stopped us in our tracks so he could pull me into his arms. "You've got that straight! You're either married to other men, or getting shot in the head, or nearly fed upon by Vampires, or kidnapped by other Werewolves! But you've got your own magic about you B, because you keep returning to me, no matter what."

"Sabre, you're not turning soft on me, are you?" I ribbed. "Where's the tribe's 'bad ass' that I mated with? Crying over an opera and then this? Oh come on!"

He chuckled as he ducked his head to kiss my neck and then my bare shoulders. "As I said before B, you're my weakness let alone the proverbial thorn in my behind."

"You know what, Declan?" I said mockingly. "I think you only put up with me because I'm your only avenue for getting laid."

"Oh, I thought you knew that's what I was doing." He joked back. "Of course it's the real reason why I tell you that I love you, B. Women use sex to get love and men use love to get sex."

I laughed out loud, "I'll tell you what, how about I walk you back to the theatre and hand you over to the gay usher? Then if you shag another male, neither of you will ever have to use the dreaded 'L' word again. You can get sex without any emotional proclamations."

"Eugh!" He almost let go in disgust. "He's so NOT my type, B!"

"Oh and what is your type exactly?"

"Give me something female; something with breasts; something that's soft and squidgy. Something that smells good like a female Lokoti Werewolf with her pheromones." He breathed in as he pulled me close.

"But being strong as the first female Lokoti Werewolf doesn't exactly make me soft and squidgy." I pointed out.

"Oh, but you are in just the right places." He moaned as he ducked his head to kiss me on the neck again.

I giggled at his words and his affection, as I wrapped my arms about his neck. I teased back, "shall we go back to our hotel room and you can show me these soft spots in the right places?"

"Purely for the sake of education, of course." He gave a mischievous grin.

"Of course, as this would have nothing to do with that 'L' word." I rubbed my nose against his.

"Or how good you feel in my arms." He growled quietly.

"I think we'd better hurry then." I started to make a move.

"Wait." He pulled me back as he looked about. "Quick! While there's nobody else around, instantaneously phase us back."

"What?" I echoed in shock to hear him suggest such a thing out in public.

"I can't wait for us to walk back!" He growled again this time in frustration. "Since there's nobody around at the moment, instantaneously phase us back."

I giggled at his sense of urgency before I too looked about. However as soon as I confirmed that we didn't have any witnesses, we disappeared from the street in a flash of light to reappear in another, in the privacy of our hotel room.

"You know this little ability you have also works in your favor." Declan said hotly as his hands worked fast to undress us both.

"I thought it might." I pushed off his jacket and then his shirt.

"I officially declare that class is in session!" He proclaimed as he picked me up to fall onto the bed underneath him.

*****

'Class' went for a good two hours, with no indication that my 'teacher' was in anyway coming to the end of his lesson plan. We rolled about the bed as the sheets were uprooted, the quilt was tossed aside and even the mattress suffered.

"And I believe these soft spots..." he lectured as he massaged intimately, "...are also called your erogenous zones."

"Oh really?" I breathed in sharply. "That explains then what the biology text book was going on about."

"B, what did I tell you about you reading?" He growled playfully in my ear before he chewed on it. "All those years you were doing the wrong kind of homework."

I giggled back, "I should have been studying in your bedroom, rather than at your dining table."

"Hey, I'm a flexible kinda guy. We could have 'studied' on top of my dining table as well as in my bedroom." He chuckled as he nuzzled my collar bone.

"I'm sure your mother would have been impressed with THAT." I growled as I felt my teeth turn elongated and sharp.

Then I used them to chew on his lower lip to taste his blood. My mate groaned as I felt his own teeth sharpen which he used to graze my jaw line. Just as our claws began to appear with our arousal, the sound of his mobile phone blasting out 'Iesha' by Death In Vegas, interrupted.

He growled in annoyance as he reached over whilst never letting go. I was pulled across the bed as he moved us closer to the bedside table to answer the call. I watched him frown when he saw the name of the caller on his screen before he hit the 'receive' button.

"Derik," he greeted seriously, "what is it?"

That's a nice way of greeting your little brother! I started to shake my head in disapproval but I stopped when a feeling of dread sunk in from seeing Declan's unhappy look. Oh oh, something bad has happened.

"OK Derik." He said somberly. "B and I will be home in thirty minutes."

Then he hung up as he looked down to say what was wrong? But he shut his mouth again as he looked like he was struggling how to say it.

"What is it?" I sat up simultaneously as he raised himself.

"It's Rachel." He said flatly. "She passed away tonight."

My mouth fell open in shock...

"Come on." He rolled out of bed first then pulled me up second.

Neither of us said anything further as we quickly dressed in sneakers, jeans and t-shirts. As we hurriedly packed up our room, we quietly passed each other. Within fifteen minutes we were ready to go home.

"I'll hand in our security card to reception so can you call Hodge Endeavor? Tell them we have to leave from a family emergency. Your Gran's PA can oversee returning our rental car and canceling the rest of our trip." He organized on his way out the door.

I nodded as he left our hotel room then I picked up my mobile phone to make the call.

*****

I instantaneously phased us and our four suitcases into Derik and Rachel's living room. In a flash of light we left Belgium and in another, we were in Alaska. We found Michael, Blanche and their spouses were sitting whilst sipping coffee. However we must have given them a fright by our sudden appearance, as they quickly stood up.

"Where's your father?" My mate asked Blanche as I hugged Michael.

"Dad's in his bedroom with Mom." She answered tearfully.

Declan patted her on the arm before he and I left the living area to walk down the small corridor. When we walked into Derik's and Rachel's room, we found him sitting on the side of the couple's bed, looking tearfully down on his late wife. She was tucked under the covers, looking like she was asleep rather than dead.

My husband walked over to pull Derik into a hug, as he held onto his grieving brother. He used his supernatural strength to hold up the elderly man, as the weaker one clung to him. His white hair shook as he openly cried.

I left my mate to comfort his brother, as I moved to sit on the other side of the bed. I looked down on Rachel's peaceful expression as my eyes stung. I took hold of her cold, limp hand and squeezed it in my warmer, stronger ones. Out of my four friends from childhood, now two of these were gone.

"How - how did she go?" I looked up.

Derik sniffed as he pulled away, but my European Werewolf mate kept his strong arm about his frail brother.

"She passed away in her sleep." My best friend said sadly. "She had a tension head ache from her bad hip so I suggested she take a nap. When I came in to tell her dinner was ready, she wouldn't wake up."

With that, Derik erupted into sobs which made his whole body shake. My mate pulled his brother into his arms again and I saw he how he was holding him up. My tearful eyes met Declan's and the expression on his face was not only bereft at his little brother's loss but it was mixed with something else.

THANK YOU FOR NEVER LETTING ME GO THROUGH THIS WITH YOU – I heard his thoughts.

Tearfully, I ducked my head as my watery eyes returned to Rachel. My hand squeezed hers which was stupid I know. She wouldn't be able to feel it as she was long gone. Rachel was well on her way to be with Mandy and everyone else who had left this life behind.

*****

Dawn arrived in Alaska right behind my husband and I. We remained at his brother's house, along with the rest of the Sabre family. Everyone was tired and emotionally wrung out and the only people who were sleeping soundly were the grandchildren, in Michael and Blanche's old bedrooms.

I left the brothers to talk quietly, as I departed the bedroom and passed through the living area to go into the kitchen. I turned on the kettle and proceeded to make several cups of coffee as I needed to keep busy. My eyes were still watering as I noticed my hands tremble slightly.

Michael walked in to say, "thanks for getting here so fast."

"Of course we'd come immediately." I said simply.

"I'm sorry that your trip was cut short." He said next.

"We were going to drive back to Paris for our flight back in a day's time anyway." I promised.

"The kids will be wanting their presents as soon as they wake up." He tried to joke but then he dissolved into tears.

"Shhh." I pulled my godson into my arms to hold him tightly. "Shhh."

He took a deep breath as he pulled away, "so I heard there was some excitement during your trip."

"But that's what trips are for, are they not?" I said wryly.

"To nearly get eaten by European Vampires and kidnapped by European Werewolves?" He snickered. "I bet Uncle Declan loved that, his own breed betraying him."

"Your Uncle may physically resemble a European Werewolf, but he's a Lokoti Werewolf at heart." I stated.

"Right." He said awkwardly as he stood back to watch me finish off the beverages.

"Would you like one?" I offered.

"Nah," he shook his head, "I've drunk too much coffee tonight as it is."

Just then Declan walked into the kitchen and headed straight for one of the mugs I'd made.

"I'll just go and give this to Derik." I picked up another.

"Don't bother," he said curtly, "I've put him to bed."

"Where's he sleeping?" I wondered out loud.

"In bed, beside her," he answered flatly, "where he should be."

Michael blinked hard, "I suppose Grandpa Wisetail will be coming soon to take Mom's body away to prepare for the funeral."

"I suppose." My mate said as he stared out the kitchen window.

The pale light of dawn made the colors in the backyard look dim, with the only exception was the green grass. We three proceeded to stand there and stare as if in a daze. Then Michael turned and walked out of the kitchen to go and sit beside his wife in the living room.

As soon as he left, I wrapped my arms about my husband's waist to hug him from behind. I buried my face in his warm, strong back as I allowed my tears to wet his t-shirt. I felt one of his hot hands cover my own and I appreciated his supernatural body heat.

"Hold me tighter." I overheard him say under his breath. So I did, as I squeezed with my all of my might to which I heard him sigh appreciatively.

Then he put his coffee down to turn around in my arms so he could meet my gaze.

"Derik's a mess and his eyes, they've turned hollow. I don't know how he's going to live without her and I don't think he knows either." He said concerned.

"We'll lend him our supernatural strength." I said softly.

"I know how he feels because if anything ever happened to you? My eyes would turn just as empty as Derik's." I looked up into his tearful face and I saw a haunted look in his usually bright eyes. "We've been married for fifty-five years but Derik and Rachel were married for fifty-seven. She WAS his life. His whole world revolved around his wife and kids. Just like you are everything to me."

I squashed my face against his wide chest as I relished his steady heart beat. Declan in turn, buried his face in my hair as I listened to him inhale my scent over and over again. He squeezed me so tightly with his greater strength almost to the point of pain...almost.

That was until the grandkids woke up loud and hungry, which made their parents come to.

"We'd better feed them before they wake Derik up." He sighed, as he released me to open up the fridge.

Blanche came into the kitchen to help him cook as I began to set the table.

"Should we wake Dad and see if he wants to eat something?" She asked as she helped prepare the bacon and eggs. Her uncle shook his head so she decided, "then I'll leave a plate for him in the oven."

"I wouldn't." He said. "The eggs will turn rubbery."

"Oh." She looked dismayed at not doing something her grieving father.

Declan paused when he saw her expression and he patted her on the shoulder. "When he wakes up, you can make him some fresh eggs but the bacon and hash browns can be kept in the oven for him."

Blanche took a deep breath as she nodded at what her uncle had said. She prepared a plate of bacon and hash brown for her father which she put in the said oven. Then she returned to the task to feeding the noisy young monsters in the shapes of her children, growling at the table to be fed.

"Anthony." Michael glared at his teenaged son who was tormenting his little sister by pulling on her hair.

He instantly released his hold, which thankfully stopped her whining.

"Pull her hair like that again and I'll pull your head off." I growled at the fiend of an older brother.

Anthony's eyes widened and he immediately sat back in his seat away from his little sister. Michael chuckled as he passed me more slices of toast to help him butter for the kids.

"I remember when Uncle Declan used to say that to me for tormenting Blanche. I used to be petrified of him during the occasions you babysat us." He reminisced.

I passed out the buttered toast triangles to the grandkids as I remembered, "yeah, you were just as bad as Anthony growing up."

Honey Dew whom was listening in, looked at my youthful appearance to her Uncle Michael with his older appearance. Although the grandkids knew how their Uncle Declan and Aunt B were 'different', I think we still fascinated her.

"Here we go." My mate came out of the kitchen to place a plate of food in front of her and her brother. Before he could return to the kitchen to bring out more, Honey Dew stopped him.

"Uncle Declan." She turned around in her chair to look up at her big grand uncle. "Did you used to say you would pull off Uncle Michael's head when he was little?"

All of the adults snickered as my mate looked on his grand niece in amusement.

"I would have done it with love, baby." He affectionately patted her on the back before he returned to work.

Michael chuckled, "that's Werewolf childrearing skills for you; tough love."

"Oh stop complaining." I smirked. "You lived, didn't you?"

Blanche exchanged a wry look with her brother as she carried out two more plates of food, before she sat down. Her husband Stuart Elm whom was Ian's grandson and another Lokoti Werewolf, chuckled along.

"I thought I had it bad with my grandfather growling at me if I didn't take out the trash." Stuart guffawed.

"Remember the summer Aunt B and Uncle Dec babysat us when Mom and Dad went away for the weekend for their wedding anniversary? We got into trouble for swimming in the river without getting permission first." Michael told the story to his wife and brother-in-law.

"Do I remember?" Blanche raised her eyebrows. "When Aunt B and Uncle Declan's eyes began to glow, I thought we were about to be eaten!"

"But you didn't go down to the river without permission again, did you?" My husband gloated as he carried out another two plates of bacon, eggs and hash browns.

He paused on his way back into the kitchen to kiss Blanche on the cheek and then to mess up Michael's hair. The grandkids all laughed at him for being man-handled by his younger looking uncle.

"OK kids, eat!" Michael's face flushed.

The youngest generation of Sabre's gladly obeyed as they tucked into their delicious breakfast. When Declan had finished doling out the plates of food, we soon found that there weren't enough chairs for everybody to sit down. So Michael kicked Anthony out of his seat to go and eat at the coffee table in the lounge room and Honey Dew willingly went along to keep him company. Then my mate took Honey Dew's vacated seat which was beside mine.

Soon he was shoveling the food into his mouth as his other hand held onto mine and we both ate with just our forks.

"This is nice thanks." I complimented his culinary skills. "You always cook my eggs perfectly; not too runny and not too hard."

"I'm a Sabre, we're naturally good cooks." He shrugged off my praise. "Plus we've been married for fifty-five years and then add on another twenty for growing up with you. I'd have to be blind not to observe your eating habits."

Blanche and I rolled our eyes as the kids laughed at their grand uncle's typical bluntness.

"You have another two hundred years of that to look forward to?" She teased. "Maybe when you're 298 years old, my Uncle who will finally look older, will learn how to say, 'thank you dear'."

The adults now had a chuckle as he gave his niece a wink.

"Thank you dear." My mate repeated, before he planted an eggy-kiss on my cheek.

"Yuck!" Immediately I dropped my fork to wipe the yolk off my cheek which had been all over his lips, sending the grandkids into another fit of hysterics.

"Notice how she drops her fork but not his hand?" Michael teased.

"I'll drop you in a second, if you put ideas like that into my wife's head." Declan growled at his nephew, which elicited more laughs.

Next, my mate winked my way as he carried on eating. I smilingly picked up my fork to continue eating, when something caught my eye. I looked up when I froze and my fork hung mid-air...

...because I was staring at Derik, who was standing by the front door but what disturbed me was for the fact that he looked young again.

My best friend looked just as he did when he was 18 years old and he was even wearing the same clothes of that long-ago era. He gave a rueful smile before he turned to walk through the closed front door. Instead of opening it, he passed through the wood like a ghost. I jumped in fright!

Omygod! That was a death omen! That was an after image of Derik's energy leaving the timeline which meant...

"...oh no!" I dropped my fork as I jumped to my feet to everyone's surprise.

They watched me run through the living room before I disappeared down the hallway. I threw open Derik's bedroom door before I froze again to stand transfixed in the doorway.

I stared upon a deceptively serene scene which simply looked like an elderly Derik was sleeping beside an elderly Rachel. She lying under the covers and he was sleeping on his side on top of the quilt, with his hand resting on her shoulder. But I didn't hear a single heart beat nor a single breath come from the couple on the bed.

My chest ached as my eyes burned, which caused my face to become a river of tears. I leant sideways on the door frame for support which gave Declan room to move past as he came after. He gingerly walked over to his little brother's form and although his hearing was just as good as mine, if not better; he wanted to be sure. I watched him gently place his fingers on his little brother's neck, to check for a pulse.

My mate looked back with his face distorted in pain, "he's still warm but he's gone."

Loud sobs escaped as the ache in my chest almost became unbearable. My legs wavered as I looked on the couple who lived their life and entered the next in the same state, which was together.

Michael and Blanche walked into the room as they approached the bed. Their uncle looked on the brother and sister who stood distraught. He spoke in a broken voice, "he went peacefully in his sleep...just like your mother did."

She immediately grabbed onto her brother for support as she cried into his shoulder, "he couldn't face life without Mom!"

He held her closely as his face looked ashen, "he lived his life, Blanche. He was a good Medicine Man as he was a good husband and father. He lived a long and happy life with Mom. It's just come to the end of his road, that's all."

Declan walked around the pair of grieving children as he went to stand in a corner of the room. His hands were on his hips as he glared tearfully at the floor. He had outlived his human brother, his human mother and his human father. He was now the last of his immediate family as well as the European Werewolves.

I noticed the veins in his neck start to protrude by how tense he was, indicating he was restraining himself. It looked like he was holding himself back from going wild with grief.

"B." He spoke in a low voice. "Say goodbye to your best friend."

Whilst sobbing, I looked from my husband to his brother, lying in the bed. I don't know how, but somehow I managed to walk over. I looked on Derik's peaceful form, with his hand on his wife's shoulder. My eyes flooded to blinding point as I vividly recalled the many years with my best friend.

The flashbacks started when Derik was a 3 year old, hiding with me under the dining table from a 6 year old Declan. Then I saw him as a 5 year old, as we helped each other to read from a book of fairy tales. I saw Derik as a 7 year old, sitting beside me in school and helping me with Math. I saw Derik as a 9 year old, chase after me, Mandy and Rachel in the woods during a game of 'tag'. I saw Derik as an 11 year old, kick the ball to me during a game of soccer. I saw him as a 15 year old, hanging out in my bedroom, listening to music. I saw him as a 17 year old, studying Biology as I studied History, before I threw my pen at him which he smilingly threw back. I saw Derik as a 22 year old come home to Rachel after setting Jonah Huntington's broken leg.

Next, I saw a 23 year old Derik proudly hold his first born his arms, as he sat beside Rachel and planted a tender kiss on her forehead. I saw a 25 year old Derik proudly introduce his daughter to Declan and I. Then I saw a 28 year old Derik along with Rachel, take Michael to his first day at school which Aunt

Susan was still running. I saw a 32 year old Derik look surprised as did Rachel, when they came to pick up their kids after one of our many babysitting adventures. "Declan, what did you do to my kids? They're...behaving themselves."

I saw a 41 year old best friend stay up late, playing cards with Declan, Rachel and I whilst we waited for Blanche to come home from her first date. "It's 10.33 PM, so she's officially three minutes late. Do you think it's grounds enough for me to shoot Stuart Elm?" He asked before Declan discouraged, "you can't go around shooting people being the tribe's Medicine Man, Derik. That's why you've got me for an older brother, I'll tear Stuart Elm to shreds!"

I saw a 47 year old Derik celebrate Michael's Housewarming as I remembered walking past the brothers as they offered their perspectives on being married. "If Lila is moody and you know it's because of that time of the month? Whatever you do, don't blurt out, 'is it that time of the month?' I once did to your mother and she's never let me live it down." He advised his son. Declan agreed, "just keep your trap shut and get the painkillers or the chocolate ice cream." Then the three shut up when they realized I was listening in.

Then I saw a 49 year old best friend celebrate Blanche's Housewarming. This time when I walked past, I overheard Derik and Declan have 'the talk' with Stuart Elm. "I've still got my shotgun and being the tribe's Medicine Man I may not ethically be allowed to kill you? But I do know where to shoot where it will hurt you for the rest of your life." Derik warned the younger Elm whereas Declan simply shrugged, "you know my story, I have no ethics or morals. If you ever hurt Blanche, I'll flat-out kill you." Stuart's face flushed but he certainly had the Elm sense of humor, "right, I got it. One wrong move and I lose my life. With all due respect Derik, your brother is still scarier than you."

I saw a middle-aged Derik proudly show off his first grandchild by Michael. I saw a grandfatherly Derik coo over Rachel's shoulder as they held their next three grandchildren from either Michael or Blanche. I saw an elderly Derik help the new generation of Sabre's with their Math, or take them fishing with Declan or Michael or Stuart. I saw how quickly he sprung into action when his wife fell over the afternoon she broke her hip. As Declan picked her up and carried her into the house, he barked out instructions of what to do as he treated his wife.

The last image to play inside my mind was of my young best friend, standing there in his clothes of old before he vanished through the front door. Now my last two friends were gone; Derik and Rachel's time has ended as their energy departed for the space time continuum. That is, until they are reincarnated whenever that will be.

"Aunt B?" I heard Blanche call. I blinked madly so I could focus again before I turned her way. She asked, "how did you know Dad was gone? Did you hear or smell something else as a Werewolf?"

Michael waited to hear my response and even Declan looked on expectantly.

"Not as a Werewolf, no." I spoke in an empty voice. "But as a Circulator, I saw – I saw – I saw -" I faltered as I couldn't blurt it out, it just seemed really cliché. I hastily said instead, "I just knew."

*****

Grandpa arrived with Grandfather, Uncle Julian and Phoenix late in the morning to pick up Rachel's body. Only now there wasn't one body to prepare for the funeral, there were two.

"Declan -" Grandfather began as he rested his hand on my mate's shoulder.

"Yeah I know, Uncle Em." He interrupted as he shook his hand off. "You're sorry, they're sorry and everybody's sorry!" Grandpa and Grandfather exchanged wary looks over his bad temper. Then my husband growled as he turned away, "let's just get this over and done with."

I stood in the bedroom doorway to watch Grandpa and Grandfather wrap both Rachel and Derik up in the traditional, woven fabrics.

"Are these the clothes that you would like them to remain in?" Grandpa asked Michael.

Earlier, Blanche and I had changed Rachel as he and Declan had changed Derik. The couple laid on top of the bed dressed in the clothes their family thought that they should be sent into the afterlife in.

"Yes." He said softly as he looked on his parent's faces one last time.

Then Grandpa and Grandfather enclosed Derik and Rachel inside of the Lokoti funeral shrouds. When Uncle Julian and Phoenix carried in two old, wooden stretchers, Declan gave a start.

"No." My husband stopped them before they could move Derik and Rachel's bodies. "I'll carry them."

Grandfather gave a nod as he and Grandpa stepped aside. Uncle Jules and Phoenix wordlessly carried the wooden stretchers back out of the room and then the house.

"I'll carry Mom if you want to carry Dad." Michael said to Declan, who gave a curt nod.

My husband carried his brother in his arms, out to Grandfather's truck. His nephew was right behind as he carried his mother in a similar fashion. Both uncle and nephew respectfully laid the dearly departed onto the stretchers which waited in the back. Blanche and I tearfully walked hand-in-hand after them, with Stuart and Lily holding onto their children's hands as they walked after us.

"Where's Granny and Granddad going?" Honey Dew asked upset.

"They're being taken to the Holy Room before the funeral, sweetie." Stuart squeezed her hand supportively.

"What's the Holy Room?" She asked confused.

"It's a special room where the deceased are kept before the funeral." Grandpa explained. "Two Lokoti painted as the Lokoti Wolf who is the protector of our tribe, stand guard to watch over them. Then the deceased are taken to the Holy Grounds on the third night after their passing. They are sent into the next life by family and the tribe as the Tribal Elders lead the funeral chant. The flames of the funeral pyre and our singing, releases their spirit and enables them to leave behind their earthly concerns. Then in the Holy Hunting Grounds, the departed will be reunited with loved ones who died before them. There they are altogether for a little while, before they come back to be reborn. This is why the deceased's ashes are sprinkled into the river, to symbolize the ongoing nature of life."

As soon as our Tribal Elder finished speaking, my European Werewolf mate blurted out, "I want to take the first watch."

"Declan," he said gravely, "you know that immediate family members cannot be guardians of the dead. Your sorrow would disrupt the dead's sleep."

My husband looked like he was about to argue, so I quickly stepped up to place my hand on his chest.

"Fine!" He snapped as he turned away to storm back inside the house.

Grandfather looked on his departure unhappily, as did the other Werewolves. I think they sensed as I did, that his sorrow was pushing his self-control to breaking point.

"Michael." Grandfather squeezed his shoulder in farewell before he climbed into the driver's seat.

"Blanche." Grandpa squeezed her shoulder too then he climbed in on the passenger's side.

Uncle Jules and Phoenix remained in the back, to watch over the bodies. I stood firm for my niece and nephew as altogether we watched the truck start up and then carry their parents away.

"Goodbye Derik," I emitted a heavy sigh, "farewell Rachel."

Lastly, I took hold of their children's hands to lead them back inside. I expected to find my mate in the living area, but he was nowhere to be found. I sniffed the air when I noticed that his scent was stale, indicating he was no longer in the house. I let go of their hands as I followed his trail back into Derik and Rachel's bedroom.

There on the floor, I found his discarded shoes and clothing. I also noted that the bedroom window was wide open. Declan must have stripped and then slipped out to change and temporarily run away from his problems.

Running through the woods in supernatural speed, sure sounded tempting right then. I wished I could run beside or maybe hunt with him to ease the tension; but I sensed that he had slipped out because he wanted to be alone. I sighed as I bent over to pick up his things before I carried them out to one of our suitcases which were still in the living area.

*****

Around 6 PM Blanche and her family went home as did Michael and his. I followed suit by instantaneously phasing to my house on top of the hill, along with the four suitcases. We decided to leave organizing Derik and Rachel's possessions for another day.

My sword sat in its' sheath, leaning against my luggage. Before we left St. Petersburg, I had used my ability to 'see' what my kidnappers had done with it, when I was unconscious. I had to instantaneously phase into a drainage tunnel to retrieve my priceless yet dangerous antique.

I lugged both the cases and weapon upstairs to the bedroom using my Werewolf muscle. As I unpacked, I put on Bruce Springsteen's album 'Devils & Dust' to listen to. Once the clean clothes were put away, I began the laundry. I worked away until 9 PM, when I finished with folding up and putting away the washing.

I frowned as I looked on Declan's digital clock, he's been gone for eight hours. Not only was I feeling worried but I missed him. We had just spent the past six weeks practically in each other's pockets on our holiday. His absence made my aching worse.

To get my mind off matters, I had my evening shower. As I stood under the water, I turned the hot water tap further until the water was almost scalding. But I needed the heat to loosen my tense shoulders. My shower went for half an hour as I used it to relax as well as to cleanse. Finally I turned the water off, stepped out onto the bath mat where I dried myself before crossing over to the sink to brush my teeth.

After my nightly ritual was complete, I went back into the bedroom to put on my new negligee I had bought in Paris. Lastly I climbed into bed before I turned off the bedside lamp. Just before I closed my eyes, I looked one last time at Declan's digital clock which read as 10.03 PM.

Where was my husband, was he going to stay out all night? He's been away for most of the day. I yawned as I rolled over as I decided not to wait up for him. Instead, I fell into an uneasy sleep...

...or until I heard the back door downstairs swing open. I looked at the time and saw it was 3.33 AM.

I listened to my mate come inside the house. I could smell it was him, as his maple syrup scent was as clear as day. He shut the door behind himself but left it unlocked, as we customarily left it when he occasionally needed to hunt in between full moons. I listened to him tread heavily up the stairs before he came into the bedroom.

My eyes were open but my back was to him. I lay still as I felt him climb into bed. That's strange, usually he wouldn't come straight to bed but he would shower first to wash off the dirt and any remaining blood. Just as I rolled over to ask him to do this, especially when I could smell fresh animal blood on his skin? His appearance startled me into silence...!

His eyes were glowing green as his teeth were jagged and sharp and the nails on his hands and feet were claw-like. But the worst of it was he was almost completely covered in blood! Blood was over most of his face, hands, feet and torso. What did he do, feed on the entire animal population inside the National Park? I heard the snarling under his breath, indicating that the bloodlust was still upon him.

"Declan -" I began to sit up in concern, when my mate growled ferociously as he pushed me back down. He tore my new negligee when he ripped it off my body. He ruined it and when I tried to object, I didn't have a chance to do this either. "Declan!"

Suddenly he pushed himself on top as well as inside his wife before falling into a hard and fast rhythm. He was still snarling as he moved, which was also worrying. When I tried to move into a more comfortable position, Declan thought I must have been trying to wriggle away so he pinned me to the bed with his clawed hands. To make matters worse, he reared his head to roar loudly before he brought his sharp mouth down to bite hard into my shoulder!

"Oow!" I tried to push him off, but his jaw was locked. This made me cry out in alarm as he's never bitten this deep before! "Declan, stop it!"

But he didn't stop, as I felt his sharp teeth not just break my skin but they embedded in the muscle. The pain in my shoulder grew to the point of agony when to top things off, I felt him drink greedily. As he drank, he sped up his movements by pushing harder. I lay there hurting and angry about it, as his bloodlust and lust was purged. At last he released his jaws as he threw back his head to howl;

"AAAAAARRRRRRROOOOOOOOOOOOOOOOAAAAAWWWRRRRR!"

Then he completely let go as he fell onto his back, panting hard with his eyes squeezed shut. It looked like he was satiated, I observed as I sat up to look onfrightenedly. I was afraid of what was happening to my husband...

Was this the same man I had one of the most romantic nights of my life in Brussels? Declan was losing his self control! I was tempted to get up, put some clothes on and instantaneously phase to Mum and Dad's place to stay tonight. However I was worried what would happen to him if I did. I was fearful he was about to lose control of the bloodlust and hunt human!

"B?" He growled out whilst keeping his eyes squeezed shut.

"What?!"

"Are you...OK?"

"I'm pissed off! But other than that I'll live."

He opened his glowing green eyes, "you're still bleeding."

I flinched when he took hold of my arms to pull me down to place his mouth over my wound. He felt this, which I heard him whimper apologetically. Next, I felt his tongue tenderly run over the bite mark, sending it numb as it started off the healing process.

"I'm sorry B." His glowing eyes turned tearful. "But you weren't in any danger, I promise. My body knows you're my mate and even my bloodlust knows you're a part of me. It's what made me crave you."

"If you ever bite me like that again, you'll find a silver sword sticking through your other lung." I warned.

He laughed softly, "understood."

His glowing green eyes started to fade into their blue colour, as I felt his claws retract as his sharp teeth returned to their human bluntness. He changed back as he was holding me in his arms, as if he were using my presence to calm himself. Appreciatively, he started to stroke the skin on my back as he laid me over him.

"You're covered in blood and dirt and you've made the bed all dirty and bloody." I said crossly. "Now we're both going to have to shower and change the sheets."

"Then I promise to wash both you and the sheets when the sun is up." Declan chuckled. "But until then, let's get some sleep."

"NOW you want to sleep?" I asked annoyed. "You damn well woke me up!"

"Let's get some sleep B." He yawned. "You can beat me up tomorrow, I promise."

"You ruined my new negligee!"

"I'll sew it up tomorrow... but let's just sleep now." His head rolled to the side as he seemed to slip into unconsciousness. "Let's... just... sleep...now."

Then he was floating somewhere in the dream world, effectively turning himself off like a light.

Great! His bloodlust is placated as he eats nearly every frickin' animal in the woods. He almost eats me as he gets his jollies and then he frickin' passes out into a stupor...? It was like he wanted to bury his pain in his bloodlust and it was more than happy to let him do this. I knew all too well what happens when a Werewolf's bloodlust gets out of control. I remember all too clearly what it was like when Grant died. Then I had thought the bloodlust was helping, but although it kept me breathing; I ended up being restrained and drugged. Declan was going through something similar in his mourning.

Eventually I settled back down to sleep by nestling my face into his warm neck. The smell of animal blood interrupted his comforting scent of maple syrup. It even made my stomach rumble as it almost ignited my own bloodlust... but I forced it back down.

I yawned as I tried to get comfortable. He sleepily shifted his hold as his body automatically adjusted to my movements. I moved lower so my cheek could rest on his chest as that way I could use his heart beat to lull myself back into sleep.

What partially surprised me was how quickly I did slip back unconscious although I was still angry. The next morning though explained it; because I had a lot of difficulty waking up. I felt weak, groggy and a little light headed which made me think that Declan drank more than I had at first thought?

"B?"

"Hmm...?"

I felt his fingers trace over my sore shoulder as he said unhappily, "frickin' hell, I'm such a jerk."

"Oow!" I recoiled.

"If your father or your grandfather saw your shoulder right now, I would be in for a beating and rightly so."

"Huh?" I forced my eyes to open. "Hasn't it healed?"

"The skin has healed over, but you've got a massive bruise where I bit you."

"You bit really hard, the deepest yet." I frowned before I tried to roll over and go back to sleep.

Next, I heard him open his mouth and bite on something but thankfully not me this time. Then I smelled something familiar and sweetly tempting waft towards me. When I opened my eyes again to see what it was? I found a bloodied wrist coming at me!

"Drink." He tried to jam it in my mouth.

"What? No!" I moved my head away.

"Drink!"

"No, Declan!" I moved away again.

"Frickin' drink B, so you can regenerate properly and get rid of that bruise!" He tried to force his way past my lips.

"Declan GET LOST!" I used my remaining strength to push him off!

Angrily, I flung off the covers as I jumped out of bed and then I stormed out of the bedroom. I stomped down the stairs as I pulled on my robe before I went into the kitchen to loudly open the refrigerator door. I poured myself a glass of OJ and once the juice was back in the fridge, I slammed the door shut.

He came down the stairs as he pulled on his robe too. He saw me down the sweet liquid in three seconds flat. He had his injured wrist in his mouth to use his saliva to kick-start his regeneration. As soon as he came into the kitchen, he used his healed-over arm to prepare himself another glass of OJ.

"My blood would be better for you right now than the vitamin C in that juice." He said sulkily.

"Enough Declan!" I lost my patience. "What are we, Werewolves or Vampires? I'm sick of blood! I don't want to see it, I don't want to smell it and I don't want to hear about it! No more blood!" He paused at my ranting to give a surprised look over his glass. "European Vampires want to drink my blood and my European Werewolf husband likes to taste my blood. Now I have to go upstairs and use a hell of a lot of stain remover to get blood off our white Egyptian Cotton sheets... NO MORE BLOOD DO YOU HEAR ME?!"

"Copy that." He said quietly as he looked on in remorse. Next, he shoved his glass of juice into my hand. "Here, you need the sugar more than I do. It will give you energy which will improve your mood."

Then he left the kitchen to make a start on soaking the sheets himself.

*****

My anger lifted as soon as my weariness did. Declan cooked up a huge breakfast as he continually topped my glass with juice. When the orange ran out, he opened the bottle of apple. Thanks to my renewed energy, I began to feel much better.

By the time I went to bed that night, the huge bruise on my shoulder had completely faded. I noted this as I looked on in the bathroom mirror, whilst brushing my teeth. When I came out of the bathroom, I found a sewn up negligee waiting on top of the bed.

Declan's workmanship was impressive as the negligee almost looked like it had never been torn. The stitches were small and obscure thanks to his years of practice with mending his own clothes. I picked the garment up and proceeded to put it on. When I finished, I noticed that I had an audience of one, watching from the top of the stairs.

"Is it OK?" He checked.

"It's fine." I gave a small smile.

The following night however, neither of us smiled as it was the night of Derik and Rachel's funeral.

My worry over my husband heightened as I sensed his overwhelming grief and his sense of isolation. Whilst I stared tearfully; Declan glared tearfully at the funeral pyre where two bodies burned in the Lokoti funeral shrouds.

The huge flames danced in the night sky, as the Tribal Elders which included Grandpa, lead the funeral chant to the drum beat.   All of the tribe stood respectfully, to farewell their second Medicine Man and their Naturopath. Derik and Rachel had been good people who earned the admiration of everyone they knew. Their good deeds as healers placed them in sainthood.

The Sabre and Elm families stood on either side of my husband and I at the front of the crowd, as the Riverclaw and Wisetail families stood directly behind to show their support.

I felt Mum affectionately rub my back as Gran gave a squeeze of my arm. Then I caught in the corner of my eye, Grandfather rest his hand on Declan's shoulder and keep it there. I could tell my husband appreciated the older Lokoti Werewolf's gesture. He momentarily turned his head to shoot him a grateful look, which made his hand tighten.

YOU ARE NOT ALONE DECLAN. - I overheard Grandfather think his way - *YOU WILL ALWAYS HAVE FAMILY, THE TRIBE AND THE PACK AS YOUR BACK UP. THE LOKOTI PEOPLE ARE YOUR PEOPLE AS YOU ARE ONE OF US.*

My European Werewolf mate gave a single nod before he turned his head back towards the burning funeral pyre, but at least he wasn't glaring anymore.

~~~~~~
~~~~~~

~ 28 ~

12th July 2195

It was just after three in the afternoon on a warm summer's day with clear blue skies and a gentle breeze. The soft wind teased the leaves or pine needles in the trees of the surrounding forest. But instead of enjoying what nature had to offer, I was stuck inside preparing myself for my next lecture at Cambridge University.

I stood in front of the full-length mirror in my bedroom as I glared at my reflection. My wardrobe wasn't the problem, it was my body itself. I looked too young! Since I wasn't aging, I've had the appearance of a twenty-something year old for the past century.

My constant youthfulness was starting to cause suspicion when I ventured into the outside world to do my guest speaking. I didn't have to worry about hiding my identity as a Circulator among my people, as the Lokoti were used to having Circulators and Werewolves who aged slowly. My tribe was well-practiced in protecting the secret identities of their supernatural members.

I was a 129 year old Circulator who didn't look a day over 29 years. My European Werewolf husband was 132 years old nor did he look a day over 29. My Circulator mother was 148 years old and she didn't look a day over 29. My Lokoti Werewolf father was 150 years old and he had the appearance of a 59 year old. My Circulator Gran was 167 years old and she didn't look a day over 29. However her husband, my 167 year old Lokoti Werewolf Grandfather looked like a man who could have been 79 years.

With my public work in the academic field, I had to start making myself look older. I've published numerous essays primarily on comparative studies of Ancient History in the Mediterranean and the Middle East. I've been invited to speak at several universities around the world. Once a month I would instantaneously phase from Alaska to an airport in a foreign city where I would pretend I had just 'flown in'. After giving the lecture, I might attend a luncheon or dinner held by the University Faculty and then I'd instantaneously phase home from a secluded location. However I could never spend more than twelve hours away, as my absence was deeply felt by my mate. Once I was away from home for eighteen hours because I was invited to a symposium with an academic dinner and Declan didn't stop ranting for a week.

For the first thirty years of my academic career, I was known as Dr. Bianca Sabre. Now I have a different identity as Dr. Bianca Wisetail as I used my maiden name. Vincent had Hodge Endeavor produce mock Death Certificates for me, Mum, Gran as well as himself so not to cause suspicion with our long lives. Then we were provided with new Birth Certificates and other forms of ID.

I knew several of the Professors who would be coming to my guest lecture tomorrow. It was now pushing twenty-five years as my persona Dr.

Bianca Wisetail and I knew that my continued youth was starting to raise a few eyebrows. The last time I saw a particular colleague ten years ago when I attended his lecture, he asked if I had any 'work' done, meaning plastic surgery. From this I thought I had better alter my appearance so I would look like a 50 year old human.

Certain Circulators can manipulate their age, as I'd heard Elisha Worthall made herself appear older. She purposefully made herself 'grow old' alongside her human husband Jarrod Worthall, who passed away at the age of 78 years. After his death she reverted back to her 'true' appearance of a young woman. If my great, great grandmother can change between young and old and back again, then so should I but the question was, how?

I had my laptop open on the bed nearby with Elisha's diary entry displayed of one of the times she altered her physical appearance. I read her description of going into phase and manipulating her molecules which were in temporal flux.

"OK," I took a deep breath as I turned back to the mirror, "let's do this."

I psyched myself up by doing a stretch before I closed my eyes. Then I put my body into phase as I turned my biological being into one made of light. Whilst I turned bright and see-through, I concentrated on reorganizing my light particles. I focused on my age, like manipulating a biological clock which made my energy field fluctuate. There, that should be it. As soon as I reformed into my solid human body, I opened my eyes again to see if it worked...

...when I jumped in fright! I stared gob smacked at my reflection in the mirror. Frickin' hell, THAT'S what I'd look like if I were a 50 year old human? Eugh, yuck! I look like absolute crap as an older woman! My human friends and family who've aged, look better than this.

My face looked worn instead of smooth and I had wrinkles around my eyes and mouth. My black hair had turned a silvery grey and when I looked down at my hands and arms, my skin looked blotchy with sunspots. I even felt different, somehow heavier and a little tired.

"B?" My husband suddenly called from downstairs.

"Yeah?" I called back when my hands flew up over my mouth in surprise. Oh no, even my voice has changed!

"I'm going fishin' with a couple of the guys." He announced. "You wanna come?"

"Er no, I can't." I flinched as I hated my new voice. "I'm um, getting ready for tomorrow."

"B," he immediately recognized that my voice had changed, "have you changed into your Werewolf form?"

"No."

"Have you got a sore throat?"

"No."

"Are you putting on a funny voice again?"

"No."

"What the hell are you doing up there then?"

"Um..." I wondered what to say?

Just then I heard his heavy footsteps as he jogged up our wooden staircase. Oh no, I didn't want him to see me like this! I knew what his reaction will be and I wasn't far wrong.

"HOLY CRAP!" His eyes almost popped out of his skull when he looked in through the bedroom doorway. "B, WHAT THE HELL HAVE YOU DONE?!"

"Um, I'm getting ready for tomorrow...?" I shrugged helplessly.

"Why, are you going to a geriatrics convention?!" He rushed up to look on worriedly.

"No, I'm going to Cambridge University tomorrow to do my guest lecture on Ancient Deities -" I began.

"And you have to look like an ancient deity?!" He interrupted.

"No, but all my academic colleagues have aged and it will look funny if I don't." I explained.

"OK..." Declan grabbed hold of my arms to sit me on the bed, "...we'll see if my blood can regenerate you."

Before I knew it, he was grabbing the manicure scissors out of my bedside draw to cut open his wrist!

"No!" I jumped up to stop him when I pulled a muscle in my back for doing so. "Oow!"

"B?" He sat me back down with his eyes wide with worry. "What is it, what's wrong?"

"Man, being old sucks coz I just hurt my back." I groaned in pain. When he positioned the scissors again, I grabbed his hand. "No wait! I'm OK, Declan."

"B, you're not OK!" He looked on frightenedly. "We have to try to make you young again and stop you from dying on me!"

That was his fear, of me aging and dying on him? I found this hilarious! It made me crack up laughing.

"It's NOT funny!" He looked on angrily. I tried to disagree but the only thing that came out was more laughter. He rolled his eyes, "great now you're getting dementia!"

My European Werewolf mate made me laugh so hard, I started to fall off the bed but my mate's quick reflexes caught me just in time. I sat in his lap as I smiled tearfully from laughing so much. I cupped his face to kiss him softly on the lips, before I tenderly rubbed my nose against his.

"Declan Domitian Sabre, I love you."

"I'll love you more if you don't die on me." He looked on fearful.

Whilst sitting on his lap, I went into phase again. Before his very eyes, I turned see-through and bright as I reverted to my younger and stronger appearance. His look of relief was overtaken by anger.

"What, you were just FAKING it?!" His quick temper triggered another laughing fit. He sat me back onto the bed as he swore, "frickin' hell!"

He slammed the manicure scissors down on top of the bedside table before storming out of the room. I knew I should go after him to apologize for giving him a fright; but I couldn't move from the bed because I was laughing so much.

~~~~~~

20th July 2195

Declan did go fishing that afternoon with Derik's grandson Anthony and his son Julius. I think Grandfather, Uncle Julian, Phoenix, Chiron and his son Stone joined them. Vincent who was visiting, also went along.

As the years passed, our Calculator's visitations increased in frequency as he stayed with Gran and Grandfather in their larger house. That was another funny thing about time; your house would empty as your children grew up, left home and had children of their own. To some, it could make a person feel a little lost and lonely which made them seek solace with other family or friends.

Although my presentation was ready, I lied to Declan and said that I needed more time. I wanted my husband to spend the afternoon with the boys and have a 'male bonding' moment.   Since Derik's death, my mate has been more appreciative of my company as I guess he relished being married to an everlasting Circulator. But I could tell he also valued the Lokoti Werewolves for their longevity. In fact, so did the other members of the pack who also lost family members due to time. I've noticed how the members bonded together through the decades as half of the pack had lost their mates from old age.

Uncle Julian lost his wife as well as his daughter from time. Phoenix lost his sister and wife from old age. Vincent lost both his wife and daughter to time, leaving him with his elderly granddaughter and her family whom we have visited at Blythe Castle. My relatives in England and Australia, all continued to be born, to live and to die. However another side effect from time was that we began to lose touch with our overseas families.

Vincent used to be the closest to the Worthall's aside from Gran, but now he felt lost amongst the new family members. It was because of this, he visited us instead to have some form of constancy in the Circulators and Werewolves. With us, he didn't feel isolated with his slower aging, as his human family members could and did, move on without him.

My father and Calculator surprisingly started to get along better too. Gone were the one-liners, barbs, dirty looks or just plain insults. Hell, Dad even growls at Vincent less which surprised Mum. The two were a lot more tolerant of each other. Now they settled their differences over chess.
~~~~~~

Sadly last winter, Grandpa passed away. However before he died, he and Dad used to play chess and their games could last for hours. My father could take a quarter of an hour before he moved one of his pieces, much to his father's amusement. Grandpa would half be watching the chess board and the other half his son. My father would be frowning deeply as he tried to guess his strategy. However he always beat Dad, even in his final weeks. His physical health may have declined, but his mind remained sharp as a tack.

In Grandpa's last weeks, we visited him everyday as we tried to spend as much time with him as possible. I could tell he appreciated the company as well as our cooking. Declan and I would come over with pre-prepared meals as did Mum and Dad or Gran and Grandfather. Sometimes it fell to the remaining couples in the family to entertain and feed the widows in Grandpa, Julian and Phoenix. When Vincent visited, this would turn into four widows to keep company.

Vincent liked to watch Dad and Grandpa's games of chess. With his Calculator's brain, he would play out the game inside his mind. Dad wanted to beat his father even just once, as Grandpa looked on his son's quiet determination with respect.

I overheard Grandfather ask his fellow elderly Werewolf quietly, "Fern why don't you let Hunter win one of your games?"

"He would sense it if I let him win." He said simply. "Also, I don't want him to stop trying. He's got a good mind as he's always been able to see both sides of the coin. I like watching him think."

One dark and icy evening as the snow lay thick on the ground, the wind blew so hard it screeched past the house. It was coming close to dinner time and Declan was in the kitchen helping Gran, Grandfather and Mum cook. I sat by the fire in the lounge room to watch one of Dad and Grandpa's chess games at the coffee table. So did Vincent but whereas I was happy to sit quietly and observe, my Calculator couldn't.

"Come on Hunter, bloody well move a piece would you?!" He rolled his eyes. "Winter is going to end before this game does!"

My father ignored his protest and after a couple more minutes, he finally slid his piece across the board.

"I wouldn't have done that if I were you." He goaded. "Now Fern can take your Queen's Bishop and that will leave your defenses vulnerable."

Dad growled annoyed, "go back to England would you Vincent?"

We snickered at the two's old rivalry before Grandpa gave a wink and returned his attention to the game. Dad got his patience from him as well as some of the retired Medicine Man's wisdom. My grandpa maintained his place on the council of Tribal Elders right up until his death.

When he passed away in his sleep, all of the family felt it. I had been fast asleep in my mate's arms, when I woke with a start. I suddenly sat upright as I looked about the dark bedroom because I felt something was wrong.

"Hmm?" He stirred to look up sleepily.

"It's Grandpa."

Declan's eyes widened as he immediately guessed. We both jumped out of bed to dress but not bothering about our hair, before we raced out of the house. When we arrived at Grandpa's, we found Gran and Grandfather also pulling up just as Uncle Julian and Phoenix did. However my parents were already there.

"Hunter sensed Fern would pass tonight." Mum came out into the freezing night air to meet us. "We never went home after dinner, so Hunter could be with him."

The women tearfully hugged each other as the men went into Grandpa's bedroom to see to Dad. My father was sitting as still as a statue by his father's side, holding onto one of his hands. His eyes were wet as they stared at Grandpa's face, whose expression was one of peace. Grandfather placed his hands on Dad's shoulders as the other Werewolves stood nearby, but Declan remained in the doorway.

"He's with your mother now, Hunter." He said softly to his grieving son-in-law.

"I know, Em..." my father managed out. "...but I'm gonna miss him, like I miss Mom."

"They'll wait to see you again in the Holy Hunting Grounds before they begin their next lives." He promised.

"Yeah, I hope so..." my father uttered bereft, "...I couldn't stand the idea of never seeing them again."

Just then my mother brushed past to walk up to her husband and scoop him into her arms to hold onto him tightly. Gran also came into the bedroom to wrap her arms about her elderly husband as I did the same to my youthful husband. Both Grandfather and Declan turned to put their appreciative arms about their youthful mates as Dad clung onto Mum. Uncle Julian and Phoenix looked on a little jealously, at the Werewolves whose mates were still present.

Mum stood strong for her desolate husband as she held onto him like she would never him let go, never in a million years. Thanks to our longevity as Circulators, it could very well be possible. I watched her tenderly smooth back his short, graying hair to deliver several soft kisses to his wet face. Dad looked like he drank up her affection.

"Thanks Jess." He looked up tearfully.

"Thanks for what?" She wondered. "Don't thank me, Hunter."

"Thanks for not aging and leaving me." He gave a rueful grin.

"Sorry husband, but that's one way you'll never get rid of me." She lovingly caressed his face.

Three days later, we all went to another funeral. The Lokoti Tribal Elders with a newly elected member on the council to take Grandpa's place, led the funeral chant to a drum beat. Our family along with the rest of the tribe, stood to pay their last respects to their tribe's honored Medicine Man, Tribal Elder and one of the pack.

I was beginning to hate the sight and smell of the funeral pyre. I was truly starting to detest the thing. So instead of watching the flames destroy Grandpa's body, I stared up at the starry sky. I imagined Grandpa and Nana together again inside of the space time continuum.

Eight months later with Grandpa gone, Vincent took his place at the chess board. During their games, Uncle Julian and Phoenix would sit around to watch. Dad won their first game of chess then with their following matches, the Lokoti Werewolf won most of them as the Calculator continually underestimated him.

"Checkmate." Dad grinned as he sat back.

"What?" Vincent blanched. "No, wait a minute here..."

"He's right." Uncle Julian verified. "Your King is prey to Hunter's Queen."

"No, but this can't be!" He objected. "I can still move my King."

"Then Hunter will checkmate you again." Phoenix proceeded to point out on the board. "See, if you move here then Hunter can move there -"

"I can see that you idiot!" He snapped like a sore loser. "But that's what I don't get, I'm a Calculator. I'm meant to calculate for every contingency in the timeline. So how the hell did a Werewolf beat ME?!"

The Werewolves cracked up laughing at the fuming Vincent!

"We're cunning, we are predators after all so we know how to stalk our prey." Declan said coolly as he came out of the kitchen.

I looked up from my seat on the couch, "is dinner ready?"

"Yup." He answered which made everyone in the lounge room move to go sit at the table.

My husband whom had helped my mother and grandparents cook, next helped them to serve up. The four carried out large plates or bowls of sliced roast pork, Great Grandma's special gravy and the cooked vegetables which continued to come from our greenhouses.

"Mmm." Uncle Julian's mouth watered at the smell of the food which was placed before us. "I love this family's knack for sticking with tradition when it comes to the kitchen."

Phoenix growled hungrily in agreement before he helped himself to putting some mint peas on his plate. The whole table became a hive of activity, as we all helped ourselves to the different vegetables or carved meat. After a moment, my cousin noticed how I sat back quietly and waited, as my husband served the both of us. When he picked up the bowl of honey cinnamon carrots, he placed some on my plate first and then his, before returning the bowl and picking up something else.

"What's this," he looked on in amusement, "not only does the man cook for you, he serves you as well? What's wrong with your hands and arms?"

When it came to food, I've always left it to Declan. I guess it's been like this for the past hundred or so years. He knows what I like or don't like, or how much I eat.

"Food is my department." My husband declared.

"That's not surprising with your European Werewolf stomach." Uncle Jules chuckled.

"You got that right." My mate smirked. "When I was little, my Mom got so tired of constantly fixing me snacks all day that when I was five years old, she started to teach me how to cook. I learned to make sandwiches first then I moved on to cutting up fruit and vegetables. When I was nine years old, we started to take turns making dinner especially when she had a lot of marking to be done."

This made us all smile on the memory of Aunt Susan and how she ran the tribe's temporary school during the years the schools in Alma were shut.

"She also taught Declan how to hand-make pasta." I proudly rested my hand on the back of my husband's neck. "He still makes our pasta as well as jars of pesto, or antipasto or even marinated olives."

"Then what do you do around the house, B?" Phoenix wondered.

"I clean and do the laundry." I shrugged. "We both tend to the vegetables in the greenhouse."

"With all the advancement in technology with cleaning equipment these days, it sounds like you have it easier than Declan." My cousin taunted.

Just as I started to open my mouth to argue, my mate jumped in instead.

"Hey don't knock what B does." He flashed the younger Werewolf whom looked older than us, a glare. "She folds up our clothes so neatly that my underwear draw must be the most perfectly organized draw in the tribe! The way she groups my different socks and boxers almost by colour-code, I can always find something. Our house must be the cleanest and most orderly house in the tribe."

What he left out though was how he assisted me with this fact. We were both pedantic about orderliness and if either of us saw something lying around where it shouldn't be, we were both quick to correct this. When we had our relatives' kids come to stay for a night here and there, we certainly didn't mind helping out with babysitting duty. But when the 'rug rat' would leave half-eaten sandwiches or toys lying around, it would grate on our nerves as we'd try to stifle our growls.

"You color-code his socks and boxer shorts?!" Phoenix laughed.

"Hell, she folds and puts away her own underwear in order of each day she'll wear them." My husband chuckled along. "Mondays are blue, Tuesdays are purple, Wednesdays are white, Thursdays are pink and Fridays are black. I know which day of the week it is just by what underwear set she's wearing."

The whole table burst into raucous laughter as my face turned bright red!

"Declan, shut up!" My hand which had been resting on the back of his neck now whacked him on the arm.

"B gets it from Hunter." My mother giggled as she looked on my father. "When we were first married, I started to notice little things. The jars of herbs on the spice rack were alphabetized or our pantry was rearranged, just like our plates had to be stacked in a certain way. However he's passive-aggressive, he'd never ask you to do something so instead he'll do it himself. In the first few years, I started to wonder if I was imagining things, because I would put something down then seconds later I'd turn around and it had moved. Before I caught him, I even wondered if our house was haunted!"

The table had another laugh as Dad patiently sat it out whilst passing me a small smile of understanding.

"You were like that when you were pregnant with Jess and Jules." Grandfather smiled tenderly on his wife.

"What's this?" My uncle looked on his parents.

"When Arabella was pregnant, she went into a cleaning frenzy as well as a food-stocking phase." He told the table. "Usually what happens when a woman mates with a Lokoti Werewolf, they can behave like a female Lokoti Wolf preparing a den for her pups. But in women it presents itself as cleaning and stocking food. Our house never smelled so much of cleaning products, or our pantry and fridge never bulged as much as it did when she was carrying the twins. It got to the stage that my grandfather was secretly giving away our excess food because we couldn't fit it all."

The other male Lokoti Werewolves exchanged looks of amusement since they had noticed this in their mates too.

"You're kidding!" Gran blushed. "Was I really that bad?"

Her husband gave her an affectionate kiss on the cheek, "Grandfather and Mom didn't mind since they had their own experiences with this. They thought it was funny."

"When Danika was pregnant with Phoenix, her nesting instinct got so strong she couldn't sit still. She'd clean the house at 10 PM! Whilst she was pregnant with Phoebe, once in the middle of the night she cooked up a complete roast dinner with all the trimmings." Uncle Julian reminisced.

My head ducked as I felt left out with all this pregnancy talk, since I would never go through it. Then I felt Declan's larger hand rest over mine under the table. I snuck a sideways look his way which he returned with a wink.

"Phoebe used to wake me up at 2 AM with her cravings when she was carrying Penelope and she always craved different things. One night it was for malted chocolate milkshakes and the next it was country fried chicken." Vincent smilingly shook his head. "But because she was a telepath, she would inflict her cravings on me and I would crave what she was craving! I'd be in a Board Meeting with Hodge Endeavor and I could tell Phoebe was craving a hamburger because that's what my mouth suddenly watered for."

All of the male Lokoti Werewolves at the table laughed in sympathy.

"Welcome to our world." Dad chuckled. "Lokoti Werewolves don't just experience their mate's cravings when they're pregnant but it's ongoing. Last night I felt Jess' craving for chocolate fudge. But because we didn't have any in the house, guess who went for a drive into Alma to procure some from the 24 hour Supermarket."

The men at the table kept on guffawing as the women rolled their eyes.

"I would have gone myself but Hunter with his overprotective nature won't let me leave tribal lands alone at night!" She huffed.

"Rightly so," Grandfather stuck up for Dad, "as there's been a small crime wave in Alma recently. Cars have been stolen and a couple of houses have been broken into."

"Hmm," the male Werewolves at the table frowned as they reminisced on their days of patrolling.

"At least your husband helps when you need something sweet." I said to her.

"Hey, I help!" Mine fired up.

"No you don't." I said coolly.

"Oh yes I do! I always bring home extra sweets than what you've put on the shopping list." He argued.

"You may but of course it doesn't help when you eat them first." I said disgruntled.

Everyone at the table chortled along since Declan's appetite was legendary.

"C'mon B, it doesn't happen all the time." My mate tried to defend himself.

"Three days ago I opened a packet of chocolate coated sultanas and nuts which I ate a couple then I put the packet in the fridge. What happened the next evening when I go to the fridge to eat a little more? It's all gone!" I said in annoyance.

"I didn't know they were yours!" He tried to use the old excuse.

"Then who's would they be, the little pink elephant?!" I retorted to the amusement of the table. "Or did you think Santa Clause or the Tooth Fairy left an open packet of chocolate coated sultanas and nuts in the fridge for you?"

"You two argue more than Jess, which I never thought possible!" Uncle Julian teased which earned a whack from Mum.

"Yeah well, at least we never get bored." My mate passed a small smile my way.

"The two of you would probably go into the next life, still arguing." Phoenix agreed with his father.

"You might be right." He smirked as he returned his attention to his food. As he ate, he gave me another wink which could still make me giggle like a schoolgirl.

"Speaking of the next life..." Grandfather began, as he and his wife shared a long look.

"...we have an announcement to make." Gran finished.

Everybody paused in their eating as we all sensed that something was afoot. Everybody but Vincent that is, maybe because as our Calculator he foresaw what they were going to say?

"Em and I are 167 years old." She stated an already-known fact.

"Yeah so?" Uncle Julian shrugged.

"Your father is elderly." Gran spoke to her children.

"Who isn't these days?" Mum shrugged dismissively.

"Arabella and I have had another discussion about the future. Soon she will turn me into a Circulator and then together we'll leave for the space time continuum." Her father announced.

A heavy silence fell on the table as nobody moved nor said a thing. Forks hung in the air, or rested on plates. We all looked on in shock except Vincent of course, who continued eating.

"Oh," Uncle Julian visibly gulped, "and when will this happen?"

"We were thinking next month." His father answered.

Declan's eyes widened as he looked on dismayed. I think my husband had been secretly hoping that the two would remain here for all his 300 year lifespan. As everybody looked like they were struggling to digest this piece of news, our Calculator carried on eating as if nothing was amiss. He even helped himself to pouring some extra gravy over his meal, much to my mate's chagrin.

"Are you right there?" He asked sourly.

"Fine thanks, how are you?" Vincent replied coolly.

My husband rolled his eyes before he looked pained towards Gran, "couldn't you turn Uncle Em into a Circulator and NOT go to the space time continuum?"

"Declan," Grandfather said gently, "it's time."

"What do you mean, it's time?" He argued. "You'll be turned into a frickin' Circulator so you'll be able to control time!"

My mother looked his way tearfully, "when Mum returned from the space time continuum, she told us that her stay would only be temporary and then she'd have to go back."

"Say what?" He looked back in surprise. "What do you mean, 'temporary'?"

"I suppose we can't complain." Uncle Jules gave his sister a sad smile. "At least Mum came back, let alone for a hundred years."

"You do know that our separation isn't for good, don't you?" Gran looked sadly on her children. "Your father and I will be waiting for you in the space time continuum when your time comes."

Uncle Jules blinked, "yeah but Mum? I'm not a Circulator, I'm a Werewolf."

"It doesn't matter, Julian. The space time continuum is the place that all souls new, old or even eternal, go when they depart from this life." His mother explained patiently. "Circulators can't be reincarnated so they live only once. But it's where other people go too, to rest before they're reborn into the timeline."

"So Circulators won't be reborn but other people like myself and Danika, will be?" Uncle Jules wanted to check.

"Yes." She gave a nod.

He stared down at his plate, "I'm a Lokoti Werewolf like my father and my sister is a Circulator like her mother. Now my Lokoti Werewolf father will also become a Circulator."

"Julian," my mother looked long and hard his way, "you're my brother so you have every right to be a Circulator too. I could turn you into one."

There was another pause as everybody watched the twin's interaction.

"No Jess," he gave his sister an achingly sad smile, "I'm a Lokoti Werewolf without his mate. I can't be turned into a Circulator because even if I do go to the space time continuum, I can't risk being separated from Danika again. If she's going to be reborn then so will I. I'll find her again and again no matter what."

Gran's eyes watered so much, she had streams of tears running down her face.

"It can happen like that, Julian." She promised. "Guy Robertson in the form of Mike Sabre found Elisha Baker again. Declan's prior incarnation was Guy Robertson's best friend, Captain Greyson and he was reborn into Guy Robertson's progeny in the Sabre family. Energy signatures are attracted to each other and follow the other through the timeline."

"Thanks for your offer, Jess." Uncle Jules said appreciatively. "I'm a Lokoti Werewolf and we don't just mate for life, but we want to be with our mate for all time. Just as I sensed Danika's cravings when she was alive, I also sense that she's waiting until I join her before she's reborn."

At the same time, the brother and sister reached across the table to hold the other's hands. The twins held a long look of understanding which was unusual to see, considering how much time was spent bickering with each other. It just proved the gravity of the situation.

~~~~~~

20th August 2195

Over the next four weeks, final plans were made and acted upon. My grandparents met with the Tribal Elders to give them the news that soon Grandfather whom was currently First of the pack, would be turned into a 'Light Person' by his mate and together they would leave. A couple of days after their meeting with the Elders, the pack convened at their house.

My grandmother respectfully made herself scarce to allow the pack privacy, so I found out when I arrived at their house with my mate just as she was leaving.

"Where are you going?" I asked in surprise.

"I'm going for coffee at the new café that's opened in Alma with Claire and Maryam." She said simply.
~~~~~~

We stood back to watch her open the driver's door of her plasma-powered four-wheel-drive. Next, she punched in the ignition code as the engine powered up. Then she reversed out of the driveway and disappeared down the hill.

"C'mon B." My husband gently pulled me up the veranda steps.

When we walked in, we found we were the last to arrive. All of the pack was here with Dad standing beside Grandfather as his faithful Second. Grandfather had been Second when Uncle Harry had been First and when Uncle Harry died, he became First and asked Dad to become his Second.

By Grandfather's side stood Uncle Julian with Phoenix, Chiron and then Stone. Ian stood on the other side of Dad along with his grandson Stuart Elm, whom had been Blanche Sabre's husband. However Stuart was now in the same boat as Ian and even half the pack; time had stolen their mates and left them widowed.

All of the Lokoti Werewolves stood in a large circle around the living room, with my husband and I coming to stand with them.

"Declan and B." My grandfather as First nodded our way.

My mate and I gave a respectful nod back and then to the rest of the men.

The 68 year old Chiron Riverclaw who had the appearance of a man in his early forties, passed me a wink which I returned with a smile. I liked Chiron, he had Uncle Julian's as well as Phoenix's sense of humor but like Grandfather, he was also patient and kind. I remembered like it was only yesterday, dancing with him at Uncle Harry's 175th Birthday Party and encouraging him to go talk to his future mate, Rain Lightfoot. Just like all the male Lokoti Werewolves, he became a faithful husband and doting father.

Rain Riverlaw was asked to join the council of Tribal Elders when Grandpa died. However Chiron was often included in many of their meetings, as his counsel was highly respected. When you asked Chiron a question, although his answers could come with a funny anecdote, it was still sound advice.

"Wolves," our First began as he deliberately looked every member of his pack in the eye, "as you are aware, I will soon be leaving this life, to join my mate in the next."

Several members of the pack growled in acknowledgement, as Declan squeezed my hand supportively.

Grandfather continued, "the history of our pack is old as we have followed the natural order of the Lokoti Wolf from the very beginning. We have always had a First to control the group will and a Second to assist the will of the First. As per the natural order when a First dies, the Second becomes First. However after a discussion, Hunter Wisetail has something to say."

Now he looked to my father to speak, just as we all did.

"Wolves," Dad began to be greeted with more growling, "Emanuel Riverclaw will follow his 'Light Person' mate Arabella Riverclaw into the next life. I too have a 'Light Person' for a mate and when the time comes, I shall leave this life with her as well. Lokoti Werewolves like the Lokoti Wolf, mate for life.”

The Lokoti Werewolves growled softly in agreement as they felt equally committed to their mates, alive or not. Several members of the pack looked curiously my way, at the third and last 'Light Person' in the tribe. This made me feel a little uncomfortable, which Declan sensed. He protectively pulled me closer as if to use his large frame to take up the view.

“It’s because of this, I am uncertain how much longer my own time will be. So when Emanuel Riverclaw leaves, I will not become First.” My father announced. This time there wasn’t any growling as the pack looked on in shock, including me. He continued to our surprise, “I will not remain as Second either. Em and I have discussed this and our will is to have a new First and Second.”

The whole pack, Declan and myself included, looked on our current First and Second in astonishment at this news. However before any questions could be asked, Grandfather’s eyes glowed as he growled out in his thunderous Werewolf voice;

“Chiron Riverclaw, step forwards.”

The pack looked on the 68 year old Lokoti Werewolf in bewilderment. I gave a puzzled look to Declan who gave a small shrug back. Although Chiron was just as taken aback as everyone was, he obeyed.

“Chiron Riverclaw,” Grandfather rumbled out, “you are strong as you are wise and Hunter and I have used your counsel in the past. It is for this reason we nominate you as First to take our place.”

After a moment, the pack began to growl softly in agreement as they looked on their new First with respect. When Chiron recovered from his surprise, he eventually gave a nod. I watched his shoulders pull back as his head rose to accept the responsibility.

“Now choose your Second.” Dad ordered.

There was a new silence as the male Lokoti Werewolves stood tall whilst they stared straight ahead. Nobody made eye-contact with anybody else, nor did they with Chiron. There was no ill will or petty jealousy among the ranks, the Lokoti Werewolf will wouldn’t allow it. Ours was tradition steeped in honor and survival. In the wild, Lokoti Wolves would fight for position of First and Second and hundreds of years ago, our pack may have done the same. But over the eons, our humanity came to reason that it shouldn’t be physical strength alone to dominate but also wisdom.

I didn’t bother to stand erect like my male kin, as I sensed the sexism in the pack wouldn’t allow a female to become Second. When the pack occasionally engaged in the odd skirmish, I was still ordered to stay home. I noticed how Declan didn’t bother to try either. He believed being a European Werewolf, he had about us much chance as I did being female. So we took a step back from the circle as Declan wrapped his arms about my waist and we contented ourselves with watching instead.

Chiron slowly walked around the circle to look long and hard on the male Lokoti Werewolves. He even sniffed a couple of times, as if to use his supernatural senses to make his decision. After five minutes, he went to stand in the centre of the circle again.

"I have made my decision." He rumbled out in his Werewolf voice as everyone looked expectant. "This Werewolf has both honor and great strength. This Werewolf is also experienced in fighting to the death for his pack, his tribe and his mate. It is through love for his mate that he is able to battle his bloodlust. He has shown great loyalty towards our First, Emanuel Riverclaw as well as respect for his Elders and the laws of our tribe."

Then my grand nephew paused as everyone waited with bated breath.

"Declan Sabre, step forwards."

What the...? My eyes bulged with surprise as did my mate's. So did the other members of the pack and even Dad's mouth fell open. My husband released his wife to obey, when Chiron placed his hand on his shoulder.

Our new First looked him right in the eye as he spoke, "Uncle Declan, you are more than an honorary member of the pack. You have hunted with us for 129 years as you have guarded these lands, to keep your mate, your family and your tribe safe. You have fought human, Vampire and foreign Werewolf foe, in protecting your loved ones. You are strong as you are loyal and you will be my Second."

Now all of the Lokoti Werewolves including Grandfather, growled softly to show their support. Declan was made speechless as he looked on Chiron before he turned to look at Grandfather. His eyes met with all of the pack's, until he looked my way.

"OK, so what's the deal here," he faced our new First once more, "do I bitch-slap anybody who gives you trouble and doesn't obey orders?"

The entire pack including myself, erupted into laughter at their new Second's bluntness.

"If you like," he smirked, "it would certainly make the long years pass interestingly."

"Remind me not to piss off our new First," Ian joked to Stuart, "otherwise I could be bitch-slapped by a bigger and stronger European Werewolf."

"That's Chiron's real reason in making Declan his Second," Stuart laughed back, "coz nobody's game to take Declan on."

Now all of male members came forwards to shake their hands in congratulations. Several more jokes flew about the room which made Declan out to be both bodyguard and 'hitman' for their new leader. I stood back and smilingly watched as I felt both proud and happy for my mate. I sensed this gesture really touched him and made him feel included. He was no longer an honorary member of the pack, he was now second in charge!

After a couple more minutes of laughter, Declan turned to look for me. He noticed that I was still standing in the same spot when he pushed his way through the crowd to come back.

"Well B, you're mated to the Second of your pack." He grinned. "Just don't get any ideas of using my status to make the pack take you shopping or whatever, OK?"

"Shut up." I laughingly rolled my eyes.

"Hey, what happened to respecting your Second?" He pretended to take offense.

"I married him." I said simply.

"Oh," He arched his eyebrows, "I guess that explains it then, as you certainly don't 'honor and obey'."

"I'll start if you start." I retorted.

Declan laughed out loud as he pulled me into a tight embrace. From across the room, the former First and Second watched our interaction. Whereas my grandfather was smiling, my father frowned.

"This should be interesting," Dad spoke quietly, "the pack has never had a Second whom was mated to another member."

"Are you worried about a conflict of interest?" Grandfather guessed. "Hunter, things usually happen for a reason and I'm guessing so has this. So far, B is the only female Lokoti Werewolf to have been created who just so happens to be mated to the last European Werewolf. This is a sign I'm sure of it, perhaps of something larger to come."

Dad cast another concerned glance our way as he muttered, "that's what I'm worried about."

~~~~~~

10th September 2195

My grandparents' 'funeral' was held differently since they didn't depart via a biological death. Instead of lighting the funeral pyre in the evening, a Remembrance Ceremony was held mid-afternoon.

It was another sunny day with the wind dancing over the surface of the river, as well as making a 'ssssshh' sound through the leaves. The trees surrounding the grassy glade which were the Holy Grounds were a variety of colours; with the dark green of the evergreen contrasted against the reds, browns and golds of the deciduous. The river looked an exceptional sparkling dark blue and all in all, it was a beautiful fall afternoon.

The weather was noted before the service by the Werewolf couple from their bedroom window as they dressed in smart casual. My European Werewolf husband pulled on his best pair of jeans, when he caught his Lokoti Werewolf wife struggle to pull up the zipper on her black cotton dress. He left his jeans unbuttoned to come over and help.

"Are you OK?" He asked softly as he zipped me up.

"I'm fine." I said briskly before I moved away to put on my shoes.
~~~~~~

Now here I was at the ceremony, standing in between Declan and Uncle Julian. Mum stood on the other side of her twin, with Dad and then Phoenix standing beside him. We were standing up the front of the assembled tribe with the generations of Riverclaw's, Sabre's and Elm's around us and then the rest of the tribe behind them.

The Tribal Elders led the service, as per normal. Rain and another Elder engraved Gran and Grandfather's names into the back of the fifth Sacred Totem whilst the Lokoti people sung the funeral chant. Although technically nobody had 'died', it was to farewell Arabella and Emanuel Riverclaw and wish them well on their way to eternity.

Although we were aware of my grandparents' plans, the afternoon they left still hurt just as much as if they had died.

It was a Sunday afternoon when Declan and I reported in to their packed up house, just as Mum and Dad did; then Uncle Julian, Phoenix, Chiron, Rain and Stone. We all assembled on the wooden front veranda where my youthful Gran and elderly Grandfather stood.

"I don't want to make this a goodbye." My grandmother blinked back her tears. "I've seen eternity as I've been there and back. This is simply a 'I'll see you soon' until we are all reunited again."

"Kids," Grandfather looked tearfully on his twins who were standing together, "behave yourselves while we're gone."

"C'mon Dad," Uncle Jules joked tearfully, "you asking Jess and I to mind our actions is like leaving a can of gasoline too close to a fire."

This brought out snickering as well as sniffling, whilst Dad rested a protective hand on Mum's shoulder.

"Have a good journey, Em. My last duty as your Second, will be watching over your loved ones." He promised.

My eyes stung with tears then as they did now, whilst I gripped hard onto Declan's hand. He squeezed mine back just as tightly, whilst glaring tearfully at the five Sacred Totems. Gran and Grandfather's names were being added to a long list of dearly departed.

I could tell my husband missed his mother and little brother keenly. He came to the Holy Grounds on a weekly basis, to look on their names which were also carved into the back of one of the five Sacred Totems. Yes you read rightly, the five Sacred Totems and not three. Another two had been carved, painted and then placed on either side of the original three, as the tribe needed more room to carve all of the names of the deceased.

In the beginning there was just the one Sacred Totem before the area was even named the 'Holy Grounds.' The land was called thus because it was reputedly where the Lokoti Wolf died whilst sharing his blood with Aru to create the first Lokoti Werewolf.

On the back of the first Sacred Totem, the names were inscribed not in English but in Lokoti symbols which were simply small pictures, similar to Egyptian hieroglyphics. When the other two Sacred Totems were added, the Lokoti picture writing changed to alphabetical letters. Then along with the names of the deceased were dates of when the person was born and then died.

However in keeping with tradition, beside their name was also a small engraving of a particular icon to represent the family the person belonged to.

For example with the Riverclaw family, beside their names and dates was a picture of a bear. With the Wisetail family, beside their names was a picture of a small owl. However with the Elm family, it was a picture of a squirrel or with the Lightfoot's it was a picture of a hare.

On the fifth Totem were Derik's, Aunt Susan's and Rachel's names, dates and engraved pictures. The Sabre family were allocated an icon when they were made members of the tribe. However their icon was a European Werewolf, to represent what happened the night they arrived. This coincided with the third Totem where the inscription 'Anthony Sabre B 2042 D 2066' with the picture. This was the Anthony Sabre whom was the father of Declan and Derik, who died from the European Werewolf attack.

I didn't visit the Holy Grounds as much as Declan did. I only came here when something significant happened, such as Joining Ceremonies or Funerals. Although this was a picturesque looking glade, this place just held too many memories, some too difficult to handle.

Ian's sisters Vine and Hannah were also inscribed into the fifth Totem, as well as Ian's wife Bec and their children. On the third Totem, his younger brother and my first husband, Grant was inscribed. Beside his name were the dates of his birth and death and the picture of the Elm family icon.

I stared blankly at the fifth Sacred Totem, which was having Gran and Grandfather's names inscribed into it along with the engraving of the bear:

Arabella Riverclaw B 2028 D 2195

Emanuel Riverclaw B 2028 D 2195

It was the same next to my Great Grandma's name and dates. Above her was my Great Granddad David Riverclaw's name, dates and family icon. I knew that in the future it would have Uncle Julian's and Phoenix's names and dates along with the same bear. However when Mum and Dad evolve, it will have the picture of the owl beside.

Uncle Julian looked tearfully on his sister who cried openly. Mum momentarily let go of Dad's hand to embrace her brother to sob into his chest. He let go of my hand to hold her back tightly whilst burying his wet face in her hair.

"I've still got you Jess just as you've still got me." My aging uncle clung to his younger looking twin.

With their parent's departure, the brother and sister finally began to let their attachment to each other show. The same thing happened last Sunday afternoon when they said their goodbyes. He resolutely held onto her hand as her husband's remained on her shoulder.

My grandparents took one last look at their children with their human eyes, before they left their biological bodies behind. Everyone watched Grandfather turn to Gran and smile softly on his mate. Then she took hold of his hands and went into phase, turning him into light along with her.

We all watched their bright and see-through forms increase in light output as their human shapes dissolved into clouds of sparkling energy. As such, they floated off the wooden front veranda and into the sky. The women cried openly as the men's watery eyes gave away their emotional states. Then Mum turned to hug Uncle Jules just as she was doing now, at their parent's Remembrance Ceremony.

I could understand why Gran turned Grandfather into a Circulator to evolve with her. Just as the two couldn't go through life without the other, nor could they in the afterlife. I'd seen first hand how mushy the pair were, almost joined at the hip as they hardly ever ventured far from the other. Now they were together forever; leaving behind this planet to exist in the eternal realm of the space time continuum.

Mum could do the same thing with Dad eventually. I didn't have to worry about this any time soon, since she wanted to be here for her twin and Dad wanted to be here for his best friend Ian. Then of course they both wanted to be here for their beloved only child.

If my name should appear on one of the Sacred Totems, I would be inscribed as Bianca Sabre with an engraving of a European Werewolf. But then I cringed at the idea of my mate's name ever being inscribed during a funeral. I couldn't bear the thought of his death at all. Declan Sabre B 2063 D 2363…picturing these words in the wood, actually sent a cold chill down my spine.

Instead would my husband come with me as a Circulator to the space time continuum? Would he agree to become my mate for all time? Could he possibly want to stay with me not just in sickness and in health, but until the Big Crunch and then another Big Bang? I knew right now probably wouldn't be the best time or place to ask, but subtlety has never been my strong suit. Perhaps it was why I suited being the mate of a European Werewolf.

"Would you come with me as a Circulator?" I rasped out.

Although I was staring at the fifth Sacred Totem, in the corner of my eye I caught Declan's head snap around to stare my way in surprise.

"Do you really have to ask?" He breathed back.

But I wanted to hear it, no I *needed* to hear him say the words… I think he saw this by my pained expression.

He growled quietly, "if I can't live without you, what makes you think that I can die the same way? Of course I'll frickin' come with you as a Circulator."

In a flash, I turned to hold him tightly with all of my might. I relished the sensation of him squeezing me back harder still, with his greater strength. My ribs objected to the force but I didn't care, as I breathed in his maple syrup scent. All that mattered was I would be ensconced in his supernaturally strong arms forever.

~~~~~~
~~~~~~

~ **29** ~

12th June 2225

It was getting late, or so Declan's digital clock on his bedside table confirmed. The time was 12.15 AM and I was home alone, going through our old photo albums. My husband was having a 'boys night out' by playing pool with a quarter of the men from the tribe, at a bar in Alma. However I didn't mind the temporary solitude, as I had only just come home from dinner at my parents'.

It was a pleasant enough evening, catching up with the other members of the Sabre, Riverclaw, Wisetail and Elm families; which also included Vincent's company. Normally Declan would accompany me, but Mum and Dad's dinner was an impromptu gathering. My mate had planned this 'boys night out' for Chiron, well over two months ago.

When he came home from work at the Garage to shower and change before going out again, he looked over as he was dressing.

"I can cancel my appearance tonight and go with you instead." He offered.

"Are you kidding? It's Chiron's Birthday so you have to go." I smiled. "You're his favourite Uncle, let alone his second-in-charge."

I too was changing clothes before heading off to Mum and Dad's. My 162 year old husband, who now looked like a man in his early thirties; paused to watch me undress. Although I was 159 years old, I still had the appearance of a woman in her late twenties. It had been within the last decade that Declan's physical appearance started to age and he looked older than me again.

"Are you right there?" I gave a funny look.

"I'm just admiring the view." He winked.

"You've seen this view for the past 135 years."

"So I'm an animal, what can I say?" He chuckled back.

Declan buttoned up his shirt over his muscled body. I have to admit, I secretly liked to watch him undress or dress, but I was better at hiding it. One of the perks being a Werewolf was our bodies remained in good shape thanks to our regular hunting.

Our bloodlust demanded that we changed at regular intervals to purge our dangerous cravings. The full moon continued to affect our brain chemistry, then running in supernaturally fast speed we chased down our quarry. The euphoria of feasting on fresh kill didn't diminish throughout the plentiful years, which ensured both our strength and longevity. The older Lokoti Werewolves like my father who was turning 180 years old, kept in good shape because of their regular hunting pattern. Dad's hair was now completely white and his skin in human form was loose and wrinkled, which gave him the appearance of a man in his seventies. But in Werewolf form, his supernatural speed and strength was still impressive.

I also found the way that Dad looked on Mum, another Circulator who too had the appearance of a woman in her twenties, awe inspiring. They had been through the wars, literally. They've fought each other, as well as along side of the other, in the difficult period after World War Three. Mum's short temper could match our bloodlust-induced anger and often poor Dad took the brunt of it. His Lokoti Werewolf will combated the sparks which flew off her aura which only supernatural creatures could see. But as I watched my parents tonight, I saw how his love for his mate of 160 years was in no way diminished.

As with most of the pack, or in particular Chiron and his mate Rain; Lokoti Werewolves aged slower than their human wives. Rain had looked like an elderly woman who could even pass as Chiron's mother much less his wife; as he appeared as a man in his mid forties. But the love that shone out of his eyes for the woman before she passed away was evident, as he used to escort her about tribal lands.

This made Mum and Dad the oddity of our tribe. With my parents, instead of seeing a Lokoti Werewolf escort an elderly wife, the tribe saw a youthful woman escorting her elderly husband. However Dad was in no way frail or losing his sensibilities, I noted this as I watched them together at dinner tonight.

My parents put together a special three course banquet for everyone. I sat at the table with Vincent, as well as Uncle Jules, Sharon Riverclaw, Claire Wisetail, Therese Sabre and Stuart Elm. Sharon and Claire's husbands were Stone Riverclaw and Peter Wisetail who were part of the pack, as Stuart was. Dad had asked Stuart over tonight since he was the grandson of his best friend Ian Elm, whom passed away last year. Although Stuart had been invited to the 'Boys Night Out' for Chiron's birthday, instead he came here to spend time with his late Grandfather's best friend. Since Stuart had also been the mate of Blanche Sabre, he was often included in many of our family gatherings.

"Wow!" His eyes widened as the entrée of Thai Fish Cakes and Cucumber & Prawn Soupcons were served. "What's the special occasion?"

"Jess and I have something to announce tonight." Dad gave a mysterious smile.

"Sounds like the two of you have a cunning plan." Uncle Jules joked.

"Yeah well, with a cheese-for-brains twin brother, anything seems cunning next to your feeble mind." Mum taunted before she returned to the kitchen to bring out a jug of orange flavoured Fanta.

The whole table made 'woah' noises at my mother's sharp tongue.

"The claws are out tonight!" Stuart chuckled to Uncle Jules. "Are you sure that your sister is just a Circulator and not a Lokoti Werewolf too?"

"Yeah but Jess doesn't need claws or teeth to draw blood." My uncle joked back. "Just look at how much Hunter is limping from all these years of being married to her."

Dad pulled a face at them as he simultaneously pulled out Mum's chair for her. As he took the seat beside, for some reason he looked at his watch. It was then I noticed there was still a spare chair at the table.

"Are you expecting anyone else?" I asked.

Immediately my question was answered when we heard another vehicle pull up outside. I listened to the plasma-powered engine shut down, before the vehicle's door opened and closed then there was a knock on the front door.

"Come in!" Dad prompted. Phoenix came in, which surprised me as I thought he would be at his son's birthday celebration? As he took his seat at the table, my father enquired, "how was it?"

"Good." Phoenix, who almost looked as elderly as his father did, nodded back. "Declan did a great job with organizing everything. There's plenty of soda and nibblies and he booked three pool tables. But mind you, nobody is game to beat a European Werewolf so he's won a game or two."

There was some chuckling at the table over my mate's temper, which I didn't get. People still think of Declan as frightening? Sure he may yell some, but he's never attacked anyone unless they started the physical altercation.

"You're scared of Declan?" I ribbed my cousin. "He's a pussy cat!"

The male Werewolves cracked up laughing at my comment.

"Look who thinks so – his wife!" Stuart pointed out.

"I think Declan is lovely." Mum took my side. "He's always quick to help out in the kitchen."

"Only because he's trying to get fed faster." Uncle Jules retorted.

"That European Werewolf is a walking bottomless pit." Dad shook his head. "If he was coming to dinner tonight, Jess and I would have had to cook up double the amount of food."

"I wouldn't have minded." She shrugged before she threw me a smile. "I don't think Declan is scary either."

"Yeah, because you're his mother-in-law so he's on best behaviour around you." Stuart pointed out.

"He's not scary to his female family members, because you're considered his territory so you're under his protection." Phoenix told her. "But if you're not family or even if you're not female? He'll occasionally let his temper boil over."

"Uncle Declan scares me." Claire spoke up.

"Me too." Therese frowned.

"Really, why?" Mum wondered.

"I was learning how to drive when I was sixteen and I accidentally cut him off at the intersection near the community centre. Although he didn't yell or anything, I saw his eyes flash green in anger and I got chills down my spine!" Claire shuddered.

Therese laughed in agreement, "when Julius proposed, I actually hesitated because I was scared of his Great, Great Grand Uncle Declan. When you marry into the Sabre family, you're marrying into Uncle Declan's family. He's almost like a European Werewolf version of 'The Godfather'." We all cracked up laughing at the analogy before Therese went on, "he always looks like he's restraining himself, especially around children. One day we were at Aunt B and Uncle Declan's for lunch when Brandon started to throw his spaghetti at the dining room wall. You know how messy toddlers are, but Uncle Declan's eyes flashed green. He picked baby Brandon up by his overalls and he put him clothes and all, into the bath tub!"

Everyone laughed so hard that we had tears coming out of our eyes!

"I remember," I heaved with laughter, "Julius laughed it off but you looked scared like Declan was about to eat your kids!"

"Julius doesn't think his uncle is scary because he grew up with him." Therese rolled her eyes. "But he scares me because with his huge muscles and temper, he always looks like he's holding back from killing someone."

"He probably is." Dad muttered to which Mum nudged him to keep quiet.

"But that's part of his charm," I told Therese and Claire, "he's a European Werewolf so he's not designed for childrearing or living in packs or even having long-term mates. But he does and it's sweet to see him battling his European Werewolf nature because he does it out of love. He may yell or slam doors or even hunt in between full moon cycles? But he's able to contain his more dangerous desires because he loves us."

"I think it's funny how you've had to replace nearly every single door in your house from the amount he's broken over the years." My mother giggled. "I still remember Dad or Hunter, constantly repairing the doors in the Sabre house which Declan grew up in."

"Well he's a kept European Werewolf, I'll give you that." Phoenix turned my way. "When he found out I was leaving early to have dinner at your parents', he tried to leave with me. But Stone and Peter talked him into staying, reasoning he couldn't leave the party he arranged."

This made me smile, "yeah, when he found out I was coming to Mum and Dad's for dinner; he offered to come along."

"Speaking of which," Uncle Jules looked at his sister, "why have we all been asked here?"

My parents shared another secretive look which Vincent was even part of, before Dad answered, "the news will come after the main course."

Then they stood up to take away the empty plates our entrées had sat on.

"Vincent," I looked his way, "is there anything that you would like to share with us?"

"Not particularly." My Calculator answered. "Jess and Hunter are holding this dinner so announcements are their department."

Uncle Jules' eyes narrowed as he regarded him before he asked, "how's Hodge Endeavor going, Vincent?"

"The same as usual," my Calculator shrugged, "the Circulate Mainframe monitors the company and I just show up for the Board Meetings."

"How is Phoebe's great granddaughter?" Uncle Jules asked after his progeny.

"Still alive." He sighed as he wearily rubbed his face.

Vincent and Phoebe's daughter Penelope married late in life and gave birth to one child, a daughter named Calliope. She in turn, was educated at the best schools and then went to study a business degree at Cambridge. She ended up on the board of Hodge Endeavor as she inherited Vincent's analytical mind and her contribution boosted the company's shares. However Calliope visited her Lokoti relatives little as she preferred to spend time with her English relations at Blythe Castle. She and her daughter, Cassandra enjoyed 23rd Century technology and 'wealthy living', as they didn't appreciate the Lokoti's old fashioned values and lifestyle.

Mum and I didn't like Cassandra either and even Vincent had to admit that his great granddaughter was a snob. All Cassandra cared about was the latest fashion and technology or how the company shares were listed on the Stock Market. Poor Uncle Jules tried hard to stay in touch with his daughter's offspring, but his invitations to come and stay were frequently turned down. As a Lokoti Werewolf, he was tied to his hunting grounds in Alaska however Mum would instantaneously phase him to Blythe for day trips so he could see them there.

"So I guess *Cassandra*," Phoenix said her name in an icy tone, "and Hodge Endeavor are interested in the new terra forming projects off world then."

"We have controlling shares in the international space ventures, yes." Vincent spoke casually.

"I wish Cassandra would pack up her family and move to another galaxy!" He rolled his eyes. "She's always looked down her nose at us, people who are closer to Earth than she is. Why doesn't she just move to another planet and make it official?"

"Phoenix," Uncle Jules emitted a low growl, "don't talk about your sister's family that way."

"C'mon Dad," he stood his ground, "the last time we saw that family was years ago."

"You're lucky then, as Mum and I have to see them every time we instantaneously phase Vincent to London." I said quietly.

"What are they like to you?" He enquired.

"Oh, they're nice to us because the Circulate retains control over Hodge Endeavor." I said snidely.

"Is it true that your late wife Danika and daughter Phoebe, were mind readers?" Therese asked out of curiosity.

"Yup, Danika and Phoebe were really something." Uncle Jules smiled sadly.

"Phoebe could get a bit annoying." Her brother chuckled at the memory. "Try having a mind reader for a little sister, because every time you did something wrong? She would read your mind and tell on you."

This got a few more laughs from the table, as Uncle Jules and Phoenix exchanged a rueful grin.

"You should try being married to a mind reader." Vincent smirked. "If you thought the woman on the other side of the room looked nice? All of a sudden your wife would whack you even though you didn't say or do anything."

Stuart laughed back, "I can beat that, try having a European Werewolf for an Uncle-in-law. On the day of Blanche's and my Housewarming, he threatened my life. Now that's what I call incentive to a successful marriage."

Claire asked next, "is Cassandra or her children mind readers?"

"No," Uncle Jules shook his head, "Penelope was the last to have telepathy and then I think Calliope had some kind of empathic range."

"I don't think Cassandra or her kids are empathic." I frowned. "You'd think empaths would be extra nice, since they can sense how their words or actions impact others? But not with THAT family."

Just then our conversation was cut short when Dad and Mum returned from the kitchen with the main meal. We were served Fillet of Beef in Green Sauce, along with Creamy Potato Bake and Stir-Fried vegetables in Oyster Sauce.

"Yum!" The male Lokoti Werewolves mouths watered in anticipation.

"Is this the same Green Sauce that Blanche borrowed the recipe for?" Stuart licked his lips.

"Yep, it sure is." Mum answered as she sat down again. Then she smiled on her husband, "Hunter made it, he has the patience to make the complicated recipes as I can't be bothered."

"I'm surprised you have patience for anything with your temper." Uncle Jules goaded.

Then we all laughed again when she whacked him on the arm.

"Try being her Calculator," Vincent joined in, "when I try to tell Jess that something is not possible? She tries to rearrange the laws of physics!"

"Sounds like my wife alright," my father chuckled as he kissed her on the cheek. "Jess' way to fix something is to break it even more."

"Watch it you two," she warned, "otherwise I'll leave you both behind."

What was that? I looked up sharply as everyone else continued on serving themselves. Nobody besides me seemed to catch the hint.

"Huh?" I stared in surprise. "Say that again?"

Uncle Jules paused whilst helping himself to the Stir-Fried Vegetables. He looked questioningly from me to Mum. Now his sister looked guilty for letting the cat out of the bag, as she looked apologetic to Dad.

Her husband supportively rested his hand over hers as he began, "I'm two years older than Jess and Julian."

"Yeah, so?" Uncle Jules shrugged.

"So, Jess and I have talked about her turning me into a Circulator soon." Dad said.

"Oh...?" Uncle Jules' struggled to hide his hurt expression. "Well, I guess since Ian's death, you've held on for as long as possible."

"Don't be an idiot, Julian." She said crossly. "We're not about to abandon you, you're my twin brother."

"Now I get it." My uncle put down the large bowl of vegetables. "You're waiting for me to 'cark it' and then you two will leave?"

"Yes," Mum said sarcastically, "so if you would be so good to die soon? Hunter and I would appreciate it."

Although we knew she was joking, everyone suddenly lost their appetites as they looked on hurt.

"But Aunt Jess and Uncle Hunter, you two are the tribe's longest married couple. Now you're leaving us?" Stuart asked disappointedly.

I think he was hurting because he had lost his wife, his children and his parents from the passing of time. When his grandfather died, he still had his grandfather's best friend in Dad. With his departure, he was afraid he was running out of family and friends.

"We'll still be married inside of the space time continuum." Dad smirked.

"Yeah, but it will be in the space time continuum and away from us." Phoenix said flatly and I saw he was feeling the same way as Stuart.

Therese looked about herself at everyone seated at the table before looking back on my parents.

"I think I understand what's happening here," she began, "that's why you asked someone from each family; the Sabre's, the Elm's, the Wisetail's and the Riverclaw's here tonight. It was so you could break the news to us and then we would pass it on to the rest of the families."

"We weren't planning on doing it tonight," Mum confessed, "but Vincent said -"

"Vincent said what?" Uncle Jules demanded.

Our Calculator cleared his throat, "I said that plans should be made."

"Why, do you see my death on the horizon?" My elderly uncle glared at the younger looking Calculator whom was actually older than him.

"Look," he took a deep breath, "it's not just Jess and Hunter that's eager to leave, but it's me too. Jess is worried about Hunter aging however he held on for Ian and now he's holding on for you and B."

I looked on my father in further surprise who returned my gaze with a loving smile.

"Of course I'm holding on for my daughter." He said simply.

"Julian, you're not the only one who's estranged from Phoebe's family." Vincent said in annoyance. "One of the reasons why I waited so long to get married was because I knew this would happen."

"You knew what?" Uncle Jules asked grouchily.

"I knew how unbearable life would become if I married and my wife died of old age!" He bit out as his eyes watered with sadness. "Everyone keeps dying and I'm sick of it! My parents died when a bomb landed on their house during World War Three. Then I became close to Bas and Yvette Worthall and their family, but they died of old age. I knew that this would happen to Calculators and Circulators, because we were different... But then I fell in love with Phoebe. I couldn't help it, no matter how I tried to resist. She was bloody brilliant with her telepathic gift, just as she was funny and a joy to be around. She gave me Penelope and those fifty years we were together was the happiest I've ever been. Now both of my wife and daughter have died and the new generations have drifted away. Do you know how transparent it can make you feel, knowing that the family line you created, only sees you as a distant relation?"

My elderly uncle's eyes watered, "yes I do know how that feels, Vincent. I was lucky, that one of my children became another Lokoti Werewolf with a supernaturally long life span. I was also lucky that my twin sister is a Circulator and so is my niece. Hunter and Jess are the luckiest pair alive, because they'll never outlive their spouse or child. But you're not alone Vincent. You married my daughter who was Lokoti which makes you Lokoti. I have the tribe, the pack and my family and so do you. You're a Riverclaw as you are a Worthall or a Moher."

My cousin added on, "Lokoti Werewolves cope with the death of their mate, by the company of the pack who are in the same situation as them."

"The pack fight together, hunt together and remain together, as does our tribe." My father looked from the male Lokoti Werewolves then to me.

"I miss my wife, but I have my grandchildren's children to look after, just as I have the pack and the tribe." Phoenix agreed before he added on humorously, "also watching Hunter beat you at chess makes my life worth while."

The tension broke as the table erupted into another round of laughter.

"He doesn't ALWAYS beat me." Vincent smirked. "He's only won just over 52% percent of the games we've played."

"Hey, that's still 2% in Hunter's favour." Stuart argued.

"Right, that's it!" My Calculator got all riled up again. "Hunter Wisetail, it's you and me at the chess board after dinner."

"Oh not again," Mum huffed, "I'm sick of chess! Why can't we play Monopoly or something else?"

"It's obvious you're sick of chess, as you want to run away and hide in the space time continuum." Uncle Jules returned. "But what are you going to do if everyone in the continuum is playing the game there?"

"I am NOT running away from anything!" She snapped. "I'll bloody well break every chess board in existence!"

"Hey hey hey!" All of the male Lokoti Werewolves objected.

"Don't even think about it!" Stuart growled warningly.

"The chess board is the perfect way to release the bloodlust for aging Lokoti Werewolves!" Phoenix exhorted.

"Yeah, we get to stalk our prey from the comfort of our own living rooms!" Stuart agreed.

"Speaking of which, I brought my chess board with me tonight." My cousin looked his way. "I'll give you a game after dinner."

"Right, you're on." Stuart clapped his hands. "Prepare to be hunted!"

"Dream on!" He retorted. "My Queen is going to kick your King's ass!"

"I'll give you a game, Jess." Uncle Jules looked to his sister.

"No way!" Mum shook her head. "I'm not playing."

"Why not?" He whined. "Hunter is playing Vincent and Phoenix is playing Stuart so I'll play you."

"No." She said staunchly.

"What's wrong Jess, are you scared?" Her brother goaded.

"Like hell I'd ever be scared of you!" She sneered.

"Then prove it!" He nudged her.

"No, Julian!" Mum flared. "Pick on B, why don't you? She's another Werewolf, so ask her to play."

Uncle Jules immediately looked in my direction, which made my eyes widen.

"Nah ah!" I quickly shook my head. "I don't know how to play."

"Yes you do." My father smirked. "I taught you when you were little and you spent hours watching your Grandpa and I play."

"Yeah but Dad, that was years ago and I've forgotten now." I frowned.

"Good, that means fresh meat for the grinder!" Uncle Jules laughed evilly.

"C'mon B, with practice you'll be able to beat Declan." Phoenix pointed out.

Beat the European Werewolf at chess? Now there's an idea... I could picture his oncoming tantrums as his bloodlust turned him into a sore loser.

"If you have some spare doors to replace the ones he'll break over it; sure why not?" I giggled, as did everyone else.

As soon as dessert was over, the games began. Mum, Claire and Therese served coffee which they were happy to drink on the sidelines. They milled around to watch the tribe's Lokoti Werewolves sit down to several rounds.

I ended up enjoying myself as Uncle Jules was a funny but patient teacher. He tried to stretch out our game for as long as possible as he didn't take advantage of my mistakes. When I started to move my Bishop, he cleared his throat loudly as a hint.

"No?" I moved my piece back to its original spot.

"Hang on B, if you had moved your Bishop then his Castle could have taken you out." Claire moved forwards to point out.

"Yeah, but her Queen could have taken Uncle Jules' castle." Therese came to stand on my other side.

"Nup," Mum shook her head whilst standing behind her brother, "in two moves, Jules would have checked B's King."

"Well whadyaknow, you're not completely useless after all." Uncle Jules peered over his shoulder at his sister.

"You wish, monkey brain!" She whacked him once more.

He started to laugh at her show of affection but then his laughter turned into coughing. For a good couple of minutes, he couldn't stop which made him gasp for breath. We all watched the elderly Werewolf with concern.

"Jess, try not to beat your elderly twin to death." Dad said dryly.

"Hey, who are you calling elderly?" Uncle Jules objected as he wheezed. "Jess couldn't hurt me even if she tried."

"How about I get my silver sword and put your theory to the test?" She taunted.

This made Uncle Jule's eyes bulge and say hastily, "it's still your turn to move, B."

As I contemplated which piece to move instead, Claire and Therese thought they'd help.

Claire pointed out on the board, "I say move your Bishop here."

"Good idea." Therese agreed. "Then it's leaving room for B to move her Queen next."

"You're playing three people at once, eh Jules?" My Calculator smirked.

"That's how good I am, Vincent." He preened.

Phoenix and Stuart chuckled as they looked over from their own game.

"With the rate you're losing, maybe you should get a couple of human females to help you too." Phoenix goaded his opponent.

"Hey!" Mum, Claire, Therese and Sharon objected.

"You're in danger of that silver sword yourself, Phoenix." Stuart teased.

"Nah, Aunt Jess would never hurt me." He scoffed. "I was always her favourite nephew."

"You were my only nephew." Mum said flatly.

"You see? I'm her favourite nephew." He guffawed as Stuart shook his head.

"So Vincent," Uncle Jules called as his eyes never left the board.

"Yes Dad?" He used the old father-in-law joke, which the two always found amusing considering the fact that Vincent was older.

"What's going to happen to the Circulate Headquarters, once you're gone?" He queried as his mind was planning strategically. "You spend a fair amount of time there maintaining the computer systems. Shouldn't you also teach B, for when you're gone?"

My Calculator and father stopped playing to look my way. This made me wonder if it had already been discussed? Even my mother passed a guilty look.

"B won't have to worry about maintaining the Circulate's systems on Mars, because there won't be a computer system to maintain." Vincent announced.

What the...? In alarm, I turned to look on my Calculator. He sat still as he calmly met my startled eyes.

"What's that supposed to mean?" I gaped.

He took a deep breath before he announced, "I'm going to set off the self-destruct mechanism to destroy the Circulate HQ on Mars."

"Excuse me?!" I fired up. "You're gonna do WHAT?!"

"You'll still have the Circulate base on Taurus Six, which will become the new Headquarters. I've already transferred most of the Martian memory banks to the data banks there. I've also programmed the Circulate Mainframe to act as your Calculator, when I'm gone. The Mainframe itself will monitor your timeline and control Hodge Endeavor in my stead. You'll be able give orders to the company via the computer or the Mainframe will tell you which Board Meeting you'll need to sit in upon occasion. You'll always have the company account as your financial back-up." Vincent promised.

"But why can't the Circulate Mainframe on Mars do this for me? I would rather the one on Mars since Taurus Six is so far away!" I complained.

"That's the reason why, B." Dad frowned.

"Huh?" I looked on confused.

"Because Taurus Six is further away, it will be some time until human space exploration reaches that far." Mum spoke up.

"But why?" I whined disappointedly. "Not only do you desert me, but you also take away my HQ as well?"

"B," my father stood up to come over to where I was sitting, "we're not deserting you. As a Circulator, you'll be able to evolve and join us inside of the space time continuum when you're ready."

I tearfully looked away to glare at my Calculator, "but I won't just be the Last Circulator; I'll be the last of the Circulate! I won't have a Calculator or a Headquarters with a Viewing Room or Props Room anymore!"

"B, stop being so overdramatic." He rolled his eyes. "You'll have the Circulate HQ on Taurus Six with the Circulate Mainframe to monitor your timeline and assist when required. You've been to Taurus Six and seen for yourself that there's also a Gate, a Viewing Room and a Props Room as it's an exact replica of the base on Mars. Remember when I made you, your mother or grandmother move a couple of the costumes as well as some other items there?"

Ah, so that's why Vincent asked us over the years to play gopher by transporting those things to Taurus Six. For a Calculator, he certainly was cunning. He must have been planning this changeover for decades now!

He continued, "the Circulate Mainframe will not only watch over you as an individual, but also your finances. Or if the Circulate Mainframe should detect that you are in any kind of trouble, it will also notify a team of specialists within Hodge Endeavor. The company can contact your relatives or they have employed Private Investigators or Bodyguards to come to your immediate aid."

"Let alone your pack who would also help one of their own." Phoenix reminded.

"The pack may act as back up for B in this era," he pointed out, "but the Circulate still maintains many safe houses in Earth's past or future. The Circulate Mainframe could send word to the trusted few of what era you're in."

It was here Uncle Jules interrupted, "I'm sorry Vincent but I have to correct you there and say this to B." When I looked his way my uncle continued, "no matter what period of time you're in, if you need help then seek out the Lokoti Werewolves. The pack will smell you're Lokoti as well as family and the pack take care of their own, no matter what."

The other Lokoti Werewolves in the room all nodded in agreement.

My uncle's words and conviction behind them warmed my heart, but for the cold abandonment I was feeling. I whined once more, "but why blow up the Circulate HQ on Mars? Why can't I keep it?"

"Think about it B," my Calculator's gaze remained steady, "the Circulate is relatively unknown with its HQ existing on another planet of the past, before telescopes were invented. There's no such thing as a Circulate HQ in this era and why? Because it ceases to exist before the timeline reaches the AD period."

"It needs to be destroyed for your protection." Mum said seriously. "If humans ever found out about the existence of beings who could phase through time and space? People would try to pull you apart to see how you work, or use you for their own gain."

"By destroying the Circulate HQ on Mars, it could prevent humans from finding out that there was a Circulate." Dad placed his hand on my shoulder. "If there is no Circulate, then there are no Circulators."

Next, Mum put her hand on my other shoulder. "When you're ready to join us B, you'll come to us in your own time and not be chased into the continuum."

"You've seen the HQ on Taurus Six," Vincent went on, "it's in a much better defensive position thanks to the nebula it's situated inside. If humans ever found the new Circulate HQ, they wouldn't be able to take a space ship inside the unstable nebula to reach the base."

I frowned in contemplation as this was another time I'd heard somebody speak about Taurus Six as a defensive outpost.

Before I could ask why, he said lastly; "trust in my ability as a Calculator, please B. Patrick O'Flannigan who was Elisha Worthall's Calculator, first modified the Circulate Mainframe to be a 'smart computer'. This thinking computer with my own modifications, will almost become sentient. It will be able to carry out self-maintenance as its sole purpose will be to look after the Last Circulator."

I let out a loud sigh as I stared disheartened down at the floor. As my eyes stung and my stomach sunk, I wished Declan was here. I could have used the feel of his hot, strong hand squeezing mine right now.

*****

Now it was past midnight and I was lying on top of the bed whilst going through the old photo albums. After what took place tonight, I needed this trip down memory lane. However I wasn't just going through my family albums, I was also going through Declan's. Aunt Susan took many pictures of her sons, as I watched my husband and his brother shoot up through the years.

I saw photos of Derik as a baby whilst playing with a baby me on the floor, with a 4 year old Declan sitting close by like he was supervising. I saw photos of a 5 year old Declan, holding a 2 year old Derik in his lap whilst posing for Aunt Susan. I saw a 6 year old Declan carry on his back a 3 year old Derik who clung onto his bigger and stronger brother. I saw numerous photos of the two posing with me and my family in Christmas photos. The Sabre's always celebrated with us since we were just few of the families in the tribe who followed the Christian holidays. In these photos, I saw pictures of a young Phoenix and an even younger Phoebe start to appear.

In these group shots, Declan as the eldest towered over the rest of us kids and he already looked bulky with his European Werewolf muscle. I also noticed how he stood off to the side in the photos. Derik and I would be pulling faces at the camera, as we had our arms about each other or Phoenix and Phoebe; but his brother would be standing apart.

I frowned as I noticed this became a common practice in the photos of the children posing together. The children would be hugging each other in front of a Christmas Tree or otherwise; but Declan would be standing off to the side, with his hands deep in his pockets. When I reached the photos of him as a 14 year old, I saw how he stood further away. He towered over the five of us put together, as his clothes looked tight over his muscled frame. Derik and I were goofing off in front of the camera and Declan looked awkward, like he didn't want to be there.

Then I recalled at that age, the European Werewolf matched the strength and speed of an adult male Lokoti Werewolf. Also when he was 14 years old, the pack had with Declan 'the talk'. He was told he could never take a human woman as a mate in fear of harming her or turning her. I could see the effects of this conversation, as the loneliness appeared in his distant demeanour. Whereas Derik and I hung out every day, Declan didn't have that. I remembered with his supernatural strength and temper, how the other kids were afraid of him. He looked downright unhappy until he was 17 years old, as he constantly stood off to the side with his hands in his pockets like he was restraining himself. Maybe he was afraid of breaking something, or someone.

My heart hurt to see how isolated my husband was then. It was no wonder he always seemed be in a bad mood or even mean; because his little brother had a best friend and Declan felt like he didn't have anybody. He had the love of his mother or my Grandfather's support; as well as the pack to take him hunting. But he couldn't play with kids his age in fear of harming them, or their greater fear of being near him.

I felt bad as I thought back on all the times Derik and I excluded him with our best friendship. I used to disappear into Derik's room to hang out and not once did we invite Declan in to listen to music with us. But to be fair, as far back as I could remember he and I fought like cat and dog. I had to admit, his fierce temper did frighten me, as he'd roar instead of shout or when his eyes glowed green. Aunt Susan repeatedly had to call on Dad or Grandfather to repair his bedroom door from the amount of times he broke it by slamming it with his supernatural strength.

Just then I saw it, in a photo I saw his emerging feelings for me as clear as day. It was taken when I was 14 years old and mucking around with Derik as per usual. We had each other in a headlock and I was winning with a 17 year old Declan grinning proudly on my feat. He was standing on my other side and this time not so far away. Then as the snapshots progressed, I saw how Declan started to stand closer and usually by my side. In more and more of the photos, sometimes I'd be sandwiched between the brothers.

However from looking on that picture, I started to recall other little things about Declan. At the time they happened, I thought he was hovering because he was checking up on his little brother. When I played soccer with Derik and the other boys in the tribe, Declan stood in the distance to watch. When Derik and I sat at his dining table to do our homework with sometimes Mandy or Rachel joining us; Declan watched from the kitchen as he made himself a snack. That or he'd walk past and throw an insult my way.

"I never hated you B." Declan stated. *"I've always been attracted to you, but because you were my little brother's best friend and girl, I resented the fact that I couldn't have you."* My eyes widened even further, this time in surprise. Our glowing eyes met and held, even if our bodies couldn't. Declan went on, *"my body has always sensed that you were different to the other girls of the tribe. My body probably sensed you were a Werewolf for years before you changed after Jack's death. My body's always wanted you. My body knew you were mine the morning I drove you home in my truck and I put my hand over yours."*

His words echoed inside my mind as I took this trip down memory lane. Frickin' hell, why couldn't I have seen all of this before? Why didn't I see his bad-ass attitude was a way of compensating for the loneliness? As I continued to turn the pages, I started to notice the sideways looks he made my way in the pictures. That was until I saw a big confirmation of his feelings for me in a photo of when Derik and I were 17 years old. I was standing in the middle of the two, as both of the brothers had an arm about me. Derik had his arm about my shoulders and Declan had his arm about my waist. It was the first photo where he was actually laughing with us. I read the caption beneath and saw that this picture was taken on his 20th Birthday.

I vaguely recalled he was less of an asshole that evening, which at the time I found surprising. We were at the Sabre's for dinner as Aunt Susan had cooked up a feast where she served lasagna, tuna bake, salad and garlic bread. The adults stood around talking as Declan chatted with them whilst Derik and I played Monopoly with Phoebe and Phoenix in a corner. At one stage though, he walked past and as he did, he tickled me.

"You're not cheating again, are ya B?" He laughingly taunted then he jogged away before I could whack him.

When it came time to eat, everyone helped themselves to the dishes which sat buffet style on the table. I stood back with Derik as we let everyone else go first and besides, I think we were in the middle of planning a movie night, or something. Then I remembered feeling taken aback when Declan out of the blue, handed me a plate of food. He even included an extra slice of garlic bread, which we used to fight over. I remember feeling shocked that he had served me at all, let alone given me extra garlic bread.

"Hey, where's mine?" Derik complained as his brother came to stand with us.

"Get it yourself, you wuss!" He smirked. "C'mon bro, you're frickin' 17 years old now. Don't you think it's time to fend for yourself?"

Then as my best friend stepped away to get his own food, he gave me a wink.

"You're a bastard." I said because at the time, I thought that he was being mean.

But was he being mean, or was he simply trying to get a minute alone with me and what do I do? I call him a bastard on his birthday even after he gave me extra garlic bread. However Declan laughed off my insult and he even gave a playful nudge.

"Only around you," he grinned.

I stared at the picture of the 20 year old Declan with his arm about my waist. He looked happier in this picture than in any other of the previous photos. His characteristic scowl was missing and he looked almost carefree in this shot. His hair was longer before his crew cut years which I think he had done shortly after this was taken. His dark blonde hair looked lighter when it was longer, as it sat just below his ears. Declan looked very handsome as his clothes bulged with supernatural muscle.

The two brothers, one Werewolf and one human with me smack bang in the middle. The brothers whom I grew up with, one as my best friend and the other my worst enemy and who did I end up with? Contestant Number Two; Mr. Scowl, Smirk and Sarcasm. Looking on that photo of a 17 year old me before my change, there was no way I would have guessed that this was how my life would turn out.

Just then I jumped in fright from the sound of the front door downstairs opening and closing loudly.

"B?" My husband called out.

"I'm up here!" I called back.

I listened to him take off his coat before he put his keys and wallet on top of the dining table. Then I heard him jog up the stairs when he paused in the bedroom doorway as soon as he saw me pouring over the albums. I looked back over his early thirties appearance, still with the crew cut.

"Do you know you've had the same hair style for the past 140 years?" I greeted. "That frickin' crew cut!"

"So?" He turned defensive. "You've never once cut your hair short as you've always worn it long. Do you hear me complaining?"

"Fine then," I said coolly, "I'll get it cut tomorrow."

"Don't you dare!" He growled as he came over to flop onto his stomach on the bed beside. He appreciatively ran his hand through my long, black hair until he saw the photo of himself with the longer hair when he blanched. "Eugh, that was when I wore my hair longer to try to fit in with the frickin' tribe!"

"Really?" I laughed. "You wore your hair longer, so you could try to look Lokoti?"

"Besides the fact that I had blonde hair, blue eyes and white skin, sure!" He laughed at himself.

"I think you look hot in this photo." I declared.

"You're kidding?" He asked pleasantly surprised.

"Nope, I like you in this pic." I verified.

"So if I had pounced on you in the woods when I looked like that, you wouldn't have minded?"

"If you had looked like that, I may not have married Grant. I would have confessed to my parents I was secretly in love with you instead." I joked.

"Cool." He grinned as he rolled onto his side to prop his head up on his hand. "Now if only we could go back in time and put this into effect."

"OK then," I too rolled onto my side so I was facing him, "you write a note to tell yourself not to cut your hair and I'll take it back in time."

Declan laughed out loud as he placed his hand on my waist, "would you have told my little brother to get lost and disappear into my bedroom instead?"

"Maybe," I smiled teasingly as I entwined my fingers with his, "but what would you have done with me in your bedroom?"

"Hmm...I can think of a couple of things, but none our parents would have appreciated." He gave a cheeky grin.

I sighed wistfully, "just imagine what our lives may have been like, if you and I dated and I never married Grant."

He sighed too as he rolled onto his back to stare up at the ceiling. I watched him fold his hands behind his head as he stretched out. But instead of looking relaxed, he was frowning.

"I don't think I could have done anything then. Well, not until you went through the change." He said matter-of-factly.

"Why, because you were scared of hurting me?"

"Yep."

"But I was always a little bit stronger or faster than the other girls growing up. Maybe it would have been alright?" I shrugged.

"Nup," he turned his head to looked my way, "your strength at least quadrupled the night you turned. I had to wait until then."

I giggled as I poked him in the side, "yeah I could tell you must have been waiting for it as you pounced within the first week of my change!"

My husband looked on guiltily, "I wasn't planning to but it was like I lost control of myself. My crush turned into this obsession which made my bloodlust boil. I finally had a sexual release by the arrival of a female Werewolf and it was the girl I was already attracted to."

I believed him as I recalled the expression on his face that afternoon in the woods. I remember in the beginning how he couldn't meet my gaze or he even turned his face away. I recalled how guilty he looked over his actions.

This made me ponder, "if I hadn't of married Grant and Derik still pursued me, what would you have done?"

"I dunno," he answered honestly as he stared upwards, "I sensed the pack wouldn't approve, but Derik was the main reason why I never asked you out. Although my bloodlust kept riding me to claim you, I tried to fight it as I tried to keep my distance. It wasn't honourable what I'd done, which is why I begged you not to tell him about what happened."

"And why you shouted out it was a one time thing?" I poked him in the side again.

"I honest-to-god hoped it would be a one time thing! I thought that now it was out of my system everything could go back to normal, or that's what I was dreaming anyways." He turned to look on my face. "That's why it cut me when you were married off to Grant. I could understand why my brother left for Cambridge to get away as I was tempted to leave too. Sexual frustration and a broken heart, made me seriously think about looking for a female of my kind."

"What would have happened if you had met either Roberta or Michelle?" I asked quietly. "They were the last two female European Werewolves around that time period."

Declan looked back up at the ceiling. "I mean, I might have paired up with either of them for a night or two of entertainment, as beggars can't be choosers. But I can't imagine a long-term coupling with a female of my kind, as you may recall that they were treacherous, psycho, serial killers."

"That does ring a bell, yes." I smirked.

"Every time a human tempts my bloodlust, I think of all the nights your Grandfather sat with me when I was little." He confessed. "Or I think of you B and how giving in to the bloodlust would jeopardize ever seeing you again. Even my Mom acted as a deterrent since she was human, I wouldn't like it if somebody tried to eat her. I was so close to leaving, I'd even discussed it with Derik when Rachel overheard us. But I didn't want to abandon Mom especially since I could hear her cry herself to sleep every now and then because she missed Dad."

I felt sorry for him, as he tried to do the right thing whilst everything went wrong for him. I vividly recalled the night I was woken by sensing his pain. This made a plan formulate in my head and I surprised him by reaching into the top draw of my bedside table to take out a pen and paper.

"What are you doing?" He gave a funny look.

"I'm writing myself a letter." I said simply.

"You're what?" He looked on as if I were mad. "Why, so you can remember this conversation later in the future?"

"Not in the future, but in the past."

"Say what?" He blinked and then he slammed his hand down on the paper. "No!"

"What do you mean, no?" I tried to pull the paper back but he wouldn't let me.

"If you send this letter back in time then you would be doing more harm than good!" Declan said indignantly.

"Why?" I objected. "But what if what I write enables us to have always been together? What if I never married Grant or I broke up with Derik -
"

"No!" He growled as his eyes briefly glowed green. He snatched up the piece of paper, screwed it up and tossed it into the small bin by the bedroom door. Then he frowned my way, "if you broke up with Derik and then started seeing me, my brother would know that I was the reason you broke up with him. It would almost be as damaging as if we cheated on him."

"We did cheat on him."

"We did it once and that once was an accident. Anyone can make a mistake once, but a fool does it twice." He said firmly. "Besides, if Derik found out I would have told him it was my fault. It was me who kissed you that first night you changed and it was me who pounced on you in the woods."

His words started to grate on my nerves as I rolled my eyes whilst rolling onto my back to stare up at the ceiling too.

"Oh shut up, Declan!" I huffed. "Stop making me into 'Little Red Riding Hood' with yourself as the 'Big Bad Wolf'. I began to develop feelings for you too."

"Really?" My husband looked on pleasantly surprised again.

"Yes, now shut up with the 'it's my fault and I'm doomed to walk alone' crap!"

He laughed out loud as he rolled on top to hug me in relief. Next, he affectionately rubbed his nose against mine, before delivering several soft kisses. I liked the feel of his hot body over mine, as I pulled him even closer.

Then my mate smiled tenderly, "neither of us are going to be alone, B. Not for the rest of our lives and not for eternity as we'll always be together."

"Just like Mum and Dad will be." I sighed sadly.

"Huh?" He wondered over my mood swing.

"My parents announced tonight that they'll be leaving soon because of how old Dad is getting. I think they're delaying their departure for as long as possible so they don't leave Uncle Jules behind."

He raised himself in anger, "why didn't you call me?!"

I gave a peculiar look back, "and say what? Declan, come quick! Leave the party you spent the last two months arranging to race here and hold my hand!"

"Exactly!" He said stroppily. "That's exactly what you were supposed to do B, and I would have raced to your side quick smart!"

"I didn't want to spoil your evening." I said flatly. "There's nothing that you could do anyway, Declan. My Mum and Dad are leaving and Vincent will be going with them."

"What, he's leaving too?" He asked confused. "Then who's gonna be your Calculator?"

It was here that my eyes watered as my feelings of shock, hurt and fear came out; "I'll be all alone, Declan. I'll not only be the Last Circulator but I'll be the last of the Circulate anything."

"Hey," my husband growled softly, "you'll never be alone B, never. As you've ensured I wasn't alone in this life, I'm gonna make damn sure you're not alone in the next either."

"But – but – but you have at least another hundred years left of your supernatural lifespan and we're going to be left here on this planet." I started to cry.

"Whadya mean, we're going to be left here?" He gently scolded as he held me tighter. "We have the pack and we have the tribe. We have all new generations of Sabre's, Riverclaw's and Elm's to look after. I know they'd miss us just as much as we miss your grandparents. After all, who else are they gonna have as their backup babysitters?"

"But – but – but it won't be the same!" I sobbed. "I'll be the Last Circulator without a Calculator. Vincent is even planning to activate the self-destruct mechanism at the Circulate HQ on Mars, so the humans won't ever find out about us." I cried harder.

"Tell him if he even looks at that proverbial red button, I'll tear him to shreds!" He snarled threateningly.

"But – but – but I can see his point of view." I sobbed. "I mean, there won't be anybody around to use the Headquarters on Mars anymore."

"What about you and me?" He complained. "If I'm going to be a Circulator one day, I'd like to have a Headquarters too!"

"We'll still have the base on Taurus Six." I sniffed as I clung to the front of his shirt. "But it won't be the same, because it's so far away from Earth."

Declan frowned as he hated seeing me upset. He held my head closer so I could dry my face on his clothes as he stroked my hair. I even caught the frustrated growl under his breath that he couldn't just go out and kill something to make his mate feel better.

After a moment, he pulled away to ask hesitantly, "B do you want to go to the space time continuum with your Mom, Dad and Vincent?"

"What do you mean?"

"I mean exactly that." He said seriously. "Do you want to turn me into a Circulator now so we can leave with your parents and Calculator?"

I looked on in surprise when I noticed his reluctant determination. I sensed he wasn't ready to leave his mortal existence behind, but I also sensed that his love for me was so great that if I wanted to rob a bank, he wouldn't let me do this alone. This gave me pause then I eventually shook my head.

"No, but thank you." I gave a small smile. "You still have a hundred years or so as a European Werewolf. We'll leave when your 300 years is up."

"Are you sure?" He examined my face closely.

"Yeah, I'm sure."

"Are you sure you're sure?"

"Declan I'm sure!" I giggled as I tickled him.

He chuckled as he quickly caught my smaller hands in his bigger ones, to hold against his chest.

"You're in no way alone, B." My mate said earnestly. "I won't allow it, just as I won't let you wane. I promise to keep you so preoccupied over the next century as I remind you of the pleasures of having a biological body."

Then he growled hungrily as he bent his head to tenderly maul my neck with his sharpening teeth. I giggled as I wrapped my arms about his large form. Soon I felt his hot hands begin to remove my garments to which I returned the favour. But in the midst of our undressing, I cupped his face so my dark blue eyes could meet his bright blue ones.

"You always do Declan, you always do." I breathed, before I pulled him in for another kiss.

~~~~~~
~~~~~~

~ 30 ~

31ˢᵗ June 2225

"No way in hell!" My mate growled.

"I WANT to do this!" I growled back.

"There is no way in hell that we're going to fork out THAT much money when we can do it ourselves!"

"But we can't do this ourselves as there's too much work to do!"

"Of course we can frickin' do it ourselves! We're Werewolves, our strength is greater than a human's!"

"I don't care! I want to hire these humans to do it."

"No!"

"Yes!"

"B," his eyes glowed green as his temper was ignited, "I said NO!"

"YES!"

"NO!"

As you can see by our arguing, the day started out as just a typical morning in the Sabre household. My European Werewolf husband was trying to dominate his Lokoti Werewolf wife, who was fighting back. We momentarily forgot our breakfast of bacon and scrambled eggs, which began to turn cold.

"YES!" I roared. "Declan Domitian Sabre, you're not going to scare me with your temper so just frickin' drop it!"

"The HELL I can't!"

"NO! N – O spells NO! No no no no no! Besides, it's my money."

"And it's my frickin' garden!"

"It was my garden first!"

"Who repairs the roof, or who repaired the broken stair or even who fixed the frickin' greenhouse?"

"That was 135 years ago!"

"I was up on that frickin' roof less than five years ago when I replaced the rotten shingles!"

"I don't care Declan, I WANT to do this!"

"B, we are NOT wasting good credit, to pay a bunch of HUMANS to do what we can do ourselves!"

"But I want professionals to do it."

"We don't need a bunch of humans from Fairbanks to come and do a frickin' garden!"

"The cost of labor is included in the quote!"

"But it will be a hell of a lot cheaper if we do it ourselves."

"No!"

"Yes!"

"Declan, I'm using MY money for the garden to be done MY way and I don't care what you say!"

"Then I'll scare them away by turning into a European Werewolf!"

"Don't you DARE!"

"I'll even put up a frickin' sign that says 'Beware of Dog' and I can't wait to see the looks on their faces when I come barreling out of the house, changed!"

"Do that and so help me I'll send you back to the dinosaur age! Then let's see how tough you are against a frickin' tyrannosaurus rex!" I fumed.

I had my laptop open beside my plate to show Declan the website for the landscape company. On the website I had downloaded the shape of the land that surrounded the house which I would like to turn into a garden. Next, I had picked the kind of trees, plants and grass that I'd like. Lastly, the landscape company designer emailed me back a design and a quote. I was pleased with the plans which I tried to show my husband, but he just HAD to object didn't he?

"Look B," he shoveled another load of food into his mouth, "I'm not disputing the idea of installing a garden, but we don't have to pay humans to do it for us! We can buy the material and the plants to do it ourselves."

"I don't want to do it myself, I want to pay somebody to do it for me!" I huffed.

"Then I'LL do it for you!" My husband rolled his eyes.

"No, Declan." I refused. "I want to pay this company to come and do a professional job on the garden and that's that!"

"But B, think about it. We live in frickin' Alaska – ALASKA! Half of these plants you've picked aren't meant to survive in this climate, even in the warmer months!"

"Look at the small print Declan," I shoved my laptop closer, "these plants are genetically engineered to be hardy in cold climates. As soon as the snow is off the ground, they'll thrive!"

I watched his eyes narrow as he glared at the writing alongside of the pictures on the computer screen. He hated to be proven wrong, as I overheard his low growl. However I on the other hand, loved to be in the right.

Stubbornly I continued on, "I'm using MY money I've earned from my academic work to pay and that's that! We're going to get grass laid and our dirt driveway will be turned into gravel. We're going to have garden plots with flowers that will bloom in the spring and summer. I'm only showing you this so you won't get a fright by seeing strangers on our property and attack the gardeners!"

My husband bad-temperedly glared down at his plate as he cursed unhappily under his breath.

"I would say, 'so was your mother' but I liked Aunt Susan." I quipped as I turned the laptop around in my direction again.

Declan's eyes glowed green at any kind of mention of his mother in relation to the insults he had just muttered, but I ignored him. Next, I selected the date to book in the landscaping company before I started to type in my Credit Card details.

Just as I hit the 'pay now' button, both my mate and I suddenly jumped from the abrupt telepathic command from my father; *YOUR UNCLE JULIAN IS SICK, COME QUICK!*

We exchanged a look of dread as we both knew what this meant. Uncle Julian was 178 years old and his failing health was due to being so elderly. Today could be the last day Uncle Julian may be alive...

We both quickly stood up from the table before we snatched up our keys and our coats on our way out. Our breakfast was left half-eaten as we rushed out the door.

*****

As soon as Declan's pick up truck pulled into Uncle Julian's driveway, I jumped out first. He was quick to power down the plasma engine, punch in the security lock for the ignition and jump out afterwards. He was right on my heels, as I burst through the front door. Inside we found the next generation of Riverclaw's sitting sadly in the lounge room.

Photos of Uncle Jules and Aunt Danika adorned the mantle piece, with more photos of him posing with his arms about his wife and children or even their grandchildren. My uncle's great grandkids and his great, great grandkids, all looked expectantly our way, from our sudden entrance.

"Everyone's in Great Grandfather's bedroom." Stone's middle-aged wife Sharon, informed.

Declan's hand clasped my own as he led the way upstairs. When we walked into Uncle Jules' bedroom, we found him lying weakened and barely conscious. Mum was sitting resolutely by his side on the bed whilst holding one of his elderly hands in both of her younger ones. On the other side of Uncle Jules sat Phoenix, as Dad stood behind Mum with his hands on her shoulders. At the end of the bed stood Chiron, his son Stone as well as Stone's teenaged son, Forrest.

My father looked just as aged as my uncle did, as their hair was completely white and their faces wrinkled. Even the older Phoenix's hair had turned silver as his skin appeared worn, like old leather. Chiron wasn't immune to time either, as he sported many a grey hair in his long, black main.

Mum, Declan and I stuck out as the only people in the room whom were over a century old but we retained our youth. Funnily, now Declan looked older than Mum, as he looked like a man in his early thirties whilst she and I retained our late twenties appearance. My mother with her long, black hair, smooth white skin and bright blue eyes which were tearful, never left her elderly twin's face.

"Jess," he looked up, "you're still here? I thought you and Hunter would have beaten me to the space time continuum by now."

"Shut up, you idiot." Her voice was light, which belied her sorrow.

"Get lost Jess, you look like someone's just died." Her brother wheezed. "Isn't it bad luck, to depress the sick person?"

"Why, are you scared that I'll jinx you and you'll cark it?" She teased.

"The way you're looking at me right now, it's like I have one foot in the grave." My uncle rolled his eyes.

"You do have one foot in the grave you loser!" She broke down into sobs.

"B, come and pull your mother together, will you?" Uncle Jules called my name in a faint voice.

Declan and I came forwards and as my youthful European Werewolf husband stood beside my elderly Lokoti Werewolf father; I came to sit beside my mother on the bed. She was crying so hard, she was shaking. My father's hands gripped her shoulders tighter, but they did little to effect her sadness.

"You're my twin brother," she sniffled, "so we're the same age but you look ancient!"

"Hey, we're not all Circulators in this family." His chest heaved. "I'm only a Lokoti Werewolf, 'Little Miss Most Argumentative Female In The Tribe'."

"You're still the biggest moron," Mum sucked in a tearful breath, "and you're gonna be the biggest loser in the space time continuum too."

"But I will see you there won't I, Jess?" He looked on worriedly.

Dad promised, "we'll be right behind you."

"Mum will be there for you and so will Phoebe." Phoenix promised his father. "You're making me jealous, Dad. While you're doing the whole family reunion I'll be left behind."

My head turned sharply towards my elderly looking cousin, who was younger than me.

"And where will I be?" I asked curtly. "You may be rid of your father, but you're not rid of Declan and I, you little drama queen!"

Phoenix's eyes brightened by my words and he gave a playful grin, "great I'm left alone with bitch-features."

"Hey, watch it!" Declan growled. "Your Grandfather used to punch you on the arm when you talked like that. He may not be here but I still am, plus I hit harder."

Uncle Jules smiled weakly, "here's the bitch-slapping Second of the pack, Ladies and Gentlemen."

"I've noticed the pack is a lot more compliant with our current First and Second." Stone joined in.

"Damn straight." Chiron grinned in good humor. "You were all wandering around like lost moose, before Declan and I took charge."

"Speaking of which," Uncle Jules looked on Forrest, "with my departure, it's a safe bet that you'll be joining the other Riverclaw men; by turning on the next full moon."

The 18 year old visibly gulped, as he looked nervous by this prospect. He asked anxiously, "does it hurt?"

"Yes," one half of the room answered whilst the other said, "no."

"Yes or no, which is it?" He looked around.

"My first change hurt, but then it didn't afterwards." Dad answered honestly.

"Same here." Phoenix nodded.

"Me too." Stone chimed in.

"My first couple of months hurt like hell," I admitted, "I lost control of myself the first night I turned, since I didn't understand what was happening."

Then I looked over my shoulder at Declan who was waiting for my gaze before he gave a small smile of understanding. He was there for me when I first turned by stopping me from turning into a murderer. I would always be grateful to him for that.

Chiron told his grandson, "It was harder for B, since she was the first female Lokoti Werewolf and the pack didn't know what to expect. I was frightened the first time I changed, but I had Dad and Granddad with me. They immediately took me hunting to appease the bloodlust."

Forrest's eyes widened in fear, "but I can't be a Werewolf, I'm a vegetarian!"

This made the whole room laugh softly, as they looked on sympathetically.

Declan smirked, "you won't be after the next full moon."

"Kids today." Phoenix humorously rolled his eyes.

"I told Sharon that insisting on the kids eat all of their vegetables was overrated." Stone played along. "But what does she do? She cooks up vegetable bakes!"

"Do you hear that Jules? You can't die yet otherwise you'll ruin the lifestyle of the family's vegetarian." Mum smiled sadly on her brother.

"Uncle Dec," Forrest looked to my husband, "does it hurt when you change?"

"Yup." My mate said simply.

"Er, which part?" He asked confused. "Do you mean the first time you changed?"

"Nope, it hurts every single time I change." Declan spoke frankly. "When my eyes glow green or my nails turn into claws and my teeth sharpen that's fine. But when I expand to my larger form? My bone structure changes as my whole body is contorted. It hurts like hell, but when you've got the bloodlust riding you, your blood boils if you don't give in."

I felt a small pang in my heart as I felt his constant tug-of-war within himself as he battled the bloodlust's constant cravings. Sometimes Declan would have this pained look on his face, when he would either make a move on me in the bedroom or if he had to hunt in between full moon cycles. He tried as best as he could to assimilate, but his differences as a European Werewolf stood out.

"Then how do you cope?" Forrest pondered, as he seemed put off by the process. "You've been a Werewolf since the age of three, right? Now you're nearly two centuries old!"

There was more laughter at his exaggeration of my mate's age.

"He's only 162 years old, thank you very much!" I objected.

My husband chuckled as he settled his hands on my shoulders and I felt his hot fingers caress the skin on the back of my neck. He said, "I cope because I have B as my mate and I have the pack."

"The pack will guide you through the process." Dad promised the soon-to-be Werewolf.

"As we have done for thousands of years when a new wolf joins the fold." Stone put his hand on his son's back.

"Just be glad you're not part Circulator too." I sighed. "My change must be the hardest yet on record."

"I wouldn't say that," Declan contradicted, "so you had a rough first couple of months? My first five years were hard as your Grandfather constantly sat with me to coax me through the hunger pains. Sometimes he had to take me hunting every night for months on end, let alone on the full moon."

"No wonder the two of you are together," Dad smirked, "as you both seem to be made for each other. Now we have the Last Circulator and the Last European Werewolf as husband and wife."

It made me smile at how my father finally said something supportive about my marriage after only being together for well over a century.

"Difficult changes, or just being difficult period?" Phoenix taunted.

Everyone laughed, which made Declan and I exchange looks of amusement; it appears our constant fighting were making us legends in the tribe.

"Yep, you can tell you three are related; the first female Lokoti Werewolf who just happens to be the daughter of the most argumentative female in the tribe. Now the most dangerous breed of Werewolf gets lumped in their family?" Uncle Julian half laughed and half coughed. "But you'll look after B won't you Declan, when B's father and I are gone?"

The room momentarily turned quiet with worry when we noticed Uncle Julian's loud breathing was shallow and uneven.

"Hey, if anybody looks at my mate wrong they'll suddenly find the jaws of a European Werewolf ripping out their throats." My husband promised.

"And Jess..." the elderly man turned his fading eyes my mother's way, "...you'll be along soon, won't you?"

"We'll leave shortly for the space time continuum." She promised. "So you better not hog all of Grandma's gravy at the dinner table in the afterlife, you have to save me some."

"Hunter, you're two years older than me but you're still goin' strong." My uncle looked up at my father. "I always thought that you'd go first, thanks to being married to Jess."

There were a couple more guffaws at his taunts, as Dad smiled sadly on his brother-in-law.

"That's a good thing about having a 'Light Person' for a mate Jules; when they're running around at the speed of light, you don't think of slowing down. Instead it makes you want to run faster to catch up."

Uncle Jules looked on knowingly, "are you sure that's the only reason why?"

What's that supposed to mean? But somehow Declan, Phoenix, Chiron and Stone seemed to cotton-on to Uncle Jules' meaning. The male Werewolves all exchanged another look.

"You do seem to have a particularly radiant glow about you today, Hunter." My husband smirked.

"It's such a healthy glow, it could be called an aura." Phoenix added on.

Did he just say an aura? Then does that mean...? No way! My head snapped around to stare upwards in shock.

My father met my startled eyes to say softly, "last night your mother made me a Circulator."

"But – but – but I thought that as soon as she did that, you'd have to go to the space time continuum! That's what happened with Gran and Grandfather." I uttered out my surprise.

"When Elisha Baker turned Mike Sabre into a Circulator, they didn't immediately go to the space time continuum, did they?" My mother pointed out.

My elderly looking father gave a large stretch to flex his muscles, which made me notice that his joints didn't crack as they usually did.

"Dad, you're a Circulator and a Lokoti Werewolf, like me!" I gawked and then my father laughed when I jumped up from the bed to throw my arms about him. He even felt like his old strong self, as he held me back tightly. I squealed excitedly, "it's like you're young again! So are you going to alter your appearance and look young too?"

"What's the point in that? I'm 180 years old and I'm not ashamed of my age. Besides, your mother and I will be leaving for the space time continuum soon." My father sighed in resignation.

Just then we were interrupted by a loud gasp. We quickly turned back around to see Mum looking ashen on her twin. Dad released his hold on me to move forwards and gravely look down.

My elderly uncle lay quietly with his eyes closed as if he were no longer breathing.

"Jules?" Mum gently shook his hand. "Julian?"

There was no response as the room turned dead silent whilst we stared agape at the figure in the bed.

Just to be sure, my father leaned over to check my uncle's pulse when suddenly Uncle Jules' eyes snapped open, giving Dad and everyone else a fright too!

"Made you look." He gave his last mischievous grin...and then he closed his eyes for good.

It was Uncle Jules' last joke, but nobody laughed nor did anybody say a thing. Like a room full of statues, we stood still with stinging eyes. It was as if we were too scared to move or we might lose our last moment with him forever.

*****

Time seemed to become lost that day. I don't recall reaching midday or afternoon, let alone evening. But never-the-less time progressed, leaving a mourning family in its aftermath.

In the early afternoon, the pack appeared downstairs as they sensed the demise of one of their own.

One at a time, each member excluding the ones who were already here, solemnly walked into the bedroom to say their goodbyes. I stood along the wall of the bedroom with Mum, Dad and Declan; as we watched the steady stream of visitors. Like mournful background music, we could hear the weeping downstairs in the newer generations of Riverclaw's. Phoenix, Chiron, Stone and Forrest sat in the lounge room to grieve with their families.

Dad gripped hard onto Mum's hand as Declan did with mine. My mother and I were standing side by side, staring vacantly off into the distance. The Circulators each sensed that Uncle Jules' death marked the end of something else as well. I knew what was coming as I could see it, smell it and I was foretold of it by the emptiness I felt; our lives were changed forever.

Mum acted like a zombie that day. She hardly spoke as she walked as if in a daze. She looked like she had stared a gorgon in the face and practically turned to stone. Her skin was pale and her eyes had an empty look about them. Usually with her youthful appearance, she would appear to be full of life and vitality...but not today.

My father watched his mate worriedly, as she struggled through the motions to walk, to speak or even to breathe. Her twin was dead; her sometime enemy, her tormentor and her outlet to be loud and annoying back, was gone.

Uncle Jules had delighted in ribbing her and with his supernatural strength, he hardly flinched at her retaliation but instead he laughed. He and Ian would guffaw when one of their jibes made Mum fire up. Dad would stand back to smilingly watch, as the Lokoti Werewolves enjoyed witnessing the sparks which came flying of my mother's aura. However if her tantrums got out of control, then he would use his will to gently calm her down.

At sunset, a Tribal Elder along with Chiron arranged to take Uncle Julian's body away. However as they were organizing, Mum reacted like something inside her snapped.

"You want to do WHAT?!" She flared.

"We have to take away Uncle Julian's body to the Holy Room to prepare for the Funeral Ceremony." Chiron said gently.

"Funeral...? You mean put Julian on the FUNERAL PYRE?!" She shouted. "Like hell you're going to burn my brother's body!"

"Jess, please..." my father tried to pull my mother into his arms, "...let the Tribe say goodbye to your brother in the traditional way."

"Get off me Hunter!" She pushed him away.

I watched her wander a little away on unsteady legs. She wavered towards the bed where she sat down heavily by her brother's side to retake hold of his hand.

"We're coming Julian," she spoke in a flat voice, "we're coming."

I felt frightened by her words as I turned to look on Declan, whom I saw was feeling the same way. Was this it? Is this really the end of my immediate family? Uncle Julian's death appeared to be the door my parents would exit by.

As Chiron and Dad carried Uncle Julian's body out of the house on the old fashioned stretcher, Mum and I followed behind. Together we stood on the front veranda when we turned into a threesome by Declan hugging us both in his larger, stronger arms. Like this, we watched Uncle Julian's body which was wrapped in a woven funeral shroud, was carefully placed in the back of the Tribal Elder's truck.

Dad rejoined us on the veranda along with Phoenix, as Chiron and Stone moved to sit in the back of the truck with Uncle Julian's body. Like this, the Tribal Elder drove off down the hill and as soon as the truck disappeared from sight, Mum turned to her husband.

"Vincent will be expecting us." She spoke crisply.

Then she pulled herself out of Declan's arms to walk back into the house. Dad shared a surprised look with Phoenix, before the four of us followed her inside.

"But Jess," my father faltered, "we're only half way through packing up the house."

"They're just possessions, Hunter!" She snapped. "It's not like we're gonna need them where we're going."

Then everyone watched her angrily grab her coat and handbag.

"Aunt Jess," Sharon wondered, "are you going somewhere?"

My mother turned on the remaining members of the family, "we're leaving."

"If you're leaving, where are you going?" Forrest queried.

"To the space time continuum." She announced.

"Huh?" He looked on blankly. "Where's that?"

But then his mother silenced him by pulling her son into her arms.

Mum glared tearfully at the new generations of Riverclaw's who returned the look with hurt expressions.

"I'm not sticking around to watch them burn my brother's body, I'm leaving for the next life to be with him instead." She said adamantly.

"But Aunt Jess, you HAVE to go to your brother's funeral." Phoenix protested. "You're the last member of his immediate family that's left alive."

Then my father stepped up to place his hand on my mother's arm. He said gently, "Jess we don't have to go right now, we can leave in three days time."

"No!" She stubbornly pulled away. "Hunter, we do have to go right now! Julian's waiting for us with Mum and Dad. They're all waiting for us."

"If they're waiting for us, I'm sure being in eternity they'd be patient about it." Dad tried to reason.

"No!" She suddenly squealed like she was frightened. "What if he's immediately recycled into the timeline? What if he's reincarnated and we just miss him? No Hunter, we have to leave now."

My elderly father let out a heavy sigh, but he stopped arguing with her. Phoenix saw by my mother's fragile state that he couldn't talk her around, so he pursed his lips together. Everyone looked on Mum right now like she was a keg of gunpowder about to go off and even Declan's eyes were wide with worry.

Subconsciously, I reached for my husband's hand who was quick to take it.

*****

Mum instantaneously phased Dad, as I instantaneously phased Declan to Circulate HQ. Once we arrived, she immediately let go of his arm however I never let go of my husband's hand.

The Circulate Headquarters on Mars appeared peacefully quiet as it usually did. The only noise we could hear was the background hum of the environmental systems inside the dome which the Mainframe maintained.

"This way," my mother ordered as she curtailed off down the hallway.

We followed her through several corridors until we came to the Viewing Room, but we didn't find Vincent there.

"Maybe he's in his quarters." She said next.

Then she spun around and stalked back down the hallway, with us in tow. We reached the personnel quarters section of the dome where we slowed upon approach of Vincent's automated door. Mum hit the door control to announce our presence, but there was no response.

"Is he here?" Her husband enquired.

"Apparently not." She said curtly.

"I mean, is he here at Headquarters?" He tried again.

"He's a Calculator, Hunter. He can't instantaneously phase like a Circulator can!" She snapped. "I dropped him off here last week, after a meeting with the board of Hodge Endeavor."

Just as I was about to ask the computer for the whereabouts of Vincent, I caught Declan sniff the air. He decided to do this the Werewolf way, by tracking our Calculator by his scent.

"This way," my mate said as he headed down the corridor in another direction.

Since Declan was still holding onto my hand, I was pulled along. However when I looked back I caught my parents look impressed at his tracking skills. Then my father must have caught the same scent, as he walked alongside of my mate with the two males leading the way.

We walked down several more hallways with their smooth black floors. We passed the futuristic computer interfaces along the walls, which were lit up and beeping busily away. The sun which was high in the Martian sky, shone through the glass dome, making the Headquarters warm and bright. We walked past the automatic doors to the Self Defense room, the Medical Lab and the Science Lab, the former Council Chambers and we even passed the Props Room.

Lastly, we approached a large set of double doors which were glass, but were thick like protective barriers. Above the door's control panel on the side was the room allocation which read; CIRCULATE MAINFRAME.

The double doors instantly parted and when we four walked inside, our eyes bulged as what we found in the centre astounded us. In the middle of the computer interface lined room, was what looked like to be a huge, crystallized three-sided pyramid which slowly turned in midair. It sparkled as numerous beams of light hit it which I guess was how the computer operated, by the light beams accessing the ingrained data inside the crystal.

Then we noticed the Calculator sitting on the floor using small, electronic tools. He seemed to be hard at work, like he had been doing this for some time. He was using one futuristic device to shine a small laser beam onto a small crystallized computer circuit. I think it belonged to one of the open computer panels which were directly below the huge, hovering crystal pyramid.

"Hallo." He greeted aloof whilst not looking up.

"Vincent, what is this?" Mum gawked.

"The Circulate Mainframe." He stated the obvious.

"You're kidding me!" She stared at the huge, hovering pyramid which seemed to be turning by itself in midair. "THAT'S the Circulate Mainframe?"

"Yes." He replied. "Usually you don't see the computer core, because it's behind protective casing. But it's exposed today, because of the downloading."

"What downloading?" Dad asked as he looked on the multiple beams of light.

"I'm doing a core transfer so every single byte of information of anything that has ever been stored in the Circulate Mainframe, will be transferred to the second computer core on Taurus Six." Our Calculator explained before he finally looked up. "Elisha Baker's SSIT Reports, the Circulate Council meetings, all of the Calculator's Reports; absolutely everything ever documented by the Circulate, will be saved for posterity. This way B will always have access to them, as the last remaining member of the Circulate."

"So it's true then," Declan asked unhappily, "that you're abandoning your Circulator and blowing this place up?"

"Yes." He said coolly as he returned to work.

Suddenly my mate leapt forwards to snatch him up by the front of his shirt, as he held him up in the air!

"You are NOT blowing up this place!" My huband roared. "So you're going to pike out and leave B behind? You're NOT blowing up her last tie to the Circulate and who she is!"

"Declan!" My parents tried to pull the enraged European Werewolf off the Calculator.

However he wouldn't budge until I stepped up. Gently, I placed my hand on my mate's shoulder and gave him a certain look which made him instantly release Vincent. My Calculator almost collapsed to the floor but Dad caught him in time.

He straightened his clothes as he threw my husband a filthy look, "I'm not leaving B all alone Declan, that's what I'm making sure of!"

"Oh yeah then how?" He challenged. "All I see is a pansy little Calculator abandoning his Circulator!"

His face reddened before he spoke icily, "B will have the second Circulate base on Taurus Six. She will have the computer core and all the information ever stored, at her finger tips. I've even programmed the Circulate Mainframe to become her Calculator! The Circulate Mainframe will watch over her finances and her timeline. As long as B continues her biological existence, so will the Circulate."

Declan looked on in disbelief, "how will a computer do all of that?"

"How about using your brain instead of your muscles for one minute and think about it," he sneered back, "the Viewing Room is tied into the Mainframe, as all of the Circulate's systems are. Elisha Baker's Calculator Patrick O'Flannigan already programmed the computer before he left in the

'Final Phase', to watch over Hodge Endeavor and to monitor Elisha Baker's progeny. All I had to do was add to the programming, to teach the 'smart computer' to focus solely on Bianca."

"What the hell was all of that supposed to mean?" My mate asked narkily.

"B," my Calculator looked my way, "speak to the computer."

"And say what?" I wondered.

"Computer," Vincent spoke instead, "acknowledge Circulate member 701."

"The Circulate Mainframe acknowledges the Last Circulator, Bianca Wisetail Elm Sabre." The female-voiced computer sounded.

"Advise Bianca and Declan Sabre of what I am currently doing." He wearily rolled his eyes.

"Circulate Member 702, the Last Calculator called Vincent Moher; has initiated a compressed data stream to the second Circulate computer core on Taurus Six. Downloading will be complete in approximately thirteen minutes. Once the download is finalized, the computer core on Mars will self-destruct. The explosion is calculated to completely annihilate the Circulate base on Mars. The destruction will remove any proof of the Circulate's existence on the Red Planet." The computer reported.

"But what about Patrick O'Flannigan's 'smart computer'?" I asked worriedly.

The computer answered, "the Circulate Mainframe will be fully operational at the new HQ on Taurus Six when the data transfer is complete. From the Circulate Mainframe's new location, the system will be available to take on the role as Calculator to Bianca Sabre."

I looked on Vincent in surprise by the computer answering my question instead of he, to which he gave a smug smile.

"You should get used to it B, the Circulate Mainframe is going to become your new best friend."

Declan possessively put his arm about my waist as he said staunchly, "B already has a best friend; me."

"But can you act as her Calculator?" He crossed his arms. "If B has to track down a person in the timeline, would you be able to do this? Or can you accurately foretell the changes in the World Wide Stock Market, to protect Hodge Endeavor's investments?"

"If B needs to find someone, I can frickin' track them for her." My mate boasted. "European Werewolves are second to Asian Werewolves with hunting down our targets."

"What if this person exists in the 5th Century?" Vincent returned. "You can only track a person in your time frame. Or what if this person moves to an off-world colony on one of the new terraformed planets? The Circulate Mainframe via the Viewing Room can hone in anywhere in the galaxy. If B had to go off-world to see this person; can European Werewolves leave Earth considering the impact celestial objects such as moons, have on your psyche?"

Here my husband faltered as he shot off a resentful look towards my Calculator. No, I don't think Werewolves in general, could risk leaving Earth thanks to the moon's influence on the bloodlust. However I as part Circulator had a little more leeway, which was the point Vincent was making. Where Declan couldn't go, the Circulate Mainframe could as my new Calculator.

"Sorry to interrupt here," Dad stepped up, "but didn't the computer say it was going to self-destruct when the transfer was complete?"

"It did," Mum nodded, "so can we save the 'pick on the Werewolf' session until later?"

"Jess and Hunter, relax. The computer is not going to blow up Headquarters when we're inside." Vincent rolled his eyes. Then to prove his point, he spoke to the Mainframe again, "computer please tell our guests that they're not going to get blown up today?"

The Mainframe responded, "the self-destruct sequence would be cancelled if motion sensors detected your presence inside of the Headquarters." Our Calculator smirked our way when the computer next chirped; "please be advised though that by suddenly halting the self-destruct process will cause a six hour delay in reinitiating the sequence."

"On that note, you'd better come with me." He led the way out of the Circulate Mainframe's room of operations.

I stared longingly at the hovering, huge, crystal pyramid which glimmered with all of the different light beams hitting it. It seemed such a shame to destroy something so beautiful, let alone technologically advanced. Declan took hold of my hand to gently tug me along and we trailed after the other three.

"Where are we going?" My mother asked as our Calculator picked up the pace.

"You'll see." He sung secretively.

We walked down the corridors towards the personnel quarters once more. He walked towards an empty set of quarters and the frosted-over, sliding glass door opened upon our approach. I took quick note of the small, lit up control panel on my way into the tiny quarters; Room 636 'E. Baker'.

"No way!" I exclaimed. "These were Elisha Baker's quarters?"

Vincent walked over to the small table by the wall to pick up a backpack which looked half full.

"Inside are Elisha Worthall's laptop with her stored personal diaries and emails, as well as a few photos which were never stored on the Circulate Mainframe." He handed me the bag. "I thought you might like to keep them on Taurus Six."

My mother's eyes widened as she watched our Calculator hand me my great, great grandmother's belongings. Quickly, I opened up the bag to peek inside.

"No way!" I exclaimed.

"What?" Mum came forwards to look too.

I pulled out an old looking photo frame with a picture inside I'd never seen before. I've seen plenty of photos of Elisha with her husband Jarrod Worthall as well as with their children and grandchildren. But this photo was of her in the arms of another man and strangely, this man looked a lot like Derik! They were almost identical, except for different hair styles and maybe their height.

"Why is Great, Great Gran being hugged by Derik?" I asked confused.

Vincent laughed as he shook his head at my obtuseness, whilst Mum, Dad and Declan crowded around to see.

"That's not Derik." She realized. "It's Mike Sabre, who is Declan's great, great grand uncle."

"The photo was taken when he and Elisha were a couple, before she married Jarrod Worthall." Our Calculator announced.

"Aaaww...!" I melted before I looked into my mother's face, "isn't that sweet? They were a couple before she married and a couple again, after her husband passed away. Now they're together forever inside of the space time continuum, never to be separated by time again."

"That sounds familiar, the before and after scenario." Declan smirked.

I smiled back at my mate, at the irony of how our relationship shared this similarity with Elisha and Mike Sabre.

Right at that moment, the computer's voice interrupted our reverie.

"Vincent, the download is complete. I am now transmitting to you from the Circulate base on Taurus Six. Would you like me to now initiate the computer core overload at the base on Mars?"

"Yes please." He answered.

"Then may I recommend your hasty removal from the premises and obtain at least 20 km's distance to be clear of the explosion?" The computer said helpfully.

"Will do," he agreed before he turned to Mum, "do you fancy instantaneously phasing us the hell out of here?"

"Hang on," I stopped him, "do you need to get anything first?"

Vincent looked on incredulous, "I don't think I can take a suitcase with me to the space time continuum, in my evolved state of energy and light."

"Oh yeah." I saw his point, but it still seemed a shame to just leave like this as the whole place was soon to disappear forever. I tried again, "do you have any photos or anything else that you want to save from annihilation? I don't mind looking after them, or even using them to remember you by."

Now my Calculator softened at my sentimentality, "thank you B. But my parent's died in World War Three and the photo albums which were taken from the rubble, are stored at Blythe. Now with the all new generations of Worthall's living there who hardly know me, or who their foremother Elisha Worthall, was? I have nothing else to tie me to this life anymore."

Frickin' hell, Uncle Julian's death really was the marking of the end of an era. I was losing an entire generation of family who were ready to move on, or evolve.

Again the Mainframe interrupted when it announced, "the computer core temperature is reaching critical point. The destruction of the Mars Circulate Headquarters is imminent. The explosion will occur in approximately 2.58 minutes and counting down."

"Jess," her husband looked on worriedly, "I may be a Circulator now but I don't know how to instantaneously phase like you and B can."

"Time to go!" Declan snatched the photo frame out of my hands to shove into the backpack. Then he slung the bag over his shoulder as he looked my way demandingly.

I retook hold of his hand, as Mum placed hers on Dad and Vincent's shoulders. In a bright flash of light we disappeared from Circulate Headquarters and in another, we were standing outside.

We stood on a cliff top 50 km's away from base, on the surface of the Red Planet. However as soon as we reappeared, all five of us started to gasp! The atmosphere of Mars 250,000 years in the past was cold and thin, making us shiver as well as try to catch our breath.

"Look." Vincent puffed as he pointed in a particular direction.

From where we were standing, we were overlooking the Mare Acidalum. Vincent was pointing to something small and shining in the distance, which was the glass dome reflecting the sun's light. It looked miniscule from this distance, but just visible.

Suddenly it looked much more obvious by a bright light engulfing it! Then the light turned yellow, then orange and then red which must have been the different stages of the explosion. We watched plumes of black smoke appear, as there were several more emissions of white and then yellow light as different parts of the Headquarters erupted into flame.

We stood quietly as we all watched the black smoke dramatically decrease for some reason, then there was a blinding flash coupled with a rumble like thunder. The light emitted was so bright, it made all of us blink. However when we opened our eyes again, what we saw next made us blink and then blink again in disbelief.

There were no more flames just as there was no further smoke, with only the wispy trails in the sky to indicate where the Headquarters used to be. All that remained now was a scalded crater in the surface of the planet.

Just like that, it was gone. Within a minute, the Circulate Headquarters on Mars was no more. As the boys from Monty Python which my great, great grandmother used to be a fan of would put it, "it ceased to be, it went to join the choir invisible, it is no more, it is an ex-Headquarters."

"Don't you just love 25th Century technology?" Vincent breathed hard. "When you program a 25th Century computer to self-destruct, it really gets the job done. No half-way suicide attempts there."

"But the crater -" Dad began.

"The crater will be seen by astronomers in the future." He interrupted from guessing his thoughts. "However it will simply look like any other crater on this planet's surface. By the time humankind terra forms Mars to establish a colony here, any forensic evidence left from the explosion will be non-existent."

"Speaking of which," Declan panted, "why is it so frickin' hard to breathe all of a sudden?"

"Mars' atmosphere is leaking into space." He looked upwards. "In another thousand years, there'll be hardly any oxygen left and definitely not enough to support life." Then he looked down as he kicked at one of the many patches of red dirt on the ground. "The vegetation is already dying out. There aren't many insects left and nearly all of the animal life has died out. This planet will die before it goes through its own reincarnation when humans terra form it."

"What, just like that?" My husband looked around in disappointment.

"It is a dead planet is it not, when the age of man begins?" Our Calculator reminded. "Besides, it's a good thing that Mars' atmosphere is leaking into space."

"It is?" Dad gave a funny look.

"Martian microbes which are biological blueprints, leave Mars to land on Earth. Mars' death adds to the evolution of our Mother Earth." Vincent looked up into the sky as if he could 'see' this taking place.

"You're saying some of the life on Earth comes from Mars?" My husband raised his eyebrows in disbelief.

"Humans share the same skepticism to the idea of Werewolves existing." Our Calculator returned.

Then Dad bent over to pluck a small, disheveled flowering plant from the ground which looked similar to a dandelion. I watched as he carefully tried to save the roots as if to keep the plant as a whole. Then to my surprise, he handed it to me.

"Here you go B," he smiled softly, "something to take away with you. It would be a shame to let all life on Mars go."

Declan looked on the plant in curiosity as he put his arm about my shoulders, "it looks like a dandelion."

"Well now you know where dandelions come from." Vincent shrugged.

"I like it." I smiled on my present. "Thanks Dad."

"If you take it home, you could pot it inside your greenhouse to keep." He suggested.

"Let's get out of here, right now the temperature feels like an Alaskan winter!" My mother shivered. Then she moved closer to my father who was quick to put his arm about his mate to share his body heat with her.

"I feel like I'm about to faint coz I can't breathe properly!" My husband said uncomfortably.

We all took a last look about the dying planet with its' orange-hue sky, before my eyes settled lastly on the steaming-hot crater.

"Good bye, cruel world." I murmured.

Mum placed her hands on Dad and Vincent's shoulders who in turn, placed their hands on Declan's and mine. Then in another blinding flash of light, Mum instantaneously phased everyone back to the Alaska of our present. However when we reappeared, it wasn't the same day we left.

Instead my husband and I found it was the evening of three days later. We found ourselves standing on the Holy Grounds, by the edge of the river. The five of us stood behind the five Sacred Totems which a funeral pyre was burning in front of. The Tribal Elders were wearing the suede clothes of old and wearing the traditional face paint, as they led the tribe in the funeral chant.

Chiron stood with the Tribal Elders, dressed as they were. I spotted the Riverclaw family standing up the front of the crowd, staring tearfully at the wrapped body which burned on top of the pyre. Declan put a supportive arm about my waist, as Dad the same to Mum whilst Vincent stood by himself. We remained as such as we listened to the mournful singing to the steady drum beat.

"I hate that bloody funeral pyre," Vincent said bitterly, "I couldn't stand it when they put Phoebe on top of it."

We all nodded in silent agreement, especially since we had all lost someone.

"I won't miss it. Thank God Mum and Dad didn't have a funeral pyre and thank God Hunter or I won't either." My mother voiced her feelings and then she took hold of my arm. She said adamantly, "B don't have a Remembrance Ceremony for your father and I. We've talked about it and we don't want one."

Declan and I looked on my parents in surprise before he queried, "how are we supposed to stop the tribe if they want to have one?"

"You're a good cook," she gave my husband a grin, "just have our families over for dinner and tell them that way."

"Break the news while you break bread, or garlic bread." Dad smirked.

"You want us to just tell them that you slipped quietly into the night with no proper goodbyes?" I asked disappointedly.

"I think they already know, B." My father sighed. "Your mother's behavior with her brother's death, made our intentions pretty clear."

"Like crystal." Declan looked back towards Uncle Julian's funeral pyre.

We saw that the Riverclaw's had spotted us. Chiron, Phoenix and Stone gave a nod to acknowledge Mum had made it to her brother's funeral after all. Both Dad and Declan gave their fellow Werewolves a nod back.

"I think it's perfectly timed that we leave now." Vincent said melancholy whilst staring at the flames. "Departing at Phoebe's father's funeral seems appropriate since we're going to see Phoebe again shortly."

His angle showed just how much he still missed his human wife, which coincided with his previous words at how there was nothing left for him here. Vincent was well and truly ready to move on and be reunited with his loved ones. This made my heart hurt as my eyes watered non-stop. I could feel their upcoming departure pressing into my chest so hard, it still made it difficult to breathe.

"Your mother and I had started to pack up the house in preparation for our departure." My father tearfully looked my way. "Feel free to claim anything you see, or pass on. Since you already have a house, I've left the place to my cousin Jake Wisetail, as a Housewarming present. Then the house can be used for another young couple's first start in life."

Then he gave his mate a tender look as I guess they were remembering when they first moved in together. She gave him a loving smile in return.

"I remember our Housewarming like it was only yesterday. I remember our first month living together and how exciting and scary it was." My mother spoke in a strained voice which gave away her emotional state. Then she looked my way, "I remember giving birth to you, inside that house."

My throat constricted, which made me emit sobbing noises as I struggled to breathe. Declan was squeezing my hand so tightly he almost crushed it, as his eyes watered too.

"It's time, Jess." Our Calculator said solemnly. "Now take me to see my parents, wife and daughter."

Then Mum, Dad and I collapsed tearfully into each other's arms.

"I love you..." I bawled to my parents, "...I love you both so much!"

There are times where you might blurt out, "I love you," to an important person in your life, as a 'just in case' it may be the last thing you say to them? But when you know it's going to be the last time in this life you'll see that person, it's the most important thing you want to impart.

"I love you B," she sniffed, "and you know that you'll see us again, don't you?"

"I know Mum, I know." I cried.

"We'll look in on you from time to time." My father cupped my face to hold my tearful gaze. "When your Gran first went to the space time continuum, she was still able to watch over her family."

"I know Dad, I know." I sobbed.

As we were saying our goodbyes, my European Werewolf mate stepped up to my Calculator and offered him his hand.

"Say hi to Derik, Rachel, Michael, Blanche as well as my Mom and Dad for me." Declan said sadly.

"Will do." Vincent shook on it. "I'm sure they already know from where they are; but you'll see them again as a European Werewolf and a Circulator."

My husband's eyebrows rose in surprise at how he knew this, since we hadn't told anyone of our conversation at my grandparents' Remembrance Ceremony. However my Calculator 'knew' a lot of things which were unspoken.

My father openly cried as he released his hold on his daughter. Then he gently pushed me backwards into Declan's awaiting arms. He looked on him long and hard, like a telepathic conversation passed between them.

"Do you really have to ask?" My mate asked offended for some reason. "You still don't trust me, even now?"

"Yes I do, Declan." My father met his angry gaze. "But B's my only child, so give me a break."

"What was that?" My mother looked from her husband to her son-in-law, but both men dismissively looked away.

My parents now waved goodbye to our remaining relations. All of the Riverclaw's, Wisetail's, Sabre's and Elm's waved back, as the rest of the tribe looked on puzzled. Chiron stepped out of the circle of Tribal Elders to give them a final salute; he used old sign which was common in Native Alaskan tribes as he told the travelers to 'go in peace'.

Lastly, Mum placed her hands on both Vincent and Dad's shoulders and put them into phase with her for their final time.

Declan and I watched their see-through forms grow brighter and brighter, as their human shapes dissolved away. When their formations became blindingly bright, they changed into three perfect circles of light. The circular shaped lights hovered before us as the brightness they emitted was so great, it was as if three spotlights lit up the Holy Grounds. Their light even dwarfed the flames of Uncle Julian's funeral pyre.

In the background, I heard the gasps come from the tribe as they looked on in amazement. The drum beat stopped as did the singing whilst everyone stared at what three of their tribal members had turned into.

I couldn't be certain, but I sensed my parents' hesitation to leave their only child behind. I tried to be happy for them, so I managed out a smile whilst the tears were streaming down my face. This seemed to have worked as the perfect circles of light understood.

All three lights hovered higher and higher into the air, raising every single person's head as we all watched their departure. At around two hundred meters in elevation, but still emitting so much light that the Holy Grounds looked like it was daylight; the three took off! Abruptly the grounds were returned to darkness, as the lights disappeared into the starry sky.

I tried to watch for as long as possible, but the three lights became camouflaged amongst the stars as if they were celestial objects themselves. My eyes remained upwards, as I couldn't look away. Although I felt sorrow over their departure, a tiny yearning began to grow inside. I felt anticipation for when it would be my time and I would do that too. Becoming lost amongst the stars, what a seductive prospect...

"B?" My husband murmured into my ear as he was holding me tightly from behind.

Next, I felt his hands raise mine to remind me what I was still holding; the dandelion-like flower. There were still some small clumps of red soil clinging to the roots, of our little piece of Mars.

"Let's take it home and plant it inside the greenhouse." Declan cajoled. "Then how about I make up some fettuccine carbonara with garlic bread for dinner? I'm starved!"

I tittered softly as I found my European Werewolf mate's constant hunger comforting. His appetite represented the fact that at least there were some things in life which would never change.

Whilst carrying the Martian plant in my right hand, Declan's own tightly clasped my left. Then with our family and friends watching, he led the way past the Sacred Totems, as we walked around the large gathering. Hand-in-hand, we walked quietly all the way home.

~~~~~~

30th July 2225

I stood on the front veranda with my coffee whilst admiring my new garden on this glorious summer's afternoon. The warm breeze teased the skirt of the light cotton dress I was wearing, which was long with thin shoulder straps.

The short, thick grass almost glowed green in the warm sunlight. My multi-coloured tulips, daffodils and gerberas looked bright in their new garden plots. Our new Jacaranda Tree which sat pride of place in the middle of the front lawn dropped its purple flowers. It made it look like there was a patch of purple snow on the ground. Everything looked so serene and dare I say, surreal?

My new garden reminded me of a diary entry written by my great, great grandmother. Elisha once observed the ending of life in contrast to new life created; when she looked on a small child at an elderly person's funeral. Right now I could relate, as the garden symbolized a new chapter in my life contrasted against the old house, which represented the family members I had lost.

Elisha had attended the funeral of Mike Sabre's grandfather, a man by the surname of Stevens. It was the day that she found out that her boyfriend was the progeny of her first love Guy Robertson, from an old family tree in the Steven's bible. Then months later she found out that Mike Sabre was in fact the reincarnation of Guy Robertson.

When I died and saw Elisha and Mike/ Guy together in the space time continuum, I found out that my mate who was a relation of Mike Sabre; was the reincarnation of Captain Greyson whom was Guy Robertson's best friend. He had fought alongside him in the Battle of Plassy under Sir Clive of India. Declan Sabre's and my coming together seemed like a series of accidental coincidences when truly it was fate.
~~~~~~

Why did Declan's parents, Susan and Anthony Sabre search out the Lokoti in Alaska after World War Three? Because they were told to, in a letter from Mike Sabre. On the night of their arrival, Anthony Sabre died and a three year old Declan was turned into a European Werewolf by a man-eating monster which had left Russia in search of humans without radiation sickness. The Lokoti Werewolves battled the foreign Werewolf who had come onto their territory and one of the pack, Yule Elm also died that night.

Yule was the father of Ian and Grant Elm; Ian was Dad's best friend and his death activated Grant's Lokoti Werewolf DNA to take his father's place in the pack. When I too turned just prior to my 18th Birthday, Grant was chosen to be my husband by the pack and the Tribal Elders. My best friend Derik Sabre who was Declan's little brother had romantic designs on me, as did Declan but in secret. Declan as a European Werewolf, was told he may never take a human woman for a mate with the risk of harming her or turning her. Then the girl he loves, turns into a Lokoti Werewolf but it took my arranged marriage to Grant to separate me from Derik, which finally gave Declan his opportunity after Grant died.

A leads to B which results in C, or so Circulators and Calculators are taught in temporal causalities. I died when I was shot in the head with a silver bullet which was meant for Declan, whereupon I meet my mate's prior incarnation as Captain Greyson. When I'm healed partly thanks to my mate's regenerative blood as a European Werewolf, Declan and I are officially called mates in the eyes of our families and tribe. Now we were embarking on a new chapter of our lives as the Last Circulator and the Last European Werewolf in existence.

Looking on my new garden, it made me think how my life right now pictured this setting perfectly. The new garden was around an old house; the garden was a fresh start as I was the old house. Declan and I have been mates for 135 years and with our supernaturally long life spans, we would be mates for many more.

I went down the veranda steps, crossed the gravel driveway and walked onto the lawn. Here I paused to slip off my shoes, so my bare feet could feel the springy grass underneath. Whilst nursing my coffee mug, I wandered until I found myself standing under the blooming Jacaranda Tree.

Right at that moment, a purple flower fell from the tree to land 'splat!' into my coffee.

Well, would you look at that… I mean, what are the chances for it to land in my beverage like that? I thought the perfect timing complimented my previous thoughts on temporal causalities. I smiled at the irony, as I dipped my fingers into the liquid to remove my spontaneous gift. Next, I dropped the sodden flower onto the grass so it could join the hundreds of others.

Then my attention was taken away from a familiar sound. I turned to see Declan's metallic black, pick up truck come up the steep road and pull into our gravel driveway. He powered down the plasma engine and looked like he was about to jump out, when he paused.

Declan sat still for a moment to observe me standing underneath the Jacaranda Tree, as a soft smile formed on his lips. Then he climbed out and shut the door behind, whilst engaging the central locking mechanism. I watched him leave the driveway to walk towards me.

I greeted with a smile, "you're home from work early."

"Yeah well, now that I own the Garage I can come and go as I please." He grinned back.

My mate came to stand before me, when he momentarily looked up at the purple flowers in the tree before he looked back into my dark blue eyes.

"I like this tree." His grin grew wider.

"So I have good taste after all, when I put together the plants for our garden?"

"I never said you didn't have good taste," he leaned in to kiss my bare shoulder, "nor did I say that you didn't taste good either."

"OK," I laughed, "now you're being TOO charming, what do you want?"

"Well..." he drawled, "...I have a business proposition for you."

"A business proposition?"

"It's kinda like a business proposition, or maybe it's just a proposition that can affect your business."

I looked on warily. "Uh huh."

"You and I are mates."

"Yeah, the past 135 years can testify to that." I smirked.

"Right," he cleared his throat, "and the Lokoti know we're mates."

"Yeah, living together for the past 135 years could give them that idea." I went on humorously.

"But when you venture off tribal lands to do your guest lectures, outsiders won't know we're mates." He frowned.

Declan cleared his throat again as he pulled out something small from the inside pocket of his denim work jacket. I saw it was a red velvet box which he opened as he held it out. Inside sat three gold rings, one which had a diamond on top, as well as two plain.

"What are those?" I looked on curiously.

"This one..." he took out the diamond ring first, "... is an engagement ring." My mate raised my left hand to slide the diamond ring onto the finger next to my middle.

"An engagement ring?" I gave a peculiar look. "After 135 years of being mates you want to demote us to being 'engaged'?"

He ignored my protest as next he took out the smallest of the two plain gold rings. He retook hold of my left hand to slide the ring onto the same finger he had placed the 'engagement ring' on.

"And this is a wedding ring." He finished as I watched him take out the last ring in the box, which he put on the same finger on his left hand too.

"Now you don't have to keep showing your ID to strangers to prove that you're married."

"Wedding rings...?" I looked on as if he were nuts. "You want us to wear wedding rings?!"

I had only seen wedding rings on Gran and Grandfather's fingers, or even on Vincent and Pheobe's because they had a Christian Wedding Ceremony. However among the Lokoti, these accessories were scarce due to the fact there weren't many of those around here. If a guy and gal moved in together, they may have a Housewarming but that was it.

"Whenever we venture off tribal lands, people will see these rings and know that you're Mrs. Declan Sabre." He declared.

This made me wonder out loud, "then will everyone who sees your ring know you as Mr. Bianca Sabre?"

Declan cracked up laughing and he laughed so hard, he started to bow over.

"Yeah B, outsiders who see my wedding ring will know me as Mr. Bianca Sabre." He guffawed. "Speaking of which, what's a couple of wedding rings albeit 135 years late, without a second honeymoon?"

Next, I watched him pull out a folded-up document from his inside pocket again to hand over.

"This isn't a marriage certificate or anything, is it?" I asked warily as I took the papers from him.

"Shut up and open it, will you?"

I huffed as if this was asking a lot, whilst I proceeded to unfold the document. However as soon as I had straightened it out, my eyes widened as my mouth fell open. Declan smiled smugly when I started to jump up and down!

"We're going to Asia!" I squealed excitedly. "We're going to Asia!"

"Oh so THIS will get a reaction out of you, but not the expensive jewelry?" He laughed again. "We're booked in next summer for six weeks of sightseeing as we visit Japan, Korea, China, Vietnam, Cambodia and Thailand."

I dropped my coffee mug onto the grass when I leapt onto my husband! Declan easily caught me with his greater strength, as I wrapped my legs about his waist and my arms encircled his neck.

"Stick with me kid, I'll take care of you." He squeezed me back tightly.

Our mouths soon found the other's as our typical passion was ignited. I felt him sink to his knees and then lower me onto the soft grass underneath. It felt nice lying in the cool shade with his hot body over mine.

He mumbled with his mouthful, "you know B, we haven't exactly 'christened' this garden of ours yet."

"Er, Dec?" I worriedly looked about how we were out in the open, "I'm not so sure of this idea."

Since our house was at the end of a cul-de-sac on top of a steep hill, nobody drove past our place. But you never know when you're going to be surprised by visitors?

"It's OK, we've got wedding rings to show people now." He chuckled back before his mouth reclaimed mine.

~~~~~~
~~~~~~

~ Conclusion ~

1st September 2340

"This is ISF London Control Tower granting clearance to shuttlecraft Trekker." The female Air Traffic Controller's voice came through the ships' communication device. "Your flight plan has been logged and approved."

I programmed the co-ordinates into the shuttlecraft's computer as the vehicle lifted up into the air. The small shuttle levitated off the Trans Port pad before the retro-thrusters engaged. As soon as they did, I felt the slight jolt as the vehicle gunned over the United Kingdom.

"Trekker to London Control Tower, I'll see you in four hours." I reported back.

"Enjoy your flight, for all seventeen minutes of it." The Controller scoffed.

"Will do, Trekker out." I laughed back.

Once I was zooming over the Arctic Ocean towards Alaska, I engaged the auto pilot to let the shuttlecraft's computer do the rest.

To say I was feeling nervous would be an understatement. I looked down at my ISF uniform and hoped it wouldn't be too pretentious arriving in these clothes. I could have dressed as a civilian, but since my graduation ceremony as an Engineer in the International Space Fleet was yesterday? I wanted to greet my rellatives as such.

'To greet my rellatives', who am I trying to fool here? I've never been to Alaska as my family has never been inclined to. However after reading the diaries, I wanted to see it. I had to see for myself if these women or in particular one woman, really existed.

To just think, I could have a distant relation who was an actual time traveler; a real live Circulator! A woman who was over two centuries old and still alive, made the temptation too great to resist. I also wanted to see if she would recognize my name and acknowledge me as kin...Jarrod Worthall.

I was named after my forefather who married Elisha Baker, the woman who started a female lineage of Circulators and one male Calculator. Our family retained Blythe Castle and its large library. On one of its many shelves, sat Elisha's academic work and copies of her SSIT Reports she made with another ancestor in the family by the name of Xavier Bell. The two befriended each other at Cambridge University where they began Supernatural Scientific Investigative Team as a kind of 'social club'. When they graduated, they turned the club into a business venture. Elisha married the future Lord Worthall of Blythe Castle and Xavier married a French telepath by the name of Belle Dupont, whom he met on an SSIT investigation. Elisha's son and Xavier's daughter ended up marrying and reproducing more of my ancestors.

Until I read Elisha's diaries and then her daughter Alexandrina's and granddaughter Arabella's; I wouldn't have believed that Circulators or Calculators existed. When I read the SSIT reports of Elisha and Xavier's encounters with hauntings, ESP, reincarnation, werewolves and vampires; at first I thought it was the stuff of fiction. But the proof was there, my ancestors did exist and now I was on my way to see Bianca, who is Arabella's granddaughter. Bianca Sabre is reportedly 274 years old and is not only called the Last Circulator, but the first female Lokoti Werewolf.

Although the Worthall family didn't maintain contact with our Lokoti relatives, we did remain tight-lipped about their paranormal qualities. Besides, who would believe that we were descended from Circulators, Calculators, Telepaths or Werewolves? The library in Blythe Castle housed many a photograph album showing our family tree; Elisha and Jarrod's wedding, of Arabella and Emanuel Riverclaw's wedding, Julian Riverclaw's visits with Vincent and Phoebe Moher and their grandchildren. When a visitor inquired of our ancestors, we simply left out the part about their supernatural differences.

Bianca was reportedly married to a 277 year old European Werewolf named Declan Sabre. He was the great, great grand nephew of Mike Sabre, the first person ever to be transformed into a Circulator. I was about to meet history and this thought both intimidated as well as excited.

"Don't get your hopes up," my cynicism goaded, "who says this woman exists? But then if she does, what if you brazenly walk up and state your name, but she doesn't want to know you? I mean, why would she? You're such a distant relation, you'd be a stranger to her."

"Nonsense!" The other side of my brain argued back. "Look at where she's still living; on the tribal lands inside the Lokoti National Park. Family, tribe and loyalty is everything to these people."

The shuttlecraft zoomed over the icy North Pole and within minutes the landmass of Alaska appeared below. The auto-pilot slowed upon our approach of the Alaska Range. As I looked out the window I saw the river system and forest-encrusted, snow-tipped mountains give way to the small settlement of Lokoti tribal lands. My heart raced in excitement, as the shuttlecraft gently touched down upon the community centre's Trans Port.

As soon as the shuttlecraft powered down, I was out of my seat and opening the pressurized door. When I stepped out, I squinted in the bright light of the afternoon's sun. It was August which meant Alaska had its extended daylight during the summer.

As I walked off the Trans Port pad, I headed towards the small general store which was next to a garage. Gone were the days of petroleum run vehicles which would have been in Bianca and Declan Sabre's early years. Instead I saw two mechanics who appeared to be Lokoti, repairing a plasma-powered hover-car, using up-to-date equipment.

The general store was open, with Lokoti entering and exiting. I couldn't resist, I had to go inside to see where Arabella, then Jessica and maybe Bianca frequented. Plus this could be an opportunity to enquire if Bianca and Declan Sabre lived around here? I walked through the automatic glass door and then I stood back to wait as a pretty, teenaged girl was serving a middle-aged man and an elderly woman.

"There you go, Mr. and Mrs. Lightfoot." The girl smiled as she stacked the milk, bread and carton of eggs into a cotton carry bag. "Congratulations again on your 50th Anniversary! You take care now."

Did she just say 50th Anniversary, as in their WEDDING anniversary?! My eyes widened as I watched this mismatched couple depart, with the middle-aged man carrying the bag of food for the elderly woman. Could he be a...? I mean, she did say the couple had just celebrated their 50th anniversary so could this man be a Lokoti Werewolf?

My heart skipped a beat as I watched the husband and wife depart via the automatic glass door. The man in turn, threw a curious look over his shoulder my way. When my eyes nervously skipped away the tall, strong looking, long-haired man returned his attention to escorting his elderly wife.

"Hi there!" The Lokoti girl grinned as she looked me over. "That's an ISF uniform, isn't it?"

"What?" My attention was called back. "Ah yes it is."

"You're far from home," she laughed lightly, "we don't have any ISF bases in Alaska. What can I do for you?"

"I'm sorry, but did you just wish that couple a happy wedding anniversary?" I asked bewildered.

"Er," she looked uneasy as if she'd been caught out, "so how can I help you today?"

I saw how quickly she changed the subject, to protect the privacy of the couple. This made me blush, "I beg your pardon, it's none of my business I'm sure."

"I wouldn't worry about it!" She laughed it of. "So soldier you're far from home, is that an English accent?"

"Quite." I smiled. "I'm here to hopefully see a relative."

"Really?" She asked out of interest. "Say, what's your name?"

"It's er...." I hesitated incase it may be a mistake, "...Jarrod Worthall."

"Oh, as in the Worthall's of Blythe Castle?" Her face immediately lit up with recognition whereas my face was a mask of surprise at how she knew that. She went on, "you're related to the Riverclaw's! I bet you're here to see Bianca Sabre, aren't you?"

"Why um, yes." I stammered out in shock.

"You walk around the sports field and follow the road out of the community centre. When you come to the intersection, head towards the hill. You can't miss it, because it's the only hill that has any houses on it. You walk up the steep road and it's the very last house at the end of the cul-de-sac." The girl directed as she illustrated with several hand movements.

"Is that Bianca Sabre's house?" I asked in anticipation.

"Uh huh."

"Bianca Sabre, as in the daughter of Jessica Wisetail?" My eyes widened with hope.

"Yup."

"Bianca Sabre, as in the granddaughter of Arabella Riverclaw?" I wanted to clarify that I was hearing this right.

"The one and only." She laughed at my reaction.

"Thank you!" I cried out as I almost bolted out of the shop in excitement.

I hurriedly walked around the sports field next to the general store, where a group of youths were having a game of soccer. The boys played with their shirts off to keep cool and work on their tans, as I saw a small gaggle of girls sitting to watch. I left the community centre with its small streets and wooden houses as I followed the road towards the hill.

As I hiked up the steep road, I observed the hill was primarily encrusted with forest, with just a couple of houses in between. I remember reading how this road used to be dirt in Arabella's time. I saw either gravel or concealed driveways run towards old wooden houses, lovingly preserved with pretty gardens surrounding them.

Whilst I walked past the houses, I stopped to look up the driveways as I wondered whose house was whose? Which house did Arabella and Emanuel live in? Or, which house was Fern and Ling Wisetail's, or which house was it that Hunter prepared for Jessica Wisetail? All of the houses were either of log cabin design or constructed of wood, with stone chimneys and nestled by forest.

After walking for half an hour, I reached the top of the hill with its' cul-de-sac and there I saw it...a beautiful garden with a gravel driveway, surrounding a two story, dark brown painted wooden house. The building was as small as a cottage, with another stone chimney.

Before I could wonder if anyone was home, I heard a loud banging. My heart pounded as I nervously walked up the driveway as the banging got louder. When I looked up, I saw two men working on the roof.

One man looked to be a Caucasian in his fifties, with short, grayish-blonde hair and bright blue eyes. He was working alongside a young man of Lokoti appearance who appeared to be in his late teens. Together they were replacing rotten shingles, which amused me by the antiquated custom. These days, buildings had concealed roofs which never needed replacing. But the old house looked like it needed constant maintenance.

Just then the hammering stopped when the man in his fifties called down, "can we help you?"

The men were looking down suspiciously, particularly at my uniform. Suddenly my mouth turned dry as I didn't know what to say. Could this older man be Declan Sabre?

Next, the older man asked sarcastically, "comprende Anglaise?"

"Oh er, pardon me." I swallowed nervously. "But I'm looking for Bianca Sabre?"

The older man's eyes narrowed, "and what do you want with HER?"

Oh dear, this wasn't how I had imagined this would go...what do I say now?

"He smells a bit like B," the Lokoti youth said quietly to the older man.

Did he just say I SMELL like Bianca? I caught the older man also sniff, but he covered it up by wiping his nose like he had a cold or something.

"Yeah, he does a bit." The older man grumbled. "He could be one of those English relatives or something."

"He does smell English," the Lokoti youth nodded in agreement.

"B!" Abruptly the older man yelled out. "B!"

"What?!" I heard a woman shout back from inside the house.

"There's somebody here to see you!"

"What?"

"There's somebody HERE to see YOU!" The older man yelled impatiently.

"Alright already!" The woman returned in annoyance. "I'm coming!"

Just then the front door opened and a beautiful, tall woman with broad shoulders, long black hair and dark blue eyes came out. She stood on the veranda, wiping her hands on a tea towel whilst staring at my ISF uniform just as I stared back. She looked like she could have been the same age as me. My heart raced at her attractiveness yet my stomach sank in disappointment.

This can't be her...she's too...young?

Her gaze settled on my face as she enquired, "yes?"

"Bianca Wisetail Elm Sabre?" I gulped.

She looked on in surprise, "yes?"

"He's an English relative." The older man called down from the roof.

"Thanks Declan, like I wouldn't have been able to work that out for myself!" She rolled her eyes.

"Yeah well, the guy seems to be having a hard time getting anything out of his mouth." The older man scoffed, making the younger one laugh.

"Don't encourage him Derik." Bianca called to the youth before she smiled my way, "you look like a Worthall."

"Why yes I am."

She looked over my uniform once more, "are you a pilot, a doctor or an engineer in ISF?"

My eyes widened further in surprise, "I'm an engineer."

"Figures."

I wondered out loud, "how did you know that?"

"Most men in your family usually end up in one of those professions." She smirked. "So, what's your name?"

I swallowed harder as my throat constricted, "er Jarrod...my name is Jarrod Worthall."

"I'm surprised you didn't end up as a doctor with a name like that." Bianca giggled.

Then she turned around and held open the front door to imply that I should come in.

"B," her husband called down to her, "can Derik and I get a couple of sodas?"

"Sure you can!" She scoffed. "You've never had to ask my permission before when you've used the fridge."

"Hey!" The older man complained. "We're up here, busting our asses repairing YOUR roof!"

"I said that you should have used roof concealer instead of more wooden shingles." She sung. "Then you wouldn't be back up there, fixing the damn thing again."

"Wooden shingles add appreciation to the property!" He snapped.

"If we put down roof concealer, we wouldn't have to fix the damn thing every ten years!" She retorted before she walked into the house after me.

I entered what looked to be a cozy living area which had country-style pine furniture, overstuffed couches and many photographs as well as antique ornaments about the place.

The ornaments looked to be international, coming from many different countries from long ago eras. There was a small jade Chinese mask, sitting next to a colourful porcelain Venetian mask. A display cabinet by the dining table held Ancient Greek pottery as well as several other expensive knick-knacks from Earth's history. There was a huge Ming Dynasty vase sitting on the floor next to the cabinet with dried sunflowers sticking out of it. Amongst the valuable trinkets, were framed family photos.

Bianca stood back and watched, as I walked up to the mantle piece over the fireplace which was completely covered with photographs.

I recognized wedding photos of Elisha and Jarrod, then of Alexandrina and Scott and even of Arabella and Emanuel, but curiously they were the only wedding photos on display. Then there were photos of couples, such as Elisha with Mike. I looked on a picture of a baby in Jessica's arms whilst Hunter as the proud father, had his arms about the two. There was also a photo of Bianca and a younger looking Declan, with the Louvre behind them indicating a visit to Paris.

I picked up a photo of an unknown man who looked a lot like Mike Sabre, posing with a pretty Lokoti woman and two kids beside them.

"Who is this?" I asked.

"That was Declan's little brother Derik and his wife Rachel, with their kids Michael and Blanche." She sighed wistfully. "The young man you saw up on the roof helping Declan, is Derik's descendent also named Derik. Declan's little brother became one of our tribe's Medicine Men as he was a gifted healer."

"Oh." I marveled over the family resemblance between Derik and Mike. "His descendant up on the roof said that I smelled English, is he a Lokoti Werewolf?"

Bianca's eyebrows rose at my enquiry, as I think my knowledge of the supernatural quality of some of the members of the tribe surprised her.

After a moment she answered, "yes he's one of the pack. Blanche married Stuart Elm and henceforth almost all the eldest sons in her line were Lokoti Werewolves."

From looking at the family tree on display, I noticed there were no other photos of her English relatives after the group shot of Vincent, Phoebe and Penelope.

"Do you have anything more recent of your English relatives?" I queried.

"No, as I haven't visited Blythe in over fifty years. I lost touch with your family." She sighed before she changed the subject, "would you like a coffee or tea or a soda or something?"

"A tea would be lovely." I smiled back appreciatively.

I watched her turn to go into the kitchen to procure this. I followed her to the entranceway where I watched her switch on a kettle and prepare two mugs putting in each a teabag of Earl Grey. Since I was used to a food synthesizer which generated my meals and beverages; I smirked at their further antiquated customs. I think it would be safe to say that the Lokoti were used to living a certain way of life.

"Are any of your relatives still telepaths?" Bianca asked as she worked.

"No." I answered as I leant on the wall. "My sister has an uncanny knack in reading people's faces, but the telepathy has been bred out of us I'm afraid."

"That's a pity," she sighed before smiled, "I remember how my cousin used to get a real kick out of embarrassing people she disliked by using her ability on them. I think Phoebe's daughter Penelope was the last to have it. After Penelope, the telepathy was watered down to empathy but it's nothing to what my aunt or cousin had."

I looked on in wonder at this seemingly young woman talk about my ancestors like she had only seen them yesterday.

"Do you know why it was only the females in Belle Dupont's lineage who were telepaths?" I asked.

"Why is it usually the males in this tribe who become Lokoti Werewolves?" She shrugged. "Some supernatural abilities are just like that, I guess."

"Except you, as you were the first female to become a Lokoti Werewolf." I smirked, but then I froze as I saw her pause mid tea preparation. Oh dear, I haven't over-stepped the boundary, have I? Hastily I added on, "I beg your pardon, I certainly didn't mean any offence."

"No offence taken." She flashed a smile as she started up again. "How do you take your tea?"

"With lemon please."

"Lemon?" She echoed whilst she turned around to open her fridge and look inside. "I don't have any actual lemons but I do have lemon juice?"

"Then as is would be fine, thank you."

Bianca handed me my cup and then I followed her into the lounge room where she carried her own and we sat down on separate couches.

"You know since my change, there hasn't been anymore female Lokoti Werewolves created." She frowned.

"Really?" My eyebrows rose in partial surprise. "So not only are you the Last Circulator, but you are the only female Lokoti Werewolf?"

"Yes."

Right at that moment, her husband walked in through the front door. He paused to look on us sitting there, sipping our tea. He complained, "aw, where's mine?"

"I didn't know you would be joining us." She shrugged.

"Man, I have to do EVERYTHING around here!" He whinged as he walked into the kitchen and we heard him open up the refrigerator.

When he walked back into the lounge room, he was carrying a small bottle of soda. I watched him flop tiredly onto the couch beside Bianca. Casually, he put up his feet onto the coffee table as well as his arm about his wife.

"Where's Derik?" She asked.

"He went home." He answered. "Uma called him in."

"Oh, you mean she called him via mobile phone?" I queried.

"Nope, she just called him." Declan said simply.

"Oh and where does Derik live?" I asked.

"Derik and Uma live in the community centre." He shrugged.

I frowned as I pondered on how this was possible, as the couple exchanged amused glances.

"Yes, Derik heard Uma call his name all the way up here, from the community centre with his supernatural hearing." She thought she should clarify.

"Oh right." I tried not to show my surprise.

"So you're an English relative, huh?" Declan moved the conversation along.

"Yes." I answered.

"And you're an engineer in ISF?" He went on.

"Yes, I've just graduated from the academy and I leave for my first posting tomorrow." I told them.

"Where are you going?" She asked out of interest.

"I've been assigned to the USS Darwin."

"Oh cool, you'll meet Purto!" Her eyes lit up.

This made my own eyes widen in surprise yet again, "you know Commander Purto?"

"He's a Circulator." She announced.

"He's a Circulator?" I echoed in astonishment. "But I thought other than yourself, there were no more Circulators because they've evolved to the space time continuum?"

"They did." She said chirpily. "You'll meet the Purto of the past, on one of his many time travels. He enjoyed visiting the 24th Century."

"But I wouldn't rock up and blurt out in a crowded room, 'so how's the Circulate going?' if I were you." He smirked.

"No of course not." My face flushed. "Oh yes, now I recall reading in Elisha's diary of a conversation she had with Purto and he told her he was in ISF."

"That's him," Bianca beamed before she turned to Declan, "I'm tempted to seek out other Circulators in the different time periods they used to visit."

"Why?" He gave his wife a funny look.

"Why not?" She shrugged back.

"How long would you be away for?" He didn't look happy at the idea.

"I don't know, a couple of days?" She shrugged again.

"No." He said firmly.

"What do you mean, no?" She asked unimpressed.

"For one, it's a full moon tonight so there's the hunt. Two, it could be dangerous. Do you remember what happened to you the last time you saw Purto?" He ranted.

But Bianca didn't buy it, as she passed a small smile my way, "we've just celebrated our 250th Wedding Anniversary and we've never been apart for more than 24 hours."

"Your 250th Wedding Anniversary?!" I gawked at the pair. "How have you remained married for so long? These days couples celebrate a five year anniversary as if it were their golden jubilee!"

"It hasn't been easy, I can tell you!" Declan rolled his eyes. "If I'm not chasing away other men because of her pheromones and youthful looks; I'm keeping away supernatural creatures who try to either feed on or claim her!"

"Stop exaggerating Declan!" She shook her head as she turned away.

"Exaggerating?!" Her older husband exhorted. "What about the time you were kidnapped by the European Werewolf, Marcus? Or when you were attacked by the European Vampires or even the South American ones?"

"At least you never got called a prostitute!" She retorted.

I almost choked on my tea when she said that! "You were called a prostitute?"

"It was during one of our trips around Europe." She put her tea down to tell the story. "When we were staying in a hotel in Paris... oh, what was it called? You know, the restored one which used to be a Royal Residence before the French Revolution."

"Hotel de Crillon." He put in as he sat back and smilingly listened to his pretty wife tell the story.

"Yes, so we're staying at the Hotel de Crillon and we're...you know, behaving as most married couples do." She inferred which made me snicker.

"But according to this human, married couples don't seem to be doing this anymore." Her husband chuckled as he took a swig from his soda bottle.

"Shut up!" She slapped his thigh. "You're jumping ahead of the story."

"Sorry." He apologized as he affectionately held her closer.

"When out of the blue we're interrupted by this knock on the door." She blushed. "Declan answered it with a sheet wrapped around his waist and he's half hidden behind the door to talk to the people on the other side. It was a hotel employee who came to tell us to keep the noise down, as a neighboring guest made a complaint."

"The guest complained it sounded like a dog fight going on with all of the banging and growling he heard. The hotel employee asked us if we had any animals which we didn't check-in." Her husband smirked. "Then he asked if he could take a look inside to make sure that we haven't trashed the place."

"I could tell Declan was getting angry as he raised his voice to the employee and the male guest standing beside him. So I quickly wrapped a towel about myself to speak to them and calm the situation."

"Big mistake!" Her husband snorted.

"The hotel employee sees this bloody bite mark on my shoulder and next he threatens to call the police on Declan for assault and battery!" She burst into laughter.

"So B had to show them I had one too, on my shoulder which was hidden behind the door." He smilingly shook his head. "The look on that hotel employee's face, it was as if he sprung a sadist-masochist orgy or somethin'."

His wife giggled along, "the employee got all embarrassed and apologized before he asked if we could please keep the noise down."

"Then the guest beside him, who's this middle aged, overweight business executive, gives B a good look up and down and asked her what she charges." He growled angrily. "I told this loser I would punch his lights out if he ever referred to my wife like that again! Then he scoffs, 'son I've been married for 12 years and I KNOW from the amount of noise you two are making that that's not how married people behave! So how much does the woman charge?'"

Bianca laughed with a red face, "I was scared Declan was about to change to literally bite the man's head off! He certainly surprised them with the threatening growl he emitted! But because of what this middle aged, sex-starved guest said, the employee apologized for the offence and threw in complimentary room service for the incident."

"Free five-star food..." her husband smiled mischievously, "...I was tempted to use you on the other middle aged men in the hotel, to see if we could get more."

"Shut up!" She whacked him harder on his thigh.

I laughed at the pair with their fiery chemistry, as it amazed me it had lasted for so long. The way the husband with his appearance of a built-up man in his fifties regarded his younger looking wife, was full of admiration and love. I saw the same in Bianca as she smiled teasingly at her mate of 250 years.

"Where else have you traveled to?" I asked with interest.

"I think the question is where HAVEN'T we traveled to." He corrected.

"After my parents left for the space time continuum, every two years or we traveled." She advised.

"The UK, Europe, Asia, South America, South Africa, Australia, New Zealand, North America, Canada, Hawaii...you name it? We've probably been there." He shook his head wearily.

"So I guess the rule that Lokoti Werewolves are tied to their hunting grounds didn't stop you then." I remarked.

"Our holidays were never more than six weeks, as we had to return to hunt." She confirmed.

"We couldn't be away for more than one full moon." He frowned. "Anything longer than that aggravated the bloodlust."

I had to admit, listening them to talk about the dangerous side of their nature, made me feel uneasy. It compounded the fact that I was sitting in a room with two supernatural creatures whose kind were known as man-eaters.

"So," I changed the subject, "did you encounter anything else supernatural on your travels?"

Declan scoffed, "traveling with this woman, it was a given!"

"Here we go again!" Bianca rolled her eyes. "It's my fault for having the aura of a Circulator and the pheromones of a female Lokoti Werewolf."

"What happened?" I asked intrigued.

The older European Werewolf said in annoyance, "in China we ran into a clan of Asian Werewolves who tried to kidnap B, to repopulate their species."

His wife stared uncomfortably into her tea cup, "that was until I called out that I couldn't breed and they broke off their pursuit."

"So it's true," I frowned, "you're not just a rarity being a female Lokoti Werewolf, you're a rarity for being a female Werewolf at all."

"I'm one of the few remaining female Werewolves left in the world." She said flatly.

"We came across a North American Werewolf who also tried to get its claws into her." He said unhappily. "Then in New Orleans a Voodoo Witch Doctor tried to cut us up to sell off our parts on the black market."

My eyes bulged when I heard this, "did you come across anything nice in your travels, in the supernatural world?"

"When we toured Scotland we met a nice Wiccan named Nairn." She smiled on the memory. "For somebody who wasn't a Calculator, she was a gifted 'seer'. She postured it could have been fate which made me unable to conceive, especially with so few female Werewolves in the world."

"Nairn had a point," he sympathetically rubbed her back, "you being unable to conceive probably protected you in more ways than one. As soon as the Asian Werewolves found out you couldn't breed, they stopped their pursuit."

"That and because they didn't like the size of you when you change." She gave him a small smile.

"The night we were in the Chinese countryside and surrounded by Asian Werewolves, they saw me as a threat but you turned into a vendetta. It wasn't until you yelled out you were barren that they broke off their attack." He disagreed.

"Alright, so you didn't scare off the Asian Werewolves but you did annihilate the North American Werewolves. You were twice their size and strength and you obliterated them." Bianca looked on her mate proudly.

I frowned in confusion, "why didn't you just instantaneously phase out of danger? I read that you, your mother and grandmother could do this. Why did you fight your way out of these situations?"

"It's a territorial thing." Declan explained. "Once the predator gets the scent of a perspective mate or prey, it pursues. The male Asian Werewolves would have followed B all the way back to tribal lands which would have put all of the tribe in danger. By dealing with the situation then and there, it was claiming the dominant position and ending the pursuit."

"So anything and everything supernatural sought the two of you out, wherever you went?" I asked concerned.

"B's aura as a Circulator can be seen by Shape Shifters or humans with ESP. When you include her pheromones, she's a three course gourmet dinner to a predator. No matter where we went, if there was something else supernatural there? They spotted her immediately like there was a bright neon sign over her head." He spoke whilst keeping a possessive arm about his mate.

"But it wasn't ALL bad." Bianca admitted. "Aside from the Wiccan we met in Scotland, we met other people with ESP in Peru. They imbibed Yaje to become one with the Puma spirit, who was an important religious figure in their culture."

"That was cool," he smiled fondly, "we took part in their hunting ceremony. They called Werewolves 'spirits of the father wolf' and on a night of the full moon, we hunted with humans who were 'one with the mother Puma'."

"Are you talking about actual possession?" My mouth fell open in shock.

"Yup." He smirked at my surprise. "Their eyes glowed yellow and looked feline. When they were 'one' with the Puma spirit, their strength and speed increased and they even saw better in the dark."

"We became honorary members of their tribe." Bianca looked proudly on her mate once more, "especially after Declan destroyed that small coven of South American Vampires who had been preying on them."

"MORE Vampires?" I sat up straighter. "How many are there in this world?"

"Don't ask." He said sourly. "They spread like disease, as there are more species of Vampires in the world than there are breeds of Werewolves."

"Yes, I read about a couple of the different species in Elisha's SSIT Report." I said seriously as I put down my empty cup.

Bianca continued, "the Shaman we stayed with in Peru came up to Alaska to meet the pack and our Tribal Elders. An alliance was formed between our people which still lasts today. That was nice, kinda becoming goodwill ambassadors like that."

"Elisha's work with SSIT lives on then, by seeking out elements of the supernatural and bringing it altogether." I observed.

"We remained in contact with Nairn for the rest of her life." She nodded. "She came to visit a couple of times, too. She and our previous Medicine Man named Meadow, would exchange recipes for poultices or other herbal remedies. Nairn was a respected midwife and healer in her town. She could 'see' what was wrong with a person, so she knew how to treat them."

"Is that why she told you that you weren't meant to conceive?" I wondered.

She frowned, "I was tempted to ask her for a fertility spell, but I knew she was right. The major factor of my inability to have children was related to being the Last Circulator."

"Why, because if you had a child it could also become a Circulator?" I guessed.

"Maybe." She sighed sadly as she leaned into her husband's side and his arm about her tightened. "I had a vision of my great grandmother telling me that I'm the last on the line."

"So am I because when I depart, there won't be anymore European Werewolves in the world." Declan declared.

"You're the last of your kind as well?" I looked on the older man taken aback.

"If I had kids I would be creating more European Werewolves." He glared upon the idea. "I still struggle with my bloodlust every full moon and I'm 277 years old. I've never turned a human as I refuse to create anymore of my kind. So I don't know how I'd cope stopping a child of mine from becoming a killer. B is my perfect mate because I don't have to worry about that."

Then the two looked on each other in absolute adoration which made me look away uncomfortably. To busy myself, I stood up to cross over to their framed photo collection on top of the mantle piece again.

As I looked on the photos of Emanuel Riverclaw as well as Hunter Wisetail, I queried; "when your grandfather and father left the pack, were two new Lokoti Werewolves created?"

"Yup." Declan replied first. "When Uncle Em evolved with Aunt Arabella, a new Lokoti Werewolf was created to take his place. The same thing happened when Hunter left with Jess and Vincent."

"Their departures were treated like a death within the pack and tribe." Bianca explained. "I guess in human terms they did end their biological existences to live for all eternity in a place where human souls temporarily rest in. Although there were no bodies to put on top of a funeral pyre, the tribe still held a service for Gran and Grandfather to wish them well in their new existence."

"Does this mean that their names are on headstones in a cemetery somewhere?" I asked out of curiosity.

"No, the Lokoti don't have burial grounds." He shook his head. "Their funeral rites involve cremating the body and then scattering the ashes into the river. The Lokoti believe at some stage the deceased will come back later in the timeline which the river represents, like reincarnation."

"Have the Lokoti always believed that?" I asked. "Elisha wrote something similar in her SSIT Report on Reincarnation."

"The tribe has always believed in reincarnation." She confirmed. "They call the space time continuum the 'Holy Hunting Grounds'. It was because of Elisha's similar beliefs and for calling her a 'Light Person', the tribe allowed her to study the Lokoti Werewolf."

"Then how are your departed remembered?" I asked disappointedly.

I was starting to worry that aside from these photos or the diaries I'd read, there was no other testament to Arabella's and Jessica's remarkable lives. I had seen Jarrod's, Bastian's, Yvette's and the other Worthall's headstones at Blythe. But how were Arabella and Jessica remembered or how could people pay their respects?

The couple exchanged a long look then after a moment, they too stood up.

"I suppose we could show him." He shrugged.

"I think it's what he's alluding to." She shrugged back.

"Show me what?" I queried.

Mysteriously, the two crossed over to where I was standing to each lay a hand on my shoulder. Abruptly I was blinded by a bright flash of light! I blinked quickly to recover my sight when next I stared in astonishment. Their living room had been replaced by a peaceful, grassy glade next to a river.

My word...I was instantaneously phased here! I was moved from indoors to outdoors within the blink of an eye and I hardly felt a thing. Well alright, I did feel a rush of warmth and a little tingly for a second. Now my eyes strained as they had to readjust to the bright afternoon sun.

I tried to get my bearings as I looked about. I saw a road ran past which went towards the distant houses of the Lokoti community centre, letting me know I was still on tribal lands. The grass in the glade was mown, which was contrasted by the surrounding wilds of the Alaska Range. However what was in the middle of the glade was the main attraction, as there stood seven tall, brightly painted Totem Poles.

"This way," Declan nodded towards them.

I followed the husband and wife team around the back of the Totems. Then Bianca pointed towards the surface of one Pole in particular and I caught on to their meaning. On the back of the seven Totem Poles was a long list of engraved names, dates and small pictures of different animals.

My eyes widened as I read off the names; ARABELLA RIVERCLAW B 2028 D 2195/ EMANUEL RIVERCLAW B 2028 D 2195 and beside their names, was an engraving of a bear.

I read onwards until I found, JESSICA WISETAIL B 2047 D 2225/ HUNTER WISETAIL B 2045 D 2225 and beside their names, was an engraving of an owl. Below their names, I saw VINCENT MOHER B 2043 D 2225 and beside his name was an engraving of a bear. On the Totem beside it, I read off the engraved names and dates of Anthony Sabre, Susan Sabre, Derik Sabre, Rachel Sabre and with them was a picture of a European Werewolf.

"Your family?" I looked to Declan, who gave a curt nod before he looked away whilst blinking hard.

Bianca stood closer to her mate as he in return, put an appreciative arm about her waist.

I turned back towards the Totem to look on all of the names of the Lokoti who were remembered here. These Totem Poles seemed to serve as seven massive headstones for the dearly departed. It was poetic when you think about it; on the front of the poles were the carved and painted icons of tribe's animal spirit guides. Then on the back, were the names of people who now resided in the spirit realm with their guides.

"These are the Holy Grounds." She explained. "In legend, this was where the Lokoti Wolf gave up his life and blood to the Warrior Aru, who became the first Lokoti Werewolf. At first there was one Sacred Totem, then the one became three, the three became five and now we have seven Sacred Totems."

My eyes widened as a feeling of awe settled upon me. I walked over to the Totem in the middle to see other engravings which weren't in English, indicating how old it was. I felt like I was truly part of something, standing here in such a place of history. Usually I only felt like this when I visited the Worthall family's headstones at Blythe. The family plot was on the edge of the grounds on the west side of the castle.

Then I wandered back over to the fifth Totem and with reverence, I reached out my hand to touch the engraved name of Arabella Riverclaw. This instilled a sense of belonging seeing my distant relations as part of the tribe. The Lokoti were my distant relations, just as Bianca Sabre was. I felt like I was just as much home here, as I was at Blythe Castle.

I turned back around to ask, "Elisha has a headstone at Blythe, just as Alexandrina and Scott Carmichael do as our family's way of remembering them. But tell me, do you know how Mike Sabre is remembered? He evolved with Elisha, Alexandrina and Scott didn't he?"

"There's a headstone in Indianapolis for Dr. Michael Sabre. It's beside his brother's headstone in the name of Anthony Sabre, the namesake of my father." He advised. "My family didn't know he was a Circulator until we came to live here. When Mike visited his older brother who was my great, great grandfather; he would make himself look older with the passing of time. When World War Three erupted, he left with the Circulate in the Final Phase. But he also left my father a letter telling him to bring his young family to live with the Lokoti. Mike Sabre knew we would be safe here from fall out and looting. The Lokoti took us in, thanks to Arabella and Emanuel Riverclaw."

"Then the night you arrived on tribal lands, your family was attacked by a European Werewolf." I remembered the entry in Jessica's diary. "The monster killed your father and turned you with its bite."

Declan gave another curt nod, as he frowned at the engraving of his parents names and the picture of the European Werewolf beside them. I saw that his memories of the event were still bitter, which would also explain his resolution to never create anymore of his kind. I think so did Bianca, who affectionately rubbed her nose against his neck, to make her mate chuckle.

I saw this was how the two coped with the loneliness a long life can bring; by each other. It would explain why the two were quite close, they were not only lovers, but they were friends as well as each other's family. They had to be.

"If you don't mind me asking…" I looked curiously on the two, "…are you both going to eventually evolve to the space time continuum too?"

"Eventually." He answered.

I studied the aging European Werewolf before asking, "but not yet?"

"Not yet." His mate smiled softly. "We'll leave when the time is right.

I swallowed nervously, "then if that's the case, may I come back to visit again?"

He chuckled at my unease which he thought was amusing, "we would think you were rude if you didn't."

A brief laugh of relief escaped at how they welcomed the stranger who abruptly arrived on their doorstep and how quickly they saw or smelled I was family.

*****

We departed the Holy Grounds and Declan and Bianca walked me back to the Trans Port, where my ISF shuttle was waiting.

As we three strolled into the community centre, we talked constantly. I told them about my upcoming mission the USS Darwin was assigned to; exploring a nearby galaxy to assess it for colonization. They both listened with interest, however I noticed Bianca's eyes sparkle to hear about space travel.

"Since the two of you have traveled all over Earth, maybe you should think about vacationing off world before you evolve." I joked.

"I can't." He said gruffly. "The Earth's moon plays an important role with a Werewolf's physical being as well as our psyche. I don't know how it would affect our bloodlust being on a planet which had two moons or even five. We might have to constantly hunt to placate the bloodlust."

"Hmm," I frowned, "I see your point."

"We'll have ample time to see the universe when we evolve." She shrugged it off. "But until that happens, we're quite happy remaining on Earth a little longer. Besides, not all of our travels have been in this era."

"Really?" I listened with interest.

Declan looked on his wife proudly, "B's an Ancient History and Mythology Professor."

"Yes I've read your work, Bianca." I smiled her way. "I found several of your papers in the Holy Spirit College Library at Cambridge University."

"I didn't know the University still had them." She said in surprise.

"It certainly does!" I laughed at her modesty. "When I was researching you before I came, I found several Universities around the world has copies of your papers."

"Cool." She giggled abashed. "As you can tell by my publishing them under different surnames over the years, I've been at it for a while."

"Jarrod?" He called back my attention.

"Yes?"

"Quit with the Bianca crap." He lightly scolded. "Since you'll be visiting on a regular basis, she's known as B. Only outsiders call her Bianca."

"Sorry, B it is." I grinned. "Does this mean you're known as 'D' then?"

"Only if you want me to eat you," the European Werewolf said shortly.

B burst into laughter when she saw my smile disappear.

"He's kidding!" She poked me in the side before she whacked her mate on the arm. "I told you your temper is scarier than mine!"

"It's just because the kid isn't psychic." He argued back. "When you were battling that Voodoo Witch Doctor in New Orleans? He was ducking for cover!"

"Yeah right!" She scoffed.

"When this girl gets angry, sparks come flying off her aura and she can make the temperature drop as well as lights flicker." He warned.

"I believe you." I smiled again as I recalled reading something similar in Elisha, Alexandrina and Arabella's diaries.

The couple escorted me onto the Trans Port pad. They stood back to watch me enter the security code into the shuttlecraft's hatch controls. When the pressurized door opened, I turned back to look on the supernatural pair once more.

"Thank you for your hospitality." I offered them my hand.

"Like I said, don't be a stranger." Declan shook it in his much stronger grip.

"When you're on leave, you have to come and visit again." B smiled and instead of shaking my hand, she placed a kiss on my cheek.

However as soon as she did, I was suddenly hit by a delicious aroma of something sweet and warm like freshly baked butterscotch pudding. My eyes widened as I inhaled deeply and my heart even began to pound. The close proximity of her scent and high body temperature made me want to put my arms about her...

"Hey hey hey!" He quickly pulled his mate away. "B, don't overwhelm the poor guy!"

"Sorry." She instantly blushed.

Were THOSE the famous pheromones I'd heard about this afternoon?

"I can see why you're so popular." My face burned in embarrassment.

"Tell me about it!" Her older husband vented. "The woman with her aura and her pheromones certainly keep me busy."

"Shut up!" She whacked her mate on the arm again. "Your temper keeps me busy! How many excuses have I made for you over the years when your green-eyed monster came out?"

"Metaphorically or literally?" I snickered.

"Both." They answered automatically.

"Well," I sighed a little disappointedly, "I guess now is the time I should depart."

"So long then," Declan said as he replaced his arm about his wife.

"Drive safely." B smiled warmly.

"Will do, the ship's auto pilot is a good driver." I joked, making them laugh again.

The pair moved back as I disappeared into the shuttlecraft and the pressurized door automatically closed behind.

I returned to the pilot's chair where I entered in the ignition sequence into the computer. The shuttlecraft's engines powered up as I sat back into my seat. When the vehicle slowly lifted into the air, I looked out the window to see the couple standing still to see me off. I gave one last wave which they returned, as the shuttlecraft turned in mid air.

Once I was twenty meters from the ground, the shuttlecraft zoomed out of Lokoti airspace. I had to hit the control to dim the front window from the glare of the Alaskan sun and then I settled back as I smiled to myself.

This afternoon turned out to be all I had hoped for and more. I met two people who were just as much part of the natural as they were in the realm of the supernatural. But most importantly, they made me feel like I was family. Indeed, it was almost like the tribe did, as I recalled the pretty Lokoti girl who worked in the store and recognized my name.

The awe I felt whilst standing in the Holy Grounds stayed with me. I momentarily closed my eyes as I remembered the feel of the old wood beneath my fingertips, like I had actually touched history itself. I couldn't wait to tell Mum and Dad and my sister Elisha tonight, at my farewell dinner back at Blythe.

~~~~~~
~~~~~~

SSIT Report On Reincarnation

With Circulate Amendments

On The Reoccurrence Of Human Energy Signatures In The Timeline

First SSIT Report Compiled By Elisha Worthall & Dr. Xavier Bell. Amendments By Patrick O'Flannigan, Genevieve Nelson, Sally Parsons and Vincent Moher

INTRODUCTION

Throughout human history, there have been theorizations, postulations, speculations and examinations in either religious or scientific circles on the concept of reincarnation.

In Christianity, the most significant example of reincarnation would be Jesus Christ, with the story of his arising from the grave or even the prophecy of his second coming. In Buddhism, it is to be expected for a person to live and then relive again. Another example would be certain Native American Tribe's belief that a person's spirit will be reborn whereby they give a newborn the name of a deceased. Different scientific communities have interviewed humans who have claimed to have experienced déjà vu from visiting a place they have never been before, or have given accurate accounts without evidence of any prior study which can explain their knowledge on a subject. The most famous example of this was the case of 'The Search for Bridey Murphy'; where a woman whom lived in the United States in the 1950's was able to recant life in Ireland in the 1800's through hypnosis with parts of her testimony both disputed or confirmed to be true.

In the human quest for the so-called 'meaning of life', often the subject of the 'after life' is raised. There are certain religions who believe a human is only granted two lives; the biological and then the spiritual. Wars have repeatedly been fought over people's beliefs however the curiosity remains; what happens to a human when they die? In the search for the after life, humans have either visited hypnotists to look for any past life remnants in their subconscious, or have visited psychics who can see into the past or future.

When the Circulator Elisha Baker, continued her work on SSIT – Supernatural Scientific Investigative Team – after graduating from University; her SSIT notes compiled on Extra Sensory Perception then led to the concept of reincarnation, which was previously visited in Circulate studies. Elisha Baker met several psychics and one telepath whom immediately 'sensed' she was a Circulator and therefore a time traveler.

When Elisha Baker and Xavier Bell were permitted to participate in Dr. Dystar's study of ESP and other modes of 'seeing' through time; an exchange of information took place. In return, not only did the telepath Belle Dupont accurately read the Circulator's mind about her travels, but several of Dr. Dystar's psychic subjects could recant information about her romantic attachment to an 18th Century English Royal Navy Captain, Sir Guy Robertson.

Calculators within the Circulate have postured the idea that certain people or their energy signatures, were attracted to other energy signatures in the timeline. However, reincarnation was only ever a vague theory in the Circulate, until Elisha Baker and Xavier Bell's research into this topic. What fascinated the Circulate's best scientific minds in the forms of its Calculator's; was the particular emphasis on Elisha Baker's personal experiences with this subject.

On two separate occasions, Elisha Baker came into contact with familiar energy patterns. The first was Guy Robertson, whom Elisha Baker discovered came back as the reincarnation of Mike Sabre. Like magnets attracting each other, the energy signature of Guy Robertson managed to seek out Elisha Baker's bio-electromagnetic frequency in his reborn self. In this form, the subject who grew up in Indianapolis in the United States and graduated from Medical School; accepts an internship at Royal Prince Alfred Hospital in Sydney, Australia. Like a positive charge attracting a negative charge, Elisha Baker who is an Australian, met Mike Sabre when she was admitted to the hospital.

The second case was Jarrod Worthall, who is the reincarnation of Vincent Worthall. When World War Two erupted, the Holy Spirit College Darts Champion at Cambridge University enlisted. Elisha Baker met the Spit Fire pilot during one of her circulations through time and they bonded whilst taking shelter during a bombing raid on London. Vincent Worthall later lost his life when his plane was shot down, however his energy signature resurfaced in the timeline as another Cambridge University student when Elisha Baker was in attendance. In a twist of irony, the Circulator in fact engaged in a relationship with Jarrod Worthall before meeting his past life identity.

Another commonality the two energy signatures of Guy Robertson and Vincent Worthall share is familial contact. Several Calculators have postulated that when an energy pattern reoccurs in the timeline, often the energy signature reappears in the same biological lineage or close to it. Guy Robertson's energy signature repeated itself in the form of his centuries later progeny Mike Sabre; whereas Vincent Worthall's reincarnation was his great grand nephew, Jarrod Worthall.

With these two examples, we have the close proximity of a third energy signature in Captain Greyson, who was later reincarnated as Declan Sabre. Captain Greyson was not related to Guy Robertson, although the closeness was in camaraderie such as brothers-in-arms. The energy pattern of Captain

Greyson attached itself to the Robertson-Stevens-Sabre lineage, to resurface later in the timeline, as part of the Sabre family. From a letter sent by Guy Robertson/ Mike Sabre, after World War Three, the Sabre family relocate from Indiana to Alaska to be united with the Riverclaw family. By this twist of irony or even lining up of circumstances, Greyson/ Declan then became the mate of the Last Circulator Bianca Wisetail. Captain Greyson befriended Elisha Baker on her very first trip back in time and later reincarnates into the lives of her lineage.

Indeed, the way the reoccurring energy signatures of certain individuals moving throughout the timeline could almost be called supernatural, by one who is not trained in quantum mechanics. In each instance, the unique energy signatures of both 'souls' were attracted to Elisha Baker's bio-electromagnetic frequency to reunite with her in what an untrained eye in temporal causalities may call, 'coincidence'. In psychic circles, this collision of energy signatures could be called 'fate'. However to the Calculators assigned to these Circulate personnel, it is called temporal causality; A leads to B which then concludes in C.

CAN ANYONE BE 'REINCARNATED'?

The Circulate's data on the reoccurring energy signatures through the timeline, indicate whilst humans can be 'reincarnated', Circulators and Calculators cannot.

Like stepping stones in the time stream, a human's energy signature may disappear due to biological death to reappear in another form at a later date, further down stream. However since Circulators and Calculator's energy is in temporal flux, this does not occur. As Calculator's and Circulator's bio-electromagnetic fields register higher than a human being's, this is attributed to the molecules being in temporal flux. A particle in temporal flux cannot be replicated and it cannot reoccur in the timeline. The only exception to this rule is in Elisha Baker's progeny which is the only case in Circulate history of a Circulator passing down their ability to circulate genetically.

With their bio-electromagnetic fields in temporal flux, results in Calculators and Circulators decreased rate in biological aging. On this note, there are certain Circulators who are able to manipulate time inside of themselves, to alter their physical appearances from young to old and back again. However, only eight Circulators in the Circulate have the ability to alter their ages by going into phase, from the high amount of particles that are in temporal flux, which are present in their bio-electromagnetic frequencies.

In the beginning, the four Circulators in the Circulate who had this ability, were Lucas Hodge, Rufus Kell, Sophie Wilmont and Elisha Baker. Now, with Sophie Wilmont's departure to the space time continuum; and including Elisha's Baker's sole ability to replicate particles in temporal flux, the eight Circulators are; Lucas Hodge, Rufus Kell, Elisha Baker, Mike Sabre, Alexandrina Worthall, Scott Carmichael, Arabella Carmichael, Jessica Riverclaw and Bianca Wisetail.

Circulators and Calculators can exist in biological form for over a thousand years. This is believed to be another reason why a Circulator and a Calculator cannot be reincarnated. Humans have a much shorter life span when their energy changes from corporeal to non-corporeal, to be reentered into the timeline in a new era. However, Circulators and Calculators who retain a biological existence for a longer period of time, can take up more room inside the timeline. This is especially so when the Calculator or the Circulator, circulates through time to visit different eras by will rather than by reincarnation.

If a Circulator changes a person into another Circulator, this is done by effectively raising their bio-electromagnetic frequency and putting it into temporal flux. In a Circulator, the heightened brain activity which controls the signals running through their central nerve system, is linked directly to their bio-electromagnetic fields. When a Circulator goes into phase to circulate through time, the electrical signals originates from their brain and is sent throughout the Circulator's body via this system. The electrical impulses activate the Circulator's bio-electromagnetic frequency, changing their biological bodies into one made of light waves.

However changing a human into a Circulator affects the timeline, as the flow of time must adjust to the absence of a mortal energy signature. As Circulators and Calculators energy signatures are separate; with such an impact, several Calculators have observed the ramifications made to time and space when a Circulator is created.

CALCULATION OF THE RAMIFICATION TO SPACE AND TIME

When Elisha Baker inadvertently changed Mike Sabre into a Circulator and then further Circulators were created; our Calculators picked up several anomalies.

The first was that the sun experienced a massive output in energy; or in layman's terms, a 'solar flare' occurred. On the 27th March 2004, the solar flare caused severe electromagnetic interference in several northern hemisphere countries, namely Canada, United States of America and Russia. The radiation from the solar flare knocked out several satellites which in turn, disrupted devices such as telecommunications, satellite television and government military monitoring installations such as the Pentagon.

Since this was the first time a Circulator was created as such, it was not linked to the occurrence. However, when Elisha Baker created another Circulator by giving birth to Alexandrina Worthall, another astronomical anomaly was reported. On the 30th May 2008, the Earth's moon shifted its orbit, causing an unusual high tide which resulted in partial flooding to several south-eastern Asian countries in the Pacific Ocean. During a meeting of the Circulate's best Calculators, Patrick O'Flannigan reported that he had 'seen' these side effects, when the Circulator he was assigned to, irreparably altered the timeline by creating two Circulators.

As more Circulators were created by birth or deliberate manipulation, several more astronomical anomalies presented itself as the timeline was affected. Similar to the 'Butterfly Effect', the more Circulators were created, resulted in the greater ramifications to the timeline. Under normal circumstances, non-ESP humans are oblivious to disruptions to space and time. However from the magnitude of disruptions in certain geographic locations on Earth, humans may physically experience the side effects, such as with the reoccurring time warp commonly called, 'The Bermuda Triangle'.

On the 12th December 2028, the Luxury Liner, 'Mistletoe' passed through a time warp in the famed seas. This coincided with the Calculators Patrick O'Flannigan and Genevieve Nelson's observations of when Arabella Carmichael was born. The 'Mistletoe' completely disappeared from 21st Century satellite relay systems for a whole 21 minutes. The Coast Guard of the United States nor Cuba could locate the massive ship as it abruptly disappeared from their sensor net. Then just as several Search and Rescue vehicles were dispatched, the ship reappeared on the human's computer sensors. However, what they could not explain was, how the ship reappeared thousands of kilometers away from its original position, now floating off the coast of Norway; in another area of sea where unexplained sightings or disappearances had occurred.

Humans have hundreds of documented cases of transport vehicles such as planes or ships disappear at sea, with certain stretches of water noted to be more hazardous than others. This creates such vernacular terms as 'Bermuda Triangle' or 'Devil's Triangle' as a device to instill trepidation in travelers who pass through these areas. The two regions which have had the most disappearances, occurred in the North Atlantic Ocean, either in the Caribbean or Northern European waters. However as human myth compounds these abnormal pieces of geography are triangular shaped, they are partly correct as the three sides represent past, present and future which occasionally collide into one. The colloquial terminology of this effect is 'lost time', however in the Circulate it is relegated as a time warp.

Calculators have compiled accounts of all the geographic locations when a time warp, time loop or a time recording occurs. Partly some of this research was compiled by Elisha Baker and Dr. Xavier Bell with their work on SSIT; but most of it has been recorded in the Viewing Room of Circulate Headquarters. Using the 25th Century technology, the Circulate has monitored, recorded and been able to predict with a 95% success rate when a warp in the timeline will occur. The Circulate Mainframe has surface maps which profile Earth's major Ley

Lines which so happens, several converge under the waters of the Bermuda Triangle in the Caribbean as well as the Devil's Triangle off the coast of Norway. Some human scientists have likened Earth as a major super conductor, being bombarded with energy from the sun and the planet generating electrical storms in its atmosphere. The Ley Lines conduct this charge until the build up electrostatic energy flares, which can cause a ripple or even a momentary hole in the timeline.

Using this principle, the Last Calculator Vincent Moher, was able to monitor further changes to time and space as several more Circulators were created. When Arabella Carmichael returned to Earth, temporarily de-evolving from her elevated existence inside the space time continuum; Vincent Moher observed the sight of the Aurora Borealis caused by the high levels of electromagnetic charge in the Earth's atmosphere. What was unusual in this scenario, was that it was the wrong time of year for Alaska to encounter the 'Northern Lights'.

However, the greater effect to space time occurred when Arabella Carmichael, altered her Lokoti Werewolf husband Emanuel Riverclaw, into another Circulator on the 7th September 2195 before departing Earth, to evolve to the space time continuum together. Vincent Moher reported that the birth of a new star he was previously observing in the Orion nebula; actually began to falter until it faded into clouds of hot gas. The Last Calculator reported that somehow the gravity field which was creating the star was 'pulled apart', effectively weakening it. This in turn, no longer created the correct gravity well strong enough to compact the gas and heavy minerals for the star to ignite.

Vincent Moher commented in his Personal Log stored on the Circulate Mainframe; "...I couldn't believe my eyes. The Viewing Room system of course sped up the time differential since a star's birth or death can take thousands of Earth years, but the Viewing Room did record a match. The approximate star's date that the gravity field in the Orion nebula was first affected, was in the Earth time of the 7th September 2195. I had read previous Calculator reports on the other Circulators, Elisha Baker and Alexandrina Carmichael, and the anomalies that coincided when they altered the timeline by creating new Circulators, but until now, I had never actually believed it. I mean, what are the chances? Is this event just pure coincidence? Then what about the particularly bright Aurora Borealis when Arabella first came back from the space time continuum...?"

From the future Calculator Vincent Moher's observations, the Circulate Council had a meeting. This was to discuss the ramifications of the Circulators Elisha Baker and her progeny, were making to the timeline and the surrounding space. As taught in temporal mechanics, the timeline is seen as 'effect' in relation to the space time continuum which is the 'cause'. Or as certain Calculators explain to the Circulators in their care; let's use the ocean metaphor.

The ocean floor is the space time continuum and the surface of the water is the timeline. If there is a tremor in the ocean floor which is the cause, then the tidal wave on top of the water which is the timeline; is the effect. What Elisha Baker inadvertently created which began as small anomalies on the planet or in our solar system; the effects can now be seen echoing out as far as the Orion nebula, or further still.

However the Circulate Council ultimately deliberated that they would not attempt to prohibit Elisha Baker or the Circulators in her lineage in using their abilities as such. The reasons involve personal liberty as well as necessity. The people Elisha Baker, as well as Alexandrina Worthall, Arabella Carmichael and Jessica Riverclaw, change into Circulators are their life partners. And since the Circulate need these Circulators to assist in elevating all of its members to the 'Final Phase', the Council decided that it would be hypocritical to say; "please do not turn any people but us into Circulators."

It is unknown if the said Circulators are aware of the kind of impact their actions are causing; however their Calculators Patrick O'Flannigan, Genevieve Nelson and Sally Parson believe that on an unconscious level, they can sense it.

Genevieve Nelson wrote on the matter; "...trying to talk logic or even reason to Elisha and her female progeny is like putting TNT inside of a Jack-O-Lantern for a Halloween trick – their heads will explode. So what I do is this, either give them a verbal 'bitch slap' and yell at them to snap out of it, or offer to buy them a clue. But to be impartial, I'll give them this. They're not exactly giving out conversions to Circulator-hood like a kissing booth at the 'country fair'. They (Elisha, Alexandrina, Arabella and Jessica) actually want the poor saps that drool all over them, to be with them for all eternity, and lucky for us that's one guy a piece..."

Sally Parson more succinctly put in her observations; "...I had a chat to Elisha about it last night over coffee and cake when Jarrod was working at the hospital 'on call'. She asked me how Josh and Petra were doing and I asked her back how was her family? Elisha told me that Alexandrina had started dating a boy in her school called Scott Carmichael and then she smiled when she said, "like mother like daughter... not only is Alex a Circulator like her mother is; but she's already decided on the man for her for the rest of her life." When I joked that she was once involved with another great love prior to Jarrod, Elisha mused, "yeah... but I don't think Jarrod is the one that I'm going to spend all eternity with." She was doing her typical scowl, indicating that she had something on her mind. Once prompted, she confessed, "I still think about Mike from time to time... and I wonder how he is. Being turned into an almost-immortal is a big deal. I don't know if I could do it again (to another person)"."

Patrick O'Flannigan put in his report; "...the way these girls (Elisha, Alexandrina, Arabella and Jessica) treat turning a person into a Circulator is with solemnity. Excluding Elisha, her Circulator progeny wait until the very last minute before they change their husband/ partner/ mate into a Circulator, as if they want their male to experience the very last drop of mortality before changing forever. Elisha changed Mike as an accident, and has felt guilty over it ever since. Sometimes even Mike behaves like he's still in shock. But it doesn't stop the idiot from nagging me every time he sees me about 'will Elisha also change Jarrod'? Like it's a huge worry for him, or even if he's biding his time for Jarrod to cark it from old age, so he can try to win the woman back. But then what will Mike do, if Jarrod is reincarnated later on in the timeline and meets up with Elisha yet again?"

According to the report by the Calculator Vincent Moher, he believes that after Jessica Riverclaw transforms her Lokoti Werewolf mate Hunter Wisetail into a Circulator, that there will be one last transformation. It is widely acknowledged that the Last Circulator Bianca Wisetail who is Elisha Baker's great, great granddaughter; will change her European Werewolf mate Declan Sabre, into a Circulator just prior to his biological death. As there will be no Calculator's present to bear witness to the astronomical repercussions, the Circulate Council is wary of what effects will result from this cause.

After the Circulate entered the 'Final Phase', the Last Calculator Vincent Moher, noted the following; "... when I learned how to access the Viewing Room logs, I found several programs running which were being maintained by the Circulate Mainframe. Two Calculators who'd been studying time differentials with the Black Hole in the constellation of Cygnus, had pre-programmed the Viewing Room computers to continue monitoring this astronomical anomaly in their absence. The Viewing Room systems reported that for an unknown reason, the gravity well of the Cygnus Black Hole, became 'stronger'. This was observed by an increased rate in which the Black Hole was destroying the galaxy. The galaxy's date that the gravity well increased in strength matches the Earth date 6th June 2062 when the Circulate entered the 'Final Phase'. A hundred quid says, it was thanks to the Circulate's evolution that buggered it up."

IS REINCARNATION A HUMAN'S WAY TO CIRCULATE?

To revisit the Circulate's data on circulating, calculating, the timeline and the space time continuum; the theory of reincarnation could be considered as the human equivalent of circulating.

Whereas Circulators can transform their biological bodies into one made of light waves, humans evidently cannot. However as this is a Circulator method of time travel, humans do so similarly in a non-corporeal form by returning to the timeline in a different time period. Although this manner is successful in human energy signatures traveling forwards, due to the 'one way' nature of the timeline they are unable to go backwards. This means that although human energy signatures can reappear in a future period, they cannot retreat to a long ago era.

The Circulate's field research in time traveling, their calculations and visions, can be seen to mirror several human scientists theories on time, space and time travel. Using the water analogy again, time is like a perfectly rounded, spherical pond. When there are ripples in the timeline, these are seen on the surface of water. Calculator's prefer this analogy, as they advise that when the circular pond is still, those with a trained eye can see clearly through the depths into the past and the future.

However, when the water is clouded or choppy, the waves in the surface disrupt their vision and for brief moments the past, present or future can seem to collide. Another of the effects of this phenomenon are time warps. Many humans attribute time recordings which are another result of time warps to be 'ghosts', when they can see the long since departed. Human witnesses jump to the conclusion that it is the dead trying to make 'contact' with them. But time recordings are also created by atmospheric conditions such as the temperature, humidity or the weather which impacts the electrostatic charge in the atmosphere, effects the geographic location which can, like a recording can imprint on a location. Then if the exact conditions reoccur later on, it can make the event seemingly replay itself. When this occurs, human's call this phenomenon a 'haunting'.

The timeline which would be the surface of the pond, is directly connected to the space time continuum, which would be at the centre of the sphere of water. In this shape, time for the most part is a circle with no beginning, no middle and no end, as they are one. On this theory, an analogy of the different eras one travels through via aging, reincarnation, or circulating; it would be as if diving into the depths and resurfacing at another juncture in the surface. This would mean that if you traveled far enough around the sphere, you could wind up where you started from.

What is monitored in the Viewing Room though, a human energy signature has never reappeared in the same juncture in the timeline it had left via reincarnation. The reason for this is because although time is curved as is space; existence follows another circular pattern of the Big Bang, the Big Crunch and then another Big Bang. As space and time curves around itself, so does the cycle and the recycle of the Universe. Eons would have passed when the energy signature had traversed the entire timeline to wind up at the originating point. By this stage a new timeline has been generated for the energy to present itself in its changed form.

The continuity of this cycle is assured by the space time continuum, the ever present 'sea bed' which upholds the timeline and body of space. However to remain impartial and keeping to known data, the true nature of the space time continuum is so far conjecture, based on calculations and observed facts. The Circulate cannot definitely know of the omnipotent presence of the continuum until actually experiencing it themselves.

~ The Circulate Series ~

By K.R. Smith

~ Book One: Circulate ~

Elisha Baker learns something new about herself when she attends the haunted international boarding school, Hamilton's College.

~ Book Two: Circulating ~

Elisha and her friends graduate from Hamilton's and the Circulate; to begin University and SSIT – Supernatural Scientific Investigative Team.

~ Book Three: Circulation ~

Armed with degrees, Elisha and her friends continue with SSIT. However adult life isn't as straightforward as they imagined, especially when an investigation into past lives interferes with a present romance.

~ Book Four: Progeny ~

Alexandrina and twin brother Bastian, grew up without a mother and a distant father. But it's to Jarrod's chagrin that his daughter mirrors his late wife, with the fact that she too is a Circulator.

~ Book Five: Ardor & Redolence ~

Arabella joins her grandmother on a SSIT case and meets Emanuel Riverclaw. Eventually they marry and create twins Julian and Jessica; a son who will become a Lokoti Werewolf like his father and a daughter who is a Circulator like her mother.

~ Book Six: Scent ~

At first the Last Circulator can't stand the tribe's most dangerous Werewolf, then Bianca and Declan's fiery arguments turn into something else.

~ Book Seven: Sororate ~

Claws come out in the marriage of the tribe's first female Lokoti Werewolf and the world's last European Werewolf; who spend their tumultuous years together traveling the world and through time.

~ Book Eight: Small Fry ~

Declan swore he wouldn't create anymore European Werewolves like himself, so his wife's new condition has his already hot blood boiling.

~ Book Nine: Alma ~

The new girl in Alma High School called Mali Roanne, suspects there's more than meets the eye with her Lokoti friends. However Mali is hiding a supernatural secret of her own.

~ Book Ten: Heterogeneous ~

In a space age, the different breeds of Werewolves are confined to Earth because of the influence of its one moon. But there's no such holds on the separate species of Vampires or even Human/ Animal Shape Shifters.

~ Book Eleven: Cohesion ~

Parents become grandparents when their children marry and procreate; with all of the different elements of the supernatural combining into one unusual family.

~ Book Twelve: Full Circle ~

The end is nigh, with answers as to why the futuristic Circulate technology never advanced past the 25th Century; because humankind doesn't.

To find out more on the series or the author please visit:

http://onaya3.blogspot.com/

http://twitter.com/onaya3

www.storywrite.com/onaya3

www.writing.com/authors/onaya3

www.facebook.com/pages/Circulate-Series-By-KR-Smith/222260061814?ref=ts

~ References ~

- Front cover photo of Matanuska Glacier, Alaska taken by Nina Ackerman and Leesa Montague, 2007

- Heacox, Kim. In Denali, A Photographic Essay Of Denali National Park & Preserve Alaska. Companion Press. Santa Barbara. 2001

- Alaska, A Scenic Wonderland. Arctic Circle Enterprises Inc. 3812 Spenard Road, Anchorage, Alaska.

- Alaskan Wildlife. Arctic Circle Enterprises Inc. Anchorage. 1995

- www.AlaskaStock.com

- www.wikipedia.com

- Animal World Mammals: Their Lives And Their Future. Issue Nine, Wolves. Marshall Cavendish Ltd. London. 1986

- Chisholm, Jane and Millard, Anne and Jackson, Ian. The Usborne Book Of The Ancient World. The Usborne Publishing Ltd. London. 1991

- Hawking, Stephen. A Brief History of Time, From the Big Bang to Black Holes. Bantam Books. London. 1988

- Bormanis, Andre. Star Trek Science Logs. Pocket Books. New York. 1998

- Goldman, Jane. The X-Files Book of Unexplained, Book 1. Simon & Schuster. London. 1995

- Goldman, Jane. The X-Files Book of Unexplained, Book 2. Simon & Schuster. London. 1996

- Pennick, Nigel. Mysteries of the Ancient World: Leylines. Weidenfeld & Nicolson. London. 1997

- Burl, Aubrey. Mysteries of the Ancient World: Stone Circles. Weidenfeld & Nicolson. London. 1997

- Warren, Joshua P. How to Hunt Ghosts: A Practical Guide. Fireside. NY. 2003

- Martin, Robyn. Quick 'n Easy Finger Food. Concept Publishing. Auckland. 1999

- Sutherland Smith, Beverly. Salads & Barbecues. Five Mile Press. Noble Park. 1998